PRAISE FOR

NIGHT FILM

"Mysterious and even a little head-spinning, an amazing act of imagination." —DEAN BAQUET, *The New York Times Book Review*

"Maniacally clever . . . [Marisha Pessl's] Cordova is a monomaniacal genius who creeps into the darkest crevices of the human psyche. . . . As a study of a great mythmaker, *Night Film* is an absorbing act of myth-making itself. . . . Dastardly fun . . . The plot feels like an M. C. Escher nightmare about Edgar Allan Poe. . . . You'll miss your subway stop, let dinner burn and start sleeping with the lights on." —*The Washington Post*

"Inspired . . . ingenious . . . If there's any justice, the first chapter of literary wunderkind Marisha Pessl's much-awaited second novel, *Night Film,* should go down in literary history as among the most notable formal innovations of this century. . . . The cumulative effect is entrancing and delightful, infusing the narrative of this whip-smart humdinger of a thriller with urgency and spookiness. It feels, above all things, new." —*The Boston Globe*

"A hair-raising mystery that's equal parts family drama, horror movie and jigsaw puzzle. As the pieces come together, it's impossible to look away."
— *People* (4 stars)

"A masterful puzzle. The vivid oddballs in Cordova's world could've been sprung from a film-noir classic, complete with the inexplicable urge to spill their secrets to strangers. [By] forcing you to sort out the clues from the red herrings, Pessl builds up real suspense."
— *Entertainment Weekly*

"Hypnotic . . . The real and the imaginary, life and art, are dizzingly distorted not only in a Cordova night film . . . but in Pessl's own *Night Film* as well."
— *Vanity Fair*

"Ambitious and multi-faceted, *Night Film* takes readers to the edges of the earth and into the darkest, most disconcerting recesses of the unknown. It's a harrowing journey, but one worth taking."
— *USA Today*

"*Night Film* has been precision-engineered to be read at high velocity, and its energy would be the envy of any summer blockbuster. Your average writer of thrillers should lust for Pessl's deft touch with character."
— *The New York Times Book Review*

"Noirish, impish and stylish, this literary thriller delivers twists, kinks and characters to care about. . . . *Night Film* gets two thumbs up."
— *MORE*

"An engrossing yarn, full of twists and cliffhangers. And Ms Pessl handles Cordova's menace superbly, keeping readers in thrall. . . . Its pace, suspense and fiendish originality win the day."

—*The Economist*

"Pessl . . . knows how to keep the creep factor simmering on low while the plot thickens. . . . *Night Film* is never boring."

—The Associated Press

"Reading this book is like sitting in a movie theater in wraparound darkness, feeling a deep chill that's part air conditioning, part anticipation. . . . I was totally happy to sit in the darkness until the very last page, and I didn't move a muscle until the lights came up."

—MEG WOLITZER, NPR

"You won't put this book down."

—*Marie Claire*

"A twisty plot, wonderfully flawed characters, and vivid writing catapult Marisha Pessl to the top of the literary-thriller class."

—*Parade*

"A very deeply imagined book . . . sprints to an ending that's equal parts nagging and haunting: What lingers, beyond all the page-turning, is a density of possible clues that leaves you leafing backward, scanning fictional blog comments and newspaper clippings, positive there's some secret detail that will snap everything into focus."

—*New York*

"A literary mystery that's also a page-turner . . . *Night Film* might be the most talked-about novel this summer." —*Time Out New York*

"A novel that is in every way bigger, more ambitious, and more satisfying than her splashy debut . . . deft and insightful."

—*The Millions*

"A shrewdly contemporary whodunit." —*W*

"Compelling . . . *Night Film* is that rare noir thriller that maintains its creepy suspense right up until the very last sentence." —*All You*

"Smoothly propulsive . . . creepily cinematic . . . Pessl is all business right from the start, and the business she's in is the turning of pages. . . . Solidly entertaining." —*Slate*

"A worthy page-turner . . . Pessl whisks the reader along with McGrath, a self-destructive and insatiably curious skeptic. . . . A gripping mystery." —*Chicago Tribune*

"Consistently sure-handed and evocative, suspenseful and fast-paced . . . a fast and furious [ride]." —*Newsday*

"Hip, smart and exquisitely brilliant . . . like a roller coaster ride through the haunted house at the wildest amusement park ever built . . . a spine-tingling journey covering deep recesses of the human psyche . . . Grade: A+." —*Cincinnati CityBeat*

"*Night Film* is structured as a mystery, about discovering the truth about the death of Cordova's daughter, Ashley. But calling it that is the same as calling your favorite film nothing more than a diversion you watch while eating popcorn. . . . *Night Film* is propelled by strong writing, the kind of prose Pessl showed in her highly regarded debut. . . . It may be true, as the opening scene of the novel says, that everybody has a story about Cordova. But it's hard to imagine any one that would be better than *Night Film*."

—*St Louis Post-Dispatch*

"Masterfully played . . . Pessl has matured into a cleverly entertaining writer who wields her strengths with greater precision than in *Special Topics*."

—*The Kansas City Star*

"Hypnotic . . . intricately plotted . . . masterfully crafted . . . Pessl makes the case for old-fashioned—and literally spellbinding—storytelling. . . . A gothic thriller that's among the best novels I've read this year."

—*Milwaukee Journal Sentinel*

"Intoxicating . . . spellbinding . . . [The] set piece at the Peak delights and terrifies; it's perfectly paced and totally freaked me out. . . . *Night Film*'s thrall is all encompassing."

—New York *Daily News*

"Fast-paced, dark and riveting . . . The suspicious death of a reclusive director's daughter drives Pessl's moody, gritty thriller. . . . [*Night Film*] does a fine job of upending your assurances."

—Minneapolis *Star Tribune*

"A quick read, thanks to Pessl's fast-paced storytelling gifts . . . Pessl has proved she has the commitment and talent to give us a lifetime of rich storytelling." —Durham *Herald-Sun*

"A mystery with literary heft . . . Pessl and her amateur detectives are wonderful guides." —*Connecticut Post*

"A smart literary thriller about artistic obsession—utterly absorbing, the kind of book that'll carry you through a summer afternoon regardless of sun or rain." —*Washingtonian*

"Pessl artfully propels the narrative forward by gradually expanding our perspective on McGrath's life as he hunts for clues about the Cordovas. . . . Pessl adeptly brings Cordova to life. . . . Captivating, a noir tour de force with enough suspense and pop-culture quirkiness to keep it interesting to the end."
—*The Charlotte Observer*

"[*Night Film*] asks readers to take some great leaps of the imagination—and rewards them. . . . A clever horror-tinged novel spiraling around a deftly woven character study of an elusive director . . . entertaining and creepy." —*The Dallas Morning News*

"Creepy good fun." —*Tucson Weekly*

"A sometimes-metafictional, always-addictive literary thriller that will probably make you forget the sun and sand and suck you completely into its dark, twisted little world. If you look up and you have a raging sunburn and it's midnight, well, you were warned."
—*Flavorwire*

"An exceptionally well-constructed, compelling story about a doomed young girl, her cult filmmaker father, the fans who are obsessed with him, and the truth about how much life imitates (truly disturbing) art."   —*DuJour*

"Gripping . . . a genre-bending page-turner . . . Pessl is nothing if not audaciously imaginative."   —*Bust*

"The kind of quirky, twisty thriller that makes you want to shut yourself away with its pages and ignore real-life people altogether. Its hairpin turns are gripping, its numerous characters over-the-top, its format inventive."   —*Bullett*

"Prepare to stay up reading well past your bedtime."   —*PureWow*

"A thrilling cinematic journey . . . moody, boldly ambitious."
                    —*BookPage*

"Expands from a seemingly straightforward mystery into a multi-faceted, densely byzantine exploration of much larger issues . . . Into this mazelike world of dead ends and false leads, McGrath ventures with his two, much younger helpers, Nora and Hopper, brilliantly portrayed Holmesian 'irregulars' who may finally understand more about Ashley than their mentor. . . . The writing is always under control, and the characters never fail to draw us further into the maelstrom of the story."   —*Booklist* (starred review)

"[A] creepy and exciting mystery . . . [Cordova's] bleak artistic vision successfully imbues the novel with an ominous atmosphere. . . . A thrilling read."   —*Library Journal* (starred review)

"Seven years after *Special Topics in Calamity Physics,* Pessl returns with a novel as twisted and intelligent as that lauded debut. . . . Pessl does wonderful work giving the hard-headed Scott reason to question the cause of Ashley's death, and readers will be torn between logic and magic." —*Publishers Weekly*

"Inventive . . . brooding, strange and creepy . . . Think Edgar Allan Poe and Stephen King meet Guillermo del Toro." —*Kirkus Reviews*

"A rare and wonderful thing—an ambitious novel that hits its target fair and square. *Night Film* is beautifully imagined, beautifully written, and hypnotically suspenseful." —LEE CHILD

"A bold, dark, complex universe of fear and art and obsession." —ELIZABETH GILBERT

"A mystery, a horror story, a love letter to the manipulative arts of cinema . . . Pessl builds a labyrinth, gives us a minotaur and a tangled ball of twine, then sends us fumbling deeper and deeper into darkness. That she ever manages to shepherd us out into the light again, after so many engaging twists and turns, is a testament to her tremendous gifts as a storyteller." —SCOTT SMITH

"Lightning indeed strikes twice. Pessl has done it again. She constructs a driving get-up-at-four-in-the-morning-so-you-can-have-time-to-read myth-tery, replete with dazzling visual aids . . . a modern and mystical masterwork from a commanding voice in the genre." —JAMIE LEE CURTIS

NIGHT FILM

By Marisha Pessl

Special Topics in Calamity Physics

Night Film

MARISHA PESSL
NIGHT FILM

A NOVEL

RANDOM HOUSE TRADE PAPERBACKS · NEW YORK

2014 Random House Trade Paperback Edition

Copyright © 2013 by Wonderline Productions LLC
Reading group guide copyright © 2014 by Random House LLC

Published in the United States by Random House Trade Paperbacks, an imprint of Random House, a division of Random House LLC, a Penguin Random House Company, New York.

RANDOM HOUSE and the HOUSE colophon are registered trademarks of Random House LLC.

Originally published in hardcover in the United States by Random House, an imprint and division of Random House LLC, in 2013.

Illustration credits appear on page 601.

Grateful acknowledgment is made to the following for permission to use the specified materials:

The New York Times: The New York Times standard logo & web page layout, copyright © 2013 The New York Times. All rights reserved. Used by permission and protected by the Copyright Laws of the United States. The printing, copying, redistribution, or retransmission of this Content without express written permission is prohibited.

Rolling Stone: Fictional *Rolling Stone* cover. Rolling Stone® is a registered trademark of Rolling Stone LLC. All rights reserved. *Rolling Stone* mock cover used by permission.

TIME Magazine, a division of Time Inc.: "Dummy Photo-Essay" created by permission of TIME Magazine, a division of Time Inc. TIME, Time.com, and "T" in Red Box Design are trademarks of Time Inc. Used with permission.

Vanity Fair: Permission courtesy of *Vanity Fair* / Conde Nast. © Conde Nast.

LIBRARY OF CONGRESS CATALOGING-IN-PUBLICATION DATA
Pessl, Marisha.
Night Film : A Novel / Marisha Pessl.
pages   cm
ISBN 978-0-8129-7978-7 (pbk.) — ISBN 978-0-679-64391-3 (eBook)
1. Suicide—Fiction. 2. Fathers and daughters—Fiction. 3. Subculture—Fiction.
4. Investigative reporting—Fiction. 5. New York (N.Y.)—Fiction.
6. Psychological fiction. [1. Mystery fiction. gsafd] I. Title.
PS3616.E825N54   2013
813'.6—dc23   2012041163

Printed in the United States of America on acid-free paper

www.atrandom.com

9 8 7 6 5 4 3 2 1

Book design by Simon M. Sullivan

In memory of my grandmother,
RUTH HUNT READINGER
(*1910–2011*)

Mortal fear is as crucial a thing to our lives as love. It cuts to the core of our being and shows us what we are. Will you step back and cover your eyes? Or will you have the strength to walk to the precipice and look out? Do you want to know what is there or live in the dark delusion that this commercial world insists we remain sealed inside like blind caterpillars in an eternal cocoon? Will you curl up with your eyes closed and die? Or can you fight your way out of it and fly?

—**STANISLAS CORDOVA**
Rolling Stone, December 29, 1977

PROLOGUE

New York City 2:32 A.M.

EVERYONE HAS A CORDOVA STORY, whether they like it or not.

Maybe your next-door neighbor found one of his movies in an old box in her attic and never entered a dark room alone again. Or your boyfriend bragged he'd discovered a contraband copy of *At Night All Birds Are Black* on the Internet and after watching refused to speak of it, as if it were a horrific ordeal he'd barely survived.

Whatever your opinion of Cordova, however obsessed with his work or indifferent—he's there to react against. He's a crevice, a black hole, an unspecified danger, a relentless outbreak of the unknown in our overexposed world. He's underground, looming unseen in the corners of the dark. He's down under the railway bridge in the river with all the missing evidence, and the answers that will never see the light of day.

He's a myth, a monster, a mortal man.

And yet I can't help but believe when you need him the most, Cordova has a way of heading straight toward you, like a mysterious guest you notice across the room at a crowded party. In the blink of an eye, he's *right beside* you by the fruit punch, staring back at you when you turn and casually ask the time.

My Cordova tale began for the second time on a rainy October night, when I was just another man running in circles, going nowhere as fast as I could. I was jogging around Central Park's Reservoir after two A.M.—a risky habit I'd adopted during the past year when I was too strung out to sleep, hounded by an inertia I couldn't explain, except for the vague understanding that the best part of my life was behind me, and the sense of possibility I'd once had so innately as a young man was now gone.

It was cold and I was soaked. The gravel track was rutted with puddles, the black waters of the Reservoir cloaked in mist. It clogged the reeds along the bank and erased the outskirts of the park as if it were nothing but paper, the edges torn away. All I could see of the grand buildings along Fifth Avenue were a few gold lights burning through the gloom, reflecting on the water's edge like dull coins tossed in. Every time I sprinted past one of the iron lampposts, my shadow surged past me, quickly grew faint, and then peeled off—as if it didn't have the nerve to stay.

I was bypassing the South Gatehouse, starting my sixth lap, when I glanced over my shoulder and saw someone was behind me.

A woman was standing in front of a lamppost, her face in shadow, her red coat catching the light behind her, making a vivid red slice in the night.

A young woman out here alone? Was she crazy?

I turned back, faintly irritated by the girl's naïveté—or recklessness, whatever it was that brought her out here. Women of Manhattan, magnificent as they were, they forgot sometimes they weren't immortal. They could throw themselves like confetti into a fun-filled Friday night, with no thought as to what *crack* they fell into by Saturday.

The track straightened north, rain needling my face, the branches hanging low, forming a crude tunnel overhead. I veered past rows of benches and the curved bridge, mud splattering my shins.

The woman—whoever she was—appeared to have disappeared.

But then—far ahead, a flicker of *red*. It vanished as soon as I saw it, then seconds later, I could make out a thin, dark silhouette walking slowly in front of me along the iron railing. She was wearing black boots, her dark hair hanging halfway down her back. I picked up my pace, deciding to pass her exactly when she was beside a lamppost so I could take a closer look and make sure she was all right.

As I neared, however, I had the marked feeling she *wasn't*.

It was the sound of her footsteps, too heavy for such a slight person, the way she walked so stiffly, as if waiting for me. I suddenly had the feeling that as I passed she'd turn and I'd see her face was not young as I'd assumed, but *old*. The ravaged face of an old woman would stare back at me with hollowed eyes, a mouth like an ax gash in a tree.

She was just a few feet ahead now.

She was going to reach out, seize my arm, and her grip would be strong as a man's, *ice cold*—

I ran past, but her head was lowered, hidden by her hair. When I turned again, she'd already stepped beyond the light and was little more than a faceless form cut out of the dark, her shoulders outlined in red.

I took off, taking a shortcut as the path twisted through the dense shrubbery, branches whipping my arms. *I'll stop and say something when I pass her again—tell her to go home.*

But I logged another lap and there was no sign of her. I checked the hill leading down to the bridle paths.

Nothing.

Within minutes, I was approaching the North Gatehouse—a stone building beyond the reach of the lamps, soaked in darkness. I couldn't make out much more than a flight of narrow stairs leading up to a rusted set of double doors, which were chained and locked, a sign posted beside them: KEEP OUT PROPERTY OF THE CITY OF NEW YORK.

As I neared, I realized in alarm, glancing up, that she was *there*, standing on the landing, staring down at me. *Or was she looking through me?*

By the time her presence fully registered I'd already run blindly on. Yet what I'd glimpsed in that split second drifted in front of my eyes as if someone had taken a flash picture: tangled hair, that blood red coat decayed brown in the dark, a face so entirely in shadow it seemed possible it wasn't even there.

Clearly I should've held off on that fourth scotch.

There was a time not *too* long ago when it took a little more to rattle me. *Scott McGrath, a journalist who'd go to hell just to get Lucifer on the record,* some blogger had once written. I'd taken it as a compliment. Prison inmates who'd tattooed their faces with shoe polish and their own piss, armed teenagers from Vigário Geral strung out on *pedra,* Medellin heavies who vacationed yearly at Rikers—none of it made me flinch. It was all just part of the scenery.

Now a woman in the dark was unnerving me.

She had to be drunk. Or she'd popped too many Xanax. Or maybe this was some sick teenage dare—an Upper East Side mean girl had put her up to this. Unless it was all a calculated setup and her street-rat boyfriend was somewhere here, waiting to jump me.

If *that* was the idea, they'd be disappointed. I had no valuables on me except my keys, a switchblade, and my MetroCard, worth about eight bucks.

All right, maybe I was going through a *rough patch, dry spell*—whatever the hell you wanted to call it. Maybe I hadn't defended myself since—well, *technically* the late nineties. But you never forgot how to fight for your life. And it was never too late to remember, unless you were dead.

The night felt unnaturally silent, *still.* That mist—it had moved beyond the water into the trees, overtaken the track like a sickness, an exhaust off something in the air here, something malignant.

Another minute and I was approaching the North Gatehouse. I shot past it, expecting to see her on the landing.

It was deserted. There was no sign of her anywhere.

Yet the longer I ran, the path unspooling like an underpass to some dark new dimension in front of me, the more I found the encounter unfinished, a song that had cut out on an expectant note, a film projector sputtering to a halt seconds before a pivotal chase scene, the screen going white. I couldn't shake the powerful feeling that she was very much *here,* hiding somewhere, watching me.

I swore I caught a whiff of perfume embroidered into the damp smells of mud and rain. I squinted into the shadows along the hill, expecting, at any moment, the bright red cut of her coat. Maybe she'd be sitting on a bench or standing on the bridge. *Had she come here to harm herself?* What if she climbed up onto the railing, waiting, staring at me with a face drained of hope, before stepping off, falling to the road far below like a bag of stones?

Maybe I'd had a *fifth* scotch without realizing. *Or this damned city had finally gotten to me.* I took off down the steps, heading down East Drive and out onto Fifth Avenue, rounding the corner onto East Eighty-sixth Street, the rain turning into a downpour. I jogged three blocks, past the shuttered restaurants, bright lobbies with a couple of bored doormen staring out.

At the Lexington entrance to the subway, I heard the rumble of an approaching train. I sprinted down the next flight, swiping my Metro-Card through the turnstiles. A few people were waiting on the plat-form—a couple of teenagers, an elderly woman with a Bloomingdale's bag.

The train careened into the station, screeching to a halt, and I stepped into an empty car.

"This is a Brooklyn-bound four express train. The next stop is Fifty-ninth Street."

Shaking off the rain, I stared out at the deserted benches, an ad for a sci-fi action movie covered in graffiti. Someone had blinded the sprint-ing man on the poster, scribbling out his eyes with black marker.

The doors pounded closed. With a moan of brakes, the train began to pull away.

And then, suddenly, I was aware, coming slowly down the steps in the far corner—shiny black boots and *red,* a red coat. I realized, as she stepped lower and lower, soaked black hair like ink seeping over her shoulders, that it was she, the girl from the Reservoir, the ghost—*what-ever the hell she was.* But before I could comprehend this impossibility, before my mind could shout, *She was coming for me,* the train whipped into the tunnel, the windows went black, and I was left staring only at myself.

NIGHT FILM

The New York Times   N.Y. / Region

Ashley Cordova, 24, Found Dead

Ashley Cordova, 24, Found Dead   *Photograph courtesy of K&M Recording*

Published: October 14, 2011 by Charles Dunbar

A body that was found in a vacant Chinatown warehouse Thursday was identified by the city medical examiner as that of Ashley Cordova, daughter of the Academy-Award-winning American film director Stanislas Cordova. She was 24.

The cause of death has not yet been determined, but the police are investigating reports that Ms. Cordova, who reportedly had a history of depression, committed suicide by jumping into an out-of-service elevator shaft, said Hector J. Marcos, the chief spokesman for the city medical examiner's office.

Ms. Cordova was a classical pianist and former child prodigy. She made her Carnegie Hall debut at age 12, playing Ravel's Piano Concerto in G Major with the Moscow Philharmonic Orchestra. Ms. Cordova retreated from music at age 14, declining further recitals, tours and public appearances.

She was raised at The Peak, her father's vast, private Adirondack estate, which served as the setting for many of Mr. Cordova's films, including his 1979 psychological thriller, "Thumbscrew." Ms. Cordova graduated from Amherst College in 2009. Unlike her half-brother, Theo Cordova, who frequently acted in his father's films, Ms. Cordova appeared only once, playing the youngest of the Stevens children in "To Breathe with Kings" (1996), adapted from the novel by August Hauer.

The Cordova family could not be reached for comment.

Cordova's Daughter Found Dead

🇫 🇴 ◀ ✉

Ashley Cordova, the 24-year-old daughter of cult shadowmaster Stanislas Cordova, has been found dead in downtown New York, a supposed suicide. This adds another dark chapter to the life of a man who has appeared to have ingeniously crafted and rejected his own infamous legend. It also prompts the obvious question: Is this just a sad coincidence or a severely cursed dynasty? We will continue to cover the story as it unfolds. [The New York Times]

GET MORE: MOVIES, STANISLAS CORDOVA, ASHLEY CORDOVA, CULT

---

809 Comments ADD COMMENT   NEWEST   OLDEST   PICKS   MOST REPLIES   ☑ Threaded

---

ANONYMOUS   !

Very sad.

Friday, Oct 14 2011 @ 11:23 PM

---

ineedcaffeine   !

R.I.P. Ashley C.

Friday, Oct 14 2011 @ 11:26 PM

Cathie   !

The man is a sociopath. People like him shouldn't make movies.

Friday, Oct 14 2011 @ 11:31 PM

Bill is a tall leprechaun   !

EXACTLY Cathie!! God forbid something be dark, freakish, and so unnerving you question your commercialised, corporate-sponsored view of the world.

Friday, Oct 14 2011 @ 11:33 PM

Cordova Fan   !

"What is now proved was once only imagined." - William Blake

Friday, Oct 14 2011 @ 11:36 PM

AWOL   !

Not surprised. Only a madman could make the mindfuck that is Isolate 3.

Friday, Oct 14 2011 @ 11:41 PM

> **Jess**   !
>
> Where did you see it?   Friday, Oct 14 2011 @ 11:43 PM

> **AWOL**   !
>
> freedom tunnel 4 am   Friday, Oct 14 2011 @ 11:48 PM

TIME **Photos**

CULTURE

The Last Enigma

Oct. 14, 2011 | Add a Comment

Stanislas Cordova, New York City, December 1977. This photo is the last known image taken of the legendary filmmaker.

Ashley Cordova, 24, daughter of the film director Stanislas Cordova, was found dead yesterday in an abandoned warehouse in Lower Manhattan.

In our modern world of tweeting, TMI, and total exposure, Stanislas Cordova is the exception. He has refused to appear in public or give interviews since *Rolling Stone*'s 1977 cover feature. Those who have worked with him maintain a strict code of silence. Cordova's 15-film body of work—gut-twisting journeys through evil underworlds— still enjoys cult status as some of the most terrifying films ever made. Equally enigmatic is the man himself, whose personal life and professional career have been dogged by controversy.

TIME takes a brief pictorial look at Cordova, the inscrutable figure who—even when staying silent and out of sight—still creates a storm.

 Like ‹ 38   Tweet ‹ 90   +1 ‹ 3   Share

The Last Enigma

Oct. 14, 2011 | Add a Comment

Beginnings

Cordova was an only child raised in the South Bronx by a single mother, though little more has been confirmed of his upbringing. When uncovering personal snapshots of the reclusive director became a cult pastime of his fans, a retired first-grade teacher at P.S. 12 claimed this picture featured Cordova (*back left*). A search of the school's attendance records revealed a boy named Stan Cordova enrolled in her class in 1948. He was given poor marks for "sullen behavior."

The Last Enigma

Oct. 14, 2011 | Add a Comment

Boss

A former Cafe Wha? waitress named Jessica Ramirez claims to have been Cordova's girlfriend between 1960 and 1962. She said Stanislas was a high-school dropout and petty criminal. After stealing a Ford Thunderbird, he made a living working as an all-night livery-cab driver for prostitutes working the seedy night world of 1960s New York, while spending his days writing the script that would become his chilling first feature, *Figures Bathed in Light* (1964). "He had alien eyes," Ramirez said. "Eyes that came at you from light-years away and turned you inside out." This is the only picture she has of herself (*left*) with Cordova (*center*).

The Last Enigma

Oct. 14, 2011 | Add a Comment

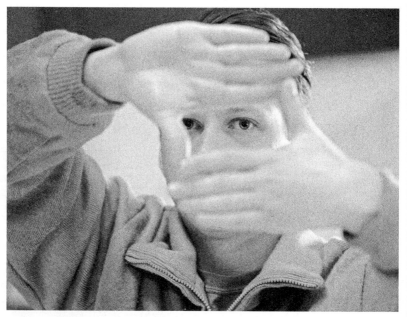

Dark Genius

Warner Bros. released this publicity still depicting Cordova on the set of his second feature, *The Legacy* (1966). The film, an unnerving tale about a 10-year-old boy's decision to kill off a malicious county sheriff, introduced the themes Cordova would explore throughout his work: a horrifying underworld lurking beneath what is beautiful and normal; the fractured nature of human identity with its unspoken fears, violent motives, and immoral sexual desires; and the *night film* itself as a spellbinding, emotionally harrowing experience. When Cordova ceased all public appearances, doubts were raised that he was, in fact, the man in this photo.

The Last Enigma

Oct. 14, 2011 | Add a Comment

Right-hand Woman

Beginning with his second feature, Cordova's most trusted collaborator has been a woman named Inez Gallo. Gallo was allegedly a Mexican housewife (*wedding photo above*) when in August 1965 she met Cordova on a Brooklyn-bound Q train. Days later, she abandoned her family in the middle of the night and for the ensuing 30 years surfaced only as "Assistant to Mr. Cordova" in the credits of his 15 films. Her sole public appearance was at the 1980 Academy Awards, when she accepted Cordova's Best Director Oscar for *Thumbscrew* (1979). Her one-sentence speech, delivered in combat boots, was a summons for people to "break out of [their] locked room[s], real or imagined." The appearance spawned rumors that she was the true genius behind Cordova's work. The clip has more than 3 million views on YouTube.

The Last Enigma

Oct. 14, 2011 | Add a Comment

The Heiress

In June 1975, Cordova married Genevra Castagnello, an Italian model and heiress to an Italian banking fortune. A year later, they purchased a sprawling Adirondack estate known as The Peak, formerly a Rockefeller vacation home. Shortly after giving birth to a son, Theodore, Genevra was found dead by accidental drowning in a lake on the property. Her death was believed to be the cause of Cordova's increasing personal isolation, and of evil as a cornerstone of his work.

 34 61 +1 32

The Last Enigma

Oct. 14, 2011 | Add a Comment

The Peak

Since 1976, Cordova has lived and shot each of his films on a 300-acre estate located in upstate New York in the remote wilderness north of Lows Lake. The isolated nature of the compound—the nearest town is Crowthorpe Falls, pop. 829—and the well-documented fact that it is protected by a 20-foot military fence have been the subject of much rumor and speculation as to the nature of Cordova's life there.

 Like 71   Tweet 25   +1 2   Share

The Last Enigma

Oct. 14, 2011 | Add a Comment

The Muse

Actress and legendary beauty Marlowe Hughes became Cordova's second wife during the making of his film *Lovechild* (1985), though the union was annulled just 3 months later. She refused to speak publicly about the man or the marriage, though her grueling performance as a politician's wife hunting down her blackmailer—who threatens to disclose her past as a child prostitute—earned her rave reviews, the best of her career. The film, rated X, was the last of Cordova's films afforded mainstream theatrical release.

 1 48 +1 54 Share

The Last Enigma

Oct. 14, 2011 | Add a Comment

Fiasco or Shrewd Marketing Ploy?

Cordova's tenth film, *At Night All Birds Are Black* (1987)—about a teenage girl who goes to horrifying lengths to find her missing father—was condemned by the Motion Picture Association of America and led to outraged picketing by Christian morality groups (*above*). When a young woman suffered a mental breakdown in the theater during a test screening, Warner Bros. refused to release the film. A few months later, word began to spread of illicit screenings held illegally in the vast network of tunnels beneath Paris, the City of Light.

The Last Enigma

Oct. 14, 2011 | Add a Comment

Urban Underbellies

Secret showings of Cordova's films—known as *red-band screenings*—began in the Parisian catacombs, a maze of subterranean passageways built during the twelfth century where, fittingly, the walls are constructed out of human bones. The underground screenings soon spread throughout Europe, America, and Japan. This marked the beginning of Cordova's emergence as a subversive sorcerer of a dark, terrifying world liberated from the commercial trappings of mainstream society.

 Like 21   Tweet 14   +1 3   Share

The Last Enigma

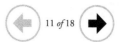
Oct. 14, 2011 | Add a Comment

Symbol of Sovereignty

In Cordova's infamous 1977 *Rolling Stone* interview—the last time he ever spoke in public—he noted his favorite shot of his films was a close-up of the killer's eye in *Figures Bathed in Light*, cryptically describing the image as "sovereign, deadly, perfect." He further admitted it was actually *his* eye, and close examination of the shot revealed a woman screaming in the iris. When Cordova vanished from the public stage, his fans—who call themselves Cordovites—used the words as a slogan and a stylized version of the shot as a symbol to organize illicit screenings of his films.

The Last Enigma

Oct. 14, 2011 | Add a Comment

Last Exit to Cordova
In a Berlin subway station on October 1, 1989, at 2:14 a.m., a young woman examines cryptic directions to a screening of *La Douleur* (1989).

The Last Enigma

Oct. 14, 2011 | Add a Comment

Prelude to Hell

Those who attend the red-band screenings rarely speak of what occurs. Some have claimed the showings—which take place in pitch darkness in condemned buildings or off-limits tunnels beneath a city—are so horrifying, audience members are known to pass out in terror. Others claim they turn into orgiastic raves that last for days. Above, an anonymous street artist in Detroit dances in anticipation of a screening of *Wait for Me Here* (1993), Cordova's first full-scale horror film about a series of unsolved murders terrorizing a backwoods South Carolina town. The street artist later claimed that to see the film was to "leave your old self behind, walk through hell, and be reborn."

The Last Enigma

Oct. 14, 2011 | Add a Comment

The Wannabe

In February 2000, the mutilated body of Amy Andrews, 8, was found in an abandoned paper mill in Kalamazoo, Mich. Authorities found injuries on the body similar to those suffered by the child victim, Alice Reinhart, in *Wait for Me Here* (1993). When the suspect, Hugh Thistleton, 22, was apprehended, pirated DVDs of Cordova's black tapes—his last five films—were found in his apartment, prompting the Andrews family to establish Amy's Light, an organization dedicated to buying and destroying all contraband copies of Cordova's work sold anonymously over the Internet.

The Last Enigma

Oct. 14, 2011 | Add a Comment

Defamation

On May 12, 2006, award-winning investigative journalist Scott McGrath appeared on *Nightline*, announcing that Cordova was his next subject. He claimed Cordova was a "predator—in the same league as [Charles] Manson, Jim Jones, Colonel Kurtz"—referencing the barbaric mass murderer in *Apocalypse Now*. McGrath further remarked that "someone needs to terminate [Cordova] with extreme prejudice." Two days after the program aired, a million-dollar slander lawsuit was filed against McGrath by attorneys representing the Cordova estate (*above*). Though the suit was settled out of court, it was later revealed the journalist's "inside source"—a former chauffeur to Cordova—was pure fiction, leading to McGrath's dismissal from *Insider* magazine.

 Like 75   Tweet 54   +1 2   Share

The Last Enigma

16 *of* 18

Oct. 14, 2011 | Add a Comment

Beautiful Child

In 1986, Cordova allegedly married his third wife, Astrid Goncourt, a French costume designer. They had a daughter, Ashley, who appeared at 8 years old in Cordova's last known film, *To Breathe with Kings* (1996). Later, she gained fame as a piano prodigy using the name Ashley DeRouin, making her Carnegie Hall debut at age 12. She was found dead in an abandoned Chinatown warehouse on October 13, 2011. She was 24.

 50 49 +1 7 Share

The Last Enigma

Oct. 14, 2011 | Add a Comment

Waiting

Since 1977, Cordova has not made a public statement. In 2003, reports surfaced that he was at work on a new film, tentatively titled *Matilde*—though there has been no evidence that production ever started. In a plea for the director to release a new movie, Cordovites have adopted the symbol of the red bird, which makes a fleeting appearance in each of his 15 films: a symbol of stark beauty, the human impulse for freedom, and in the face of unimaginable horror, the possibility for transcendence.

 Like ‹ 78   Tweet ‹ 21   +1 ‹ 12   Share

The Last Enigma

Oct. 14, 2011 | Add a Comment

Final Whisper

Rumors about the director are dissected and analyzed across an invisible Internet fan site known as the Blackboards. While reports persist that the director has been stricken by insanity or a disfiguring disease, or is even dead, a small hint of his whereabouts came on June 2, 2008, when an anonymous employee at Christie's International in London leaked to the press a bill of sale following their contemporary art auction. The document revealed that Francis Bacon's *Self-portrait* (1971) was sold for an undisclosed eight-figure sum to one *S. Cordova*.

1 | A LARGE CHANDELIER showered golden light on the crowd as I surveyed the party in the bronze mirror over the mantel. I was startled to spot someone I barely recognized: myself. Blue buttondown, sports jacket, third or fourth drink—I was losing count—leaning against the wall like I was holding it up. I looked like I wasn't at a cocktail party but an airport, waiting for my life to take off.

Infinitely delayed.

Every time I planted myself at these charity soirees, lost scenes from my married life, I wondered why I kept coming.

Maybe I liked facing a firing squad.

"Scott McGrath, great to see you!"

Wish I could say the same, I thought.

"Working on anything cool these days?"

My abs.

"Still teaching that journalism class at the New School?"

They suggested I take a sabbatical. In other words? Cutbacks.

"Didn't know you were still in the city."

I never knew what to say to *that one*. Did they think I'd been exiled to Saint Helena, like Napoleon after Waterloo?

I was at this party thanks to one of my ex-wife Cynthia's friends, a woman named Birdie. I found it both amusing and flattering that, long after my wife had divorced me, swimming on to bluer seas, a dense school of her girlfriends swirled around me as if I were an interesting shipwreck, looking for a piece of rubble to salvage and take home. Birdie was blond, forties, and hadn't left my side for the better part of two hours. Every now and then, her hand squeezed my arm—a signal that her husband, some hedge-fund guy (*hedge fungi*) was out of town and her three kids Guantánamoed with a nanny. Only a summons from the hostess to show Birdie her newly renovated kitchen had pried the woman from my side.

"Don't go anywhere," Birdie had said.

I'd done *precisely* that. *This wreckage wanted to stay submerged.*

I drained the rest of my scotch, was about to head back to the bar, when I felt my BlackBerry buzzing.

I slipped through the door behind me onto the second-floor landing. It was a text from my old attorney, Stu Laughton. I hadn't heard from Stu in at least six months.

Cordova's daughter found dead.

Call me.

I closed the message and Googled *Cordova*, scrolling the returns.

It was true. And there was *my* goddamn name in quite a few articles. "Disgraced journalist Scott McGrath . . ."

I'd be a marked man, peppered with questions, the moment this latest news circulated the party.

Suddenly, I was sober. I slipped through the crowd, down the spiral marble stairs. No one said a word as I grabbed my coat, walked past the bronze bust of the hostess (which, in a shameless use of artistic license, made her resemble Elizabeth Taylor), out the front door, and down the townhouse steps onto East Ninety-fourth Street. I headed to Fifth, breathing in the damp October night. I hailed a taxi and climbed in.

"West Fourth and Perry."

As we took off, I unrolled the window and felt my stomach tighten as the reality of it settled in: *Cordova's daughter found dead.* What was the unfiltered sound-bite I'd blurted on national television?

Cordova's a predator—in the same league as Manson, Jim Jones, Colonel Kurtz. I have an inside source who worked for the family for years. Someone needs to terminate this guy with extreme prejudice.

That inspired tidbit cost me my career, my reputation—not to mention a quarter of a million dollars—but that didn't make it any less true. *Though I probably should have stopped talking after Charles Manson.*

I couldn't help but laugh at myself for feeling like a fugitive—or maybe the more apt comparison was a *Most Wanted* radical. Yet I had to admit there was something electrifying about seeing that name again—*Cordova*—in the possibility that maybe, *just maybe,* it was time to start running for my life again.

2 TWENTY MINUTES LATER, I let myself into my apartment at 30 Perry Street.

"I said I had to be out of here by *nine,*" a voice announced behind me as I closed the door. "It's after one. What the *hell?*"

Her name was Jeannie, but no sane man would ever dream of her.

Two weekends a month when I had legal visitation with my five-year-old daughter, Samantha, my ex-wife, in an eighteen-year two-for-one promotion, decreed it compulsory I also take custody of Jeannie, the nanny. She was a twenty-four-year-old Yale graduate studying education at Columbia and clearly relished her powerful position as the designated bodyguard, the private escort, the *Blackwater detail* for Sam whenever she ventured into my dangerous custody. In this equation, I was the unstable Third World nation with a corrupt government, substandard infrastructure, rebel unrest, and an economy in free-fall.

"I'm sorry," I said, throwing my jacket over the chair. "I lost track of time. Where's Sam?"

"Asleep."

"Did you find her cloud pajamas?"

"No. I was supposed to be at a study group *four hours* ago."

"I'll pay you double, so you can hire a tutor." I took out my wallet, handed Jeannie about five hundred bucks, which she happily zipped into her backpack, and then I moved deliberately around her, heading down the hall.

"Oh, and Mr. McGrath? Cynthia wanted to know if she could switch weekends with you next weekend."

I stopped outside the closed door at the end, turning back. "Why?"

"She and Bruce are going to Santa Barbara."

"*No.*"

"No?"

"I made plans. We'll stick to the schedule."

"But they already made the arrangements."

"They can unmake them."

Jeannie opened her mouth to protest, but clamped it shut—sensing, quite rightly, that the territory between two people who were *once* soul mates but were *no longer* was akin to wandering into Pakistan's tribal region.

"She's gonna call you about it," she noted quietly.

"Good night, Jeannie."

With a dubious sigh, she let herself out. I entered my office, switched on the desk lamp, and nudged the door closed behind me.

Santa Barbara, my ass.

3 MY OFFICE WAS a small, neglected, green-walled room of filing cabinets, photographs, magazines, and piles of books.

There was a framed picture on my desk of Samantha, taken on the day she was born, her face ancient and elflike. Hanging on the wall was a movie poster of a debonair but exhausted-looking Alain Delon in *Le Samouraï*. The print had been a gift from my old editor at *Insider*. He'd told me that I reminded him of the main character—a lonely French existentialist hit man—which wasn't a compliment. Across the room, left over from my Phi Psi frat-house days at the University of Michigan, was a sagging brown leather couch (on which I'd both lost my virginity and pounded out every one of my best stories). Hanging above that were framed covers of my books—*MasterCard Nation, Hunting Captain Hook: Pirating on the Open Seas, Crud: Dirty Secrets of the Oil Industry, Cocaine Carnivals.* They looked faded, the dust jacket designs *very* late-nineties. There were also a few copies of my more famous *Esquire, Time,* and *Insider* articles: "In Search of El Dorado." "Black Snow Inferno." "Surviving a Siberian Prison." Two giant windows opposite the door overlooked Perry Street and a banged-up poplar tree, though it was too dark to see it now.

I walked to the bookshelf in the corner, beside the photograph of me in Manaus with my arm around a *hecatao* river trader, looking irritatingly *happy* and *tan—snapshot from a past life*—and poured myself a scotch.

I'd bought six cases of the Macallan Cask Strength during my 2007 three-week road trip through Scotland. The trip had been taken at the inspired suggestion of my shrink, Dr. Weaver, after Cynthia had informed me that she and my nine-month-old daughter were leaving me for Bruce—a venture capitalist with whom she'd been having an affair.

It was just months after Cordova slapped me with the slander lawsuit. You'd think out of mercy Cynthia would have rationed the bad news, told me first that I traveled too much, *then* that she'd been unfaithful, *then* that she was madly in love, and finally, that they were each divorcing their respective spouses to be together. Instead, it all came on the same day—like a quiet coastal town *already* hit by famine, further hit by a mudslide, a tsunami, a meteorite, and, to top it all off, a little alien invasion.

But then, maybe it was better that way: Rather early in the chain of disasters, there was nothing left standing to destroy.

The purpose of my trip to Scotland had been to start anew, turn the page—get in touch with my heritage and hence *myself,* by visiting the locale where four generations of McGraths had been born and flourished: a tiny town in Moray, Scotland, called Fogwatt. I should have known simply from the *name* it'd be no Brigadoon. Dr. Weaver's suggestion turned out to be akin to learning my ancestors had arisen from the criminally insane ward at Bellevue. Fogwatt comprised a few crooked white buildings clinging to a gray hill like a couple of teeth left in an old mouth. Women trudged through town with the hardened faces of those who'd survived a plague. Silent red fat men blistered every bar in town. I thought things were looking up when I'd ended up in bed with an attractive bartender named Maisie—until it occurred to me she could feasibly be my distant cousin. Just when you think you've hit rock bottom, you realize you're standing on another trapdoor.

I downed the scotch—instantly feeling a little more *alive*—poured another, and moved to the closet behind my desk.

It'd been at least a year since I'd ventured in there.

The door was jammed, and I had to force it open, kicking aside old sneakers and blueprints of the Amagansett beach house I'd considered buying Cynthia in an eleventh-hour attempt to "work things out." *The million-dollar marital Band-Aid, never a wise idea.* I pried loose what was obstructing the door, a framed photo of Cynthia and me, taken when we were touring Brazil on a Ducati, searching for illegal gold mines, so in love, it was impossible to fathom a day it might not be the case. *God, she was gorgeous.* I chucked the picture aside, pushed back piles of *National Geographic*s, and found what I was looking for—a cardboard box.

I pulled it out, hauled it over to my desk, and sat back in my chair, staring down at it.

The duct tape I'd sealed it with was unsticking.

Cordova.

The decision, five years ago, to take the man on as a subject had been accidental. I'd just come back from an exhausting six-week sojourn in Freetown, a Sierra Leone slum. At about three in the morning, wide awake, jet-lagged, I found myself clicking onto an article about Amy's Light, the nonprofit dedicated to scouring the Internet for Cordova's *black tapes,* buying them, and destroying them. A mother whose daughter had been brutally killed by a copycat murderer founded the organization. Like the central murder in *Wait for Me Here,* Hugh Thistleton had kidnapped her daughter, Amy, from a street corner, where she was waiting for her brother to return from a 7-Eleven, took her to an abandoned mill, and fed her through the machinery.

An organization dedicated to keep Cordova from infecting our youth, declared the website. This mandate I found to be poignant for its sheer impossibility—trying to rid the Internet of Cordova was like trying to rid the Amazon of insects. Yet I didn't agree with it. As a journalist, freedom of speech and expression were cornerstones—principles so deeply embedded in America's bedrock that to surrender even an inch would be our country's undoing. I was also staunchly anticensorship—Cordova could no more be held responsible for Amy Andrews's gruesome death than the beef industry for giving Americans fatal heart attacks. As much as some people would like to believe, for their own peace of mind, that the appearance of evil in this world had a clean cause, the truth was never that simple.

Until that night, I'd hardly given Cordova a second thought beyond enjoying (and getting creeped out by) some of his early films. Wondering about the motives of a reclusive director was not my professional aim or my specialty. I tackled stories with stakes, where life and death were on the line. The most hopeless of all hopeless causes was where my heart tended to go when on the lookout for a new subject.

Somehow, at *some* point that night, my heart got into it.

Maybe it was because Sam had been born just a few months before and, suddenly faced with fatherhood, I was more susceptible than usual to the idea of protecting this beautiful clean slate—protecting any child—from the destabilizing horrors that Cordova represented. Whatever the reason, the longer I clicked through the hundreds of Cordova blogs and fansites and anonymous message boards, many of the postings by kids as young as nine and ten—the more insistent my sense that *something* was wrong with Cordova.

In hindsight, the experience reminded me of an alcoholic South African reporter whose path I'd crossed at the Hilton in Nairobi when I was there in 2003 working on a story about the ivory trade. He was on his way to a remote village in the southwest where a Taita tribe, close to the Tanzanian border, was dying out and was considered *walaani—cursed*—because no child born there could live longer than eleven days. We'd met at the hotel bar and after commiserating over the fact that both of us had recently been carjacked (validating the city's nickname, *Nairobbery*), the man told me he was thinking about missing his bus the following morning, abandoning the story altogether, because of what had befallen the three reporters who'd gone before him to the village. One had apparently gone mad, wandering the streets stuttering nonsense. Another had quit and a week later had hanged himself in a Mombasa hotel room. The third had vanished into thin air, abandoning his family and a post at the Italian newspaper *Corriere della Sera*.

"It's infected," the man mumbled. *"The story.* Some are, you know."

I'd chuckled, assuming such dramatics were a side effect of the Chivas Regal we'd been guzzling all night. Yet he went on.

"It's a *lintwurm.*" He squinted at me, his bloodshot eyes searching my face for understanding. "A tapeworm that's eaten its own tail. No use going after it. Because there's no end. All it will do is wrap around your heart and squeeze all the blood out." He held up a tightened fist. *"Dit suig jou droog.* Some stories you should run from while you still have legs."

I never *did* find out if he made it to that village.

Cordova's daughter found dead. The thought pulled me back to the present, and I opened the old box, grabbed a stack of papers, and started through it.

First: a typed list of all the actors who'd worked with Cordova. Then a list of shooting locations from his first film, *Figures Bathed in Light.* Pauline Kael's review of *Distortion,* "Unraveling Innocence." A film still of Marlowe Hughes in bed in the closing shot of *Lovechild.* Typed transcripts of my notes from Crowthorpe Falls. A photo I'd snapped of the fencing surrounding Cordova's property, The Peak. Wolfgang Beckman's syllabus for his Cordova class, taught a few years ago at Columbia film school, though he was forced to cancel it after only three classes due to outcry from parents. ("Special Topics in Cordova: Darkly Alive and Totally Petrifying," he'd impishly called the class.) A DVD of the PBS documentary on Cordova from 2003, *Dark's Warden.* And then a transcript from an anonymous phone call.

John. The mysterious caller who proved to be my undoing.

I pulled the three pages out of the pile.

Every time I read through them, transcribed within minutes of hanging up—I tried and failed to find the moment in the conversation where I'd lost my head. *What,* exactly, had prompted me to disregard twenty years' experience and *jump the shark* during a television appearance not twenty-four hours later?

SM: Hello.
Caller: Is this Scott McGrath, the reporter?
SM: It is. Who's this?

No immediate answer. Voice is older, mid-sixties or seventies.

Caller: I hear you're investigating Cordova.
SM: How'd you hear that?
Caller: Word gets around.
SM: Are you a friend of his?

No answer. He sounds nervous.

Caller: I don't want this call recorded.
SM: It's not. What's your name?
Caller: John.

Not his real name. I am tempted to turn on my phone recorder--a necessary precaution--but plugging in the TP-7 jack makes a clicking noise on the line. I don't want to scare him off.

SM: What's your connection to Cordova?
Caller: I drove him.
SM: You were his chauffeur?
Caller: You could say that.
SM: Where?
Caller: Upstate.

Upstate New York. "John" is breathing oddly--having second thoughts about talking.

SM: Are you still there?
Caller: Sorry. I don't know how I feel about this now.
SM: Take your time. How did you come to work for him?
Caller: I don't like all the questions.
SM: You're the one who called me, John. Would it be easier if we met?
Caller: No.

Thirty-second pause.

Caller: Most of the time I drove the woman, the Mexican, who works for him into town. But one night he called me and asked if I'd drive him.
SM: You live close to his estate in Crowthorpe Falls?
Caller: I don't want to say.

Caller:	He wanted me to pick him up in the middle of the night. 3 A.M. He asked me to come up slow to the mansion with my lights off. I had the feeling he didn't want to wake anyone at the house. When I got there, he was waiting for me on the steps.
SM:	Was he alone?
Caller:	Yes. He got into the car. The backseat.

A pause.

SM:	Where did you take him?
Caller:	To an elementary school.
SM:	An elementary school.
Caller:	Yes.
SM:	Which one?
Caller:	No specifics.
SM:	Okay. I'm listening.
Caller:	He asked me to drive into the parking lot, turn off the engine, and wait. I watched him walk across the lawn into the children's playground. At first he was very still. And then, he moved around the swings. Pushing one so it swung out into the air, empty. Then he went around the seesaw, tipping it so it bobbed up and down. Then he went into the sandbox and sat down.
SM:	He sat down in the sandbox.
Caller:	I couldn't see what he was doing. But it wasn't right, you understand?
SM:	What was he doing?
Caller:	At first I was scared he was doing something sexual. But it looked like digging.
SM:	Digging?
Caller:	That's what it looked like. When he came back to the car, he was hiding something in his coat.
SM:	What?
Caller:	I couldn't see. I just drove him home.
SM:	Did he say anything?
Caller:	No. But a few weeks later he called me again, asked the same thing.
SM:	To take him to the elementary school?
Caller:	A different one this time. This time he headed out across the athletic field. He slipped up into the bleachers, searching for something. When he came back, again he had something in his coat. When I drove back to the mansion, I saw what it was when he climbed out.
SM:	What was it?

A long pause.

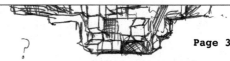

Caller: A child's <u>gym uniform.</u> Tiny yellow shirt. Blue shorts.
It made me sick. I asked what he wanted with it. He
only looked at me hard from behind those glasses. Got
out of the car. Next day I heard from the Mexican. My
services were no longer needed. But I know for a fact he
hired someone else to drive him at night. A young guy.
He paid him a lot of money to do it. For years.

SM: Why?

Caller: There's something he does to the children.

SM: What?

A pause.

SM: How? He hurts them?

No answer.

SM: Who else knows about this?

No answer. I'm losing him.

SM: Anything more you can tell me? John?

No response.

SM: There's nothing to be afraid of.

The line goes dead.

4

THERE'S SOMETHING HE DOES TO THE CHILDREN.
Even now, I remembered the old man's terrified voice on the phone.

I don't remember much about my interview on *Nightline*—except that I did most of the talking. My purpose for appearing on the program was to discuss prison reform. Much to the delight of *Nightline*'s host, I veered *way* off topic, bringing up Cordova. After we wrapped, oblivious to the shit storm about to ensue, I was filled with satisfaction, the kind a man feels only when he's finally told it like it is.

Then the calls started coming: first, my agent asking what I'd been smoking, then my attorney saying he'd just heard from the brass at ABC.

"You put a *hit* out on Stanislas Cordova."

"What? *No*—"

"They just faxed me the transcript. I'm reading here, you interrupted Martin Bashir to announce Cordova should be terminated 'with extreme prejudice.'"

"I was being *ironic*."

"There's no irony in television, Scott."

Needless to say, I never heard from *John* again. He vanished.

Cordova's attorneys contended I'd not only put their client's life and his family at risk, but I'd actually fabricated the anonymous call—that I'd walked to the pay phone a block from my apartment and phoned *myself* in order to establish record of a fictitious source.

I laughed at the preposterous allegation—then ate my own words when I realized I couldn't prove otherwise. Even my attorney was vague on whether or not he believed me. He suggested John was real but had been scared off by my *rogue behavior*.

I had no choice but to settle the lawsuit, conceding my guilt of not *actual malice,* but *reckless disregard for the truth.* I paid the Cordova estate $250,000 in damages, a fair chunk of what I'd saved from my books and stories, building a career on the notion of uncompromising integrity, which was now in shreds. I was fired from *Insider,* my column nixed at *Time.* I'd been in preliminary talks at CNN about hosting a weekly investigative news show. Now the idea was laughable.

"McGrath's like a revered sports hero who's been caught doping," declared Wolf Blitzer. "We need to question everything the man's written and everything he's said."

"You should think about teaching or becoming a life coach," my agent informed me. "In journalism, you're untouchable at the moment."

It was a moment that lasted. *Disgraced journalist* became cemented to my name like *ex-con.* I was a "symptom of the sloppy state of American reporting." A mash-up video of me appeared on YouTube in which I repeated thirty-nine times (my voice Auto-Tuned) *terminate with extreme prejudice.*

I abandoned the investigation. The night I made that decision, packing my notes away, I was embroiled in the slander lawsuit. Cynthia and Sam had moved out, leaving a silence so total it felt as if I'd undergone surgery without my consent. Though I was alive, I was left with the vague suspicion something was permanently *off* inside me. It was beyond my reach, some vital nerve twisted, some organ accidentally put back upside down. I felt only rage toward Cordova—neatly concealed behind his lawyers—an anger especially gutting because it was really toward *myself,* for my own arrogance and stupidity.

Because I knew my downfall was no accident. Cordova, displaying a foresight and intelligence I hadn't anticipated, had outmaneuvered me. I was down, knocked out, the fight over, a winner declared—before I'd even stepped fully into the ring.

I'd been masterfully set up. John had been the bait. Seeing I was coming after him, Cordova had designed a booby trap using this anonymous caller, knowing, with almost superhuman clairvoyance, the man's haunting suggestion—*there's something he does to the children*— would strike a nerve with me, and then he sat back as I dug my own grave.

And yet if Cordova had been that concerned about my investigation to go to such lengths to get rid of me, what was he actually hiding— something even more explosive?

I'd resolved to let it go, leave it alone, focus instead on getting some semblance of a *life* back.

But here I was again. I downed the rest of the scotch, grabbed another stack of pages, and within minutes, I found what I'd been looking for.

It was a thin manila envelope. *Ashley* was scribbled across the front.

I unclasped it, pulling out the contents: a sheet of paper and a CD.

Ashley Cordova '09 practices in the Arms Music Center.

CLASS ACT *(continued)*
plans to return to Denmark, after completing a double major in Biochemistry and Computer Science.

Ashley Cordova '09 is another talented freshman, hailing from upstate New York. Her father just so happens to be legendary filmmaker Stanislas—about whom she says little: "We are a very private family," she explains—though she is an incredibly accomplished woman in her own right.

Using the professional name Ashley DeRouin—DeRouin is a surname from her French mother's side of the family—at eleven years old she won first place at the International Tchaikovsky Competition in Moscow playing his Piano Trio in A minor, beating out Juilliard-trained musicians six years her senior.

She toured the international concert circuit—including a recital at Carnegie Hall.

At fourteen, she recorded her first and only solo album, *Ashley DeRouin Plays Maurice Ravel's Gaspard de la Nuit,* or *The Devil in the Night,* winning critical acclaim for her creative and emotional rendering of the work—one of the most challenging solo piano pieces ever written.

Though she no longer plays professionally, her piano is still a pleasure in which she indulges daily. "It's wonderful to get lost in a piece of music. To forget your name for a while."

Gaspard remains one of her favorite pieces not just for its technical difficulties—figurations, cadenzas, quicksilver chromatic runs the pianist performs with a single hand—but because of Ravel's source of inspiration: three Bertrand poems that range in subject from a water sprite luring a man to come live with her in the water, to a hanging corpse, and a devil who dances in the night, wreaking havoc on human lives.

"It's wonderful to get lost in a piece of music. To forget your name for a while."

"It's a gift to play these pieces," she says. "Ravel was very modest. He never called himself a composer—only that he tried and a piece was finished when he could not try anymore. As you play the sonatas you're transported to a world of great cruelty, yet there is also yearning for love, sadness, a fear not of death but a wasted life. It's all there in his music."

In spite of her virtuosic musical abilities, Ashley is looking to move beyond piano during her time at Amherst, planning to major in Anthropology or History. And after she graduates? "Maybe living abroad. Traveling. Finding the spot where the earth ends. There's a life for me beyond music."

Spoken like the daughter of a true master.

Lucy Polk '09 is another woman who wastes no time going after what she wants. When she was only four she started selling lemonade and by twelve founded her own lemonade brand by *(continued on p. 44)*

5 YEARS AGO, focused on Cordova, I'd barely given this article about outstanding freshmen a second glance. I hadn't even bothered to listen to the CD.

I tore off the plastic, loaded the CD into my stereo, and pressed *play.* There was a long stretch of silence and then: the piano.

The first few bars were high-pitched, insistent, so fast and assured, it seemed inconceivable that the person playing was just fourteen years old. The notes rippled, softened for a moment before stirring up into a furious outburst, like a machine gun exploding sound into the air.

As I listened, the minutes ticked by, and suddenly I became aware of soft footsteps along the wood floors outside my office.

It was Sam. Recently she'd fallen into the habit of waking up in the middle of the night. The knob turned, and my daughter appeared in the doorway, half asleep in a pink nightgown.

"Hi, honey."

Rubbing her eyes, she only padded over to me. She'd inherited Cynthia's beauty, including the showstopping blond ringlets straight off a Sistine Chapel angel.

"What are you doing in here?" she asked in a low, serious voice.

"Research."

She propped her elbows on the desk, doing some strange backward kicking with her foot. She was at that stage where she was always bending, knotting her arms, *winding up* as if involved in an ongoing game of Twister. She squinted at the Amherst article.

"Who's *that*?" she asked.

"Ashley."

"Who's Ashley?"

"Someone in trouble."

She looked at me, concerned. "Did she do something bad?"

"Not that kind of trouble, honey. The kind that's a mystery."

"What mystery?"

"Don't know yet."

This was our dynamic. Sam launched questions into the air and I scrambled to answer them. Due to Cynthia's ironclad custody schedule and Sam's busy life of playdates and ballet, unfortunately I didn't get to see her very much. The last time was more than three weeks ago for an outing to the Bronx Zoo, during which it was clear she trusted every lowland gorilla in the Congo Forest—including the four-hundred-pound silverback—a hell of a lot more than she trusted me. She had her reasons.

"Come on." I stood up. "Let's get you back into bed."

I held out my hand, but Sam only frowned, an unmistakable look of *doubt* on her face. She seemed to already know what took me forty-three years to figure out, that even though adults were *tall*, what we knew about anything, including ourselves, was *small*. The jig had been up since she was about three. And like an innocent convict who'd simply been in the wrong place at the wrong time, Sam was resigned to patiently serve out her sentence (childhood) with her inept wardens (Cynthia and me) until she was on parole.

"How about we go upstairs and find your *cloud pajamas*?" I asked.

She nodded eagerly, allowing me to escort her down the hall and upstairs, where she sat patiently on her bed as I dug through her closet. The *cloud pajamas*—blue flannel, covered in cumulus clouds—were the one thing I'd done right. I'd bought them at a hip children's store in SoHo, they were Sam's favorite, and sometimes she cried if she couldn't wear them to bed—forcing Cynthia & Co. to purchase *second* and even *third* pairs of the hit pajamas to shore up Sam's sleeping on their end—what I took to be a small but powerful personal victory.

I went through every inch of Sam's closet, finally locating them on a back shelf. I dramatically unveiled them—Sam liked when I did a lot of Rudolph Valentino–style silent-film acting. We put them on and then I tucked her in.

"Tighter," she ordered.

I tucked.

"Want me to leave the light on?" I asked.

She shook her head. She was the one child on earth who wasn't afraid of the dark.

"Good night, sweetheart."

"Good night, Scott."

She'd always called me *Scott,* never Dad. I could never remember when this started, its origin as impossible to discern as the chicken and the egg.

"I love you more than—*how* much again?" I asked her.

"The sun plus the moon." She closed her eyes and seemed to fall instantly, magically, to sleep.

I headed back downstairs. The CD was still playing, the music erratic and wild. I sat at my desk, rereading the Amherst article.

To forget your name for a while, Ashley had said.

She had to mean Cordova.

There's something he does to the children. What had he done to his own daughter? How had she ended up dead, an apparent suicide, at twenty-four?

I could feel it starting again—the dark undertow toward Cordova. Forget my fury toward him, which still simmered—this was a chance for absolution. If I went after him again and proved he *was* a predator—what I'd believed in my gut—all I'd lost might come back. Maybe not Cynthia, I couldn't hope for that, but my career, my reputation, my life.

And unlike five years ago, now I had a lead: *Ashley.*

There was something violent in the comprehension that this stranger, this wild magician of musical notes, was gone from the world. She was lost now, she'd been *silenced*—another dead branch on Cordova's warped tree.

She could be his fragile corridor.

It was a covert line of attack described in Sun Tzu's *The Art of War.* Your enemy expected the direct approach. He prepared for it and fiercely fought it off, resulting in severe casualties, the expenditure of major resources—and, ultimately, your own defeat. And yet, occasionally, there was another entrance, *the fragile corridor.* Your enemy never expected advancement via this route because it was labyrinthine and treacherous, and he often didn't even know it was there. But if your army managed to make it through, it would deliver you not just behind your enemy's lines but to his inner chamber, the heart of his heart.

A tapeworm that's eaten its own tail, that old journalist had warned me. *No use going after it . . . All it will do is wrap around your heart and squeeze all the blood out.*

No, I never found out what happened to him—but I knew the answer. For all his grumbling, the next morning, surely as the sun rose, he climbed out of bed, packed his bags, and rode a bus straight into that damned village.

He wouldn't have been able to stay away from the story.

Neither would I.

6 A LITTLE OVER a week later, at 3:00 A.M., I boarded a Harlem-bound M102 bus—#5378, as Sharon Falcone had instructed— and took a secluded seat in the back.

If the city had one spot where murmured conversations and dubious glances went ignored, it was *this bus* at three in the morning. Whatever passengers were present, they were likely to be dead tired, strung out, or involved in shady dealings themselves—so you could bet they wanted to remain as incognito as you did. I'd never understood how Sharon had arranged it, but now, I swore it was the same driver from the last time we'd done this, some nine years ago.

I first met Detective Sharon Falcone back in 1989 when I was a green reporter for *The New York Post* and she was a rookie cop helping out on the Central Park jogger case. Even now, more than twenty years later, I still knew just snippets about her, but those bits went a long way, like a pinch of Cajun powder in your food. She was forty-six and lived alone in Queens with a German shepherd named Harley. For the past decade, she'd worked for the Manhattan North Homicide Squad, a specialized unit that helped other precincts with homicides that occurred north of Fifty-ninth Street, and she served her deceased victims with a devotion that seemed old-fashioned in its selflessness and dedication.

The bus turned west onto East One hundred sixteenth, passing abandoned housing projects, empty lots, tattered churches—SALVATION AND DELIVERANCE, read a sign—men loitering on corners.

Something must be wrong, I thought to myself. *The last time we did this, Sharon had boarded by now.* I checked my phone, but there was no missed call, no text. The conversation we'd had the day before had not been promising, nor had she made any real commitment to helping me.

"Tomorrow night. Same place and time," she'd said curtly and hung up.

The bus was turning down Malcolm X Boulevard and I was just beginning to think she'd blown me off, when we abruptly pulled over in front of a ramshackle townhouse, a lone figure standing by the curb. The doors opened, and within seconds Detective Sharon Falcone was hurrying toward me—as if she'd known precisely where I was sitting all along.

She looked the same: still 5'3" and grim, lips thin and unsmiling, a button nose that curved up at the tip like a wood shaving. She wasn't *un*attractive. But she was *strange*. Sharon could pass for a pale nun staring out from a fifteenth-century portrait in the Flemish painting wing at the Met. Only the artist hadn't *quite* mastered human proportions, so he'd given her an elongated neck, uneven shoulders, and too-small hands.

She slid next to me, eyeing the other passengers, letting the black shoulder bag fall to her feet.

"Of all the M102s in all the towns in all the world, you walk into mine," I said.

She didn't crack a smile. "I don't have much time." She unzipped the bag, pulled out a white 8 x 10 envelope, handing it to me. I slid out the thick stack of papers, the first page, a photocopy of a file.

Case No. 21-24-7232.

"How's the investigation going?" I asked, slipping it back and tucking the envelope into my pocket.

"Fifth Precinct's handling it. They're getting a hundred calls a day. Anonymous tips, but they're bullshit. Last week Ashley was spotted at a McDonald's in Chicago. Three days before, a Miami nightclub. Already they got two homicide confessions."

"Was it homicide?"

Sharon shook her head. "No. She was a jumper."

"You're positive?"

She nodded. "No sign of a struggle. Fingernails clean. She took off her shoes and socks, placed them together at the edge. That kind of methodical preparation, very consistent with suicide. They haven't done a postmortem. Not sure they will."

"Why not?"

"The family attorney's all over it. Religious reasons. If you're Jewish it's a sacrilege to desecrate the body." She frowned. "I noticed some shots missing in the file. Front and back torso. My guess is they're being held in a separate file so some creep doesn't leak them to The Smoking Gun."

"The cause of death?"

"Standard for any jumper. Massive hemorrhaging. A broken neck, lacerated heart, multiple broken ribs, and a skull fracture. She was there for a few days before they found her. She'd been admitted last month to some swank private hospital upstate. They filed a missing-person's report for her ten days before she jumped."

I stared at her in surprise. "Why? She ran away?"

She nodded. "A nurse confirmed Ashley was in her room, lights off, at eleven o'clock. At *eight* the next morning, she was gone. Somehow she appeared on just *one* security camera—crazy, because the place is outfitted like the Pentagon. You can't see her face. She's just a figure in white pajamas running across the lawn. A man was with her."

"Who was he?"

"They don't know."

"Why was she at the hospital? A drug problem?"

"I don't think they knew *what* the hell was wrong with her. A few pages of her medical evaluation are in there."

"When did the hospital report her missing?"

"September thirtieth. It's in the report."

"And when did she jump?"

"Late night on the tenth. Eleven, twelve midnight."

"Where did she go during those ten, eleven days in between?"

"No one has any idea."

"Any activity on her credit cards?"

Sharon shook her head. "Cell was off, too. She must have known not to turn it on. Seems like she didn't want to be found. There was just one confirmed sighting in those ten days. When they found the body, she was wearing just jeans and a T-shirt. They found a plastic ticket in her pocket. A tree insignia on the back. It was traced to the Four Seasons Restaurant. You know, that little shack on Park Avenue?"

I nodded. It was one of the most expensive restaurants in the city, though it played out more like a rare wildlife reserve. One paid an exorbitant entry fee ($45 for crab cakes) to observe—but never *disturb*—New York's privileged and powerful as they fed and fought among themselves, displaying all the recognizable traits of their species: hardened expressions, thinning hair, gun-gray suits.

"A girl working the coat check identified her," Sharon said. "Ashley came in around ten but left minutes later, *without* her coat, and never came back. A few hours later, she jumped."

"She must have been meeting someone."

"They don't know."

"But someone will look into it."

"No. There's *no crime* here." She eyed me sharply. "To get to that elevator shaft the girl had to enter an abandoned building, which is a notorious squatters' hangout, the *Hanging Gardens*. Then, on the roof, she squeezed through a skylight about a foot wide. Few are small enough to get through such a narrow opening, much less if they were holding someone against their will. They combed the place for trace evidence. There's no sign anyone was there but her." Sharon continued to watch me—or perhaps the right word was *investigate*, because her brown eyes were slowly moving over my face, probably in the same methodical grid pattern she used with a widespread search party.

"This is when I ask *why* you want this information," she said.

"Some unfinished business. Nothing for you to worry about."

She squinted at me. "You know what Confucius said?"

"Remind me."

" 'Before you embark on a journey of revenge, dig two graves.' "

"I've always found ancient Chinese wisdom overrated." I took out an envelope and handed it to her. It contained three thousand dollars in cash. She shoved it inside her bag, zipping it closed.

"How's your German shepherd?" I asked.

"He died three months ago."

"I'm sorry."

She brushed her spiky bangs off her forehead, scrutinizing an elderly man who'd just boarded.

"All good things must come to an end," she said. "We done here?"

I nodded. She looped the strap of her bag over her shoulder and was about to get up when I thought of something else and grabbed her wrist.

"What about a suicide note?" I asked.

"They didn't find one."

"Who identified Ashley at the morgue?"

"An attorney. The family hasn't said a word. I hear they're out of the country. *Traveling.*"

With a look of regret but little surprise, she stood up, moving to the front of the bus. The driver instantly pulled over. Within seconds, she was scurrying down the sidewalk, though she didn't walk so much as *plow*, shoulders hunched, eyes fixed on the ground. As the bus took off again with a belch, veering into the road, Sharon became just a shadowed figure moving past the closed stores and barred windows, swerving quickly around a corner—and she was gone.

BH
Briarwood Hall

NEW PATIENT ASSESSMENT

Patient Name	Ashley Brett Cordova		Date of Birth	12.30.86
Address	1014 Country Road 112			
City	Crowthorpe Falls	State	NY	Zip	12847
GP	Patient claims not to have a family doctor.		GP Phone	N/A
Briarwood Physician	Annika Angley M.D.			
Date of Assessment	9/5/11	Dates Seen	8/31, 9/1, 9/2, 9/3

Description of Presenting Complaint / Problem

Patient presents with sullen mood and is unresponsive to questioning. Patient can be combative and seems to have paranoid ideation -- specifically related to strangers. Patient has been known to experience violent outbursts when left alone and/or in the dark (first noted on 8/31). Patient displays no interest in others or in socializing and appears unmotivated with respect to her ADL's. In contrast to above, patient's demeanor changed when she was allowed to play the piano during social hour. During this time she played without cessation for two hours -- R/O manic tendencies.

Further evaluation is recommended along with 3 hours of daily treatment -- both group and individual.

Description of Presenting Complaint / Problem	Family History of Mental Illness
Patient claims never to have been treated.	None claimed.

Social History (including substance, or other, abuse) including Current Relationships, Job

A former musical prodigy. Current job and relationship status unknown.

Current Medications	Relevant Medical Conditions / Investigations / Allergies
None	None

Mental Status Examination *(Please indicate relevant details)*

Appearance	Unkempt, pale, suggestive of anemia	Mood		Angry, paranoid, combative
Thinking	Clear	Affect		Blunted, flat
Perception	Good	Sleep		Good, but requires all room lights on
Anhedonia	No	Appetite		Poor
Attention / Concentration	Good	Motivation/Energy		Poor
Memory	Good	Judgment / Insight		Can be paranoid
Orientation	Good	Speech		Clear

Risk Assessment *(if answer is Yes to plan, intent, or risk to others refer to CODE SILVER Team, CST, on 9211 3911)*

Suicidal thoughts	Yes ☑ No ☐	Suicidal ideation	Yes ☑ No ☐
Current plan	Yes ☐ No ☑	Risk to Others	Yes ☑ No ☐

ICD – 10 Provisional Diagnosis

Patient is suitable for:

F1 Alcohol & Drug Use disorder	☐
...ychotic Disorder	☑
	☑
	☐
	☐

Depression group	☑
Panic and avoidance group	☐
Co-morbidity group	☐
Individual therapy	☑

INITIAL INCIDENT / OFFENSE REPORT

DETECTIVE'S INCIDENT SUMMARY

Time and Date of This Report	TIME	DATE
	14:02	10.14.11

CASE #	LEAD DETECTIVE ASSIGNED TO CASE	TYPE OF CRIME / INCIDENT
21-24-7232	Detective Mike Wu NYPD, 5th Precinct	Death Investigation

RELATED CASE / INCIDENT	Missing Persons Report, NY 12-388 Shandaken Police Dept. Ulster County
ALSO PRESENT AT SCENE	Sgt. Frank Bryant; Officer Joseph Anderson; Phil LaRock, photographer for Office of Chief Medical Examiner; Dr. Sanja Inratis, Assistant Medical Examiner; Crime Scene Investigator Richard Davis; Dr. Lisa Bennett, Associate Medical Examiner
LOCATION OF INCIDENT	9 Mott Street

DECEDENT'S NAME _____

WITNESSES

NAME	RACE	GENDER
No eyewitnesses known.		

INCIDENT

INITIAL SCENE INFORMATION

At approx. 15:22 PM, October 13, 2011, Anthony Pellman, a general contractor, arrived at 9 Mott Street to inspect the building. Gut renovation work had ceased for 7 days due to contractual disputes and Pellman arrived to appraise the space before work was scheduled to resume October 14th. Upon entry Pellman was struck by a foul odor and after a search, located the decedent, believed to be female, in an obsolete freight elevator shaft. He dialed 911 to alert authorities.

Decedent was found by first responder, Officer Joseph Anderson, to be fully clothed, slim build, dark hair, lying on left side, approx. southeast to northeast orientation. Appearance of heavy bleeding wounds. Major cranial injury to left side of skull. Possible dislocation of left jaw and shoulder. Bloodstains under head and neck area indicate profuse bleeding. Pooling is dry, red to brown in color, measures approx 22" by 18" inches. Decedent appears to have fallen from a high elevation and bled out where found. Body displays lividity to left side facial area. Appears to have deceased at least 48 hours prior to discovery. Early signs of decomposition on face. Hands open, no evident defense wounds.

Decedent is wearing dark blue jeans and black T-shirt with an angel on the front. Bare feet, evident tattoo on top of right foot. No jewelry. No weapons found.

A pair of black boots and black socks believed to belong to decedent were located on the top floor of 9 Mott Street, seven stories above position of body. No immediate sign of foul play. Due to lack of functional stairs or lift, decedent is believed to have reached the shaft by entering the building via the skylight accessed from the roof of 203 Worth Street—the Hanging Gardens, a known squatters' residence and crack den.

MISSING / UNIDENTIFIED PERSON REPORT

PO 336-151 (Rev. 2-94)-ht

CERTIFICATION ON REAR TO BE COMPLETED AFTER DETACHING

TEAR OFF

TYPE OF CASE	JURISDICTION / REPORTING AGENCY
☒ MISSING ☐ UNIDENTIFIED	Shandaken

Time and Date of This Report	TIME	DATE
	22.04	9.30.11

CASE #	OFFICER ON DUTY	TELEPHONE
12-388	HELMS	845-555-9022

LAST NAME	FIRST	OTHER	
CORDOVA	ASHLEY	BRETT	

AGE	Time and Date Missing Since	TIME	DATE
24		8:12 A.M.	9.30.11

SEX	RACE	HEIGHT	WEIGHT	EYE COLOR	HAIR COLOR/ LENGTH	BLOOD TYPE
F	CAUC	5' 9"	117	GRAY	DRK BRN.LONG	UNKNOWN

LOCATION LAST SEEN	PROBABLE DESTINATION
9.29.11, 11:10 P.M. ROOM MH-314, BRIARWOOD HOSPITAL	UNKNOWN

VEHICLE INVOLVED ☐ YES ☐ NO IF YES:	UNKNOWN	SS # 438-38-2219	DL 79-894 791

LICENSE #	MAKE / COLOR	YEAR

FINGERPRINT CLASS (if known)

MARKS / SCARS / TATTOOS   Color tattoo on right foot and ankle of horse/goat creature shows only the head and front legs. Back half missing. Burn scar on top of left hand.

VISIBLE DENTAL WORK ___ None

GLASSES / CONTACTS ☐ YES ☒ NO IF YES:	FRAME TYPE	PRESCRIPTION

CLOTHING DESCRIPTION   Subject last seen wearing white cotton pajamas.

WAIST SIZE ___20 in.___   SHOE SIZE ___8___   JEWELRY DESCRIPTION ___None___

SUSPICIOUS CIRCUMSTANCES / FOUL PLAY   Unknown

ADDITIONAL CIRCUMSTANCES / INFO   Subject seen on surveillance video leaving clinic grounds with unidentified Caucasian male.

UPON COMPLETION, PLEASE RETURN TO: SHANDAKEN POLICE DEPARTMENT - ULSTER COUNTY 64 NEW YORK 42 SHANDAKEN, NY 12480
ATTENTION: SPECIAL FEATURES - MISSING PERSONS UNIT

7

"*WHO IS ZIS?*"

The woman's voice—thick, with a Russian accent—came out scratchy over the intercom.

"Scott McGrath," I repeated, leaning toward the tiny black camera above the door buzzers. "I'm a friend of Wolfgang's. He's expecting me."

It was a lie. This morning, after reading through Ashley Cordova's NYPD file, I'd spent the last three hours trying to track down Wolfgang Beckman: film scholar, professor, rabid Cordovite, and author of six books on cinema, including the popular tome on horror movies *American Mask.*

I'd tried his office in Columbia's Dodge Hall, got his class schedule from the office, only to learn he was teaching just one class this semester, "Horror Topics in American Cinema," Tuesday nights at seven. I'd called his office and cell but they clicked to voicemail, and given our *last* encounter more than a year ago—when he'd not only told me he hoped I rotted in hell, but had taken two wild, vodka-induced swings at me—I knew he'd sooner call back the pope. (There were two things Beckman truly loathed in life: sitting in the first three rows of a movie theater and the Catholic Church.) My last resort was to show up *here,* a run-down building on Riverside Drive and West Eighty-third, where I'd spent many an evening listening to him lecture in his mole burrow of an apartment, joined by his fleet of cats and a crowd of students who drank in his every word like kittens lapping up cream.

To my surprise, there was a scratch and a loud buzzing, letting me inside.

When I knocked on the door marked in tarnished numbers, 506, a tiny woman answered. She had cropped black hair that sat on her head like a cap on a pen. She was Beckman's latest housekeeper. Ever since his beloved wife, Véra, had died years ago from cancer, Beckman, totally unable to take care of himself, hired a multitude of petite Russian women to do it for him.

They were uniformly short, severe, and middle-aged, with blue eyes, chapped hands, hair dyed the color of artificial candy, and Bolshevik *Don't even sink about it* personalities. Two years ago, it was Mila, in stonewashed jeans and rhinestone T-shirts, who spoke relentlessly of a son back in Belarus. (And when she wasn't talking about Sergio, most of what she said could be summed up with a single word: *nyet.*)

This one had a hawk-beak nose, wore pink dishwashing gloves and a long black rubber apron, the kind welders in factories wear for forging steel. She appeared to be wearing it to mop Beckman's kitchen.

"He's expecting *you?*" She inspected me from head to toe. "He's at *denteest.*"

"He asked me to come in and wait."

She squinted, skeptical, but shoved the door aside.

"You like *tea?*" she demanded.

"Thank you."

With a final look of disapproval, she disappeared into the kitchen and I stepped down the hall into the living room.

The place hadn't changed. It was still dark and morose, smelling of dirty socks, festering humidity, and *cat.* Faded fleur-de-lis wallpaper, the ceiling sagging like the underside of a sofa—at Beckman's, one always had the persistent feeling water was about to come seeping up through the wood floors. Never had I been inside an apartment so *scrubbed* (Beckman's housekeeper was always armed with mop and bucket, cans of Lysol, Clorox wipes) that still felt so insistently like a bog deep in the Everglades.

I strolled to the mantel, framed pictures lined up along its edge. They, too, hadn't changed. There was a color photo of Véra on her wedding day, beaming with joy. Next to her was a signed photograph of Marlowe Hughes, the legendary beauty and Cordova's second wife, star of *Lovechild.* Beside this was a picture of Beckman's son, Marvin, the day he graduated from law school; he looked shockingly normal. Next to him: a still from Cordova's *Thumbscrew,* when Emily Jackson eyes her husband's mysterious briefcase; a photo of Beckman, Indian-style, enthroned like a gleeful Buddha on Columbia's Low Library steps, surrounded by fifty worshipful students.

Hanging to the right of the mantel was the framed poster of the wrinkled and creased close-up of the Cordovite's eye. The poster had been here as long as I'd known Beckman. He'd torn it off a Pigalle Métro station wall after attending a red-band screening for Cordova's *At Night All Birds Are Black,* held back in 1987 in the Parisian catacombs, one of the first events of its kind. Scribbled along the bottom by hand was the designated meeting spot: *Sovereign Deadly Perfect N 48° 48′ 21.8594″ E 2° 18′ 33.3888″ 1111870300.*

A few feet to my right, in the corner, was a wooden desk and Beckman's old Apple computer. It was humming, which meant it was actually *on.*

"Your tea."

The housekeeper had materialized behind me. She slid the tray across the coffee table, glaring at me as she shoved aside a black Chinese wooden box and piles of newspapers, then stalked back into the kitchen.

I waited for her to resume cleaning, then tapped the keyboard. I wasn't exactly *proud* of myself, snooping on an innocent man's computer, but desperate times called for desperate measures.

I clicked onto Firefox, then *View History.*

Oral surgery complications—Google search
Tooth extractions what can go wrong—Google search
Potential side effects from novocaine—Google search
The New Republic online
The New York Post
Russian Soulmates.ru
Russian phrasebook
Ashley Cordova—Google search
Ashley Cordova, 24, Found Dead—nytimes.com

The next entry read simply: *blackboards.onion.*

I clicked on the link. The site took a moment to load, the home page featuring a fog-drenched forest, which I recognized as the opening shot of Cordova's *Wait for Me Here.* The URL was long, yet buried within the string of symbols and punctuation were three key words: *sovereign deadly perfect.*

It was the Blackboards, the Deepnet website for Cordova fans. Entry was fiercely guarded, for authorized Cordovites only. The site had a secret URL on Tor, the anonymous Internet—so it never appeared on Google and couldn't be spotted by standard browsers. Years ago, when we'd first met, I'd tried bribing Beckman for the URL to no avail. He said it was "the last hidden corner," a black hole where fans could not only hash over all things Cordova, but express their every dark urge and dream without judgment.

I heard keys jangling, the front door banging open. A mop clattered to the floor. *Madame Tolstoy had to be alerting Beckman he had a guest.*

I pulled out my BlackBerry, took a quick photo of the URL, and clicked the browser closed, stepping back to the mantel just as I heard footsteps racing down the wood floors.

"*Cocksucker,*" a voice bellowed behind me.

Beckman appeared in the doorway. He was wearing a tightly belted trench coat, which gave him the appearance of a potato tucked into parcel paper.

"Get out."

"Hold *on*—"

"The last time we spoke I made it *quite clear* you were dead to me. *Olga!* Call the police and tell them we have a dangerous intruder."

"I'd like to patch things up."

"One cannot *patch* a friendship that's been *blown* to smithereens."

"You're being ridiculous."

He glared at me. "Betrayal isn't ridiculous. It's the reason empires fall." He unbelted his trench coat, threw it over the chair—a dramatic gesture reminiscent of a Spanish matador tossing away his red cape—and strode toward me. Thankfully, he didn't notice his computer, the corner bright from the lit-up screen.

As *livid* as he was, it was impossible for Beckman to be physically intimidating. He was wearing gray dress slacks too short in the leg and round gold eyeglasses, behind which his small, kind eyes blinked like a chipmunk's. He also had a gung-ho hairline. It couldn't *wait* to get started, beginning an overeager two inches above his eyebrows. His right cheek was badly swollen as if stuffed with cotton balls.

"I want to talk to you about Ashley," I said.

The name jolted him as if he'd been shocked by a live wire. He muttered something under his breath and moved over to an armchair, sitting with a faint whoopee-cushion wheeze. He removed his shoes, propping his feet—sporting bright yellow argyle socks—on the leather ottoman in front of him.

"*Ash Cordova,*" he repeated, rubbing the slackened, novocained side of his face. He turned, barking over his shoulder, "*Olga!*"

She appeared in the doorway on the phone, seemingly with the police.

"For God's sake, Olga, *what're* you—put the phone down. My *God.* This is my dear friend McGrath. Could you bring him something besides *tea?* Tea doesn't make a *dent* in the man." He looked at me. "Still drinking heavily in daylight?"

"Of course."

"Glad you've retained your personality's best quality. Bring the premium vodka, would you?"

Olga disappeared, and I sat down on the couch. Beckman still hadn't noticed the glowing computer screen, diverted by the three cats that had just materialized from wherever they'd been hiding. There were eight in the apartment, some very exotic Eastern breed with blue eyes, black faces, fur like shag carpeting, and irritating Greta Garbo personalities, deigning to make public appearances *only* when Beckman was present.

He bent down to stroke one as it rubbed the ottoman.

"Which one is that?" I asked, feigning interest because there was a direct ratio between your interest in Beckman's cats and his good mood.

"McGrath, you've met him on *countless* occasions. This is One-Eyed Pontiac. *Not* to be confused with Peeping Tom or Boris the Burglar's Son." He arched an eyebrow. "I just got another kitten, you know. Found another trademark. It's quite embarrassing I missed it."

"*Nine cats?* They can send you to prison for that."

He pushed his glasses back on his nose. "I'm calling him Murad, after the cigarettes."

"Never heard of them."

"They're an obsolete Turkish brand, popular in the 1910s and '20s. *Murad* means 'desire' in Arabic. The *only* brand that ever appears in a Cordova film is *Murad.* There's not one Marlboro, Camel, or Virginia Slim. It goes further. *If* the Murad cigarette is *focused upon* by the camera in any Cordova film, the very *next* person who appears onscreen has been devastatingly *targeted.* In other words, the gods will have drawn a great big *X* across his shoulder blades and taped an invisible sign there that reads FUCKED. His life will henceforth never be the same."

Murad. Every one of Beckman's cats was named after some very specific detail in Cordova's films, a trademark or silent signature. They ranged from split-second walk-on roles (similar to Hitchcock's cameos) to tiny props within the mise-en-scène that symbolized looming devastation (much as the appearance of an orange in *The Godfather* films foreshadowed death). Most weren't obvious but extremely obscure, like One-Eyed Pontiac and Boris the Burglar's Son.

I slid forward to sip my tea, stealing another glance at the computer, *still shining*. Beckman rolled up his sleeves and, frowning, seemed on the verge of following my gaze.

"What have you heard about Ashley?" I asked.

His face darkened. "Tragic." He took a deep breath, settling back into the armchair. "You remember Véra and I saw her perform years ago. Weill Recital Hall. A stunning experience. The concert was to begin at eight. Everyone was waiting. It was eight, eight-ten, eight-*twenty*. A bearded man stepped onto the stage and nervously announced, 'The concert will begin shortly. Please be patient.' The minutes trickled by. Eight-thirty, *forty*. Was she *going* to arrive? People were getting angry. 'With what we paid for *tickets*?' Naturally, *I'm* looking around to see if her father showed up. A lone figure in the back, army fatigues, gray hair, the all-seeing expression, and his usual round black glasses turning his eyes to dead black *coins*."

Beckman, eyes wide, actually turned to the empty doorway as if he hoped to see Cordova there. He turned back, sighing.

"*He was a no-show*. Suddenly, this child in black tights, bright red taffeta dress enters fast through a stage door. We thought she was going to make an announcement. 'The concert is canceled.' Instead, she hurries over to the Steinway, sits without taking the slightest interest in us. She sweeps her hands back and forth along the keys like a master chef dusting off a cutting board. Then she begins, without waiting for the audience to stop talking. It was Ravel's *Jeux d'eau*."

Olga was now at the coffee table, pouring chilled vodka from a black bottle painted with crude Russian letters. Beckman and I clinked glasses and drank. It was some of the best vodka I'd ever tasted: crisp and light, dancing down your throat.

"The notes weren't played," he went on. "They were *poured* from a Grecian *urn*. People went from indignation to shock to dazed worship. None of us could believe a mere *child* could play in such a way. The dark depths to which she had to descend . . . *alone*."

"The police are saying suicide," I said.

He looked pensive. "It's possible. There was something about her playing . . . a knowledge of darkness in the most extreme form." He frowned. "But it's quite common, isn't it? What you tend to find in the personal lives of brilliant men is devastation akin to a nuclear bomb going off. Marriages mangled. Wives left for dead. Children growing up as deformed prisoners of war—all of them walking around with holes where their hearts should be, wondering where they belong, what side they're fighting for. Extreme wealth, like the kind Cordova married into, only magnifies the size and scope of the fallout. Perhaps that's how it was for Ash."

"*Ash?*"

"It's what they called her in the musical world. Ash DeRouin. The ashes from ruins. She was thirteen. But she played like someone who'd lived six lifetimes. Six births. Six deaths. And all the sadness, love, and yearning grasped at and lost in between." He frowned, his thick eyebrows twitching together. "*That* level of skill and feeling, compounded with the fact she was, without doubt, the most beautiful living child I'd ever seen. When we were leaving the concert hall, Véra, wiping away her tears, said she couldn't be human. She meant that without exaggeration."

"Do you know anything about her childhood?" I asked, pouring more vodka. "What she was like? You remember that anonymous phone call."

He eyed me skeptically. "You mean, your mystery caller, *John?*"

I nodded.

"You know I never believed in John. You were the victim of a prank. Someone pulled your leg. What would Cordova want with children's clothes? On the *other* hand. A girl surrounded by daisies, Shetland ponies, and doting parents named Joanie and Phil could not play music in such a fashion. There *is some* dark cloud hanging over the family, I give you *that*. But covering what, how dense—if it's simply smog, a category-five hurricane, or a black hole out of which no light has ever escaped—I don't know."

"Have you ever heard that Ashley had mental health problems? She was admitted to a clinic upstate in late August called Briarwood."

He looked puzzled. "No."

"She escaped the grounds with an unidentified male and died in the warehouse ten days later. Have you heard any rumors on the Blackboards?"

"Good God, McGrath, the *Blackboards*?" Chuckling, he flung back his vodka, slapping the glass on the table. "I stopped logging on to that site years ago. I'm too old for such histrionics."

This phony demurring was everything I expected from Beckman. Questioning him was always a rain dance around a campfire, requiring a delicate touch and three or four bottles of this *vodka*, which was more potent than opium and doubtless had origins in some Siberian bathtub.

"Where do you think Cordova is now?" I asked him.

He raised an eyebrow. "Don't tell me you're back in your little motorboat, traveling alone up the Amazon. Is it revenge this time, because you ruined your career over him, or just nagging curiosity?"

"A little of both. I want the truth."

"Ah, the *truth*." Beckman's eyes fell onto the black hexagonal box on the coffee table. He was about to say something, but instead turned around and stared directly at his computer. The screen was still lit, and one of those goddamn cats—One-Eyed Pontiac, whatever the hell its name was—was rubbing against the legs of the desk.

He sat up in alarm. *"Olga!"* he bellowed. "Bring a plate of those Spanish sardines, would you? Boris has low blood sugar." He turned back, his eyes blinking rapidly behind his glasses. "You know, I did hear something recently you might find helpful. *Peg Martin.*"

"Peg Martin?"

"She had a small role in the first twenty minutes of *Isolate 3*. Plays one of the custodians at the Manhattan law firm. That very gawky girl with her arm in a cast. Frizzy red hair. Flat nose. She disappears down the stairwell and never comes back. She did the *Sneak* magazine interview in the mid-nineties and talked about Cordova."

I remembered. Five years ago, I'd dug up the article in my research.

"One of my students this semester has a terrier. She takes him to group obedience school in Washington Square Park, Sunday evenings at six. She told me, toward the end of the hour class, a wiry redhead enters the dog run with an ancient black Labrador and they sit shoulder to shoulder on a bench, watching the others wrestle and romp and play and laugh." Beckman was sitting on the edge of his chair, playing the part of Peg Martin. "She speaks to . . . no one. Looks at . . . *no one.* Neither does the dog. Well. My student told me *that* woman is Peg Martin."

"So?"

"So go down there. Talk to her. She might know something about the family. She was a junkie for fifteen years, so she might not be as steadfast as the others about remaining silent." He frowned. "I'd also go through that 1977 *Rolling Stone* article. Cordova's last interview before he plunged underground. I've heard there's something crucial in there. I've looked through it, couldn't find a thing. Maybe you can."

"And Cordova? Where is he?"

Beckman drained his glass. "Hiding, probably. I imagine he's brokenhearted. It's funny to consider, given the horrors of his work. But I've always suspected the dark was there to reveal the light. He saw the mental suffering of people and hoped his films might be a refuge. His characters are ravaged, beaten. They walk through infernos and emerge charred doves. The fact that people don't learn these days, that they're weak, petty, so apathetic about this gift of life as if it were all a mere Pepsi commercial—I don't blame him for going underground. Have you *seen* the world lately, McGrath? The cruelty, the lack of connection? If you're an artist, I'm sure you can't help but wonder what it's all for. We're living longer, we social network alone with our *screens,* and our depth of feeling gets shallower. Soon it'll be nothing but a tide pool, then a thimble of water, then a *micro drop.* They say in the next twenty years we're going to merge with computer chips to cure aging and become immortal. Who wants an eternity of being a *machine?* No wonder Cordova hides." Abruptly he fell silent, looking rather deflated in his chair.

The computer had at last gone dark. I checked my watch. It was after six. I had to get going.

"Thanks for the vodka," I said. "I also want to formally apologize."

Beckman said nothing, distracted by some gloomy thought, though after a moment his bright eyes again fell on the black Chinese box on the table. He reached forward, testing the lid with an index finger—but of course it would not open.

"Surprised you didn't try to crack it open while I was out," he muttered.

"I do have *some* scruples."

He raised a quizzical eyebrow.

Humoring him, I reached over and picked up the box—it was in the shape of a hexagon, quite heavy. I shook it, immediately recognizing the infamous *dry thuds* clunking inside. I didn't know what they were— *no one did,* except the unidentified person who'd locked them in there.

Beckman had purchased the locked box from a black-market memorabilia dealer. It was allegedly a prop stolen from Cordova's film set *Wait for Me Here.* In the film, it's a personal possession of the serial killer, Boyd Reinhart. Though the audience never learns what's locked inside, it's supposed to hold the object that caused him to kill, something that had mentally broken him as a boy. Yet, according to the collectibles dealer, due to a problem with the provenance documentation, there was a possibility that the box hadn't come from the film set at all, but had been stolen from the FBI evidence files for Hugh Thistleton, the copycat killer who'd mimicked Boyd Reinhart from his way of murdering down to his flamboyant clothing.

Beckman loved showing the box to people, letting them pass it around. "There it is," he'd say reverentially. "The box represents the mysterious threshold between reality and make-believe. Is it Reinhart's? Is it Thistleton's? Or is it *yours?* Because every one of us has our box, a dark chamber stowing the thing that lanced our heart. It contains what you do everything for, *strive* for, *wound* everything around you. And if it were opened, would anything be set free? *No.* For the impenetrable prison with the impossible lock is your own head."

The last time I was here, when Beckman disappeared into the kitchen for another bottle of vodka, I—quite bombed and egged on by one of his attractive female students—had the brilliant idea of jimmying the lock with a penknife to find out what was inside, once and for all.

The tarnished brass lock didn't budge.

Beckman had caught me in the act. He'd thrown me out, shouting, *"Traitor!"* and *"Philistine!"* His final words to me before slamming the door in my face were: "You couldn't even see where it opened."

Olga was carrying in two platters piled with sardines—enough food for the entire otter exhibit at SeaWorld. She set them down on the faded carpet, the cats sniffing them.

"The problem with *you*, McGrath," said Beckman, draining the bottle into our glasses, "is that you've no respect for *murk*. For the blackly unexplained. The un-nail-downable. You journalists bulldoze life's mysteries, ignorant of what you're so ruthlessly turning up, that you're mining for something quite powerful that"—he sat back in his chair, his dark eyes meeting mine—"does *not* want to be found. And it will not."

He was talking about Cordova.

"Anyway," he added softly, "a man's ghoulish shadow is not the man."

I nodded and held up my glass. "To the murk."

We clinked and drank. I stood up, bowed deeply at Beckman—he had a soft spot for royal treatment—and stepped past him. He said nothing, slumped helplessly in his chair, trapped in the avalanche of his thoughts.

As I rode down to the lobby, I found myself not only guilty over what I'd done, browsing so brazenly on his computer, but also regretting the direction of the conversation. Thanks to that vodka, I'd been a little *too* candid. Beckman would have no doubt now that I was back on the trail, after Cordova once again, and I had no idea what he'd do with that information.

I checked the photo I'd taken of his computer screen and couldn't believe my luck. The picture was blurry, but I could still make out the convoluted URL. In all the years I'd known Beckman, it was the most useful piece of information I'd ever extracted from the man.

I closed the photo and made a quick note in my calendar.

Peg Martin. Washington Square Park. Sunday at 6 P.M.

8 | THE GIRL IN THE FOUR SEASONS coat check was eating handfuls of colored jelly beans and reading a thin yellow paperback.

I'd read in the witness report in Ashley's police file that the coat-check girl's name was Nora Halliday and she was nineteen.

Every time a party of diners arrived—midwestern tourists, finance dudes, a couple so elderly they moved like they were doing a form of tai chi—she whisked off her black-rimmed eyeglasses, hid the book, and with a cheerful *"Good evening!"* took their coats. After they moved upstairs to the restaurant, she put her glasses back on, brought out the paperback, and started reading again, hunched over the counter of the stall.

I was watching her from the opposite side of the lobby on a seat by the stairs. I'd decided it was best to wait *here*, because I was slightly more bombed than I realized, thanks to the jet-fuel vodka back at Beckman's. At one point, she glanced curiously in my direction. No doubt assuming I was waiting for someone, she smiled and resumed reading her book.

According to the police report, she'd been working here only a few weeks. She was about 5'7" and scrawny as a question mark, with pale blond hair in a French twist—curls around her face channeling alfalfa. She wore a brown skirt and brown blouse too big for her—the restaurant's uniform—visible shoulder pads sitting unevenly on her frame.

At last, I stood up and walked over to her. She closed the book, turning it facedown on the counter, though *not* before I glimpsed the title.

Hedda Gabler by Henrik Ibsen.

A tragic play featuring what was widely believed to be the most neurotic female protagonist in all of Western literature.

I had my work cut out for me.

"Good evening, sir," she said brightly, removing her glasses, revealing big blue eyes and delicate features that would have made her an "it girl" about four hundred years ago. But this being the era of fish pouts and spray-on tans, she was *pretty,* certainly, but old-fashioned—a turn-of-the-century Twiggy. She was wearing harsh pink lipstick, which didn't look like it'd been applied in good light or within two feet of a mirror.

She *did* look *friendly,* however. And easy enough to get talking.

She grabbed one of the silver hangers off the rack and held out her hand for my coat.

"I'm not checking it," I said. "You must be Nora Halliday?"

"I am."

"Nice to meet you. Scott McGrath." I removed my business card from my wallet, handing it to her. "I was hoping we might chat, at your convenience."

"Chat about what?" She squinted at the card.

"Ashley Cordova. I understand you were the last person to see her alive."

She glanced back at me. "You're police?"

"No. I'm an investigative reporter."

"What are you *investigating*?"

"I've done cover-ups, international drug cartels. I've been getting some background on Ashley. I'm interested in your perspective. Did she say anything at all to you?"

Biting her bottom lip, she set my business card down on the stall door and carefully shook multicolored jelly beans into her hand from a bag that contained about four kilos of them. She shoved the pile into her mouth, chewing with her lips clamped closed.

"Everything you tell me can be off the record," I added.

She covered her mouth with her hand.

"Have you been drinking?" she asked.

"No."

She seemed to take issue with this, swallowing with a gulp. "Are you dining with us this evening, sir?"

"No."

"Are you meeting someone at the bar?"

"Probably not."

"Then I'm going to have to ask you to leave."

I stared at her. She was *definitely not* from New York. This one screamed *Recent grad of Ohio State with a degree in the dramatic arts.* Something told me she'd probably played a Pink Lady in some abysmal production of *Grease* and when someone asked her who she was, she said *I'm an actor* in the same breathy voice I'd seen people in AA announce *I'm an alcoholic.* Girls like her moved here by the truckload, hoping to be discovered and to meet Mr. Big but too often ended up in bars in Murray Hill wearing black dresses from Banana Republic, Band-Aids over the blisters on their heels. They'd get their *I'll Take Manhattan* taken off them soon enough. To live in this city for any extended period of time required masochism, moral flexibility, skin like an alligator's, and mad jack-in-the-box resilience—none of which these faux-confident twenty-very-*littles* could even *begin* to wrap their heads around. Within five years she'd be running home to her parents, a boyfriend named Wayne, and a job at her old high school, teaching movement.

"If you continue to loiter I'm going to call my manager. Carl will be happy to address any complaints or requests."

I took a deep breath. "Miss *Halliday*," I said, taking a small step toward her so I could see her pink lipstick had skidded off her upper lip. "A young woman was found dead. *You* were the last person to see her alive. The Cordova family knows this. A *lot* of people know this. The NYPD isn't keeping your name anonymous. People are wondering what you did and what you said to her, which caused her to end up dead hours later. I'm not jumping to conclusions. I just want to hear your side."

She stared back at me, then plucked the phone off the wall behind her, dialing a three-digit number.

"It's Nora. Could you come down? There's a man here, and he's . . ." She blatantly stared at me. "Mid-fifties."

It *wasn't* the reaction I'd hoped for. I exited the lobby swiftly. Outside under the awning I looked back. Little Miss Streep had put her glasses back on and was leaning over the door of the stall, observing me.

A man in a blue suit hastily appeared from upstairs—*Carl to the rescue,* I assumed—so I turned and headed back to Park Avenue.

That hadn't gone well. I was rusty.

I checked my watch. It was after eight o'clock, cold, the night sky streaked with clouds that whitened and dissolved like breaths against glass.

I might be a little *off my game,* but I wasn't going home.

Not yet.

9 | Fifteen minutes later, I was in a taxi, cruising through Chinatown, past the shabby walk-ups and restaurants, dirty signs advertising BACK FOOT RUB and THE PEOPLE'S PHARMACY, awnings jumbled with English and Chinese. Men in dark jackets hurried past storefronts lit up in lethal colors—cough-syrup crimson, absinthe green, jaundiced yellow, all of it bleeding together in the crooked streets. The neighborhood felt thriving yet empty, as if the area had just been quarantined.

We passed a brick church—TRANSFIGURATION CHURCH, read the sign.

"Right here," I told the driver.

I paid him and climbed out, gazing up at the building. It was a seven-story derelict mess with peeling white paint, construction scaffolding, every window boarded up. It was the warehouse where Ashley Cordova had been found dead. Flowers and handmade cards were piled around the front entrance.

There were bouquets of roses and carnations, lilies and candles, pictures of the Virgin Mary. *Rest in peace, Ashley. God bless you. YOUR MUSIC WILL LIVE ON FOREVER. Now you're in a better place.* It was always surprising to me how ferociously the public mourned a beautiful stranger—especially one from a famous family. Into that empty form they could unload the grief and regret of their own lives, be rid of it, feel lucky and light for a few days, comforted by the thought, *At least that wasn't me.*

I gently moved aside some of the flowers to reach the steel door. It was secured with two padlocks, CAUTION and DANGER signs. The PO-LICE LINE DO NOT CROSS tape remained intact.

Behind me, a maroon sedan with a loud muffler cruised past, the dark silhouette of the driver hunched low. I stepped back, staying hidden in the shadows of the scaffolding as it coasted to the end of Mott, made a left, and the street went silent again.

Yet I had the unmistakable feeling that someone else was present—or had just been here.

I zipped up my jacket, and after surveying the sidewalk—deserted, except for an Asian kid darting into a store called Chinatown Fair—I turned and walked to the end of Mott where it intersected Worth. I rounded the sharp right, passing a red awning reading COSMETIC DEN-TISTRY, a dented chain-link fence spanning an empty dark lot. When I reached the next building, a mangy walk-up, and the one after that, 197 Worth, I knew I'd gone too far.

I backtracked, noticing that by the dentist's office there was a hole cut in the wire fence. I made my way over, crouching down. A tiny black rag had been tied there—clearly to mark some kind of entrance. I could make out a narrow dirt path that twisted deep into the lot, leading toward an abandoned building.

That had to be it. *The Hanging Gardens,* Falcone had called it—*a known squatters' residence and crack den,* according to the incident summary in Ashley's file. Police had concluded Ashley entered 9 Mott from *here,* a building at 203 Worth, then climbed up a flight of stairs all the way to the roof, entering the adjacent Mott Street building from a skylight. Though the police's canvass of the area turned up no witnesses and none of her personal belongings, this meant nothing. Detectives were notoriously lazy when they concluded early in a case that the death had been a suicide—often overlooking crucial details that told an entirely *different* story.

That was the reason why *I* was here.

I ducked through the opening, the rancid smell of garbage overpowering, unseen animals scurrying away as I made my way along the path. It was probably just New York's mascot: *the cat-sized rat.* As my eyes adjusted to the dark, I could see the crumbling brick exterior of the building, a door to my left. I stepped toward it, tripping on an old bicycle, some plastic bottles, and pulled it open.

It was a large warehouse, dim light trickling in from somewhere illuminating walls covered with indecipherable graffiti. The place was putrid and filled with *junk,* newspapers and cans, Sheetrock and insulation, sweatshirts and boxes, pots and pans. Squatters had clearly been living here—though they appeared to have vacated, probably from the recent police presence. I stepped inside, letting the heavy door screech closed behind me.

Now that Beckman's deadly vodka had worn off, I realized how unwise this was, coming here without so much as the switchblade I used on my Central Park jogs. I hadn't even thought to bring a flashlight. I took a deep breath—ignoring the voice in my head reminding me, *Didn't we just establish you were off your game?*—and headed to the back in search of some stairs.

They were corroded. I grabbed the railing to see if I could pry the structure off the wall, but the bolts were surprisingly sturdy.

I started up, the metallic echoes of my footsteps jarring. I paused every now and then to look around, make sure I was alone, taking a few snapshots with my BlackBerry. With my every step, the old building seemed to growl and cough, protesting my scaling its rusted spine. *This was where Ashley had climbed.* If her intention had been to commit suicide—a conclusion I didn't accept as gospel, no matter what Falcone said—*why had she come here, to this derelict place?*

I passed the sixth floor and then climbed the final, steepest flight into a claustrophobic attic space, a stained futon slung across the floor. Where the sloping ceiling met the wall, there was a square hatch. I heaved my shoulder against it, the door gave way with a gasp, and I hoisted myself outside.

It was a deserted rooftop, a mangled sofa in the far corner. Landscaping the view was lower Manhattan's bristled bed of skyscrapers: blunt stumps of low-income housing, fat municipal building boulders, water towers sprouting like buds of black thistle—all of it fighting for a piece of the night sky.

The back of 9 Mott Street abutted this building, the space between them only a foot wide but cutting straight down to the street. I stepped onto the low wall ringing the roof's perimeter, and after making the mistake of *looking down*—if I fell, I'd die lodged like human parsley between brick teeth—I jumped onto the adjacent roof.

I made my way around a massive water tower—and there was the skylight. It was a rectangular pyramid, most of the glass missing. I walked over to it and, crouching down, looked through one of the shattered casements.

About twelve feet below me was a dark floor. Farther to my left, I could see directly into the empty shaft of a freight elevator, which extended seven stories below, the concrete brightly lit at the very bottom. It was like gazing down a throat, a corridor between two dimensions. The fall looked to be about a hundred feet. Even from this high angle, I could make out patches of rusty stains on the floor. *Ashley's blood.*

She'd allegedly climbed in through this skylight, removed her boots and socks, and stepped to the elevator's ledge. It must have been so fast, wind in her ears, her dark hair protesting in her face—and then nothing.

Falcone was absolutely right. The skylight's blown-out metal casements were so narrow, it would've been hard to force Ashley down there against her will. Hard, but not *impossible.*

I stood up, inspecting the ground. There was no evidence, no cigarette butts or scraps, no debris of any kind. I was about to leave, heading back to the Hanging Gardens, when suddenly something moved,
far below at the bottom of the elevator shaft.

A shadow had just swept across the floor.

I waited, wondering if I'd imagined it, staring at that empty, lit-up
space.

But then, *again,* a silhouette slowly slid into view.

Someone was standing in the mouth of the elevator, his shadow
tossed in front of him. He remained there for a minute, immobile, and
then stepped all the way inside.

I spotted dirty-blond hair, a gray overcoat. *He had to be a detective,
back to inspect the scene.* He ducked down, ostensibly to study the
blood patterns on the concrete. Then, to my surprise, he actually *sat
down* in the corner, propping his elbows on his knees.

He didn't move for some time.

I leaned forward to get a better view, dislodging a shard of glass. It
fell, smashing to the landing just below.

Startled, he looked up, then scrambled out of sight.

I lurched to my feet and took off across the roof.

He couldn't be a detective. No detective I knew—with the exception
of Sharon Falcone—moved *that* quickly.

10 I RACED AROUND THE CORNER back to 9 Mott Street, fully
expecting to find the entrance unsealed.

But the police tape remained intact, the door still padlocked.

How had he gotten in? *And who the hell was it? A Cordovite? Some
death-scene gawker?* I checked the windows—every one nailed shut.
The only other possibility was a narrow alleyway blocked with mountains of garbage. I pushed some of it aside, trying not to inhale, squeezing through. Sure enough, in the very back was an open window casting
light on the opposite wall.

Whoever he was, he'd used a crowbar—lying on the ground—to pry
away the old boards, leaving a space just wide enough to crawl through.

I stepped over, looking inside.

It was a brightly lit construction site, bare white neon bulbs dangling from an unfinished ceiling, plastic barrels and tarps piled by the front entrance. Hundreds of studs for building walls lined the expanse. Toward the back, on the right-hand side, a band of yellow POLICE LINE tape was strung across the elevator's entrance.

There was no sign of the man.

"Hello?" I called out.

Silence. The only noise was the insect buzz of the lights. I grabbed the crowbar—*just in case*—and scrambled through, falling into a pile of concrete bags.

It was a wide-open expanse. Along the back wall there was just a stack of metal beams and mixing barrels, a plastic tarp covering *something.*

I stepped cautiously toward it and yanked it aside.

It was a wheelbarrow.

"Anyone here?" I called out, looking around.

There was no answer, no movement.

The guy probably got scared off.

I stepped toward the police tape, was about to duck it, when suddenly a hand seized my shoulder and something hard hit me on the side of the head. I wheeled around but was shoved to the ground, dropping the crowbar.

My eyes went white, blinded, though I managed to make out a man staring down at me. He shoved his foot onto my chest.

"Who the fuck are you?" he shouted. It was a young voice, slurred with rage. Bending over me again, he reached out as if to grab my throat, though I wrenched free, pushing him off balance, grabbed the crowbar, and socked him with it in the shoulder.

It wouldn't exactly have made Muhammad Ali proud, but it worked. He tried to grab a metal stud for support, missed, and stumbled backward.

I staggered over to him. To my surprise, he was too wasted to stand. He reeked of booze and cigarettes, and he was just a *punk*—midtwenties, shaggy hair, dirty white Converse sneakers, a faded green T-shirt that read HAS-BEEN. His eyes were watery and bloodshot, seemingly unable to focus as they stared up at me.

"My turn," I said. "Who the fuck are *you*?"

He closed his eyes and appeared to pass out cold.

My first impulse was to strangle the kid. Touching the spot where he'd cracked me on the head, I could feel blood. He wasn't a cop, so that left random derelict or a Cordovite. *Or, he knew Ashley.*

I pulled his gray tweed coat out from under him, checking his pockets. There was a pack of Marlboros, three cigarettes left, a lighter, a set of apartment keys. I put them back. In the other, I pulled out an iPhone, the screen cracked, locked with a security code, the background a snapshot of a half-naked blonde.

I checked the inside pocket. It was empty. Yet, I felt *something else* and realized there was another compartment sewn into the ripped lining.

I reached inside, pulling out two tiny Ziploc bags. Both contained pills, one set yellow, the other green, letters and numbers stamped on the sides—oc 40 and 80. *OxyContin.*

So, he was a *drug dealer*—and pretty small-time, given the fact that he was snoozing through a body search. I returned the pills to the pocket and stood up.

"Can you hear me, Scarface?"

He didn't answer.

"Hands in the air. FBI raid!" I shouted.

Nothing.

As gently as I could—though I don't know *why* I bothered; he'd siesta through an apocalypse—I rolled him onto his side, removing his wallet from his back pocket. No driver's license, no credit cards, only *cash*—seven hundred and forty bucks, mostly twenties.

I put the money and wallet back, but zipped his iPhone into my own pocket. Then I stepped around him to inspect the elevator.

There was nothing there but the dark pools of dried blood, a few tendrils spreading into the cracks of the concrete.

I took a few shots and then moved back to the kid, checking his breathing. He appeared to be only *drunk*—not on anything else. I pushed him deeper onto his side, so he wouldn't suffocate if he got sick, and headed back to the window and climbed out, darting through the alley and back onto Mott Street.

I assumed I'd learn nothing more about him until tomorrow, when he discovered his phone missing. Yet during the cab ride home and even hours later, after I'd taken a shower, downed two Tylenol (given the immense pain from Beckman's vodka and getting cracked in the side of the head, I should have swiped an OxyContin)—the kid's phone was bombarded with texts.

> Where r u?

That was Chloe. She wrote again six minutes later.

> W8ting 2 hrs 4 u wtf ???

Then it was Reinking (I couldn't help but visualize *her*: Nordic, legs like ice picks):

> Johns out come over now

Two minutes later:

> I want u

Twelve minutes later:

> I'm so hot 4 u. U downstairs yet?

Then she appeared to *sext* a picture, which I couldn't open. It was followed with:

> Hello? Nothing??
> Fuck u

Then a text from Arden:

> U out? Come to jimmys

Interspersed with all of this, a highly obsessive girl named Jessica called eleven times. I let her go to voicemail.

Then Arden again:

It had to be his name. *Hopper.*

Small-time drug dealer in a faded coat, crouched in the corner of that freight elevator—he'd have something to tell me about Ashley, whoever he was.

11 "HELLO?" I ANSWERED. I heard plates clattering on the other end.

"Hey. You found my phone."

"So I did." I took a sip of my coffee.

"*Cool.* Where?"

"Backseat of a taxi. I'm in the West Village. You want to come pick it up?"

Twenty minutes later, my buzzer rang. I pulled aside the living-room curtains, the window affording a clear view of the front stoop. There he was, *Hopper:* wearing the same coat from last night, the same faded jeans and Converse sneakers. He was smoking a cigarette, his shoulders hunched against the cold.

When I opened the door for him, I realized in the stark light of day, even with the greasy hair, the brown eyes hollowed out from booze, *women*—who knew what else—he was a good-looking kid. I didn't know how I'd missed it before. It was as glaring as a silver silo piercing a cornfield horizon. He was about 5'10", a few inches shorter than me, slight, with a mangy scruff of beard and the raw, beautiful features of some brooding actor from the fifties, the ones who cry when drunk and die young.

"Hey." He smiled. "I'm here for my phone."

He clearly had *no* recollection of the previous night; he was looking at me as if he'd never seen me before.

"Right." I stepped aside to let him enter, and after sizing me up and apparently deciding I wasn't going to jump him, he shoved his hands in his coat pockets and came in. I closed the door, heading into the living room, indicating his phone on the coffee table.

"Thanks, man."

"Don't mention it. Now, what were you doing at that warehouse?"

He was startled.

"In Chinatown. Your name's Hopper, right?"

He opened his mouth to speak—but stopped himself, his eyes flitting past me to the door.

"I'm a reporter, looking into Ashley's death." I gestured toward the bookcase. "Some of my old cases are there, if you want to take a look."

With a doubtful glance, he stepped to the bookshelf, pulling out *Cocaine Carnivals*. " 'A page-turning tour de force,' " he read, " 'about the drug's billion-dollar business and the millions of mangled lives it sucks into its deadly machinery.' " He glanced at me. "Sounds *epic*."

He'd said it with sarcasm.

"I try."

"And now you're gonna write about Ashley."

"Depends on what I find. What do you know?"

"*Nothing*."

"What's your connection to her?"

"Don't have one."

"Then why'd you break into the warehouse where she died?"

He didn't answer, only returned the book to the shelf. After browsing a few other titles, he turned back, shoving his hands in his coat pockets.

"What magazine do you work for?" he asked.

"Myself. Anything you tell me can be off the record."

"Like attorney-client privilege."

"Absolutely."

He smirked skeptically at this, but then his face fell as he stared at me. It was a look I knew well. He was dying to talk, but he was trying to decide if he could trust me.

"Got some free time?" he asked quietly, rubbing his nose.

12 I FOLLOWED HOPPER up the stairs of a dingy Ludlow Street walk-up and into his apartment, #3B. Slinging his gray coat over a beach chair, he disappeared into a back bedroom—there didn't seem to be anything *in* there except a mattress on the floor— leaving me by the front door.

The place was tiny, with the woozy, stale air of a flophouse.

The sagging green couch along the far wall was covered with an old blue comforter where someone had recently crashed—maybe *literally*. In a plate on the coffee table there was an outbreak of cigarette butts; next to that, rolling papers, a packet of Golden Virginia tobacco, an open package of Chips Ahoy!, a mangled copy of *Interview*, some emaciated starlet on the cover. His green HAS-BEEN T-shirt from last night was flung on the floor along with a white sweatshirt and some other clothes. (As if to expressly *avoid* this pile, a woman's pair of black pantyhose clung for dear life to the back of the other beach chair.) A girl had kissed one wall while wearing black lipstick. An acoustic guitar was propped in the corner beside an old hiker's backpack, the faded red nylon covered with handwriting.

I stepped over to read some of it: *If this gets lost return it with all contents to Hopper C. Cole, 90 Todd Street, Mission, South Dakota 57555.*

Hopper Cole from South Dakota. He was a hell of a long way from home.

Scribbled above that, beside a woman named Jade's 310 phone number and a hand-drawn Egyptian eye, were the words: *"But now I smell the rain, and with it pain, and it's heading my way. Sometimes I grow so tired. But I know I've got one thing I got to do. Ramble on."*

So he was a Led Zeppelin fan.

Hopper emerged from the bedroom carrying a manila envelope. With a wary glance, he handed it to me.

It was addressed to: *HOPPER COLE, 165 LUDLOW STREET, 3B*—the address scribbled in all caps in black permanent marker. It had been stamped and mailed from New York, NY, on October 10 of this year. I recognized it as the last day Ashley Cordova had been seen alive by the girl in the Four Seasons coat check. The return address featured no name, reading simply *9 MOTT STREET*—the address of the warehouse where Ashley's body had been found.

Surprised, I looked at Hopper, but he said nothing, only watched me intently, as if it were some sort of test.

I pulled out what was inside. It was a stuffed monkey, old, with matted brown fur, stitching coming out of its eyes, a red felt mouth half gone, its neck limp, probably from some child's hand clamped around it. The whole thing was encrusted with dried red mud.

"What is it?" I asked.

"You've never seen it before?" he asked.

"*No*. Whose is it?"

"No clue." He moved away, yanking aside the blue comforter and sitting on the couch.

"Who sent it?"

"*She* did."

"Ashley."

He nodded and then, hunching forward, grabbed the package of rolling papers off the table, pulled one out.

"Why?" I asked.

"Some kinda sick joke."

"Then you *were* friends with her."

"Not exactly," he said, reaching across the table for his gray coat, fumbling in the pockets for the pack of Marlboros. "Not friends. More like *acquaintances*. But even that's a stretch."

"Where'd you meet her?"

He sat back down, tapping out a cigarette. "Camp."

"Camp?"

"Yeah."

"What *camp*?"

"Six Silver Lakes Wilderness Therapy in Utah." He glanced at me, brushing his hair out of his eyes as he began to dissect the cigarette, peeling the filter away from the paper. "You've *heard* of this first-class institution."

"No."

"Then you're missing out. If you have kids, I highly recommend it. Especially if you want your kid to grow up to be a great American maniac."

I didn't bother to hide my surprise. "You met Ashley there?"

He nodded.

"When?"

"I was seventeen. She was, like, *sixteen*. Summer of '03."

That made Hopper twenty-five.

"It's one of these juvenile therapy scams," he went on, sprinkling a pinch of the Golden Virginia tobacco along the rolling paper. "They advertise help for your troubled teen by staring at the stars and singing

'Kumbaya.' Instead, it's a bunch of bearded nutjobs left in charge of some of the craziest kids I've ever seen in my life—bulimics, nymphos, cutters trying to saw their wrists with the plastic spoons from lunch. You wouldn't believe the shit that went on." He shook his head. "Most of the kids had been so mentally screwed by their parents they needed more than twelve weeks of *wilderness*. They needed reincarnation. To *die* and just come back as a grasshopper, as a fucking *weed. That'd* be preferable to the agony they were in just by being alive."

He said this with such pissed-off defiance, I gathered he wasn't talking about any of the campers but about himself. I stepped around the white sweatshirt on the floor to one of the beach chairs—the one with pantyhose climbing up the back—and sat down.

"Who *knows* where they found the counselors," Hopper went on, tucking the filter into the end, leaning down to lick the paper. "Rikers Island, probably. There was this one fat Asian kid, Orlando? They *tortured* him. He was some kind of born-again Baptist, so he was always talking about Jesus. They made him go without eating. Kid had never gone ten minutes without a Twinkie in his life. He couldn't keep up, got *heat* stroke. *Still,* they kept telling him to find his inner strength, ask God for help. God was busy. Didn't have anything for him. The whole thing was *Lord of the Flies* on steroids. I still get nightmares."

"Why were you there?" I asked.

He sat back against the couch, amused. He stuck the hand-rolled cigarette into the side of his mouth, lighting it. He inhaled, wincing, and exhaled in a long stream of smoke.

"My uncle," he said, stretching his legs out. "I'd been traveling with my mom in South America for this missionary cult shit she was into. I ran the fuck away. My uncle lives in New Mexico. Hired some goon to track me down. I was crashing at a friend's in Atlanta. One morning I'm eating Cheerios. This brown *van* pulls up. If the Grim Reaper had wheels it'd be *this* thing. No windows except two in the back door, behind which you just knew some innocent kid had been kidnapped and, like, *decapitated.* Next thing I know I'm in the back with a male nurse." He shook his head. "If *that* dude was a licensed nurse, I'm a fucking congressman."

He paused to take another drag of his cigarette.

"They took me to base camp in Springdale. Zion National Park. You train there for two weeks with your fellow fucked-up campers, making Native American dream catchers and learning how to scrub a toilet with your spit—*real vital* life skills, you know. Then the group sets off on a ten-week trek through the wilderness, camping at six different lakes. With every lake you're supposed to be inching closer to God and self-worth, only the reality is you're inching closer to becoming a psychopath 'cuz of all the mind-fucking shit you've been exposed to."

"And Ashley was one of the campers," I said.

He nodded.

"Why was she there?"

"No *clue*. That was the big mystery. She didn't show up till the day we were setting out on the ten-week hike. The night before, counselors announced there was a last-minute arrival. Everyone was pissed because that meant whoever it was had been able to bypass basic training, which made *Full Metal Jacket* look like *Sesame Street*." He paused, shaking his head, then, eyeing me, he smiled faintly. "When we saw her though, we were down."

"Why?"

He gazed at the table. "She was *hot*."

He seemed on the verge of adding something, but instead leaned forward, ashing the cigarette.

"Who dropped her off?" I asked.

He looked up at me. "Don't know. Next morning, breakfast, she was just *there*. Sitting by herself at one of the picnic tables in the corner, eating a piece of cornbread. She was all packed and ready to go, red bandanna in her hair. The rest of us were totally disorganized. Running around like deranged chickens to get ready. Finally we left."

"And you introduced yourself," I suggested.

He shook his head, tapping the cigarette on a plate. "Nope. She kept to herself. Obviously, everyone knew who her father was and that she was the little girl from *To Breathe with Kings,* so people were all over her. But she iced everyone out, said nothing beyond yes, no." He shrugged. "It wasn't like she was *sulking*. She just wasn't into making friends. Pretty soon there was resentment, especially from the girls, about all the get-outta-jail-free cards she got from the counselors. Every night around the campfire *we* had to wax poetic about all the shit we'd done to end up there. Burglary. Suicide attempts. Drugs. The rap sheets of some of these kids, longer than *War and Peace*. Ash never had to say a *thing*. They'd skip over her, no explanation. The only clue was this ACE bandage on her hand, which she had when she first arrived. Couple of weeks into the hike she took it off and there was a bad burn mark. She never said what it was from."

I was surprised to hear this. *That* very burn mark, along with her foot tattoo, were mentioned in the missing-person's report as her only identifiable markings.

"Two days into the hike we made a bet," Hopper continued. "First kid to sustain a conversation with Ashley that lasted longer than fifteen minutes would get the two hits of ecstasy one of the kids from L.A., Joshua, had smuggled in taped into the hollow shoelace tip of his hiking boot." He tilted his head back, quickly exhaling smoke at the ceiling. "I decided to hold back, get my game together, let the others jihad themselves. And they did. Ashley blew them all off. One by one."

"Until you," I said.

It was easy to imagine: two gorgeous teenagers finding each other in the wilderness of adolescence, two orchids blooming in a desert.

"Just the *opposite,* actually," he said. "She blew *me* off, too."

I stared at him. "You're kidding."

He shook his head. "About a week after everyone else had crashed and burned, I made my move. Ashley always walked in the back, so I did. I asked where she was from. She said New York. After that it was just one-word replies and a nod. I struck out."

He stubbed the cigarette out on the coffee table and tossed it on top of the other butts, sitting back against the couch.

"Ashley didn't say anything to anyone for *ten weeks?*" I asked.

"Well, she *did*. But nothing more than the bare bones of conversation. Everyone broke down at some point, had their fifteen-minute Shawshank Redemption where they howled at the sky. The hiking, the counselors, voyeuristic fucks, they made you dredge up all this shit from your past. Everyone broke. Half of it was real and half of it was to get them off your back. Everyone took their Oscar-nominated turn, howling about parents, how all they wanted was to be *loved*. Except Ashley. She never cried, never complained. Not *once*."

"Did she ever mention her family?"

"No."

"What about her father?"

"Nothing. She was like the Sphinx. That's what we called her."

"So that was *it*?" I asked.

He shook his head, clearing his throat. "Three weeks into the hike, Orlando, the fat Asian kid, was a *mess*. He was so sunburned he had blisters all over his face, which the counselors dealt with by handing him a bottle of calamine lotion. Crusty pink shit all over his face, crying all the time, he looked like a leper. So one night Joshua slips him one of the pills of X, a *gift,* you know, to lift his spirits. He must have taken it when we started out the next morning, because at nine A.M. suddenly Orlando was out of his goddamn *mind,* hugging people, telling them they were beautiful, eyes dilated, shuffling his feet like he was John Travolta in a twist contest. At one point we lost him, had to backtrack, and found him twirling around a field, smiling at the sky. Hawk Feather, the head counselor, went apeshit."

"Hawk Feather?" I repeated.

He smirked. "The counselors insisted we address each other with Native American tribe names even though most of us were white, fat, and about as *of the earth* as a Big Mac. Hawk Feather, one a' these tightly wound Christian assholes, he hauled Orlando away, demanding to know what he was on and where he got the drugs. Orlando was so ripped all he did was laugh and say, 'It's just a little Tylenol,' over and over. 'It's just Tylenol.' "

I couldn't help but laugh. Hopper smiled, too, though the amusement quickly left his face.

"That night, everyone was scared shitless," he went on, brushing his hair out of his eyes. "We didn't want to know what Hawk Feather was gonna do to Orlando or the rest of us on his mission to find out who'd smuggled in the X. That night, Hawk Feather announces if someone doesn't come forward to explain who brought the ecstasy he was gonna make our lives hell. Everyone was scared. No one said a word. But I knew it was just a matter of time before someone ratted out Joshua. Suddenly, though, this low voice announces, *'It was me.'* We all turn around. No one could believe it."

He fell silent, still amazed, even now.

"It was Ashley," I said, when he didn't continue.

He glanced at me, his face solemn. "Yeah. At first, Hawk Feather didn't believe her. She'd had all this preferential treatment. But then she produces the *second* pill of X, which somehow she stole from Joshua's hiking boot. She says she'll accept whatever punishment he had in mind." He shook his head. "Hawk Feather went ballistic. He grabbed her, hauled her away from the campsite. He ended up taking her to some far-off site in the middle of nowhere and made her sleep there by herself in just her sleeping bag, totally alone. She wasn't allowed to come back in the morning till he went and got her."

"No one challenged this guy?" I asked. "What about the other counselors?"

He shrugged. "They were afraid of him. We were beyond civilization. It was like laws didn't exist." He reached forward and snatched the pack of Marlboros off the table, tapping out another cigarette.

"The other part of her punishment was putting up all of our tents and collecting firewood. We weren't allowed to help. When she was slow, Hawk Feather would scream at her. She'd just stare him down with this look on her face, like she couldn't care less, like she was so much stronger than him, which only made him *more* pissed. Finally, he let up. One of the other counselors warned him he was going too far. So, after the seven nights of sleeping on her own, she was allowed to join the rest of us at the campsite."

He smiled, an unreadable look on his face. He then shook his head and lit the cigarette, exhaling.

"The first night she's back we all wake up at three in the morning because Hawk Feather is screaming like he's being *stabbed.* He runs out of his tent in nothing but his underwear, this fat fuck stammering like a child, crying that there's a rattlesnake in his sleeping bag. Everyone thought it was a joke, that he'd had a nightmare. But one of the female counselors, Four Crows, she went and got it, unzipped it right in front of us, shaking it out. Sure enough, a *rattlesnake,* five feet long, fell onto the ground and whipped right across the campsite, disappearing into the dark. Hawk Feather, white as a sheet, about to piss his pants, turned and stared *right* at Ashley. And she stared back. *He* didn't say a fuckin' *word,* but I know he believed she put it in there. We all did."

He fell silent for a moment, gazing out into the room.

"After that, he left us alone. And Orlando?" He paused, swallowing.

"He *made* it. His sunburn healed. He stopped crying. He became, like, this *hero.*" He sniffed, wiping his nose. "When we finally made it back to base camp, we were supposed to have one night all together where we held hands and marveled at our accomplishments—which was more like thanking God we hadn't *died.* 'Cause that was the thing, the whole time, death was a possibility. Like, it was always waiting for us beyond the rocks. And the person that prevented it was Ashley."

I couldn't see his expression—he was now staring at the floor, hair in his eyes. "About an hour before dinner," he went on, "I looked out the cabin window and saw her climbing into a black SUV. She was leaving early. I was disappointed. I'd wanted to try and talk to her. But it was too late. A driver collected her stuff, put it in the back, and they drove off. It was the last time I saw her."

He lifted his head, staring at me challengingly, yet saying nothing.

"You never heard from her again?"

He shook his head, pointing the cigarette at the envelope in my hand.

"Not until *that.*"

"How do you know she sent it?"

"It's her handwriting. And the return address is where . . ." He shrugged. "I thought she was messing with my head. I broke in a couple of nights ago, wondering if there was some kind of message or *sign* in there. But I haven't found anything."

I held up the monkey. "What's the significance?"

"I've never seen it before. I *told* you." He stubbed out his cigarette.

"You have no theory as to why she'd send it?"

He glared at me. "I was kinda hoping *you* would. You're the reporter."

The red mud encrusting the stuffed animal looked like the kind found out west, certainly throughout Utah, which made me wonder if perhaps it had belonged to one of the kids at the camp—maybe Hopper himself. But he looked more apt to carry around a worn-out copy of *On the Road* as a security blanket.

It was helpful, his insight into Ashley's character. It had allowed her to come briefly into focus, revealing her to be a kind of ferocious avenging angel, a persona entirely in keeping with the way she played music. I couldn't fathom why she mailed Hopper the monkey on the day she died—if it *had* been she.

Hopper appeared to have fallen into an irritated mood, slumped way down on the couch, arms crossed, his faded white T-shirt—GIFFORD'S FAMOUS ICE CREAM, it read—twisted around him. He reminded me of a teenage hitchhiker I'd once met in El Paso; we were the only two at a diner counter at the crack of dawn. After we got to talking, swapping stories, he said goodbye, hitching a ride with the driver of a BP oil truck. Later, I got up to pay my bill only to realize he'd stolen my wallet. *Never trust a charismatic drifter.*

"Maybe there's something inside," I said, turning the stuffed animal over. I took out my switchblade, cutting an incision down the back of the monkey. I pulled out the stuffing, yellowed and crusty, feeling around the inside. There was nothing.

I realized my cell was buzzing, the number a 407 area code.

"Hello?"

"May I please speak to Mr. Scott McGrath?"

It was a woman, her voice crisp and musical.

"This is he."

"It's Nora Halliday. From the coat check? I'm at Forty-fifth and Eleventh Avenue. The Pom Pom Diner. Can you come? We need to talk."

"Forty-fifth and Eleventh. Give me fifteen minutes."

"Okay." She hung up. Shaking my head, I stood up.

"Who was that?" Hopper asked me.

"A *coat-check* girl, last person to see Ashley alive. Yesterday she nearly had me arrested. Today? She wants to *talk.* I have to go. In the meantime, I'll hold on to the monkey."

"That's okay." He snatched it back, giving me a wary look, before shoving it back into the envelope and disappearing with the package into the bedroom.

"Thanks for your time," I called over my shoulder. "I'll be in touch if I hear anything." But suddenly Hopper was slipping out into the hall right behind me, shrugging on his gray coat.

"Cool," he said. He locked the door and took off down the stairs.

"Where are you off to?"

"Forty-fifth and Eleventh. Gotta go meet a *coat-check girl.*"

As his footsteps echoed through the stairwell, I berated myself for mentioning where I was headed. I worked *solo,* always had.

But then—I started down the stairs—maybe it wasn't such a terrible idea to team up with him, this *once.* There was quantum mechanics, string theory, and then there was the most mind-bending frontier of the natural world, *women.* And in my experience with that thorny subject—which included decades of trial and error, throwing out countless years' worth of shoddy results (Cynthia), the sad realization I'd never be a leader in the field, just another middling scientist—they really had only one identifiable constant: Around guys like Hopper, icebergs turned to puddles.

"*Fine,*" I shouted. "But I'm doing the talking."

13 | THE POM POM WAS AN OLD-SCHOOL DINER, narrow as a railroad car.

Nora Halliday sat in the back by a wall-sized photo of Manhattan. She was slumped way, way down on the seat, her skinny legs stretched out in front of her. Yet she wasn't just *sitting* in the booth. She looked like she'd put down first and last month's rent, plus a security deposit, plus an exorbitant broker's fee, signed a lease, and moved *into* the booth.

On one side of her were two giant Duane Reade shopping bags, on the other a brown paper Whole Foods bag and a large gray leather purse, unzipped and sagging open like a gutted reef shark, inside of which you could see all it had ingested that morning: *Vogue,* a green sweater still attached to knitting needles, a sneaker, a pair of white Apple earphones wrapped around not an iPod but a *Discman. It might as well have been a gramophone.*

She didn't notice us walking toward her because her eyes were closed and she was whispering to herself—apparently trying to memorize the block of highlighted text from the play in her hands. On the table in front of her was a plate of half-finished French toast floating like a houseboat on the Mississippi in a pool of syrup.

She glanced up at me, then Hopper. Instantly—probably from the jolt of his good looks—she jerked upright.

"This is Hopper," I said. "Hope it's okay he joins."

Hopper said nothing, only slid into the booth across from her.

She was wearing a strange outfit: stonewashed jeans straight from an eighties movie, a wool sweater so hot-pink it scalded the eyes, black wool fingerless gloves, lipstick a livid shade of red. Unlike last night, her pale blond hair was down, parted in the middle and surprisingly long, hanging all the way to her elbows, stringy on the ends.

"So, you're an actress?" I asked, sliding in beside Hopper.

She smiled, nodding.

"What have you acted *in*?" Hopper asked.

This caused her eyes to skid confusedly over to him, then swerve back to me. Even *I* knew that was one of the rudest questions to ask an actor.

"Nothing. *Yet*. I've only been an actress five weeks. That's how long I've been in the city."

"Where'd you move from?" I asked.

"Saint Cloud. Near Narcoossee."

I could only nod, as I didn't know what *Narcoossee* was. It sounded like an Indian reservation and casino where you could play craps and watch a Crystal Gayle lookalike sing "Brown Eyes Blue." But Nora smiled without shame, closing the play, touching the cover like it was a sacred Bible—yet it was David Mamet's *Glengarry Glen Ross.*

"Sorry I was so rude last night," she said to me.

"Apology accepted," I said.

With a tiny frown, she swept her hands officiously over the surface of the table, brushing a few toast crumbs onto the floor. She then turned and opened up the Whole Foods bag, peering inside as if there were something alive in there. She reached in with both hands and gently pulled out a bulky red-and-black bundle, placing it on the table and sliding it toward me.

I recognized it immediately.

It was a woman's coat. And for a moment, the diner and everything in it dissolved. There was only that article of clothing, so ferociously *red,* staring me down. It looked like a costume, ornate, faintly Russian—red wool fabric, the cuffs black lamb, black cord embellishing the front.

The woman I'd encountered at the Central Park Reservoir, weeks ago, had been wearing it.

The soaked dark hair, the ambling in and out of lamplight, the coat lighting like a flare, alerting me to—*what*? Had she simply been toying with me? How the woman had managed to follow me down into the subway as quickly as she had defied logic. The incident had been so odd, when I came home that night I couldn't sleep, infected by the strangeness of it. I climbed out of bed more than a few times to pull aside the curtains, half expecting her to be there, her slender form like a red incision in the sidewalk, her face turned up to me with hard black eyes. I'd actually questioned my sanity, wondered if *this* was *it*: the substandard past few years had finally led to a mental break with reality, and now, floodgates open, there'd be no limit to the fiends I'd encounter. They'd simply crawl out of my head, down into the world.

But the sidewalk had no red tear. The street, the night, remained flawless and still.

I'd actually started to forget the entire episode—*until now.*

It had been Ashley Cordova.

The realization was startling, and it was quickly followed by the paranoid feeling something was wrong, including this awkward coatcheck girl. She had to be involved in some kind of setup. But the girl only smiled innocently back at me. Hopper, on the other hand, must have seen something on my face—complete shock—because he was squinting at me suspiciously.

"What is it?" he asked, nodding at the coat.

"Ashley's coat," she said. "She was wearing it when she came into the restaurant." She picked up her knife and fork and cut into her French toast. "She left it with me. When the police came later, asking about her, I gave them a black coat from the lost and found and said *that* one was Ashley's. If they found out I was lying, I was going to say I'd mixed up the tickets. But they never came back."

Hopper slid the coat toward him, unfolded it, holding it up by the shoulders. For all its elaborate stitching, the coat looked worn, even seemed to smell of the city, the dirty wind, the sweat. The inside was lined with black silk, and I noticed, sewn into the back collar, a purple label. LARKIN, it read in black letters. Rita Larkin was Cordova's longtime costume designer. I was about to mention this detail when I noticed there was actually a long dark *hair* stuck to the sleeve in an elongated S.

"Why'd you lie to the cops?" Hopper asked Nora.

"I'll tell you guys. On one condition. I want to be part of the investigation." She looked at me. "You said last night you were investigating Ashley."

"It's nothing that formal," I said, clearing my throat, managing to look *away* from the coat and at Nora. "I'm really investigating her father. And Hopper's just here today. We're not partners."

"Yeah, we are," he countered, shooting me a look. "*Absolutely.* Welcome to the *team.* Be our friggin' *mascot.* Why'd you lie to the police?"

Nora stared at him, taken aback by his intensity. Then she looked at me, awaiting my response.

I said nothing, because I was adjusting to what it meant, this encounter with Ashley. I took a deep breath, trying to at least *pretend* I was considering her request. For the record, it'd be over my dead body that I'd ever employ a sidekick—particularly one who'd just crawled out of the Florida boonies.

"This is not the adventure of a lifetime," I said. "I'm not Starsky. He's not Hutch."

"If I'm not involved from beginning to end when we find out *who* or *what* made Ashley die *before her time*"—she articulated all of this decisively, as if she'd rehearsed it sixty times in front of the bathroom mirror—"then I'm not telling you what she was like or what she *did,* and you can both get lost." She slid the coat back and began to mash it inside the bag.

Hopper looked at me expectantly.

"There's no need to be so black-and-white about it," I said.

She ignored me.

"*Okay.* You can work with us," I said.

"You swear?" she asked, smiling.

"I swear."

She extended her hand, and I shook it—mentally crossing my fingers.

"It was a quiet night," she went on eagerly. "After ten. There wasn't anyone in the lobby. She walked right in wearing *that,* so of course I noticed her. She was *beautiful.* But really thin, with eyes almost clear. She looked right at me and my first thought was, *Oh wow, she's pretty.* Her face was more in focus than everything else in the room. But as she turned and started walking toward me, I felt scared."

"Why?" I asked.

She bit her lip. "It was like, when you looked into her eyes the human part was detached and there was something else looking out."

"Like *what*," Hopper prompted.

"Don't know," she said, gazing down at her plate. "She didn't seem to blink. Or *breathe*, even. Not when she pulled off that red coat, not when she handed it to me, not when I gave her the ticket. As I hung it up on the coat rack, I could feel her eyes on me. When I turned back, I *thought* she'd still be standing there, but she was already disappearing up the stairs."

I'd witnessed the same startling movement when she'd suddenly appeared in the subway.

"At that point, other people came in. As I was checking their coats I noticed she was coming back down the stairs. Without looking at me she headed outside. I figured she'd gone out to smoke. I didn't see her come back, so I figured I'd been so busy I missed her, but at the end of the night her red coat was still hanging there. The only one left."

She took a quick gulp of water.

"Three days went by," she went on. "Every night when I closed the coat-check booth I put her coat in the lost and found. When I returned the next day, I'd take it out and hang it up. I was *sure* she'd come back for it. But I dreaded it, too." She paused, tucking her hair behind her ears. "At the end of my shift on the fourth night it was cold out and I only had this navy windbreaker. So after I closed up, instead of returning her coat to the lost and found, I put it on and I walked out wearing it. I could have taken any of the coats from the lost and found. But I took hers."

Nora stared down at her hands, her face flushed. "The next day when I arrived at the restaurant, the police were there. They saw me walk in wearing her coat. When they told me what happened, I was so upset, *what I'd done*. I was afraid they'd think I had something to do with it. So, I took the Yves Saint Laurent coat out of the lost and found and said *that* one was hers." She took an agitated breath. "I thought for sure they'd find out I lied, that they'd show it to her family. But . . ." She shook her head. "No one came back to ask me anything. Not yet, anyway." She looked at me. "Only *you*."

"What else did she have on?" I asked.

"Jeans, black boots, a black T-shirt with an angel on the front."
The same clothing Ashley was wearing when she died.

"Did she speak to you? Mention if she was meeting someone?"

Nora shook her head. "I said my usual 'Good evening' and 'Will you be joining us for dinner?' There's a little script they like you to memorize to be welcoming. But she didn't answer. Every night since I met her—before I knew she'd passed away—I've had nightmares. You know the kind where you wake up fast and sounds are echoing through the room but you have no idea what it was you'd just screamed out loud?"

She was actually awaiting an answer, so I nodded.

"That's what *I've* had. And my grandmother Eli on my mom's side of the family said the Edges are in tune with stuff from fourth and fifth dimensions."

I sensed it was compulsory to intervene now before we were treated to more wisdom from Grandma Eli.

I smiled. "Well, I'll look everything over and be in touch."

"First we need to exchange numbers," Nora said.

She and Hopper gave each other their info. I was just starting to wonder how I was going to *auto-eject* myself out of here, when Nora glanced at her watch and let out a squeak, scrambling out of the booth.

"Shoot. I'm late for work." She grabbed the check, digging through her purse. "Oh, *no*." She looked at me, nibbling a fingernail. "I left my wallet at home."

"Don't worry. I'll take care of it."

"Really? Thanks. I'll definitely pay you back."

If *that* was indicative of her acting talent, not even a daytime soap would hire her. She zipped up her purse, heaved it onto her shoulder, and grabbed the Whole Foods bag.

"I can take the coat. So you don't have so much to carry."

She glanced at me with a flash of mistrust, but then reconsidered, handing me the bag.

"See ya later," she called out cheerfully as she jostled away, bags banging her shins. "And thanks for breakfast."

I climbed out of the booth and, reading the check, saw that the girl had actually consumed *two* meals: the French toast and coffee, but also scrambled eggs, a side of bacon, half a grapefruit, and cranberry juice. *So the string bean Dame Dench had the appetite of a sumo wrestler.* It had to be the reason she'd decided to talk, so I'd subsidize breakfast.

"What'd you think?" asked Hopper, sliding out behind me.

I shrugged. "Young and impressionable. Probably made most of it up."

"Right. That's why you looked so bored and nearly tripped over yourself to get your hands on that coat."

I said nothing, only pulled two twenties from my wallet.

"For one thing," he said, "she's got no place to live." He was staring out the window where Nora Halliday and her many bags were still visible, far across the four-lane street. She was using a building's mirrored reflection to fix her hair into a ponytail. She then picked up the bags and vanished behind a delivery truck.

With a last hard look at me—clearly indicating he didn't trust me *or* particularly like me—Hopper put his phone to his ear.

"Keep those eyes open, Starsky," he said, heading out.

I held back, waiting for him to duck past the window. I doubted I'd see him again—*or* Hannah Montana, for that matter. When New York took over, both of them would fall by the wayside.

That was the magnificent thing about the city: It was inherently Machiavellian. One rarely had to worry about follow-*throughs*, follow-*ups*, follow the leaders, or any kind of consistency in people due to no machinations of one's own but the *sheer force* of living here. New York hit its residents daily like a great debilitating deluge and only the *strongest*—the ones with Spartacus-styled *will*—had the strength to stay not just *afloat* but on course. This pertained to work as much as it did to personal lives. Most people ended up, after only a couple of months, far, far away from where they'd intended to go, stuck in some barbed underbrush of a quagmire when they'd meant to head straight to the ocean. Others outright drowned (became drug addicts) or climbed ashore (moved to Connecticut).

Yet the two of them had been helpful.

All those nights ago, it had been Ashley Cordova. I thought I'd decided on my own to look into her death, and yet incredibly she'd come to me first, wedged herself like a splinter into my subconscious. I'd have to review the timing, but I remembered the Reservoir encounter was a little more than a week before her death. When I saw her it must have been just a few days *after* she'd escaped from the mental-health clinic, Briarwood Hall.

How had she known I'd be there? No one knew I went to the park to jog in the dead of night except Sam. One evening months ago, while tucking her into bed, she'd announced that I was "far away" and I'd answered I *wasn't,* because I went up to her neighborhood to run. With every lap, I could look up to her window and see she was snug in her bed, safe and sound. This was a *stretch,* of course; I could no more see Cynthia and Bruce's ritzy apartment on Fifth Avenue than the Eiffel Tower, but the thought had pleased her. She'd closed her eyes, smiling, and fell right to sleep.

The only possible explanation, then, was that Ashley had been following me. She would have known about me after her father's lawsuit. It was conceivable she'd tracked me down in order to tell me something, something about her father—John's ominous words immediately came to mind, *There's something he does to the children*—but had lost her nerve.

But after what Hopper had told me, shyness didn't seem an underlying part of Ashley's personality. *Quite the opposite.*

I had to get back to Perry Street: first, to make arrangements to drive upstate to Briarwood so I could learn about Ashley's stay there. I also wanted to check out the URL of the Blackboards I'd swiped off of Beckman's computer.

I grabbed the Whole Foods bag, exiting the diner. The sun was out, splattering brash light over the cars speeding down Eleventh Avenue. It did nothing to lighten the unease I felt over the simple, startling fact that the red coat, that blood red stitch in the night from the Reservoir, had appeared one last time in front of me.

It was in my own hands.

From: **Elizabeth J. Poole <ejpoole@briarwoodhospital.org>**   📎   Hide
Subject: Re: Tour
Date: Oct 25 2011 06:24:44 PM EDT
To: Dr. Leon Dean <leoncdean@gmail.com>

Dear Dr. Dean:

Thank you for your inquiry.

I would be delighted to give you a guided tour of our state-of-the-art health facility and also to answer any questions you may have. I've penciled you in for tomorrow at 11:30 AM.

In the meantime, please browse our website and the attached literature about Briarwood and its esteemed history.

Please call me at your earliest convenience.

Very truly yours,

Elizabeth J. Poole
Director of Admissions

Briarwood Hall Hospital

Restoring Mental Health since 1934

http://tunnelstaircase8903-5493r89jidfj9w0129e61)??)*#(((sovereigndeadlyperfect.blackboards.onion

WELCOME TO THE BLACKBOARDS

This is the Cordovites' premier wormhole, where time ticks backward, trees grow down, light eats itself, fear is an opening, and life is sovereign, deadly, perfect.

WARNING: THIS WEBSITE CONTAINS GRAPHIC IMAGES FROM THE WORLD OF CORDOVA AND THE REAL WORLD.
IF YOU CAN'T HANDLE IT, KEEP YOUR EYES CLOSED.

ENTER >

◀ ▶ 👁 http://tunnelstaircase8903-5493r89jidfj9w0129e61)??)°#(((sovereigndeadlyperfect.blackboards.onion/interlope

| PARKING | CORDOVA | FILMS | FREAK | RED BAND | STRANGERS | CLIMB IN |

**WHOEVER YOU ARE,
YOU SHOULDN'T BE HERE.**

GET OUT.

ENTER >

14 | THE FOLLOWING MORNING, an hour before I was set to leave for the three-hour drive upstate to Briarwood, I was in my kitchen making a fresh pot of coffee when there was a knock on my front door.

I walked into the foyer and checked the peephole.

Nora Halliday was at my door.

I didn't know how in the hell she'd found out where I lived, but then I remembered: It was on that damn business card I'd given her back at the Four Seasons. Someone must have buzzed her in. I considered pretending I wasn't at home, but she knocked again and I knew the old wood floors of my apartment squeaked with every step, so she could hear me standing there.

I unlocked the door. She was wearing a tight black wool jacket with a collar of ostrich feathers, black tights, boots, and a zebra-print nylon miniskirt, which looked like a figure-skating costume from the Lillehammer Olympics. She had no shopping bags with her, only that gray leather purse, her long blond hair braided into two cords wrapped around her head.

"Hi," I said.

"Hi."

"What are you doing here?"

"I'm ready to work."

"It's eight o'clock in the morning."

She picked at something crusty on the hem of her jacket. "Yeah, well, I thought maybe you could use someone to bounce ideas off of."

I was about to tell her to come back tomorrow—then obviously I'd have to *move* or join a Witness Protection Program—but I remembered that observation Hopper had made, that the girl didn't have a place to live. She did look pale and faintly exhausted.

"You want to come in for a cup of coffee?"

She beamed. *"Sure."*

"I'm about to leave for an appointment, so it won't be long."

"No problem."

"What exactly are you wearing?" I asked, leading her through the foyer into the living room. "Your mother doesn't let you walk around like that, does she?"

"Oh, sure. She lets me do whatever. She's dead." She slung her purse beside the couch—it had to contain at least one bowling ball.

"Then that grandmother you mentioned, she doesn't let you walk around like that."

"Eli?" She really pronounced the *hell* out of the name: EEL EYE. "She's dead, too."

Something told me I should stop while I *wasn't* ahead.

"What about your father?"

She leaned forward to study the painting above the fireplace.

"He's at Starke."

"Starke?"

"Florida State Prison. They have an Old Sparky there."

Old Sparky—it was the nickname of the electric chair. I waited for her to clarify that her dad wasn't destined to *meet* Old Sparky, but she moved to the bookcase, inspecting the books, leaving that strand of the conversation dangling like the end of a party streamer she didn't bother to tape up.

"How do you like your coffee?" I asked, retreating into the kitchen.

"Cream, two sugars. But only if it's not too much trouble."

"It's no trouble at all."

"You wouldn't have anything to *eat*, would you?"

I set the girl up in my living room with coffee, two toasted English muffins piled with butter and marmalade, and a copy of my book *Cocaine Carnivals*. After making sure there was no cash lying around or any other valuables she could feed to her carnivorous purse, I went back into my office to print out directions to Briarwood Hall.

I also tried logging on to the Blackboards website again, but I was tossed back to the exit page, as I'd been before.

My IP address appeared to have been blocked.

When I returned to the living room, Nora had settled in. She'd taken off her boots, pulled a wool blanket over her legs, and drained some of the contents of that purse onto my coffee table: two stage plays, a tube of lipstick, that beat-up Discman.

"Who's C.L.M.?" she asked, turning back a few pages to stare at the dedication page.

"My ex-wife."

She was astonished. "*You* have an *ex-wife?*"

"Doesn't everybody?"

"Where's she?"

"Probably working out with her trainer."

"Got any kids?"

"A daughter."

She thoughtfully considered this. I figured it was as good a time as any to bring up the mystery of her living arrangements.

"So where exactly do you live?" I asked.

"Hell's Kitchen."

"Where in Hell's Kitchen?"

"Ninth and, like, Fifty-second."

"*Like* Fifty-second?"

"I just moved in, so I forget the cross-street. Before I was on a friend's pullout." She resumed reading.

"Any roommates?"

She didn't look up. "Two."

"And what do they do?"

"What d'you mean?"

"Are they pimps, drug addicts, or working in the porn industry?"

"Oh, *no*. I mean, I don't know what they do during the day. They seem nice."

"What are their names?"

She hesitated. "Louisa and Gustav."

Those were imaginary roommate names if ever I'd heard any. Living in New York for more than two decades, never had I once come *close* to meeting anyone with those names.

I looked at my watch. *I was out of time to babysit.*

"I have to leave for a doctor's appointment," I said. "So you'll need to go. But we can talk tomorrow."

I collected her plate and coffee mug, Nora watching with wide eyes, and carried them to the kitchen, loading the dishwasher.

"Thank you for the coffee," she called out.

"Don't mention it."

There was a stretch of rather dubious silence.

I was about to go check on her, but then heard her purse unzipping and zipping. She was packing up her things—*thank Christ.* But I knew this was buying me only a little time; she'd be back again tomorrow.

The girl was like one of those tiny fish that swam relentlessly under a great white shark's chin *for miles*. I'd have to phone some old contact, someone in one of the unions or in banking, twist his arm to get her gainfully employed twelve hours a day at some Capital One bank in Jersey City.

"What's Shandaken?" she abruptly shouted.

"What?" I stepped out of the kitchen.

"You have directions to a place in *Shandaken,* New York."

She was in the foyer, inspecting the folder containing the directions to Briarwood and my emails with the admissions director, which I'd put on the table next to the Whole Foods bag containing Ashley's coat.

"You're getting a tour of the facility?" she asked, glancing up in amazement. "What *facility?*"

I snatched the folder from her and, checking my watch—I was supposed to be on the New Jersey Turnpike ten minutes ago—I strode to the closet, grabbing my black jacket, pulling it on.

"A mental hospital." I moved back into the hall, switching off the lights.

"Why do you want a tour of a mental hospital?"

"Because I might *admit* myself. We'll catch up tomorrow." I grabbed the directions and Nora's bony arm, escorting her to the front door and giving her a gentle *push* so she was launched outside, then stepped after her, locking the door.

"You lied in that email," she said. "You said your name's Leon Dean."

"A typo."

"You're going there to investigate Ashley."

I took off down the hall, Nora hurrying after me. "No."

"But you're taking her coat. *I* should come."

"No."

"But I could be your daughter you're thinking of admitting. I could play, like, a dark and brooding teenager. I'm really good at improv."

"I'm going there to get information, not play charades."

I stepped outside into the bright morning, holding the door for her— she had a fast, lopsided walk, though I couldn't tell if it was scoliosis or a result of that leaden bag.

"This place has the security of the Pentagon," I said, jogging down the steps. "Over the years I've developed a method of interviewing that allows people to trust me. It's because I work alone. Deep Throat never would have talked to Woodward if he'd been shadowed by a teenage Floridian."

"What's Deep Throat?"

I stopped dead, staring at her. She was legitimately puzzled.

I took off again across the street. "You've *at least* seen the *movie. All the President's Men.* Robert Redford, Dustin Hoffman? You know who *they* are, don't you? Or aren't you aware of any movie stars older than Justin Timberlake?"

"I know them."

"Well, they played Woodward and Bernstein. Legendary journalists who exposed Watergate. They forced a president of the United States to admit wrongdoing and resign. One of the most powerful acts of patriotism by two journalists in the history of this country."

"So you'll be Woodward. And I'll be Bernstein."

"That's not—okay, yes, they were a *team,* but they each brought something substantive to the table."

"*I* can bring something to the table."

"Like what? Your deep knowledge of Ashley Cordova?"

She stopped dead. "*I'm coming,*" she announced behind me. "Or I'll call the hospital and tell them you're a fake using a fake name."

I stopped in my tracks, turning around to survey her. There it was, that Teflon personality I'd gone *mano-a-mano* with at the Four Seasons. That was *women* for you—always *morphing.* One minute they were helpless, needing shelter and English muffins, the next they were ruthlessly bending you to their will like you were a piece of sheet metal.

"So it's blackmail."

She nodded, her stare fierce.

I walked the remaining yards to my car, a dented silver 1992 BMW parked along the curb.

"Fine," I muttered over my shoulder. "But you're staying in the car."

Nora, squeaking with excitement, hurried around to the passenger side.

"You'll do everything I say at all times." I unlocked the trunk, shoved the Whole Foods bag inside. "You'll be a silent operative with no personality. You'll simply process and execute my orders like a machine."

"Oh, *sure.*"

I climbed in, yanking on my seatbelt and starting the car.

"I don't want *feedback*. Or yammering. I don't *chit*, and I sure as hell don't *chat*."

"Okay, but we can't leave yet." She leaned forward, turning on the radio.

"Why not?"

"Hopper's coming."

"No. He's not. This isn't a fucking fourth-grade class trip."

"But he wanted to meet up with us. You really hate people, huh?"

I ignored that comment, inching out onto Perry, though a taxi barreling down the street behind me laid on the horn. I slammed on the brakes and was forced to retreat meekly *back* to the curb as a motorcade of cars passed, piling up at the light, trapping us in the space.

"You remind me of this man back at Terra Hermosa."

"What the hell's Terra Hermosa?"

"A retirement community. His name was Hank Weed. At mealtimes he'd always take the good table by the window and put his walker against the empty seat so no one else could sit down and see the view. He died like that."

I didn't answer, silenced by the sudden realization that I had absolutely no idea if any of what came out of this girl's mouth was true. Maybe she *was* really good at improv. I couldn't be certain she *was* nineteen or that her name really *was* Nora Halliday. Maybe she was like one of those sweaters with an innocent little thread hanging off of it: One pull, the whole thing unraveled.

"Do you drive?" I asked.

"Sure."

"Give me your license."

"Why?"

"I have to make sure there's not an Amber Alert out for you. Or that you weren't profiled on *Dateline* as some kind of tween criminal."

Smirking, she leaned forward, dug around in that hulking bag, removing a green nylon LeSportsac wallet, so stained and filthy it looked like it'd floated for a couple of years down the Nile. She flipped through a few snapshots encased in plastic—deliberately turning the wallet away so I couldn't view them—and slipped out the license, handing it to me.

In the picture she looked about fourteen.

Nora Edge Halliday. 4406 Brave Lane. Saint Cloud, FL. Eyes: blue. Hair: blond. Born June 28, 1992.

She *was* nineteen.

I handed it back, saying nothing. Both Edge as a middle name and Brave Lane—not to mention the year of her birth, which was pretty much *yesterday*—were enough to render me mute.

The light turned green. I put the car in drive, easing out.

"If you want to wait for Hopper, be my guest. I have work to do."

"But he's here," she yelped excitedly.

Sure enough, *Hopper* was shuffling down the sidewalk in his gray coat. Before I could stop her, Nora reached over and repeatedly honked the horn. Seconds later, in a blast of cold air, cigarette smoke, and booze, Hopper collapsed in the backseat.

"What's up, *cholos*?"

The kid was bombed again.

I accelerated through the yellow light, speeding across Seventh Avenue. Hopper muttered something incomprehensible. A half-hour later he asked me to pull over on the side of the New Jersey Turnpike and got sick.

It didn't look like he'd been home all night; he was still wearing the white GIFFORD'S FAMOUS ICE CREAM T-shirt from yesterday. TRY OUR 13 HONEY-PIE FLAVORS! it whispered in faded letters. When he finished, he seemed to want to sit down on the guardrail and watch the traffic blasting inches from my car like cannonballs, so Nora climbed out to help him, guiding him back to the car. She did this with remarkable tenderness and care. I couldn't help but sense she'd done such a thing many times before. *For whom? The dead mother? The convict father possibly awaiting Old Sparky? Grandmother Eel Eye?*

Why the hell did she care about Ashley Cordova—about any of this? And Hopper—was a stuffed monkey anonymously mailed to him *really* why he chose to be with me on a Wednesday morning, not in bed with Chloe or Reinking or some other downtown girl reeking of cigarettes and indie bands?

These two kids clearly knew a hell of a lot more than they let on. But if they were hiding something, I'd learn what it was soon enough. *Secrets*—even in hardened criminals, they were just air pockets lodged under debris at the bottom of an ocean. It might take an earthquake, or you scuba diving down there, sifting through the sludge, but their natural proclivity was always to head straight to the surface—*to get out.*

Nora loaded Hopper into the back. He mumbled something as she removed his sunglasses, and then, stretching out across the seat with a boozy sigh, he slung his arm behind his head and conked out. Nora resumed scanning the radio. She stopped on a folk song—"False Knight on the Road," read the display—and sat back, staring out the window at the ragged fields.

The morning seemed to tiredly sponge off the sky, washing the road signs and windshields in dull, bathwater light as the rhythm of the highway thumped under the tires.

I didn't feel like talking, either. I was too surprised at where I found myself: with two total strangers, an assortment of stories behind us and who the hell knew *what* in front of us, but for the time being, our lives three frail lines running side by side.

We made our way toward Briarwood.

15 | "WE DON'T THINK of our guests as *patients,*" Elizabeth Poole told me as we strolled down the sidewalk. "They're part of the Briarwood family for life. Now, tell me more about your daughter, Lisa." She glanced back at Nora—known for the time being as *Lisa*—who'd fallen twenty paces behind us. "What year is she?"

"She *was* a college freshman," I said. "But she dropped out."

She waited for me to elaborate, but I only smiled and tried to look uncomfortable, which was *easy.*

Elizabeth Poole was a short, plump woman in her fifties with such a sour expression I initially assumed she was sucking on some type of hard candy, only to realize as the minutes ticked by that expression showed no sign of subsiding. She wore high-waisted mom jeans, her thin brown hair slicked into a ponytail.

Nora and I had left Hopper passed out in my backseat and found Poole's office on the ground floor of Dycon, a redbrick building that housed Briarwood's administration, which didn't so much *sit* on the pristine hill as *nail it down* with long boxy annexes and gray tendrils of sidewalks. I'd taken just one look at Poole—then, as it jingled out from behind her desk, her snow-white, pink-barretted Maltese, Sweetie, who glided around her office like a tiny Thanksgiving Day parade float—and immediately wanted to call off our ruse.

Making matters considerably worse was Nora's acting ability—or alarming lack thereof.

As we'd sat down, I'd explained that my daughter, Lisa, had disciplinary issues. Nora had grimaced and stared at the floor. I was sure the many hard, knowing looks Poole shot me were not compassionate but coolly accusatory, as if she knew my daughter was a sham. Just when I was certain she was going to order us off the premises, however, Poole—and panting, tingling Sweetie—had kick-started the tour, leading us out of Dycon and across Briarwood's sprawling grounds.

"What sort of security do you have in place?" I asked her now.

Poole slowed to consider Nora again, who was glowering at the sidewalk (a look Sue Ellen gave Miss Ellie throughout season twelve of *Dallas*).

"I'll go over the specifics with you in private," Poole said. "But in a nutshell, every patient is assigned a level of surveillance, which ranges from *general* observation, when the patient is checked by staff every thirty minutes throughout the day and night, to *constant* observation, when the patient must remain within arm's length of a trained technician at all times and may use only a spoon at mealtimes. When she arrives, Lisa will be evaluated and assigned the appropriate level."

"Have there been any recent incidents of escape?" I asked.

The question caught her by surprise. *"Escape?"*

"Sorry. Don't mean to make it sound like Alcatraz. It's just, if Lisa sees an opportunity, she'll make a run for it."

Poole nodded. If she was reminded of Ashley Cordova's breakout, she gave no indication.

"We have forty-six acres," she said. "The perimeter is fenced in and secured with video surveillance. A twenty-four-hour detail at the gatehouse entrance monitors every vehicle entering or exiting." She smiled thinly. "Patient safety is our biggest priority."

So *that* was the official statement on Ashley's escape: It *never happened.*

"The funny thing is," she continued, "once people settle in it's harder to get them to leave than stay. Briarwood is a sanctuary. It's the real world that's brutal."

"I can see that. This is a beautiful place."

"Isn't it?"

I smiled in agreement. *As beautiful as an injection of morphine.*

A vast, immaculate lawn spanned out on either side of us, smooth, flat, and ruthlessly green. Far off to our right stood a massive oak tree, an empty black bench beneath it. It looked like the front of a condolence card. The grounds were eerily deserted, except for an occasional smiling nurse striding past us in purple pants with a matching festively patterned shirt—*to distract you, no doubt, as she fed you your meds.* Farther off, a bald man hurried purposefully between brick buildings.

Though Poole had explained that at this hour everyone in the clinic—*clinic* seemed to be code for *psych ward*—was in a behavior therapy session, the place had a creepy, muzzled feel. Any second now, I wouldn't have been surprised to hear a man's gut-wrenching scream pierce the chirping birds and the breeze. Or to see one of those doors fly open—a door to one of the buildings Poole had expressly *skipped* on our tour; "Just another dormitory," she'd said when I'd inquired what it was—and some patient in white pajamas come out, trying to make a run for it before he was tackled by a male nurse and hauled off to his electroconvulsive therapy session, leaving the landscape stiffly serene.

"How many patients do you have?" I asked, glancing back at Nora. She was lagging even farther behind.

"One hundred and nineteen adults between our mental health and substance abuse programs. That doesn't include outpatients."

"And psychologists work closely with each person?"

"Oh, yes." She stopped walking to bend down and brush off a brown leaf that was stuck in Sweetie's fur. "Upon admission, each resident is assigned a personal health-care team. That includes a physician, a pharmacologist, and a psychologist."

"And how often do they meet?"

"It depends. Often daily. Sometimes twice daily."

"Where?"

"In Straffen." She pointed to our left at a redbrick building half concealed by pine trees. "We'll head over there in a minute. First, we'll take a look at Buford."

We veered off the path, heading toward a gray stone building, Sweetie trotting along right by my feet.

"This is where residents dine and meet for extracurricular activities." Poole moved up the steps, opening the wooden door ahead of me. "Three times a week we have professors from SUNY Purchase give talks in the auditorium on everything from global warming to endangered species to World War One. Part of our philosophy for healing is giving our patients a global perspective and a sense of history."

I nodded and smiled, looking over my shoulder to see where the hell Nora was. She'd stopped following us, standing back at the center of the lawn. She was shading her eyes, surveying something behind her.

"I can see your trouble with her," Poole said, following my gaze. "Girls can have a tough time at her age. Where's *Mrs.* Dean in all of this, if you don't mind me asking?"

"She's out of the picture."

Poole nodded. Nora looked like she was debating making a run for it. But then she shuffled toward us with slumpy posture, stopping to give Poole a Dr. Evil look before skipping up the steps. Poole led us through the foyer, which smelled strongly of disinfectant, and into the dining hall. It was a large, sunlit room with round wooden tables, arched windows. A handful of female staff were busy arranging place settings.

"This is where residents take all meals," said Poole. "Obviously we promote physical health as well as mental, so the menu has a low-fat option, also vegetarian, vegan, and kosher. Our head chef used to work at a Michelin-star restaurant in Sacramento."

"When do I get to meet the people who *live* here so I know they're not all psychotic?" asked Nora.

Poole blinked in shock, glanced at me—I stared back sheepishly—and then, recovering, she smiled.

"You won't be meeting anyone *today,*" she said diplomatically, holding out an arm to usher us down the hall, as Sweetie floated along beside her, nails clacking on the floor. "But if you come, you'll find the people here are as diverse as the people anywhere."

Poole stopped abruptly beside a dark alcove and, after a pause, switched on an overhead light. The walls were covered in bulletin boards decked with sign-up sheets and photos of activities at Briarwood.

"As you can see," Poole said, gesturing inside, "people are really quite happy. We keep everyone busy, physically and mentally."

Scowling, Nora stepped inside. "When were these pictures taken?" she asked.

"The last few months," said Poole.

Nora glared skeptically, then inspected the pictures, her arms crossed over her stomach. I figured she'd *really* lost it, decided to do an imitation of Angie in *Girl, Interrupted,* when I realized what she was doing.

She was looking for Ashley.

It wasn't a bad idea. I moved past Poole to take a look. The photos were of patients involved in relay races, nature hikes. A few looked legitimately happy, though most appeared too thin and fatigued. *Ashley would be obvious, wouldn't she?* The dark-haired girl a little bit alone, with a challenging gaze. I scanned photos of a music recital, but seated at the piano was a man with dreadlocks. There were quite a few shots of a summer barbecue on the main lawn, patients crowded around picnic tables, eating burgers—no sign of Ashley anywhere.

I glanced back at the doorway and realized Poole was looking at us, faintly alarmed. We must have been inspecting a little *too intently.*

"Everyone looks so happy," I said.

She coolly stared back. "Why don't we move along?"

I stepped out of the alcove, that little doily of a dog twirling in circles as it stared up at me, panting as if I had beef jerky in my pocket. Nora was flipping through the pages of a sign-up sheet for Briarwood Book Club, noticeably reading all the names.

"*Lisa,*" I said. "Let's *go.*"

Poole led us back outside, across the lawn to Straffen Hall, where we headed straight to the second floor—devoted to music, painting, and yoga. It was clear from Poole's clipped descriptions and tightened tone that she really didn't care for me or my huffy daughter. I tried to fawn over the facilities, but she only smiled stiffly.

As we passed the reflection room—candles, photos of meadows and sky—a two-note chime sounded over a loudspeaker. It was shrill and reverberating, the musical equivalent of a stubbed toe.

"I have to go to the bathroom," Nora announced petulantly.

"Certainly," said Poole, stopping beside a water fountain, pointing at the door marked WOMEN in the middle of the corridor. "We'll wait for you here."

Nora rolled her eyes and took off. The corridor walls were bright, painted half white, half kitten-nose pink, but the place felt clinical and claustrophobic, like a train compartment. *The Disoriented Express headed toward Crazytown. All aboard.*

Patients started to flood out of classrooms. They wore jeans and baggy cotton shirts—*no belts or shoelaces,* I noticed—a surprisingly wide range of ages. One guy with spiky gray hair staggered out of an art room—he looked about eighty. Most avoided eye contact as they walked past me. Various eggheads and shrinks milled about, too, conferring, nodding, looking constructive. They were easy to spot because they were all dressed in L.L.Bean fleeces and barn jackets, wool sweaters in earth tones—*probably so patients would mistake the place for Vail.*

Poole was fussing with the barrette in Sweetie's hair.

"I've heard very good things about Dr. Annika Angley," I said.

She stood up, holding the dog in her arms.

Annika Angley was the psychologist who'd completed Ashley's new-patient assessment, which had been included in the NYPD file.

"A friend of mine recommended her," I went on. "She's apparently very good with young women who have depressive disorders. Is there any way I could speak to her?"

"Her office is on the third floor. That area isn't open to visitors. And discussion of Dr. Angley or *any* physician at this stage is premature. If Lisa comes, she'll be assigned a team of health professionals that suits her needs. Which reminds me. I'm going to go check on her."

She put Sweetie down, smiling at me, the implication of which was *Don't you dare move,* and marched down the hall, her black orthopedic shoes squishing on the linoleum.

When she appeared a minute later, her face was beet red.

"She's not in there," she announced.

I blankly stared back.

"*Lisa* is *missing*. Did you see her?"

"No."

Poole spun on her heel and stomped down the hallway.

"She must have exited the *other end*."

Sweetie and I—mutually stunned by this recent development—took off after her, though as I passed the ladies' room I couldn't help but open the door and call out: "*Lisa? Honey?*"

Poole shot me a look over her shoulder. "She's not there. *Really*."

She barged past patients, thrusting open the door at the end and storming into the stairwell. I followed close behind. She paused, squinting up at the next flight—sectioned off by a metal gate and a sign that read AUTHORIZED PERSONNEL ONLY—then turned, stomping down the stairs. We blasted out onto the ground floor, jostling a man carrying a stack of folders, Sweetie's paws skidding on the slick wood floors as she rounded the sharp turn. We followed Poole into an office marked DRUG AND ALCOHOL EXTENSION PROGRAM.

"Beth, did you see a five-forty-six wandering around? Skinny blonde? Micro-mini? Hair in Heidi braids?" She eyed me icily. *"Feathers?"*

"No, Liz."

Poole, muttering to herself, marched back down the hall.

"What's a five-forty-six?" I asked.

"A *prospective*. I'll have to review the security monitors. She likes to run away, does she? Any idea where she might go?"

"If she makes it to the main road she might try to hitchhike."

"Unless she has *wings* and can *fly* over a thirty-foot *electrified fence*, that girl's not going anywhere."

"I'm terribly sorry about this."

We exited through the glass doors. Outside, across the lawn, patients—quite a few escorted by nurses—streamed down the sidewalks, heading to lunch. There was no sign of Nora anywhere. With the getup she was wearing, she'd be easy to spot. I had no idea where she was; this wasn't part of the orders I'd given her. She'd gone rogue.

A minute later, Poole deposited me on the floral couch in her office. "You wait here," she said. "I'll be right back with your daughter."

"Thank you."

She only glared at me and slammed the door behind her.

16

I WAS ALONE WITH SWEETIE. The dog had gone over to her pillow bed by the potted plants and returned with a squeaking hotdog.

The chime *ding*ed over the loudspeakers for the second time.

I studied the ceiling. *No visible camera.*

I stood up and moved over to Poole's desk.

There was a screensaver on her computer monitor. Unsurprisingly, it featured floating shots of Sweetie, though every now and then there was the presence in the background of a thin bald man who looked baffled. *Mr. Poole.*

I tapped the keyboard and was prompted for a password.

I tried *Sweetie.* It didn't work.

On the corner of the desk were stacks of papers in IN and OUT trays. I flipped through them: thank-you notes, admission applications, a signed confidentiality statement, an email from Dr. Robert Paul announcing his retirement. Surely, there had to be some kind of internal administrative memo about Ashley Cordova. It'd be written by some hospital head, filled with phrases like *This is a very delicate matter* and *It's critical to the reputation of this hospital*—and so on.

I opened the desk drawers.

They were filled with office supplies, a Pottery Barn catalog, and strewn with wrapped hard mint candies. I moved to the row of filing cabinets along the back wall. They were all locked and no sign anywhere of the keys.

I moved back over to the door, opened it, and looked out.

The hallway was empty, except for two nurses standing about halfway down in front of Dycon's main entrance.

Nora is getting me thrown out anyway. I might as well go down like a kamikaze. Suddenly, Sweetie was gnawing the hotdog on my foot. A nurse stopped talking to glance curiously in our direction.

I reached down, launched the toy across the room—it lodged in the leaves of a giant potted corn plant by the window; Sweetie would have to scale the six-foot stalk to reach it—and checked outside again.

The nurses had quietly resumed talking. I slipped out, walking straight through the side door.

Outside, I headed toward Straffen.

The grounds were quiet again, a few stragglers making their way toward the dining hall. I hurried across the lawn, heading up the front steps, where patients were chatting and smoking cigarettes. They only glanced at me idly as I entered the building and headed straight for the elevator banks.

Stepping inside one, I pressed 3. But the number didn't light.

I needed some type of code. I was about to exit when a gray-haired woman stepped in, her eyes glued to her BlackBerry. Without acknowledging me, she pressed a four-digit code into the panel. It didn't work, clearly because I'd pressed a button. Frowning, she pressed reset, typed the code again, and the doors closed. We began to rise. She'd pressed 6. I stepped forward, tried 3 again. This time it lit up.

She turned to me, curiously looking me over.

The doors opened on 3. I exited, sensing the woman was now wondering who the hell I was, but before she could react, the doors closed.

I was alone.

The third floor of Straffen looked identical to the second, except the overhead neon lights were pinker, the linoleum shinier, the walls painted spearmint green. Black doors spanned the hall in both directions. They were doctors' offices. I moved along them, outside each one, a plaque printed with a name. I could hear low voices and bamboo-whistling music, the kind you hear at a spa while getting a massage. Midway down the hall, there was a small windowed sitting area where two young men sat stretched out on couches, writing in notebooks.

They didn't notice me as I walked past.

I spotted the plaque, ANNIKA ANGLEY PH.D. I knocked lightly and, hearing nothing, tried the knob. *Locked.* I strolled back to the young men.

"Excuse me?" I asked.

They looked up, startled. One was blond with a soft, uncertain face. The other had brown curly hair, his skin red and pockmarked.

"Maybe you can help me," I said. "Did either of you know a former resident who was here recently named Ashley Cordova?"

The blond kid glanced hesitantly at the other boy. "No. But I just got here."

I turned to him. "What about you?"

He nodded slowly. "Yeah. I heard about her."

"What did you hear?"

"Just that Cordova's daughter was here."

"Did you ever meet her or see her?"

He shook his head. "She was Code Silver."

"What's Code Silver?"

"The acute-care unit. They all live in Maudsley."

"Excuse me," a male voice called out behind me. *"Can I help you?"*

I turned. A short, portly man with a dense brown beard was in the hallway, staring at me.

"Hopefully," I said. "I'm looking for my daughter, Lisa."

"Come with me." He held out his arm, beckoning me to step away from the boys with a rigidly pissed-off smile. I nodded my thanks to them and followed the man around the corner.

"This floor is prohibited to everyone but residents and physicians. How did you get up here?"

I explained as confusedly as I could that I'd been on a campus tour with Poole and had lost my daughter.

Looking me over with great distaste—though seemingly buying into my stupidity—he stepped toward an office, fumbling with his keys. He shoved the door open, switching on the lights.

"Please wait with me in here until I speak with Elizabeth."

"Actually, I know the way. I'll just head back myself."

"Sir, get in here *now* or I'll call security."

He was Jason Elroy-Martin, M.D., according to his plaque. I entered, sitting on his leather couch as he, with increasing frustration, dialed phone numbers off a contact sheet taped to the wall beside his medical diploma from the University of Miami. After leaving two messages for Poole, he finally reached her, and swiftly his face—what was *left* of it; his beard had overrun his cheeks—was flushed with outrage.

"He's in front of me," he said, staring me down. "He approached two one-seventeens. They were free-writing in their journals. Yes. *Yes.*" He paused, listening. "No problem."

He hung up the phone and sat back in his swivel chair, interlacing his fingers.

"Am I dismissed?" I asked.

"You're not going anywhere."

He continued to frown at me until there was a knock on the door.

It opened, revealing two large uniformed security guards.

"Scott B. McGrath," one of them said, "you'll have to come with us."

The fact that he'd said "*B*"—which stood for my middle name, Bartley—was not promising.

17 | THEY ESCORTED ME across the grounds to the Security Center, a boxy cinder-block bunker away from the other buildings at the edge of the woods. We entered a stark lobby, where a toad-faced guard sat behind glass. I was led down a hall past rooms buzzing with monitors, each displaying jumpy black-and-white shots of corridors and classrooms.

"Is this the part where I get waterboarded?" I asked.

They ignored me, stopping beside the open doorway at the end.

Nora was there, hunched on a metal folding chair at the center of a yellow-carpeted room with plywood walls. Thankfully, she appeared to be *out* of character, biting her nails, staring wide-eyed up at Elizabeth Poole—now so red-faced she appeared to be radiating thermonuclear heat. Beside her, perched on the edge of a desk, was a tall man with salt-and-pepper hair. He was wearing ironed khaki slacks and a bright Easter egg–blue sweater.

"Scott," he said, rising and extending his hand. "I'm Allan Cunningham. President of Briarwood Hall. Very nice to meet you."

"Pleasure's all mine."

He smiled. He was one of those beaming men not merely clean-cut but *spick-and-span*, with the unblemished complexion one usually finds on babies and nuns.

"So, *Nora,*" he said, looking down at her and smiling—she actually smiled back—"whose pseudonym today I understand has been *Lisa*. She's been explaining that you guys aren't potential guests, as you claimed, but here to dig illegally for information on a former patient."

"That's right," I said. "Ashley Cordova. She escaped from your care and died ten days later. We're trying to determine if there was misconduct on the part of the hospital, which directly resulted in her death."

"There was no misconduct."

"You admit, then, Ashley Cordova was a patient here."

"Absolutely not." It was taking considerable effort for Cunningham to keep that broad grin on his face. "But I will say there have been no breaches in patient safety."

"If Ashley was *authorized* to leave with an unidentified male in the middle of the night, why did the hospital file a missing-person's report the next day?"

He looked incensed, but didn't answer.

"She was Code Silver. The *acute-care* unit. They're not authorized to leave without a guardian. So someone at the hospital must have been asleep at the wheel."

He took a deep breath. "Mr. McGrath, this is not a public hospital. You're subject to trespass laws. I could have you both taken straight to jail."

"Actually, you *can't.*" I unzipped my pocket, handing him a folded brochure. "You'll find that, in addition to our concerns about Ashley, Nora and I are here to distribute materials about our religion, as we are legally allowed to do under *Marsh versus Alabama,* the Supreme Court ruling that upholds, under constitutional Amendments One and Fourteen, state trespass statutes do *not* apply to those involved in the distribution of religious literature, even if it takes place on private grounds."

Cunningham surveyed my old Jehovah's Witness brochure.

"Cute. *Very cute,*" he said. "You'll be escorted off the premises. I'll file a complaint with police. If I hear you or your friends—*including* the person sleeping in your car—try to enter our grounds again, you'll be arrested."

He crumpled up the brochure, making a nice rim-shot with it in the trashcan by the door. I was about to thank him for his time, when sudden movement in the window behind him caught my attention.

A woman was racing through the woods along the dirt path encircling a deserted construction site, her red hair flashing in the sun. She was wearing pink nurse's scrubs with a white cardigan and appeared to be in a serious hurry, heading straight for our building.

Cunningham glanced over his shoulder out the window, but then turned back, nonchalant.

"Do I make myself clear, Mr. McGrath?"

"Crystal."

Cunningham nodded at the guards, and they escorted us outside.

We filed down the sidewalk around the construction site. *Lisa,* for all her bad-girl scowling, certainly looked docile now. As we walked between the two guards she shot me countless freaked-out, *what-are-we-going-to-do-now?* looks—all of which suggested she was relishing this clash with authority. If you could even *call* these security officers *authority.* They looked like La-Z-Boys.

Farther down the path, I noticed that *nurse* again—the same redhead I'd spotted out the window. She'd just stepped out of nowhere and was rushing toward us, staring emphatically at the ground. But when we were just a few yards away, she jerked her head up, staring agitatedly *right* at me.

I stopped in surprise.

She only picked up her pace, veering onto another route leading around the back of a dormitory.

"*Mr. McGrath.* Let's go."

When we reached the parking lot, news of a security breach appeared to have traveled around the hospital, because we had a handful of onlookers—nurses, administrators, shrinks—standing on the front steps of Dycon, watching our procession.

"A going-away party," I said. "You shouldn't have."

"Kindly make your way to your vehicle," the guard ordered.

I unlocked the car, and the two of us climbed in. Hopper was *still* passed out in the back. He looked like he hadn't moved.

"Why don't you make sure he has a pulse?" I muttered, starting the engine.

I eased out of the parking space, edging the car toward the exit. There were people still milling around Dycon, watching us, but no sign anywhere of that redhaired nurse. *Had she wanted me to follow her?* Surely she'd have seen with the security guards it was impossible.

"He has a pulse," chirped Nora happily, turning back. "That was a close call, huh?"

"*Close? No.* I'd call that a bull's-eye."

I made a right, accelerating out onto the main road that would get us the hell out of here, a dizzying two-minute drive through the woods.

"You mad or something?" Nora asked.

"Yes. I'm *mad.*"

"How come?"

"Your little Houdini act back there? You didn't just draw attention to us. You drew a red circle around us and added a *They are here* arrow. Next time bring a mariachi band."

She huffed, fiddling with the radio.

"Right now Cunningham's on the phone with Ashley's family—Cordova *himself*, probably—telling him a reporter named Scott McGrath accompanied by a white cracker Floridian is snooping around his daughter's medical history. Any hope I had at keeping this investigation quiet is gone now, thanks to you, *Bernstein*. Which brings me to your *acting*. I don't know if anyone's told you this, but you need to rethink your life purpose."

I checked the rearview mirror. A blue Lincoln had just appeared behind us—in the front seats, the unmistakable boxy forms of the security officers.

"Now we've got Mumbo and Jumbo tailing us," I muttered.

Nora excitedly whipped around in the seat to look. The girl was about as stealthy as a semi hauling a wide load.

We sped down the hill, rounding a grove of trees. I counted about fifteen seconds between the time our car rounded a curve and the blue sedan appeared behind us. I pressed harder on the gas, racing around another bend.

"Bet I got more on Ashley than *you*," Nora announced.

"Oh, yeah? What've you got?"

She only shrugged, smiling.

"*Bupkis.* Exactly."

We sped around another turn, the road straightening and intersecting with a dirt service road. I paused at the stop sign and was just starting to floor it when suddenly Nora screamed.

That *woman*—the redheaded nurse—was crashing out of the steep wooded bank just to our right, running directly in front of our car.

I slammed on the brakes.

She fell forward against the hood, red hair spilling everywhere. For a horrified moment I thought she was hurt, but then she lifted her head, racing around the car to my side, leaning in an inch from the window.

She stared in at me—her brown eyes bloodshot, her freckled face desperate.

"Morgan Devold," she shouted. "Find him. He'll tell you what you want to know."

"What?"

"Morgan. *Devold.*"

She lurched back in front of the car and ran to the shoulder, scrambling up the steep embankment just as the blue sedan appeared behind us.

Frantically she was crawling on her hands and knees up the hill, sliding in the leaves and dirt. She reached the summit and wrapped her cardigan around herself, pausing to stare down at our car.

The guards had pulled up behind us and beeped.

They hadn't seen her.

I took my foot off the brake and—still intoxicated with shock—we continued down the drive, though in the rearview mirror, just before we rounded the next bend, I saw the woman was still standing on the hill, a gust of wind whipping that red hair into her face, blotting it out.

18 A STONE-FACED GUARD OPENED the electronic gate and we accelerated through, the Lincoln behind us doing a U-turn, heading back to the hospital.

"Oh my God," said Nora, exhaling, pressing a hand to her chest.

"What was the name she said?" I asked.

"Morgan Devold?"

"Write it down. D-E-V-O-L-D."

Nora hurriedly dug through her purse for a pen and bit off the cap, scribbling the name on the top of her hand.

"I saw her before when we were in the Security Center," she said. "And then she passed us on our way out. She wanted to talk to us."

"Apparently so."

"What's going on?" mumbled a hoarse voice from the backseat.

Hopper was up, yawning. He rubbed his eyes, staring out at the rural landscape speeding by, unsurprised.

I handed Nora my phone. "Google *Morgan Devold* and *New York.* Tell me what you get."

It took a few minutes, due to the patchy cell service.

"There's nothing much," she said. "Just one of those genealogy web-sites. A man named Morgan Devold lived in Sweden in 1836. He had a son named Henrik."

"Nothing else?"

"The name turns up on a site called Lawless Legwear."

We accelerated past another road sign. BIG INDIAN 5.

"Where the hell are we?" asked Hopper, rolling down the window.

Nora turned around, eagerly filling him in on what had transpired in the last four hours.

"We were about to be arrested," she went on. "But Scott was a total rock star. He whipped out this brochure that read across the front, 'The Greatest Man Who Ever Lived. Questions About Jesus Christ for Young People.'" She giggled. "It was *classic*."

As she explained what had just happened with the nurse, I spotted a Qwik Mart approaching on our right. I braked and made the turn.

"Go inside," I said to Nora, pulling up beside a gas tank and cutting the engine. "Ask if we can borrow a phone book. And pick up some snacks." I handed her twenty bucks and set about filling the tank.

Hopper emerged from the backseat, stretching.

"What'd you find out about Ashley?" he asked hoarsely.

"Not much. Apparently, she was a Code Silver patient, which is the most critical level of care."

"But you didn't find out what was wrong with her."

"No."

He seemed about to ask me something else, but instead turned, strolling across the parking lot, pulling out his cigarettes.

It was after four o'clock. The sun had loosened its grip on the world, letting the shadows get sloppy, the light, thawed and soft.

Directly across the street, a white farmhouse stood in the middle of a wild lawn, the grass strewn with garbage. On a drooping telephone wire sat two black birds, too tiny and fat to be crows. The Qwik Mart door dinged behind me and I turned to see an old man in a green flannel shirt and workman's boots, heading to a pickup, a brown mutt in the bed. The man climbed behind the wheel and they pulled out, swerving to make a right extremely close to Hopper, the muffler backfiring.

Hopper didn't react. He was staring in a sort of melancholic trance out at the middle of the road, oblivious to the cars speeding by.

Maybe that was the point—he was imagining stepping in front of one. He looked like he was at a river's edge, about to throw himself in. It was a melodramatic thought—probably residual paranoia from the appearance of that nurse. I could still see her anxious, freckled face staring at me, her lips chapped, the window clouding over from her breath, erasing her mouth.

Hopper took a drag of his cigarette, brushing his hair from his eyes, and looked up at the sky, squinting at those birds on the telephone wires. More had appeared out of nowhere. Now there were seven— seven tiny black notes on an otherwise empty piece of sheet music, the lines and bars sagging, giving up as they stretched between poles and twisted on down the road.

Another ding and Nora emerged, her arms laden with coffee cups, jelly beans, Bugles, and a phone book. She spread it all out on the hood.

"I got Hopper some coffee," she whispered, holding up the jumbo-sized cup and squinting worriedly across the parking lot at him. "He looks like he needs caffeine."

"He looks like he needs a hug."

She set the cup down, flipping through the phone book.

"It's here," she whispered in amazement.

I walked over, staring down at the page.

19 "It's the next driveway," said Nora, squinting at the phone. The drive to Livingston Manor was an hour and a half of snaking backcountry roads. It was already getting dark, the sky fading to a bruised blue. There were no street signs along Benton Hollow Road, no house numbers, no streetlights, not even any lines—just my car's faded headlights, which didn't so much push back the advancing dark as nervously rummage through it. To our left was a wall of solid shrubbery, barbed and impenetrable; to our right, vast black land stretched out, rumpled pastures and faded farmhouses, a lone porch light punctuating the night.

"This is it," whispered Nora excitedly, pointing at an opening in the shrubs.

There was a metal mailbox, but no number and no name.

I made the turn.

It was a constricted gravel drive straight uphill through dense foliage, an opening barely wide enough for a *man*, much less a *car*. The incline grew steeper, so I had to floor it, the entire car shimmying uncontrollably like the space shuttle trying to break the sound barrier. Spindly branches slapped the windshield.

After about a minute, we inched over the crest of the hill.

Instantly, I hit the brakes.

Far in front of us, across a scruffy lawn, wedged back between tall trees, sat a tiny wooden house so decrepit it rendered us mute.

The white paint was cracked and flaking. Shingles were missing from the roof, exposing a raw black hole, windows along the attic floor punched out and charred black. Strewn across the yard among the dead leaves and a large fallen tree were a child's toys—a wagon, a tricycle, and, farther off, along the edge of the yard where it was dark, an old plastic kiddie pool looking like a popped blister.

There was something so inherently menacing about the house as it loomed there, poised in the shadows, I automatically turned off the engine and headlights. A lone lit bulb by the front door illuminated a porch swing half on the ground and an old air conditioner. Another light was on in one of the back rooms—a tiny rectangular window lit with mint-green curtains pulled tightly closed.

It occurred to me we had no context whatsoever for this man—*Morgan Devold*. We were following the tip of a total stranger, a Briarwood nurse—who, recalling the way she'd thrown herself in front of the car, hadn't appeared exactly rational.

Parked beside the house in front of a wooden shed were a pickup truck and an old gray Buick, a plastic tarp hanging out of the trunk.

"Now what?" Nora said nervously, biting her thumbnail.

"Let's go over the plan," I said.

"*Plan?*" Hopper said with a laugh, leaning forward between us. "It's simple. We talk to Morgan Devold and find out what he knows. Let's go."

Before I could say a word, he'd climbed out, slammed the door, and was making his way across the yard. His gray wool coat caught the wind, flapping out behind him, and with his head down, his walk deliberate as he headed straight for the house, he resembled some kind of moody comic-book character about to unleash brutal vengeance on the inhabitants.

"He's certainly come back from the dead," I muttered. "What'd you put in his coffee?"

Nora didn't answer—she was too busy fumbling for the door handle like an eager kid sister who didn't want to be left behind. Within seconds she scrambled out, dashing right after him.

I held back, waiting. Let *them* be the scouts—*the lowly privates who checked for land mines before the general arrived.*

Their footsteps were the only sounds—soft crunches through the leaves and grass strewn with sticks. Maybe it was the peeling paint, giving the house scaly skin, but the place looked reptilian and alive, poised beyond the trees, waiting—that lone lit window like an eye watching us.

Somewhere far away, a dog barked.

Hopper was already at the front porch, so I climbed out of the car. He stepped around the air conditioner, pulled open the screen, and knocked on the door.

There was no answer.

He knocked again, waiting, a blast of wind sending a cluster of leaves across the lawn.

Still no answer. He let the screen bang closed and jumped down into the flower bed spiked with dead stalks and a tangled garden hose. Shading his eyes, he peered in one of the windows.

"*Someone's* home," he whispered. "There's a TV on in the kitchen."

"What are they watching?" I asked quietly, striding over the giant fallen tree trunk and then, past Nora, inspecting something lying facedown in the grass. It was an old teddy bear.

"Why?" whispered Hopper, glancing back at me.

"We'll be able to tell what type of people we're dealing with. If it's hardcore Japanese anime, we've got problems. But if it's a Barbara Walters special—"

"It looks like a rerun of *The Price Is Right*."

"That's even worse."

Hopper stepped gingerly back up onto the porch, this time noticing a dirt-encrusted doorbell. He pressed it twice.

Suddenly there was the jumble of locks turning, a chain sliding, and the front door *gasped* open, revealing a middle-aged blond woman behind the screen. She was wearing baggy gray sweats, a stained blue T-shirt, her peroxide-streaked hair in a ponytail.

"Good evening, ma'am," Hopper said. "Sorry to disturb you during the dinner hour. But we're looking for Morgan Devold."

She surveyed him suspiciously, then craned her neck to look at me.

"What do you all want with Morgan?"

"Just to chat," Hopper said with a laid-back shrug. "It should only take a few minutes. We're from Briarwood."

"He's not home," said the woman rudely.

"Any idea when he'll be back?"

She squinted at him. "You all get off our property or I'm callin' the cops."

She was about to slam the door, when a man materialized beside her.

"What's the matter?"

He had a soft, mild-mannered voice, in startling contrast to the woman, who appeared to be his wife. He was considerably shorter than she, and looked younger—early thirties—stocky, wearing a faded blue flannel button-down tucked neatly into his jeans, the sleeves rolled up. He had brown hair in a crew cut and broad, reddish features that were neither unattractive nor handsome, only ordinary. It was the face of a million other men.

"Are you Morgan Devold?" asked Hopper.

"What's this about?"

"Briarwood."

"You all got *some nerve* showin' up here," said the woman.

"Stace. It's all right."

"*No more communication.* You heard the lawyer—"

"It's fine."

"It's not *fine*—"

"Let me *handle* it." He said it with a sharp, raised voice, and suddenly somewhere in a back room, a baby started to cry.

The woman darted out of the doorway, though not before glaring at him.

"Get rid of them," she said.

Morgan—it appeared this *was* Morgan—stepped forward with an apologetic smile. As the baby wailed, he said nothing, and the way he stood there, stranded behind the screen door, reminded me of my last visit to the Bronx Zoo with Sam; she'd pointed out with great concern a chimpanzee staring dolefully out at us from behind the glass—such profound sadness, such resignation.

"You guys are from Briarwood?" he asked uncertainly.

"Not exactly," said Hopper.

"Then what's this really about?"

Hopper stared at him for a second before answering. "*Ashley.*"

It was surprising, the knowing way he said her name. In fact, it was *ingenious*—implying Ashley was some incredible experience both of them had had, so memorable, any mention of a last name was unnecessary. She was a magnificent hidden island, a secret house on a rocky cliff, visited by only a privileged few. If it was a deliberate trap on Hopper's part, it worked, because instantly a look of recognition appeared on the man's face.

Glancing furtively over his shoulder—where his wife had just disappeared to tend to the baby—he turned back to us. With a guilty smile, he extended his index finger and, careful not to make any noise, pushed it against the screen, quietly opening the door.

"Out here," he whispered.

20

WE FOLLOWED MORGAN DEVOLD to the edge of the yard, where there were dense trees, close to the children's pool filled with black water and leaves. The baby was still crying, though away from the house now the wind acted as a balm on the sound, easing it, folding it into the cold shivers of the night.

"How'd you find me?" Morgan asked rather resignedly, hooking his thumbs in his jean pockets.

"Through a nurse at Briarwood," said Hopper.

"Which one?"

"She didn't tell us her name," I said. "But she was young. Red hair and freckles."

He nodded. "Genevieve Wilson."

"Is she a friend of yours?"

"Not really. But I heard she made a stink to administration when I got the ax."

"You used to work at Briarwood?"

He nodded again.

"Doing what?"

"Security."

"For how long?"

"'Bout seven years? Before that, I did security at Woodbourne. I was all set for a promotion at Briarwood. Thought I was going to be assistant head." Smiling sadly, he looked up, staring past me to his own house. He looked bewildered, as if he didn't recognize it or couldn't remember how he'd come to live there.

"Who are you guys?" he asked.

"Private investigators," said Nora with evident excitement.

Somewhere Sam Spade just rolled over in his grave. I was certain Morgan would call us out on this obvious lie, but he nodded.

"Who hired you?" he asked solemnly. "Her family?"

He meant Ashley.

"We work for ourselves," I said.

"Everything you tell us can be off the record," added Nora.

He seemed to accept this, too, staring into the dark water of the pool. I realized then, he didn't care *who* we were. Some people were so burdened by a secret they'd give it away free to any willing stranger.

"Stace doesn't know a thing about it," he said. "She thinks I was fired 'cause Briarwood found out we're Adventists."

"It'll stay that way," said Hopper. "How did you know Ashley?"

But Morgan was no longer paying attention. Something had caught his attention in the kiddie pool. Frowning, he stepped a few feet away, picked up a fallen tree branch, and extended it into the water, trawling through the decaying leaves and mud.

A bulky object was actually floating there, bobbing along the bottom. He snagged it on the branch, pulling it toward him.

I thought it was a drowned animal—a squirrel or possum. So did Nora; she was staring at me with a stricken, horrified face as Morgan reached right in and pulled the thing out, dripping.

It was a plastic baby doll.

It was missing an eye, half bald, seeping blackened water, yet still smiling manically with puffy cheeks, what remained of its yellow hair matted with leaves. It was wearing a ruffled white dress, now mottled black, some kind of fungus growing like rancid heads of cauliflower out of the neck. Its fat little arms reached out at nothing.

"Last few weeks I turned the house upside down looking for this thing," mumbled Morgan, shaking his head. "My daughter cried for three days straight when it went missing. Couldn't find it. Was like the doll got fed up, walked clear outta the house. I had to sit her down, tell her it was gone now, went to be with God in heaven. Whole time, it was just out *here*."

He chuckled at the irony of it, a tight, frustrated sound.

"How did Ashley break out of Briarwood?" Hopper asked, glancing at me, indicating he sensed something was off with the man.

"With me," Morgan answered simply, still staring down at the doll.

Hopper nodded, waiting for him to go on. But he didn't.

"How?" Hopper prompted in a low voice.

Morgan glanced at us again, as if remembering we were there, smiling sadly. "It's funny how the night that changes your life forever starts out like all the others."

He let his arm fall to his side, holding the doll by its leg, its dress hanging over its head, exposing frilly underwear and drooling black water on the grass.

"I was coverin' for a buddy of mine," he said. "Working the night shift. Nine to nine. Stace hated when I took all-nighters, but I liked to watch the monitors at night. It's easy work. I'm the only one in the back rooms of the center. Patients are asleep, the corridors so still and quiet, it's like you're the last man alive." He cleared his throat. "I guess it was about three in the morning. I wasn't paying much attention. I had some magazines. Wasn't supposed to, but I'd done it a million times before. Nothing happens. There's nothing ever going on except the nurses checkin' the Code Reds."

"And what are the Code Reds?" I asked.

"Patients on suicide watch."

"What about Code Silver?" asked Hopper.

"Those are the patients kept apart 'cause they can hurt themselves and others. I'd been watching all night. It was like every other. Quiet. I'm flipping through a magazine when I glance up and something catches my eye on the monitor. One a' them music rooms in Straffen. There's somebody *in* there. As soon as I seen that, it switches to another. Video feeds are on a ten-second rotation. You can break the sequence to take a longer look at any live feed. I break, go back to that music room. I see there's a *girl* in there. She's a patient, 'cause she's wearing the authorized white pajamas. She's at the piano. Camera's high in the corner of the ceiling, so I'm lookin' down on her, a little over her shoulder. All I see are her skinny arms moving fast, her dark hair in a braid. Never seen her before. I work day shifts mostly, and you get to know the patients. I channel in audio, turn up the speaker . . ."

He fell silent, running a hand over the top of his head as if he couldn't believe what he was about to say.

"What?" I asked.

"It freaked me out."

"Why?"

"It was like a recordin'. Most times we got patients poundin' out 'Heart and Soul.' My first thought, she was one a' those *polter*—uh—"

"Poltergeist," interjected Nora eagerly.

"Yeah. Somethin' not real. She was playin' *violent*-like, head down, hands flippin' so fast. My second thought was I was *losin'* it. Seein' somethin' strange. I'm set to sound the alarm, but somethin' makes me hesitate. She ends that music, starts another, and before I know it even though I got my finger on the switch to call a breach, a whole half-hour goes by, then another. When she stops playin' she's quiet for a long time. Then, *real slow,* she lifts her head. I could just see the side of her face, but it was like . . ."

He fell silent and shuddered uncomfortably.

"Like *what*?" Hopper asked.

"She knew I was there. Watching."

"What do you mean?" I asked.

He gazed at me, serious. "She *saw* me."

"She saw the camera in the ceiling?"

"It was more than that. She stood up, and when she got to the door she turned and smiled *right at me*." He paused, incredulous, as he remembered. "She was like nothin' I'd ever seen before. A black-haired angel. She slipped right out. And I tracked her. Watched her move down the hall and outside. She moved fast. I'm havin' a hard time keepin' up with her on all the different video feeds. I follow her down the paths all the way back to Maudsley. I figured for sure she was going to get caught, but she enters, and for some crazy reason, there's *no officer* at the front desk."

He shook his head in disbelief. "She hurries in and up the back stairs so fast it's like her feet don't touch the ground. She goes all the way up to the third floor, races inside her room. I can't believe *that,* either. She's Code Silver, which means she's got a round-the-clock nurse detail. I keep watchin'. Twenty minutes later, I see the security officer and the nurse in charge of the third floor. They come smiling upstairs from the basement and something tells me they weren't down there doin' laundry. They got a little *thing* goin'. Somehow the girl knew about it." He paused, wiping his nose. "First thing I do is wipe the tapes. They're never checked, anyway. Not unless a problem's reported. But I erase 'em, just in case. The next morning I put in a request for extra night shifts."

"Why'd you do that?" asked Hopper with faint accusation.

"I had to see her again." He shrugged bashfully. "She went there to play piano every night. And I watched. The music . . ." He seemed unable to find the right words. "It's what you'll hear in heaven if you're lucky enough to get there. The whole time she ignored me, 'cept for the very end, when she'd *look* at me." Morgan smiled to himself as he surveyed the ground. "I had to find out who she was. I wasn't authorized to look into the files of patients. But I didn't care. I had to know."

"What'd you find out?" I asked.

"She had a fear of darkness. This thing called *nycta* somethin'—"

"*Nyctophobia?*" blurted Nora.

"That's it. I looked it up. People who got it go crazy in the dark. They start shakin'. Convulsin'. Think they're drownin' and dyin'. Sometimes they pass out. Or kill themselves—"

"Wait a minute," I interrupted. "Wasn't Ashley in the dark when you watched her on the camera?"

Morgan shook his head. "Briarwood's bright at night. The sidewalks and central grounds are kept lit for security purposes. Interior building lights are on energy-saving motion detectors, so they'd light up around her as she came and went. Some of them are on a delay. I began to notice she'd wait for a light to go on before she'd continue. When she was outside she'd keep to the bright side of every path. Like she couldn't step on a shadow or she'd melt or somethin'. She was real careful about it."

I frowned, trying to imagine such a manner of moving, skipping from one patch of light to another. I recalled the ascent through the Hanging Gardens up to the roof of the warehouse in Chinatown—had there been enough weak light to step through all the way up? And yet around the Central Park Reservoir, where she'd flickered in and out of the lamplight in that red coat, it was mostly pitch black.

"The other thing I found out," Morgan went on, "was the doctor treatin' her sent out a hospital-wide memo barring her from playing the piano. Said it brought on manic episodes. The date the order went out was the first night I saw Ashley. So, it was like she *had* to play. Like nothing could stop her from it."

He fell silent for a moment.

"On the eighth night I watched, on her way out of the music room I noticed she removed something from her pocket and stopped for a second right over the top of the piano. It happened fast. I wasn't sure what I'd seen. I rewound the tape and saw she'd stuck something in there. I waited till the end of my shift and headed over to Straffen, up to the music room on the second floor. When I walked in, the smell of her, the *feel* of her was still there. A perfume and like a warmth, I guess. I went over to the piano, checked under the lid. Inside, tucked in the strings, was a folded-up piece of paper. I took it but waited until I was safe in my car to read it."

He paused, visibly uneasy.

"What did it say?" I asked.

"*Morgan!*"

A screen door slammed.

"What're you still doin' out here?"

Stace was on the front porch, cradling the baby against her chest, shading her eyes in the glare of the light. Stepping after her was *another* child, a little girl of about four, wearing a white nightgown covered with what appeared to be cherries.

"They're not *gone* yet?"

"Everything's fine!" Morgan shouted. He turned to us, whispering, "Drive down the driveway and wait for me there, okay?"

He hurried back across the lawn.

"Oh my God. I told you to get *rid* of them!"

"They're from Human Resources. Doing a survey. Hey. Look what I found."

"But we're not supposed to—what *is* that?"

"*Baby.* I just rescued her from the pool."

"Are you *insane?*"

The little girl screamed, no doubt upon taking a look at that *doll.* Nora and Hopper were already making their way across the grass. I headed after them, and when we climbed back into my car the Devolds had returned inside, though their shouting could still be heard above the wind.

21 "IT'S OBVIOUS MORGAN FELL IN LOVE with Ashley," Nora said. "Can you blame him?" I asked. "He *is* married to *It*. I'm referencing the Stephen King book."

"He's a freak is what he is," said Hopper.

I turned around to him in the backseat. "You remember Ashley having nyctophobia at Six Silver Lakes?"

Glaring at me, he exhaled cigarette smoke out the window. "*No way.*"

We were in my car, sitting at the end of Devold's driveway. We'd been waiting for him to reappear for forty-five minutes. Apart from my headlights illuminating the unmarked road, which twisted around the dense shrubs in front of us, it was pitch black out here, totally deserted. The wind had picked up. It whistled insistently against the car, making the branches nervously tap the windshield.

"He's probably not coming back," I muttered. "*Stace* put the guy's muzzle back on and returned him to his cage in the basement."

"She wasn't *that bad*," said Nora, shooting me a look.

"Let me bear witness as the only person in this car who's *been* to the dark side of marriage and survived. She's *bad*. She makes my ex-wife look like Mother Teresa."

"He's coming back," muttered Hopper. "He has to."

"Why?"

"He's dying to talk about her."

He ground out the cigarette on the window, flicking the butt outside.

Suddenly, Nora gasped as the man himself stepped into the headlights.

I didn't know how we'd managed *not* to hear his footsteps. There was something odd in the way he stood there in his faded blue flannel shirt, blinking at us uneasily, his head held down at a strange, shy angle. None of us said a word. *Something was wrong.* But again, Hopper and Nora were unlocking the doors, scrambling out. I held back to observe the guy for a few seconds longer. In spite of his sudden appearance, the ghostly pallor, he looked uncomfortable—*wounded,* even.

I climbed out, leaving the headlights on.

"I only got five minutes," Morgan said nervously. "Otherwise Stace'll get out the shotgun."

It had to be a joke, yet he said it with unnerving seriousness.

Blinking, he held out a folded piece of paper.

Hopper immediately snatched it, shooting him a suspicious look as he opened it in the beam of light. When he finished reading, his face giving away nothing, he handed it to Nora, who read it with wide eyes and passed it to me.

It was torn from a legal pad.

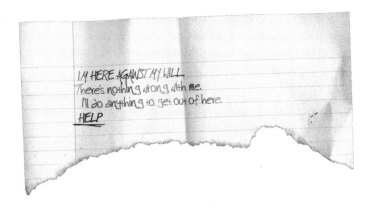

I'M HERE AGAINST MY WILL
There's nothing wrong with me.
I'll do anything to get out of here.
HELP

"It took three weeks to plan," Morgan said. "I'd use all prerecorded tapes. They'd play, not the live feed. The time code would be wrong, but no one ever checked. I went down into storage, where they keep all the patients' personal belongings until they check out, and I got hers from her locker and kept it for her in a box in my house. All she had was a red-and-black coat. Real fancy."

"That was it?" I asked, noting the odd, rather fastidious way he'd said it. I couldn't help but imagine him silently slipping out of his bed in the middle of the night while Stace slept, creeping down into his own dark basement to open up the cardboard box, staring in at her red coat—*that coat.*

"Yeah," he said. "She didn't have anything else."

"No cellphone? No handbag?"

He shook his head. "No."

"What about clothing?"

"Nothing. See, her father's famous. He makes Hollywood movies. I figured she'd want some nice clothes, so I left her a note asking for her sizes. Then I took a day off, went up to Liberty, bought her some jeans, black boots, and a pretty black T-shirt with an angel on the front."

Ashley was wearing the same clothing when she died.

"Once I had the details worked out," he went on, "I went to the music room and left Ashley a note tucked between the piano strings right where she did. It said when she was ready, she should play 'Twinkle Twinkle Little Star.' That'd be my green light. It'd mean the very next night I'd come for her at two A.M. when her nurse and the guard were gettin' it on in the boiler room."

"Why that particular song?" I asked.

"She'd played it before." He smiled. "It reminded me of her. That night, Stace ended up in the hospital and was put on bed rest. I had to transfer back to days. I didn't see Ashley for a week. I was worried I missed her playin' it. But the first night I was back on the night shift she darted into that music room and I was freaking out because I wasn't sure she was going to play it. But then she *did*. Right at the end. I knew then we were on."

He stared at us, flecks of light brightening his small eyes. He was newly animated, remembering it.

"The next night, around one, I get the prerecorded tapes going. Then I tell the officer on duty who sits out front, Stace's having another pregnancy scare and I had to head home. I go straight to Maudsley, thinking I'm going to have to slip up to Ashley's room to get her. But if she isn't already standing out in front waiting for me in those white pajamas. My heart's beating like *crazy*. I'm nervous as a goddamn schoolkid because, you know, it was the first time I was seeing her in the flesh. She just took my hand, and together we ran across the lawn, simple as that." He grinned sheepishly. "It was like *she* was leading *me*. Like *she'd* planned it. I opened my trunk, she climbed in, and we drove out of there."

"But wasn't it dark inside the trunk?" Nora asked. "If Ashley had nyctophobia she wouldn't have climbed in there."

Morgan smiled proudly. "I took care of it. I had two flashlights in there for her so she wouldn't be afraid."

"Did they stop you at the gatehouse?" I asked.

"Sure. But I said my wife was having another emergency and he let me through. As soon as we were out of there I pulled over so Ashley could get out of the trunk. I brought her back here so she could shower and change. I also had to put my daughter to bed. Stace was still in the hospital, so our neighbor was watching the baby. I asked Ashley where she wanted to go and she said the train station because she had to get to New York City."

"Did she say why?" I asked.

"I think she was meetin' someone."

"Who?" Hopper asked.

"Don't know. She was shy. Didn't talk much. Just looked at me. She liked my little girl, Mellie, though. Read her a bedtime story while I was on the phone with Stace at the hospital."

"Where was Ashley going in the city?" I asked.

"Walford Towers? Somethin' like that."

"She told you this?"

He looked guilty. "No. She'd asked to use the Internet while she was here. When she was in the bathroom I checked the browser to see what she looked for online. It was a website for a hotel on Park Avenue."

"The Wal*dorf* Towers?" I suggested.

Morgan nodded. "That sounds about right. When she was dressed, she put on that red coat and she looked like the prettiest thing I'd ever seen. I drove her to the station. We got there 'bout four in the morning. I gave her some cash, then left her in the car while I went and bought two tickets to Grand Central."

"*Two* tickets?" I asked.

He nodded, embarrassed.

"You hoped to go with her."

He stared down at the ground. "Seems crazy now. But I'm romantic. I thought we'd go together. She kept *smiling* at me. But when I got back to my car with the tickets, she was gone. I saw a train had pulled in. I ran up to the platform, but the doors had already shut. I moved down it, searching for her in every car, feelin' sick about it until I found her. She was sitting right by the window. I knocked. And slowly, she turned to me, stared at me. I'll never forget the look she gave me, not for the rest of my life."

He said nothing for a moment, his shoulders hunched.

"She didn't know me."

He exhaled, his breathing unsteady.

"You were fired shortly afterward?" I asked quietly.

He nodded. "Soon as Ashley was found missing it was all traced back to me."

"When did you find out that she'd died?"

He blinked. "Head of the hospital called me in."

"Allan Cunningham?"

"Yeah. He said nothing would happen in terms of the law if I signed a confidentiality paper sayin' I'd acted alone and never, ever talk about it—"

"*Morgan!*"

It was Stace again. Her voice startled all of us, not just by its shrillness but its close proximity. We couldn't see her, but heavy footsteps were coming nearer, heading down the dark gravel drive.

"*Morgan!* Are those people still here?"

"You'd better go," Morgan hissed at us.

Before I could stop him, he'd snatched the paper from me, racing back up the driveway.

I took off after him.

"That paper—we'd like to *keep* it—" I shouted.

But he was sprinting with remarkable speed. I could barely keep up.

Stace abruptly appeared at the top of the hill. I froze. She wasn't brandishing a shotgun, but even *more* terrifyingly, she was brandishing *children.* The half-naked baby was still in her arms, and the girl wearing the nightgown was holding her mother's hand, sucking her thumb.

"They're going right now," Morgan said. "They needed directions to the highway." He put his arm around her, saying something inaudible as he moved them back toward the house, shoving the paper into his back pocket.

Damn. I'd wanted to keep it, compare the handwriting with that on the envelope mailed to Hopper.

They moved out of sight, though I could hear them walking through the leaves, Stace angrily saying something, the baby whimpering.

I turned, making my way back down the drive, Hopper and Nora in the beam of the headlights, waiting for me. I hadn't taken ten steps when a rock scuttled behind me.

I turned around, startled, and saw I wasn't alone.

That little girl in the nightgown was following me.

Her face in the darkness looked hard, her eyes hollowed black.

She was barefoot. The white of her nightgown glowed purple; the cherries looked like chain links and barbed wire. She was also, I realized, holding that rotten doll Morgan had exhumed from the swimming pool—*Baby*—clutching it in the crook of her arm.

My first reaction was revulsion, followed by the urge to *run like hell.*

She suddenly extended her arm. A chill shot down my spine.

Her hand was in a tight fist, her stare pointed. She was holding something black and shiny in her fingers. I couldn't see exactly what it was, but it looked like a tiny doll.

Before I could react, she spun around and scampered back up the drive, vanishing over the top in a streak of white.

I stood there, staring at the empty space on the hill, sensing, for some reason, she'd reappear.

She didn't. And yet it was oddly silent.

There was no trace of Stace's harsh voice—no baby whimper, no footsteps, no screen door swinging open followed by a slam, nothing but the wind shoving through the shrubs.

Even that lonely hound in the distance had gone quiet.

I turned, jogging the rest of the way to the car.

"What was that?" asked Hopper.

"His little girl followed me."

I unlocked the car, climbed in, and within minutes we were speeding back down Benton Hollow Road. They didn't say so, but I suspected all three of us were relieved to be rapidly putting some *serious distance* between ourselves and the Devolds.

22 "THAT'S WHAT HAPPENS when you marry the wrong woman," I said. "A wife sets the ambience of a man's life. He can very easily get stuck listening to Michael Bolton Muzak droning in a loop from tin-sounding speakers for the rest of his life, if he doesn't keep his *wits* about him. You can't blame the guy for wanting to run."

"He was a total loser," said Hopper from the backseat.

"That's another way to put it." We were hashing over Morgan Devold and all we'd learned about Ashley at Briarwood, now driving down the New Jersey Turnpike, minutes from the city.

That was the wonderful thing about New York: You might spend a few nervous hours in rural landscapes with nurses who threw themselves in front of your car and strange families, but the closer you came to Manhattan and took one look at that bristling skyline—*then* took a look at the guy who just cut you off in a pimped-out Nissan blasting Tejano-polka—you realized that all was right with the world.

"Ash played him," Hopper went on, without looking up from his phone, buzzing with texts. "She knew someone was watching her on the camera. So, she decided, whoever he was, he was her best bet for breaking out of there."

"What about this fear of the dark?" I asked, glancing at Nora. "Which reminds me. How did you know that term, *nyctophobia*?"

She'd dismantled her hair from those long braids and was absent-mindedly staring out the window, untangling the ends. "Terra Hermosa," she said. "A gentleman on the second floor named Ed. He used to go down this phobia list and boast about all the ones he'd had. He'd never had nyctophobia. But he had *automatonophobia*."

"What's that?"

"Fear of ventriloquist dummies. Anything with a waxy face. He went to see *Avatar* and had to be hospitalized."

"He should definitely stay away from the Upper East Side."

"It's bullshit," said Hopper, shoving his hair out of his eyes. "Ash wasn't scared of the *dark*. She probably just put that act on for the doctors, so they'd leave her alone."

"What about the way she looked at Morgan from the train?" asked Nora. "Maybe she *didn't* know him. Maybe she had amnesia or short-term memory loss."

"No," Hopper said. "He'd served his purpose and she was done with him. That was it."

"One other thing kind of worried me," Nora added.

"Only *one* other thing?" I asked.

"Morgan said Ashley read his daughter a bedtime story."

"So?"

"You don't let a stranger you just broke out of a mental hospital spend time with your child. Do you?"

"He's not winning any awards for Father of the Year. What about that Bride of Chucky he fished out of the kiddie pool? *Baby.* Not to mention that little *tyke* that tailed me down the drive. When she grows up she's going to need a long sojourn at Briarwood."

Nora tilted her head. "You don't think Morgan hurt Ashley, do you? When he took her to his house to change clothes—there was something about the way he described it, it gave me the creeps."

"He didn't lay a hand on her," interjected Hopper.

"How do you know?" asked Nora, turning around to him.

"Because if he *had,* he'd be severely maimed right now."

I glanced at him in the rearview mirror, startled by his tone of voice. He was staring out the window, his face gilded by lights of the passing cars. One thing I'd gathered in the past few hours was that his knowledge of Ashley—*Ash,* he'd called her—was significantly more intense than the casual acquaintance of years ago he'd claimed. He knew her better than he let on, or else he'd once observed her carefully, maybe even from a distance like Devold. I was tempted to press him on it, try and get him to admit he hadn't been forthcoming, but decided against it—for the time being. He'd probably only glower and become defensive, and that wouldn't get me anywhere.

I checked the clock on the dashboard: 9:42 P.M.

"So, where am I dropping you two off?" I asked.

Nora turned to me. "We're *not* done *yet.* We still have to go to that hotel, the Waldorf, see if somebody noticed Ashley. He said she was going there. So we should go."

"Sounds like a plan," muttered Hopper, meeting my eyes in the rearview mirror.

"It's a long shot," I said. "But sure. Let's check it out."

23 | LIKE MOST NEW YORKERS, I went out of my way to avoid the Waldorf Astoria. It was like a very rich, very large, and mercifully very *distant* great-aunt who had three rolls of fat under her chin, wore taffeta, and had a personality so bossy you only needed to not *see* her but *hear* about her once to have your fill of her for the next fifteen years.

If you decided to venture inside, however, through the Art Deco revolving doors past the businessmen from Milwaukee and the Unitarian Church group, then took a breather before beating your way through the crowd up the carpeted stairs past the line into Starbucks and the woman rolling her carry-on suitcase over your shoes, instantly you were assaulted by the bloated luxury of the place. There were vaulted ceilings. There were palm trees. There were gilt clocks. There was marble. If there was a wedding reception—and there usually was, the bride and groom, Bobby and Marci of Massapequa, *Lawn Guyland*—the lobby throbbed like a gymnasium on prom night.

Hopper and Nora followed me through the lobby, ducking around an extended family wearing matching Red Sox sweatshirts toward a discreet wooden doorway. It was labeled with a tiny gold plaque, THE WALDORF TOWERS—so tactful its obvious aim was to go unseen.

I strode down the corridor to the elevator banks, stepping inside, Nora and Hopper right behind me.

"You really know your way around here," said Nora, as I pressed *G.*

I *did,* unfortunately.

The Waldorf Astoria was only a distraction from the section of the hotel where the *important* people stayed, the more exclusive Waldorf Towers, hotel of choice to presidents, the Duke and Duchess of Windsor, Saudi princes, and various high-rolling Wall Street businessmen when they rendezvoused with their mistresses, which, sadly, was something along the lines of how *I* knew the place.

I wasn't proud of it—and I sure as hell didn't recommend it—but there was a six-month hellish stretch when, shortly after my divorce, I saddled myself with an affair with a married woman. And I met her here, at the Waldorf Towers, a total of *sixteen times,* though this was only after she'd sent me feedback emails in the bitter tone of an unsatisfied boss informing me the *first* hotel I'd chosen for our trysts, one I could actually *afford,* the generic Fitzpatrick Manhattan on Lex—known by its devoted clientele as *The Fitz*—was too close to her office, the rooms didn't get enough light, the sheets stank, and the man at reception gave her a funny look after he asked if she needed help with luggage and she announced she didn't have any, she'd be there for only forty-five minutes.

The elevator doors opened, spilling us into the Waldorf Towers lobby, small, elegant, and totally empty.

The three of us walked around the corner to the reception area, where a young man of Middle Eastern descent stood alone behind the front desk. He was tall, with a narrow build, dark eyes. His nametag read HASHIM.

I briefly introduced myself. "And we were hoping you might help," I went on. "We're searching for information on a missing woman. We think she came here sometime in the last month."

He looked intrigued. He also, thankfully, made no sign of needing to go fetch his manager.

"Mind taking a look at her picture?" I asked.

"Certainly not." It was a bright, genial voice, gilded with a British accent.

I removed Ashley's missing-person's report from my inside coat pocket, folded so only her picture was visible, and handed it to him.

"When was she here?" he asked.

"A few weeks ago."

He handed it back. "I'm sorry. I've never seen her before. Of course, it's hard to tell from the picture. If you like I can make a photocopy and post it in the back, in case any other staff met her or remember her."

"Nothing was reported out of the ordinary?"

"No."

"Do you videotape the lobby?"

"We do. But that would require a warrant. I assume you've contacted police?"

I nodded, and Hashim smiled with flawless five-star sorrow at being unable to help me further—*and it was time for us to be on our way.*

"She would have been wearing *this*," said Nora, pulling Ashley's coat out of the Whole Foods bag and setting it, folded, on the leather desk pad.

He looked down at it and was about to shake his head when something about the coat visibly stopped him.

"You recognize it," I said.

He looked puzzled. "*No.* It's just, a member of housekeeping reported an incident. It was a while back. But I think it *did* have something to do with a person in a red coat. The reason I remember is the matter came up *again* this morning, when the same housekeeper refused to clean one of the floors. It caused a disruption because we're at capacity."

Hashim, looking up, noticed all three of us were leaning with great intensity over the desk.

He took a step back, alarmed.

"Why don't you leave a number and my supervisor can speak with you?"

"We don't have time for a supervisor," said Hopper, jostling Nora as he moved closer to Hashim. "With a missing person, every minute counts. We need to talk to the housekeeper. I know it'd mean you bending a few *rules,* but . . ." He smiled. "We'd appreciate it."

It'd been my suggestion back in the car to allege that Ashley was *missing,* not dead; the missing, I'd found, prompted a greater sense of haste and willingness to help. This strategy seemed to work. Or perhaps it was just Hopper's looks cranked up and turned blazingly onto the man, because Hashim stared at Hopper, a few seconds too long. And I saw the brief yet brazen look of male desire flash on his face, unmistakable as an oil tanker blinking a light at another ship. The man picked up the phone and, tucking the receiver under his chin, swiftly dialed a number.

"Sarah. Hashim at the front desk. Guadalupe Sanchez. That episode she reported a few weeks back. Wasn't there something about a red coat? Isn't that what—*oh.*" He fell silent, listening. "Is she still on duty tonight?" He listened. "Twenty-nine. All right, thank you."

He hung up.

"Come with me," he said with a curt smile at Hopper.

24 WE FOLLOWED HASHIM into an elevator, where he inserted a white keycard into the slot and pressed 29.

We rose in silence, though quite a few times Hashim glanced swiftly at Hopper, who was staring down at his Converse sneakers. I wasn't sure *what* was going on in this silent communication, but it was working; the doors opened, and Hashim exited briskly, making his way down the cream-colored hallway.

A housekeeping cart was parked at the end. We made our way toward it, Nora hanging back to inspect the few black-and-white photographs hanging on the wall, pictures of Frank Sinatra and Queen Elizabeth.

Reaching the cart, Hashim knocked sharply on the door marked 29T, slightly ajar.

"Miss Sanchez?"

He pushed it open. We filed after him into a suite's empty sitting room: blue couches, blue carpet, an extravagant mural painted on the walls, featuring Greek columns and a blue-skinned goddess.

Hashim stepped through a kitchen alcove, the three of us following.

It led into a bedroom where a petite silver-haired woman was in the process of making up the bed. She was Hispanic, wearing a sea-gray housekeeping dress. She didn't react because she was listening to music—a mint-green iPod strapped to her arm.

She moved around the bed, tucking the sheet, and spotted us.

She cried out shrilly, clamping a hand over her mouth, eyes bulging.

You'd have thought we just filed in wearing hooded robes and wielding scythes.

Hashim spoke in Spanish, an apology for scaring her, and the woman—Guadalupe Sanchez, I gathered—removed the earbuds from her ears, and in a raspy voice muttered something back.

"How's your Guatemalan Spanish?" Hashim asked brightly.

"Spotty," I said.

Nora and Hopper both shook their heads.

"I'll do my best to translate, then." He turned officially back to her and fired off some immaculate Spanish.

She listened with keen interest. Occasionally her gaze left Hashim to study us. At one point—it must have been when he explained why we were there—she nodded almost reverentially and whispered, *Sí, sí, sí.* She then stepped around the bed toward us slowly, nervously, as if we were three bulls that might charge her.

Seeing the woman only a few feet away now, her face was round and girlish with the fat cheeks of a toddler, yet her caramel skin was so finely wrinkled, it looked like a brown paper bag once tightly wadded in a hand.

"Show her the picture," Hashim said.

I removed it from my coat pocket.

She took a moment to carefully unfold her glasses, setting them on the end of her nose, before taking it. She said something in Spanish.

"She recognizes her," Hashim said.

Nora, who'd been fumbling with Ashley's coat in the Whole Foods bag, finally shook it loose, holding it up by the shoulders.

The woman took one look at it and froze, whispering.

"She thinks she's seen it before," Hashim said.

"She *thinks?*" I said. "She looks pretty convinced."

He smiled uncomfortably, turning back to the woman and asking her a question. She responded, her voice serious and low, eyeing Ashley's coat as if worried it might come alive. Hashim interrupted to ask a question, and she heatedly responded, taking a few steps *away* from the coat. She talked for several minutes, so *dramatically* at times I wondered if she were a popular telenovela actress on Venevisión. I tried to dig through the stream of Spanish to find a word I might recognize, and, abruptly, I did.

Chaqueta del diablo. The devil's coat.

"So?" I asked Hashim when she stopped talking and he made no effort to translate.

He looked irritated. "It happened weeks ago," he said. "Five o'clock in the morning. She was on the thirtieth floor, starting her morning rounds."

Guadalupe was watching him closely. He smiled back thinly.

"She'd just unlocked a room when she noticed something at the end of the hall. A red form. She couldn't see what it was. She'd left her glasses at home. It was just a ball of *red.* She thought it was a suitcase." He cleared his throat. "Forty-five minutes later, after she finished cleaning the room, she came out again. It was still there, this *blurry red thing.* Yet, it *moved.* Guadalupe wheeled her cart down the hallway and as she came nearer she realized it was a young woman. The same one in your picture. The girl was crouched on the floor, her back against the wall. She was wearing *that coat.*"

"What else?" asked Hopper.

"That's it, I'm afraid."

"Did Guadalupe speak to her?" I asked.

"No. She tried shaking her, but the girl was in a drug-induced stupor. Lupe ran away to alert security. When they returned, the girl was gone. She hasn't been seen since."

"Can she remember the *specific date* that this happened?" I asked. "It would be helpful."

"She can't remember. It was a few weeks ago."

Guadalupe smiled sadly at me, and then, seemingly recalling something new, added something, extending her right arm in front of her. It was a strange gesture, her hand forming a sort of *claw*—as if grabbing an invisible doorknob in the air. She then pointed at her left eye, nervously shaking her head.

"What's she saying now?" I asked.

"It was all very disturbing for her," he said. "It's unusual to come across a vagrant passed out in our halls. Now, if you don't *mind*, we should let Lupe return to work."

His five-star customer service had deteriorated into about a one-star. Not even Hopper was enough to sway him from ending the interview. In fact, Hashim seemed to deliberately avoid looking at him.

"Downstairs you said she wouldn't clean her assigned floor this morning," I said. "What was that about?"

"The girl frightened her. We need to return to the lobby. Any further questions you should address directly with the police." He added a few words to Guadalupe and strode to the door.

Nora stuffed the coat back inside the bag—as Guadalupe nervously watched—Hopper and I moving behind her, though when Hashim continued on, I covertly darted back into the bedroom.

I wanted a few private moments with Guadalupe—maybe get her to add something I could translate later. I found her in the bathroom, standing in front of the mirror by the pink marble sink. Spotting me in the reflection, her gaze jumped off her own face onto mine. It was such a panicked look, it shocked me. She opened her mouth to say something.

"*Sir,*" snapped Hashim behind me. "You need to leave *now,* or I'm calling security."

"I was just thanking Guadalupe for her time."

With a last glance back at her—Hashim had scared her, because she was already crouching over the tub, her back to me—I followed him out.

25 "THE POLICE CAN BE of further help," said Hashim as he deposited us outside the hotel's entrance on East Fiftieth Street. "Best of luck."

He watched us walk to the corner of Park Avenue by Saint Bartholomew's Church, then said something to the doorman—doubtlessly orders to alert security if we came back—and vanished inside.

It was after eleven now, a cold, clear night. Taxis and town cars were roaring down Park, though the wide sidewalks stretching north were quiet and deserted, the grand buildings nothing more than hollow cathedrals standing in the sky. In spite of the traffic, it felt lonely. The church's entrance was strewn with the dark immobile forms of men in bulky overcoats, asleep on cardboard boxes. They might have been dark whales, caught unaware by a tide that suddenly receded, leaving them stranded on the steps.

"What do you think?" Nora asked me.

"Lupe? She was a bit *dramatic* but had to be telling the truth. Her version of it."

"Why would Ashley be on the thirtieth floor, just *sleeping* there?"

"Maybe she was staying with someone. Didn't have a key. Or she was meeting someone."

"Did you see the way she stared at the coat? It was like she thought it was going to lunge at her or something."

"She called it the devil's coat. Hashim forgot to mention that."

"He forgot to mention a lot of things," interjected Hopper. He'd been squinting back at the entrance to the hotel, but now he stepped over to us, fumbling in his coat pockets. "He made half that shit up."

"So you do speak Spanish," I said.

"I lived since I was seven in Caracas. Then wandered Argentina and Peru for about a year." He announced this offhandedly as he tapped out a cigarette, turning his back to the wind to light it.

"Like Che Guevara in *Motorcycle Diaries*?" asked Nora.

"Not really. It was hell. But I'm glad it was good for something. Like knowing when someone's trying to con me."

I was surprised, to say the least. I hadn't expected the kid to be bilingual. But then I remembered a detail he'd let slip when he was telling me about Six Silver Lakes back in his apartment. *I'd been traveling with my mom in South America for this missionary cult shit she was into. I ran the fuck away.*

"I wanted to see if he was on the up and up. And he wasn't." Hopper exhaled a long stream of smoke. "I didn't like that guy."

"He certainly liked *you*."

He didn't respond, seemingly bored by the comment.

"So, what did she *really* say?" I asked.

"It was kinda tough to follow because she was speaking in a Guatemalan dialect. *And* she was bat-shit crazy."

"Why was she bat-shit crazy?" asked Nora.

"She believed in ghosts, spirits, like, they're all floating around us like pollen. She went on for like fifteen minutes about how she came from a long line of *curanderas.*"

"What's that?" I asked.

"Some folksy medicine-woman bullshit. I've heard of them, actually. They cure bodies and souls. A one-stop shop for all your troubles."

"So, what did he lie about?"

"He was right about the housekeeper seeing Ashley on the thirtieth floor. But the second he got to the part where she was wheeling the cart down the hall, he took all kinds of liberties. She actually called her *espíritu rojo,* a red spirit. She never thought it was a person sitting there, but some kind of confused soul or something, trapped between life and death. The nearer she got, she felt something, like some change in the gravitational pull of the Earth. When she crouched down in front of Ashley she said she was *inconsciente.* Unconscious. But not from *drugs.* She called her *una mujer de las sombras.* A woman of shadows." He shrugged. "No *clue* what that meant. She touched her, and Ashley was like ice, so she shook her by the shoulders and when she opened her eyes, she saw *la cara de la muerte* staring back at her. The face of death."

He fell silent, thinking it over. "She said Ashley was marked," he added.

"In what way?"

"By the devil. *Told* you the woman was nuts. She said there was a second pupil in her left eye, *some* shit, and it was . . ." He tossed his cigarette to the ground. "She called it *huella del mal.*" He ground the butt out with his heel, and when he glanced up again, he seemed surprised by our expectant faces, waiting for him to translate.

"It means evil's footprint," he said.

"That's why she pointed at her left eye," I said.

Nora was staring at Hopper, speechless. She rolled the Whole Foods bag containing Ashley's coat even tighter, as if to make sure whatever *aura negativo* attached to it remained securely inside.

"Then what happened?" I asked. "Stigmata appeared on Guadalupe's palms?"

"She was scared, ran to the basement, got her things, and went to church for the rest of the day. She *didn't* call security, which was why Hashim was pissed. She didn't follow housekeeping protocol. Hashim thought Ashley was homeless, and he told Guadalupe he was going to speak to her boss about her handling of the situation. So after all that, I think we got the woman in trouble."

It made perfect sense. When I saw Guadalupe staring at herself in the bathroom mirror with that odd look on her face, it had to be because she feared she might lose her job.

Hopper now looked rather dismissive of the entire episode. He'd taken his phone from his pocket, scrolling through messages.

"I gotta bounce," he said. "Catch you guys later."

With a slipshod smile, he turned, stepping off the curb.

Even though cars were racing down Park, surging toward us, he jogged right out in front of them, oblivious, or else he didn't care if he was hit. A taxi braked and honked, but he ignored it, hopping right up onto the median, waiting for the cars to pass on the other side, and then he dashed across the street, Nora and I looking on in silence.

26 | NORA DIDN'T WANT ME to drive her home, but I insisted, so she told me to drop her off at Ninth and Fifty-second Street. As I drove, neither of us spoke.

It'd been a *long day,* to say the least. I hadn't eaten anything but jelly beans and Bugles. Hopper's chain-smoking had left me with a dull headache. Everything we'd uncovered about Ashley—the escape from Briarwood, the housekeeper's apparent sighting—was too fresh to make sense of at this hour. My immediate plan was to go home, pour myself a drink, go to bed, and see how it all looked in the morning.

I made the left onto Ninth, pulling over in front of a Korean deli.

"Thanks for the ride," said Nora, grabbing the strap of her purse and opening the door.

"Did you miss work tonight?" I asked. "The Four Seasons?"

"Oh, *no*. My last day was yesterday. The normal girl came back from maternity leave. Tomorrow I'm starting as a waitress at Mars 2112."

"Where's your apartment?"

"Down there." She pointed vaguely over her shoulder. "Guess I'll see you later." Smiling, she heaved her bag onto her shoulder, slammed the door, and took off down the sidewalk.

I stayed where I was. After she'd gone about ten yards, she glanced back—clearly checking to see if I was still there—and continued on.

See you later.

I pulled out onto Ninth Avenue, stopping at the red light. Nora was still walking down the block but slowed to glance over her shoulder again. She must have seen me, because she immediately skipped up the front steps of the nearest cruddy building.

Jesus Christ. Sartre *really* wasn't kidding when he said *Hell is other people.*

The light turned green. I floored it to get in the right-hand lane but was immediately cut off by an articulated bus. As usual, the driver was driving like he thought he was in a goddamn Smart car, not a block-long centipede on wheels. I braked, waiting for him to pass, turned right onto Fifty-first Street, again onto Tenth and then Fifty-second.

I pulled over behind a truck and spotted Nora immediately.

She was sitting back along the ledge of the front steps of the apartment building she'd seemingly disappeared into, checking her cell. After a minute, she stood, peered around the columns to take a furtive look at the spot where I'd just dropped her off. Seeing I was now gone, she skipped down the steps, heading *back* to the corner.

I edged into the street. Reaching the deli, she strode past the rows of fresh flowers—saying something to the old guy sitting there—and entered.

I pulled over again to wait. A minute later, she emerged carrying those two giant Duane Reade shopping bags she'd had back at the Pom Pom Diner as well as—oddly enough—a large, white wire cylindrical birdcage.

She crossed the street with this luggage, heading south down Ninth.

I waited for the light to turn green and made a right, watching her jostle down the sidewalk in front of me. I slowed, so as not to pass her—a taxi behind me laying on the horn—and saw her stop at the door of a tiny, narrow storefront. PAY-O-MATIC, read the sign. She pressed a button to enter, waiting, and vanished inside.

I accelerated, making a fast right onto Fifty-first Street, parking in front of a fire hydrant. I locked the car and headed back to Ninth.

The glass façade of PAY-O-MATIC was covered in signs: WESTERN UNION, CHECKS CASHED, 24-HOUR FINANCIAL SERVICES. The shop was tiny, with brown carpeting and a couple of folding chairs, boxes piled on the floor. Along the back wall there was a teller window with bulletproof glass.

I rang the buzzer. After about a minute, the back door opened and a large bald man stuck his head out.

He was wearing a black short-sleeved shirt and had a face like a piece of pastrami. He pressed a switch on the wall and the entrance clicked open.

As I stepped inside, he moved into the teller window, wiping his hands on the front of his shirt, which I now saw had branches of red bamboo sewn all over it. As a rule, I didn't trust men who wore embroidery.

"I'm looking for a young woman with shopping bags and a birdcage."

He made a bogusly confused face. "Who?"

"Nora Halliday. Nineteen. Blond."

"It's just me here." He had a thick New York accent.

"Then I must be Timothy Leary tripping on serious *acid,* because I just saw her walk in."

"You mean Jessica?"

"Exactly."

He stared at me, worried. "You a cop?"

"What do you think?"

"I don't want trouble."

"Neither do I. Where is she?"

"The back room."

"What's she doing there?"

He shrugged. "She gives me forty bucks. I let her crash here."

"Forty bucks? That's it?"

"*Hey,*" he said defensively. "I've got a family."

"Where's the back room?"

Without waiting for his answer, I stepped to the only door and opened it.

It led down a cluttered, dark hallway.

"I don't want trouble." He was right next to me, his heavy cologne nearly knocking me over. "I did it as a favor."

"To whom?"

"*Her.* She showed up here six weeks ago, crying. I helped her out."

I stepped past him into the hall. Muffled rap music throbbed on a floor above, giving the building a thudding heartbeat.

"*Bernstein!*" I shouted.

There was no answer.

"It's Woodward. I need to talk to you."

At the end of the hall were two closed wooden doors. I moved toward them, around a janitor bucket filled with dirty water, passing a kitchenette, a half-eaten sandwich sitting on top of a folding table.

"I know you're in here somewhere," I called out.

The first door was slightly ajar. I pushed it open with my foot. It was a bathroom, a crumpled issue of a skin magazine and a ribbon of toilet paper stuck to the floor.

I moved past it, knocking on the second door. When there was no answer, I tried the handle. It was locked.

"Nora."

"Leave me alone," she said quietly. It sounded as if she were mere inches away, behind a piece of cardboard.

"How about opening the door so we can talk?"

"I'd like you to leave, please."

"But I want to offer you a job."

She didn't answer.

"I'm looking for a research assistant. Room and board included. You'd have to share the bedroom every few weekends with my daughter and her stuffed animal collection. But otherwise, it's yours." I glanced over my shoulder. The big guy from out front was eavesdropping, his fat frame plugging the hallway.

"What's the starting salary?" she asked from behind the door.

"What?"

"Of the *job*. The salary."

"Three hundred a week. Cash."

"Really?"

"Really. But you'll handle your own money laundering."

"What kind of health benefits?"

"None. Take echinacea."

"I won't sleep with you or anything."

She noted this as if announcing a food allergy. *I won't eat shellfish or peanuts.*

"No problem."

"Everything okay back here?" The guy from the front was now behind me.

The door suddenly opened, and Nora was there, still wearing that ice-skating skirt but with her long hair down around her shoulders, her face solemn.

"Yeah, Martin," she said. "I'm leaving."

"With a *cop?*"

"He's not a cop. He's an investigative journalist. *Freelance.*"

That seemed to *really* disturb the guy—not that I blamed him. Nora smiled at me, suddenly shy, and turned back inside, leaving the door open.

It was a large walk-in closet, a bare bulb shining overhead. Spread out in the corner were a sheet and an army blanket. Along the wall were a bag of hotdog buns, a folded pile of T-shirts, a bag of Forti Diet Bird Food, plastic forks and knives, and anthills of tiny salt and pepper packets—probably swiped from a McDonald's. Beside the birdcage—there didn't seem to be anything *in* there—was a blue yearbook that read, HARMONY HIGH SCHOOL, HOME OF THE LONGHORNS. Beside the makeshift bed were two tiny colored photos taped to the wall—close to the spot where she'd put her head. One was of a bearded man, the other a woman.

It had to be the dead mother and convict father.

I took a step inside to get a better look and realized the man was actually *Christ,* the way he appeared in Sunday-school classrooms: milky complexion, starched blue dressing gown, a beard trimmed as painstakingly as a bonsai tree. He was doing what he was always doing: cupping blinding light in his hands like he was trying to warm up after a long day of downhill skiing. The woman taped next to him was Judy Garland in *The Wizard of Oz*. They made quite a pair.

Nora shoved a stack of shirts into the plastic bag. "If I take this job, you're not allowed to ask me tons of questions. *I'm* none of your business." She grabbed a pair of discarded gold sequined hot pants tossed in a ball in the corner, stuffing them inside the bag. "This is just till we find out about Ashley. After that I'm doing my own thing."

"Fine." I bent down to check out the birdcage. Inside, there was a live blue parakeet, though the thing was so still and faded it looked like taxidermy. Ornate toys were strewn all over the newspaper in front of him—colored balls, feathers and bells, a full-length mirror—but the bird seemed too exhausted to summon any interest in them.

"Who's this guy?" I asked.

"Septimus," she said. "He's an heirloom." She stepped over, smiling. "He's been inherited so many times no one remembers where he came from. Grandma Eli got him from her next-door neighbor, Janine, when she died. And he was bequeathed to Janine from Glen when *he* died. And *Glen* inherited him from a man named Caesar who died of diabetes. Who he belonged to before Caesar, only God knows."

"He's not a bird, he's a bad omen."

"Some people think he's got magical powers and he's a hundred years old. Want to hold him?"

"No."

But she was already unlatching the door. The bird hopped over and *chucked* himself into her hand. She took mine and slipped the bird into it.

He was not long for this world. He looked like he had cataracts. He was also trembling faintly like an electric toothbrush. I'd have assumed he was catatonic, if he didn't suddenly jolt his head to one side, staring up at me with a cloudy yellow eye that looked like an old bead.

Nora put her face up to him.

"Promise not to tell anyone?" she asked quietly, glancing at me.

"About what?"

"This. I don't want anyone to feel sorry for me." Her eyes moved off of the bird and onto me, her gaze steady.

"I promise."

She smiled, satisfied, and resumed packing, collecting every one of those salt and pepper packets, sprinkling them into the Duane Reade bags.

"I actually have condiments at my place," I said.

She nodded—like I'd just reminded her to bring her pajamas—and set about pulling down black stockings and bras hung to dry along the top shelves, crazy leopard and zebra prints tacked down by Black & Decker drills and paint cans.

The girl was like one of those picture books with pages that unfold and unfold all the way out, which caused children's eyes to grow wide. I suspected she'd never stop unfolding.

After Nora packed up her clothes, she set about peeling Jesus and Judy Garland off the wall. Jesus came off easily. Judy, predictably, took a bit of coaxing. She grabbed the *Harmony High* yearbook, opened it, carefully tucked the two pictures inside, and then returned Septimus to his cage.

I realized, staring at the army-green blob he'd left, the bird had taken a shit in my hand.

"It's best if you let that dry first, then flick it off," said Nora, glancing at it. I'm ready. *Oh.* Almost forgot."

She rummaged through her purse and handed me a colored photograph. I assumed she was showing me a member of her family, but then realized with surprise it was a photo of Ashley.

Her gray eyes, hollowed by dark circles, seemed to fasten onto me.

"When I disappeared from the tour at Briarwood and got in trouble? *That's* what I went back to get. I saw it on those bulletin boards by the dining hall under 'Weekly Picnic.' It's her, isn't it?"

La cara de la muerte, the Waldorf maid had said. The face of death. I understood what she meant.

27 | THE NEXT MORNING, I was woken at 5:42 A.M. by creaks outside my bedroom door. Footsteps retreated down the hall, followed by the sound of water pipes shrieking, more creeping *back* into Sam's room, and then downstairs, where plates and glasses clattered in the kitchen as if someone were starting preparations for a dinner party of twenty-five.

In spite of my wondering if, when I *did* wake up, I'd find my apartment stripped of all valuables, I fell back to sleep, only to be woken again by a soft knock on the door.

"Yeah," I mumbled.

"Oh. Did I wake you?"

The door creaked open, followed by silence. I cracked open an eye. The clock read 7:24. Nora was peering at me through the doorway.

"I was wondering when we were going to get *started.*"

"I'll be right down."

"Cool."

Sweet Jesus.

I groggily pulled on a bathrobe and shuffled downstairs, where I found Nora curled up on my living-room couch wearing a Marcel Marceau striped black-and-white shirt and black leggings. She was picking at the shell of a hard-boiled egg and scribbling in a leatherbound journal, which I realized, after a dazed moment of recognition, was *mine.* I'd found it in a bookbinding shop in Naples. An eighty-year-old Italian named Liberatore had crafted it with his arthritic, trembling hands over the course of a year. It was the very last of its kind because he was now dead, his shop replaced by a Fiat dealership. I'd been saving it for the day when I had something substantial and profound to write inside it.

"You like to sleep in, huh?" She stopped writing to smile up at me. I saw she'd scribbled ASHLEY CORDOVA CASE NOTES at the top of the page, followed by indecipherable handwriting.

"It's not even eight o'clock in the morning. That's early."

"If Grandma Eli was here she'd say the whole day was wasted. I made you breakfast."

With slight trepidation, I stepped into the kitchen.

There was a plate of scrambled eggs and toast on the counter. She'd *cleaned,* too. Not a dirty dish or glass in the sink.

I stepped out of the kitchen. "Don't cook for me. Or clean. This is a black-and-white working relationship."

"It's just *eggs*."

"I'm forty-three. I don't need help feeding myself."

"*Not yet.* There was this man, Cody Johnson, at Terra Hermosa? He showed signs of dementia around thirty-nine."

"I think I've heard this story before. He died alone?"

"Everyone dies alone."

There was little to add to *that.* Whenever the girl brought up Terra Hermosa it was like spraying DDT on the conversation—an instant *killer.*

I poured myself a cup of coffee and motioned for Nora to follow me.

"Inside this box is everything I know about Cordova," I told her as we stepped into my office. "Organize it by published date and subject matter. Keep all information on his *films* together. Pull out anything you think might help us understand Ashley's personality, music, hobbies, her background—any mention of family life or the Adirondack compound, The Peak."

I noticed a thin set of papers sticking out, a photo of The Peak I'd found from an old *National Geographic,* printed and clipped to the front. I yanked it loose, handing it to Nora.

"You can start by reading this. When I began investigating Cordova five years ago, I went up to Crowthorpe Falls, wandered around, asked locals what they'd heard. Everything I found is in there."

I moved to the door, leaving Nora sitting Indian-style on the sofa, studiously tucking her hair behind her ears as she settled in to read.

Trip to Crowthorpe Falls, NY, and The Peak Estate
S. McGrath
April 3 — 13, 2006

Crowthorpe Falls, New York.   Harrison, Taylor & Woods, Architects
THE PEAK, THE HOUSE OF EDWARD ROBB ROCKEFELLER, ESQ. · THE ENTRANCE FRONT.

The Peak, c.1912

The Peak

The estate known as The Peak, once a Rockefeller vacation property
and designed by the architects Harrison, Taylor, & Woods, sits north of
Lows Lake in the wilderness of the Adirondacks in upstate New York.

The nearest town is Crowthorpe Falls, one of the poorest in the
region. Mobile home parks, abandoned barns and parking lots, motels,
roadhouse saloons, and topless bars comprise the town proper (nicknamed
Crow by locals). To make one's way through Crow to The Peak one must
know the area well: Almost all of the roads are unpaved and unmarked.

Stanislas Cordova and his first wife, Genevra, a descendant of the
Italian Castagnello family, purchased the property in foreclosure
from British aristocrats, Lord and Lady Sludely of Sussex. Shortly
after moving in to the estate in 1976, Cordova began the construction
of massive soundstages throughout the 300-acre grounds where he could
shoot, edit, and sound mix his films without ever leaving the property.

With the termination of his production deal with Warner Bros.,
Cordova started self-financing his films, turning The Peak into his
official one-man studio—and only adding to the mystique of the director
as an agoraphobic recluse and madman.

Source: Wikipedia.org/wiki/Stanislas_Cordova

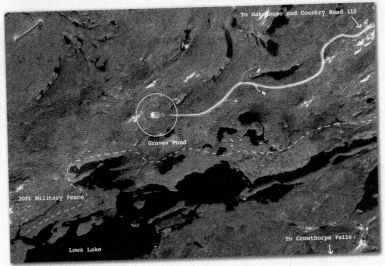

The Peak mansion sits in dense wilderness atop a high ridge just north of Graves Pond, a smaller pond north of Lows Lake.

The entirety of the property—which extends north past Darning Needle Pond close to Cranberry Lake—is surrounded by a twenty-foot military fence.

December 2004
Medical Equip?

   Garcia is Stanislas Cordova's closest next-door neighbor, a seventy-eight-year-old retired apple farmer originally from Lafayette, New York. Since 1981, he has lived in the rust-colored single-wide trailer on a patch of land across from the overgrown driveway that leads to The Peak. He claims never to have met or even seen the Cordovas—due to his type 2 diabetes he rarely ventures into town, having a nurse visit and bring supplies three times a week. But he did have a few interesting incidents to tell me about his infamous neighbor.

   "We used to have street signs all around here, but the mailman told me they removed them," he said.

   "Who do you mean by *they*?" I asked.

   "The people who live up there."

   "You mean the Cordova family?"

   He nodded.

   "Why would they remove the road signs?" I asked.

   "They don't want people up there. They like to keep to themselves. That's what I heard around town. I used to see all kinds of fancy cars driving in and out from midnight till all hours of the morning. Especially in the eighties and nineties. Limos. A Rolls-Royce once. A few times I heard helicopters landing in there. Music, too. But starting in early 2000, it's been quiet. Never see a soul go in or out."

   According to Garcia, in early December 2004, he received a series of UPS deliveries that were intended for The Peak but, by mistake, were delivered to him. The first was a massive box stamped with a label reading Century Scientific.

Century Scientific, Inc., based in Scranton, Pennsylvania, is a company that specializes in medical equipment. They vend beds, wheelchairs, stretchers, and other therapeutic devices to private hospitals.

"My daughter sometimes sends me packages, so I signed for it," Garcia told me. "After the boy drove off, I realized it wasn't mine."

"Who was it addressed to?" I asked.

"Someone named Javlin Cross. And the address said 1014 Country Road 112. I'm 33 Country Road 112. I didn't open it. But it was heavy. I could barely lift it. About four feet high. I guess it was some kind of chair—that was the shape of the box."

Garcia called UPS and within the hour the package was picked up.

A week later, the driver delivered another box, again for Mr. Javlin Cross.

"The return address said something or other 'Pharmaceuticals,'" Garcia said. "I told the boy he'd made a mistake. He apologized, said he was new on the job. And that was really the last of it. For a month or two, though, once a week in the afternoon, I'd see the truck drive by and turn in there, bringing them God knows what. I'd wait a few minutes and then I'd hear the real shrill scream of the iron electronic gate opening to let the truck drive up. A piercing hinge so shrill it hurt to listen to. You'd think it'd shatter the TV." He shook his head. "My guess is someone was sick up there. Or injured."

Garcia told me he'd probably have forgotten about the mix-up had he not noticed something else strange about a week after the accidental deliveries. He drove his garbage to the Dumpster at the end of the road and noticed a strange odor emitting from the other plastic bags.

"Never smelled anything like it. It was foul. Like burned plastic."

Garcia said only he and the Cordovas used the disposal site. The week after this observation, he noticed no other trash bags had appeared, and to this day, he's the lone user of the bin.

"Now they set fire to all their garbage," he said. "You can smell it when it's hot at night. Burning. And sometimes when the wind's blowing southeast I can even see the smoke."

I asked Garcia if he's ever seen any of Cordova's films. He shook his head.

"I'll get nightmares," he said.

"In his film *Isolate 3*," I explained, "there's a man being held in captivity against his will. A former convict that the main character has to hunt down and free. His name is Javlin Cross—the name on those packages you received."

Garcia nodded, thinking this over.

"What's the consensus in town about the Cordovas?" I asked.

"What d'you mean?"

"What do people say about him? About the property?"

"No one likes to talk about it. Don't know why. But they don't. See, how it works up here is, everyone minds their own business."

He had nothing more to add and looked ready to settle in watching *Wheel of Fortune*, so I thanked him for his time and left.

May 28, 2003
5:30am

On May 28, 2003, at 5:30 AM, sixty-two-year-old Kate Miller was walking along deserted Old Forge Road in Bainville, New York, a small resort town a hundred miles north of Albany and forty-five minutes from Crowthorpe Falls.

It was the end of a long night. Miller worked at the front desk during the all-night "witching shift" at Forest View Motel, a vacation resort south of town. Every morning, regardless of rain or snow, six days a week, Miller hiked the two miles from the motel to Bainville's Main Street in order to catch the Trailways bus that took her twenty miles north to Danville, where she lived with her husband and twelve-year-old grandson.

Old Forge is a narrow two-lane road that heads toward town at a steep incline. Its hairpin curves are notorious spots for car accidents—mostly local teenagers or tourists. Miller told me she was two miles from town, walking on the left side of the street, facing oncoming traffic, when a silver sports sedan careened past her in the right-hand lane.

"I thought it was a drunk driver [because] he was all over the road," she said. "He disappeared around the bend, there was silence, then a crash, glass shattering, and a cracking noise. The horn was going off, too."

She hurried toward the accident, though the arthritis in her knees prevented her from running. Less than a minute later she saw what had happened: Miscalculating a turn, the driver had lost control of the car and collided with a hemlock standing at an eight-foot drop off the road.

The car was severely smashed, and a blond woman in her fifties was crawling on her hands and knees up the dirt bank to the street. She was badly shaken, but didn't appear to be injured apart from scrapes on her face and arms.

"She was crying. And shaking all over. I asked if she had her phone on her but she said she'd left it at home. I've never had a cellphone.

So I said I'd go straight into town and call an ambulance. I asked if there was anyone else with her, and she shook her head."

Miller continued down Old Forge, but not before she stepped to the road's edge and looked inside the car again.

"This time I noticed there was someone lying in the backseat," she said. "A large man all in black, unconscious, covered in bandages. They were all over his arms and face. They looked bloody. But I didn't stop to argue—she'd just been in a wreck after all and probably didn't know what she was saying. I decided to get help as fast as I could."

Fifty minutes elapsed between the time Miller walked the two miles, dialed 911 from a gas station, and an ambulance and police arrived at the scene. They found a woman who identified herself as Astrid Goncourt. The car, a silver 1989 Mercedes, was empty.

Goncourt admitted she'd been speeding, submitted to a Breathalyzer test, and passed. Police saw no sign anyone else had been with her in the car. She was treated at a local hospital for minor cuts and scrapes, and hours later, discharged.

The following day, the New York *Daily News* and Albany's *Times Union* reported that Mrs. Cordova had been in a car accident driving home from a friend's birthday party and suffered minor injuries. The fact that The Peak is an hour's drive from Bainville (a lengthy drive to begin at 5:00 AM) failed to alert police, though it was unclear if this was Astrid's story or simply a case of lazy reportage.

Three weeks after the accident, Miller re-contacted police. She'd read about Astrid and her famous husband in the intervening period—"I'm not into horror movies," she explained, when I asked her why, initially, the names meant nothing to her—and she now identified the person she'd seen in the car as Stanislas Cordova.

The Bainville Police Department took her statement and showed her the door.

Miller's claim was never investigated further.

Trip to Crowthorpe Falls, NY, and The Peak Estate
S. McGrath
The Drive up — April 13, 2006 2:14 P.M.

Obviously, I was due to pay my own visit to The Peak.

I climbed into my car and made the left turn that was the entrance to 1014 Country Road 112—according to the GPS—accelerating down the unmarked drive.

It started out scarred with tire ruts and mud, but about six yards in, it flattened into a surprisingly meticulous gravel road. Some sort of caretaker must regularly attend the path; not a stray limb, shrub, or weed marred the way. On more than a few tree trunks, lower, offending branches had been visibly sawed off.

On my right I passed a small but conspicuous red-and-white sign: *Private Drive, No Trespassing.* It was a warm, unthreatening spring afternoon— overhead, sunlight drooled through the trees; the day had an idle, drowsy feel.

I accelerated around a bend. I was deep in the woods now. The foliage overhead was so dense it felt like I was inside a wool sweater: heavy, knotty, and only now and then a tiny gap where you could see through to the blue sky. The air suddenly reeked of gasoline—my car in need of a tune-up, probably—but something else, too: *burning.*

I accelerated past a bizarre tree, three voluptuous trunks writhed around each other in pleasure or in pain. They looked pornographic. *My God,* I asked myself, *could it be this easy?*

I only made it a few more yards.

I rounded a curve, and directly in front of me loomed a gatehouse, seemingly deserted, overrun with ivy. There was no way around it, either in the car or on foot. Beyond the wrought-iron gate, a massive military fence cut through the forest in either direction. I inched the car closer. Two surveillance cameras hung like wasps' nests at opposite corners of the gate. I rolled down the window, staring up at one. I swore I saw the lens move, that little Cyclops eye focusing in on me.

"Any chance I could come up for a cup of coffee?"

My words sounded lame, flat, in the warm, poised afternoon.

How did he *live* up there? Was the property his version of Michael Jackson's Neverland Ranch, Elvis's Graceland, Walt's Magic Kingdom? Were the rumors about his lunacy all simply part of the myth and he was no dark prince, but simply an old man who hoped to live the remainder of his life in peace and solitude?

Maybe the truth was something else entirely. Maybe Kate Miller was right; maybe she *had* seen Cordova in the backseat of the car in the early morning of May 28, 2003. Maybe he was critically injured from an accident up at The Peak, maybe even killed. Kate Miller, the lone witness, was manipulated to leave the scene. Astrid probably did have a cellphone and immediately called someone—a friend or one of Cordova's children, Theo or Ashley—and in the intervening minutes, they extracted Cordova from the car and drove him away. Is Cordova alive at The Peak? Is he bedridden, unconscious, confined to a wheelchair? It would explain the series of medical deliveries received by Nelson Garcia more than a year later.

I climbed out of my car, took a photo of the gatehouse, then took off, speeding back down the driveway and out onto Country Road 112, passing

Garcia's trailer and the garbage disposal site. My foot didn't let up from the gas until I was back in the gridlocked traffic of the FDR in Manhattan.

Whatever the truth about Cordova, within fifteen horrifying films, he taught us how our eyes and minds perpetually deceive us—that what we know to be certain never is.

Now we can only hope one day he might return—so we can see, once again, how blind we've been.

Nelson Garcia
Phone # (518) 555-1493

28 "THE NUMBER'S BEEN DISCONNECTED," said Nora, hanging up. She'd tried calling the old man, Nelson Garcia, using the phone number in my notes.

"He's probably dead," I said. "When I talked to him he could barely get up off the sofa."

Nora said nothing, only picked up the transcript of the anonymous caller, John, squinting as she read through it.

It was after eight-thirty. I'd just returned from an early dinner down the street at Café Sant Ambroeus with an old friend—Hal Keegan, a photojournalist from *Insider* I used to work with, though we'd seen little of each other in the past few years. I'd opted not to tell him what I was working on. I trusted Hal, but despite getting caught by security at Briarwood, I hoped to keep my investigation quiet. For all their hard-nosed rationale, journalists were a superstitious bunch. There was an unspoken understanding that when a reporter chased a story, hunches and theories became airborne and other reporters could catch them like a cold. It was usually just a matter of time before your competitors had all the same inklings about a case that you did. I was under no delusions that I was the sole journalist looking into Ashley Cordova's death. But there was no glory in being the second or third to crack a case. There was only *first*.

When I returned home, Nora was in the same place I'd left her, still at work organizing my papers. I'd brought her some pesto linguini, but after saying, "Gosh, thanks, that looks tasty," she'd barely touched it, and instead continued scouring with complete absorption Beckman's syllabus for his obsolete Cordova class. I was surprised by her focus. She'd been in my office for twelve hours *straight,* stopping her reading only to lavish attention on that prehistoric parakeet, Septimus, whose cage she'd set on the bookshelf by the window—"He loves to people-watch," she'd said.

Though she'd said nothing *specific,* I was gathering Nora had been raised by a pack of free-spirited geriatrics at this place she was always peppering her conversations with: *Terra Hermosa*. She seemed preternaturally *wired* to the elderly's barn-animal hours and feeding times. She'd asked what I was doing for dinner at 4:45 P.M.—the legendary hour of senior suppertime—and used some telling McCarthy-era expressions: *gracious, jeepers, Holy Moses,* and *don't flip your wig.*

"How soon after you went up to Crowthorpe Falls did you receive the anonymous phone call?" Nora asked me, setting aside the transcript.

"A few weeks later." I was on the leather couch typing up notes on my laptop, detailing our trip to Briarwood and the Waldorf.

"It has to mean what you uncovered up there was *real.*"

"You mean Kate Miller and Nelson Garcia?"

She nodded. "It had to be why John called you. Cordova probably got a clear picture of your face from the security camera when you drove up to his gatehouse. And John was a trap."

"I tend to agree, but I've never had confirmation."

"Maybe Cordova *was* hurt in the car that night. And someone *was* sick up at The Peak, which was why they were receiving that medical equipment."

"I didn't mention this in my notes," I said, setting aside my laptop and sitting back against the cushions. "But I always thought Kate Miller's ID of Cordova a little suspect. Six months after I talked to her, she tried to sell her story to the *Enquirer,* but they wouldn't touch it. There could be no corroboration for anything she said, and they didn't want to get tied up in litigation. Now, if the *National Enquirer* won't touch you because you're dirty, that means you're really filthy." I downed the rest of my scotch. "Anyway, Miller could never explain how she knew what Cordova looked like. Because *no one* really knows. The *Rolling Stone* pictures of him appear to be doctored. The infamous close-up of him on the set of *The Legacy* isn't believed to be him, but a stand-in."

"Maybe he's disfigured like the Phantom of the Opera," Nora whispered excitedly. "Or maybe it was a dead body Kate Miller saw in the car."

"We can't conclude we're dealing with homicidal maniacs without proof."

She didn't appear to hear me. "The Cordovas might have some kind of mystical powers. There was what the Waldorf maid told us yesterday. Even *Morgan Devold* mentioned it—that Ashley somehow *knew* he was watching her. For a second, he thought he was watching something already dead. In your notes Garcia says that no one will talk about The Peak." She picked up Ashley's CD case, staring at the cover. "Even the music she recorded. It means 'The Devil in the Night.' "

"You'd be shocked how many people go for the *paranormal* when they can't explain something," I said, striding to the bookshelf to refill my glass. "They reach for it like reaching for the ketchup. I, on the other hand, and hence, *you,* as my employee, will be dealing with cold, hard facts."

Even though I was firmly *not* a believer in the paranormal, there was *still* the nagging remembrance of how Ashley had appeared the night at the reservoir. I hadn't told Nora about it. I hadn't told anyone. The truth was, I was no longer certain of what I'd seen. It was as if that night could be separated from all the others as a night without logic, a night of fantasy and strangeness, born of my own lonely delusions, a night that had no place in the real world.

Nora had picked up the 8 x 10 envelope containing Ashley's police file—the one given to me by Sharon Falcone—and pulled out the stack of papers, loosening a page from the front and handing it to me.

It was one of the colored reproductions of photos taken of Ashley's body when she'd arrived at the medical examiner's office. There were a variety of shots—clothed and unclothed, though Sharon was correct in mentioning that any pictures that would be particularly graphic, full-frontal and rear shots, were missing from the file. This shot featured the upper portion of Ashley's face, her gray eyes blotched red and yellow, staring out, dulled.

"Look at her left eye," said Nora.

Within the iris there was a black freckle.

"*This?* It's concentrated pigmentation in the iris. It's very common."

"Not like *that.* It's across from the pupil, perfectly horizontal. It has to be what Guadalupe talked about. Her *mark.* I can't remember the Spanish word Hopper said, but it meant evil's footprint."

"*Huella del mal.*"

"And then there's what happened to Cordova's *first* wife."

"Genevra."

Nora nodded.

"I already looked into it." I handed her back the photo and returned to the couch. "So did the police and about a hundred other reporters and gossip columnists at the time. She'd learned to swim only two months before. Her family—a bunch of snobs from Milan who *loathed* Cordova, considered him a working-class heathen—even *they* conceded it had to be a terrible accident. Genevra had a history of being impulsive. She announced to her son's nanny she was going down to the lake to practice her swimming. She was asked to wait, but refused. It was an overcast day and it began to rain, which soon became a thunderstorm. She must have become disoriented. Couldn't tell the direction of the shoreline. After a search, she was found tangled in the reeds at the bottom of the lake. Cordova was busy with postproduction for *Treblinka* and had a dozen alibis, his entire crew and his producer from Warner Brothers who spoke to the press, Artie Cohen. Five months later, he gave his final interview to *Rolling Stone*. He never appeared in public ever again."

Nora didn't appear to be listening. She was biting her lip, vigorously digging through the papers again. She pulled an article from my old notes, printed from microfiche, handing it to me.

I recognized it as something I'd printed out years ago from a library archive. It was dated July 7, 1977, the Albany *Times Union*.

CASTAGNELLO'S DROWNING ACCIDENTAL, POLICE SAY

By JASON MONTERSON

Genevra Castagnello, the wife of film director Stanislas Cordova, found dead early Sunday morning in a lake on her Adirondack estate, accidentally drowned, according to authorities.

Arthur Bailey, chief forensic investigator with the St. Lawrence County Medical Examiner's Office, ruled following an autopsy that Genevra Castagnello, 31, died as the result of accidental drowning.

Castagnello went missing late Saturday afternoon after she went swimming in Graves Pond, one of the many lakes on her property. She was reportedly last seen wading into the water at 4 p.m. in a red bathing suit. When she didn't return to the house an hour later when it began to thunder and rain, authorities were called. After a fifteen-hour search, her body was found in the lake early Sunday morning by St. Lawrence County Fire and Emergency Services.

WNYT-TV reported that Castagnello had only recently learned to swim, having finally overcome a lifelong fear of drowning.

"I'm in shock," said Anoushka Ponti, a childhood friend of Genevra's visiting from Italy, who was staying at the house at the time of her death. "I had lunch with her a few hours before. She went down to the lake to swim and relax after the baby was put down for a nap. She'd been melancholy. It's so sudden, I can't understand it. She was a beautiful person."

Lt. Jason Restig, public information officer for St. Lawrence County Fire and Emergency Services, said that although the investigation remains open, what happened appears to be self-explanatory, adding, "We don't suspect any foul play, no drugs, no alcohol. This was just a very unfortunate tragedy."

Genevra married Stanislas Cordova in 1975, after meeting the director during a screening of *Somewhere in an Empty Room* at the Venice Film Festival. She was a former model in Milan and

BELLA ITALIA. Castagnello was married to the film director Stanislas Cordova for two years. She drowned Saturday in a lake on her property.

heiress to a legendary banking fortune dating back to the 19th-century association with the C M de Rothschild & Figli bank.

She leaves her husband, Stanislas, working on his sixth film, *Treblinka*, and a four-month-old son, Theodore.

Albany Times Union

Dated July 7, 1977

FAIR HOUSING SUPPORTERS PLAN STATE-WIDE RALLY

"Even if it *was* an accident," said Nora, "for your first wife and your daughter to die by accident—that's not a good track record in terms of karma. But what really stood out was what her *friend* said."

"That she was melancholy."

She nodded. "Genevra might have committed suicide. If Ashley did, too, what does that say about Cordova?"

"He's toxic. On the other hand, for a mother to commit suicide, orphaning her infant child, goes against the primal impulses of motherhood."

"It was from being around *him*." Nora leaned forward, staring dubiously down at the stacks of papers. "I read your other notes, but you didn't get too far in terms of anyone talking about him."

"Thanks for the memo."

"What about *Matilde*? Ever hear anything about it?"

"Cordova's supposed final film?" I was surprised she knew the title. Only diehard Cordovites knew about *Matilde*.

She nodded.

"Apart from a few unsubstantiated rumors that the script was a thousand pages and had driven him mad, no," I said.

She nibbled her thumbnail, sighing. "We need a new direction."

"I did have something promising. But I haven't been able to crack it."

"What?"

"The Blackboards. The invisible Cordovite network on the onion. A community for his hardcore fans."

"What's the onion?"

"The hidden Internet. You download a plug-in for Firefox to access it. I managed to get the URL from a professor friend, *tried* logging on. It kicks me out every time." I carried my laptop over to the desk to show her, attempting to log on to the site, but again I was thrown back to the WELCOME TO THE BLACKBOARDS page.

"Well, that's your problem," Nora said. "The user name you're trying is Sire of Fogwatt. We should try something Cordova-related."

Nora unplugged my wireless router in the corner, waited for five minutes, explaining that this would give me a new IP address, which wouldn't be recognized and barred by the site. When she plugged it in again, she made it to the CLIMB IN page, where she typed in new registration details.

"For a user name, let's try Gaetana Stevens 2991."

Gaetana Stevens was the name of Ashley Cordova's character in *To Breathe with Kings* (1996), Cordova's last film, one of the *black tapes*.

I was amazed. Few people had actually *seen* it. I'd only managed to do so at Beckman's, five years ago. He had one bootleg copy, which he'd refused to loan me because there was an impenetrable lock on the DVD prohibiting any type of copying or downloading—and Beckman suspected, probably rightly, that I'd never give it back.

To watch the film *once* was to be lost in so many graphic, edge-of-your-seat scenes that when it was over, I remembered feeling vaguely astounded that I'd returned to the real world. Something about the film's darkness made me wonder if I *would*—as if in witnessing such things I was irrevocably breaking myself in (*or just breaking myself*), arriving at an understanding about humanity so dark, so deep down inside my own soul, I could never go back to the way I was before. This anxiety, of course, subsided as ordinary life took over. And even now that terrifying tale in my memory was little more than a collection of darkly lit, chilling images, punctuated by the presence of Ashley Cordova, whom I remembered as a beautiful, gray-eyed child who wore her hair in a red-ribboned ponytail.

She spends the film in silence, running in and out of drawing rooms, hiding under stairs and in maids' closets, peering through keyholes and wrought-iron gates, blasting her bicycle fast across the lawn, leaving lurid slash marks on the grass.

The film's plot was straightforward—as most of Cordova's plots were, employing the general storyline of the odyssey or hunt. It was adapted from an obscure Dutch novel, *Ademen Met Koningen,* by August Hauer. The wealthy, corrupt Stevens family—a gorgeous clan of dissipated Caligulas living in an unnamed European country—is calculatingly butchered, one by one, confounding police. Though the inspector assigned to the case eventually arrests a tramp who did landscaping work for the family, the movie's final hairpin twist reveals the killer is actually the family's youngest child, the mute, watchful eight-year-old Gaetana—played, of course, by Ashley. By the time the inspector pieces this grisly truth together, it's too late. The little girl has vanished. The last scene shows her strolling along the side of the road, where she's picked up by a traveling family in a station wagon. In true

Cordova style, it's left ambiguous if this family is destined to meet the same horrific fate as her own, or if she simply made herself an orphan so she could be raised by a happier family.

"How did *you* manage to see *To Breathe with Kings?*" I asked Nora.

She'd finished registering on the Blackboards, pressed *I'm ready,* and we were waiting to see if the page would successfully load.

"Moe Gulazar," she said.

"Who's Moe Gulazar?"

"My best friend." She blew a strand of hair off her face. "He was an old horse trainer who lived down the hall. He loved everything about Cordova. Had black-market connections, too, so one day he traded all his horse trophies for a box of the black tapes. He held secret midnight screenings in the Activity Room all the time." She looked at me. "Moe was a triple threat."

"He could sing, dance, and act?"

She shook her head. "He could speak Armenian, saddle break a stallion, and pass for a female in drag."

"That *is* extremely threatening."

"When he got dressed up, even you'd think he was female."

"Speak for yourself."

"He used to say when *he* was gone, it'd be the end of a rare species. 'There'll never be another of me, not in captivity or the wild.' That was his anthem."

"Where's old Moe now?"

"Heaven."

She said it with such wistful certainty, it might as well have been Bora Bora.

"He died of throat cancer when I was fifteen. He chain-smoked cigarillos since he was twelve because he grew up at the racetrack. But he bequeathed me his whole wardrobe, so he's always with me."

She twisted around, yanking her arm out of the bulky gray wool cardigan to show me a red label sewn into the neck with elaborate black lettering. PROPERTY OF MOE GULAZAR, it read.

So a geriatric Armenian drag queen was behind her flamboyant wardrobe. My first thought was that she had to have made it up: She'd probably found a box full of the clothes at Goodwill, all with the same mysterious label, and invented a fantastic scenario for how she'd come to have them. But as she returned her arm into the sleeve, I noticed her face was flushed.

"I miss him every single day," she said. "I hate how the people who really *get* you are the ones you can never hold on to for very long. And the ones who don't understand you *at all* stick around. Ever noticed that?"

"Yes."

Maybe it *was* true, then. And anyway, I supposed when one was confronted with the choice to believe in the existence of an Armenian drag-queen horse trainer or *not* to believe, one will believe.

"Is that the reason you wanted to be on this investigation?" I asked. "Because you know so much about Cordova's films?"

"Of course. It was a *sign*. Ashley gave me her coat."

To my amazement, the webpage had actually loaded successfully, reading at the top: YOU MADE IT.

I pulled a wooden chair beside Nora and sat down, noticing as I did she smelled of musky men's cologne, dramatic as a hint of dark chocolate in the air, and I couldn't help but imagine that was the proof I needed, a whisper of old Moe Gulazar, always with her.

| PARKING | CORDOVA | FILMS | FREAK | RED BAND | STRANGERS | CLIMB IN |

YOU MADE_IT

If you found this hidden website it's because someone
thought you worthy of being here.

Congratulations, this is the beginning of your life.
You are also a Cordovite. This is the place where you
can do anything, reveal anything, but you cannot lie.
GO lie somewhere else on the Internet and put a fake
smile on your face and dumb yourself down into a series
of idiot choices like LIKE and DISLIKE. Here, while
there is total anonymity, there is the belief only in
the unassailable truth of things. The Cordova truth:
the complexity of the human mind and resilience of the
human spirit. The desire for terror. The desire for
love. The desire for emotional experiences that rip
you apart.

This site is a terrifying reality. A sacred
worksplace. A dangerous wood. A place where you
can discuss and question everything your family and
friends, your religion, your society is threatened
by and afraid of. This is a world away from what is
glossy and commercialized. A place that is dirty and
eerie and horrifying, messy and ugly and fascinating.
A place that has no bottom and no walls. There is only
the fight for something worthy here. Something honest.
Cordova, that is what he urges us to find within
ourselves in all of his work. Our honest selves.

Cordova has nothing to do with this site. He might
not even know it exists. This was created by his most
serious fans as an extension of what he—whoever he is
—has done for us: point the way down the dark tunnel
that will set us free. Fear is the first step.

WARNING: If we find that you in any way are debilitating
this raw and wild space, there will be consequences. We
believe in freedom of expression and complexity but we,
the creators of this blacked-out corner, will fight to
keep it black.

The Creators of the Blackboards

Sovereign, deadly, perfect_

?

FREAK THE FEROCIOUS OUT

Parking
Leave behind what you came in with

Cordova
What Little We Know
His Philosophy:
Freaking the ferocious out of you
The Final Interview:
December 29, 1977,
Rolling Stone

Red Band Experiences

Forum
Talk to Strangers

The Films

Figures Bathed in Light (1964)
The Legacy (1966)
Chasing the Red (1968)
Distortion (1972)
Somewhere in an Empty Room (1975)
Treblinka (1977)
Thumbscrew (1979)
A Small Evil (1982)

Lovechild (1985)
At Night All Birds Are Black (1987)
La Douleur (1989)
A Crack in the Window (1992)
Wait for Me Here (1993)
Isolate 3 (1994)
To Breathe with Kings (1996)

| CLIMB IN | DIG FOR SOMETHING | ? | IF YOU ARE LOST CLICK HERE |

| PARKING | CORDOVA | FILMS | FREAK | RED BAND | STRANGERS | CLIMB IN |

SEARCH RESULTS FOR "REAL CORDOVA PHOTOS"   *Result 1 of 243 results*

Cordova

POSTED BY Beckett Reinhart   12/12/1999 11:39 P.M.

My grandmother was a well-known New York City socialite in the
fifties and sixties. Her name was Gwendolyn "Dottie" Howard
and she was married to L. P. Howard, a clothing manufacturer
and millionaire. Dottie was considered one of Truman Capote's
original "swans." In 1966, she attended Capote's infamous
Black and White Ball in the Grand Ballroom of the Plaza Hotel,
which Capote threw to celebrate the success of *In Cold Blood*.

Dottie was leaving the ladies' room after freshening up, when
abruptly a man grabbed her wrist. With a knowing smile, he
led her away from the crowd to a private alcove where he
handed her a glass of champagne and told her to "drink."
Dottie was stunned by his brazen behavior. She'd never seen
him before. He was tall and quick-moving, with piercing dark
eyes behind scholarly spectacles. Yet, she found herself
doing exactly what he said, downing the entire glass while
he watched, saying nothing. When she finished, he wiped her
mouth with his thumb, leaned in, and kissed her. Just when
Dottie was forgetting herself, when she knew she'd disappear
with him into the night if he ordered her to, the man pulled
away, took her hand, and led her back to the dance floor where
he delivered her to her husband, announcing simply: "Your wife
was lost."

Needless to say, Dottie was lightheaded and skittish for the remainder of the evening—searching the crowd for this strange, mysterious man. Around 3:00 A.M. when the festivities were winding down, she spotted him disappearing alone into a waiting cab.

"But who is that?" she blurted.

"Cordova," someone answered. "He's a film director."

Dottie never forgot that night. She said later she felt as if she were an hors d'oeuvre he'd taken one bite of, then put back on the tray.

I've combed through every photo taken at the ball and I think I found Cordova.

NEXT >>

PARKING	CORDOVA	FILMS	FREAK	RED BAND	STRANGERS	CLIMB IN

Stan Cordova
Hollywood, CA 1962

POSTED BY Sometimes You Must Get On Your Knees 2/12/2000 2:03 A.M.

I found this photo at a garage sale in Beverly Hills, CA,
in 1999. It was in a box filled with old family pictures and
maps. I asked the owner of the sale where the photo had come
from. She didn't know. She was packing up her stepfather's
house. He had just died at 82 years old. She said he was an
accountant for different businesses around Hollywood, many of
which were illegal, including a notorious Beverly Hills madam
at the center of a high-end prostitution ring that served both
men and women.

I've read here on the Blackboards that when Cordova set out
to make his first film, *Figures Bathed in Light*, he went to
Hollywood and worked there as a gigolo to raise the money he
needed. My guess is—and this is just a shot in the dark—this
was stolen from the Beverly Hills madam's files, a picture she
showed to potential clients.

NEXT >>

PARKING	CORDOVA	FILMS	FREAK	RED BAND	STRANGERS	CLIMB IN

SEARCH RESULTS FOR "REAL CORDOVA PHOTOS"   *Result 22 of 243 results*

Lola & babe 8½ months

POSTED BY Axel   **10/12/2001 4:18 A.M.**

My mother owned a series of low-rent apartment buildings in
the Bronx near Morris Avenue. Mostly Italian and Spanish
immigrants lived there, many illegally.

| PARKING | CORDOVA | FILMS | FREAK | RED BAND | STRANGERS | CLIMB IN |

One of her tenants cleared out suddenly in 1967, leaving no word. This photograph was all that was left, caught under the carpeting in the living room. The unit—2E, a studio—was rented by an Italian woman for more than twenty years who barely spoke English. When the woman first took the room in 1944, she had just emigrated from Spain and had an infant son but no husband. She listed her name on the lease as *Lola Cordova*. I think this must be a photograph of Cordova's mother with Stanislas, taken shortly after their arrival in America. My mother later told me the woman was quiet, neat, paid her rent on time, and worked tirelessly at two jobs—one as a hotel maid in Manhattan, the other as a cleaning woman to the wealthy. My mother, busy with running four buildings, doesn't remember seeing the little boy grow up or playing in the courtyard like some of the other kids. To this day, she does not know where the woman went or what happened to her.

NEXT >>

PARKING	CORDOVA	FILMS	FREAK	RED BAND	STRANGERS	CLIMB IN

SEARCH RESULTS FOR "REAL CORDOVA PHOTOS"   *Result 59 of 243 results*

Harvey Koon Antiques

POSTED BY Emily Jackson Is Not Crazy   8/02/2002 12:39 A.M.

I worked the summer of 2001 at the offices of the New York City
antiques dealer Harvey Koon. Koon specializes in bizarre
antiques, from Spanish Inquisition torture devices to old marine
equipment. He has a lot of wealthy and strange clients, many
anonymous. One day, while compiling client invoices, I came
across a shipping address I recognized: 1014 Country Road 112,
Crowthorpe Falls, NY.

It's the address of Cordova's estate, The Peak.

Intrigued, I checked the history of items that were purchased
and sent there. The latest was a pair of thumbscrews—a torture
device that dates back to medieval times, which was used to break
prisoners' fingers and toes. It is also the device Brad Jackson,
the Medieval Studies professor, has in his possession in Cordova's
film of the same name, *Thumbscrew*.

The other two items purchased and sent to this address were
a Siebe Gorman Royal Navy diving helmet and a very expensive
fifteenth-century Romanian impaler, a vertical steel spear on
which prisoners were skewered like pigs—used notoriously by Vlad
the Impaler, otherwise known as Dracula. It's obvious Cordova—
or someone in his household—is a collector of these eccentric
antiques.

The day after I made this discovery I was let go due to "budget
problems." I never knew if it was because my boss found out I'd
been snooping and learned Cordova was a client—or if it was just
a coincidence.

NEXT >>

| PARKING | CORDOVA | FILMS | FREAK | RED BAND | STRANGERS | CLIMB IN |

SEARCH RESULTS FOR "REAL CORDOVA PHOTOS"   *Result 85 of 243 results*

1.24.79

James,

Cordova is considering you for a part in his next film: A Small Evil.

If it suits you, call me to make arrangements to come to his home to discuss the part.

— Inez Gallo

POSTED BY Truth Is a Tall Order   **11/22/2003 4:19 A.M.**

My father was a talent manager in the 70s and 80s at Discover
Management. He represented the film star James Coburn.
Growing up, my dad had a story that he received correspondence
from Cordova's assistant, Inez Gallo, which included a
disturbing picture of the director wearing a gas mask. I
always thought my father—prone to trickery—was joking. When
my dad died of a heart attack in 1994, I went through his desk
and found this in his papers. It is an 8 X 10 headshot, the
writing scribbled on the back in permanent marker.

The other thing I remember my dad saying about Cordova was
that *people who knew* whispered there was something wrong with
the director's eyes—they had a condition called *photophobia*,
which means they're sensitive to open air and light—and thus
he often wore sunglasses with pitch black lenses or old-
fashioned British driving goggles.

NEXT >>

SEARCH RESULTS FOR "REAL CORDOVA PHOTOS"   *Result 104 of 243 results*

POSTED BY If You See a Dead Bird   8/9/2004 12:39 A.M.

In 1991, I worked as an assistant for the film producer Artie Cohen.
One night Artie announced he was staying late. It was unheard of;
he loved to be home by six so he could have dinner with his kids.
He was on edge, told me to go home—suggested I take my girlfriend
out for dinner. Knowing he was Cordova's longtime producer, I knew
something was up. I said goodbye and raced home to get my camera.
I returned to our office building in TriBeCa, went up the back
stairwell, found a position by the window with a view of the street,
and waited.

NEXT >>

PARKING	CORDOVA	FILMS	FREAK	RED BAND	STRANGERS	CLIMB IN

And waited. After four hours, I dozed off. When I woke, I went down to check Artie's office and saw his light was still on. Artie was alone. Not only that, he was drunk—talking to himself. I returned to my lookout. Finally, at 2:37 A.M. a lone man appeared around the corner and crossed the empty street. It was too dark to see much, but I knew it was Cordova. I took pictures of the figure *blindly*, unable to see out of the viewfinder, it was so dark. He vanished inside our building. I figured I'd follow him when he left, get more pictures. I waited. Soon the sun came up. Bewildered, I checked Artie's office. It was locked up, totally dark. They must have left by a back entrance. Or had I dozed off for a few minutes without realizing it? I went home, dejected, and developed the film. The pictures I'd taken were blurry and black—except for this single photo.

Artie never mentioned the incident. I asked him why he stayed late, but his answers were nervous. "I was here all by myself," he assured me. In the end, this photo was all I needed for proof of Cordova's existence and that for some reason, he only comes out at night.

NEXT >>

PARKING   CORDOVA   FILMS   FREAK   RED BAND   STRANGERS   CLIMB IN

SEARCH RESULTS FOR "REAL CORDOVA PHOTOS"   *Result 172 of 243 results*

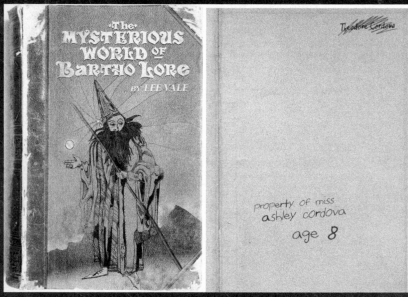

POSTED BY Somewhere Soon There'll Be Laughter   10/28/2006 1:48 A.M.

This was left behind in a hotel room where the legendary
actress Marlowe Hughes stayed on July 25, 1996. It was Hôtel
du Cap-Eden-Roc in Cap d'Antibes. The day after it was found
on the bedside table, a woman called to ask if we had found
it. I was working the front desk and took the call. I lied,
telling the woman that no book had been found in the room.

The name Theodore Cordova is scribbled out at the top in light
pencil.

NEXT >>

SEARCH RESULTS FOR "REAL CORDOVA PHOTOS"   *Result 218 of 243 results*

POSTED BY Specimen 919   5/11/2008 11:28 P.M.

I believe that Inez Gallo, Cordova's longtime assistant, and
Stanislas Cordova are the same person. There is a tattoo of
a wheel on the back of her hand when she accepted Cordova's
Academy Award for *Thumbscrew* (1979).

The same tattoo can be seen on Cordova's hand in the original Warner Bros. publicity still that was sent out for his first film, *Figures Bathed in Light* (1964).

NEXT >>

PARKING | CORDOVA | FILMS | FREAK | RED BAND | STRANGERS | CLIMB IN

SEARCH RESULTS FOR "REAL CORDOVA PHOTOS"   *Result 243 of 243 results*

POSTED BY Diane from the Writing Class   2/21/2011 3:06 A.M.
What happens to you when you watch a Cordova film.

NEXT >>

http://tunnelstaircase8903-5493r89jidfj9w0129e61)??)*#(((sovereigndeadlyperfect.blackboards.onion/films

POSTED BY Crowboy123   **12/23/2006 11:27 P.M.**

I live in Long Lake, a town 13 miles south of Crowthorpe
Falls.

One night in June 1992, I was eating at a diner when I noticed
a young Mexican teenager sitting in a booth in extreme
distress. He spoke no English. I am a Spanish teacher at the
local high school, so I asked him if he needed help. He told
me he had just witnessed an appalling act.

He said he was part of a group of migrant workers who had been
transported over a month ago to Crowthorpe Falls from Mexico
for the purpose of working crew on a private film. I sensed he
was illegal but I didn't press him on this as he seemed scared
to talk. He explained to me that day they were shooting a
driving sequence with two actors in the woods. They had been
shooting for a few hours when a stranger—a young teenage boy—
came running into the shot, screaming. After much confusion,
it was discovered that the boy was the director's son who
had been servicing a motorboat on a lake nearby and he had
accidentally severed three of his fingers.

The boy was holding the bloody fingers in his hand, screaming
in pain, asking his father if he could call an ambulance.

The director said no. Instead, he fired one of the actors and
made his son play the part.

The director had his son shoot sixteen complete takes before the boy went unconscious. An ambulance was finally called. But by then too much time had elapsed to reattach the fingers.

After telling me this the Mexican grew fearful and after wiping his tears, he left the restaurant. I called the police in Crowthorpe Falls, asking them to look into the incident, but no one ever followed up with me.

I was haunted by this story for years. I managed to track down on the Internet a copy of the horror film that Cordova made around that time, *Wait for Me Here*. I was horrified to see that the role of John Doe in the beginning is played by Cordova's son, Theo. I believe everything the Mexican told me is true. The devastating pain on Theo's face is real and if you stop the film exactly at the 5:48" mark you can see the raw bone of the severed fingers on his left hand dangling there.

NEXT >>

29 | Nora and I stayed up most of the night on the Blackboards. It was like fumbling through a pitch-black funhouse with trapdoors and tunnels, voices calling out from rooms with no doors, stumbling down rickety staircases that twisted deep into the ground with no end.

Every time I was about to suggest we head to bed, continue sifting through this endless Cordova archive with rested eyes in the morning, there was *one more* anecdote to click onto, another uncanny incident, rumor, or strange photo.

Freak the ferocious out—there were quite a few pages on the site devoted to Cordova's supposed life philosophy, which meant, in a nutshell, that to be terrified, *to be scared out of your skin,* was the beginning of freedom, of opening your eyes to what was graphic and dark and gorgeous about life, thereby conquering the monsters of your mind. This was, in Cordovite speak, *to slaughter the lamb,* get rid of your meek, fearful self, thereby freeing yourself from the restrictions imposed on you by friends, family, and society at large.

Once you slaughter the lamb, you are capable of everything and anything, and the world is yours, proclaimed the site.

Sovereign. Deadly. Perfect.

These three words, which Cordova had mentioned in his infamous *Rolling Stone* interview while describing his favorite shot in his films— a close-up of his own eye—was a slogan on the Blackboards and for life itself. *Sovereign:* the sanctity of the individual, regarding yourself as princely, powerful, self-contained, wrestling authority for yourself away from society. *Deadly:* constant awareness that your own death is inevitable, which means there is no reason not to be ferocious, now, about your life. *Perfect:* the understanding that life and wherever you find yourself at the present are absolutely ideal. No regret, no guilt, because even if you were stuck it was only a cocoon to break out of—*setting your life loose.*

I'd known Cordova's fans believed him to be an amoral enchanter, a dark acolyte who led them away from what was stale and tedious about their daily lives deep into the world's moist, tunneled underbelly, where every hour was unexpected. Combing through the Blackboards' whispers and suspicions, the sheer density of anonymous comments— which veered from reverential to frightened to supremely twisted and depraved—only underscored what I'd long suspected, that Cordova was not just an oddball eccentric along the lines of Lewis Carroll or Howard Hughes, but a man who also inspired devotion and awe in a vast number of people, not unlike a leader of a religious cult.

By 3:45 A.M. Nora and I—blank-eyed and delirious—were in the living room, digging out my pirated copy of *Wait for Me Here*—purchased for seventy-five bucks from Beckman—watching the terrifying opening scene, which featured Jenny Decanter, played by twenty-two-year-old Tamsin Polk, driving alone down the dirt forest road in the dead of night.

Abruptly, Theo Cordova—cast as John Doe #1—came crashing out of the trees, causing Jenny to scream, slamming on the brakes, sending her car spinning into a ditch, the engine stalling.

I'd always thought Theo Cordova looked like a deranged Puck: strung-out, half naked, eyes glassy, blood and what looked to be human bite marks covering his bare chest. He looked even more horrendous *now*, given Crowboy123's anecdote on the Blackboards. As he knocked on the car window, trying the door, and said his only line—*"Help me, please,"* words barely audible over Jenny's screams—his voice oozed out like some strange sap.

Nora, standing beside the flat-screen, paused it.

Frame by frame, she inched toward 5:48, where it was possible to see that Theo was missing three fingers.

"There."

"It's a movie. It could be special effects, makeup, prosthetics—"

"But the look on his face is real *pain*. I *know* it."

She pressed *play,* and Theo's hand dropped out of sight.

Jenny managed to get the car started, and, nearly running over this strung-out, wounded boy, she barreled back into the road, tree branches cracking the windshield, tires squealing. As she blindly took off, petrified, blinking away tears, she watched him in the rearview mirror.

The boy's half-naked figure glowed red in her taillights, quickly faded to a thin black silhouette, and then—*fast as an insect*—he darted out of the road, vanishing from view.

Nora scrambled back to the couch, pulling the wool blanket over her legs and reaching down to pick up Septimus from the coffee table, as if that ancient bird would protect her from the horror about to unfold on-screen.

"Want me to make some popcorn?" I asked her.

"Definitely."

We ended up watching all of *Wait for Me Here.*

Cordova's films were addictive opiates; it was impossible to watch just one minute. One craved more and more. Around 5:30 A.M., when my head was soaked with gory imagery and that hellish story—not to mention echoing with whispers of those anonymous voices calling out from the Blackboards—Nora and I called it a day.

30 | THE NEXT MORNING I woke up to learn *Vanity Fair* was reporting that *they* had "the inside scoop" on Ashley Cordova and the article was due to be published on their website within days. This meant not only that other reporters were hot on the trail, but it was probably just a matter of time before *they* ended up at Briarwood Hall—and on the doorstep of Morgan Devold. Whatever advantage I'd had, thanks to Sharon Falcone and getting my hands on Ashley's police file, would be gone.

And unfortunately, my own investigation had stalled.

We'd learned about Ashley's escape from Briarwood and her diagnosed affliction, *nyctophobia,* "a severe fear of the dark or night, triggered by the brain's distorted perception of what would or could happen to the body when it's exposed to a dark environment," according to *The New England Journal of Medicine.* We'd had a small coup by logging successfully on to the Blackboards, able now to ransack through the rumors of his staunchest fans.

Yet there was no new lead to follow.

Ashley had come to the city by train after leaving Morgan Devold, but *why,* or where she'd gone during the ten days before her death—besides the thirtieth floor of the Waldorf Towers—was still a mystery.

I *could* bribe an employee at the hotel for a list of every guest staying on that floor within the time frame—September 30 to October 10—but from personal experience I knew I needed *something more,* a filter for the names. The list would be substantial, many of the guests doubtlessly wealthy tourists who wouldn't appreciate—or feel any obligation to honestly *answer*—questions about what they were doing at the hotel.

By the time I tracked everyone down, showing them Ashley's picture, I'd probably have little to go on and, even worse, the exercise would take up a hell of a lot of time.

"Maybe we could take Ashley's picture to businesses around the Waldorf," Nora said, after I explained some of this to her. "Ask if someone noticed her. She'd stand out with that red coat."

"I might as well take her picture to Times Square and ask random passersby if they noticed her. It's too vast. We need specifics."

She suggested we watch Cordova's films. "Maybe we'll spot a hidden detail, like Theo's three missing fingers."

With no immediate alternative, I dusted off the box set of the eight films released by Warner Bros.—*The Legacy* (1966) through *Lovechild* (1985)—packaged to resemble the infamous Samsonite briefcase in *Thumbscrew* (1979), and we pulled the living-room shades, made more popcorn, and settled in for a Cordova marathon.

Nora called Hopper, inviting him to join, but he didn't respond. I actually wouldn't have been surprised if we never saw him again. I sensed from his restlessness—whatever his relationship with Ashley—his desire to be involved in the investigation would be as erratic as his moods. He seemed to veer between intense interest and a desire to forget the entire thing.

As we settled in to watch *Thumbscrew,* I was in the kitchen making more popcorn when the buzzer to my apartment rang.

"I'll get it!" sang Nora.

After a minute, when I noticed nothing but silence, I stuck my head out. To my shock, Cynthia and my daughter, Sam, were in the foyer, staring in bewilderment at Nora.

It was my weekend for custody. I'd forgotten.

Seeing my ex-wife was still a jolt to the system. *Jeannie* was the designated go-between for Sam. The appearance of Cynthia in my home was akin to a grizzly wandering into my remote campsite: a life-threatening scenario I'd *considered,* but only as a worst-case disaster.

She looked stunning as usual in a cream-colored wool coat and jeans, a sweep of blown-out ash-blond hair. She was a dealer at an exclusive contemporary art gallery on Madison Avenue and often scrutinized oddly dressed strangers as if they were 99-cent airbrushed Elvis portraits.

"Hi, honey," I said to Sam. "Mrs. Quincy. To what do we owe this pleasure?"

She turned to me. "You didn't get my messages? Jeannie's in the hospital. She's come down with mono and has to go home to Virginia until she's better. It'll be six weeks at least."

I looked down at Sam, tightly gripping the handle of her *Toy Story* suitcase and staring, wide-eyed and opened-mouthed, up at Nora.

"Sweetheart, did you meet my new research assistant?" I asked.

She didn't answer. She tended to become speechless out of *pure awe* when encountering a stranger. She took a shy step behind my ex-wife.

"Can I talk to you in private?" Cynthia asked me, smiling thinly.

"Certainly."

"Sam, I want you to stay here. I'll be right back."

Cynthia led the way down the hall. We entered my office, and she closed the door behind me.

"Who is *that?*" she asked.

"Nora. She's helping me out with a story."

"How *old* is she? Sixteen?"

"Nineteen. And extremely mature for her age." I'd have loved to imagine Cynthia was jealous, seeing me with another woman, but these questions had nothing to do with me. She was worried about Sam.

She looked around, frowning at the papers and notes piled all over the floor, doubtlessly thinking, *Some things never change.*

She was still beautiful. It was awful. I'd been waiting for Cynthia to venture deeper into her forties so she'd wake up to wrinkles like a maze of molehills screwing up a legendary lawn. But *no,* her green eyes, those cheekbones, the expressive little mouth that broadcast her every mood with the diligence of a UN translator, were still youthful and bright. Now Bruce woke up every morning to that face. I still couldn't believe *that* man—fifty-eight, with a paunch, hairy wrists, and a yacht in Lyford Cay named *Dominion II*—was allowed to live daily with such beauty. He had a *knack* for spotting deals in the marketplace, I'd give him *that.* When Cynthia sold him a Damien Hirst called, rather aptly, *Beautiful Bleeding Wound Over the Materialism of Money Painting,* Bruce noticed she, too, was a work of art to look at for a lifetime. That she allowed herself to be bought along with the *painting*—that I didn't see coming.

When I met Cynthia our sophomore year at the University of Michigan, she was flighty and poor, a French studies major who quoted Simone de Beauvoir. She wiped her runny nose on her coat sleeve when it was snowing, stuck her head out of car windows the way dogs do, the wind fireworking her hair. That woman was gone now. Not that it was her fault. Vast fortunes did that to people. It took them to the cleaners, cruelly starched and steam-pressed them so all their raw edges, all the dirt and hunger and guileless laughter, were ironed out. Few survived real money.

"So, you and that girl are only working together," Cynthia said, turning back to me.

"Yes. She's my research assistant."

"Well, research assistant to *you* can mean any number of things."

I let that one hit me square in the gut. It was true, after our divorce I'd ended up in a *slight relationship* with my last research assistant, Aurelia Feinstein, age thirty-four—though, let me state for the record, it was not as hot as it sounded. Making love to Aurelia was like rummaging through a card catalog in a deserted library, searching for one very obscure, little-read entry on Hungarian poetry. It was dead silent, no one gave me any direction, and nothing was where it was supposed to be.

"It's all very G-rated around here, so what's really the problem?"

"You didn't even remember Sam was coming today."

"That's not true. She'll have a great time. If there's any trouble, I'll call you and you can airlift her out by Black Hawk."

"What about Nancy?"

"*Nora.* She'll be out of here by ten." *It wasn't the time to mention Sam had a roommate.*

Cynthia sighed, a familiar look of surrender on her face. "Have her home by six on Sunday. And Bruce and I rescheduled our Santa Barbara trip for *next* week, so you'll have Sam for a long weekend." She eyed me skeptically. "Unless you can't handle it."

"I can handle it."

"We're going with friends, so you can't suddenly change your mind."

"You have my word. I want the extra time with her."

She seemed to accept this, sweeping her blond hair over her shoulder, staring at me expectantly, waiting for me to say something more.

This had been one of the great enigmas of our marriage. In the sixteen years we were together, Cynthia often waited for me to say something more, as if there were very specific words that would unlock her, state-of-the-art vault that she was. I never came close to deciphering the combination. *I love you* did not work. Neither did *What are you thinking?* or *Tell me what you want to hear.*

She'd wait for a minute, maybe longer, and when she understood she was going to remain locked until further notice, she'd walk away, lost in sealed-tight silence. This was what she did now, opening the door and striding back down the hall.

I was about to head after her, when I felt my cell ringing in my pocket. It was Hopper.

"Come to Fifty-eighth and Broadway," he shouted as a police siren ripped into the receiver. *"Now."*

"What?"

"I found someone who saw Ashley a few days before she died."

I glanced back down the hall. Cynthia was taking off Sam's coat.

Shit.

"Give me twenty minutes," I said and hung up.

So Hopper couldn't stay away after all. The kid was proving to be quite the trump card.

31 | SAM STARED SULLENLY back at me. Even though I'd just explained, crouched down on her level with as much drama as I could muster, that her dad had some *top-secret business* to attend to and needed to run, so she was staying with Mommy—she didn't say a word.

"Next weekend we'll be spending four *days* together," I said. "Just the two of us, okay?"

Still, the silence. But then, seemingly thinking something quite serious, she reached her right hand way up and *patted* me on my head. She'd never done that before. Cynthia, her face flushed, shot me a look—*Great parenting*—but, smiling agreeably for Sam's sake, she extended the handle of the *Toy Story* suitcase, handing it off to Sam, who dutifully wheeled it to the door like a tired stewardess learning she had to fly an extra leg to Cincinnati.

"Bye, sweetheart," I said. "I love you more than—*what* was it again?"

"The sun plus the moon," she answered, heading down the hall.

"I'll make it up to her," I said to Cynthia.

"Of *course.*" She swept her hair over her shoulder and smiled, stepping after her. "We'll put it on your tab."

I strode to the hall closet, trying to ignore the tsunami of guilt flooding through me.

"Hopper called," I said to Nora over my shoulder. "We're meeting him uptown *now.* He has a lead." I grabbed my keys, but Nora didn't move from the living-room doorway. She was staring at me, wide-eyed.

"What's the matter?" I asked.

"That was *bad.*"

"What was bad?"

"*That.*"

"My ex-wife? Yes, I know. Can you believe *that woman* used to live to karaoke on a Saturday night? In college, we called her Bangles. You couldn't pay her to stop singing 'Walk Like an Egyptian' in public."

"*She's* not what I'm *talking* about."

I was helping Nora into her coat. "Then *what* are you talking about? And tell me quickly, because we need to get going."

"You think you're subtle, but you're not."

I was jostling her into the hallway, locking the door. "Subtle about what?"

"That you're crazy mad in *love* with her."

"*Hey.* No one's crazy or mad or in love with anyone here."

She put a hand on my shoulder, a look of evident pity.

"You need to move on with your life. She's *happy.*" And with that, she took off merrily down the hall, leaving me staring after her.

32 HOPPER WAS WAITING for us on the corner by the HSBC bank, smoking a cigarette, the serious, hollowed-out expression on his face suggesting that he'd barely slept in the two days since we'd seen him.

"What are we doing here?" I asked him.

"Remember what Morgan Devold said? He thought Ashley had to play the piano every day?"

"Sure."

"Yesterday I started thinking, if Ashley came into the city to track someone down, if she wanted to play, where would she go?"

"Jazz clubs. Juilliard. A hotel lobby? It's hard to say."

"None of those places would let a stranger off the street just sit down and start playing, uninterrupted. But then I remembered, I got a friend who's big into the classical music scene. If you're really good, the showrooms on Piano Row let you come in and play as long as you like. This afternoon I went into a bunch, asked around, and a manager in one of the shops actually recognized her. Ashley came in twice the week before she died."

"Nice work," I said.

"Right now he's waiting to talk to us. But we have to hurry because they're about to close." He chucked the cigarette onto the pavement and took off down the sidewalk.

I'd never heard of Piano Row. It was a splinter of Fifty-eighth Street between Broadway and Seventh Avenue, where delicate piano stores had tucked themselves between hulking sixties apartment buildings like a few sparrows living among hippos. We hurried past a small shop called Beethoven Pianos, posters taped in the windows advertising Vivaldi concerts and voice lessons. Inside, identical shiny baby grands were lined up, lids open, like hefty chorus girls awaiting a cue. Hopper shuffled past the Morton Williams supermarket and crossed the street, passing a fire station, and then pausing in front of a shop with a dirty green awning that read KLAVIERHAUS.

I held the door open for Nora and we entered. Unlike Beethoven Pianos, there were only three pianos on display. The store was empty, without a single customer or employee. It appeared in the Internet age, *pianos, like physical books, were fast becoming culturally extinct. They'd probably stay that way unless Apple invented the iPiano, which fit inside your pocket and could be mastered via text message. With the iPiano, anyone can be an iMozart. Then, you could compose your own iRequiem for your own iFuneral attended by millions of your iFriends who iLoved you.*

Hopper emerged from a door in the very back with a middle-aged wisp of a man sporting brown corduroys and a black turtleneck, a weedy patch of gray hair sprouting off his balding head. He looked like a classical music man-child. You could spot these Mahler-loving men within a ten-block radius of Carnegie Hall. They tended to wear earth tones, have on DVD all of public television's Great Performances series, live alone in apartments on the Upper West Side, and have potted plants they spoke to daily.

"This is Peter Schmid," Hopper said.

"The manager of Klavierhaus," Peter added with pride.

Nora and I introduced ourselves. "I understand Ashley Cordova came in here a few weeks ago," I said.

"I had no idea who she was at the *time*," Peter said eagerly, clasping his hands together. "But based on Mr. Cole's description, yes, I believe she came to Klavierhaus."

He was one of those people you initially believed had a foreign accent, though it turned out he was American, only spoke *delicately,* as if every word were something to be carefully dusted off and held up to the light.

"Did the police come here to ask about her?"

"No, no. We've had no police. I had no inkling of who she was until Mr. Cole came in this afternoon. He gave me her description, and I recognized her immediately." Peter glanced at Hopper. "The dark hair. The red coat with the black detailing along the sleeves. The beauty."

"When exactly did she come in?" I asked.

"You need the precise date?"

"It'd be helpful."

Peter hurried into the administrative alcove along the opposite wall. After fumbling down behind the counter, he produced a large leather calendar stuffed with papers.

"It was almost certainly a *Tuesday,* because we'd just had our weekly concert salon," he mumbled, flipping open the cover. "Usually it's over by ten-thirty. On *this* night, around eleven, I was in the back cleaning up when suddenly I heard the most exciting interpretation of Ravel's *Valses nobles et sentimentales.* I'm sure you know it?"

We shook our heads, which seemed to concern him.

"*Well.* I'd forgotten to lock the door." Scrutinizing the calendar, he frowned, thoughtfully pressing a finger to his lips. "It was October *fourth.* Yes. That has to be it."

Smiling, he slid the calendar around for us to take a look, tapping the day in question with his index finger.

"I hurried into the showroom, and I saw her at the piano."

"Which one and where?" I asked.

He pointed toward the front. "The Fazioli. There in the window."

I strolled over to it, Nora following me.

"Is it a good one?" I asked.

Peter chuckled as if I'd made a joke, heading after us. "Faziolis are the best in the world. Many professionals find them superior to Steinways."

I studied it. Even by my amateur eyes, it was a gorgeous, intimidating instrument.

"Pianos are like people," Peter noted softly. "Every one has a different personality. They take time to get to know. And they can get lonely."

"What personality does this one have?" Nora asked.

"Her? Oh. *She's* a bit of a diva. If she were in high school, she'd be the prom queen. She can be moody, imperious. Take over if you're not careful. But if you show her a firm hand, she'll dazzle you. All piano soundboards are made of spruce. Well, *Fazioli* uses spruce from the Val di Fiemme forest in Northern Italy."

He awaited our amazed reaction, but we could only stare back blankly.

"It's the same timber the Stradivari family used to craft their legendary violins in the seventeenth century. It produced an opulent velvet sound that can't be replicated by any other manufacturer today. It's why Stradivarius violins today sell in the millions."

"What did you do when you heard her?" I asked.

"I intended to tell her she'd have to come back tomorrow. We were closed, after all. But her playing was"—he shut his eyes and shook his head—"*electrifying.* I could tell she'd been trained by a European, due to her take-no-prisoners, blustery articulation perfectly balanced with profound intimacy, which brought to mind some of the greatest pianists of all time. Argerich. Pascal Rogé. I couldn't bear to interrupt. Genius doesn't keep to business hours, *n'est-ce pas?* I didn't speak to her until she was finished."

"How long was that?" I asked.

"Approximately a minute and a half. She looked so familiar, in a very distant way. Like a tune you suddenly recall from childhood and yet you can't remember the lyrics or really anything beyond a handful of mysterious notes." He sighed. "*Now* I realize it was Ash DeRouin. All grown up. I'd heard from one of our owners, Gabor, that she used to come in here and play years ago, as a teenager. But I didn't make the connection." He paused, his face pensive. "When she finished, she asked me politely if she could play the entire suite, the *Assez Lent* through the *Epilogue*. The performance takes about fifteen minutes. Naturally I said yes." He smiled. "If she'd have asked to play every one of Beethoven's sonatas, I'd have agreed. When she finished, she raised her head, gazing at me. She had a very piercing stare."

"Did she say anything?"

"She thanked me. She had a low voice. Hoarse. A sort of swanlike way of moving. Immaculate surface. No idea what's going on beneath. She sat there a moment saying nothing. I sensed it was difficult for her to speak. I wondered if English wasn't her first language. She picked up her bag, and then . . ." His eyes drifted away from the piano, as if imagining Ashley there now, walking to the door. "I *tried* getting her to stay, but when I asked her name she said, 'No one.' And then she left."

"What was her demeanor?" I asked.

"Demeanor?"

"Did she seem depressed? Mentally unwell?"

"Apart from her hesitation with talking? No. Not *this* time. This time she was quite satisfied when she finished. The way one might feel after a vigorous swim in the Pacific. Musicians feel that way after a good practice." He cleared his throat, turning to stare out the window at the empty street. "I watched her drift down the sidewalk, as if she weren't quite sure where she was going. Finally she moved west toward Broadway and was gone. That night when I got home, I remember very distinctly I couldn't sleep, not the whole night. Yet I felt great calm. I'd been dealing with some personal issues of late, the details of which I'll certainly spare you. But her sudden appearance for me was a gift. Part of it was because only *I'd* seen her. She could very well have been a figment of my imagination. One of Debussy's *demoiselles*. I doubted I'd ever see her again."

"When did she come back?" I asked.

He seemed saddened by the question. "Three days later."

"That would be October the *seventh*," I said, making a note of it in my BlackBerry. "Do you remember the time of day?"

"An hour after closing. Seven o'clock? Again, I was the last one here. Even our intern had disappeared." He turned, gesturing at the large antique-looking leather notebook open on a table along the back wall. "We ask everyone who comes into Klavierhaus to sign the guestbook. If an artist has signed the Klavierhaus guestbook, it's believed to help future recitals and technique. A sort of baptism, if you will. We've had all the legends sign it. Zimerman. Brendel. Lang Lang. Horowitz."

When it was clear the names meant little to us, he inhaled sharply, disheartened, and pointed over his shoulder to the administration alcove.

"I was typing up the addresses and names when there was a knock on the glass. Technically, we were closed. But when I saw who it was, of *course* I let her in. As soon as I unlocked the door, however, I realized something was terribly wrong."

"What?" asked Hopper.

Peter looked uncomfortable. "I don't think she'd had a shower—perhaps hadn't even taken off that *coat*—since I'd last seen her. Her hair was disheveled. She reeked of dirt and sweat. The cuffs of her jeans were filthy. *Mud from the country,* I thought to myself. She seemed drugged. It occurred to me she must be homeless. We've had quite a few vagrants enter the shop. They wander down here after sleeping on the steps of Saint Thomas on Fifth. The music draws them in." He sighed. "She asked if it was all right if she played. I said yes. And she sat down right there." He indicated the same lustrous Fazioli piano, gazing down at the empty brown leather seat. "She ran her hands over the keys and said, 'I think Debussy today. He's not so mad at me.' Something to that effect. And then she—"

"Wait a minute," I interrupted. "She talked about the composer as if he were an *acquaintance*?"

"Sure," Peter said with a blithe nod.

"Isn't that a little strange?"

"Not at all. Concert pianists get to be quite chummy with dead composers. They can't help it. Classical music isn't just *music*. It's a personal diary. An uncensored confession in the dead of night. A baring of the soul. Take a modern example. Florence and the Machine? In the song 'Cosmic Love,' she catalogs the way in which the world has gone dark, disorienting her, when she, a rather intense young woman, was left bereft by a love affair. 'The stars, the moon, they have all been blown out.' *Well.* It's no different with Beethoven and Ravel. Into their music these composers poured their fiercest beings. When a pianist memorizes a piece, he or she gets to know the dead man *intimately*— giving rise to all the pleasures and difficulties such an intense relationship implies. You learn Mozart's trickery, his ADD attention span. Bach's yearning for acceptance, his intolerance for shortcuts. Liszt's explosive temper. Chopin's insecurity. And thus when you set out to make their music come *alive* in concert, on *stage,* in front of thousands, you very much *need* the dead man on your side. Because you're bringing him back to life. It's a bit like Frankenstein resuscitating his monster, you understand? It can be an astonishing miracle. Or it can all go horribly wrong."

I glanced at Hopper. He continued to stare at Peter, the look on his face something between absorption and skepticism. Nora was spellbound.

"What happened this time?" I asked.

"She began playing. The opening parallel fifths of *La cathédrale engloutie*—"

"The opening parallel *what?*" interjected Nora, frowning.

"*La cathédrale engloutie.* The Sunken Cathedral."

Peter, noting our obvious ignorance, *beamed,* unable to restrain his delight.

"Claude Debussy. The French impressionist. It's one of my very favorite preludes. It tells the story of a cathedral submerged at the bottom of the sea. On a clear day, it rises up out of the churning waves and fog, bells chiming ecstatically, to rest for mere *seconds* in the air, shimmering in the sun, before sinking down again in the fathomless depths, out of sight. Debussy instructs the musician to play the final chords pianissimo, at half-pedal, so it truly sounds as if there are church bells deep underwater, notes colliding, before fading and ending as all things do—as *we all do*—with a few reverberating chords and then silence."

He paused, his face darkening.

"She couldn't do it. Her playing—so revelatory before, such melting lyricism, such romance—was disturbing now. She tore into the music, but the notes eluded her. It was erratic. *Despairing.* And when she looked up at me, I . . ." He swallowed loudly. "Her eyes were bloodshot.

They actually looked to be bleeding. I was filled with such horror by her face, how it had transformed so from the time I'd seen her before, I instantly left to phone the police. I left her playing here in front. But just as I entered the back room, she stopped. There was only silence. I peeked my head out. She was sitting very still, *watching* me with those eyes, as if she knew what I was doing. Suddenly she grabbed her bag and left. Like *that*." He snapped his fingers. "It was what truly frightened me."

"Why?" I asked.

He wrung his hands, uneasy. "She moved like an animal."

"An *animal*?" Hopper repeated.

Peter nodded. "It was too fast. It certainly wasn't normal."

"Which direction did she go?" I asked.

"I don't know. I returned to the front, but there was no sign of her. I even stepped outside to take a look. She wasn't *anywhere*. I locked up the shop immediately. I didn't want to be in the store alone."

He lapsed into melancholic silence, staring at the floor. "She never came back. I *thought* about her. But I hadn't told anyone until you came in." He looked at Hopper. "I was relieved when you asked about her, so happy to know I hadn't dreamt her out of thin air. I've . . . I've been under some pressure of late." He flushed. "To say the least, it was nice to know I wasn't going crazy." His gaze returned to the piano. "She was a bit like that cathedral. Rising up, stunning me, decaying, and then vanishing, leaving only her echo. And me, so uncertain of what I'd seen."

"Do you have video surveillance in the store?" I asked.

"We have an alarm system. But no cameras."

"Did she mention anything else? Where she was staying?"

"Oh, *no*. We didn't speak beyond what I told you."

"And she left nothing behind? No personal items?"

"I'm afraid not."

Nora had moved over to the small table along the wall with the open guestbook, turning back the pages.

"That's really all—oh, *do* be careful with that." Peter scurried after her. "The pages are quite fragile, and it's our only copy."

"I'm just wondering if she signed it," said Nora, Peter looking on nervously over her shoulder.

Hopper had stepped up to the Fazioli that Ashley had played, solemnly running his hand along the gleaming keys, playing a few sharp notes.

I strode over to Nora. Having found the page marked October 4, she was running her finger down the list of scribbled names and addresses.

"Daniel Hwang," she read. "Yuja Li. Jessica Song. Kirill Luminovich. Boris Anthony." She turned the page rather roughly, and Peter touched his forehead as if he might faint. "Kay Glass. Viktor Koslov. Ling Bl—"

"What did you say?" I asked.

"Viktor Koslov."

"Before that."

"Kay Glass."

I stepped closer, incredulous, staring down at the page.

It was scribbled in black pen, that familiar handwriting, identical, I was certain, to the note that Morgan Devold had shown us—and maybe even the envelope mailed to Hopper.

"That's her," I said.

33 THE STREETS WERE NARROW, shriveled bodegas and faded walk-ups packed shoulder to shoulder. Upstairs windows, filled with plants and shampoo bottles, were lit up like dirty fish tanks in electric greens and blues. Every now and then we passed someone walking alone, usually Chinese, carrying orange plastic shopping bags or hurrying along in a down jacket. Almost everyone turned to stare in at us as if they knew—probably because we were riding in a taxi—we were trespassing.

Our driver turned onto Pike Street, a wide, four-lane boulevard. To our left was a low brick building—MANHATTAN REPAIR COMPANY, read the sign—and on our right, what looked to be a public school.

"That's Henry Street," Hopper said suddenly, craning his neck to make out the street sign. The cabdriver made the left turn.

HONG KONG SUPERMARKET. JASMINE BEAUTY SALON. It was after seven o'clock, and every shop was closed, metal grates pulled down, padlocked.

"There's ninety-one," said Nora, leaning forward to survey the deserted street. "Eighty-three is coming up on the right."

Ashley had written in the Klavierhaus guestbook—and Peter Schmid was at a loss to explain *when* exactly she had done so:

Kay Glass was the name of the missing friend in *A Small Evil*—the unseen woman who invites her new coworker, Alexandra, and Alex's fiancé, Mitchell, to her parents' beach house for the weekend. In the opening minutes of the film, Alex and Mitch, having argued during most of the drive from the city, arrive at the house a little after midnight. They find it entirely in the dark and deserted, the friend—Kay Glass—nowhere to be found. An initial search of the home—a modernist glass structure standing at the edge of the ocean like a monument to nihilism—reveals that a horrific crime has taken place moments before their arrival, and the perpetrators—masked, dressed head-to-toe in black—are still there.

I'd recognized the name because not only were the Blackboards rife with theories and the occasional shrine to the elusive Kay Glass, I'd also heard Beckman give a detailed lecture on the name and its meaning. He contended *Kay Glass* meant chaos. Beckman further argued that the missing woman—the question of what had happened to her—was, in fact, a metaphor for the inescapable darkness in life. The figure was a Cordova trademark, and Beckman had named one of his cats after it: *Shadow.*

"Kay Glass is the Shadow that hounds us relentlessly," Beckman said. "It's what we chase but never find. It is the mystery of our lives, the understanding that even when we have everything we want it is one day to leave us. It's the something unseen, the lurking devastation, the darkness that gives our lives dimension."

The fact that out of all the potential pseudonyms, Ashley had chosen *that one*—a missing woman from her father's film—led to all sorts of psychological conclusions, the most obvious being that her father's stories were a part of her day-to-day reality, maybe even overshadowed her sense of self. What was her response when Peter Schmid had asked her who she was?

No one, she'd said.

It reminded me of the profile in the Amherst newsletter. *It's wonderful to get lost in a piece of music,* she'd said. *To forget your name for a while.*

Our taxi eased down the deserted street. In front of us, the Manhattan Bridge extended at a diagonal like a massive fallen tree no one had bothered to remove. Dingy walk-ups had sprouted up around it.

"There," Hopper said, indicating a building on our right.

The awning out front read 83 HENRY STREET in white letters, followed by a few Chinese characters. Metal grates had been pulled down on either side of the front entrance—a green door with a small rectangular window.

I paid the driver, and we climbed out.

It was oddly silent and still, the only sound the faint moans of unseen cars racing across the bridge. I stepped up to the door, looking through the window.

Inside, a derelict hallway spray-painted with graffiti extended beyond a row of mailboxes.

"Look," Nora whispered, pointing at the label beside the buzzer for #16. It read K. GLASS.

"*Don't* press it," I said. I stepped back to the curb, staring up at the building: five stories, crumbling red brick, a rusted fire escape. All of the windows were dark except two on the second floor, another on the fifth with frilly pink curtains.

"Someone's coming," Hopper whispered, moving away from the door, darting around the corner, where there was a parking lot. Nora lurched backward, hurrying down the sidewalk. I stepped around the trash bags piled on the curb, heading across the street.

Seconds later, I heard the door open behind me, rapid footsteps.

An Asian man wearing a blue jacket had exited, walking toward Pike Street. He didn't appear to have seen us—not even Hopper, who'd slipped past him and managed to catch the door before it closed.

"*Nice,*" Nora whispered excitedly, rushing inside after him. "Number sixteen must be the top floor."

"Hold on a minute," I said, stepping after them.

But Hopper was already racing down the hall and out of sight, Nora right behind him. I held back, inspecting the mailboxes. Apart from Glass at #16, there was only Dawkins in #1 and Vine in #13.

I slipped down the hall, a TV babbling somewhere close by. Hopper and Nora could already be heard clanging upstairs. Because of a bright light somewhere beyond the corridor, their dark, elongated shadows were suddenly tossed against the wall in front of me—two long black tongues sliding down it, licking the cracked brown tiles and vanishing.

I headed after them, the steps strewn with trash and ads for Asian escorts, mostly in Chinese. One flier, wedged into a filthy window-pane, read ASIAN GIRL-MASSAGE and featured a naked Korean wearing rubber chaps shyly peering over her shoulder. MEET YUMI, it read.

Hopper and Nora had disappeared somewhere along the top floor. As I started up the next flight, kicking aside a Tsingtao beer can, there was a sudden *bang* somewhere below me.

I stared over the metal railing.

No one was visible. Yet I swore I could hear *breathing.*

"Hello?" I called out, my voice echoing through the stairwell.

There was no answer.

I moved up the remaining flights, pulling open the door marked 5, spotting Hopper and Nora at the end of a long dim hallway outside #16. As I caught up, they both turned, startled, at something behind me.

A woman had just appeared at the opposite end.

34 THE SINGLE NEON BULB on the ceiling drenched her wide nose and forehead in sickly yellow light. She was quite fat, wearing a long green skirt and black T-shirt, straggly brown hair covering her shoulders.

"What d'you think you're doing?" she asked in a croaky masculine voice.

"Checking in on a friend," I said.

She scurried toward us, hunched shoulders, flip-flops rapidly slapping her bare feet.

"*What* friend?"

"Ashley."

"Who?"

"Kay," Nora interjected. "He means *Kay.*"

The name made the woman stop short, unwilling to approach further. She had to be in her fifties, with mottled skin, also missing some teeth, giving her face the countenance of a crumbling statue.

"Where the hell *is* Kay?" she demanded. "You tell her she owes me three weeks' rent. I'm not running a free shelter here."

Hopper reached into his coat pocket, unfolding a piece of paper.

"Is this her?" he asked. It was a black-and-white photograph of Ashley. He must have printed it off the Internet, because I'd never seen it before—unless it was from his own collection, a snapshot taken at Six Silver Lakes. The woman didn't move to look at it, only jutted out her chin.

"You're cops?"

"No," I said. "We're friends of Kay's."

"When was the last time you saw her?" blurted Nora.

The woman glared at us. "I don't talk to cops."

"We're *not* cops," said Hopper, removing his wallet from his back pocket. The instant he flipped it open, the woman's small black eyes swarmed it like flies over a turd. "Answer our questions, we'll make it worth your while." He held out three twenties, which she grabbed instantly, counting them, then sticking them down the front of her T-shirt.

"Is this Kay?" asked Hopper again, holding out the picture.

"Sure looks like her."

"When did you last see her?" I asked.

"*Weeks* ago. That's how come I came up. Heard all the creepin' around, thought she came back to get her stuff and was trying to sneak past me. Any idea when Her Highness plans to show?"

"Not really."

The news infuriated her. "I coulda rented this room five times over. Now I gotta get a locksmith up here. Clean out her shit."

"Why a locksmith?" I asked.

She nodded at the door. "I don' got the key to her room. She changed the locks on me."

"Why?"

"Hell if I know."

"What was she like?" asked Nora.

The woman grimaced. "Had duchess airs, if you ask me. Had a way of demanding things, like she thought she was a queen a' England. Wanted me to fix the lights in the bathrooms 'cuz it was too dark for her, then the hot and cold tap. Musta mistaken this place for a fuckin' Marriott."

"Do you know what she was doing in the city?" asked Nora.

The woman squinted as if faintly insulted. "You pay me on time, what you do in the room is your business. She *did* do me a favor once. I had to run out, and she watched my nephew a coupla hours. That I *did* appreciate. But then she changes the locks, runs out, stiffs me on the rent. I'm runnin' a business. Not a charity." She stared resentfully at the door again. "Now I gotta pay for a locksmith."

"How long has she been living here?" I asked.

"'Bout a month. But I haven't seen her for weeks."

"And how did she hear about it?"

"Answered my ad. I got fliers posted around Port Authority."

"How much to break the door down?" Hopper asked, running his hands along it. "We'll also cover whatever Kay owed you in rent."

"Uh, that'd be—oh, *one-fifty*. Plus any damage to the door."

"Here's three hundred." He shoved a wad of bills at the woman, which she hastily grabbed, then he strode to the end of the hall, where there was a door with a grimy pane of glass—some sort of communal bathroom—and a fire extinguisher. He pulled the extinguisher free and moved back, raising it over his head and slamming it hard against the deadbolt.

He did this five times, the wood splintering, and then—with a laid-back ease that hinted he'd done this before—he tossed aside the canister, took a few steps back, and side-kicked it. The door flew open, cracking against the wall, and then closed, stopping so it was ajar about an inch.

For a moment, no one moved. Hopper pushed the door wider.

It was pitch-dark inside, light from the hallway barely illuminating the scarred concrete floor, walls of flaking blue paint.

There was also a noticeable *stench*—something rotten.

I turned, intending to ask the landlord when she'd last been inside Kay's room, but she'd actually backed away.

"Gotta get downstairs," she mumbled, then turned, flip-flops hammering her feet as she hurried down the hall. "Gotta check on my nephew." She darted out, and within seconds could be heard clanging back downstairs.

"She's afraid of something," I said.

"It's that *smell*," whispered Nora.

35

HOPPER TOOK A STEP INSIDE. I followed, sliding my hands along the wall, trying to find a light switch.

"*Fuck*," he said, coughing. "The smell's really bad."

There was a grating *screech* as he accidentally tripped on something—a metal folding chair—then, fumbling with a lamp, the room was suddenly drenched in pale light.

It was small and stark, with a faded brown rug, a window with a torn shade, a sagging metal cot in a corner. Something about the way the sheets were thrown back, a green blanket dangling on the floor— a discernible *dent* in the pillow—seemed to suggest Ashley had just climbed out of it, moments ago. In fact, the entire shabby room hinted she'd just been here, the musty air still filled with her breathing.

The rank stench, a combination of sewage and *burning*, seemed to seep out of the walls. A brown stain covered the ceiling by the window, as if something had been slaughtered on the roof, then left to slowly bleed down into the rafters. The floor, strewn with a few plastic wrappers, was sticky from some type of dark soda that had spilled.

"Didn't Devold say Ashley was wearing white pajamas when he broke her out of Briarwood?" Hopper asked.

"Yes," I said.

"They're right here."

Sure enough—a pair of white cotton drawstring pants and a top had been tossed in a heap on the sheets.

Hopper seemed reluctant to touch them. I picked up the pants, noting with surprise not just that *A. Cordova MH-314*—her room number at Briarwood—had been printed along the inner waistband, but the legs still held her form. So did the top; cut in the boxy shape of surgical scrubs, the left sleeve still twisted around her elbow.

I put them back on the bed, stepping toward a small closet. There was nothing in there—just four wire hangers on a wooden rod.

"Something's under here," Hopper said. He was looking under the bed.

We grabbed the cot, carrying it to the center of the room, and then all three of us stared, bewildered, at what had just been exposed.

None of us said a word.

36 My first thought was that it was some type of target. And if I ever found such a thing under my *own* bed, I probably couldn't help but wonder if the Grim Reaper had put it there, a reminder that I was due to be picked up in a matter of days—*or I had enemies who wanted to scare the living daylights out of me.*

Four concentric circles made out of black ashes had been meticulously laid out on the floor. At the center—almost directly beneath where Ashley's torso or heart would be, I noticed, if she were lying flat on the bed—was a pyramid of charcoal. It stood about six inches, the rocks white and crumbling, the concrete beneath it charred black.

"What is it?" Nora whispered.

"The ashes are what smells," said Hopper, crouching beside it.

After taking photos, Nora found a sandwich bag in her purse, and, turning it inside out, we collected a sample of the powder. It looked like finely chopped leaves, dirt, and bone. I sealed the bag and tucked it into my coat pocket.

"Holy shit," Hopper whispered behind us. "Check this out."

He was by the door, staring at something lodged above it—a cluster of sticks. They'd been carefully positioned deep in the corner, *as if to deliberately escape notice.*

Hopper pulled them down, holding them in the light from the hallway. They looked like *roots*—some thick, others thin, others tightly coiled in spirals, though they all looked to be from the same plant. Each one had been knotted neatly with white string and tied to another.

"Looks like some kind of occult practice," I said, carefully taking the bunch from Hopper. I'd come across some bizarre religious customs over the years—baby-tossing in India; Jain monks who walked around naked, *wearing* the air; tribal boys forced to wear gloves filled with bullet ants, a ritual to enter adulthood. This seemed to be something along those lines.

"Why would it be over the doorway?" asked Nora.

I looked at Hopper. "You remember Ashley being involved in any unusual practices or beliefs?"

"No."

"Let's do another walk-through. See if there's anything we missed. Then let's get the hell out of here."

Nora and Hopper nodded, glancing warily around the room. I was about to head over to the bedside table, when out of the corner of my eye I saw something *green* streaking past the doorway followed by staccato slapping. *Flip-flops.*

I stuck my head out. The landlord was scampering down the hall. *The old crone had been spying.*

"Wait a minute!" I shouted, stepping after her.

"I don't know nothing," she growled.

"You must have noticed that *smell* coming out of her room."

She stopped dead at the end of the hallway, turning, her skin glistening with sweat.

"I don't know *what* that girl did with herself."

"Have any of the residents said anything?"

She didn't respond. She had an off-putting, *lizardlike* way of moving, remaining stone still—as if knowing she'd be camouflaged by the grim light and cracked walls around her—then hastily scuttling away. Now she was absolutely immobile, staring at me with her head cocked.

"She scared people." She grinned. "Don't know *how,* 'cuz she's a skinny thing. And some a' the numbers who take my rooms, *they're* usually the ones who do the *scaring.* But I don't make it my business. People can do what they want, long as they pay me."

I was halfway down the hall now, but stopped because a small boy—

no more than five or six years old—was peering at me through the stairwell door. After a pause, he slipped out, standing sullenly behind the woman. He was in a dirty T-shirt, cotton pants too short in the leg, and socks meant for much larger feet.

"Is that your nephew?" I asked.

She surveyed him coldly and turned back to me, saying nothing.

"You mentioned Kay watched him once when you were out. Can he tell me anything about her?"

She pointed at me. "For a *friend,* you don't know too much."

I noticed then a shard of light was coming out of a room beside me, the door moving. *Someone was eavesdropping.* Before I could see who it was, there was a loud clanging. The landlord and boy had just disappeared into the stairwell. I took off after them.

"Hold on!"

"You leave us alone."

I raced down the steps, tripping on fliers, catching up on the next landing. Without thinking, I grabbed the boy's arm. He emitted a *bloodcurdling squeal,* as if I'd just branded him with an iron.

Startled, I let go, yet he continued to scream as he watched something—some kind of action figure he'd just dropped—careen down through the metal railings, bouncing on the steps, skidding across the tiles on the ground floor. With a whimper, he took off after it.

"Look what you done now," the woman mumbled furiously, heading after him. "Take your *friends* and get out of here. We don't know nothin'."

When I reached the ground floor, I found the two of them frantically scouring the hallway. The boy stood up, turning to the woman, his fingers working fast in the air. *He was speaking in sign language.* He was deaf. *And I'd traumatized him.*

Guilty, I turned, searching the tiled floor, kicking aside fliers and wrappers. I soon found it in a rectangle of light under the stairwell.

It was a tiny wood carving of a snake—three inches long, mouth open, tongue extended, twisted body. It felt oddly heavy.

Suddenly beside me, the landlord snatched it, handing it back to the boy. She then seized his arm, hauled him toward an apartment door. I caught a glimpse of a cluttered room, a TV playing cartoons, as she shoved the boy inside, darted in after him, the door slamming.

Nora and Hopper were racing downstairs, the building growling with the noise. They ran straight down the hall, Nora turning, silently beckoning me to hurry. I exited after her into the cool night, realizing I was gasping for breath, as if I'd just wrenched free of something—something that, without my knowledge, had been suffocating me.

37 "DID YOU TAKE THE ROOTS over the door?" I asked when I caught up with Nora and Hopper across the street.

"Yep," she said, opening up her purse to show me.

"Okay, let's grab a cab—"

"We *can't*. A neighbor of Ashley's is coming down to talk to us."

I recalled that shard of light I'd seen outside room #13.

"While you chased the landlady, this other woman stuck her head out, upset by all the commotion. Hopper showed her Ashley's picture, and she recognized her. She's coming down to talk to us in two seconds."

"Nice work."

"Here she comes," whispered Nora, as a figure emerged from 83 Henry.

The woman was tall, wearing a white zip-up sweatshirt and sneakers. She carried a black duffel bag over her shoulder, and whatever was in there—*assault rifles,* by the shape of it—appeared to be quite heavy, making her walk stooped over. She hurried across the street toward us.

"Sorry I took so long," she said breathlessly, skipping up onto the curb in a potent blast of perfume. "Couldn't find my keys. I'm off to work, so I don't have much time. What'd you want to ask me?"

Her face was quite pretty, fringed with bleached blond curls, though wearing so much makeup, it was difficult to know where she ended and her illusion began. She looked about thirty, though I noticed she stood deliberately away from the streetlight and kept her hands shoved in the pockets of her hoodie, shoulders hunched, as if not entirely at ease with people getting a close look at her.

"Just a few questions about your neighbor Kay."

She smiled. "Oh, yeah. How's she doing? Haven't seen her."

"Fine," I answered, ignoring Nora's look. "We're friends of hers and want to know about her stay here. What'd she do with herself?"

"Gee, I wouldn't know. We barely talked." Setting the duffel down on the sidewalk—mysterious metallic clangs—the woman removed a ball of Kleenex from her pocket and blew her nose. "*Sorry.* I'm just getting over a bad cold. I only saw Kay, like, once."

"When?" I asked.

"A month ago? I was just getting in from work. About five, six in the morning. I went into the bathroom to take my makeup off. There's only one per floor. Everyone shares. I was in there, like, forty-five minutes, brushing my teeth, probably even talking to myself, when all of a sudden there was a *splash* behind me." She shuddered. "Scared the shit out of me. I screamed. Probably woke up the whole building."

"Why?" I asked when she didn't go on, but paused to blow her nose again.

"She was right there," she said, giggling, a high-pitched, jingle-bell sound. "*Kay.*"

"Where?"

"In the bathtub. She'd been behind me, taking a bath, the whole time."

I glanced at Hopper and Nora. They seemed to be thinking what I was—the disturbing nature of the scene she'd just described was entirely lost on the woman.

"I introduced myself," she went on, sniffing. "She told me her name but leaned her head back against the tub, closing her eyes like she'd had a long day and didn't feel like talking. I finished putting on my wrinkle creams, said good night. After I heard her leave the bathroom, I went back because I'd left my toothpaste on the sink. She hadn't drained the tub, so I stuck my hand in to unplug it." She shook her head. "I don't know *how* she was in there without her legs and arms freezing off. It was like *ice.*"

"You never saw Kay again?" I asked.

"No. I *heard* her, though. The walls are like paper. She seemed to keep the same hours as I did."

"What hours are those?"

"I work nights." She said it vaguely, gazing past us at the deserted street. "You know what? There *was* another time. Sorry. My mind's stuffy from this cold medicine. It was my night off, so it musta been on a Saturday. I was coming back from the supermarket and passed Kay on the stairwell. She was on her way to a club. I don't remember the name." She shook her head. "It was feminine. Kinda French? I *think* she said it was being held in an old jail on Long Island. She wanted to know if I'd ever been, but I hadn't."

"An old jail?" I repeated.

She shrugged. "It was a five-second conversation. You know what? Last week I did see two guys outside her door. They stared at me like they wanted me to mind my own business, so I did."

"What did they look like?"

"Just *guys*. One was older, the other in his thirties? Later I heard Dot come upstairs and get rid of them. She doesn't like strangers."

"Dot?"

"Yeah. You were talking to her."

"A little boy lives with her?"

"Lucian. He's her nephew."

"How long has he been living here?"

"Long as I've been at Henry. About a year." She sniffed and pulled back her sleeve, checking her watch. "Shit. I gotta run." She grabbed the duffel, heaving it, clanging, over her shoulder. "You'll tell Kay I said hi?"

"Of course."

"How can we get in touch if we have more questions?" asked Nora.

After a slight hesitation, the woman unzipped the duffel, handing Nora a black business card. Then she smiled and took off down the sidewalk toward the Manhattan Bridge. Nora handed the business card to me without a word.

IONA, it read. BACHELOR PARTY ENTERTAINMENT.

38 "A NIGHTCLUB ON LONG ISLAND," I said. "It has a French name. It might be held in an old jail or abandoned building. Ring any bells?"

I was on the phone with Sharon Falcone, standing outside Gitane, a temperamental little French-Moroccan café on Mott Street. After leaving 83 Henry, we'd taken a cab here to grab a bite and debrief. When a

Google search of *club, Long Island, French,* and *abandoned jail* elicited no breakthrough, I decided to call Sharon on the off chance she knew what the club could be.

"Don't tell me you're harassing me because you need help with your social life," said Falcone on the other end.

I could hear phones wailing, a TV droning *NY1*, which meant she was still at her desk at the police station, sitting in her beat-up swivel chair, poring over the details of a case her colleagues had long given up on, glasses perched on the tip of her nose.

"Not quite," I said. "It's a lead."

"I know Long Island like I know my kitchen. I understand it's there for my pleasure and enjoyment, but somehow I never manage to go there. Can't help you. Can I get back to work now?"

"What about occult worship in the city? How prevalent is it?"

"Does worshipping money count as occult?"

"I mean, strange practices, rituals. How often do you come across that kind of thing at a crime scene? Would it surprise you?"

"*McGrath.* I got stabbings. I got gunshot wounds. I got a rich kid who knifed his mother in the neck, a six-month-old baby shaken to death, and a man who was castrated at the InterContinental in Times Square. *Sure,* we got occultism. We got it all. There might be a Starbucks on every corner and an iPhone at every ear, but don't worry, people are still fucking crazy. Anything else?"

I was about to say no and apologize for bothering her, when I thought of something.

"I might have a case for Child Protective Services."

She didn't immediately respond, though I could practically see her jerking upright, unearthing a yellow legal pad out of the piles of witness testimonies and lab photos, flipping through her illegible scribbles to a blank page, grabbing a pen.

"I'm listening," she said.

"I just left a woman who's the guardian of a young deaf boy. It doesn't look right. The building's a shithole, might be a brothel."

"What's the address?"

"Eighty-three Henry Street, between Pike and Forsyth. The woman's name is Dot. She runs the place."

"I'll have someone look into it."

"Thank you. Now, when am I taking you out for a drink?"

"When this city gets all warm and fuzzy inside."

"So, never?"

"I keep hoping." A phone bleated on her end. "I gotta take—"

She hung up.

It was after ten o'clock now, a Friday night. Groups of twentysome-things crowded the sidewalk, stumbling toward bars and hookups. Across the street, where the sloping redbrick wall surrounding Saint Patrick's old cathedral cut sharply around the corner, I noticed a man in a black leather jacket talking on a cellphone, his hand cupped over the receiver.

He was staring at me and I couldn't shake the feeling it was *me* he was *speaking* about.

He looked away, past the Ralph Lauren store on the corner, still muttering into his phone. I headed back into Gitane.

I was just being paranoid.

39 | "I WAS JUST TELLING HOPPER," said Nora, as I sat down in the window seat beside her. "I found a receipt in Ashley's trashcan."

Hopper was inspecting the small piece of yellow paper, and with a doubtful look, he handed it to me.

It was a handwritten receipt from Rising Dragon Tattoos, located at 51 West 14th Street. Someone—I could only assume Ashley, though no name was listed—had paid $363.24 in cash for an "American flag / portrait tat" on October 5, 2011, at 8:21 P.M. I knew from the coroner's photos that the tattoo Ashley had on her right foot predated this receipt. So it was a mystery what *American flag / portrait tat* referred to.

"We'll go there tomorrow," I said. "See if someone there recognizes her picture."

"We'll also have to find someone who can tell us what those circles are that she put under her bed," said Nora, taking a bite of avocado toast.

"We don't know *she* put them there," interjected Hopper. "Any kook could have planted that."

"I agree," I said. "The landlord eavesdropping—she could have easily been lying about the key. There are also the two men Iona saw outside Ashley's door. I wonder if she was hiding from somebody, possibly her family. Why else would she take the room under a pseudonym and change the locks?"

"It's almost like there are two Ashleys," said Nora thoughtfully.

"Meaning?" I asked.

She shoved her fork through the tower of couscous on her plate. "There's the pianist. The woman who was fearless and wild. The girl Hopper met at Six Silver Lakes. Then there's this other one people keep talking about. This creature with supernatural tendencies."

"Supernatural tendencies," I repeated.

She nodded, her face serious. "There's what Guadalupe said at the Waldorf Towers. That she was *marked*." She looked at Hopper. "In the coroner's photo we saw a black dot in her left eye just like she said. Think of how she manipulated Morgan Devold without saying a *word*. She hypnotized him. And then Peter at Klavierhaus? He said she moved like an animal."

"She was admitted against her will to a *mental hospital*," said Hopper, sitting low in his seat. "Who *knows* what meds they gave her? I've seen people on that shit, trying to come *off* that shit. They don't know what they're doing half the time."

"One other thing I noticed," Nora continued in a subdued voice. "Ashley had some kind of weird interest in children."

I was impressed. I'd noticed the same thread myself.

"Ashley read Morgan Devold's daughter a bedtime story," she went on. "She also babysat the landlord's nephew. If she came to the city, hoping to meet someone at the Waldorf—and now this nightclub— why would she take the time to do that?"

"Maybe she liked kids," said Hopper.

"That's some *serious* interaction with children in a span of just a few days. Remember that doll Morgan Devold fished out of the pool? He told us it'd been missing for a few weeks."

"So?" said Hopper.

"That'd be around the time Ashley was at his house."

"You think *Ashley* hid the doll in the pool?"

"Maybe. Why would she put that dirt in circles under her bed? Or those roots over her door?"

"We already *established* she probably didn't do that." He said it so angrily, a couple of models at the table beside us stopped speaking to stare at him. He leaned in, lowering his voice. "I'm sure you *love* the idea that Ashley was some kind of Blair Witch, cooking up stews with puppy-dog tails and little kids' toes or whatever the *fuck*. But it's a *joke*. Her family's responsible. *They're* the wackjobs who put her in Briarwood. She wanted to get away from them. Probably died trying." He muttered these last words to himself, shoving his hair out of his eyes and stabbing his fork into his baked eggs, too irritated to eat.

Nora shot me a look and mutely resumed eating. I said nothing. The way she phrased it—*Ashley had some kind of weird interest in children*—reminded me of my anonymous caller from five years ago. *John. There's something he does to the children,* he'd said, words that had haunted me.

What did it mean? That the entire family, or at least father and daughter, had a fixation on children? *Why?*

Simply posing such a question, the mind automatically answered with the darkest responses imaginable. This dichotomy was a major theme in Cordova's work: the malignance of adulthood, the purity of youth, and the collision of these two charges. *Somewhere in an Empty Room, Thumbscrew, The Legacy, Lovechild* all dealt in some way with it, though in *To Breathe with Kings,* Cordova turned this equation on its head, allotting depravity to the child character, sanctity to the adults. There was a line spoken by Marlowe Hughes in *Lovechild,* a slight variation on a quotation by William Blake:

Better to murder an innocent child and be done with it, than mistreat one and give rise to a monster.

I thought suddenly of Morgan Devold's daughter, Mellie, how she'd silently tiptoed after me down the driveway and held out her hand, holding something black.

Had I misread her? Had she silently been pleading for help, begging me not to leave? I was glad I'd told Sharon Falcone about that boy at 83 Henry Street. With a little more research, I wouldn't hesitate making the same call for the Devold children. The thought was so unsettling, I found myself sending Cynthia a text, apologizing for the change in plan, telling her I was looking forward to having Sam for the weekend while she was in Santa Barbara.

"That's the third time that guy's walked by looking in at us," Hopper said, staring out the window behind me.

I turned, following his gaze. It was the *same man* I'd noticed before— tall, dark hair, black leather jacket. He was across the street again, a few yards from where I'd first spotted him.

"He was watching me before, when I was outside," I said.

Hopper suddenly leapt out of his chair, jostling a waitress, who nearly dropped her tray of food as he ran past her and outside. Seeing him coming, the man darted around the corner. I stood up and took off after them.

40 | HOPPER WAS HALFWAY DOWN THE BLOCK, running in the middle of the street. I caught up with him at the corner of Lafayette.

"He just took off," he yelled, pointing at a cab accelerating toward Houston. Hopper stepped into the traffic, trying to flag down another, and I headed after the taxi.

Far ahead at the intersection, the light turned yellow, and the cab, swerving into the center lane, was flooring it. *He was going to fly right through—and that would be that.* But then suddenly the taxi slammed on its brakes, coming to an abrupt halt at the red light.

I had seconds. I weaved between the cars, darting along the right-hand side. I could see the man—a dark silhouette in the backseat, looking over his shoulder—probably to see if Hopper was behind him. I tried the door.

He whipped around, startled. His shock quickly gave way to *cold calm* as he realized the doors were locked. He looked distantly familiar.

"Who are you?" I shouted. "What do you want?"

He shook his head, shrugging as if he had no idea who I was. *Did I have the wrong taxi?* The cab crept forward, the man's face slipping into the shadows. Then the light turned green and the taxi shot across Houston, cars honking as they swerved around me.

Just as the cab pulled away, his left hand had slipped into the light. The man was missing three fingers.

41 | BACK AT GITANE, I explained to Hopper and Nora what had happened, that I was certain it was Theo Cordova who'd been watching us.

"It changes everything," I said. "The family is on to us now, so we'll have to assume our every move is being watched."

They responded with somber acceptance, Hopper almost immediately throwing a few crumpled bills on the table and taking off in answer to a text, Nora and I heading home. She went to bed, though I poured myself a Macallan scotch and looked up *Theo Cordova*.

There were at least a thousand returns in Google images, every one a Cordova film still. He'd played small roles in *At Night All Birds Are Black* and *A Crack in the Window,* though most of the photos were from the opening scene in *Wait for Me Here,* when he runs half naked into the road.

The more I scrutinized the photos, the more certain I was that it was the same man, the same long, thin nose, same pale brown eyes. I checked my notes for his birth date: born in St. Peter's Hospital in Albany on March 12, 1977, which made him thirty-four.

There was little more about Theo on the Blackboards. In the world of Cordova, it appeared the man's son was basically an afterthought. According to one source, for the past eleven years he'd been living a life of total obscurity in rural Indiana, working as a landscaper, and had changed his name to Johnson.

After scrolling through a few more pages, I had an idea. I set up a simple post in the TALK TO STRANGERS section, asking for assistance identifying and privately accessing a mysterious club on Long Island with a French name, "held in a former jail or forgotten prison."

Then I put the computer to sleep and headed to bed.

42 | I WAS EXHAUSTED but couldn't sleep. I had the gnawing feeling that he was still out there somewhere, watching me.

Theo Cordova. The feeling was so acute I climbed out of bed, yanked up the shade, and looked out the window. But Perry Street remained silent and solemn, packed with shadows, no movement except the trees trembling in a faint freeze. *Now I was turning into some para-noid nutcase straight out of Dostoyevsky.*

I went back to bed, pulling the sheet up over my face, furiously *will-ing sleep,* shoving my pillow over to the cool side. Within seconds it was hot and clammy. The sheets were scalding, too, untucking from the mattress so they bunched around my waist like carnivorous plants try-ing to strangle me. Whenever I closed my eyes, Theo's face was there, half-drowned in the dark of the taxi, his dull eyes and deformed hand pressing against the window as if trying to tell me something, plead with me, warn me, as disturbing and elusive a presence as Ashley that night at the Reservoir.

Somehow, around three in the morning, I must have fallen asleep because I was awakened by soft knocking on my door.

I cracked open an eye. The clock read 3:46 A.M.

"Can I come in?" whispered Nora.

Without waiting for an answer—thank *Christ* I had on pajama bottoms—she crept inside. I couldn't see much of her in the dark, but she appeared to be wearing a white long-sleeved nightgown, which made her look like a ghost that had just wafted into my room, now hovering at the end of my bed, sizing me up, trying to decide if I was worth haunting.

"I was just thinking . . ." she began, but didn't continue.

"Why are you thinking at four in the morning?" I asked, bunching the pillows underneath me and leaning back against the headboard. "This better be good."

"It's Hopper. Before I couldn't put my finger on it, but . . ." She propped her feet on the railing of the bed, slipping the nightgown over her knees. "How did he know to go to that piano store? Out of the whole city he found the *one* place she went to? It's too incredible."

I agreed with her. It'd been such a stroke of luck, Hopper chancing upon an eyewitness for Ashley at Klavierhaus. When something ap-peared to be a wild coincidence, nine times out of ten it wasn't.

"And when I suggested that Ashley put that stuff under her bed, he got so mad."

"I noticed."

She bit her thumbnail. "You think he's responsible in some way for what happened to her?"

"Not sure yet. But he's definitely hiding something."

"I don't think he likes us, either."

"A *terrible* flaw. There's also the chain-smoking, the morose scowling, the bad-boy hair. It's like he thinks he's the rebel in a John Hughes movie."

She giggled.

"We'll pull a choice move from the McGrath playbook. The Corleone. We keep him close. Eventually he'll reveal himself. Works every time."

She tucked her hair behind her ears, making the bed shake, but said nothing.

"May I ask you something?" I asked.

She turned to me, her face a milky blur in the dark.

"Terra Hermosa. How were you allowed to live there? Surely there was some kind of age requirement."

"*Oh.* It was illegal. But I couldn't leave Eli. She raised me. The worst day of my life up till then was when she fell in the parking lot of Bonnie Lee's Fried Chicken and the doctors said she had to go into a home."

"How old were you when you moved in?"

"Fourteen."

"What about your parents?"

She fiddled with the frilly sleeves of her nightgown. "My mom died when I was three. She had a heart problem. My dad had been put away for twenty years by then."

"What was he put away for?"

"Mail fraud, wire fraud, identity theft, credit cards. He was real hardworking at being illegal. Eli used to say if my dad put half the energy he did into cutting corners into just driving *around* the corner, he'd be a billionaire."

I nodded. I'd known such men, had investigated more than a few.

"For a while I'd spend the day there, leave, then sneak back in at night. But after I got caught, I was all set to go into foster care. But Eli got together with the other seniors on her floor, and they made a big stink. The president ended up surprising everyone, because she didn't want a senior uprising. She said if I stayed out of sight when the state evaluators came I could live there till I finished high school. There was always a room coming available, because someone was always dead.

When Eli died of cancer I left without saying goodbye to anyone. I figured if I didn't do it then, I never would."

She paused, clearing her throat. "She died in the hospital on a Sunday, and I went back to her room to collect her things. There's a waiting list, so I knew someone was going to be moving in. If the family doesn't take away the personal items they just chuck them, and within seconds the room looks like you were never there in the first place. Just an old bed and chair, a window waiting to be stared out of by the next person. I was getting her stuff together when all of a sudden Old Grubby Bill who lived right across the hall whistled at me through his teeth."

"*Old Grubby Bill?* You haven't mentioned him."

"Everyone called him Grubby Bill because he always had black dirt under his fingernails. He'd fought in World War Two, and he bragged to everyone he was right beside Hitler's bunker when it exploded. So, people used to whisper some of the debris from that *bunker* was *still* under his fingernails, which was why they were so filthy."

She paused, sniffing. "He whistled at me to come into his room. He was always whistling at people. I was scared to go in there. Nobody ever did, because it smelled. But he dug under his bed and pulled out a Rockport shoebox. He told me he'd been saving up money for my dreams. It had six hundred dollars in it. He handed it to me and said, '*Now's your chance to make something of yourself. Scram, kid.*' So I *scrammed.* I walked to the Kissimmee station and got on a bus to New York. People don't realize how easy life is to change. You just get on the bus."

She fell silent. For a while, neither of us spoke, letting her story drift like a raft between us.

"I was *lucky,*" she went on. "Most people just get one mom and dad. I got a whole crowd."

"You were very lucky."

She seemed pleased, tucking her hands inside the long white sleeves.

"It's easy to be yourself in the dark. Ever noticed that? Guess we should probably get some sleep." The bed shook as she hopped off and darted out of the room. "'Night, Woodward."

"'Night, Bernstein."

VF DAILY
Culture, Society, Politics

FEATURED STORIES

John & Yoko Talk Beatles Break-Up   Suicide Bomber Targets NATO   Occupy London Gets Loud

MOST POPULAR

1. The Dark Sides of American Novelists
2. Stanislas Cordova Photo Essays: Macabre and Madness
3. The Enchanter's Daughter
4. The Nightwatchmen: The Next Generation of Lee Harvey Oswalds?
5. Proust Questionnaire: Cher

CULTURE ▶ WEB EXCLUSIVE ▶

The Enchanter's Daughter
OCTOBER 29 2011

 Like ⟨ 16   Tweet ⟨ 2   💬 COMMENT (0)   ✉ EMAIL

Fans of reclusive cult film god Stanislas Cordova were rocked two weeks ago when news broke that his 24-year-old daughter, Ashley, was found dead in a New York City warehouse, an apparent suicide. *Vanity Fair's* LIZ KRUGER tracks down Ashley's freshman roommate at Amherst College and learns that the auteur's glam, wild-spirited daughter leaves in her tragic wake as many alarming questions as her notorious father.

Photograph courtesy of K&M Recording

"We lived together almost the entire year and I can't say that I knew her," says Emma Banks, Ashley's roommate freshman year at Amherst College from 2005 to 2006. "She was wild. I'm from Moline, Kansas, population 371. We didn't *have* girls like Ashley in my town. I mean, she had a crazy Japanese tattoo on her foot and drank whiskey while she wrote her term papers."

The fact that I'm sitting in Pastis on a Wednesday morning, having croissants with a woman who actually knew Ashley Brett Cordova, feels a bit surreal. Ever since news broke of her alleged suicide in a run-down Chinatown warehouse—the first report of anything Cordova-related in years, not withstanding the slander scandal surrounding investigative journalist Scott McGrath some five years ago—I'd been trying to track down Ashley's friends, neighbors, people she worked with, to hear what they had to say about her, if they could explain such a tragedy, to no avail.

{ 1 2 3 4 5   NEXT }

CULTURE   WEB EXCLUSIVE

The Enchanter's Daughter

OCTOBER 29 2011

Ashley used no social media—which in this day and age means you don't exist. Google gives rise only to her childhood music career and her role in her father's last film, *To Breathe with Kings*, a bootleg copy of which I can find exclusively on Craigslist for $1,950. Contacting The Spence School (where I hear she spent half a semester) and Amherst College (where she graduated) to obtain her academic transcripts proves impossible—her records have been sealed.

So far, my wild-goose chase leads me only to Emma Banks, 25, formerly of Moline, Kansas, currently of Chelsea, New York City. An economics major at Amherst, she now works as an analyst at JPMorgan Chase.

"Ashley read things like *Interview* and Lord Byron," Banks continues, thoughtfully pulling apart a croissant. "Sometimes she stayed up all night composing music. I'd wake up at four in the morning and see she was awake in bed with a flashlight, her pencil scratching away. The rest of us freshmen wandered around in big awkward groups, you know, worried about grades, who our friends would be, fitting in. She

When Banks moved out of their dorm room at the end of the 2005-2006 school year, she found this photo—one of three photographs that had fallen behind Ashley's dresser.

already knew who she was. And *nothing* scared her."

When I ask what she means by this, Banks tells me about an incident halfway into the fall semester when she and a friend attended an off-campus party. When they arrived, there was a commotion in a back room. Making her way through the crowd, Banks saw everyone was watching a strip poker drinking game, which consisted of Ashley Cordova and eight men, all seniors.

"I would have been *so* intimidated," says Banks. "They were on the lacrosse team,

CULTURE ▸ WEB EXCLUSIVE

The Enchanter's Daughter
OCTOBER 29 2011

economics majors, *super*-arrogant. All of them thought they were the next George Soros. Ashley drank them under the table. Four had to excuse themselves to go throw up all over the lawn. Soon it was just her and this rich kid named Carson. He was a third, a total asshole. You know those guys who use words like *attenuate* in conversation and talk about summers on the Vineyard? Well, within an hour, he was stripped to nothing but his tightie-whities, so wasted he staggered out of his chair and fell to the floor unconscious. Ashley was totally sober. She had all their money, and the only thing she'd had to take off was her *sweater*. That was the moment every guy on campus fell in love with her."

The second of the three Polaroids that Ashley left behind.

Banks describes another incident, when she came home late one night from the library to find Ashley holding a "Truth or Dare?" party in their room. "Ashley refused to do truth, only dares," says Banks. "The dares became more and more insane, and she wouldn't hesitate. At one point, someone dared her to put out a cigarette with her fingers. She did it on her *tongue*. When they were daring her to climb onto the roof and she climbed right out, walking along the edge—we were on the top floor of Appleton—I felt sick and had to leave the room. When I came back an hour later, the party had broken up and she was in bed, reading. Like nothing had happened."

I ask Banks if Ashley ever talked about her home life— her father, in particular.

"No, she was private. But at a party just before Christmas break I remember seeing her making out with this junior soccer player, Matt, who every girl on campus was obsessed with. She went off with him, I think, because she didn't come back to the room for four days. When she did, she was curled up on her bed, sobbing. It scared me because I'd never seen her like that, so I asked what was wrong and she said, 'A demolished heart.' That was *so Ashley*. Her heart wasn't just broken, it was demolished, you know? She said she was

The Enchanter's Daughter

OCTOBER 29 2011

in love with someone and there was no hope. I figured Matt had blown her off. But Matt started calling all the time, trying to see her, so I don't think it had to do with him. It was something else. Someone else. I never knew who."

Banks was an economics major and spent most nights in the library. Soon she had a boyfriend and rarely spent time in the room—though when she *was* there, Ashley never was.

"I think she was taking the train all the time into Manhattan, doing her own thing, as well as her schoolwork. In spite of all her running around, she made better grades than me. I remember seeing her semester average printed out on her desk and it was all A's. She did everything to the max, *blew it out of the ground*—an expression she used. She hated things that were wishy-washy and weak and cautious, which was probably how she saw me."

Banks knew nothing about Ashley's family, except that they called regularly, like her own parents. "Most times it was her mom. She had a thick French accent. Very glamorous. But one time I picked up when Ashley wasn't there and a man with a deep voice asked for her. I asked who was calling, and he said, 'Her father.' That was it."

This state of affairs continued until about midway through spring semester when Ashley abruptly disappeared from Amherst—with no word as to why.

"There were a series of phone calls for her," Banks tells me. "I didn't recognize the voice. It was a man, though. And suddenly Ashley was *gone*. This Hispanic woman came a week later to pack up her stuff. I wasn't there, but people saw her. I came back to the room and it was stripped bare. The only thing left were three photos I found months later when I was

The last of the three Polaroids that Ashley Cordova left behind.

The Enchanter's Daughter
OCTOBER 29 2011

moving out for the summer. They'd fallen down behind her dresser. She had an old 1970s Polaroid camera she was always taking pictures with. It was three of them."

I ask Banks where she thought Ashley had gone.

"People whispered that she'd gotten pregnant," she tells me. "Or she'd done something illegal or was into hard drugs and had to go to rehab. No one knew. But then, spring of my sophomore year she was back. She'd gotten permission to live off campus. I'd lost contact with her. But I remember seeing her once alone in the library reading at the end of senior year. I wanted to go up to her to say hi but I didn't. I guess I was still intimidated."

Banks says she was saddened to hear of Ashley's death. (At the time of this article's publication, the NYPD have yet to release the medical examiner's official ruling, though preliminary inquiries point to suicide.) Banks admits her stunning, free-spirited roommate awed her. Now she feels only regret, wishing she'd taken the time to get to know her, see what was behind Ashley's daredevil attitude and thirst for living.

"If I learned anything about her it was that she lived with a vehemence most of us never have the courage for," Banks tells me. "But there was something about her that precluded an ordinary existence. In some ways I'm not surprised she's dead. A job, husband, kids, a beach house? That wasn't her. I can't explain why, except she was more like a force that whipped through life, defying logic, scaring you, even hurting you because she was everything you wanted to be, but you knew you'd never have the guts—and then she was gone. That was my experience of Ashley Cordova."

Banks falls silent, her uneaten croissant pulled to flaky tatters on her plate.

"'It was many and many a year ago, / In a kingdom by the sea, / That a maiden there lived whom you may know / By the name of Ashley C.'"

She smiles with embarrassment. "Spring semester, after she was gone so suddenly, someone on our floor—I never found out who—wrote that on the dry erase board hanging outside our door. I left it up, because it was amazing. No one would ever rewrite an Edgar Allan Poe poem for me, you know?"

Banks checks her watch. She pulls on her gray jacket and slings her JPMorgan Chase bag over her shoulder. "That's all I know," she says, draining the rest of her cappuccino and gently returning the cup to the saucer. She sighs. "Guess I have to get back to my life now."

43 | I CLOSED the *Vanity Fair* article on my BlackBerry. It was after ten A.M., and we were in a taxi speeding down Avenue A.

I was actually reassured by the piece—published on the website early this morning. The reporter hadn't made much headway in her investigation, *thank Christ,* and a Google search of news for Ashley Cordova revealed no other reporter had uncovered the critical lead, that Ashley had been admitted to Briarwood—which meant we were still ahead of the game. *At least for now.*

I made quick note of one odd detail: Ashley's unexpected leave from Amherst during her freshman year.

"There it is," Nora said suddenly, and the driver pulled over.

We'd turned down East Ninth Street, and Nora was indicating a narrow storefront sunken some five feet down from the sidewalk, a black front gate and a beat-up red metal awning, a single word painted across it in purple letters:

ENCHANTMENTS

On its website, Enchantments called itself *New York City's Oldest and Largest Witchcraft and Goddess Supply Store.*

We climbed out of the cab, heading down front steps encrusted with dead leaves and cigarette butts, stepping inside.

Immediately, a tall, freckle-faced orange-haired kid moved out from behind the cash register, shouting, *"Zero, come back here!"*—Zero being a white Persian cat that had run toward the open door, though I closed the door before it could escape.

"Thanks, man," said the kid.

There was an overpowering smell of incense, the ceiling low, narrow brick walls slanting inward like a corridor in an M. C. Escher print. They were lined with wooden shelves crammed with mystical knick-knacks. In Enchantments it seemed all holy items were created equal. The store was arranged as if Christ, Buddha, Mohammed, Vishnu—plus a couple of random pagans—had gotten together to hold a garage sale.

Mini witch cauldrons (in Tall, Grande, and Venti) were brazenly stacked next to Saint Francis, Mary, and a few Catholic saints. Beside them was a much-paged-through paperback on display, *Jewish Kabbal*

Magic, which sat next to a Bible, which was beside tarot cards, sachets of potpourri called *Luck & Happiness Ouanga Bags,* a basket of carved wax crucifixes, ceramic frogs, and plastic vials of *Holy Water* (on sale for $5.95).

Apparently many New Yorkers had given up on shrinks and yoga and thought, *Hell, let's try magic,* because the store was crowded. Toward the back, a group of thirtysomething women was swarming around a tall bookcase crammed with hundreds of colored candles, choosing them with a frantic intensity. A tired middle-aged man in a blue button-down—he looked alarmingly like my stockbroker—was carefully reading the directions on the back of a Ouija board.

I stepped around Nora and a solemn boy with stringy brown hair paging through a pamphlet—I glanced at the title over his shoulder: *Guide to Planetary and Magical Significance*—and walked over to the display case. Inside were silver necklaces, pendants, and charms carved with hieroglyphics and other symbols I didn't recognize. Hanging from the ceiling above the cash register was a five-pointed star surrounded by a circle, a pentagram—the symbol for Satanists, if I remembered correctly from my college days. Beyond that on the back wall were framed 8 x 10 black-and-white headshots of men and women who had the severe expressions and dead raisin eyes of serial killers—legendary witches and warlocks, no doubt.

A small faded handwritten sign was taped beside them.

We do not sell black magick supplies, so don't even ask.

The orange-haired kid who'd chased Zero to the back of the store shuffled over to us.

"Need some help?"

"Yes," said Nora, setting a book she'd been leafing through—*Signs, Symbols & Omens*—back down on the stand. "We were hoping someone could help us identify some herbs and roots that we found in strange patterns in our friend's room."

He nodded, totally unsurprised, and pointed his thumb toward the back.

"Ask the witches on call," he said. "They know everything."

I hadn't noticed it when we'd entered, but in the back of the store there was a wooden counter, a young Hispanic kid sitting behind it.

Nora and I made our way to him, filing around the women fussing over the colored candles. One with frizzy red hair was holding a purple, a yellow, an orange, and a green. "Should I get Saint Elijah and San Miguel, too?" she asked her friend.

"Don't mess this up," Nora whispered. "I know you don't believe in this stuff, but it doesn't mean you can be rude."

"Me? What are you talking about?"

She shot me a look of warning before stepping behind a young woman quietly discussing something with the Hispanic kid. He was perched on a tall stool, industriously carving into a green candle with a large hunting knife.

He didn't *look* like a *witch*—but that was probably the same dim observation as a neighbor telling the *Evening News* old Jimmy who lived in his mother's basement and was rarely seen in daylight didn't *look* like a homicidal maniac. This male witch had shaggy black hair and was wearing an army-green workman's shirt, the kind popularized by Fidel Castro and Che Guevara, giving him a sort of socialist tropical authority.

Cluttering the wooden counter in front of him were colored candles, sachets of herbs, bottles of oils and dark liquids, box cutters, string, switchblades. On a clipboard hanging off the side of the counter by a rope was a cluster of tattered pages. I grabbed it—ENCHANTMENTS CUSTOM CARVED MENU, it read—flipping through.

"Win at Court. This candle allows you to win in all legal matters great and small."

"Purple Wisdom. Used for overcoming obstacles, known or unknown— and for prophetic decisions. It is for gaining wisdom in the ancient sciences such as astrology, hermetic magic, Qabbalism, and other magickal systems."

"Come to Me. This candle works on people who are full of sexual desire and brings them together. It is a VERY POWERFUL SEXUAL candle and should be used with caution."

I should have come here *years* ago.

The woman in front of us stepped aside, and we moved to the counter.

"How can I help you?" the kid asked without glancing up. Nora, in a lowered voice, tactfully explained why we were there, removing two Ziploc bags from her purse, one containing the dirt sample, the other with the cluster of roots tied together with white string.

"We found *this* under our friend's bed in a series of strange circles," she said, holding up the dirt sample. "We need help identifying what it is and why it was put there."

The kid set down the knife, taking time to carefully wipe his hands on a rag before taking the bags. Without opening it, he rubbed the dirt between his fingers, inspecting it under the small desk lamp in front of him. He then opened it, sniffing, blinking from the stench. He re-sealed it, set it down, hopping off the stool. He grabbed a small stepladder shoved into the corner and set it down in front of the shelves to our right. They spanned all the way to the ceiling and were jam-packed with row upon row of giant glass jars filled with herbs, each one with a faded label.

I stepped forward to read a few.

ARROWROOT. BALM OF GILEAD. BLADDERWRACK. DEER'S TONGUE. DRAGON'S BLOOD CHUNKS. FIVE FINGER GRASS. HIGH JOHN THE CONQUEROR ROOT. QUEEN OF THE MEADOW. JOB'S TEARS.

The kid climbed the ladder, reaching up on his tiptoes to collect a jar from the top shelf.

VALERIAN ROOT, read the label.

He returned to the counter with it, opened the lid, using a spoon to scoop some of the dirtlike substance into his palm.

He compared it to the contents in the Ziploc bag.

"Same texture, same smell," he whispered to himself.

"What is it?" asked Nora.

"Vandal root."

"What's that?" I asked.

"An herb. Its magical reputation is pretty dark."

"Its *magical reputation*?"

He nodded, unperturbed by my skepticism. "Sure. Vandal is used a lot in black magic. Hexing. Forcing love. Uncrossing. It's *kinda like* coming across a gimp costume in your best friend's closet. There's no explaining that shit away, know what I mean?"

I wasn't sure I *did*, but I nodded anyway.

"You said it was laid out in a specific pattern?" he asked.

"Yes." I showed him the photos on my BlackBerry.

"We also found these twigs tied together," added Nora, indicating the other bag on the counter. "They were hidden along the doorjamb of her front door." The kid, frowning at it, reached into a box on his left, donning a pair of latex gloves, and pulled out the clump of sticks.

"Where'd you find all this?" he asked uncertainly.

"In a friend's room that she was renting," I answered.

He squinted at the root in the light, twirling it in his fingers. "This looks like some really high-level shit, so you should talk to Cleopatra. Lemme see if she's available."

He yanked aside a heavy black velvet curtain in the back wall, and as he disappeared, I caught a glimpse of another room with dim red light and a few candles.

"Hang on to your *wallet*," I said to Nora. "We've been marked as whales. We're about to be granted access to the high-rollers room. They're going to be offering us glimpses of our future, contact with the dead, and other soul-cleaning paraphernalia that's going to save us from bad vibes and set us back a couple thousand bucks."

"Shhh," she admonished as the Hispanic kid stuck his head out.

"She'll see you," he said and held aside the curtain for us.

Nora grabbed the plastic bags, eagerly stepping after him like she'd just been granted a one-on-one with the pope in the Vatican's inner chambers.

With a silent Hail Mary, I followed.

44 IT WAS A SMALL BACK ROOM lit with gloomy red light, crumbling brick walls draped with black fabric, a circular wooden table with a few folding chairs, a red stained-glass lamp suspended over it.

A woman—*Cleopatra*, I could only assume—was standing in the back beside a messy counter, talking on a cordless phone, her back to us. She was tall and pudgy, wearing a black peasant blouse, jeans, old red Doc Martens. Her shoulder-length jet-black hair, streaked with chunks of purple, sat atop her shoulders like a lampshade.

"Have a seat," the Hispanic kid said, pulling out the chairs for us around the table. "I'm Dexter, by the way."

"Yeah, let's try that on him," Cleopatra said into the phone, her voice flat and clinical. "The Juniper berries. See how he reacts. If he doesn't call you to set up the third date, we'll try something more potent."

She set the phone down and turned around.

She was Asian—*Korean,* I guessed—with a stark, chubby face, late forties. She wore a long clip of bluebird feathers in her hair and so many silver bracelets, cuffs, dangly skull earrings, necklaces—one pendant a four-inch tooth from the mouth of a tiger—as she strode toward us, she rattled and clanged.

"I'm Cleo," she announced flatly. "Hear you found evidence of a black trick."

"We don't know *what* it is," said Nora.

Cleo, clearly having heard this many times, pulled an upholstered armchair set against the wall over to the table, foam crumbling out of the seat. She sat down, folding one leg under her, the other knee up, linking her arm around it, so when she was finally still she was in a warped pose—something between an extreme-level yoga position and a dead twisted insect one finds along a windowsill.

"Get me up to speed?" she asked Dex with a touch of impatience.

He picked up the Ziploc bags and my BlackBerry and walked her through the evidence like an intern showing a specialist a confounding MRI.

"But see this?" he murmured, pointing at something. "And *here?* I—I didn't understand the symmetry. First I thought anvil dust or maybe rabbit feces? But then *that?* I've never seen . . ." His voice trailed into doubtful silence. She grabbed the phone, narrowing her eyes as she zoomed in on one of the pictures.

"I got it," she said with a glance at Dex. "You can go now."

He nodded, and with a final look back at us—what appeared to be genuine worry—he darted around the curtain back into the store.

Cleo inspected the pictures for another minute, ignoring us.

She picked up the herbs, sniffing them—unaffected by the rank smell—and then studied the roots, the strand of feathers clipped into her hair rolling along her cheek as she leaned over the table.

"Tell me where you found all of this," she said in a low voice.

"Inside the room that a friend of ours was renting," said Nora. "The circles and the charcoal were under her cot."

"Who is this friend?"

"We'd like that to remain anonymous," I said.

"Man or woman?"

"Woman," answered Nora.

"And where is she now?"

"That's also something we don't care to discuss," I said.

"How is she?"

"Fine," I answered. "Why?"

Cleo had been closely inspecting the bouquet of roots, but now she looked up at me. She had black eyes, so deeply embedded in her plump face I couldn't see the whites, only the black irises sparking with light in spite of the dimness of the room.

"Your friend has a pretty severe curse on her."

She didn't elaborate, only set down the branches and sat back in the chair, patiently waiting for us to say something.

I stared back at her in silence. So did Nora.

Normally I would have shrugged off such a pronouncement, thinking it was pure superstition. Yet there was something about Cleopatra—her point-blank certainty—that wasn't so easy to shrug off. First of all, the woman looked like Confucius's punk sister. She also spoke in a bland expert neurosurgeon's monotone.

"What type of curse?" I asked her.

"Not sure," Cleo answered. "It wasn't a simple jinx." She grabbed my BlackBerry, holding up one of the pictures. "She performed a high-level uncrossing ritual. Vandal root in a circle mixed with sulfur, salt, insect chitin, dried human bones, probably some other stuff that'd make your stomach turn. All of that encircling asafoetida burned on a perfect pyramid of charcoal. There was probably a really repulsive smell."

"*Yes,*" answered Nora quickly.

"That was the Devil's Dung. Asafoetida. It repels evil and brings harm to enemies. Another way to undo a trick is to mix it with vandal root, black hen feathers, black arts powder, and a strand of hair off the person who cursed you. You urinate into it, put the mixture into a glass jar, and bury it in a place you know they'll walk over again and again, like their front porch or garage. After that, they'll pretty much leave you alone for the rest of your life."

"Does it work on ex-wives?" I asked. "If she lives in a Fifth Avenue co-op, can I just leave it with the doorman?"

Nora shot me a look of rebuke, but Cleopatra only cleared her throat.

"If you don't have access to a location where they'll be," she went on patiently, "you do what your friend did. Set up a Vandal Circle."

"Did it work?" asked Nora. "Did it remove the curse from her?"

"No idea. Spells are like really crude antibiotics. You have to try different ones to see what's responsive. Super-spells can be resistant like a strain of bacteria, one that constantly morphs to stay firmly attached to and thriving on the host. Have you talked to your friend lately? How's she feeling?"

Nora eyed me uncomfortably.

"What about these twigs we found over the door?" I asked.

Cleo reclined in the chair as she considered the cluster on the table. "It's Devil's Shoestring. A natural-occurring root from the honeysuckle family. It grows in wild fields and forests. It's used for protection. In the deep American South people make anklets out of it. Or they douse them in whiskey and bury them in the ground. You can also do what your friend did. Take nine pieces, some white string, tie a single knot around each piece—nine roots, nine knots—and then you stick it somewhere by your front door or under your porch. Some people bury it in their front yard."

"What does it do?" I asked.

She stared at me for a moment before answering, her face unreadable.

"It trips up the devil."

"*Trips* him?"

"Stops him. Gives him pause."

"I see," I said, picking up the roots. "I don't know why the U.S. spends six hundred billion on national defense. We should just make sure every American family has a set of these."

Cleo was clearly used to—and totally unfazed by—skeptics and nonbelievers. She didn't react, only interlaced her ring-laden fingers—skulls, Egyptian ankhs, a cat's head—atop her raised knee.

"Did your friend take baths before sunrise?" she asked.

"Yes," said Nora. "In really icy water."

I was about to ask Nora what she was talking about when I suddenly remembered the strange incident Iona had described—the early morning when she'd come upon Ashley bathing in the tub.

"So she did cleansing rituals," said Cleo, nodding.

"What are they for?" I asked.

"They grant purification from evil. For a *time*. They're not permanent. More of a temporary Band-Aid. Did she wash her floors?"

Nora glanced at me. "We don't know."

"Was she cold to the touch?"

"No idea," I answered.

"Did you notice if she had difficulty communicating? Almost as if she had a mouthful of peanut butter or sand?"

"We wouldn't know."

"What about an alarming heaviness?"

"Meaning?"

Cleo shrugged. "I've heard of some people, if they're under a particularly severe curse for an extended period of time, when they step onto an ordinary scale they can weigh up to three hundred, sometimes even four hundred pounds, even though visibly they've grown very, very thin."

"We wouldn't know that, either," I answered, though I had a sudden, unnerving vision of the first and only time I'd ever seen Ashley in person, when she was wandering around the Reservoir—that strange, trancelike bearing, the heavy sound of her footsteps cutting resoundingly through the rain.

Cleo, suddenly struck by a new thought, grabbed my BlackBerry again, frowning as she scrolled through the pictures.

"One thing I don't see here is a reversal. When you're dealing with black magic, you have to uncross but also *reverse,* so the curse boomerangs back onto the perpetrator." She glanced up at us. "Spells are nothing more than energy. Think of it as charged particles that you've attracted to one concentrated place. You have to put them somewhere. Energy is neither created nor destroyed, but transferred. It's the transfer I don't see evidence of, and that's troubling." She tilted her head, thinking, twirling the tooth pendant in her fingers. "Notice any reversing candles in the room?"

"What are reversing candles?" Nora asked.

"White wax on the bottom, black at the top."

Nora shook her head.

"What about a cardboard box filled with objects?"

"No."

"No mirror box," whispered Cleo to herself.

"What's a mirror box?" I asked.

She glanced at me. "For straightforward reversals. You get a black candle, inscribe the enemy's name into it, bury it in a graveyard with pieces of a broken mirror. Whatever negativity or evil aimed at you will reflect back onto them." She cleared her throat, raising an inky black eyebrow. "Let's go back to her room. Were there any powders or chalk marks on the floor?"

"It was dark inside," Nora said. "But no. We would have noticed something like that."

"But the floor was sticky," I added.

Cleo looked at me. *"Sticky?"*

"As if a soft drink had been spilled all over it. Plus a couple of plastic wrappers."

Cleo unwound herself from the twisted way she was sitting, leaning across the table, jutting out her chin.

"Did you *pick up* one of the wrappers?" She demanded it so intensely I caught a whiff of her breath, hot and garlicky and pungent, like she'd been drinking some strange herbal tea. She had small tobacco-stained teeth crowded together, quite a few in the back capped in gold.

"No," I said.

"Then how do you know they were plastic wrappers?"

"That's what they sounded like."

She took a deep agitated breath. "Did you go *inside* the room?" she asked, sitting back in the chair.

"Of course. How do you think we found that thing under her bed?"

"How long ago was this?"

"Just last night."

She looked underneath the table. "Are those the shoes you were wearing?"

"Yes."

She stood up and strode to the back counter, returning with a pair of latex gloves and a pile of faded newspapers. She snapped the gloves onto her hands and spread the newspaper across the table's surface.

"Take one shoe off and slowly hand it to me, please."

Glancing at Nora—she looked stricken—I pulled off one of my black leather boots, handing it to Cleo.

Carefully—as if handling a rabid animal—she placed the boot on its side on the newspaper, the sole facing her. She fumbled in her jean pocket and produced a four-inch pocket knife, the handle intricately carved out of some type of animal bone. She opened the blade with her teeth and, holding down the boot with her other hand, scraped it slowly along the sole. She did this for minutes, ignoring us, and when she stopped, inspecting the blade inches from her nose, there was a thick brownish-black paste collected along the edge. It looked like dried molasses.

"This is the reversal," she whispered. "It's a sophisticated foot-track spell. I've never seen anything like it."

"What's a foot-track spell?" asked Nora.

"Something for your enemy to walk through. A trap."

"But *we* walked through it," I said.

Cleo's eyes darted from the knife to me.

"Does she have any reason to believe *you're* her enemy?" she asked.

"No," I said, though as soon as I *did*, I felt an uneasy chill. I had the sudden memory of Ashley stalking me at the Reservoir, her hard face staring down at me when she'd appeared abruptly by the gatehouse. Had she considered me a threat? *But what had I ever done to her, to her father, except seek the truth?* Maybe that alone made me an adversary. But how could the family be so hypocritical, when nearly every hero in a Cordova film was desperately searching for the same thing? Didn't that matter? Didn't the art in some albeit small way reflect the values of the creator's life? *Not necessarily.* People had an illogical, self-serving rationale when it came to interpreting the behavior of others.

"Whatever her reasoning," Cleo whispered, as if reading my mind, her gaze returning to the dark glue coating the knife, "one thing is clear."

"What?" I asked, my mouth suddenly dry.

"You've been *crossed*."

45 "YOU MIND EXPOUNDING ON THAT?"

Cleo only carefully set down the knife and stood up, striding to the bookcase at the back of the room.

"Look," whispered Nora, inspecting the cracked soles of her own motorcycle boots. They were spangled with the same dark blotches, like wads of black gum. She yanked off one, scrutinizing the sole in the overhead light. I could see sand and thread, maybe even fingernails, mixed into the paste, glittering splinters of what looked like glass.

Cleo returned with a hulking stack of encyclopedias. *Hoodoo—Conjuration—Witchcraft—Rootwork* by Harry Middleton Hyatt, read the spines. They looked ancient, with orange covers tied together with a frayed black ribbon. She sat down, picking up volume one and flipping to the contents page, slipping her index finger down the entries. When she came to the end—apparently not finding what she was looking for—she slammed it shut, moving on to volume two.

I grabbed the book she'd just put down. It reeked of mildew, the pages yellowed. It was published in 1970, and a splotch of red liquid—tomato sauce *or blood*—had dried along the seam of the title page. *Hoodoo—Conjuration—Witchcraft—Rootwork. Beliefs accepted by many Negroes and white persons, these being orally recorded among Blacks and whites.*

General Description of Beliefs p.1. Belief in spirits, ghosts, the Devil, and the like p. 19. Timing of spells and recurrence of the effects of spells over time p. 349.

The book appeared to be an encyclopedia of spells, some of the entries short, others extensive. They were transcribed interviews with backwater southerners with thick accents, their accounts written out phonetically. For example, on p. 523 under the title heading *Mojo hands grouped somewhat alphabetically according to their major ingredient (e.g. buckeye nuts, needles, black cat bone)* was the following entry:

> **669.** Jest a — yo' see yo' git a snake — yo' can take a rattle-snake an' dry his haid up, pound it up, an' den yo' kin go to work an' use dat as goofer dust. Kill anybody.
> [*Waycross, Georgia*]

"I found something similar," muttered Cleo, inspecting the bottom of my boot before returning her attention to the page in front of her. I craned my neck to read what she was looking at.

Volume four, *More conjure work utilizing human body parts and waste.*

" 'The Black Bone trick,' " she whispered, tucking a chunk of purple hair behind her ears. " 'Frayed hemp rope, gum arabic, and goofer dust.' Your friend used a slight variation. I see some dark brown sand in here, some seaweed, too. She must have picked this up someplace exotic. You put it down on the floor in a *quincunx,* which is a makeshift crossroads. Your enemy unknowingly walks through it. Immediately it sticks to his shoes, and within hours it's eating away at his life."

"Eating *away*?" I asked. "What does that mean?"

She shrugged. "I've heard of comas. Heart attacks. Abruptly losing everything you love, like your job or family. Sudden paralysis from the neck down." She raised an eyebrow. "Have you felt any strange sensations in your legs?"

"I woke up with my foot asleep this morning," said Nora worriedly.

Cleo nodded as if expecting this bad news. She then tilted her head, grabbing that tiger-tooth pendant around her neck, rolling it in her fingers.

"One thing that troubles me is something you said before. The plastic wrappers all over the floor. I don't think they were plastic wrappers."

"What were they?"

"Probably snakeskins. If they were filled with graveyard dirt, she combined all of this with a killing curse."

"And that's . . ."

"Like it sounds. It'll kill you."

"The surgeon general says the same thing about cigarettes."

She only stared at me. "With cigarettes death takes decades. With this you could be dead within weeks."

Nora looked stricken.

"Anyone ever told you your *witchside* manner was a little harsh?" I asked.

"There's no point sugarcoating black magic."

I tried smiling at Nora for reassurance, but she ignored me, staring at the curse-riddled sole of her shoe as if it were a cluster of malignant tumors.

"Graveyard dirt," I said. "That means our friend collected dirt from a graveyard?"

"Yeah. And it's not easy to get. You have to do it at a certain time of night. Under a certain moon. You have to know whose grave you're taking it from. How the person died. Some witches believe the best dirt to use comes from either a murderer, a baby less than six months old, or someone who loved you beyond all reason. You also have to know where you're digging in relation to the body, if it's above the head, heart, or feet. You have to leave something behind, too, as a token of appreciation. Money or whiskey usually works. You mix the dirt into the snake sheds and goofer dust."

"What's goofer dust?" asked Nora.

"The H-bomb of spell materials. When you goofer someone, you're spiritually poisoning them. It comes from the Congo, the word *kufwa*, which means to die. The powder's usually a yellowish color, but you mix in the graveyard dirt so it's dark and can't be spotted. It's really powerful because it eats away at your mind without you even realizing it, poisoning your reasoning and your love. It pulls apart the closest friends, isolates you, pits you against the world so you're driven to the margins, the periphery of life. It'll drive you mad, which in some ways is worse than death."

"So our friend had something like a PhD in witchcraft," I said.

"She had a major proficiency in dark magic. Absolutely."

"And what *is* dark magic? Voodoo? Hoodoo?"

"It can mean any number of things. It's a blanket term for all magic that's used for evil purposes. I'm not an expert. My training is in Earth goddess, fertility spells, spiritual cleansing, that kind of thing. A lot of the black stuff's underground. Passed down through generations. Secret meetings in the middle of the night. Old leather-bound journals filled with spells written backward. Attics stockpiled with the really obscure ingredients, like deer fetuses, lizard feces, baby blood. This stuff is not for people with queasy stomachs. But it *works*. Does your friend come from a family of occultists?"

"It's possible," I said.

"Well, she *thought* she was cursed. She tried hard to stop it, reverse it back onto the executioner. She wanted to kill him. *That's* what it looks like to me. So maybe she didn't expect you to walk through it, but someone else, maybe someone who put the curse on her. I suggest tracking your friend down and asking her."

Nora shot me a wary look.

"Here's what I *can* tell you," Cleo went on, clearing her throat. "Scrape the trick off with a knife or razor blade. Make sure it doesn't touch your skin. Wrap it in newspaper and throw the materials away at a crossroads or a freshwater river."

"Guess that rules out the Hudson."

"I'll also give you some reversing candles." She headed to the back again, crouching beside a cabinet, digging through shelves. "Again, I really don't have experience with this. You should consult a witch doctor with a specialty in black magic."

"Where do we find one of those? Disney World?"

"Google it. Some names will come up. But all the really legit ones are in the Louisiana bayou." Cleo returned to the table, handing Nora two candles, black by the wick, white at the base.

"How much are those setting us back? A couple hundred bucks?"

"No charge. It's unethical to charge people who come in suffering from dark magic, kind of like someone coming into the emergency room with a fatal gunshot wound. You do what you can to save their life. Money's irrelevant."

Thoughtfully rolling her tiger's-tooth pendant between her fingers, Cleo watched us pull on our shoes. Nora, collecting the candles, explained that it had actually been *three* of us who'd been inside the room, so Cleo dug out a third reversing candle and then escorted us back through the store.

It was even more crowded. A dapper elderly couple inspected the skull candles. Four teenage girls browsed incense. A young man with the desperately preppy look of an unemployed Wall Street analyst perused a pamphlet: *Enchantments' Fall Class Schedule.*

Magic was all fun and games until you had the H-bomb of spell materials on the bottom of your shoes.

Dexter must have given the orange-haired kid at the register the lowdown, because they stared in fascination as we filed past them.

Cleo opened the door for us, shooing away the Persian cat.

"Good luck," she said.

"Thanks," said Nora bleakly, stepping outside. I paused.

"What if I don't *buy* any of this? I was raised Catholic."

Cleo stared at me blankly, though for a moment, I swore I caught an amused gleam in her black eyes.

"Then I guess you have nothing to worry about."

She slammed the door closed with a preoccupied expression and darted through the milling crowd, doubtless racing to her red-light lair at the back of the shop.

46 "YOU THINK WE'RE GOING TO *DIE*?" asked Nora nervously as we moved up the Enchantments steps.

"Everyone tends to."

"In the *next few days.* That goofer stuff she was talking about. She said it can kill you without you even realizing."

"Ex-wives do the exact same thing. The most interesting thing she said was the knowledge of dark magic passed from generation to generation."

"You think that's what the Cordovas are hiding? That they're all *witches* or something?"

I said nothing, the notion sounding absurd. *But then*—Cordova was a creative eccentric holed up in an isolated estate, basically a petri dish for cultivating the weird and outlandish. Cleo had testified that Ashley was quite proficient in *spells.* She'd learned how to assemble those materials from *someone.*

But for whom had she intended this Black Bone killing curse—*me?*

Had she laid it knowing I'd investigate her death and eventually show up at Henry Street? What about Hopper? He'd been sent that stuffed monkey and had somehow known she'd frequented Klavierhaus. *Or did she intend it for someone else entirely?* Iona, if she could be believed, claimed she'd seen two men outside Ashley's door. One might have been Theo Cordova. Maybe it was her family Ashley considered the enemy and she'd put down the killing curse for *them*. Hopper's inclination was to hold them accountable. Maybe they'd been chasing her, trying to find her, fearing she was on the verge of exposing them. She had, after all, been following *me*—which doubtless would have made the family quite nervous.

Nora was thinking it over, nibbling her thumbnail. "It could be why Ashley took her life. She couldn't handle the guilt of what the family had done for years, practicing black magic." She wrinkled her nose. "Maybe that's what the housekeeper at the Waldorf noticed when she saw that mark in her eye. Maybe she could tell Ashley practiced black magic."

"At this point, it's all conjecture."

Closing the metal gate behind us, I realized my phone was buzzing. I assumed it was Hopper, but instead it was an email notification from the Blackboards, indicating someone had answered my post, though to read the response I needed my laptop with the Tor browser.

"You might think this magic stuff is hogwash, but *I* don't," Nora said, scraping the soles of her boots on the curb. "This curse is like cement."

"We need to go back to the apartment." I stepped onto the street, hailing an approaching cab.

"What about going to Rising Dragon tattoos and asking about that receipt?"

"We'll do it later. Someone on the Blackboards answered my post."

PARKING | CORDOVA | FILMS | FREAK | RED BAND | STRANGERS | CLIMB IN

TALK TO STRANGERS - HELP
POSTED BY Gaetana Stevens 2991   10/29/11 2:11 A.M. VIEWS 9332

I need assistance identifying and privately accessing a mysterious private club on Long Island. I'm told it has a French name and is held in a former jail or forgotten prison.

Any direction offered much appreciated. Thanks.

REPLY TO: HELP: OUBLIETTE
Posted by Special Agent Fox 10/29/11 10:24 A.M. VIEWS 189

It's called Oubliette
The party you seek.
The butterflies that swarm there
Make decent men weep.

Women are verboten
In this cellar of sickness.
The sentences carried out
No good girl should witness.

If you were a Member, such a question
You wouldn't bother to pose.
My guess is you're a fraud
The lost way in I'll now disclose:

Drive midnight tonight to Montauk
Walk east down the shore.
When you spot Duchamp's staircase
Proceed to the door.

Oubliette is a madhouse
A hell, an attack.
Partaking or gawking
You must watch your back.

If you're exposed or you're weak
You'll be lost from the day.
And all those who love you
Will be left to pray.

REPLY >>

47 | OUBLIETTE.

There was no mention of it as a private nightclub on the Internet, nothing to verify the claims of Special Agent Fox. According to Wikipedia, the word derived from the French verb *oublier* and meant *forgotten place*. Historically, an oubliette was the most claustrophobic and hidden section of a castle dungeon, where there was only an iron trapdoor in the ceiling and no light—a cell so minuscule, it was often impossible for the prisoner to turn around or even *move,* a casket for the alive but damned. It was reserved for the most reviled prisoners, those the captors wanted to forget.

My guess was it was some type of sex club. It didn't appear to make for a particularly *fun-filled* Saturday night, but Iona had claimed Ashley was going to the club, so it was certainly worth a shot to try and find someone there who'd encountered her.

At eight o'clock that night, the October weather chilly and overcast, Nora and I left Perry Street to pick up Hopper. He'd finally responded to our messages and wanted to join, which was fine by me; with that coup he'd produced with Klavierhaus, he was proving to be an unexpected asset to the investigation.

He told us to pick him up at the corner of Bowery and Stanton. We waited more than twenty minutes, and just when I was thinking we'd have to leave without him—it was a three-hour drive to Montauk, the easternmost town of the Hamptons on Long Island—Hopper emerged from the Sunshine Hotel.

It was an infamous place, one of the city's last flophouses where rooms—more like *stalls* suited for barnyard mules—went for $4.50 a night. I could only assume Hopper had been doing business there, dropping off *candy* for quite a few customers with a sweet tooth, because the men around the entrance smiled with jittery appreciation as he ambled past them.

"How's the Sunshine?" I asked as he sank into the backseat.

Not bothering to acknowledge us, he took out a wad of crumpled bills, counted them, and then tucked them inside his coat pocket.

"Awesome," he muttered.

Within minutes, we were speeding down the Brooklyn-Queens Expressway, Nora breathlessly filling Hopper in on everything we'd learned at Enchantments, including the Black Bone killing curse we'd stepped on, thanks to Ashley. She pointed out the splotches on Hopper's own Converse sneakers—he had a sizable black wad on his left heel. His reaction was little more than cynical disbelief.

"What about that tattoo parlor?" he asked her. "Rising Dragon."

"We didn't make it there *yet*," she said. "When we saw we'd gotten a response on the Blackboards about Oubliette, we headed straight back to Perry Street."

Hopper said nothing, squinting thoughtfully out the window.

Three hours later, Hopper was passed out cold in the backseat and Nora was scanning satellite radio. I was doing eighty on Route 27, the empty highway like a gray tear ripping through the salt marshes and brackish meadows. I'd been out here quite a few times back in my married days, but never at five after midnight on a mission like this.

"I want to come," said Nora.

"We went over this," I said.

"But Ashley went. *I* can easily pass for a boy. I brought pants to change into and a baseball cap."

"This isn't *Boys Don't Cry*. And after your performance at Briarwood, we've established you're no Hilary Swank."

Within minutes, we were driving through Montauk, so dark, and still it looked like an evacuated fairground, the brightly lit sidewalks strewn with sand and empty plastic bottles, deserted. Shingled beach cottages, so cheerful in the summer, now hunched sullenly on the hill, dark and dour, bracing themselves for the winter. Even the locals were nowhere to be found.

I made a right onto South Emery Street and a left onto Emerson, accelerating past darkened shops and inns, Ocean Resort, Born Free Motel, signs reading SEE U NEXT YEAR, and then: the Sea Haven Diner, its blue twenty-four-hour neon sign bright in the window, a few cars parked in the lot out front. I sped past it and turned onto Whaler's Way, edging past a cluster of beach condos and pulling up behind a dented pickup.

When I cut the engine, I could hear the roar of the ocean, somewhere in the dark in front of us.

"Okay, troops," I said. "Let's move."

We climbed out, Hopper yawning and stretching. I locked the car and handed the keys to Nora as we headed back to Emerson Street.

"You want Hopper to go in with you?" I asked her.

"I can handle it," she said, incensed. Slinging her gray purse onto her shoulder, she spun on her heel and shuffled away.

We watched her go, her footsteps crunching down the sidewalk, the hem of her dress flashing green as she passed under the streetlight. She was dressed like Lily Munster meets Cinderella by way of *punk* in a pea-green velvet dress, black crocheted tights, Moe's motorcycle boots, and black fingerless gloves.

"Maybe you should catch up with her," I said. "Make sure she's okay waiting in there."

Hopper shrugged. "She'll be fine."

"Glad to know chivalry's not dead."

He only squinted after her. Nora pulled open the door to the diner, disappearing inside. When she didn't emerge, I zipped up my jacket.

"Let's get going," I said.

48 WE WALKED DOWN WHALER'S WAY, along the wood fence to the beach, beyond the reach of the streetlamps. I took out my pocket flashlight. We trudged through the sand and up the sloping hill, a freezing headland wind hitting us hard, slicing right through my clothes. Not knowing Oubliette's dress code, I was wearing all black—leather jacket, slacks, button-down—hoping the Russian *vor* look (*vor* being Russian slang for crime lord) would be enough for people to sense I should be left alone.

The wind grew stronger, the rumbles of the Atlantic deafening as we crested the knoll. The beach looked deserted. The ocean was rough, choppy with whitecaps, the waves crashing along the shore violently, their white explosions the only interruption in the dome of darkness surrounding us.

Staring eastward, far ahead of us down the coast, were condos and houses—all of them looked dark, boarded-up for the winter—and beyond the streetlights of town, Montauk's steep cliffs rising along the shore.

Duchamp's staircase.

It was an ambiguous clue, to say the least. I knew the modernist Cubist painting of 1912 it seemed to refer to: Marcel Duchamp's *Nude Descending a Staircase, No. 2.* Nora and I had Googled the work before leaving Perry Street, though how I was going to associate *that* with something on *this beach,* I had no idea.

I turned to Hopper, but he'd wandered down to the water, standing there, immobile, his coat whiplashing behind him, seawater frothing inches from his feet. He looked so dark and melancholy, contemplating the thundering waves, I wondered if he was considering walking right into them—letting them swallow him.

"It's this way!" I shouted, my voice scarcely audible above the wind.

He must have heard me, because he turned and started after me.

The walk was slow going.

The sand was littered with debris after a recent storm—tangled ropes of seaweed, smashed shells, bottles and rocks, long bony arms of driftwood reaching out of the sand. The wind picked up as we trudged on, trying to shove us back, the salty air abrasive and biting. We hiked past blocks of boxy condos with empty porches and parking lots, motels with dark welcome signs. I scrutinized every battered flight of stairs leading down to the beach, looking for *some sign* of life—but there was nothing.

We were alone out here.

After twenty minutes, we'd walked beyond the town of Montauk and had reached Ditch Plains, the surfing beach. It was empty, nothing but a surfboard's lost ankle strap half buried in the sand. As I scaled some rocks, I didn't move out of the way in time as a wave crashed to shore and I got soaked up to my shins in icy water. I could forget about a Russian *vor;* I was going to look like Tom Hanks in goddamn *Cast Away* by the time I arrived.

If I arrived.

Here, the beach narrowed considerably, the massive cliffs like muscular knotted shoulders bulging down the coast. Ahead, there were only multimillion-dollar beachfront estates, and it certainly wasn't a stretch to imagine that a secret party took place at one. But looking far ahead, my eyes watering in the fierce wind, I could see black silhouettes of beach houses perched high on the bluffs, but not a single light.

Oubliette. The forgotten place.

Maybe that meant they partied in the dark.

Hopper had moved ahead of me. He'd been silently striding along with dogged resolve, staring at the sand—unaware, it seemed, of the cold or the tide drenching his Converse sneakers, the hem of his coat now soaked. I picked up my pace to catch up, my flashlight whipping over the rocks, empty crab shells, the chains of seaweed. I could see he'd stopped and was waiting for me beside a flight of wooden steps.

They stretched from the sand up the cliff to a house, hidden high above us over the precipice.

"Think this is it?" he shouted.

There was nothing about those stairs that reminded me of the painting.

I shook my head. "Let's keep going!"

We moved on and within ten minutes, we reached the next flight, this one half demolished. Though at first glance I saw nothing here either that brought to mind *Duchamp,* I inspected it with the beam of the flashlight and saw with surprise that the steps above actually *did* look Cubist. Pieces of splintered driftwood had been nailed crudely together, zigzagging randomly up the sheer rock face and disappearing over the top. It wasn't so much *stairs* as a rickety ladder barely attached to the rock.

It was, however, the second staircase we'd passed. And the title of the painting included *No.* 2.

"This might be it," I shouted.

Hopper nodded and leapt up onto the first step. It was five feet off the ground, the lower stairs, including part of the railing, strewn in mangled pieces across the sand. The structure shuddered dangerously under his weight as he climbed farther up, eventually reaching a part where the handrail was intact so he could use that to balance himself.

I stepped up onto the first platform and, making a mental note not to look down, took off after him. Every wooden plank felt damp and rotten, sagging under my feet. At one point, a plank Hopper stepped onto snapped in half, his leg going through two more rotten planks below *that,* so he hung by the railings and I had to duck so the wood didn't nail me in the face as it careened past, crashing onto the beach below.

He managed to scramble onto the next step, which held his weight, and took off climbing up again. Within minutes Hopper had vanished over the top. When I made it, it was a white-knuckled pull-up, as the last few steps were completely out. I stood up in tall beach grass, switching off the flashlight.

We were in someone's backyard.

Beyond manicured grass, a covered swimming pool, and clusters of black cherry trees sat a massive cedar-shingled mansion—entirely dark and still.

I checked my watch. It was after one.

"Maybe we're too late," I whispered.

Hopper eyed me. "Sounds like you need to get out more."

He took off deliberately through the shadbush onto the path, making his way toward the house. I followed him, though when we were some twenty yards from the back patio, without warning, a door opened. Dense, throbbing music filled the air. Pale white light flooded the flagstones.

Hopper and I froze, pressing our backs into the hedge along the path.

A lanky kid sporting a black bar apron emerged, dragging numerous garbage bags.

He hauled them across the patio, tossing each one against a low wall stretching around the side of the house, the sound of shattering glass bottles exploding through the night. After he tossed the last bag, he retreated back into the mansion, slamming the door hard.

Silence again engulfed the house.

Hopper and I waited for a minute, the only noise the wind, the faint roar of the ocean far below.

With a nod to each other, we sprinted the final distance to the patio and up the steps. Hopper tried the door. It opened easily, and we slipped inside.

49 IT WAS SOME KIND of backroom storage area.
The overhead lights had been switched off, and it was freezing inside. We appeared to be alone. Stacked all around us were large wooden crates and boxes, a two-wheeled cart propped against the

wall. I stepped over to the crates to read the labels. RÉMY MARTIN. DIVA VODKA. CHATEAU LAFITE. WRAY AND NEPHEW LTD. JAMAICAN RUM.

Not too shabby. Spanning the wall was a row of oversized steel refrigerators, and beyond that in an alcove, hanging from a line of hooks, black pants and shirts—some type of waiter's uniform. There was a long wooden table at the center of the room cluttered with supplies, and I stepped over. Piled across it were cellophane-wrapped blocks of what had to be cocaine, each one about a kilo. There were at least a hundred, plus four padlocked cash boxes chained by a metal cable to the table legs.

"It's an airport duty-free shop in Cartagena," I muttered.

Hopper stepped beside me, raising his eyebrows. "Or some billionaire's outfitted his bunker really nicely for the end of the world." He grabbed one of the bricks of coke, tossed it into the air like it was a football, he a seasoned quarterback. He caught it and stuffed it into his coat pocket.

"Are you *nuts?*"

"What?"

"Put it back."

He shrugged, wandering over to the refrigerators. "It's market research." He wrenched open one of the steel fridge doors, the shelves packed with foam cartons and trays.

"I've crashed parties like this before." He rummaged through the containers. "It's underwritten by a Saudi prince, maybe a Russian. All this shit for them is like Bud Light and pretzels to us. Would you give a shit if a couple bags of Fritos go missing?"

I picked up a box of Cuban cigars. *Cohiba Behikes.*

Hopper, scrutinizing a black glass jar, returned it to the shelf. "There's more caviar here than the Black Sea."

"Help yourself. I'm getting out of here before the Saudi prince needs a pick-me-up." I stepped over to the door on the opposite side of the room. I could hear house music, throbbing like the gears of the Earth as it turned, shimmering, relentless.

I opened the door a crack and peered out. It took a moment of adjustment to understand what I was seeing.

It was a party. And yet the floor—black-and-white geometric inlaid tiles—rippled like a sea. It spanned an immense circular atrium, ringed with Corinthian pillars, yet there was no ceiling, just a bright blue cloud-filled sky. *How the hell was it a perfect summer day in here?* In the distance, beyond stone arches covered in ivy and dark doorways lead- ing down dirt paths, there was a luscious bloom-filled garden where stone Greek statues reclined in the sun. An egret waded in a shining stream. Red-and-green parrots soared through the jungle, sunlight fil- tering divinely through the canopy.

As my eyes madly searched for some semblance of reality, my mind short-circuited, both entranced and trying to form some rational con- clusion as to what the hell it was: *a biosphere, a staged play, an adult Disney World, a portal to another planet.* And then I caught a flaw in the tropical paradise: Along the floor, about a foot from where I stood, there was a *light socket.*

All of it was painted, a photorealist trompe l'oeil of such detail and beauty, in the dimmed amber light it was all somehow *alive, thriving.* At the sunken center of the room, seated on the leather couches, standing around the marble tables, was a dense crowd. *They* were real, I was certain. They were middle-aged men, most with the battered gargoyle faces of self-made tycoons (a few with the flabby demeanors of those who'd inherited their wealth), most of them Caucasian, a few Japanese. Women drifted among them, dripping in gowns and jewels, though due to the liquid floor, they seemed to float in a pool of water, snagging on a group of men like scraps of paper caught on a branch before spinning across the room on another mysterious cur- rent.

There was a *strict dress code*—which the person who'd answered my post on the Blackboards had failed to mention. The men were in suits and ties. Hopper and I were certainly going to *stick out*—not to men- tion the fact that I had chalky rings of saltwater on my pants.

Hopper moved behind me, and I stepped aside so he could take a look.

"Jesus Christ," he whispered.

"It's got to be some kind of cult. Anyone offers you Kool-Aid or a hot shower, say *no.* And don't forget the reason why we're here. Find some- one who saw Ashley."

He turned to me and extended his hand. "See you on the other side."

We shook hands, and I exited the storage room.

50 A BLACK MARBLE BAR spanned the far wall, a handful of men seated there—one vacant red stool on the farthest-right side.

That would be a perfect vantage point for me to wait until I understood just *what* I was dealing with, so I strode casually toward it around the atrium, passing the columns—*those were real*—feeling slight vertigo from the shifting floors and the teeming landscapes surrounding me.

The ceiling was high as a cathedral's and the mural of the sky so realistically painted, it looked infinite, glaringly blue. Staring up made me light-headed, and I nearly collided with a short, fat man with thinning black hair who'd abruptly crossed in front of me. He expressly avoided eye contact, making a beeline toward the stone garden wall. He pushed a moss-covered urn atop a post and it smoothly opened into a door. I caught a fleeting glimpse of a black-and-white tiled bathroom, a male attendant in a black uniform standing beside the sinks, hands clasped, eyes discreetly on the ground, before it all vanished again into that empty garden.

I slid onto the vacant stool at the very end of the bar, relieved to feel it was sturdy and *real,* and turned to observe the scene.

Waiters in black slacks and Asian tunics moved among the marble tables, balancing drinks on silver trays. There was a deejay up high in a bell tower. He was wearing a purple T-shirt, headphones around his neck, his hair in dreads that reached to his waist. He looked relatively normal, straight from Brooklyn or the Bay Area, though I noticed he kept his eyes averted from the crowd below as he expertly worked the controls on a synthesizer and two MacBooks.

He must have been told not to stare at the guests.

I returned my attention to the crowd. The women were stunning. They were all different races, many of them dark-skinned and exotic, their unifying attributes a height of about six feet and a thinness that made them resemble insects swarming, feeding insatiably on the dark suits and balding heads. They looked young. As one turned, her blond hair so pale it seemed to float like a gleaming white halo around her face, she tipped her head back, smiling, and I caught sight of a prominent Adam's apple.

Christ. She was a *man.*

Ignoring an irrational feeling of alarm, I scrutinized another wandering through the crowd in a blue sequin dress. After speaking with a group of men, she—*or he*—touched one on the shoulder. She had long fingernails painted black, her arms laden with jewelry. Very slowly, as if to move suddenly in this place was prohibited—would puncture the dream—they detached from the group. She took him by the wrist, led him up the steps along a crumbling stone wall, the Aegean stretching beyond it. They slipped through an arched doorway and down a dirt path, vanishing. There were at least twelve identical entrances around the room. They led to—*what? A crying game.*

It had to be a high-end bondage club. *Never underestimate the desire for wildly successful men to torture themselves for fun.*

"May I bring you something, Mr. . . . ?"

I turned to see the bartender standing across from me. Though he was dressed in a slick gray suit like everyone else, a double-Windsored blue silk tie, he was muscular, with a crew cut, craggy features, and an iron-rod posture that made me guess he was ex-military.

"Scotch, straight up," I said.

He didn't move, the friendliness draining from his face. *I was doing something wrong, revealing myself as a sham.* I didn't react. Neither did he. He was so brawny from anabolic steroids he looked like an action figure, as if his arms might not bend at the elbows and his head could pop off from heavy play.

"Any preference of scotch?" he asked.

"Your choice."

He grabbed the bottle of Glenfiddich from the shelves.

As he poured my drink, a hidden door opened beside the bar—a pastoral scene of a Tuscan landscape—and the young kid I'd seen outside hauling trash slipped in carrying a crate of glasses. His head lowered—he, too, seemed to have been told not to make eye contact—he began stacking them on the mirrored shelves.

The bartender returned with my drink and stood there expectantly.

"Your *card*?" he prompted.

"Which one?" I made a production of fumbling for my wallet.

"*Membership.*"

"Yeah, I don't have one of those. I'm a guest."

"Whose guest?"

"Harry, can I have a glass of water, quick? I feel dizzy."

I couldn't have timed it better. One of the women—or *boys,* if that's what they were—had slunk up beside me. She had a pouting doll pro-file, long blond hair, a purple silk dress so tight it looked like it'd been poured over her.

The bartender, Harry—he *looked* more like Biff—shot her a furious look, indicating she was breaching serious protocol by asking such a thing.

"Try downstairs," he said with a tight smile.

"I can't. I—I just need some water and I'll be fine."

He glared at her, and with a hard look at me—*I'm not done with you yet*—he stepped away.

"He's fun," I said, turning to her.

She eyed me uncertainly, her hands—they, too, had those long black painted fingernails—tightly holding the edge of the bar as if to keep herself moored there; otherwise, so skinny, she'd waft to the ceiling like a helium balloon. Her blue eyes, heavily made up, looked watery, the pupils dilated. She'd done something to her mouth to make it puffy, injected it with something, which made it exaggerated and sad like a clown's.

"What's your name?" I asked.

That prompted an immediate *Game Over.* She cast me an icy look. I was sure she was going to move away, but instead she tilted her head.

"You're a friend of Fadil's," she said.

"Where *is* Fadil? Haven't seen him."

"Back in France, isn't he?"

Harry banged the glass of water onto the bar. She grabbed it, gulping it down, a drop of water trickling out the edge of her red mouth, sliding down her chin. She set the empty glass down, wobbling unsteadily on her heels, and the bartender wordlessly moved away to refill it. *He'd been through this drill with her before.*

She wiped her mouth with the back of her fingers.

"Sure you're all right?" I asked in a low voice.

She didn't answer me, instead inspected the plunging V-neckline of her dress, her puffy mouth in a clownlike frown as she straightened the fabric.

"You should eat something. Or go home. Get a decent night's sleep."

She glanced at me in drowsy confusion as if I'd again said something off-putting. Harry shoved the second glass in front of her, and without a word she guzzled it.

I cleared my throat, smiling at him. "As I was saying, I'm a friend of Fadil's."

The name—Arabic—meant something to him. He nodded grudgingly and moved to the other end of the bar, where a short, fat man signaled to him.

I leaned in toward the woman.

"Maybe you can help me."

But her attention was on the young busboy stacking glasses under the bar in front of us. With shaggy brown hair, freckles, he looked no older than sixteen, like he'd just popped out of a Norman Rockwell painting.

"Hey," she whispered. "Do me a favor? Get me a vodka cranberry?"

He ignored her.

"Oh, *fuck*. Don't worry about Harry. He's a pussycat. I'm dying."

Her pleading, threatening to get shrill, caused the boy to look up at her reluctantly, then down to the other end of the bar, where Harry was busy fixing another drink. The kid must have felt sorry for her because he turned, grabbing a bottle of Smirnoff.

"You're an angel-boy," she whispered.

He added the juice, set it in front of her, and resumed stacking the glasses.

"Any chance I can get some ice?" I asked, sliding my drink forward.

He nodded. When he brought it back, I slid a folded hundred-dollar bill into his hand. He glanced at me, startled.

"Don't react," I said, glancing down the bar at Harry. "I need some information." I took out the photo of Ashley from my pocket, slipping it across the bar.

"You recognize her?"

He kept his head lowered, stacking the glasses.

"Take it off the bar," he whispered. "They got cameras."

I stuck it back into my wallet. If someone was watching, I hoped they'd assume I'd just showed the kid a picture of my daughter—or, given the clientele here, my jailbait Eastern European girlfriend who spoke no English.

"Can you help me out?" I asked.

The boy squinted off to his right and scratched his cheek. "Uh, *yeah,* she was the breach."

"The *what?*"

He resumed arranging the glasses. "She was the security breach from a few weeks ago. They got her picture posted downstairs."

"What happened?"

"I'm sorry. I can't do this. I'll be up shit's creek if—"

"This is life or death."

The kid eyed me nervously. He looked better suited for a paper route, leading a band of Boy Scouts, than working in this place. I reached into my pocket for another hundred-dollar bill, leaned over the bar to grab a black drink stir, and dropped it at his feet.

He bent down and picked it up, then set about ordering the stacks of red cocktail napkins emblazoned with a single black *O,* though the more I stared at the letter I realized it was an open mouth, a *screaming* mouth.

"She attacked a guest," the kid said under his breath.

"Attacked?"

"She, like, *went after* him. That's what I heard."

"How?"

He didn't seem to want to elaborate—or didn't know.

"Which guest?"

He looked apprehensively at Harry and picked up a towel, wiping down the bar.

"He's called the Spider."

"*What?*"

He shrugged. "That's his nickname."

The words had an odd effect on the girl. She'd been sucking down her drink, ignoring us, but now she swiveled around on the stool, trying to focus her bleary eyes on me.

I turned back to the kid, now replenishing with a pair of silver tongs the crystal jar of maraschino cherries on the bar. The cherries, I noticed with surprise, were *entirely black,* including the stems, and every one was a connected twin, one tied to another.

"What's his real name?" I asked, casually sipping my drink.

The kid shook his head. *He didn't know.*

"Is he here tonight? Can you point him out to me?"

He nervously licked his lips, was on the verge of answering me, but then spotted something over my shoulder. He turned, grabbing the empty crate on the counter, and scooted out the door with it, eyes averted, vanishing into that Italian countryside.

I looked to see what made him bolt.

A middle-aged man with spiky silver hair was striding through the crowd, his eyes glued to the woman beside me. He stepped right behind her and whispered in her ear.

She jerked upright in shock. He then grabbed her bare arm and wrenched her off the stool so hard she spilled her drink, leaving an ugly dark wound down the front of her dress. She sullenly mumbled something in a foreign language, the music too loud to hear what it was. Then she sprang away, lurching into the main lounge, fighting through the crowd and up the steps, fleeing down one of the dark pathways.

I turned back to the bar, sipping my scotch, ignoring the man, still standing behind me, his attention now squarely on *me*.

"I don't think we've met," he said.

51 | "You think right," I answered.
| "Let's remedy that."
| "I'm a guest of Fadil's."

He hesitated, taken aback. He had to be the manager of the place. He wore an expensive suit, an earpiece, and had the overinflated posture of all short, insecure men in positions of power. I sensed he was about to leave me alone, but then, looking me over, frowned at the saltwater ring on my pants.

"How are you acquainted with Mr. Bourdage?" he asked.

"Ask him."

"Come with me, please."

"I'd like to finish my drink."

"Come with me or we're going to have a serious problem."

I studied him with bored indignation. "You sure?"

"Do I look like it?"

I shrugged, taking time to down the rest of my scotch, and stood up.

"It's your funeral," I said.

If this unnerved him even *a little,* the man gave no indication. He stepped stiffly to the steps leading down into the main lounge, waiting for me to follow.

This isn't going to end well. I headed after him and as we moved down into the crowd I felt another unnerving surge of vertigo. It was like sinking into another dimension, hitting a snag in reality. The trompe l'oeil murals must have been painted to be viewed from this central vantage point, because every one came into greater focus. Coastal towns bustled. Sunflower fields rippled in the wind, a flock of crows exploding over them—yet unable to fly away. Jungle bromeliads shook, a dark animal stalking through them. A snake writhed over a wall. Even the pulsing music seemed to converge onto me. I could actually feel the sun beating down on my neck. As we jostled our way through the crowd, the suits and ties, the girls, *boys* in those dresses, which down here looked to be made not of fabric but fish scales, I caught snippets of conversations over the music: *be here, sometimes, I agree, water ski.*

I had to stay calm and make an exit—pronto. We appeared to be heading toward one of those dark passageways and I'd be damned if I was going to follow him down there and get my legs broken, maybe worse.

My eyes scanned the atrium's periphery for the door back into the storage room, but it was lost in the glinting scenes around me.

The manager was a few feet ahead, glaring as he waited for me to catch up. But suddenly a tall, blond man tapped him on the shoulder, greeting him, shaking his hand.

I held back a few seconds. *This was probably my chance.*

The man introduced a friend beside him. The manager turned and I hastily did a 180, barging away from him through a large group, accidentally ramming the back of a waiter. A cocktail slid out of his hands, exploding onto the floor.

I picked up my pace, my eyes averted. The women were wearing stilettos, and their toenails were painted *black,* filed into *points,* like bizarre thorns. Abruptly, I spotted something out of place: *dirty white Converse sneakers.* A waiter was wearing them.

Hopper.

He'd actually put on one of the uniforms from the storage room. He was wielding a silver tray, wandering among the guests like he owned the place. I slipped beside him.

"I need to get the fuck out of here. I've been caught."

He nodded. "Follow me."

We cut sharply left, elbowing through the crowd, skipping up the marble steps, Hopper striding deliberately toward the crumbling stone wall that ringed the entire plaza.

There was *no* visible door. But he extended his hand, pressing the face of a reclining stone statue of a woman covered in moss.

Nothing happened. Frowning, he ran his hands over it, pressing the weathered statue's arms, legs, bare feet, trying to find whatever the hell opened the door.

I glanced over my shoulder.

Two guests sitting in the lounge were watching us, alarmed. One of them turned around, signaling to a waiter.

And then I saw the manager. He was pushing aggressively through the crowd, whispering into his earpiece, scanning the atrium's perimeter.

He was seconds from spotting me.

"Any chance we can speed this up?" I muttered.

"I swear I just walked out of here."

I stepped beside him, sliding my hands over the wall, and Hopper moved left toward another reclining statue. He pressed her hands, face, breasts, eyes, and *thank Christ,* she unexpectedly gave way into a regular rectangular door, which led into a long corridor with white walls and orange linoleum.

We sprinted down it, two stainless-steel doors visible at the end.

"And you thought *I* was getting our asses kicked," Hopper said over his shoulder.

"Fallout from obtaining vital information."

"Oh, yeah, what's that?"

"Ashley crashed this party a few weeks ago. She went after a member known as the Spider. That's what you call *skills.*"

"The Spider? What's his real name?"

"Didn't get it."

We charged through the swinging doors into an industrial kitchen. It was lively, with cooks in uniform, bubbling pots, smells of roasted meat and garlic. A few glanced up curiously as Hopper and I raced around the counters, the stoves with sizzling pans, wheeled carts, dessert trays.

We flew out of a second swinging door into another empty corridor. Hopper stopped, panting, pointing.

"Take it all the way to the end, make a right, the door leads outside."

I took off, turning around when he didn't follow.

"You're staying?"

He was heading back into the kitchen. "Just getting started."

"Be careful. And thanks for saving my ass."

He smiled. "It's not saved yet."

52

I REACHED THE END of the hall, followed it right, running toward the emergency exit door at the end. An alarm began to sound from an intercom.

The manager must have alerted a security breach.

I shoved it open, sprinting outside.

It was a brightly lit loading area, the driveway packed with supply trucks, two black Escalades. A lone waiter sat on a crate, smoking a cigarette. He smiled as I walked casually past and jogged down some steps, then along a stone pathway winding around the side of the house.

It had to be the eastern side.

Rounding the corner, I stopped dead.

In front of me was the mansion's entrance, an elaborate columned porte cochere crowded with security guards dressed in black. A silver Range Rover was parked out front, the backseat window unrolled—*whoever* sat there clearly being checked on a guest list. The driveway curved left through dense trees, probably heading north toward Old Montauk Highway—*the way out of here.* Visible farther to my left beyond the foliage was a lawn, quite a few cars parked there.

I couldn't make it out this way. The guards had obviously been alerted, because they were fanning out, heading inside. One turned in my direction, motioned to another—*taking off toward me.*

I backtracked and broke into a sprint, dashing past the loading dock again and the lone waiter. He stood up, shouting something as I raced past, veering around the next rambling wing of the mansion, the windows dark, though for a split second, maybe it was the wind through the brush, I swore I heard a man's *dull, prolonged moan.*

Christ. I kept going, racing toward the backyard through flower beds and shrubs, rounding the corner.

I froze.

The back lawn was flooded with light. Guards were milling around the patio and pool, two of them far across the lawn, inspecting the stairs where Hopper and I had climbed up.

I whipped around, checking behind me. I could hear the guards' footsteps, getting closer.

I scrambled past the piles of garbage bags, up onto the stone wall, racing across the strip of grass into a tall hedge, forcing my way through, the branches so dense it was like fighting through a tightly woven net. I crouched down, breaking the limbs with my hands, crawling through headfirst.

There was shouting behind me cutting through the rumbles of the ocean.

I tore free on the other side and stumbled to my feet.

I wasn't in another backyard as I'd hoped, but in an empty expanse of moorland—no house or lawn, only darkness and tangled shrubbery shoulder high, impossible to walk through. I slipped along the hedge I'd just crawled out of, where the understory wasn't as thick, fighting through what felt like holly or rosebushes, heading in the direction of the ocean.

I had to find another flight of stairs down to the beach. I reached the bluff, squalls of wind barreling off the Atlantic. I headed unsteadily along it, but could see within minutes there were no stairs.

This had to be a wildlife preserve. I was trapped. There wouldn't be another flight of steps or a house for miles.

I checked behind me. The hedge was shaking, black forms emerging through the branches, flashlight beams sweeping the gnarled thickets, heading in my direction.

They were still coming. The manager had probably declared a fatwa on my ass.

I scrambled to the edge of the cliff. It wasn't a sheer drop to the water, but a slight incline, jagged with shrubs. Grabbing a plant to brace myself, I began to slide down it, feet first, creating an avalanche of loose rocks and sand. Flashlights were already inspecting the vegetation directly above me, the men's shouts barely audible over the waves. I pressed my back against the rocks, waiting until they moved farther down, then hurriedly continued on, many of the shrubs pulling out in my fists so I dropped in a free fall until I managed to seize a root that held my weight.

I reached a rock promontory jutting out over the beach.

The tide had come in. There was no beach—only five-foot waves, which receded for a few seething seconds, exposing spiky crags along the cliff's base, before they somersaulted aggressively forward, erupting in wild explosions against the rocks.

I waited, checking above me for movement.

I was safe. No one would be idiotic enough to follow me down here.

Yet the instant I figured this, I could see two dark figures bending down, clamoring after me.

I groped my way down a few more feet, reaching some boulders. I began crawling between them, heading westward, moving quickly when the waves receded. After a few minutes, I could make out the spindly skeleton of what had to be Duchamp's staircase, far ahead, rising out of the waves.

I edged toward it. Flashlights suddenly appeared at the top of the cliff, searching the shoreline, the beams sliding along the rocks just a few feet from where I was crouched.

They were waiting. The light slipped right over me.

Shouting cut through the waves. I took off again, faster, half expecting a ricochet of bullets clattering against the rocks around me.

When I reached the bottom of the stairs, I wedged my boots between two rocks to steady myself and looked up. A guard was actually attempting to climb down, the whole structure trembling under his weight. I seized the most rotten of the beams and after a few attempts managed to wrench it loose, a large section of the railing detaching with it. I threw it into the water behind me and took off across the rocks, drenched by another onslaught of waves.

After another few yards, I quickly checked behind me.

The guard on the staircase had fallen through a section of stairs above what I'd dismantled and was clinging to the cliff face, seemingly awaiting help. I moved on, scaling a precarious section of the cliffs where there wasn't much to hold on to and had just started to let myself think that I *might* be *home free,* when a massive wave suddenly lobbed itself against the rocks.

I lost my grip. I fell backward, my ears filled with deafening thunder as I was tossed upside down, choking on salt water. I managed to fight my way to the surface, gasping for air, but within seconds, another wave surged forward, pulling me back before throwing me toward the cliffs. Kicking as hard as I could, I was shoved against another boulder and managed to sling myself up onto it, coughing up salt water.

I lifted my head, my eyes burning. I was alone in a narrow inlet. I sat crouched on the rock, waiting for one of the guards to appear.

No one came.

When the sky was turning a silvered gray, I saw, as I squinted down the beach, a ribbon of sand. I dropped down onto it, breaking into a jog, trekking past silent condos and along the wooden fence bordering Whaler's Way, the deserted alley coming into washed-out focus in the pale morning.

I stopped, staring at the empty parking space.

My car was gone.

Bewildered, I headed to Emerson Street and the Sea Haven Diner, scanning the parking lot. There was no sign of my car, only a silver pickup and a Subaru. Entering, I saw the place was empty, apart from an old man in a back booth and a redheaded waitress slumped over the counter, reading a magazine.

"You look shipwrecked," she said as I approached.

"I'm looking for a young woman. Blond. Green dress. Was she here?"

She smiled in recognition. "You mean Nora?"

"Exactly."

"Sure, she was here."

"Well, where the hell is she?"

"Beats me. Got up and left about an hour ago."

I slid onto one of the counter stools, pulling off my leather jacket, still drooling salt water.

"I'll have some coffee, three eggs easy, bacon, toast, orange juice."

The waitress disappeared through the swinging doors. When she returned with my coffee, she sighed heavily, crossing her arms.

"She got a call from some guy. Ran out of here real excited."

I glanced at her, taking a sip. "A call on her cell?"

"*No*. Cell service sucks out here. Just one bar. He called the diner, asked for her by name. You're her dad, I take it, comin' to pick her up?" She didn't wait for my response, only nodded knowingly. "Don't know how you dads put up with it. Girls always going after the bad boys. Then there's the Internet, which makes it ten times worse with the stalkers and the sex predators."

My breakfast came quickly, *thank Christ*.

A few locals wandered in, but there was no sign of Hopper or Nora.

After I ate, I tried calling them—I was surprised to see my cell still worked—but the waitress was right: no service. I used the phone at the cash register, but for both of them it rang and went to voicemail.

When I boarded the 9:45 A.M. Long Island Rail Road train, taking me back to civilization—if you can call Manhattan *that*—I'd conked out cold before we left the station.

53 WHEN I ARRIVED in the city, it was after noon. There was still no word from Hopper or Nora. I took a cab back to Perry Street. Nora had a spare set of keys, so I wondered if she'd somehow been unable to get in touch and had beaten me home. But the apartment was empty, no messages on my home phone.

I took a shower, considered going back to bed, but felt too strung out, too uneasy—*too annoyed*.

They'd left the general for dead on the battlefield. Or had something happened? I didn't have time to worry about it, because my cell buzzed, reminding me that Peg Martin, one of the actors in *Isolate 3*, would be in the Washington Square Park dog run tonight at 6 P.M. It was the lead Beckman had given me almost a week ago.

I headed into my office, feeding Septimus some birdseed, and pulled Peg Martin's 1995 *Sneak* interview out of my box of notes. After Cordova's 1977 *Rolling Stone* piece, it was the only time anyone who'd worked with him had spoken candidly about the experience.

FRESH FACE OF THE MOMENT

PEG MARTIN

Sneak sits down with the eighteen-year-old star of HBO's first-ever original drama series, *New Found Glory*, to talk about her character and address the swirling rumors that her first role was in a Cordova picture.

"Why the secrecy? I don't know."

We heard a rumor that you got your big break in Cordova's latest film, *Isolate 3*, which can only be seen underground and is said to be so frightening, to watch it is like passing through hell. We are dying to ask: Is any of this true?

PM: I don't want to say too much about it. But yeah. I was Vivian Jean in *Isolate 3*.

How did you get to be in a Cordova film?

PM: I was working after school at a Baskin-Robbins in Vienna, New Jersey, when a woman came up to me and said she liked my look. I spoke to Cordova once on the phone. A day later he called and told me I got the part.

"She has a natural empathy and you can't take your eyes off her," says Brendan Fraser, her costar on the HBO drama **New Found Glory.**

January 23, 1995

Publicity still for HBO's *New Found Glory.*

That's a modern version of Lana Turner getting discovered at Schwab's drugstore in Hollywood. What was it like to work with him?

PM: I had a tiny role. My three scenes were shot in two days in a warehouse in upstate New York. I played a cleaning lady and an abused wife. My left arm was meant to be broken and in a cast. The costume department put a real cast on my arm so I would get used to being handicapped. My boyfriend, William Bassfender, had a much larger role, though. He's the criminal trapped in the Isolate trying to get out. He shot for three months, but won't talk about it.

"He never talked directly to me."

Why will no one talk about Cordova?

PM: When you work with him you sign an intense nondisclosure agreement. Which reminds me, I don't have anything else to say about this or I'll probably be whacked by a hit man or something.

Why the secrecy?

PM: I don't know.

There are so many rumors about Cordova,

that he isn't one man but many different men. Others say he's actually a woman. What do you say?

PM: He's one man. But then, he never talked directly to me. He gave me scene directions through his assistant, Inez Gallo.

You never actually saw him up close?

PM: No.

Where can we score a copy of *Isolate 3*?

PM: It's impossible. Copies are pretty well guarded. I haven't even seen it.

You haven't seen your own film?

PM: No. I don't like to be scared.

Where does Cordova live—at his estate, The Peak?

PM: Can we talk about my drama series on HBO? That's what I'm supposed to be promoting.

Sure—but one last question about Cordova. What is he working on?

PM: My final line in *Isolate 3* is, "Scientists look for aliens in the universe, but they're here. Aliens who pass for men. They've already invaded. For our own safety we should leave them be." That kind of says it all.

She was seventeen when she'd appeared in Cordova's film, which today would make her thirty-five.

I Googled her name and a few stills from *Isolate 3* appeared. She had only three scenes in the film, a grainy version of one of them posted on YouTube. Peg played Vivian Jean, one of the maids who worked all night cleaning the midtown offices of the law firm Milton, Bowers & Reid, ends up disappearing into a back stairwell, and is never seen again. Moments before she vanishes, she says *Scientists look for aliens in the universe, but they're here. Aliens who pass for men. They've already invaded.* She was talking about her abusive husband, how monstrous the people you loved could be. I'd always found interesting the fact that Martin in the interview used *that* line to describe Cordova.

According to IMDb, after appearing in HBO's *New Found Glory*—a modern remake of *It Happened One Night,* canceled after one season— Peg Martin appeared in the ABC TV Western *Dust Up,* costarring Jeff Goldblum. After 1996, she had no more credits. There was no current information about her and no indication of what she'd done with her life, though I did recall Beckman had mentioned she'd been a heroin addict—probably the reason she'd had such a brief film career.

I checked my watch. It was almost five. I needed to get going. But a lone man wandering a public park being friendly, asking too many questions—it would set off all kinds of alarm bells.

I needed a decoy.

54 "Mrs. Quincy called to alert me *you'd* be here," announced Dorothy, surveying me skeptically over the rim of her glasses. "But *not* a half-hour early. Samantha's in the midst of her *Nut-cracker* audition."

Dorothy was the gray-haired czarina who ruled the Manhattan Ballet School with an iron fist. I'd encountered her before, and every time she treated me like I was an escapee from a Siberian gulag.

"Okay, but we have a reservation at the Plaza for a father-daughter tea."

"If you pull her out *now,* she won't be in the running for getting a doll from Herr Drosselmeyer. She might not even make it to the party scene."

"Come on, Dorothy. Sam has to make the party scene. She *is* the party scene."

Dorothy sighed, relenting. "Go ahead."

Winking at her, I turned, striding down the hall to the ballroom where they held the classes, the wood floors creaking under my feet. I'd called Cynthia to ask if I might spend a few quality hours with Sam this evening—to make up for my postponing her visit—and miraculously, she'd agreed to it. I didn't exactly go into detail as to *what* we'd be *doing* during these quality hours, but no matter what happened with Peg Martin, Sam would enjoy the dog run, and afterward I'd treat her to a dinner and a hot-fudge sundae at Serendipity 3.

I found Sam at the end of the hall in a sunlit studio blaring Tchaikovsky. She was dancing in a flock of five-year-olds. They were all holding their arms over their heads, jumping. Sam looked ready for the Bolshoi: leotard firebird red, white tights, slippers, and white tutu. She was right in front, watching the ballet mistress demonstrate the steps.

I knocked on the glass door.

The children froze. The mistress craned her long neck, surveying me imperiously.

"*Yes,* sir? May I help you?"

I stepped inside. "I'm here for Samantha."

55 EVEN THOUGH IT WAS GETTING DARK, Washington Square Park was crowded with students and skateboarders, doting couples, a break-dancer with an eighties boom box who'd attracted a crowd. Most of the women stopped mid-conversation to beam, dazed and enchanted, as Sam nimbly plodded past them, tightly holding my hand. Though she'd agreed to put on her black coat and pink Rapunzel backpack, she'd refused to take off her tutu, tights, or ballet slippers.

"She's a very nice woman," I said. "We're going to chat with her and visit her dog for a few minutes. Okay?"

Sam nodded, brushing her gold curls out of her face.

"What's wrong with your hand?" she asked.

After my cliffside escape from Oubliette, my hands were cut up badly.

"Don't have to worry. Your dad's *tough*. Now give me the four-one-one on Mommy. Is she still working at the gallery?"

Sam thought it over. "Mommy has a problem with Sue," she answered.

"The manager. They've always butted heads. What about your step-dad?"

"Bruce?" she clarified.

Good. He was still a proper noun like me. Thank Christ he wasn't *Dad*.

"Yes, Bruce. Has the SEC investigated him yet? Any arrests for insider trading I should know about?"

She squinted at me. "Bruce has a spare tire."

"Mommy said that?"

Sam nodded, hanging heavily on my arm. "Mommy makes him drink green juice, and Bruce goes to bed *hungry*."

So Old Man Quincy had put on a couple of lbs. and was suffering through one of Cynthia's infamous juice cleanses. Suddenly I felt fantastic.

"Does Mommy ever mention *me*?"

Sam considered this for a minute and then nodded.

"Oh, yeah? What does she say?"

"You need *serious help*." She even mimicked Cynthia's self-righteous inflection. "And you're off the rail and you're acting out a *teenage foozy*."

Gone off the *rails*. *Shacking up with* a teenage *floozy*. I should have stopped asking questions after the *spare tire*.

I bent down, scooping Sam into my arms because we'd reached the dog run, a fenced-in area along the south perimeter of the park. It was packed with romping dogs and their mute owners, who hovered around the periphery like overbearing stage parents, nervously watching, armed and at the ready with leashes, balls, pooper-scoopers, and treats.

"Okay, toots. We're looking for a big black dog and a lady with red hair, mid-thirties. When you spot them, keep it on the down low. No pointing. No screaming. *Be cool*. Ya got it?"

Sam nodded, looking. Then suddenly, she squeaked shrilly and kicked me. She made a face, pointing, but only with her *pinkie*.

"You see them?"

She nodded again.

Sure enough—in the remotest section of the dog run, there was a gaunt woman with red hair and an old black Lab hunched on the bench beside her.

"Stellar surveillance work, honey. They could use you at Homeland Security."

I took a moment to glance behind us, making sure there was no one watching. I'd been keeping a vigilant eye out, ever since I'd been back in the city, in case there was further sign of Theo Cordova, but I'd noticed nothing out of the ordinary.

I unlatched the gate, and we stepped inside.

56 I WATCHED SAM carry out her orders with precision and poise. *The girl would make one hell of a Green Beret.* She actually made the whole thing look random. First, on her way around to Peg Martin, she stopped and crouched next to a white teacup Chihuahua decked in more lamé than a Newark hooker. She said hello to *that* dog for a minute before stepping over to the black Lab. Cynthia had clearly drilled into her that she must ask permission before she touched any strange animal, because I heard her politely ask both Peg Martin and then the dog himself if they minded her petting him.

Both must have said no, because very gently and respectfully Sam began to touch the top of the dog's old grayed head, his eyes weary and unblinking. She started with just her pinkie, petting the quarter-inch right between the dog's eyebrows.

I strolled past the other owners standing around the fence and moved toward them.

"It's all right if she pets him?" I asked, approaching Peg Martin.

"Of course," she answered, glancing at me.

"He doesn't bite?"

Her attention was back on the dogs in front of her.

"No."

It was Peg Martin, all right.

Her hair was thinner, dyed a synthetic shade of red, something between dying autumn leaves and beets. She'd been such a vibrant, kooky presence in *Isolate 3*. All these years later, she appeared muted and washed-out, with an exhaustion that seeped from her bones.

"What's your name?" Sam asked the dog, though he didn't respond.

"What's his name?" I asked Peg.

She looked irritated to be addressed again.

"Leopold."

"*Leopold,*" said Sam. She was petting the top of his head with her hand rigidly flat like a spatula. *She might have been carefully spreading icing.*

"You look familiar," I said, glancing at Peg. "You don't teach Sunday school at Saint Thomas, do you?"

She looked flustered.

"Uh, *no.* That, uh, definitely wouldn't be me."

"My mistake."

She smiled thinly, returning her attention to the dogs.

I took a minute to watch them, too, so as not to appear forward. A hyper Dalmatian was the leader of the pack. That white hoochie-mama Chihuahua was making her rounds—yipping, desperate for a john—but every dog was besotted with a soggy tennis ball.

"Okay," I said. "This is a long shot, and you're probably going to think I'm crazy."

She glanced at me, wary.

"*Isolate 3.* The maid with the broken arm. It was you, wasn't it?"

She blinked in surprise. She was never recognized. I was certain I overplayed it, sounding a little too amazed, but she nodded.

"That's right."

"You were great in it. The only thing that kept me from losing my mind."

She smiled, her face flushing.

It is a truth universally acknowledged that no actor ever tires of hearing they were brilliant in a role.

"I have to ask. What was he like? Cordova."

Her smile vanished like a match blown out. Glancing at her watch, she grabbed the strap of her backpack, pulling it into the crook of her arm, about to leave. But then, to my relief, Sam had managed to fully woo Leopold. He was wagging his tail. It moved like a windshield wiper. Seeing this—and Sam, quietly discussing something of great importance with the dog—she hesitated.

"It's tragic what happened to his daughter," I noted.

Peg scratched her nose.

"But then, I'm not surprised," I went on. "To create a body of work that twisted and visceral, the man has to be horrifying in his personal life. You have to be. Look at Picasso. O'Neill. Tennessee Williams. Capote. Were these shiny happy people spreading sunshine? No. Only the greatest of personal demons can force you to do powerful work."

I figured if I steamrolled the woman with words she might not get up and leave. She was sitting back against the bench, studying me with an absorbed expression.

"Maybe," she said. "You can never tell how a family is from the outside. But I just . . ."

She fell silent because that goddamn tennis ball had just rolled exactly behind her feet. She bent down, grabbing it, the dogs freezing in incredulity, mouths closed, ears perked. She threw it, sitting back again as they took off in a stampede across the gravel.

"You just . . . ?" I prompted quietly.

Good God, let her speak. And calm down, for Christ's sake.

"When they first started shooting *Isolate*," she said, glancing at me, "he invited my boyfriend to spend the afternoon with his family up at the house. The Peak. He never did things like that. He was private. At least that's what I'd heard. But his wife was organizing a picnic. They did it all the time in the summer. Billy was invited. So I got to tag along."

He was private. She actually meant Cordova.

And Billy—it had to be William Bassfender, the boyfriend she'd mentioned in the *Sneak* interview. He was the muscular, tattooed Scottish man who'd played the prisoner in the Isolate, Specimen 12. If I remembered correctly, after *Isolate 3* Bassfender went on to do a play on London's West End and had been about to appear in Oliver Stone's *Nixon,* when he was killed in a car accident in Germany.

I turned my gaze back to the dogs so she wouldn't realize I was hanging on her every word.

"It was surreal. Granted, any family that was together, not shouting or stumbling-down drunk, would have been surreal to me. But even now I think there was more love and joy in that family than I've ever seen before or since." She shook her head in disbelief. "They had their own language."

I stared. "What?"

"Cordova's son, Theo, *invented* a language for the family. They spoke it to each other, telling jokes and laughing, which made them even *more* intimidating. I remember Astrid explaining it to me like it was yesterday. 'The Russians have sixteen words for love. Our language has twenty.' She brought out all of these notebooks Theo had done. He'd written his own dictionary thick as a Bible, filled with grammar rules and conjugations of irregular verbs he'd made up. Astrid taught me some of the words. I've never forgotten them. One was *terulya*. It meant deep-diving love, a love that excavates you. It's something you have to have before you die in order to have lived. I remember being shocked a teenage boy came up with this stuff. But that's how they all were. They mopped life up with themselves. None of them were encumbered by anything. There were no limits."

She fell silent, wistful, maybe even slightly jealous of this family she was describing. She crossed her arms, frowning out at the dogs again.

"A *picnic*," I repeated, a prompt for her to keep talking.

"It was a bright day. Once you turned onto the property you continued along a long drive through woods. And at the end, the house rose up, an enormous manor commanding the hill like a castle out of a fairy tale. It was deserted. Billy and I pounded on the door and wandered around the house and the gardens. There was no sign of anyone. Finally, after twenty minutes, the massive front door opened and a Japanese man stood there. He'd just woken up and didn't speak any English. He was wearing green silk pajamas and a sword around his waist, and he wandered out, rubbing his eyes, yawning, saying something in Japanese as he beckoned for us to follow him. He led us down to the lake. That's where everyone was. A group sitting on white blankets under white umbrellas. Everyone was there, except Cordova. He was working that day. At least, that's what they said."

She took a deep breath. "It was like wandering into a painting. A dream sequence. There were movie stars, Jack Nicholson and Dennis

Hopper, but they weren't the star attraction. There were astronauts talking about deep space. A former member of the CIA living off the grid who kept in his wallet the *New York Times* article reporting his death. A famous playwright. A local priest who'd wandered the world for fifteen years and come home. Cordova's son, Theo, was there. He was sixteen and gorgeous, photographing everything with an old Leica camera, standing waist-deep in the marshes to capture shots of warring dragonflies. He was having a very intense love affair with a woman named Rachel, ten years older than he. She was there, too. I remember someone saying she'd been in one of Cordova's films."

"Which one?"

"I don't remember." She smiled wistfully. "Cordova's set designer had built the family a fleet of brightly colored sailboats—*pirate ships,* everyone called them—to sail around the lake. There was a pack of dogs, half wolf. One of the guests told the story of how the Cordovas had rescued them in the middle of the night from a farmer who'd been breeding them for dogfights. *These* were the true stories they were telling. Cordova's mother was there. She didn't speak English, was dying of cancer. They were so gentle with her, folding her into a deck chair so she could sit under an umbrella, drinking Limoncello. I swore to myself if I was ever so lucky to have a family, I wanted it to be like *that.* It was the living experience of a fantasy. I spent most of the afternoon with a philosopher from France and Astrid, who was teaching everyone to oil paint. We all had our easels along the lake's edge, standing in the wind, painting. When Billy and I left, the sun was going down and I felt a terrible sense of mourning, as if I'd spent the afternoon on an island paradise and now the ocean was pulling me out to sea and I'd never be able to make my way back."

"Sounds like Shangri-la," I said, when she didn't go on.

She glanced at me distractedly, saying nothing, and I regretted speaking, for fear I'd punctured the spell she'd been under, recounting that day. The words had sputtered, then to my immense surprise blasted out of her like a fountain, one that'd been dry for years. Now she seemed sorry that she'd said anything at all.

"What year was this?" I asked nonchalantly.

"The year of *Isolate* production. Spring of '93, I think."

Ashley's birthday was December 30, 1986. If this was the spring before, then she was six years old at the time.

"Did you meet Ashley?" I asked.

Peg nodded, reluctant to go on, but then, it seemed she couldn't leave such a vibrant question dangling in the air.

"She was beautiful. Short dark hair, almost black. Like a sprite. Pale gray eyes." She smiled, suddenly animated. "I was seventeen. Wasn't into kids at all. But totally out of the blue, Ashley took my hand and brought me down to a deserted part of the lake where there was a willow tree and tall grass, the water emerald green. She asked me if I could see the trolls. I still remember the names. Elfriede and Vanderlye. By the time she let go of my hand and took off across the field chasing a butterfly—a butterfly that was huge, bright red and orange, like this property had their own insects—I believed in trolls. I still do."

She fell silent, seemingly embarrassed by her zeal. Sam, I noticed, was staring at Peg, listening intently.

It was dark now in the park, the strangers standing along the fence, faceless. The giant elm trees with their outstretched limbs were sinking deeper into the darkness, slipping away. The pack of dogs was still going strong, a white-and-brown blurry squall of panting and flying gravel.

"I've held on to that day," Peg continued in a thin voice, "like some faded postcard. Something you put in a scrapbook to remind yourself of perfect happiness—that it *does* exist, for one moment, like a sudden streak of lightning through the sky. When I read what happened to Ashley, I couldn't believe it. I didn't know her at all, but . . . it seemed so sudden. And *wrong.* If you have a family like that and you still can't withstand this world, what hope is there for the rest of us?"

She smiled sadly, looking away.

"What was he like to work with?" Silently I cringed at the probing question. Thankfully, she just shrugged.

"I had such a small part. I was only on the set for two days. I understood nothing that was going on, really, because the crew was Mexican and Cordova's assistant gave them all their directions in Spanish."

"His assistant—you're talking about Inez Gallo?"

"Yeah. But the crew all called her *coyote.*"

"*Coyote?* Why?"

"No idea," she answered.

"Do you still keep in touch with Cordova? Or anyone from that time?"

Peg shook her head. "After he'd gotten your performance, extracted what he wanted like a surgeon harvesting organs, he was done with you. After my two days of shooting, that was it."

She turned away from me to unzip her backpack, taking out a dog's leash, clipping it to Leopold's collar.

"I actually have to get going."

She was seconds from walking away. I wanted more time, was tempted to throw caution to the wind and keep riddling the woman with questions, anything to get her to keep talking, to tell me more. Yet I sensed her candor was fleeting, the moment already gone.

She stood up, stooping over to help her dog off the bench. He moved like an old man with arthritis. She actually picked up his back legs for him, placing them on the ground, and turned to me with a perfunctory smile.

"Take care."

"You, too," I said.

And then she and Leopold were walking away, two slow-moving figures impervious to the pack of dogs charging past them.

"Is she a nice lady?" Sam asked me, wiping her curls out of her eyes.

"Very nice."

Sam climbed up onto the bench beside me, sitting close, staring fixedly up at my face.

"Is she sad?" she asked.

"No, honey. She's lived-in."

Sam seemed to accept this. It was one of the things I loved about her. I could make some ambiguous observation about human beings, about their failings or hypocrisies, their deep-seated pain—and she took in the comment like an old diamond dealer handed a raw stone, turning it over in her palm, then pocketing the gem to be examined and cut later, moving on.

Sam scratched her cheek and interlaced her fingers in her lap—copying the way *my* fingers were interlaced—and we watched them go in silence.

Leopold waited at the gate as Peg unlatched it, and he ambled through. The dog then paused, turning his head to watch as Peg locked the gate behind them, shoving her hands into her pockets—all of it, a slow choreographed movement only the most longtime of couples could do, only after years.

They strolled out into the park, and the farther they went, the more they had nothing discernible about them except the fact that they were together. And even at the greatest of distances, when they were just two dark shapes moving away, side by side, you could still see they were a remarkable pair.

57

"Ms. Quincy is *coming down*," said the doorman, hanging up the phone.

I bent down to Sam. Her ballet slippers were scruffy and her tutu was slightly crushed, but otherwise she looked all right.

"I'm proud of you, toots," I told her.

The elevator doors opened, Cynthia emerging in a crisp white blouse, jeans, dazzling swish of gold hair, Tod's suede driving loafers. I could see from her smiling face that she was furious.

"Hi, love," she said to Sam. "Go wait for Mommy by the elevators."

Sam blinked up at her and padded obediently across the marble lobby.

Cynthia turned to me. "I said *six*."

"I know—"

"She was auditioning for *The Nutcracker*."

"I worked it out with Dorothy. She's going to make the party scene."

She sighed, heading back across the lobby. "Just don't forget Thursday," she added over her shoulder.

"Thursday?"

She turned. "Bruce and I are going to *Santa Barbara*?"

"Right. Sam is staying with me for the weekend."

Shooting me a warning look—*Don't mess this up*—she took Sam's hand and they stepped into the elevators. I held up a hand, waving, and Sam smiled just as the doors closed.

58 | THE AFTERNOON PEG MARTIN HAD DESCRIBED at The Peak sounded almost too idyllic to be real. But she'd been only seventeen at the time, doubtlessly insecure and impressionable, so it was possible she'd taken creative liberties with the memory without even realizing it. Given Cordova's terrifying subject matter, for his home and workplace to be such a blissful paradise seemed unlikely. *How close was an artist's real life to his work?* Doctoral students wrote dissertations on the subject. Yet when Peg had described Ashley leading her down to the lake where the *trolls* lived—there was something undeniably honest about the episode, also when she'd described Cordova as a surgeon harvesting organs, leaving his actors for dead.

Within every elaborate lie, a kernel of truth.

I let myself into my apartment, noticing music coming from the living room. I threw my coat on the chair, striding into the living room, finding Nora curled up in the leather club chair, Septimus the parakeet perched on her knee. Hopper was slouched on the couch, looking over some papers. The three reversing candles Cleo had given us at Enchantments were burning on the coffee table in front of him beside a pizza box.

"You're home!" Nora announced brightly.

"Don't tell me," I said. "You *both* lost your cellphones and gale-force winds uprooted every landline on the East Coast."

"We're *sorry*. But we had a good reason to go MIA." She looked meaningfully at Hopper and he smiled, some shared excitement between them.

He held out the papers, and I took them. It was fifteen pages, about two thousand names. Many were LLCs or bizarre aliases like Marquis de Roche.

"It's the Oubliette membership list," said Nora excitedly.

"I can see that. How did you get this?"

"It wasn't easy," said Hopper proudly, stretching his hands behind his head. "The place turned into the Gaza Strip after *you* took off. But I was in the waiter uniform, so no one glanced at me twice. I talked to one of the girls, 'least I *think* she was a girl. She told me how to get down to the basement where the offices are. I found one empty, got on the computer, searched the hard drive for *membership*. Some Excel files came up. I logged on to my email, sent the files to myself, cleared the cache, and got out. Only they'd apparently reviewed the security footage and saw *me* saving your ass, so, two guards chased me outside onto a neighbor's property. I had to break into the house, called Nora to come pick me up. I managed to describe to her where the hell I was."

"It was a real getaway," Nora chimed in. "Tires screeching. I felt like Thelma and Louise."

"I thought you were Bernstein," I said.

"Nora pulled up, headlights off," Hopper went on. "I climbed out a window, booked it across the yard, and we got the fuck out of there."

"What time was this?"

Nora glanced at Hopper uncertainly. "Four?"

"I waited at the diner until nine. What'd you do for five hours?"

"We went back to Oubliette because I wanted a look," she blurted. "We hid next door, hoping to talk to some of the guests when they left, ask them if they recognized Ashley, but we couldn't approach any of them. They all looked exhausted, shuttled away by housekeepers in expensive cars and limos. One guy in a wheelchair looked *dead*. There were too many guards, anyway."

"You didn't think to call? You abandoned the boss, *El Jefe,* in the field without a single communication?"

Hopper stood up, yawning and stretching. "I'll see you guys bright and early tomorrow."

"Bright and early?" I asked.

Nora nodded. "Tomorrow we're posting missing-person signs for Ashley around 83 Henry Street." She handed me a flier with the scanned photo of Ashley that Nora had found at Briarwood.

HAVE YOU SEEN THIS GIRL? SERIOUS REWARD OFFERED FOR REAL INFORMATION. PLEASE CALL ASAP.

"We'll weed through the phony reports by asking what color coat Ashley was wearing."

Hopper took off, and I headed into my office, leaving Nora scribbling in her notebook. Hopper obtaining a copy of the guest list was *stellar* investigative work, much better than anything *I'd* come up with lately—*not* that I was going to admit this. I spent the next few hours cross-referencing the Oubliette guest list with a list of Cordova's actors, anyone associated with his world, in the off chance *one* name appeared on *both*—to no avail. But it did rule out one possibility: The person

Ashley had gone to Oubliette to find—*this Spider*—was probably *not* associated with her father's work. *Was he a friend of hers? A stranger? Someone connected to her death?*

I switched out the lamp, rubbing my eyes, heading back down the hall.

The apartment was quiet. Nora had blown out the reversing candles before going upstairs, but oddly enough, I noticed the wicks were still smoldering orange, as if they refused to be extinguished, *three orange pinpricks in the dark.* I grabbed them and dumped them in the kitchen sink, running the tap until I was certain they were out, then headed to bed.

59 "HOPPER PROMISED TO BE HERE," said Nora, squinting down the empty block. "Posting the fliers was his idea."

It was 9:00 A.M., and we were back at 83 Henry Street armed with a hundred missing-person fliers. We decided to split up: I covered the blocks west of the Manhattan Bridge up to East Broadway and the Bowery, while Nora handled everything east of the bridge.

The neighborhood was predominantly Chinese, so I doubted our English-language flier would get us very far. Posting leaflets, as if Ashley were a lost cat, wasn't exactly my style, but it couldn't hurt. With Theo Cordova following us, I could no longer hope to keep the investigation quiet. So why not go in the opposite direction, brazenly carpet-bombing the neighborhood with Ashley's picture, and see where *that* got us?

I taped the flier to lampposts and phone booths, mailboxes, Learning Annex stands. A Chinese woman on a bike, orange shopping bags swinging from the handlebars, braked to see what I was doing, scowled at me, and rode on. Quite a few men in bodegas refused to let me post the missing poster after they saw what it was, shaking their heads, shooing me out of the store.

When this happened for the *sixth* time, I wondered if they were worried a missing Caucasian woman would bring them bad luck—or if they'd seen something in Ashley's photo they didn't like. Or perhaps there was an even more disturbing reason: *I looked like I worked for Immigration and Customs.*

It was the opposite reaction at Hao Hair Salon on Madison Street. The teenage receptionist, the female manager, two stylists, and a client (pink robe, hair in tinfoil) surrounded me, smiling, and speaking in excited Cantonese. They took great care taping Ashley's flier to the window beside a faded poster for eyebrow threading, and when I left, they waved as if I were a beloved relative they wouldn't see for forty years.

And yet the longer I walked the streets, past Chinese restaurants, gift stores, unisex hair salons, orange and white koi drifting in pet store windows, I had the sense I was being watched. But every time I checked behind me—once, even popping into a Laundromat and looking out—I noticed nothing suspicious.

I wondered if the feeling came from the strength of Ashley's stare, so alive and insistent, gazing out from the white page. All "missing" fliers were unsettling, the lost person smiling out from some candid photo taken at a birthday party or happy hour, so ignorant of their fate. Yet Ashley, alone on that picnic table at Briarwood, had a gravity, an understanding even, as if she knew what awaited her within weeks.

As I walked on, however, I realized I was absolutely right. I *was* being watched—*by the entire neighborhood.* Hopper's idea to post these fliers wasn't so simplistic, because if *I* stood out this much, attracted this many hostile looks and slow drive-bys—once I looked up at an old walk-up and saw an old woman had pulled aside her lace curtains to stare down at me—Ashley was noticed, too.

They all must have seen her, watched her, wondered about her as she wandered their sidewalks in her red coat.

Now all we needed was one of them having the courage to call.

60 "TOM-*MAY*!" the guy at the front desk bellowed in a thick New York accent, turning toward the dozen tattoo artists at work behind him. "These guys got a question for ya!"

Rising Dragon was a fluorescent, spacious tattoo studio on the second floor of a walk-up on West Fourteenth Street. It was cheerful inside, without the aggressive *Easy Rider* feel of some of the other tattoo parlors in the city, where the handle-jawed thugs wielding the tattoo guns looked like ink was just a side job, their main work, contract killings.

The light was clean and clinical, walls decorated with tracing paper and framed stencils of full-body tattoos, skulls, Buddhas and warriors, Maori tribal patterns, shelves cluttered with bottles of colored ink and iodine. Nirvana's "Heart-Shaped Box" blared loudly from speakers.

"Ask 'em if they're cops!" The answering male voice sliced through the wasp-buzz of the tattoo guns. Yet every artist remained bent over a client.

I had no clue who'd just spoken.

"Are ya cops?" the guy asked us, wincing at the awful thought.

He had peroxide white-blond hair and the permanently stunned face of a Malibu surfer facing an unexpectedly large wave. Wolf tattoos snarled all over his biceps.

"No," I said.

The kid took this in a moment before turning around again.

"They're *not cops!*"

"Tell 'em to come over!"

The kid, bobbing his head to the music, pointed to an alcove in the farthest corner.

"You can go talk to Tommy, the manager."

Tommy appeared to be a large middle-aged man wearing black latex gloves. He was bent over, working intently, though at this distance it looked like he was doing an autopsy on a sperm whale. His client was facedown on a black massage table and was at least three hundred pounds, bald, naked, whiter than a slice of Sunbeam. As I stepped through the shop toward them, Nora right behind me, I saw the tattoo in progress was a massive lotus tree, a gnarled trunk growing out of the guy's ass crack, up his spine, flourishing all over his back, twisted branches reaching around his chest, a couple of birds—not yet colored in—alighting on his forearms.

"What can I do you for?" asked Tommy, without looking up.

"Do you recognize her?" I asked, holding out the picture of Ashley. "She came into your shop a few weeks ago."

He ignored me until he'd finished coloring in a pink lotus blossom.

Grown men with baby names—Bobby, Johnny, Freddy—there had to be some unspoken law that they looked meaner than the rest of us. He had a wide, thuggish face, salt-and-pepper hair. Unidentifiable tattoos peeked out of the neck and sleeves of his skintight silver polyester shirt. He had an easy confidence, as if he were used to people filing through the store to get to his station in the very back—*tattoo parlor equivalent of the chairman's corner office in the sky*—asking for his *take* on things as we were now.

He dully looked us over, then the photo, and bent back over his client.

"Sure. She came in a few weeks back."

"What color coat was she wearing?" Nora asked.

"Red coat. Black on the sleeves."

Nora shot me an astonished look.

"Did she come in for a tattoo?" I asked him.

"Nah. She wanted her after picture."

"Her *after picture*? What's that?"

Tommy stopped working to stare up at me. "*After* we finish your tat, we *take* your fucking picture." He gestured toward a far wall, covered with photographs of smiling people showing off with their completed tattoos.

"She had a tight twofold of a kirin on her ankle," he went on, resuming his work. "She wanted to know if we still had the after."

"A *twofold*?"

"One tat on two people. When they're apart it don't look like much. But together, when their arms are around each other, hand in hand, lovesick and shit, it turns into somethin'. A very *Jerry Maguire* 'you complete me' kinda thing."

Of course—Ashley's tattoo on her ankle featured only half of the animal, the head and front legs.

"You said her tattoo was of a kirin?" I asked.

"It's popular with Jap tat fanatics. A mystical beast."

"Did she say who had her other half?" asked Nora.

"Nah. But it's big with lovers, newlyweds, prom dates, couples 'bout to be split up, like one's gotta serve time. I did one last week. Couple in their seventies. They drove up here from Fort Myers for their fiftieth wedding anniversary. I got the after picture somewhere."

Turning off the ink gun, he spun in his swivel chair to search the messy desk behind him, the black latex gloves making his every gesture faintly dramatic, like a cat burglar or mime. He found the photo, handed it to Nora, turning on the gun again, but bent over to inspect his client's face under the massage table.

"How you doin' down there, Mel?"

"I'm cool."

Mel didn't *look* cool. He was drooling on the floor.

Nora handed me the photograph. It featured two grinning retirees, their arms around each other, wearing matching yellow polo shirts and khaki Bermuda shorts. On the top of *her* right foot and *his* left was a tattoo of a red heart with wings. With their feet side by side, it was whole.

It was a bit schmaltzy for *my* taste, but Nora was enraptured.

"I tell all my clients who come in wanting a twofold," Tommy went on cheerfully, "be a thousand percent sure. Can't tell you how many times girls come in cryin' a month later, want the work redone 'cuz her true love ran off with her best friend. At first I thought that's what your friend wanted." He nodded at the photo of Ashley. "But she just wanted the picture."

"Did she say why?" I asked.

"Nah."

"And did she get it?" asked Nora.

"Uh-uh. She had the art done a while ago, 2004, when I was at my old location at the Chelsea Hotel. With the move, things got lost. I let her go through our files in the back. She stayed a coupla hours, lookin'. But she couldn't find it."

"We have a receipt stating that she bought something," I said, removing it from my coat pocket.

He didn't bother looking up.

"There was a young soldier in here on leave. Wanted a portrait of his wife over his heart. She was also a soldier and got killed in Afghanistan. He was a mess, but what he wanted was a *real job*. Didn't have the cash. We decided on just her name. But your friend took care of it. Didn't make a big deal."

Nora looked at me, astonished.

"Did she behave strangely?" I asked him.

"Apart from not talking much? Not really."

"Did she look unwell?"

"A little pale?"

"Do you know who did her tattoo back in 2004?"

"One a' my old employees. Larry. I could tell from the work."

"And where can we find Larry?"

Tommy chuckled. "Somewhere between heaven and hell."

He wiped the finished blossom with a tissue, closely inspecting it, and moved on to the next.

"One minute Larry was slingin' ink? Next minute he's passed out on my floor, blood shooting outta his nose like the Bellagio fountains in Vegas. Died in the ambulance. Aneurysm." He frowned, bending to survey his client. "Sure you're all right, Mel? You're a cadaver down there."

"I'm listening," said Mel.

Tommy frowned, tilting his head up at us and sighing.

"So, this is the *thing*. I go home the night after your friend came in. And I think back to what happened to Larry coupla weeks before he died. This is back, like, summer of '04. Now for you to understand what I'm about to tell you, you got to understand *Larry*. He was a *big* motherfucker. Bigger than a fridge, bigger than a Barcalounger, I swear on a stack of Bibles."

"Bigger than me?" asked Mel in a muffled voice from under the table.

"*Not* bigger than you. But close." Tommy resumed his work. "He was a helluva artist. Studied in Yokohama under a Horiyoshi. Guy could pound skin, *grind* with the best of 'em. He could do a mean *Tebori, Horimono, Irezumi,* you name it, which was how come I had him in the shop. Because he was an *asshole*. I'm not sayin' nothin' I wouldn't say to his face. He *embraced* his assholeness. Hated kids. Called 'em larvae. Had four girlfriends. None of them knew about each other. His whole life was like that. Buncha lies and dodges, un-returned calls and let-downs. So, one day I come in and the shop's quiet. All the lights are off and Larry's just sitting in the dark by himself like he felt sick or somethin'. I ask him what's the matter and he's all down and shit, tells me his life's crap. He's a coward, he tells me. He's a cheat. Says he's made so many mistakes. He says he's going to change his *priorities*. First time I ever heard him use a four-syllable word. So I humor him. Ask what the hell brought on his salvation. He said he'd just done a Japanese twofold for two teenagers. They'd just left the shop ten minutes before. He said they were in love and it was like an electric current. Like that lightning that comes out of the blue when there's not even a storm going on, just a crazy crack in the sky. With something like that right in front of you, you can't help but feel there's new possibilities out there. He started goin' on about life and love and promise." Tommy glanced up at us, grimacing. "Suddenly, he was Shakespeare. I'm not payin' attention. I'm pissed as hell 'cuz he did an illegal tattoo on two *kids*, which means I could get my license revoked. And anyways this is *Larry* we're talking about. He'll go back to being an asshole in a few days, *guaranteed*. A week later I come into the shop." Tommy shook his head, rubbing his chin. "And there's a *kid* in here. I don't allow kids in here, but there's a *kid* in here. She's real weird-lookin'. *Big.* Arms and legs so long they got tangled when she walked. Braces. Frizzy hair out to here." He gestured a foot off his head. "Freckles everywhere like something exploded on her. I ask who she belongs to. She's *Larry's*. Turns out she's the daughter he skipped out on a coupla years before when he was slingin' ink in Kentucky. He tells me he's gonna be a real dad now." Grinning, Tommy shook his head, returning to the tattoo. "A *real dad*. It was a coupla days before he croaked. Who knows if those two teenagers actually turned him around. I like to think they did. I like to think it was forever. Why *not*? Sometimes people *can* surprise the hell outta you. Sometimes they can tear your heart out and turn it to putty, can't they?"

He asked this so adamantly, his voice cracked. He fell silent for a moment, faltering, clearing his throat, and, bending over his work again, began to ink the last pink blossom.

"That night after your friend came in I went home, thought about it. I wondered if she was one a' those kids Larry talked about. One a' the runaways. 'Cause that's what he called them. They were goin' somewhere together. *Where,* I don't know. Probably Timbuktu."

Tommy stopped working and stared up at us, a surprisingly tender expression on his face.

"So, who was she?" he asked.

The Japanese kirin is believed to be the most powerful creature that has ever lived, mightier than dragons, the minotaur, the phoenix—and even man. While physically powerful, the kirin's true supremacy lies in its kindness, for it uses its strength only to defend the innocent. The kirin is a guardian and protector, the champion of all that is good. It is so kind that it doesn't hunt, but thrives on the wind and the rain, and when it walks it does so without disturbing the grass under its feet.

In the face of malevolence and deceit, however, the kirin unleashes a devastation that knows no bounds. It lights the sky on fire, creating the reddest of sunsets, and leaping into the air, emits a roar so deafening birds go hoarse, oceans freeze. The ground has been known to shake for a year.

They have the head of a dragon, the body of a deer, the scales of a fish, the legs of a horse, and the tail of a bull. They usually have antlers or a single horn. The kirin is often depicted with fire all over its body.

In repose, the kirin is quiet, allowing itself be seen only by the pure of heart. Those who have had a kirin sighting claim it is a lightning-quick creature, with a dragon's head and horse's body, often covered in the luminescent scales of a fish. By all accounts it is an incredible creature to behold, for in whatever spot on Earth it has just left, observers swear that the clouds are always parting, revealing golden sky and sun.

61 I HANDED THE PRINTED PAGE back to Nora. "Why would Ashley go back to Rising Dragon for the photo?" Nora asked. She was sitting on the couch, Septimus fluttering along the armrest.

"Maybe the photo had a *clue* in it," I said. "Something to help her track down this Spider."

"The Spider might have the missing half of the tattoo."

I leaned forward, scanning the timeline of Ashley's movements I'd typed on my laptop. "Devold broke Ashley out of Briarwood on September thirtieth. She turned up at Klavierhaus and played a Fazioli piano on October fourth. Rising Dragon Tattoos on the fifth. Two days later, on the seventh, she reappeared at Klavierhaus. According to the manager, Peter Schmid, she looked unkempt and behaved strangely. On the tenth, she mailed Hopper the package, visited the Four Seasons bar, and hours later fell or jumped or was pushed to her death that night. Somewhere within this eleven-day time frame she checked into 83 Henry Street and appeared at Oubliette and the Waldorf Towers."

And last but not least—*she went to the Reservoir.*

"It's almost as if she was visiting important places a final time," Nora said, "tying up loose ends, taking a last look around, just before she . . ." She was unable to finish the thought.

"Before she killed herself," I finished.

She nodded reluctantly.

"Or before someone she was hiding from—or chasing—caught up to her."

"Someone like the Spider," Nora said.

There had to be some hidden reason that would give perfect logic to Ashley's wanderings, a reason that *wasn't* a resolve to commit suicide. What had Peg Martin said about the family? *They mopped life up with themselves. None of them were encumbered by anything. There were no limits.* A desire to die at twenty-four wasn't in keeping with that or anything we learned about Ashley. *And if the Cordovas weren't afraid of what I might uncover, Theo Cordova wouldn't have been following me.*

I grabbed my phone, buzzing with an incoming email.

To: Scott B. McGrath

From: Stu
FW: Your Client
31 Oct 2011 13:59

McGrath:

This morning I received an interesting request.
See below.

Fondly,
Stu

P.S. Are you alive?

To: Stuart Laughton
From: Assistant
Subject: Your Client

Dear Mr. Laughton:

Mrs. Olivia Endicott du Pont would like to
speak with your client, the investigative
reporter Scott McGrath. Could you forward
this email to him so he might get in touch?

Ms. du Pont has a matter of the utmost
importance she would like to discuss with him.

Very truly yours,
Louise Burne

Personal Assistant to Mrs. Olivia E. du Pont
(212) 555-9290

I hadn't heard from my attorney, Stu Laughton, since I was ma-rooned at that charity cocktail party weeks ago. He'd sent me a text alerting me to the news of Ashley's death, asking me to call him.

I hadn't. Stu was a British aristocrat and inveterate gossip, and if I gave him the slightest hint that I might be returning to my investiga-tion of Cordova, everyone from here to McMurdo Station, Antarctica, would know.

I dialed his office.

His assistant answered. After putting me on hold, she informed me, "Mr. Laughton is in a meeting," which meant Stu was sitting at his desk eating an egg-salad sandwich, playing computer solitaire, and would call me back when he was in the mood.

To my surprise, it was just two minutes later.

62

"YOU TALKED," I said.

"Haven't said a word," insisted Stu on the other end.

"You must have mentioned my name in connection with Cordova at one of your power lunches, because nothing else explains this."

"You'll find it difficult to fathom, McGrath, but I have other clients and I don't *always* discuss you at every hour of every day, though I admit, it's terribly tricky to pull off, you're so *damn* captivating."

It was always a mental adjustment talking to Stu. As a posh Englishman, he was so well educated, with such an expansive vocabulary, his briefest conversations peppered with irony and wit and deep knowledge of current events—it was like communicating with Jeeves if he ever anchored the BBC.

"How do you explain it, then?" I asked.

"Damned if I know. *If,* by some miracle of God, Olivia Endicott wants you to ghostwrite her autobiography, take the job. To quote Captain Smith, 'Grab what you can and fight your way to a lifeboat.' Everyone associated with the slow printed word is fast becoming the Great Crested Newt of the culture. First it was the poets, the playwrights, then the novelists. Veteran newspapermen are next."

"Is that supposed to make me nervous?"

"Grab the work when it comes, my man. Your competition is now a fourteen-year-old in pajamas with the username Truth-ninja-12 who believes fact-checking a story is reading his subject's Twitter feed. Be afraid."

Assuring Stu I'd call Endicott, I hung up.

"A means to track down Marlowe Hughes just fell into our lap," I said to Nora, rearing back my desk chair. "The timing can't be a coincidence. Someone's been talking. Someone we've talked to or bribed."

Nora looked bewildered.

"Olivia Endicott du Pont wants to meet with me."

Nora frowned. "Who's Olivia Endicott du Pont?"

63

"THEY WERE SISTERS. They were actors. And they *loathed* each other."

This was how Beckman always began his favorite true Hollywood story—the Tale of the Warring Endicott Sisters—intoning that last sentence with such Old Testament severity, you could practically feel the sky turning gray, clouds turning inside out, and a black mist of locusts swarming the horizon.

I'd heard Beckman recount the story at least five times, always after three in the morning after a dinner party at his apartment with his students, when he was amped up on vodka and rapt attention, his black hair falling into his face glistening with sweat.

I was always game to hear the Endicott story for two reasons: One, feuding sisters fueled the imagination. As Beckman liked to say: "Marlowe and Olivia Endicott make Cain and Abel look like the Farrelly brothers."

Unlike the infamous feuds between Bette Davis and Joan Crawford, Liz Taylor and Debbie Reynolds, Olivia de Havilland and Joan Fontaine, Angie and Jennifer, the Endicott sisters' bad blood was kept entirely out of the press—apart from a few blind items in Bill Dakota's *Hollywood "Confidential" Star Magazine*—a dead silence that only emphasized its evident ferocity.

Second, for all of Beckman's flair for dramatics, his propensity to act out all of the parts as if he were on stage at the Nederlander, on each occasion, every detail remained *exactly the same,* without any new aspect or embellishment. The story was like a precious jeweled necklace; every time Beckman brought it out, each gleaming detail was cut and meticulously set in the exact same pattern it always had been.

I'd fact-checked it myself when I was first researching Cordova five years ago, and, by association, Marlowe Hughes. She was his leading lady and former wife of three months, star of Cordova's harrowing *Lovechild.* Every name, date, and location Beckman mentioned flawlessly corroborated with public record, so I'd come to believe that this tale of fighting sisters, however wild it sounded, must be true.

Born in April 1948, Olivia Endicott was Marlowe Hughes's older sister by just ten months.

Naturally, Marlowe Hughes wasn't *born* Marlowe Hughes. She was born Jean-Louise "J.L." Endicott on February 1, 1949, in Tokyo.

Most people enter the world looking like red, shriveled trolls. J.L. resembled an angel. When the nurses spanked her so she'd take her first breath, rather than squealing like a monkey, J.L. sighed, smiled, and fell asleep. From the moment she was brought home from the hospital, it was as if Olivia had become a piece of furniture.

"Olivia wasn't ugly," Beckman said. "Far from it. With dark hair, a sweet face, she was pretty. And yet from the time she was ten months old, she might as well have been chintz curtains when her sister was in the room."

They were army brats. Their mother was a nurse, their father a medical doctor at Iruma Air Base. In 1950, the family left Japan for Pasadena, California, though within a few months, their father, John, deserted the family, leaving them in deep debt and forcing their mother to take on work cleaning rooms at a motor hotel and washing dishes. Years later, Marlowe would hire a detective to find her father, learning he'd moved to Argentina with a male retired army colonel with whom he still lived.

Neither sister would speak of their father ever again.

The rivalry was there, even in grade school. Olivia cut up J.L.'s clothes and peed on J.L.'s toothbrush. For retaliation, J.L. would only have to *show up* anywhere Olivia *was*—at ballet school, at choir—in order to render her "a tiny tear in the wallpaper," as Beckman put it. Because J.L. could dance, too, *and* sing. And while Olivia was shy, uptight, and nervous in temperament, J.L. cracked dirty sailor jokes and laughed with her head back. She was a blond Ava Gardner: green eyes, faint cleft chin (as if God, wanting to sign *this* particular work, had proudly pressed his thumb in there), a face like a heart. The reaction was always the same, from the ballet teacher to the choir director to Olivia's own friends: *besotted.*

Olivia secretly referred to her sister as Jail Endicott, a verbal smearing of her initials.

They attended different middle and high schools—their mother's attempt to diffuse the tension—but any boy Olivia brought by the house was unfailingly smitten by J.L. Was she doing it on purpose? Were her looks her fault?

According to Beckman, it couldn't be helped.

"If you're given a free Aston Martin, you're going to take it for a wild ride to test how fast it goes. Naturally, as a teenager Marlowe overdid it. If Olivia had done something to *her,* like steal her math homework or put mayonnaise in her Pond's cold cream, J.L. would drape herself on the couch and watch *The Ford Television Theatre,* wearing shorts and a halter top right in front of Olivia's boyfriend. When Olivia suggested they move into another room, the poor delirious kid wouldn't even hear her."

Olivia resolved to keep friends away from the house, but to keep her sister out of sight was like trying to keep the sun down.

"So what could Olivia *do,* a mere mortal chained by way of genetics to a goddess?"

She ran away from home.

In 1964, at sixteen, Olivia moved to West Hollywood with two girl-friends from Miss Dina's Ballet School. Within three months, Olivia had an agent and a small walk-on role in the 1965 film *Beach Blanket Bingo.* She was hardworking, diligent, rehearsing more than anyone else. Olivia had finally found her voice and her calling, landing roles in television, including *Run for Your Life* and *Death Valley Days.*

"For the first time in her life, she felt she existed," Beckman said.

At that point, acting wasn't even on J.L.'s radar.

She'd discovered sex, having lost her virginity to a science teacher. But when Olivia was the focus of a short write-up in *Variety* called "Rising Stars," for the hell of it, J.L. cut school and went to an open call for the television series *Combat!* The casting director fell in love with her but knew she needed a better name than the thorny mouthful *J.L. Endicott.*

He happened to be reading Raymond Chandler's *The Big Sleep* at the time, featuring the famous detective Philip Marlowe. There was also a ten-cent Los Angeles scandal tabloid in front of him, *Confidential: Uncensored and Off the Record,* open to an article about Howard Hughes's rumored narcotic addiction.

He stitched together a name fit for a movie queen: *Marlowe Hughes.*

Marlowe received her big break in 1966 as Woman in *The Appaloosa,* starring Marlon Brando (having a brief affair with Brando himself), while Olivia languished in bad TV, appearing in bit parts on *The Andy Griffith Show* and *Hawk.* By 1969, Marlowe was a star, appearing in four films, her name emblazoned across billboards over Sunset Boulevard. Olivia retreated to New York to try the stage. In 1978, at Warren Beatty's bungalow party at the Beverly Hills Hotel, Marlowe was introduced to the dashing Michael Knight Winthrop du Pont, a Princeton-educated football player, war hero, one of the heirs to the Du Pont fortune, and the basis for Beatty's dashing millionaire character Leo Farnsworth in *Heaven Can Wait*. Everyone called him Knightly, due to his perfect looks and old-fashioned charm. Within three months, Marlowe and Knightly were engaged.

As Marlowe's life burned so bright one needed shades, Olivia's dimmed into nonexistence. Her only booked job was as an understudy in the 1972 Broadway production of *Ring Around the Bathtub,* which closed the very night it opened.

The sisters had allegedly not spoken in over thirteen years. But it seemed with one on the West Coast, the other on the East, at last there was enough space between them.

And then on October 25, 1979: a fateful accident.

While Marlowe was horseback riding with friends in Montecito, a lawnmower spooked her horse. It reared and bolted, leaping over a fence and onto Highway 101, throwing Marlowe from the saddle. Miraculously, she sustained only multiple fractures to her left leg, though it was so severe doctors ordered her to stay at Cedars-Sinai hospital in traction for two months.

Every afternoon, Knightly came to her bedside to read to her. When the months were finished, doctors decided she needed another few weeks. Knightly continued his visits—until one day he was late and the next day, later, and on the third day, he didn't show up at all. After a ten-day absence, during which Marlowe heard *nothing* from him, he finally appeared at the hospital.

He announced their engagement was off. Apologizing, sobbing out of his own sadness and guilt, he presented Marlowe Hughes with a black pearl ring, the platinum band inscribed with four words: *Fly on, beautiful child.*

Marlowe was devastated. Nurses claimed she tried to throw herself out of the window in her room. Four weeks later, two days after she was released from the hospital, *The New York Times* made the stunning announcement: "Du Pont Heir 'Knightly' Marries Olivia Endicott, Actress."

It was a private ceremony at the family's estate in the Hudson River Valley.

No one, not even Beckman, had any idea how Olivia had pulled it off—where she'd met Knightly or how she'd transferred his affection for Marlowe, one of the most beautiful women in the world, onto *her,* an ordinary woman. Some suggested it was hypnosis, even a deal with the devil, starting with the fateful horseback-riding accident.

Or was it simply an unfortunate coincidence?

Marlowe never spoke publicly of the incident, though years later, when she was asked about her sister in an interview, she said: "I wouldn't piss on Olivia if she were on fire."

She did *fly on*—or at least *tried to.* Marlowe married three times: to a set designer in 1981, to Cordova in 1985—their union lasting just three months, though he was able to extract a stunning performance from her in *Lovechild.* She married a veterinarian in 1994; they divorced just four years later. She had no children. In her forties, Ms. Hughes found herself sliding down that character arc of so many movie goddesses before her: She became mortal. She aged. Roles stopped coming. There was plastic surgery, whispers of a painkiller addiction, and after an embarrassing appearance in *Superman IV: The Quest for Peace,* in which her makeup looked like it'd been applied with crayons, a quick cane-tug exit from the public stage.

Olivia remained married to Knightly. They had three sons. For the past twenty-seven years, she sat on the board of the Metropolitan Museum of Art, the most socially exalted position in the city, and still does.

"Marlowe got the fame, Olivia the prince," Beckman would intone in a low voice, his eyes sparking in the firelight. "But who *won* at *life?*"

The consensus was Olivia.

"Perhaps," Beckman would say. "But who knows what jealousies have eaten away her insides like acid on old pipes?"

There was one final detail. It concerned Cordova.

Even after she was married to Knightly, Olivia Endicott continued to work here and there on Broadway throughout the eighties, though she gave up the stage in order to fulfill her role as a mother, wife, and philanthropist.

Yet she remained a rabid Cordova fan.

According to Beckman, Olivia wrote the director letter after letter, hounding him with mad persistence. She begged to work with him, audition for him, take even a silent walk-on role. At the very least, she hoped to *meet* him. Cordova appeared to be the last thing she required—the final pie piece—to wholly vanquish her sister.

"And to Olivia's every letter, Cordova responded with the same type-written sentence," Beckman said.

At this point in the story, Beckman stood up, steadying himself on his Persian ottoman. Then he'd shuffle over to the dark, dank corner of his living room, where he'd brutally jerk open a desk drawer stuffed with papers, receipts, Broadway *Playbills*, rooting around the contents. A minute later, when he staggered back to the gathering, he'd be holding a pristine cream-colored envelope in his hands.

Slowly, he'd present it to the nearest student, who would nervously open it, pulling out a letter, silently reading it before blinking in awe and passing it to the kid next to him.

Beckman claimed he'd found the copy randomly at an estate sale.

November 11, 1988
My dear du Pont:

If all of the people on Earth were dead but you, you would still not appear in my picture.

Cordova

64 RELAYING THE TALE to Nora, I was nowhere near as theatrical in the telling as Beckman.

" 'Fly on, beautiful child'?" she repeated. "That's the saddest goodbye in the world. Do you think it's all true?"

"I do."

"Call Olivia. *Immediately.*"

I dialed the number.

"Of course, Mr. McGrath," said the secretary on the other end. "Are you available tomorrow? Ms. du Pont is off to Saint Moritz the following day. She was hoping you'd forgive her for the late notice and squeeze her into your busy schedule, as she won't be back for four months."

I agreed to meet Olivia at her apartment at noon the following day. The address was about as close to an American Buckingham Palace as you could get: 740 Park Avenue. It'd been the childhood home of Jackie Kennedy and countless other legendary heirs and heiresses, and was pure old rich New York: staunch, graying at the temples, secretive, and snooty as hell.

As I hung up, I realized that my cellphone was buzzing.

I didn't recognize the number, *Golden Way Market, Inc.*

"Who is it?" asked Nora.

"I suspect it's the first person calling about Ashley's missing-person flier."

65 GOLDEN WAY WAS A CHINESE GROCERY that ignored the English language so aggressively, standing in one of the narrow aisles, pungent with smells of fish and sesame, I could convince myself I was in China's Chongqing province.

There were shriveled whole chickens strung up by their talons, trillions of noodles, black teas, and lethal-looking produce—red chilies that'd numb your tongue for a year; greens so spiky, they looked like they'd slit your throat as you swallowed them. Outside, the store looked like an underworld heavy lurking on the sidewalk—a dirty red awning pulled low over its cruddy windows and stands of bruised fruit.

I headed after Nora, who'd disappeared in the back, finding her alone in front of a table piled with what appeared to be packets of potato chips, until I read the label: ROAST DRIED SQUID SHAVINGS.

She shrugged, puzzled. "I just spoke to a man, but he disappeared through there." She pointed at a set of steel doors beside a few fish tanks, gray fish drifting inside.

When I'd answered the call, a man who barely spoke English announced he had *informations*, though he was unable to explain what exactly it was. Finally, a woman came on the line to bark an address: 11 *Market Street*. The address was near East Broadway, only a block and a half from 83 Henry, so it was certainly feasible Ashley had come in.

At this moment, a slight middle-aged Chinese man emerged, followed by what had to be his entire extended family: his wife, his daughter of about eight, and a grandmother who looked to date back to the days of Mao Zedong.

Hell—maybe it *was* Mao. She had his long forehead, his tired face and gray workman's pants, the flip-flops on her bare feet, which resembled two dry chipped bricks that'd fallen off the Great Wall.

The family all smiled eagerly at us and set about getting a stool for the old woman, helping her sit. The wife then handed her a piece of crumpled paper, which I recognized as the missing-person flier.

"We have information," the little girl announced in perfect English.

"About the girl on the poster?" I clarified.

"Did you meet her?" Nora asked.

"Yes," said the little girl. "She came here."

"What was she wearing?" I asked.

The family conferred heatedly in Cantonese.

"A bright orange coat."

That was close enough.

"And what did she do when she was here?" I asked.

"She talked with my grandmother." The little girl indicated Mao, who was carefully inspecting the flier as if it were a speech she was about to present in class.

"In English?"

The little girl giggled as if I'd made a joke. "My grandmother doesn't speak English."

"She spoke to her in *Chinese?*"

The girl nodded. *Ashley spoke Chinese.* That was unexpected.

"What did they talk about?" I asked.

For the next few minutes, there was so much wild Cantonese flying back and forth Nora and I could do nothing but watch. Finally, the entire family hushed quickly because Mao had at last spoken, her parched voice scarcely audible.

"She asked my grandmother where she was born," explained the girl. "If she missed her home. She bought chewing gum. And then she talked to a taxi driver who comes in here for dinner. He said he'd take her where she wanted to go. My grandmother liked her very much. But your friend was very tired."

"Tired in what way?" I asked.

The girl conferred with Grandmother Mao. "She was sleepy," she answered.

"This taxi driver, do you know who he is?"

She nodded. "He comes in here to eat dinner."

"What time?"

This resulted in more debate, during which the girl's mother did most of the talking.

"Nine o'clock."

"Will he come tonight?" asked Nora.

"Sometimes he comes. Sometimes he doesn't."

I checked my watch. It was eight.

"Might as well wait," I said to Nora. "See if he shows."

I explained this to the girl, who relayed it to her family. I thanked them, and, smiling, the whole family came forward to shake our hands, moving aside so we could shake Mao's hand, too.

Removing my wallet, I thanked the father and tried to give him a hundred dollars, but he refused to take it. This back-and-forth went on for a good ten minutes, though I noticed *his wife's* eyes were *glued* to the money. I *had* to get the guy to take it; if I *didn't,* judging from the look on his wife's face, he wouldn't survive the night.

He finally relented and I turned back to Grandmother Mao with the intention of asking her a few more questions. Yet the old woman had silently moved off the stool, disappearing through the doors and into the back of the store.

66 | "Fuck, man," said the taxi driver, "you scared the shit outta me. I thought you were here to deport me." He cackled with laughter, revealing a set of blinding white teeth, a few capped in gold. He scratched his red-and-yellow Rasta cap as he studied Ashley's picture.

"Yah, sure. I did pick her up here."

"When?" I asked.

"Coupla weeks ago?"

"What color coat was she wearing?" interjected Nora.

He thought it over, rubbing the gray stubble on his chin.

"Greenish brown? But I'm color-blind, man."

He called himself Zeb. He was black—from Jamaica, I guessed from his slight accent—6'6", lean yet disheveled and slouched, like a palm tree after a mild hurricane.

During the past hour, as Nora and I waited, we'd managed to stitch together some basic information. He came to Golden Way five nights a week for dinner. He ate outside, leaning against the hood of his cab, playing loud music with the windows unrolled, and then took off, doubtlessly resuming his all-night driving shift, which ended at 7:00 A.M.

"When I got here," Zeb went on, scratching his head, "she was in da back talkin' to da old lady. I got my dinner. She followed me outside."

"And you drove her somewhere?"

"Yah."

"Do you remember where?"

He thought it over. "Some big-ass house on the Upper East."

"Could you take us there now?"

"Oh, no." He held up a hand. "Da stops and starts all bleed together when you drive."

"We'll pay you," blurted Nora.

He perked up. "You'll pay da meter?"

Nora nodded.

"Okay. Sure. We can do that."

Grinning, as if he couldn't believe his luck, Zeb cheerfully grabbed a foam container and began to load it with noodles, egg rolls, sesame chicken—if it *was* chicken; the gray meat looked like the *siopao* or *cat in a steamed bun* I'd once eaten by accident in Hong Kong. *Astonishing how quickly money jogged a man's memory.*

Nora and I headed outside to wait.

"This is going to be *expensive*," I muttered, squinting farther down Market Street, where a lone man was shuffling toward us. Instantly I recognized the gray wool coat and the cigarette.

"Look who decided to make an appearance."

Nora, unabashedly worried, grilled him on why he'd stood us up this morning. "We waited for you. I almost called the police."

"I had things to do," Hopper said unconvincingly.

He looked like he'd been up all night. I was beginning to realize the key to his behavior could be found in his own description of Morgan Devold: *He's coming back. He has to. He's dying to talk about her.*

Nora eagerly filled him in on the latest. In no time, the three of us were tearing up Park Avenue crammed into the backseat of a taxi with a steering wheel covered in blue shag and a rearview mirror wearing more gold chains than Mr. T. I leaned forward to study Zeb's picture ID—his full name was Zebulaniah Akpunku—noticing a worn-out paperback, *Steppin' Into the Good Life,* on the passenger seat beside him.

"Did you notice anything unusual about the girl?" I asked Zeb through the bulletproof window.

He shrugged. "She was a white girl. They all kinda look alike." He guffawed happily, quieting only to take a bite of his food.

"Did she talk to you? Anything you can tell us about her?"

"No way, man. I got one rule as a driver."

"What's that?"

"Never look in da rearview mirror."

"Never?" We drifted into the left-hand lane, cutting off a cab.

"It's not healthy to keep a' watchin' what you leavin' behind."

Ten minutes later, we were weaving our way up and down every street in the East Sixties between Madison and Lexington. The meter ticked from twenty dollars to thirty, *forty.*

"Oh, yeah, *dis* is right," Zeb would say, leaning forward to scrutinize the quiet rows of townhouses until he'd reach the end of the block. "*Shit.* I got it wrong." He'd sigh in apparent frustration, then cheerfully help himself to more sesame chicken. "No worries, man. It's da next block."

But the same thing happened on the next block. *And the next.*

After another fifteen minutes, the meter was $60.25. Nora was gnawing her fingernails, and Hopper hadn't said a word the entire ride, slumped against the seat, staring out the window.

I was about to call it off when, as we were cruising down East Seventy-first, Zeb abruptly slammed on the brakes.

"Dat's it!" He was indicating a building on our left.

It sat entirely in the dark, a massive townhouse that looked more like an embassy than a residence—pale gray limestone, twenty-five feet wide. It was weathered and run-down, dead leaves strewn across the front steps, the double doors littered with takeout menus—a sure indication no one had been there for weeks.

"We already drove down here," I said.

"I'm telling you. Dat's the *house.*"

"All right." I opened the door, and we climbed out. I handed Zeb eighty bucks.

"Peace out, brother."

Zeb happily tucked the money into his shirt pocket, alongside what looked to be a gigantic half-smoked joint. He turned up the Rolling Stones, and though there was a yellow light at the intersection—yellow lights to Zeb were cues to *floor it and pray*—he barreled out into Park Avenue in a noisy clanging of loose parts and stuttering transmission, the trunk thudding as he blasted over a pothole and swerved south, leaving us on the quiet street.

67 | WE CROSSED THE STREET to get a better view. It was dim on that side, with just a streetlamp and a high-rise apartment building, its entrance around the corner on Park, so it afforded some privacy to watch the townhouse.

It was after eleven o'clock, the neighborhood deserted. New York might be the city that never slept, but the well-heeled residents of the Upper East Side got tucked into their bespoke sheets around ten.

"Doesn't look like anyone's lived there for years," I noted.

I noticed Hopper was staring intently at the place, the expression on his face unreadable, though I sensed a sort of deep-seated hostility, as if within its hulking grandeur he saw something he detested.

It *was* unapologetic in its opulence, five stories, a garden on the roof—tree branches could be seen reaching over the top cornice. Every window was dark, a few adorned with heavy curtains, the panes dirty. A narrow covered balcony extended outside the windows on the second floor, detailed with an oxidized copper roof, black iron latticework along the sides and railing. And yet in spite of its lavishness, or because of it, the townhouse had a cold, lonely demeanor.

"Are we going to knock?" whispered Nora.

"You two stay here," I said.

I headed across the street and skipped up the marble steps strewn with leaves and bits of trash, a deli napkin, a cigarette butt. I rang the bell, noting the black bubble of a security camera above the intercom. I heard it ring inside—a strident clanging straight out of nineteenth-century England—but there was no response.

I pulled out the papers wedged through the mail slot, a Burger Heaven menu and two ads for a twenty-four-hour locksmith. They were faded, warped from the rain. *They'd been there for months.*

"Some loaded European probably owns it," I said, moving back to Hopper and Nora. "He uses it two days a year."

"Only one way to find out," said Hopper. He took a last drag of his cigarette, chucked it to the ground, and, pulling up the collar of his coat, crossed the street.

"What's he *doing?*" whispered Nora.

Hopper stepped right up to the townhouse, grabbed the black iron grating over the arched window on the ground floor, and began *to climb.* Within seconds, Hopper was twelve feet off the ground. He paused for a minute, looking down, then stepped on top of one of the old lanterns flanking the front doors and, straddling about five feet of space, grabbed ahold of the concrete ledge of the second-floor balcony.

He hoisted himself higher, *dangling* there for a few seconds, his gray coat floating around him like a cape. He hooked his right leg over the railing and fell sideways onto the balcony. Immediately, he scrambled to his feet and, with another furtive glance down at the sidewalk, crept along the narrow veranda to the window on the farthest right. Crouching, he shielded his eyes to look through the glass, then fumbled inside his coat for what appeared to be his wallet. He cracked the casement, probably using a credit card, *slid the window open,* and without the slightest hesitation, he *crawled inside.*

There was a moment of stillness. He reappeared as a silhouette, slid the window closed, and disappeared.

I was stunned, expecting at any moment now a maid's bloodcurdling scream or sirens. But the street remained silent.

"What the *hell?*" whispered Nora, clamping a hand over her chest. "What do we *do?*"

"Nothing. We wait."

As it turned out, we didn't have to wait long.

Hopper had been inside not ten minutes when a lone taxi coasted

down the street toward us, slowing and stopping directly in front of the townhouse.

"Oh, no," whispered Nora.

The backseat door opened and a heavyset woman emerged.

"Text Hopper," I said. "Tell him to get the hell out of there."

As Nora fumbled for her phone, I slipped between the parked cars, aiming for the woman who was moving up the townhouse steps, digging through her purse, trying to find her keys.

68

"Excuse me?"

She didn't turn. She jammed the key in the lock, pushing open one of the doors.

"Ma'am, I'm looking for the nearest subway."

She darted inside, switching on a light. I caught a fleeting glimpse of a white entryway, a black-and-white checked floor, and as she whisked around, *the woman herself*, before she slammed the door hard.

A deadbolt clicked, followed by the seven-digit beep of an alarm.

I froze in shock. *I knew her.*

Suddenly, the lamps over the entrance switched on, bathing me in bright light. *She wanted a good look at me in the security camera.*

I moved up the steps and rang the doorbell.

There was no response.

I rang it a second time, then a third. *Not* that I expected her to open the door—it was to alert Hopper. It would signal to him to get the hell out. I jogged swiftly down the steps, heading toward Park. At the corner, I crossed north, finding Nora where I'd left her.

"He's *still inside*," she whispered. "I texted him but haven't heard back—"

"You're not going to believe this. That was *Inez Gallo*. Cordova's assistant for years. The Cordovas must own this place."

It was *stupefying*—not just that Hopper had broken *in*, but he was now *trapped inside* a personal residence of Cordova's.

Nora, amazed, turned back to the townhouse, where a bright light had just illuminated the second floor, revealing a dark, wood-paneled library, the shelves lined with books.

"Now he has no way out," Nora whispered. "Should we call nine-one-one?"

"Not yet."

"But we have to do something. She might *shoot* him—"

"We need to give him time to look around."

"How long?"

Distant wails of sirens answered her question. They grew louder, and suddenly three police cars came barreling down the street, screeching to a halt in front of the townhouse. Four policemen jumped out, hastening up the steps, Gallo opening the door, and they disappeared inside. Two cops remained on the front steps, staring suspiciously down the street.

"Time to get the hell out of here," I said.

"But we have to make sure he's okay—"

"We'll be more help to him *out* of jail."

But suddenly there were loud voices, and the cops reemerged, leading Hopper down the steps.

He was handcuffed, and his gray coat had been confiscated, but otherwise, in his faded blue T-shirt and jeans, he looked rather undaunted by the proceedings. His eyes purposefully *avoided* our direction, though I swore I caught a faint smile on his face as they shoved his head down and pushed him roughly into the backseat.

69 | At home, I called an old friend, a criminal defense attorney named Leonard Blumenstein. I'd never needed him—*not yet, anyway*—but he'd pulled plenty of people I knew out of rocks and hard places. Apparently, you could call Blumenstein a couple of hours after killing your wife and, in a voice silkier than an Hermès scarf, he'd assure you it was all going to be fine. Then he'd give you a directive, as if the issue were simply that you'd lost your passport.

I left a message with his answering service: Someone assisting me with some research had gotten *carried away* and broken into a private residence—though he'd been unarmed and stole nothing—and was now in police custody.

The woman assured me she'd have Blumenstein call me back.

Nora and I then moved into my office to research Inez Gallo.

"What do we know about her?" asked Nora, curling up on the couch beside the box of research.

"Not much," I said. "She was supposedly Cordova's longtime assistant."

After digging through the papers, I pulled out Inez Gallo's wedding photo. The picture always turned up whenever her name appeared in the press. In it, she looked like every other beaming newlywed, which only made it tragic. Years later, she'd abandon this very husband and her two children to go work alongside Cordova.

"We also found that page on the Blackboards," noted Nora. "The one that contends she and Cordova are the same person. They both have a tiny wheel tattoo on their left hands. Are you *sure* it was a woman?"

"Positive."

We dug around YouTube and found the grainy film clip of Gallo's infamous acceptance speech on behalf of Cordova at the 1980 Oscars.

It began with co-presenters Goldie Hawn and Steven Spielberg announcing, "And the Oscar goes to . . . Stanislas Cordova, for *Thumbscrew*."

The audience gasped because it was a startling upset. Best Director was believed to be a shoo-in for Robert Benton, the director of *Kramer vs. Kramer*. In fact, Benton was so convinced he was going to win, he actually got out of his seat, making his way to the stage before his wife jumped up and physically restrained him. There was a long, confused pause during which the audience, disconcerted, was whispering, looking around, wondering if it was a mistake, if Cordova had *actually showed*.

Then the cameras focused on Inez Gallo, who was quickly making her way down the narrow side aisle of the Dorothy Chandler Pavilion. They had her sitting in the back, away from the real stars, Jack Lemmon, Bo Derek, Sally Field, and Dudley Moore.

Gallo was black-haired and heavyset, with strong, brawny features— undeniably similar to Cordova's in his early photographs—dressed in a black T-shirt and combat boots. Later, people in the audience would profess to thinking she was crashing the event like the 1974 streaker, Robert Opel, who jogged across the stage naked when David Niven was about to introduce Elizabeth Taylor—or when Marlon Brando, at the 1973 ceremony, sent Sacheen Littlefeather to turn down his Best Actor award for *The Godfather* on behalf of exploited Native Americans. Awkwardly, Inez Gallo took the Oscar from Spielberg and said into the mike, two feet too tall for her: "This is a summons to those watching to break out of your locked room, real or imagined."

She then ran offstage, and the network cut to a commercial.

We watched the speech a few times, then logged on to the Blackboards. Most of the discussion of Inez Gallo concerned rumors about the exact nature of her relationship to Cordova, that she was his sister, his puppeteer and Svengali, his female doppelgänger, an obsessive caretaker and enabler who catered to Cordova's every need and desire, a custodian who cleaned up his every mess.

Combing through one rumor after the next, Nora's eyes were closing, so she headed to bed, though I stayed up a few more hours reading.

Maybe it was simply my shock at encountering her, but there had been something unaccountably bizarre about Gallo's wide chiseled face, the hard features, the embittered voice.

Maybe the key to all of this was exactly what Cleo had said at Enchantments: *Dark magic passed from generation to generation.*

I searched on the Blackboards for mention of it, *witchcraft* and *Inez Gallo,* or another reference to the wheel tattoo that both she and Cordova supposedly had on their left hands, but other than a brief mention of her being from Puebla, Mexico, and her selfless devotion to the director being the stuff of legend ("There's nothing Gallo won't do to protect him," claimed one poster)—there was nothing else there.

70 "WOODWARD?"

I cracked open an eye. The clock read 4:21 A.M.

"Are you asleep?"

"Yes."

"Can you talk?"

"Sure."

Nora opened the door, slipping through the darkness. She was again wearing that ghostly nightgown, a pale blur perched on the end of my bed.

"What's the matter?" I asked, propping myself up on the pillows.

She said nothing. She seemed nervous. She had a way of being quite talkative, then suddenly growing silent and still, so you studied her face like some hard blue desert sky, waiting for some sign of life, however distant, a hawk, an insect.

"You're going to have to give me more to go on," I said, after a moment. "I'm a *guy*. I'm illiterate when it comes to reading between lines."

"Well . . ." She sighed, as if it were the *end* of the conversation rather than the beginning. This meant, because she was a *woman,* she'd probably already had this discussion umpteen times in her head.

"Is it about Hopper?" I asked. "Are you worried about him spending the night in jail? Because he'll be fine."

The bed jerked.

"Did you nod? It's too dark to see in here."

"It's *nothing* to do with him. It's something I said that I feel bad about."

"What?"

"That I wouldn't sleep with you."

"No need to clarify it. It goes unsaid. And it's nothing I haven't heard before." I did *not know* where Bernstein was going with this, but I had a bad feeling. It was crucial to get the girl *out* of my room, back to her own bed, *stat.* Adding *sex* to *investigative reporting* was as inspired an idea as Ford unveiling *the Pinto*—what was meant to be fun, sexy, and practical was actually a nightmare, causing great personal injury on all sides.

"You're *handsome,*" Nora said. "If you were at Terra Hermosa, the ladies would *die.*"

"Isn't that what they do anyway?"

"I didn't want any professional lines to be crossed."

"You were *right.* I can't tell you how many women I've crossed *all kinds* of lines with and afterward felt terrible."

"*Really?*"

"Like I'd just been given a prognosis of a few weeks left to live."

She giggled.

"Started my very first time when I was fifteen. Lorna Doonberry.

Talk about *lines;* she played bridge with my mother. I got carried away. She fell into a shower curtain. You know that little soap holder in bathtubs?"

"Sure."

"Her face hit it. She lost two teeth. Blood everywhere. Lorna went from a perfectly attractive fortysomething divorcée to a lead character in *Night of the Living Dead.*"

"*My* first time was Tim Bailey."

I waited for more information. None came.

"Don't tell me he was a resident at Terra Hermosa."

"Oh, *no.* He worked at Premier Pool Services. He cleaned the pool every Friday."

"How old was he?"

"Twenty-nine."

"How old were *you*?"

"Sixteen. But an *old* sixteen. He had a wife and two kids. I felt awful about it. It's a terrible thing, to lie. It's a field you keep seeding and watering and plowing, but nothing will ever grow on it." She wrapped her arms around her knees, fidgeting her shoulders. "I tried to end it a couple times, but Tim and I would go out behind the kitchen when everyone was at Wine and Cheese, and he'd dance with me to the country music coming through the kitchen window. He was a *good dancer.* But he was sad. He dreamed of just taking off and starting over, pretending his life never happened in the first place."

"Did he?"

"Don't know. Can I tell you something?"

"Of course."

"You won't make a big deal out of it?"

"I promise."

"When I first got to New York at Port Authority it was three in the morning. Septimus got stolen."

She paused, clasping her hands between her knees.

"One of the people on the bus did it. I knew who it was. He got on at Daytona Beach, and he sat behind me and Septimus the whole way. He smelled like alcohol, and he tried hard to make conversation during the ride, but I just put on my headphones and pretended to be asleep. Something was wrong with him. Mentally, you know? But when we got to Port Authority I let my guard down when we were all getting off. This lady needed help getting one of her kids into a stroller. I helped her, then went to the underneath part to get my bag, and when I went back to the curb Septimus wasn't there. His cage was gone. I went crazy. I told the driver, and he told me to report it to the main office, but all I could think was that I was going to die. I was going to die without Septimus. I couldn't *think*. By then all the other passengers had left. I exited the lot into the part where all the shops are and it was quiet. The next thing I knew, that same man was walking behind me. He whispered he had my bird. He said he wanted to give him back. All I had to do was give him a blowjob in the bathroom."

I stared at her. I felt as if the wind had been kicked out of me, so sudden was this confession. I was careful not to do anything at all, not even to move.

"I said I didn't believe him, so he brought me behind a Villa Pizza and into the women's bathroom. Septimus's cage was there on the floor, but it was empty. And then I saw that the man had stuck him in one of those silver containers in the stalls. You know, where you throw stuff away? He was fluttering around in there, going crazy. Because he *hates* the dark. Always has. You're supposed to put a sheet over the cage to calm a bird, but Septimus doesn't like it. He *has* to *see*. The man said all I had to do was *that* and he'd let him go. I got into the stall with him. There was actually a lady getting dressed in the back, but she didn't say anything when I called out to her. He unzipped his pants and leaned back with his fist clamped hard on the lid of the silver thing. So I did it. I thought of trying to get Septimus out, biting the man, but there wasn't the chance. When I stopped, the man punched me in the face. He kept calling me Nancy over and over. Nancy. Nancy. When it was done, he smiled and took out Septimus, holding him really tight in his fist, squeezing him like toothpaste. I screamed and screamed, and when I couldn't take it anymore he laughed and threw him out of the stall. I didn't know where he was at first. But then I found him on the floor under the radiator. I got his cage and my bag, and I ran as fast as I could. The place was deserted with closed-up shops, only a few people staring at nothing like a bunch of ghosts. I took the escalator up to the street. I went over to the taxi stand, climbed in, and I asked the driver to take me to the center of everything. Madonna did it, when she first came to New York. She asked the cabdriver to take her to the center of everything."

She looked over at me as if asking a question.

"He didn't know where that was. I said Times Square. He took me right there. There were people everywhere, lights like it was the middle of the afternoon. And I knew I was going to be fine. Because I was right where I was supposed to be. I'd spent my whole life feeling like I was waiting to be someplace else. For the first time, I *didn't*." Nora turned to me, her hands clasped over her knees. "I never told anybody."

"I'm glad you told me," I said.

It took a moment to hear it all; the story seemed like a toxic vapor wafting through the room that needed time to dissolve. I felt at once sick to my stomach and an overwhelming need to make sure she was all right, to extract the memory of such a thing from her head. It was never the act itself but our own understanding of it that defeated us, over and over again.

"You didn't want to go to the police?"

She shook her head. "I didn't want to waste another minute on it. My life was meant to *begin*. The bad things that happen to you don't have to mean anything at all. And anyway, he'll answer to God for what he did."

She announced this with great certainty. For a girl with nothing to her name but a parakeet, to have such unwavering belief in the reckoning of evil in the world—a belief I could never bring myself to have, having seen, time and time again, depravity go unchecked—it awed me, and it was some time before I could bring myself to speak.

Outside, a car cruised down Perry Street, and the night's stillness made it sound drowsy and relaxed; it might have been a rowboat wafting by.

"You are a magnificent and powerful person," I said.

I hadn't intended to say that, *exactly*—it'd never been my strong suit, whipping out the right words to mend that ever-present wound in a woman's heart—but it made Nora smile. She slipped toward me, mattress creaking, kissed me on the cheek, and hopped off the bed, a blurred blueish figure floating through the dark.

"I'm a *fan*," I added. "And that's an unconditional lifetime warranty. I'm like Victorinox luggage and Darn Tough socks."

She laughed sleepily, slipping out of the room. "Night, Woodward," she whispered over her shoulder. "Thanks for listening."

I don't know how long I sat there, staring into the darkness, the hardened shadows thawing as the minutes passed, the only sounds night-shivers of the city outside. After a while, when I was half asleep, her presence lingered as if some wild creature had been inside my room, a fawn or iridescent bird, or maybe a *kirin*.

71 "HE WAS HELD OVERNIGHT in the Tombs," Blumenstein informed me over the phone. "I sent a junior associate downtown to get him out. They dropped burglary in the second degree, but he's facing criminal trespass. Bail will be around five thousand dollars."

"Why so high?" I asked, wedging the phone against my ear as I pulled my coat out of the closet and pulled it on.

"He has three priors. Assault of a police officer in Buford, Georgia. Petty theft in Fritz Creek, Alaska."

"Alaska?"

"And two years ago. Possession of a controlled substance for the intent of sale. This was in Los Angeles."

"What was the substance?"

"Marijuana and MDMA. He served two months, did a hundred hours community service."

I told Blumenstein I'd cover the bail, then, hanging up, quickly relayed the conversation to Nora as we prepared to leave for the meeting with Olivia Endicott. I'd made Nora an omelet this morning, but as soon as she saw it, she announced she wasn't hungry, her face red. I chalked this up to that bizarre black box of feminine behavior that defied explanation, until I realized—cursing my *stupidity*—it was because of what she'd told me last night. She didn't want me to treat her with kid gloves, didn't want to be handled like some fragile thing with a crack through it. So I brutally chucked out the omelet and announced that Moe Gulazar's black sequin leggings and *Captain Sparrow blouse* didn't suit a meeting with one of New York's most elegant swans. I ordered her to change her clothes, which made her smile with relief as she raced upstairs to do so. Within minutes, we were out the door, hurrying down Perry Street.

It was a gray day, the sky threatening rain. We headed for the subway because we were already late. And if there was one thing I knew about New York's wealthiest, they loved to keep *you* waiting, not the other way around.

72

"MR. MCGRATH. *WELCOME.*"

The woman who greeted us at the door of apartment 17D was in her fifties, dressed in a dust-gray suit. She had the dimmed-bulb face of someone who'd lived a life in servitude. Her eyes moved inquiringly to Nora.

"This is my assistant. I hope it's all right if she joins us."

"Certainly."

Smiling, the woman ushered us into the foyer, where an old codger wearing a rumpled burgundy jacket appeared—seemingly from the walls—to take our coats. Wordlessly he drifted with them back down another dim hall.

"Right this way."

She led us in the other direction down a dark gallery. The wine-colored walls were plastered with paintings, the way scaffolding downtown was covered with ads for concerts: only these happened to be Matisses and Schieles, Clementes, the odd Magritte, each painting sporting its own bronze lamp like a miner's helmet. Between these masterpieces were dark open doorways, and I slowed to glance inside. Every room looked like a grotto, dank and stalactited with brocade curtains and Louis XIV chairs, vases and Tiffany lamps, busts in marble, ebony sculpture, books. We passed a formal dining room, the walls celery green, a crystal chandelier like a frozen jellyfish floating midair.

The woman led us briskly into a large sitting room. The windows framed a northwestern view, turning the city into a serene concrete still life with gray sky. A helicopter hovered over the Hudson like an errant fly.

The woman gestured for us to sit on the yellow chintz couch in front of a coffee table covered in miniatures: porcelain schnauzers, sheepherders, finger bowls. Fresh yellow and red tulips exploded out of a Chinese vase. They matched the yellow walls and the red jackets of the riders in the giant foxhunt oil painting looming behind us.

Nora sat down stiffly beside me, folding her hands in her lap. She looked nervous.

"May I offer you some tea while you wait? Mrs. du Pont is finishing up a telephone call."

"Tea would be nice," I said. "Thank you."

The woman slipped out of the room.

"This is what you call *jumbo rich*," I whispered to Nora. "These people are their own strange breed. Don't try to understand them."

"Did you see the shining armor on the way in? Real shining armor just *standing* there, waiting for a knight."

"The two percent of the world's richest people have over half of the world's wealth. *I* think it's all in this apartment."

Nora, biting her lip, pointed at the small end table on my right, where there was a black-and-white photograph in an antique silver frame. It was Olivia standing with her husband, Knightly, probably some twenty years ago. They had their arms around each other, posing beside an antique Bentley in front of a colossal country manor. They looked happy, but, of course, that didn't say much. *Everyone smiles for a photograph.*

Abruptly, Nora sat up.

A woman was entering the room. I stood up immediately, Nora following my lead, fidgeting to straighten her skirt.

It was Olivia.

She didn't walk so much as *float,* three Pekingese dogs shuffling alongside her feet. The room had obviously been designed with her in mind, or vice versa. Her chin-length brown hair, streaked with silver— worn in a rich candy swirl around her face—matched the Persian rug, the carved lion-paw legs of the table, even the silver cigarette case with the elegant initials engraved on the lid—OPE—the fine lettering like tangled strands of hair clogging a shower drain.

I wasn't sure what I'd expected—some grande dame blistering with jewelry—but she was surprisingly light and airy, devoid of ornamentation. She wore a simple gray-and-black dress, plump pearls roped twice around her neck. Her oval face was attractive and soft, neatly made up, long splinters of eyebrows framing her bright brown eyes, an elegant neck like a stalk on a flower *just* starting to wilt. *How many times had Marlowe Hughes dreamed of wringing that thing?*

As Olivia moved toward us, smiling, I realized her right arm hung limply in a sling fashioned out of a black-and-red floral scarf. The hand hung there like a broken wing, but she seemed resolved to pull off this handicap gamely. The fingernails on that withered hand were perfectly painted tomato red.

On the ring finger of her *functioning* hand, which she now extended to us, was a pale blue diamond, at least twelve karats. It stared out, unblinking, like a mesmerized eye.

"Olivia du Pont. I'm so pleased you could come, Mr. McGrath."

"My pleasure."

After shaking her hand, we all sat down, including her three Pekingese, which resembled fat girls stuffed into fur suits. Olivia settled into the white couch opposite, extending an arm over the white throw draped across the back, and the dogs piled around her as if to form some sort of fluffy stronghold, then stared at us expectantly as if we were meant to entertain.

"I'm sorry to have kept you waiting. It's quite *mad* around here with the move."

"You're leaving the city?" I asked.

"Just for the season. We spend the winter in Switzerland. The whole family comes out. My grandchildren love to ski and hike, though Mike and I tend to just laze around. We really sit down in front of the fire and don't budge for four months."

She laughed, a crisp, elegant sound, bringing to mind a spoon tapping a crystal glass before some dignitary made a toast.

Boy, had the apple fallen *far* from the tree. It was astounding how a woman, when she struck marital gold, procured not just a new wardrobe and new friends but a new voice straight out of a 1930s gramophone (brittle, mono-stereo) and a vocabulary that reliably included *laze, season,* and *terribly sorry.* I had to actively remind myself Olivia was an army brat who'd grown up so impoverished, her mother had a third job cleaning the bathrooms of the very public high school she attended. Now Olivia probably had six estates and a yacht as big as a city block.

"My grandson, Charlie, is a huge fan of yours, Mr. McGrath."

"Scott. Please."

"Charlie's in eighth grade at Trinity. He read your first book, *Master-Card Nation*, over the summer. He was *quite* impressed. Now, he's reading *Cocaine Carnivals* and wants to be an investigative reporter."

I assumed she was about to ask if I would please read some marvelous story he'd posted on his blog or else she wanted me to give him a job, thus coming to the reason behind this invitation.

"I never doubted you, you know," Olivia said, arching an eyebrow. "That hoopla a few years back about you and Cordova, your fictitious chauffeur, the outrageous assertions you made on television. I knew exactly what was going on."

"*Did* you? Because it was a *mystery* to me."

"You'd done something to provoke him." She smiled at my look of surprise. "Surely you've noticed that the space around Cordova *distorts*. The closer you get to him, the speed of light slackens, information gets scrambled, rational minds grow illogical, *hysterical*. It's warped space-time, like the mass of a giant sun bending the area surrounding it. You reach out to seize something so close to find it was never actually there. I've witnessed it firsthand myself."

She fell silent, pensive, just as her three uniformed maids entered with the tea. They set about arranging it before us on the coffee table, fine china, a five-tiered silver tower laden with cakes, petits fours, mini-cupcakes, and triangular sandwiches. Olivia slipped off her velvet heels—from Stubbs & Wootton, I noticed, *the billionaire's Nike*—curling her black stocking feet underneath her. As the maids poured the tea, I noticed Nora was blinking in shock at the elaborate setup.

"Thank you, Charlotte."

Charlotte and the other girls nodded demurely and darted away, their shoes silent on the carpet.

"You must be wondering why on earth you're here," said Olivia, sipping her tea. "You've resumed work on your investigation of Cordova, have you not?"

Her eyes met mine as she set down the teacup. They were bright as a schoolgirl's.

"How did you hear that?"

"Allan Cunningham."

The name rang a bell.

"The director of Briarwood Hospital? I've done some charity work for them. He told me he caught you digging rather shamelessly around the grounds last week. Posing as a potential guest."

Of course—Cunningham had hauled me into the Security Center and threatened to have me arrested.

"How *is* the investigation going?" she asked.

"It hasn't been easy getting people to talk."

Returning the teacup to the saucer, she sat back, staring at me.

"*I'll* talk," she announced.

I couldn't help but smile, amused by her directness. "About?"

"What I know. It's quite a lot, believe me."

"Because of your sister?"

Her smile faltered. That was unexpected; I'd have assumed she'd gotten over Marlowe long ago, had put her away in some safe-deposit box of childhood and locked it, tossing the key. But the mention of her sister visibly irked her.

"I haven't spoken to Marlowe in forty-seven years. I don't know what she thought of Stanislas or what her experiences were. I had my own encounters. And I've never wanted to speak about them. Until now."

"Why the change of heart?"

"Ashley."

She said it matter-of-factly. Nora was leaning forward, nervously eyeing the petits fours, as if worried they'd scurry away if she went for one.

"Police think it was suicide," I said.

Olivia nodded. "Perhaps. But there's more to it."

"How do you know?"

"I met her once." She paused to sip her tea, and when she set the teacup down, she looked at me, her eyes piercing. "Do you believe in the supernatural world, Mr. McGrath? Ghosts and the paranormal, unexplained forces we can't see yet nonetheless affect us?"

"No, not really. But I do believe in the human mind's ability to make something like that seem very real."

"Stanislas and his third wife, Astrid, have an estate in the Adirondacks near Lows Lake."

"Yes, I know. *The Peak.*"

She arched an eyebrow. "You've been?"

"I *tried* stopping by to pay my respects five years ago. Never got past the security gate."

Olivia smiled knowingly, sitting back against the couch. "I went there the first week of June in 1977. I was a struggling actress. Twenty-nine years old. Cordova was preparing his next film, *Thumbscrew.* His assistant, Inez Gallo, wrote to my agent and said Cordova had seen me in *Saint Valentine's Day Massacre* and was very impressed by my work." She smiled with visible embarrassment.

"I had a rather pitiful walk-on role, *my back* to the camera the entire time. So it seemed a cruel joke. But the assistant insisted he loved my look and was considering me for a very unusual part, which he'd written *specifically* with me in mind. He invited me to stay for the weekend at The Peak so we might discuss the role. I lived in the East Village then. I borrowed money from a girlfriend to rent a Packard station wagon, and I drove all the way up there, all by myself. I hadn't booked a job in over a year. I was desperate. As I drove I made a pact with myself that I'd do anything—*absolutely anything*—for the role."

She paused for a moment, her hand idly stroking one of the dogs.

"The drive in was quite beautiful. When you're past the woods and the security gate, it becomes a leisurely drive through oak trees and undulating hills. There wasn't a soul around. It was bright, *hot.* The sun was out, and yet I remember feeling so nervous, it soon slipped into *terror,* as if I were entering a graveyard in the dead of night. Every now and then I could hear a flock of birds, *crows,* screeching overhead. But when I slowed the car and looked up, there was nothing in the sky or the trees. *Nothing.*"

She sipped her tea.

"When I arrived at the house, a dark, colossal mansion straight out of—I don't know—a *Poe* short story, I parked by the other cars. There were quite a few, as if other actresses had been summoned as well. Yet I found myself unable to get out of my car. It was a terrible feeling. But I wanted that part. I *needed* it. To be in a Cordova picture was really the *ultimate,* you see. I'd heard it could not just make your career, but *your life.*"

She paused to smile ironically at this last comment.

"I climbed out and knocked on the front entrance and immediately found myself greeted by a stunning Italian woman who acted oddly withdrawn. Without saying a thing to me, she beckoned me to lunch, already under way outside on a loggia draped with wisteria. There was a large group eating there—no one I recognized. Cordova's groupies, I imagined. But there was no sign of the man himself. *Not* that I had a clear picture of what he looked like. I asked someone where he was and was duly informed he was working. They pulled up a chair for me to sit at the table. They were all talking about this object someone had just purchased at a private auction. They were passing this object around. Eventually it came to me. And for some reason when I had it everyone went very silent, and they asked me what I thought it was. It was odd. It looked like a sort of dagger. The bronze handle was intricately carved, the blade narrow, about five inches long, with a strange loop in the middle of it. A young blond man in clerical garb sitting at the very end of the table—he was beautiful, like an Adonis—suggested that I should stick it in my wrist to see what happened, and they all erupted in loud laughter. The only person who didn't laugh was the gorgeous Italian woman who'd answered the door. I came to understand that she was Cordova's wife, Genevra. She only stared back at me with a haunted look, like a prisoner too terrified to speak. I felt so emotional and upset, for a moment I thought I'd burst into tears, but then someone snatched it from me and the lunch was finished. Later, I looked it up and discovered what it was."

"What was it?" I asked when she didn't immediately go on.

She looked at me, her face somber. "A *pricking needle.* They were used in European witch-hunts of the sixteenth and seventeenth centuries. They're made of precious metals, artfully engraved. The 'pricker' would use it to stab the accused woman, usually stripped naked, all over her body. When he at last found a spot that didn't bleed or cause pain, he'd found the witch's mark. If he found such a place, it was of course because she could no longer scream. She'd been stabbed by this needle some three hundred times and was unconscious, slowly bleeding to death. These things, archaic instruments of torture, have a vibrant market today for certain willing collectors."

Nora was so captivated she'd forgotten to chew the rather large piece of cake in her mouth. A crumb fell from her lips, which she hastily collected from the hem of her sweater. She swallowed with a loud gulp.

"But I soon put the bizarre lunch out of my head, because some-one—a masculine-looking hausfrau with a sweaty face and gleaming black eyes—announced that Cordova was ready to meet with me. I was escorted through various corridors, into a large room filled with filing cabinets and a long dining-room table. A man sat at the very end. He was like a king on a throne, stacks of papers and photographs of locations, costumes, scene notes, piled all around him. He was fat, but not grotesque in the way Orson Welles became, or Hitchcock, or even Brando. His massiveness was somehow *distinguished*. He had a round face with thick black hair, and he wore glasses, the lenses round and black as ink. He was handsome. At least I *think* he was. He had one of those faces that captivated you. And yet you couldn't remember it a minute later, as if your brain just couldn't memorize the features, the way it can't memorize an infinite number. Possibly this was due to the glasses, the lack of *eyes*. For a moment I thought he was blind, but he wasn't, because he stared at me without saying a word and then in-formed me I had parsley on my lip. I *did*, much to my chagrin. And then he asked if I wanted to be in his picture. Obviously I eagerly said yes, oh, *yes*. I'd been a huge fan since *Figures*. He smiled. Then he began to ask me a series of pointed questions, all of which became in-creasingly personal and unsettling. He asked if I had family, a boy-friend, if I was sexually active, how regularly did I go to the doctor, who was my next of kin. Was I healthy? Was I easily spooked? That was *quite* a preoccupation. He wanted to know what I was afraid of: heights, spiders, drowning, the sea. How much physical pain had I ever en-dured? What was my worst nightmare? I began to suspect the underly-ing purpose of the questions wasn't so much to know me or see if I was right for the part but to learn how isolated a person I was, who would notice if I ever vanished or *changed* in some way. I kept asking what the part was. I very much wanted to see the script. He greeted such re-quests with only silence and a knowing smile. Finally another person came in—a woman—and escorted me out. It felt like I'd been grilled for over an hour. It was only fifteen minutes."

Olivia took a deep breath and poured us more tea with her function-ing hand. When she grabbed the tongs for a sugar cube and dropped it into her cup, I noticed with surprise her fingers were trembling. *She was nervous.*

"It became clear," she went on, "that there would be further discussion of *Thumbscrew* after supper. I agreed. A maid brought me to my room. It was an enormous house, and my room was a suite, a wall of windows with gauzy curtains like long bridal veils and a view of a lake far down the hill. I'd never seen such a beautiful room. I lay down on the bed, intending to shut my eyes for just a moment, but fell into a deep sleep. I must have been more exhausted from the drive than I realized. Three hours later, I woke up very suddenly in the dark, gasping for air, my throat hurting as if someone had been strangling me. My wrists and arms felt as if they'd somehow been pinned down. They *ached*. But there was no one, no sign of any restraints. And then I saw with horror my suitcase was empty. All of my clothes had been neatly hung up in the closet. Even my underwear had been folded into meticulous piles in the dresser drawer. A dress of mine that I was seemingly meant to wear down for dinner was laid out for me, including earrings and a silver comb for my hair. The windows were open, too, the curtains blowing every which way. They'd been closed when I fell asleep. Every hair on my arms was standing up, as if I were about to be struck by lightning. I had only one thought. *I had to escape.* Dinner was starting at eight o'clock, and there were more guests arriving. I didn't care. I threw my clothes into the suitcase and hurried out, managing to find a back staircase, running outside into the night. My car was exactly where I'd left it, and I drove out without turning on my headlights. At first I was sure someone was following me. There were headlights a few turns in the road behind me. But they were gone by the time I reached the gate. It was closed. I got out, unlocked it myself, and frantically drove away. I didn't stop for six hours. But that *feeling*— a weight, a suffocation, as if my entire body had been put in some sort of vise—it didn't go away for four days. I came very close to checking myself into a hospital."

Olivia paused to take two orange petits fours from the tea stand, feeding one to herself, the other to a Pekingese. When she looked back at us, she smiled ruefully.

"Of course, the more time that went by, when I thought back to that incident I felt humiliated. Time leeches most horror and pain from our memories. All that so-called terror I'd felt, I reasoned it'd been my youth, an overwrought imagination. *Distortion,* his picture about the teenagers' contagious insanity—it had made a deep impression on me. I'd gotten mixed up. I'd confused the art with the life. I wrote Cordova three notes of apology shortly after the episode and heard nothing back from him except a very churlish response."

"What was it?"

"Something to the effect of, if I was the last person on Earth, he'd never cast me in one of his pictures. I suppose that invitation to The Peak was my audition and I'd blown it."

I couldn't help but smile. What she said corroborated seamlessly with Beckman's letter from Cordova to Endicott, the one he passed around to his students.

She shrugged dismissively. "It was fine by me. Two years later, I was a married woman. I had a family, real love, a real life. I'd long given up my actress dreams, dreams of fame, which I understood was nothing more than consigning oneself to a cheap carnival where one lives forever in a cage, applauded and ridiculed by equal measure. Then, in 1999, I received an invitation quite out of the blue. It was from Cordova. He was inviting me to a private dinner at his home, this time in the city. This was a few years after his final film, *To Breathe with Kings*, long after he'd buried himself underground, when he was more secretive and chilling a figure than ever before. I was hesitant to accept, but then again, it *was* Cordova. I was still a fan. I'd gone to considerable lengths to obtain copies of his contraband work. To me he was more of a magician, a hypnotist in the vein of Rasputin. Not a filmmaker. All these years later, I still felt unrequited about him. It gnawed at me, ever so slightly, this question about him I needed answered. The location of the dinner was almost next door, just across Park Avenue on Seventy-first Street. If I felt uncomfortable I could leave at any time and simply walk home."

I glanced at Nora, and she nodded imperceptibly, making the same connection I was. The townhouse Hopper had broken into last night was on East Seventy-first; Olivia had to be referring to that very house. I also recognized the sentiments she described, the unrequited feeling about Cordova, the need for a resolution, for an *end,* how it nibbled at you over the years; I had it myself.

"By then, I was fifty years old, no longer the skittish ingenue. I'd been married for twenty years, had raised three boys. It would take a hell of a lot more to terrify me."

She leaned forward, taking another cake. The three Pekingese's eyes were glued to it. To their evident heartbreak, she placed it in her own mouth, chewing.

"It was a beautiful dinner, but oddly enough Cordova wasn't even there. There was only his wife, Astrid, who explained her husband had gotten waylaid working in the country and wouldn't be able to make it. I was thrown by this. I suspected something was wrong, as if it were a trap. And yet it was a wonderful mix of people, two of whom I knew from my old theater days. Whatever reservations I had about being there soon dissipated. A Russian opera star, a Danish scientist, a French actress known for her immense beauty—and yet the unmistakable center of attention was Cordova's daughter, Ashley. She was cultivating a rather stellar piano career at the time. She was twelve, the most beautiful child I'd ever seen, eyes almost clear. She played for us. Shubert, a Bach concerto, a movement from Stravinsky's *Petrushka,* and then she joined us for dinner. Oddly enough, she chose to sit *right* beside me. Immediately, I felt disconcerted. Her eyes, they were so beautiful and yet so . . ."

Olivia clasped her hands, frowning.

"What?" I prompted.

Her eyes met mine. "*Old.* They'd seen too much."

She paused to take a deep breath, smiling ruefully.

"Dinner was fantastic. The conversation, fascinating. Ashley was charming. And yet when she fell silent she seemed absent, as if she'd slipped off somewhere else, into some other world. When dinner was over, Astrid suggested we play a Japanese game that she claimed the family often played after dinner, having learned it from a real Japanese samurai who apparently lived with the family. It was called The Game of One Hundred Candles. Later, I looked up the Japanese term. *Hyakumonogatari Kaidankai* is what it's called. Have you heard of it?"

"No," I said, shaking my head.

"It's an old Japanese parlor game. It dates back to the Edo period. The seventeenth, eighteenth centuries. One hundred candles are lit, and each candle is blown out after someone tells a short *kaidan. Kai-*

dan is Japanese for ghost story. This continues, the room gradually getting darker and darker, until the final candle is blown out. It's at this moment that a supernatural entity is finally inside the room. It's usually an *onryō*—a Japanese ghost who seeks vengeance."

Olivia took a long breath, exhaling.

"We began to play, all of us fairly drunk on port and dessert wine, each of us grasping at our stories, but when Ashley told hers they were perfectly succinct tales. I assumed she'd memorized them—unless at twelve she could speak so eloquently, right off the top of her head. Her voice was leisurely and low, and at times it sounded like it was coming from somewhere else in the room. Every story she told was riveting, some disturbingly violent. One I remember described a master raping a poor servant girl and leaving her for dead on the side of the road. I was amazed at how easily her lips formed the words as if she were talk-ing about something perfectly natural. At times I had a sense of being outside myself as she talked, some*where* else. And then—I don't know how exactly it turned out that way—there was one candle left and Ashley was up to tell the final story. It was a tale of unrequited love, a Romeo and Juliet tale of illness and hope, a girl dying young, thereby setting her lover free. Everyone was mesmerized. She blew out the candle, and it was pitch-black in the room. *Too* dark. People were gig-gling. Someone told a dirty joke. Suddenly, there was a sucking noise and I felt a cold finger touching my forehead. I was certain Ashley had reached over and touched me. I shrieked, tried to stand, yet both of my legs had fallen asleep. To my utter humiliation, I tumbled out of my chair, right onto the floor. Astrid, apologizing, helped me to my feet and turned the lights on. Everyone was laughing. Ashley sat there, without looking at me, but *smiling*. That feeling I'd had all those years ago when I was at The Peak, that pressing, as if my insides were being taken hold of, it was there again. I waited a few moments, feeling ill, then made my excuses and left. I went home, fixed myself some tea, and went to bed. But hours later, when Mike woke up beside me, I was in a coma. I'd had a stroke. I regained consciousness in the hospital and realized I'd lost the use of my right arm."

Olivia gazed down at her limp arm cradled in the scarf, almost as if it were separate from her, the gnarled albatross she was forced to carry.

"I'd had a brain aneurysm. Doctors said it was my stress over the incident that must have triggered it. I'm a practical woman, Mr. McGrath. I am not prone to drawing hysterical conclusions. What I *do* know is that they did something to her, to Ashley, to make her behave in such a way."

"Who?"

"Her family. Cordova."

"And what exactly do you think they did?"

She looked thoughtful. "Do you have children?"

"A daughter."

"Then you know she was born innocent, yet soaks up everything around her like a sponge. Their way of life at The Peak, my own encounter there all those years ago, the questions he asked me. It was as if I were an experiment. They must have done that to Ashley. Except, unlike me, she couldn't run away. At least not as a child."

I glanced at Nora. She looked spellbound. What Olivia said fit in with my assumption, that at the time of her death Ashley had been on bad terms with her family, hiding under an assumed name, searching for someone known as the Spider. What I couldn't understand was why she returned to the townhouse, unless it was to meet with Inez Gallo. Perhaps Gallo lived there.

"Have you heard of someone connected to Cordova with the nickname the Spider?" I asked, sitting forward.

"The Spider." Olivia frowned. "No."

"What about Inez Gallo? It wouldn't be her nickname, would it?"

"Cordova's assistant? Not to my knowledge. But I don't know anything about her, except I believe she was the woman who escorted me in to see Cordova. And while he interviewed me, she sat on his right side, as if she were his henchman or bodyguard, or perhaps his subconscious."

I nodded. This subservient, looming position certainly backed up what was written about Inez Gallo on the Blackboards.

"Why doesn't anyone talk about Cordova?" I asked.

"They're terrified. They ascribe a power to him, real or imagined, I don't know. What I *do* know is that within that family's history there are atrocious acts. I'm *certain* of it."

"Why haven't you looked into it? You're obviously quite passionate about the matter. Surely you'd have a vast array of resources at your disposal."

"I made a promise to my husband. He wanted me to put the business behind me, given what happened. If I ruffled feathers, trying to get to the bottom of it, would I lose the use of my *other arm?* And then my legs? Because a part of me *actually* believes, you see, that yes, there was something in that room summoned by that girl, and what I was brought there for, an act of revenge, had happened *exactly* as they'd planned. I'd been made to pay for some perceived offense I'd done against my sister."

I couldn't help but think of the killing curse. Technically, my life *had* grown more hazardous since we'd walked through it; I'd nearly drowned. *It eats away at your mind without you even realizing it,* Cleo had told us. *It . . . isolates you, pits you against the world so you're driven to the margins, the periphery of life.* I could actually understand such a phenomenon happening to someone going after Cordova.

Olivia sighed. She looked tired, the intensity gone from her face, leaving it drained of color.

"I'm afraid I don't have much more time," she noted, glancing across the room at the doorway. I followed her gaze and realized I'd been listening so attentively I hadn't noticed that the woman in the gray suit who'd greeted us—Olivia's secretary, I assumed—had stuck her head into the doorway, silently alerting her mistress to her next pressing appointment.

"You mentioned Allan Cunningham," I said. "Ashley was a patient at Briarwood prior to her death. I wanted to know the circumstances of her being admitted there, but Cunningham gave me a hard time. Any way you could help me out with him?"

Olivia smiled, bemused. "Allan assured me Ashley was never a patient there. But I'll certainly ask again. We'll be in Saint Moritz through March." She sat forward, slipping her feet into her shoes. "The number you have reaches my secretary directly. Contact her if you need me for anything at all. She'll be able to get me a message."

"I appreciate that."

She stood up from the couch—her three Pekingese plopping onto the carpet around her feet—and arranged the silk scarf around her immobile arm. As Nora and I rose, Olivia reached out and took my hand with a disarmingly warm smile, her brown eyes gleaming.

"It's certainly been a pleasure, Mr. McGrath."

"Pleasure's been all mine."

We started for the door.

"But one last thing," I said.

She stopped, turning. "Of course."

"If I wanted to speak with your sister, where might I find her?"

She looked irritated. "She can't help you," she said. "She can't even help herself."

"She was married to Cordova."

"And the whole time she was addicted to barbiturates. I doubt she remembers a *thing* about the marriage—except maybe fucking Cordova a few times."

There it was—beneath the flawless elegance—*the scrappy army brat.*

"It would still be invaluable to talk to her about what she saw up there, what the man was like, how he lived. She was an insider."

Olivia stared me down imperiously, not accustomed to being disagreed with. Or perhaps it was exasperation that again, even after all these years, her sister's name still came up in her presence.

"Even if I gave you the address, she'd never see you. She doesn't see anyone except her maid and her drug dealer."

"How do you know that?"

She took a deep breath. "Her maid comes here every week to give me her bills and an update on her health. My sister doesn't know she's bankrupt, that *I've* been paying for her care and drugs for the last twenty years. And if you're wondering why I haven't sent her away to Betty Ford or Promises or *Briarwood,* I assure you I have. Eleven times. It's no use. Some people don't want to be sober. They don't want reality. After life trips them, they choose to stay facedown in the mud."

"All right," I said. "But if what you told us is *true*—"

"It *is,*" she snapped.

"Marlowe might be able to give me even more. The most unreliable witness still has the truth inside them."

Olivia surveyed me challengingly, then sighed.

"The Campanile. Beekman Place. Apartment 1102." She turned, swiftly gliding to the door, her furry entourage panting to keep up. "Speak to the doorman, Harold," she added over her shoulder. "I'll phone him this afternoon. He'll make the arrangements."

"I appreciate that."

"When you *do* see her, don't mention me. For your own well-being."

I swore I caught a faint satisfied smile on her face as she said this.

"You have my word."

She escorted us through the gallery to the entrance hall, the old codger already waiting with our coats. He looked so stiff I couldn't help but imagine he'd been standing there for more than an hour.

"Thank you," I said to Olivia, "for everything. It's been invaluable."

"Hopefully you can *do* something about it. Avenge that girl. She was special."

Nora stepped inside the elevator, and though I entered behind her, I stuck out my hand to prevent the doors from closing.

"One more question, if you don't mind, Mrs. du Pont."

She turned, her head inclined at that artful angle between curiosity and superiority.

"How did you meet Mr. du Pont? I've always wondered."

She stared me down. I thought she was going to icily pronounce it was none of my business. But to my surprise, after a moment, she smiled.

"Cedars-Sinai hospital in Los Angeles. We got into the same elevator. We were both on our way to visit Marlowe on the eighth floor. The elevator got stuck. Something to do with a bad fuse. When it got *unstuck* an hour later, Mike no longer wished to go up to the eighth floor to visit Marlowe."

She met my eyes with a look of triumph.

"He wanted to come *down* to the lobby with *me*."

With a soft smile, Olivia turned coolly on her heel and vanished down the shadowy hall, her dogs at her feet.

73 | WHEN NORA AND I STEPPED OUTSIDE under the pale gray awning onto Park Avenue, I was surprised to find it raining quite hard. I hadn't noticed it upstairs with Olivia, probably because I'd been so absorbed by what she was saying. Unless her apartment was so elegant it simply *edited out* bad weather as if it were a terrible faux pas.

The doorman handed me a golf umbrella and, opening one for himself, raced into the street to hail a taxi.

"She wasn't what I expected," I said to Nora. "She was frank and fairly convincing."

Nora shook her head, breathless. "All *I* could think about was Larry."

"The tattoo artist?"

She nodded vigorously. "Remember what happened to him?"

"He died."

"*Of a brain aneurysm.* Don't you see? It's a *trend.* Olivia had one, and Larry. *Both* after they'd encountered Ashley."

"So, what are you saying, she's the Angel of Death?" I meant it facetiously, though suddenly I recalled the incident Hopper had described at Six Silver Lakes—the rattlesnake found in the counselor's sleeping bag, the widespread belief that Ashley had put it there. *And, of course, her appearance at the Reservoir.*

"Olivia described the same thing Peg Martin did," I said. "A visit to The Peak. But their experiences were so different. One was petrifying. The other was some kind of childhood fantasy dream sequence."

"Wonder which one's true."

"Maybe both. The incidents occurred almost twenty years apart. Olivia said she went in June 1977. That's a year after Cordova had purchased The Peak with Genevra and a month before she drowned. Peg Martin's picnic at the estate was in 1993."

"It was scary how Olivia described Genevra, his first wife, don't you think?"

"The prisoner too terrified to speak."

She nodded. "And what about that witch-pricking needle?"

"It actually corroborates what Cleo back at Enchantments suggested, that Ashley comes from a dynasty of black-magic practitioners."

Nora nibbled her fingernails, apprehensive. "I bet if we ever broke *into* The Peak, that's what we'd find up there."

I knew exactly what she was thinking; somehow Cleo's words had engrained themselves in my head when she'd described the lurid realities of those working with black magic. *Old leather-bound journals filled with spells written backward. Attics stockpiled with the really obscure ingredients, like deer fetuses, lizard feces, baby blood. This stuff is not for people with queasy stomachs. But it* works.

The doorman had found a taxi, so we raced out from the awning, scrambled into the backseat. I saw I had a missed call from Blumenstein and two from Hopper. He'd also sent a text.

I'm out on bail. A million thanks. Heading to your apt

Good. I couldn't wait to ask him what he'd seen inside the townhouse—not to mention the question *How in the hell had he known how to break in?*

74

As Nora and I entered my building, she stopped in alarm and grabbed my arm, pointing at the lock on my front door.

It was smashed, the wood splintered.

Slowly I pushed the door. It was dark inside, no noise but the pounding of the rain.

I stepped into the foyer.

"Don't," whispered Nora. "Someone might still be here—"

I pressed a finger to my lips and crept farther down the hall, my every step creaking on the wooden floors. Suddenly I heard a muffled *thud* coming from the living room.

I raced to the doorway just in time to see a man climbing out the window, violent rain pummeling his black coat and knit cap as he scrambled over the flower box and jumped out of sight.

I wheeled past Nora and back down the hallway, seeing the intruder streak past the building, heading west down Perry.

I ran outside and took off after him. He was already halfway down the block, charging past a pedestrian—who I realized was *Hopper.*

"Catch that guy!" I shouted.

Seeing me barreling toward him, Hopper spun around and took off after the man, who'd just disappeared onto West Fourth.

The intruder was too short to be Theo. It had to be someone else.

Hopper disappeared around the corner. When I reached the intersection seconds later, he was already chasing the man around the block onto Charles. I ran after them, dodging cars, chained bicycles, people hauling shopping bags. The intruder made the light at Hudson, Hopper racing after him, shouting, though the resounding cracks of thunder drowned out the words. Within minutes, I'd made it to the West Side Highway, where there was a pileup of cars. Hopper tore across the median, reaching the other side, though I was forced to wait as the light turned green.

The man was hightailing it north down the bike path along Hudson River Park, past a few police barricades. Suddenly, he swerved left, heading toward Pier 46, and then vanished.

The light turned yellow, and with a break in the traffic, I sprinted across, catching up to Hopper on the bike path.

"I lost him," he said, panting.

I stared down the track, shielding my eyes from the rain. Apart from a couple walking a German shepherd, it was deserted. But the pier, a popular recreational spot, was busy, some thirty or forty people strolling the promenade, armed with slickers and umbrellas.

"He's on the pier," I said. "I'll check this end. You search the other side." I took off, passing a family of tourists in plastic ponchos; a young man walking a Jack Russell; a pair of teenagers giggling, huddled under a brown coat.

No sign of him.

I moved past a crowd of joggers in raingear stretching on the railing and spotted a lone man at the very end of the pier.

He was seated on a bench, staring at the Hudson River, his back to me. He wore a khaki coat, a bright red umbrella over his head. Yet there was something strange about him, and as I approached I saw what it was: Not only was his thinning gray hair disheveled, as if he'd just yanked a knit cap off, but his shoulders were rising and falling, *as if he was out of breath.*

Casually, I stepped alongside the bench beside a trashcan, some six feet away, and turned to see his face.

It was just an old man, his hand resting atop the handle of a quad orthopedic cane, his jeans soaked. There was a large blue JanSport backpack beside him, and the remains of a Subway sandwich.

I must have seemed brazen, studying him so intently, but he only glanced at me and smiled, muttering something.

"What was that?" I shouted.

"Think we'll need Noah's Ark?"

I smiled blandly and stepped in front of him, walking to the end of the pier. The downpour was so severe now, there was barely a difference between the swelling gray river and the rain.

I turned to check out the old man again, *just to be sure.*

But he was still hunched there harmlessly, the rain streaming in a gurgling waterfall off the red umbrella around him.

He smiled again, beckoning me to approach, and I realized from his excited expression he'd actually mistaken my stares for some kind of sexual overture.

He was some old gay geezer, out here cruising.

Jesus Christ.

"Would you like to share?" he shouted at me, looking up at his red umbrella, which made his complexion pink. "Actually, I think I have an extra." Licking his lips, he unzipped the backpack, fumbling inside.

I held up a hand, waving him off, and moved quickly down the walkway just as a resounding crack of lightning struck, followed by another rumble of thunder. As I reached the northern side of the pier, I saw that there was a commotion, a small crowd forming back along the bike path. I sprinted toward it, jostling through the onlookers to find Hopper, as well as another man, helping an elderly African American woman to her feet.

The poor woman was sobbing and completely drenched, wearing only a thin pink housedress, clutching her arm in pain.

"What happened?" I asked a woman next to me.

"She just got mugged. The asshole even stole her cane."

No sooner had she said the words, I was fighting my way through the crowd, racing as fast as I could back along the pathway.

The old man was already gone.

When I reached the empty bench, I could only stare down at it in anger.

There, abandoned, was the red umbrella, the backpack, the orthopedic cane and trench coat, the Subway sandwich wrappers. *The cunning son of a bitch had probably taken them out of the trashcan so he'd appear to be enjoying a leisurely lunch.*

Exactly where he'd been sitting was a small white scrap, facedown on the bench.

I picked it up. It was my business card.

75

I RETURNED THE BELONGINGS to the woman.

Every item was hers: the blue JanSport backpack, the red umbrella, the cane and coat. No money was missing. Her assailant had come from behind her, brutally wrenching her things away, shoving her down on the sidewalk.

"*No way* that was an old man!" Hopper shouted over the downpour as we jogged across Greenwich Street, heading back to Perry.

"I'm telling you. It *was.*"

"Then he's been eating his friggin' *Wheaties,* because he had the torque of a Suzuki. What'd he steal?"

"We're about to find out."

We picked up our pace. I could hardly calm myself to *think,* it had happened so quickly. Yet I had a feeling I shouldn't have been so cavalier about leaving Nora alone. I hadn't stopped to consider if the intruder had an accomplice.

We raced into my building. She wasn't in the hallway.

"*Nora!*"

I shoved open the door, racing through the foyer. Nothing in the living room had been disturbed. I hurried down the hall to my office and stopped dead.

It looked like there'd been an earthquake. Papers and boxes, files, entire shelves had been ransacked and dumped on the floor. A window was open, rain pouring in. Nora was moving frantically around the wreckage.

"What's the matter? Are you hurt?"

"*He's gone.*"

"What?"

She was panicked. "Septimus. I can't find him."

I spotted the empty birdcage on the floor.

"*Where the hell's my laptop?*" I shouted.

"Everything's been stolen. Someone else was here. I heard him go out the window, but I didn't see him." She moved to the closet, the wooden door hanging off the runner.

I scaled through the mess to the window, angrily slamming it closed. My filing cabinets were pulled open, the papers looted. My old framed *Time* articles had been pulled off the wall. The *Le Samouraï* poster was hanging cockeyed, so Alain Delon—*usually* gazing out coolly in his fedora at something beyond the room—now contemplated the floor. *Was that some type of cryptic message? A hint that I was shortsighted, wasn't seeing straight?*

I righted the frame, seized the leather cushions, and threw them to the couch. I grabbed one of the fallen shelves and heaved it upright, stepping on a picture frame lying facedown. I picked it up, seeing with a twinge of horror that it was my favorite shot of Sam, taken when she was hours old. The glass had been smashed. I shook out the shards, set it on my desk, then stepped over to the overturned box of Cordova research.

I almost laughed.

It was empty—except for the *Meet Yumi* escort flier that I'd pocketed back at 83 Henry. The half-naked girl stared mischievously at me, as if to whisper, *Are you really that surprised?*

I couldn't fathom my stupidity. I'd *known* we were being followed, yet like some reckless fool, I'd taken no precautions, which now seemed *especially idiotic,* considering that the last time I'd gone after Cordova, my life had collapsed around me like a cheap vaudeville set. Now my notes were in the hands of the very subject of my investigation. Cordova would be reading my every note, every brainstormed thought and scrawl. *He'd be perusing my head like a department store.* My laptop had a password, but any decent hacker could override it. Now Cordova would know everything we knew about Ashley's final days.

Whatever edge we might have had after breaking into Oubliette, the Waldorf, Briarwood, knowing that Ashley had been searching for this person called *the Spider*—it was gone.

I picked up my stereo, putting the receiver back on the shelf, and saw with disbelief Ashley's CD was gone, too. This gave way to another alarming thought.

"Where's Ashley's police file?"

Nora was still digging through the closet.

"Ashley's file that I got *illegally* from Sharon Falcone—you were reading it two days ago. Where is it?"

She turned, her face distraught.

"I don't know."

She began to cry, so I started trawling through the rubble myself. I couldn't imagine the ripple effect of that file going public: Sharon losing her job; her career ending in disgrace due to my own folly; my name appearing in print *yet again* as something toxic. It made me so furious, it took me a moment to realize that Hopper was shouting for us.

We found him in the kitchen, standing by the open oven door.

The parakeet was inside, frantically fluttering around the fan.

Nora rushed forward, gently capturing the bird. He was alive but trembling violently.

"Was the oven *on*?" she asked Hopper.

"No."

As she tended to the bird, Hopper looked meaningfully at me.

He was thinking what I was. This was no act of clemency. It was a threat. Sparing the bird sent a clear message: They were in control. They wanted to toy with the bird, play with it, petrify the fragile thing a little longer. But if they'd wanted to, they could have killed it.

And so the same was true for us.

76 WE SPENT THE NEXT FEW HOURS cleaning up my office, while a locksmith replaced the bolt on the front door. Everything about Ashley and Cordova had been taken, with a few exceptions—my old Crowthorpe Falls notes, Iona's *Bachelor Party Entertainment* business card. We found these items under the couch, which suggested that my study had been trashed first, *then* scoured for information on the Cordovas.

In another stroke of luck, they'd left behind Ashley's coat—we found it still crammed into the Whole Foods bag behind the door, probably assumed to be garbage. We also found Sharon Falcone's police file. Two days ago, Nora had taken it upstairs to review before bed. It was still on her bedside table—a sign the intruders had never made it upstairs.

I kept thinking about Olivia Endicott. It was certainly *convenient* that while we were uptown listening to her, the intruders had unmitigated access to my apartment. I couldn't help but wonder if I'd misread her. Had she been in on the whole thing from the start and tipped them off to the appointment? *Why? What motivation did Olivia have to protect Cordova?*

There was also an unsettling symmetry to what had happened. We were following Ashley's footsteps; Theo Cordova had followed ours. Hopper broke into *their* home last night; today, they broke into mine. Searching for the man on the pier, I'd only encountered myself, *my* business card. Were they genuinely threatened by what we were doing? Or were they treating it as a game, mirroring our actions, boomeranging them back onto us, one violation of the Cordovas' privacy resulting in one of mine, one invasion for another?

I didn't know what any of it meant, but at least one thing Olivia had said seemed about right: *The space around Cordova* distorts . . . *the speed of light slackens, information gets scrambled, rational minds grow illogical,* hysterical.

I went upstairs and took a shower, gave Hopper some towels so he could, too. I was planning to order some Chinese food and then quiz him about the townhouse—he'd briefly mentioned he hadn't seen very much before he was caught. I left Nora monitoring Septimus and retreated to my bedroom to clean out the old safe in my closet. I hadn't used it in years, but going forward, all notes and evidence would have to be locked inside.

I was clearing out some old redacted files when there was a knock behind me.

Nora was in the doorway, her face ashen.

"What's the matter? Is it Septimus?"

She shook her head, beckoning me to follow her.

She'd put on deafening music in the living room, the volume turned up so loud it drowned out our footsteps. She crept to the very end of the hallway, pointing at the bathroom door—open just a crack.

Hopper was inside, the faucet running. I wasn't in the habit of spying on men in bathrooms, but she animatedly gestured that I take a look.

I leaned forward. Hopper was at the sink, brushing his teeth, a towel around his waist.

And then I saw it.

77

"WHAT'S GOING ON?" asked Hopper, stepping into the living room.

"Have a seat," I said. "We're going to have a little chat."

"Right. The townhouse."

"Not the townhouse," said Nora crossly. "The tattoo on your foot."

He froze, astonished. "What?"

"Ashley's kirin," she said. "*You* have the other half."

He eyed the door.

"Hopper, we saw it. You lied to us."

He glared at her, then suddenly darted for the doorway, but I was ready. I grabbed him by the back of his T-shirt and shoved him hard into a club chair.

"That tattoo on your fucking ankle. Start talking."

He appeared to be too shocked to speak, or else was trying to think up another excuse. After a minute, Nora rose and poured him a glass of scotch.

"Thanks," he muttered sullenly. He took a sip, staring into the glass. "To know her and then *not*," he said, his voice low, "is like serving a life sentence. You see everything at a distance, through thick glass and telephones and visiting hours. Nothing tastes like anything. Bars everywhere you look." He smiled softly. "You can never get out."

He raised his head, gazing at us intently, as if remembering we were there. He actually looked relieved.

And just like that, he began to tell us all about her as the rain beat the windows like an army trying to get in.

78

"I DIDN'T LIE TO YOU," Hopper said. "Six Silver Lakes *was* how I met Ashley. And it was true, that bet we made. She did blow me off. And that incident with that kid everyone made fun of. Orlando. When he took the ecstasy and Ash took the blame for all of us. That *happened*, okay? What I *didn't* tell you was I'd been planning to break the hell out."

"Of Six Silver Lakes?" I asked.

He nodded. "I'd had it with the entire operation. Even after the rattlesnake incident, we still had another six weeks. I wasn't about to keep swallowing the bullshit. Sure, thanks to Ash, Hawk Feather was scared shitless, but so what? Every day it was a hundred degrees. The kids were budding Ted Bundys, the counselors perverted *fucks*. At night you could hear one of them, Wall Walker, jerking off in his tent. It was only a matter of time before he tried to get someone to join him. The only girl worth talking to, Ash, didn't give me the time of day. So I thought, *Fuck it*. One of the female counselors, this headshrinker, Horsehair, she was always checking out this map she kept hidden in her backpack, thinking she was covert about it. One night, when she was having a one-on-one with one of the girls, I stole it. I saw on the map that if you made it out of Zion National Park, there was an interstate pretty close that could take you west into Nevada. If I got to the road I could easily hitch a ride with a truck driver. I'd traveled with truckers before. Most hate cops, so they're trustworthy as hell. The others are so hyped up on meth they don't know who the hell's tagging along with them. My plan was to get to Vegas.

"Horsehair made a big stink about her stolen map and there was a major inquisition around the campfire. People's backpacks got searched, but they didn't find a thing. The counselors figured Horsehair had lost it. But I'd hidden it under the foot insert in my hiking boot. I came up with an escape plan. I'd ration my food, keeping the extra in the bottom of my sleeping bag. I'd wait for us to reach the camping spot in closest proximity to that highway. From what I calculated, we'd reach it in three days. From there, the highway was half a day's hike. I'd sneak off after everyone was asleep. This one counselor, Four Crows, was supposed to keep an all-night watch, but she secretly retired around one, so I'd have no problem. But there *was* something I hadn't considered. Orlando."

Hopper ran his hands through his hair. "We shared a tent. You get assigned a tentmate at the outset. Orlando was mine. One night I was up studying the map, and all of a sudden I heard in the dark, 'Hopper, whatcha looking at?' He'd woken up and was spying on me. I didn't know for how long. I told him I thought I saw a lizard and to go the fuck back to sleep. But he was a sly kid. He was *used* to people lying to him. The next morning when I woke up he'd gone through all of my things and found the map. He said he knew I was planning to run away, and if I didn't take him with me, he was going to tell the counselors."

He paused to take a long sip of scotch.

"I don't think he'd ever had anyone be nice to him without him having to blackmail them into it. He wanted me to promise on Jesus Christ—he was from North Carolina, his parents born-again Baptists. He was always mentioning Jesus like he was his next-door neighbor, someone he did a little yard work for. So I said *Cool*. No problem. Great. I swore in the name of Jesus Christ I'd take him with me. I swore that we were a team. Like Frodo and Sam."

He glanced at me. "I had *no intention* of taking him. I might as well try to escape with an L-shaped *couch* on my back. He was a total liability."

He seemed anxious saying this, brushing his hair out of his eyes, resuming his concentrated stare at the coffee table.

"Within days, it was the night. We'd set up our camp in the *exact* location I needed to be. And I remember when everyone went to bed there was a clear night sky and a *silence* I'll never forget. Usually there were insects and shit screaming in your ears all night. But on this night it was still, like everything alive had run away. I set my watch to wake up at midnight. Instead, I was woken up by a counselor. The *entire group* was awake. There was a torrential downpour. The whole campsite was flooded, all of us sleeping in about three inches of rain. It was mayhem. The counselors were yelling at everyone to pack up their tents. We had to move to higher elevation because they were worried about flash floods. Not that they gave a fuck about *our* well-being, they just didn't want to end up dead themselves. People were screaming, freaking out. No one could find anything. I realized it was a blessing because in the chaos, it'd be so easy to slip away. I knew where I had to go, where the path was. I helped Orlando pack up the tent, but as I did, I noticed Ashley. She already had her tent together, was waiting for the rest of us. The beam of someone's flashlight slipped onto her face, and I saw she was across the campsite, just staring at me. The *look* on her face—it was like she *knew* what I was about to do. I didn't have time to think about it. Some of the kids were starting to make their way up the path to the next campsite. I fell in behind them. I held back, and when they were far enough ahead, I turned off my flashlight and stepped off the path, heading down a slope in the rocks, waiting. I could see some of the kids walking along the ridge, others still freaking out over the tents. The rain was coming down so hard in the pitch-black dark you couldn't see more than a foot in front of you. They wouldn't notice I was missing until morning. I turned my flashlight back on and took off."

He paused to take another drink.

"I hadn't walked ten minutes when I turned and saw another flashlight right behind me. It was Orlando. I was *pissed*. I shouted at him to go back, but he refused. He kept saying, 'You promised. You promised to take me.' He wouldn't stop. I lost it. I said I couldn't stand him. I told him he was fat, that everyone made fun of him. I said he was pathetic and weak, and even his own mother secretly didn't love him. I said no one in the world loved him and no one ever would."

At this, Hopper began to sob, a tortured choking sound that seemed to tear through him. "I wanted him to hate me. So he'd go back. I didn't want him to like me. I didn't want him to look up to me."

He took a deep breath and fell silent, his head in his hands. After a minute, he wiped his face in the crook of his arm, hunching forward in the chair, visibly determined to keep talking, fighting his way through the story or he'd get lost in it, drown inside it.

"I took off. A minute later, when I looked back I could see his flashlight, a tiny white light in the dark behind me, so far away. It looked like it was getting smaller, like he was heading back up the path. But then I actually couldn't tell if it was moving toward me or away. Maybe he was still coming after me. I continued on. But an hour later, I realized I had no way out. The trail I was supposed to follow was through a canyon called The Narrows, and as I came into it, slipping in the mud, I saw there was a raging river where the trail was supposed to be. There was no way across. I had to turn back. It took forever because the path was pretty much a mudslide. I wasn't even sure I'd make it, and I probably wouldn't have if I hadn't had the map. It felt like I stumbled forever through the dark. Three hours later, I made it to the ridge and the new campsite. It was about five in the morning, still pouring. Everyone was asleep. No one had noticed I was gone. I unrolled my sleeping bag, slipped into one of the other tents, and collapsed. When I woke up the counselors had taken a head count. There was no sign of Orlando. By the afternoon they'd called the National Guard. I remember it was this beautiful day. A huge blue sky, so bright and beautiful."

He leaned forward, taking a deep, uneven breath, staring at the floor.

"They found him eleven miles away, drowned in a river. Everyone thought it was an accident, that he'd gotten lost in the commotion. But I knew the truth. It was because of what I'd said. He was walking and saw the river, and he threw himself in. I did it. I killed that sweet kid who hadn't done anything except be himself. There was nothing wrong with him. It was me. I was the loser. I was the waste of flesh. I was the one that no one loved. And no one ever would. See, Ashley had saved Orlando," he whispered. "And I destroyed him."

He closed his eyes. He looked so anguished whispering this, it was as if the words cut into him. After a moment, he forced himself to look up, his eyes watery and bloodshot.

"They helicoptered us out, back to base camp," he continued. "The outraged parents descended. The counselors faced negligence charges. Two served jail time. Some of their discipline methods came out, and the camp changed its name to, like, Twelve Gold Forests a year later. No one knew I had anything to do with what had happened. Except Ash. She didn't say anything. I just could tell from the way she looked at me. We were the last two to leave. A black SUV came for her, no parents, just a woman driver wearing a suit. Before she climbed into the backseat, she turned and she looked in at me, where I was watching inside the cabin. It would've been impossible for her to actually see me, but somehow she did. She knew everything."

He seemed on the verge of crying but wouldn't let himself, angrily wiping his eyes in the crook of his arm.

"You were supposed to be checked out by your parents," he said, his voice hoarse. "My uncle couldn't make it. But things were nuts with police, the local news, Orlando's family; finally the cops just turned to me and said, 'Go.' I could just walk the fuck *out*. And that's what I did."

I'd been so absorbed listening to him, I'd hardly noticed Nora had darted across the living room. She retrieved the box of Kleenex off the bookshelf, smiling as she handed it to Hopper, slipping back to the couch.

"The next five months were a blackout," he said, pausing to blow his nose. "Or a black *hole*. I hitchhiked. I went into Oregon and up into Canada. Most the time I didn't know *where* I was. I just walked. I spent nights in motels and parking lots, strip malls. I stole money and food. I bought some heroin once and locked myself in a motel room for weeks at a time, floating away in a haze, hoping I'd find the end of the Earth and just float off. When I reached Alaska, I went into this one town, Fritz Creek, and stole a six-pack of Pabst from a convenience store. I didn't know every mom-'n'-pop shop in Alaska keeps a shotgun behind their register. The owner shot two inches from my ear, right into a display of potato chips, then pointed the barrel right at my head. I asked him to please pull the trigger. He'd be doing me a favor. Only goading him like that, like a madman, I probably scared the shit out of him, because he lowered it and, visibly freaked out, he called the police. A month later, I was at Peterson Long, a military boarding school in Texas. I'd been there about a week, and I remember I was in the library—it had bars on the windows—wondering how the hell I was going to break out, when I got this email out of the blue."

He smiled reluctantly, staring off somewhere, as if even now surprised by it.

"All it said in the subject line was 'Do I dare?' I didn't know what that meant or who the hell sent it. Until I read the email address. Ashley Brett Cordova. I thought it was a joke."

"Do I dare?" I repeated.

Hopper glanced up at me, his face darkening. "It's from Prufrock."

Of course. "The Love Song of J. Alfred Prufrock." It was a T. S. Eliot poem, a crushing description of paralysis and unrequited romantic longing in the modern world. I hadn't read the poem since college, though I still remembered some of the lines as they burned into your head the moment you read them: *In the room the women come and go / Talking of Michelangelo.*

"That's kind of how our friendship started," Hopper said simply. "Writing to each other. She didn't talk about her family. *Sometimes* she mentioned her brother. Or what she was studying. Or her dogs, a couple of rescued mutts. Her letters were the reason I didn't break out of there. I worried we'd somehow lose touch if I did. Once she wrote that maybe I should stop running from myself and try standing still. So that's what I did." He shook his head. "When spring break came, I was *dying* to see her. I think a part of me didn't think it was actually Ashley that I'd been writing to, but some figment of my imagination. I knew she was in the city, so I went online and found a spot in Central Park, the Promenade near the Bandshell. I told her to meet me there, April the second, seven o'clock sharp. Cheesy as *fuck*. I didn't care. She didn't answer my email for two days. And when it came, her response was one word. The best word in the English language."

"What's that?" I asked, when he didn't immediately go on.

"Yes." He smiled sheepishly. "I took three buses to get to New York. I arrived a day early, slept on a park bench. I was so goddamn nervous. Like I'd never been with a girl before. But she wasn't a girl. She was a wonder. Finally, it was seven o'clock, seven-thirty, *eight*. She didn't show. Blew me off. I was friggin' *embarrassed* for myself, and I was about to take off when all of a sudden I hear right behind me in her low voice, 'Hello, Tiger Foot.'" He glanced up, wryly shaking his head. "It was my goddamn *tribe name* from Six Silver Lakes. I turn around and, of course, she was there."

He fell silent, thinking about it, amazed.

"And that was it," he noted quietly. "We were up the whole night just *talking,* walking the city. You can walk those blocks forever, take a break on the edge of a fountain, eat pizza and snow cones, awed by the human carnival all around you. She was the most incredible person. To be next to her was to have everything. When it was daylight, we'd been sitting on a stoop watching the street get light. She mentioned the light took eight minutes to leave the sun and reach us. You couldn't help but love that light, traveling so far through the loneliest of spaces to get here, to come so far. It was like we were the only two people in the world."

He paused, looking up at me with a penetrating stare. "She told me her father taught her to live life way beyond the cusp of it, way out in the outer reaches where most people never had the guts to go, where you got hurt. Where there was unimaginable beauty and pain. She was always demanding of herself, *Do I dare? Do I dare disturb the universe?* From *Prufrock*. Her dad revered the poem, I guess, and the entire family lived in answer to it. They were always reminding themselves to stop measuring life in coffee spoons, mornings and afternoons, to keep swimming way, *way* down to the bottom of the ocean to find where the mermaids sang, each to each. Where there was danger and beauty and light. Only *the now*. Ashley said it was the only way to live."

After this feverish outpouring of words, Hopper paused to collect himself, taking a deep breath.

"It *was* how she was. Ash not only rode on the waves and dove every day down to where the mermaids sang, she was a mermaid herself. By the time I walked her home, I loved her. Body and soul."

He admitted this evenly, his face bare and unafraid. I sensed it was the first time he had truly talked about her. There was a feeling in his unsteady voice, in the words used to describe her, that they'd been submerged inside him for years; they were musty and purpled and fragile, practically dissolving as soon as they hit the air.

"You walked her back to East Seventy-first Street?" I asked.

He eyed me. "Where we were last night."

"*That's* why you knew how to get in," whispered Nora, astonished. "You'd climbed in before."

"After the first night we were together, when she didn't come home, her parents were furious. They kept a pretty tight rein on her. They insisted she be home by one in the morning or they were going to take her away or something, to their house upstate. So, every night that week, I'd drop Ash off at her house at one, wait for her across the street, where we stood last night. At about one-thirty, Ash would climb out and we'd take off, heading to the docks or the Carlyle or Central Park. At six in the morning, she'd climb back in. She'd cut the wires so the sensors on that window weren't rigged for the alarm. Her parents never knew about it. They *still* obviously don't. When I saw the place last night it looked exactly the same. I half expected to see Ash come climbing out."

He dropped his gaze to the floor and drained the glass of scotch.

"When that week was over," he went on quietly, "I went back to school and the first thing I did was write a letter to Orlando's parents, telling them what had happened. She'd given me the courage, even though she never said a word. When I put it in the mail, I felt like a noose had been removed from my neck. It took them a few weeks to write back to me, but the letter, when it finally arrived—it awed me, I guess. They blessed me for coming forward, telling the truth. They asked me to forgive myself, said that they'd pray for me and I'd always have a place in their home."

Hopper, still awed by this, shook his head. "For the next couple of weeks, Ash and I wrote every day," he went on. "In late May, for a week

I didn't hear. I went crazy, worried something had happened. Then I got a phone call. It was Ash. I'll never forget how she sounded. She was desperate, sobbing. She said she couldn't live with her parents anymore and wanted to go where they couldn't find her. She asked if I'd come away with her. And I said—*well*, I said the best word in the English language."

"Yes," I whispered.

He nodded. "I borrowed money from one of my teachers to buy the tickets. June the tenth, 2004. Nine-thirty-five P.M. United, Flight 7057. JFK to Rio de Janeiro, Brazil. There was a city way in the south on Santa Catarina Island that I'd been to once. *Florianópolis*. The most beautiful place I'd ever seen, second to *her*. A buddy of mine ran a bar down there on the beach. He said he'd help us out with work till we knew what our plan was. Summer break arrived, and I traveled on those three Greyhound buses all the way back to the city to see her. The moment I *did*, I knew it was *on*. We were going to leave it all behind. Best night of my life was when we got those tattoos. I'd heard about Rising Dragon. But the *kirin* was her idea."

"Did Larry do it?" asked Nora.

"Yeah. He was a big guy. It was just the three of us in the shop. The design was intricate. You were supposed to do that kind of thing over a month's time to handle the pain. But our flight was the next day, so it was that night or nothing. When it was over, she threw her arms around me, laughing, like it hadn't hurt at all, and she said she'd see me tomorrow. Tomorrow it would all begin."

Hopper took a deep breath, interlacing his fingers, staring beyond us and out the window, where the rain still whipped against the glass. He seemed suddenly very far away, lost in a bottomless crevice of the past he couldn't pull himself out of. Or perhaps he was recalling a detail he chose not to disclose to us, words she'd said or something she'd done, that would remain forever between them.

When he looked back at us, he seemed reluctant to continue.

"Mind if I smoke?" he asked quietly.

I shook my head. He stood up to retrieve his cigarettes from his coat pocket, and I glanced at Nora. She was so mesmerized, she hadn't moved a muscle in fifteen minutes, elbow on the armrest, chin planted in her hand.

He sat back down and tapped out a cigarette, lighting it fast. There was a long silence, his face dark and pensive, cigarette smoke clinging to the empty space around him.

"That was the last time I ever saw her," he said.

79

"NEXT DAY, WE WERE DUE TO LEAVE," he went on. "June the tenth. Ash was meeting me at six P.M. at Neil's Coffee Shop. It's a diner on Lex, a block from her house. Then, together we'd head to JFK. Six o'clock came and went. There was no word from her. Soon it was seven. *Eight.* I called her cellphone. *No answer.* I went to her house and rang the bell. Usually there were lights on. It was dark. I knocked. No one came to the door. I climbed up there, exactly the way Ash did, up the iron bars to the second-floor balcony and in the far-right window. The place was luxurious, a palace, but it'd been packed up. And in a *hurry.* Like a bunch of criminals had decided to run for their lives. The furniture was covered with sheets, randomly, so they were half on the floor. Beds stripped. Milk and fruit and bread tossed out on the sidewalk in piles of garbage bags. I found Ash's room on the third floor. There were a few photographs, books, but a lot of her things had obviously been taken, thrown in bags really fast. The lamp was tipped over on her bedside table. But inside her closet, hidden beneath blankets on the top shelf, I found a small leather suitcase. I pulled it down, unzipped it. It was packed with her clothes, sundresses, T-shirts, *cash,* sheet music, a *Lonely Planet* guide to *Brazil.* She *was* planning to go. I knew then her parents had found out, and they'd taken her away, probably to that estate where she'd been homeschooled her entire life."

He paused, anxiously twirling the end of the cigarette with his thumb.

"I was all set to go to the police, when I heard from her. She sent me an *email.* She was *sorry,* but she'd made a mistake. We were just a couple of delusional kids, caught up in the moment. She didn't want to be tied down to anyone. She said she loved our time together, but it was over, simple as that. She told me to keep riding the waves seaward, keep searching for the goddamn chambers of the *fucking sea,* where the *mermaids* sang . . ."

He irritably cut himself off, taking a long drag on the cigarette.

"I was sure her parents had put her up to it," he went on, exhaling smoke in a fast stream. "I wrote back, said I didn't believe her. I was going to find her and she could say it to my face. She asked me not to contact her. I wrote back *again*. If this was *my Ashley,* what was the address of the stoop we'd sat on that first night, when the sun was rising over the block? She wrote the right answer back, in *seconds. 131 East 19th. And I'm no one's Ashley,* she wrote. It was a dagger to the heart. A year later, I found out she was attending Amherst. So she was fine. It had been her decision."

He brushed his hair out of his eyes, leaning back in the chair, his face calm, even slightly dazed.

"Did you ever hear from her again?" Nora softly asked him.

He nodded imperceptibly, his eyes shifting to her, but said nothing.

"What did she say?" Nora whispered.

"*Nothing,*" he answered tersely. "She sent me a stuffed monkey."

Of *course,* the *monkey*—that faded toy with loose stitching, covered in dried mud. I'd almost forgotten about it.

"Why?" I asked.

He stared at me. "It was *Orlando's.* He slept with it. I don't know how Ash had it or where she'd found it. But when I pulled it out of that envelope, I was sick. *She* was *sick,* sending it, when she knew every day I thought about that kid, lived every day with the horror of this thing I'd done. I went to the return address she'd written on the envelope, thinking I'd find a reason why she did such a thing." He looked at me. "That's when I ran into you."

"No wonder you didn't trust me," I said.

He shrugged. "I thought you might be working for her family."

"How did you know to go to Klavierhaus?" asked Nora.

"I went there with Ash once. She used to practice there."

Nora bit her fingernails, frowning. "And you didn't come with us to Rising Dragon *because* . . . ?"

"I was paranoid I'd be recognized. It was a long time ago, but . . . I didn't want to take the chance. Or be reminded." He stared with resentment down at the tattoo. "I used to have dreams about cutting off my foot so I wouldn't have to look at that thing."

"Why didn't you tell us?" I asked. "At some point, you must have noticed we were just as ignorant as you were as to what was going on."

He shook his head. "I didn't know *what* to think. I didn't recognize the Ashley I knew in any of this, this *witch* we've been tracking. Curses on the floor? Nyctophobia? Ashley wasn't afraid of the *dark*. She wasn't afraid of anything."

"Maybe she didn't send it," Nora suggested.

"It's her handwriting on the envelope."

"Someone in her family might have copied it. Maybe they're afraid of something she told you and they sent it to scare you off."

"I've been racking my brain for weeks. Trying to think of *something* she told me. But I never met anyone in her family, and she rarely talked about them, though I definitely sensed, particularly from that one phone call, she and her dad did *not* get along."

"Nothing about witchcraft?" I suggested.

He looked puzzled. "The idea Ash would be involved in something like that is *crazy*."

"What about why she was sent to Six Silver Lakes?"

"She told me she'd lost her temper and burned herself on a candle. She had a bad burn scar on her left hand. That was it."

"What about when you were inside the townhouse last night?"

He stared at me with evident unease before answering. "*It was the same.* Like no one had set foot there since I'd broken in seven years ago. Same exact sheets tossed randomly over the furniture. Same Chopin music on Ashley's piano, the lid open. The same rugs rolled up, same *books* piled on top of the tables, same drinking glass on the mantel above the fireplace, only there was about *three inches of dust* on everything. And this *mildewed* smell like a tomb. I was heading up to Ashley's bedroom to see if she'd ever come back. I honestly expected to find her suitcase still packed and hidden in the closet where I'd left it. That was when the doorbell rang and I had to turn back. I was almost at the window when the lights came on and I heard a woman ordering me to put my hands up. She was wielding a fucking shotgun."

"Inez Gallo," I said. "Had you ever seen her before?"

He frowned. "I *thought* for a second I recognized her as the driver who picked up Ashley back at Six Silver Lakes. But I'm not positive."

"Ashley went back to Rising Dragon for the picture of you together," said Nora. "She wanted to have it, even though it was lost."

He stared at her. "It's not." Slowly he reached into his back pocket and took out his wallet, removing a paper from the billfold.

He handed it to me.

It was a photograph, crinkled and worn, taken out and stared at a thousand times.

Even now, after everything he told us, it was startling to see them together, as if two people from two different worlds had collided. They sat in one folding chair, hands clasped. It was a captured moment of youth, of joy—a moment so free the camera couldn't even hold on to it. It rendered them in streaks and blurs, hinting that they were so new and light there were no words to describe them, their ankles forming that fighting creature on fire, leaping to its death or its life.

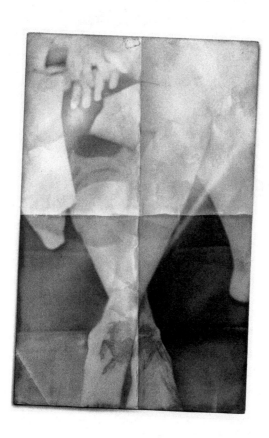

80 I GAVE HOPPER A PILLOW and blankets so he could crash on the couch. The rain was still coming down, and he didn't seem to want to go home.

Nora drowsily said good night, slipping into Sam's room.

I headed to bed myself. I was mentally and physically drained, though before turning out the light, I looked up *Six Silver Lakes* on my BlackBerry, just to verify the details of Hopper's story. There were quite a few articles about the drowning, which had occurred July 2003, many of the actual newspaper clippings scanned and posted on a site called Thelostangels.com.

INVESTIGATION UNDER WAY IN ZION WILDERNESS CAMP DEATH

By Stacey Liu

ZION NATIONAL PARK, UTAH Five counselors at a private camp for troubled youngsters have been arrested and a sixth resigned after a 15-year-old boy died in a flash flood in the park late Monday.

Counselors of Six Silver Lakes Wilderness Therapy failed to account for Orlando Wang, 15, during a campsite move away from Canyon Overlook trail during a heavy storm late Monday.

Wang was not discovered missing for seven hours as more than five inches of rain fell on the area, causing flash flooding. Park dispatch received an emergency call just after 7 a.m. Tuesday. After a widespread search, the park SAR team recovered the boy's body from the North Fork of the Virgin River.

The counselors are facing criminal charges of negligence and mistreatment and have refused to take a polygraph test.

I read the other articles, every one confirming what Hopper had told us.

So, he had loved her. Of course, I'd known it already.

Ashley.

How elusive she was, how she shape-shifted, seemed composed of as many rival creatures as the tattoo. Head of a dragon, body of a deer. *Inclinations of a witch.* She was Orlando's flashlight in the dark behind us, a pinprick of light in the violent downpour, dogging Hopper, dogging *me.* She was a beacon of mysterious origin and intention, impossible to determine if heading toward me or away. What, really, was the difference between something hounding you and something leading you somewhere?

I turned out the light, closing my eyes.

Do I dare?

I jerked upright, my heart pounding. The bedroom was dark, empty, and yet I had the distinct feeling someone had just whispered those words in my ear.

I grabbed my phone off the table, Googling *Prufrock,* my eyes blearily reading the poem.

It was as searing and sad as I'd found it to be in college—maybe more so, now that I was no longer an arrogant young man of nineteen, now that the lines about time and *I grow old . . . I grow old . . .* meant something. The poem's narrator, Prufrock, was a sort of insect specimen, mounted and pinned, still squirming, to his tedious little life, a world of endless social gatherings and parties and inane observations; the modern equivalent would probably be man alone with his phones and screens, Tweeting and friending and status updating, the ceaseless chatter of Internet culture. The man's thoughts veered between resignation, the stuttering, delusional belief that he had time, and a profound longing for *more,* for murder and creation.

The whole family lived in answer to that poem, Hopper had said.

If that was true, it was doubtlessly a ferocious, intoxicating way to live. It even corroborated the mystical afternoon Peg Martin had described at the dog run and some of those early stories about Ashley. But it could also be an enslavement, *a hell,* to keep searching for *the enchanted,* keep plunging down, down to the lonely chambers of the sea. *To seek mermaids.*

It was a tragic thing to do, like looking for Eden.

I closed my eyes, my limbs so heavy they seemed to melt into the bed, my mind untying all thoughts so they flew into the air, unattached and disordered.

She attacked a guest. He's called the Spider. Knowledge of darkness in the most extreme form. You've no respect for murk, McGrath. The blackly unexplained. Within that family's history there are atrocious acts. I'm certain of it. Sovereign. Deadly. Perfect.

The only sound was the rain, playing like an exhausted orchestra on the windows. Only when I was drifting to sleep did the storm let slip a few delicate notes—strands of some new song—and abruptly disband.

81

"THAT'S HIM," I said.

I left Nora and Hopper seated on the guardrail at the dead end of East Fifty-second Street—just outside The Campanile, an elegant limestone apartment building overlooking the East River—and walked swiftly down the sidewalk toward the approaching man wearing the gray doorman's uniform.

He was very short and very bald, carrying a small deli coffee cup, an impish spring in his step. He might have been Danny DeVito's cousin.

I caught up to him under a gray awning. "You must be Harold."

He smiled cheerfully. "That's me."

I introduced myself. He nodded in immediate recognition. "Oh, *right*. The hotshot reporter. Mrs. du Pont said you'd be stopping by. So, you, uh . . ." He raised his chin to glance over my shoulder, lowering his voice. "You want to get in to see Marlowe."

"Olivia said you could arrange a time for me to talk to her."

He smirked. "You don't *talk* to Marlowe."

"What do you do?"

"What do you do with *any* man-eating beast? Tiptoe around and pray they're not hungry." He laughed again and then sobered when he saw my confusion. "Come back tonight. Eleven o'clock sharp. I'll take you up. But, uh, then you're on your own."

"What's that supposed to mean?"

"I make a rule never to go past the laundry room."

"I'd like to *speak* to Marlowe. Not break into her apartment."

"Yeah, *that's* how you speak to Marlowe. It's how Mrs. du Pont visits. Mrs. du Pont pays for the big spread, so technically she's sneaking into her own place."

"Olivia *sneaks* into her sister's apartment in the middle of the night?" I found it difficult to imagine Olivia du Pont *sneaking* into anything.

"Oh, yeah. Marlowe Hughes and daylight's a *bad combo*. At night she's, uh, more *chill*."

"And why's she *chill* at night?"

"Her dealer comes at eight. Coupla hours later? She's riding a magic carpet over Shangri-la." He grinned, but then, seeing my reaction, shook his head defensively. "I swear it's the *only* safe way to enter. That's when we do repairs, take out her trash, make sure she hasn't left on a gas burner or clogged the toilet with her fan mail. Once a week Mrs. du Pont takes up fresh food and flowers. If she did it during the *day*, there'd be carnage. *This* way, when Marlowe wakes up, she thinks she's been visited by Santa's elves."

He took a sip of coffee, squinting at something over my shoulder. I noticed one of the other doormen at The Campanile had wandered outside.

"Artie needs to go on break. Just, uh, come by at eleven and I'll get you up there. But . . ." He squinted. "You know those electric tiger prods they use in circuses? You might want to bring one." He guffawed heartily at his own joke, taking off down the sidewalk. "'Course, it proved ineffective for Siegfried and Roy," he added over his shoulder, "so no promises."

82 FIFTEEN MINUTES LATER, we were sitting in the window of the Starbucks at Second Avenue and East Fiftieth.

"It's an ideal situation," said Hopper. "If Hughes is out cold, we'll have plenty of time to look through her place."

I was relieved to see this morning Hopper seemed to be all right after everything he'd told us. After disclosures such as his, it was difficult to gauge how the person would react afterward. But he appeared to be more focused.

"It's like having secret access to Marilyn Monroe's house," said Nora. "Or Elizabeth Taylor's. Think of the photos and letters and love affairs with presidents no one *knows* about. She might even know where Cordova is."

"As enticing as it sounds to ransack Marlowe's home while she's in a drug-induced coma," I said, "this operation is possible because of Olivia. I don't want her to find out I rummaged through her sister's apartment like a yard sale."

"We'll work fast," said Hopper, "leave the place exactly as we found it."

I said nothing, squinting across the street. A few yards from a restaurant, Lasagna Ristorante, a suspicious-looking white-haired man wearing a black coat was loitering by a brick wall. For the past five minutes, he'd been standing there, having an intense argument on the phone, but every now and then he glanced pointedly *right at us.*

"It's time to get the Waldorf guest list," I said, keeping an eye on him. "We'll get the name of every guest who stayed on the thirtieth floor between September thirtieth and October the tenth, the days Ashley was in the city. We'll compare that to the Oubliette membership. If one name appears on both, that's the person Ashley was looking for. That's the Spider."

The white-haired man outside hung up and took off, heading north on Second. I waited to see if he'd circle back or cross the street, but he appeared to be gone.

"But how do we get the names?" asked Nora.

"The only way." I drained the rest of my coffee. "Corruption and intimidation."

83

I STROLLED into the Waldorf Towers lobby to do some reconnaissance.

Today, behind the front desk there was an attractive woman, thirties, with long shiny black hair—her nametag read DEBRA—and a young Japanese man, MASATO. After answering the phone a few times, Debra fumbled under the desk and produced a large Louis Vuitton bag, a good sign; it meant she liked luxury goods, would welcome some extra cash to buy more. This, while Masato stood stoically at the other side of the desk, doing and saying nothing, like a Kendo warrior proficient in the Way of the Sword.

The single girl and the last samurai—it didn't take a genius to decide who'd be amenable to bribery.

I caught up to Nora and Hopper on the steps of Saint Bartholomew's, across from the hotel. I gave them Debra's description and put the three of us on a surveillance rotation, so we could catch her alone as soon as she left the hotel. One of us monitored the employees' entrance from Saint Bart's while the other two waited at a Starbucks down the block.

Four hours passed. And though quite a few employees exited—crossing the street to discreetly smoke a cigarette—Debra never appeared.

At four, I did another drive-by and realized Debra must have ducked out another entrance, because only Masato remained.

"Everyone has their price," Hopper said, when I explained this unfortunate development.

"Yeah, well, from the look of this guy, his price is three hundred beheadings and a katana sword."

At the stroke of six, Nora alerted us that Masato was leaving the hotel. I managed to flag him down.

"Sure, I'll do it," he announced in a flawless American accent, after I explained. "For three thousand dollars. Cash."

I laughed. "Five hundred."

He stood and walked out of the Starbucks. I was certain he was bluffing, but then he was on the subway escalator descending into the dense crowd.

"Eight hundred," I said, fighting shopping bags, women giving me dirty looks, to reach him. Masato didn't turn. *"One thousand."* I jostled an owl-looking girl in tortoiseshell glasses to get beside him. "Complete with home addresses."

Masato only put large blue deejay headphones over his ears.

"Twelve hundred. My final offer. And at *that* price we should know what nuts they ate from the minibar."

It was a *deal.*

Minutes later, Masato, displaying a fairly impressive poker face, ducked *back* inside the Waldorf, I went around the corner to an ATM, and then returned to the Starbucks. An hour passed, the crowd of commuters, once a flash flood, had drained to a meager trickle of women with tired faces and men in rumpled suits. Another half-hour, and there was still no sign of Masato. I was beginning to think something had happened, when suddenly he entered, pulled a thick envelope out of his bag.

There were more than two hundred names, alphabetized according to date, complete with calls made from the hotel phone. I handed him the cash, which he counted in plain sight. Apparently, this Starbucks was used to underworld transactions, because the employees behind the counter who'd witnessed us skulking in the window all day dully carried on taking orders.

"Quad venti soy latte!"

Masato stuck the envelope into his shoulder bag and left without a word, donning his headphones and vanishing into the subway.

The three of us ordered coffees, sat down at a table in the back corner, and started combing through the names, checking them against the Oubliette membership.

We'd been doing this for more than an hour, taking turns reading aloud, when Nora excitedly jerked forward in her seat, eyes wide.

"How do you spell that? The last name you just said?"

"Villarde," Hopper repeated. "V-I-L-L-A-R-D-E."

"It's *here*," she whispered in amazement, holding out the paper.

I stared down at the name on the Oubliette list.

Hugo Gregor Villarde III.

On the Waldorf list, he was *Hugo Villarde.*

Villarde was a guest in room 3010 for one night on October the first. He made no phone calls. His home address was in Spanish Harlem.

175 East 104th Street.

I Googled the name on my BlackBerry.

Not a *single result* came up.

"*That's* the scariest result of all," said Nora.

"Try Googling his address," said Hopper.

A business listing came up, a shop called The Broken Door. It had no website, only a bare-bones listing on Yelp.com, which described it as a shop for "discerning connoisseurs of oddity antiques."

"Open Thursday and Friday, four to six," Nora read over my shoulder. "Those are weird hours."

"We'll go there tomorrow when it opens," I said.

Staring down at the single name on both pages, I felt a wave of exhilaration and relief. At long last, *a decent break*—a minute *crack* to wedge my fingers into to pry the whole thing wide open: *the man Ashley had been searching for in the days before she died.*

84 | "You have nothing to worry about," Harold explained, stopping on the tenth-floor landing to wipe his bald forehead, drenched with sweat, before continuing up the flight behind us. "Her dealer came by at eight tonight so she's deep in Candy Land."

"Does she stay conked out the whole night?" Nora asked him.

"If you keep *quiet*. Coupla months ago we sent up a workman to do some repairs. She sat up in bed and started talking to him like he was her ex-husband. Accused the poor guy of screwing around. All he wanted to do was replace a radiator valve. But she's weak and needs a wheelchair to move even a *few feet,* so don't worry about her getting physical."

I stopped to make sure he was joking, but he was only wheezing heavily as he cleared the last step onto the eleventh-floor landing, catching up to us. He dug in his pants pockets for the keys and stepped toward one of two white doors marked 1102.

"If you need me for an emergency, there's an intercom in the kitchen."

"What kind of emergency?" I asked.

"Just be careful. Try not to touch anything. She hates her things moved." He twisted the knob, gently opening the door, but it was locked on the inside with a chain.

"She must be extra-paranoid tonight," he muttered, slipping his hand through and nimbly sliding the chain loose. "Lock the door from inside when you leave." He took off back down the stairs. "Good luck to you."

The three of us exchanged bewildered glances.

"I feel sorry for her," said Nora. "Locked up in here."

The only sound was the neon sizzle of the bulb in the stairwell, the steady thuds of Harold's footsteps retreating below.

We slipped inside, entering a dim laundry room reeking of body odor and baby powder. I switched on the overhead light. Mountains of silk robes and pajamas were piled everywhere, on top of the washing machine, spilling out of laundry baskets, heaped on the floor. One looked like something worn by the King of Siam, billowing sleeves, a red sash. I cracked the door opposite, staring into a long, dark hall.

It was silent. The only light came from an open doorway at the very end, *Marlowe's bedroom,* according to Harold's instructions.

"She must sleep with her lights on," whispered Nora, beside me.

"We'll check in on her," I said. "Then take a look around."

We moved into the hall, the walls covered, salon style, with framed photos. There was just enough light to make them out: Marlowe reclining poolside surrounded by palm trees, a wide-brimmed black hat on her head; Marlowe at the premiere of *The Godfather II* with Pacino on her arm; wearing an eighties wedding dress (puffed sleeves like flotation devices), smiling up at a nondescript groom who looked rather shell-shocked to be marrying such a knockout. It had to be the veterinarian she'd married after Cordova. Beckman had just one thing to say about him: "A man so far out of his league he suffered from altitude sickness." I looked, but there was no evident shot of Cordova or her time at The Peak. After a photo of Marlowe on the film set of *Lovers and Other Strangers* sitting in Gig Young's lap, exactly midway down the hall was the centerpiece: a giant black-and-white print of her glorious profile, her head tipped back, soaked in shadows and light. Her beauty was astounding, so high-decibel it blew out lenses and lightbulbs, made the mind short-circuit and stutter *impossible*. A signature graced the corner: *Cecil Beaton, 1979.*

We passed three dark open doorways, though I couldn't see anything. The curtains had to be pulled.

Outside Marlowe's bedroom, we stopped, stunned by the vision in front of us. Never before had I seen such decayed tropical splendor.

It looked like a dried-up lagoon, a flamingo habitat for a zoo that had gone bankrupt years ago. Two giant fake palms dolefully touched the ceiling. Black mold spangled the faded pink floral wallpaper, giving the room a five-o'clock shadow. There was a strong stench of Glade air freshener on top of mildew on top of chlorine from a motel pool. A tiny brass lamp drenched rose light all over antique wooden dressers and end tables carved and gilded. Porcelain figurines were sprinkled everywhere—drummer boys and pugs and swans with chipped beaks. Vases bulged with fake flowers that made no attempt to look real, the leaves shiny and plastic, the giant blooms colored like synthetic candy. Dominating the far side of the room, floating there like an old docked ferry, was a baroque king-size bed.

Right in the center, submerged under ripples of pink satin sheets, was a tiny curled-up form.

Marlowe Hughes. *The last flamingo.*

She was so small and bony, it was almost inconceivable there was actually a *woman* under there—certainly not the one *Life* magazine had proclaimed "a swimming pool in the Gobi." Spiky tufts of platinum-blond hair sprouted out of the sheets like dune grass.

I tiptoed inside, Hopper behind me, our footsteps silenced by the carpet, which looked to have once been pale cream, now browned in deeply treaded pathways around the room. I stepped over to the bedside table on the left, littered with orange prescription bottles; a glass bottle filled with a strange, neon yellow liquid; an ashtray filled with cigarette butts, many smudged with maroon lipstick. A red fire extinguisher stood beside the bed. *In case she accidentally incinerated herself.*

Her face was entirely concealed under the sheet. There was something so vulnerable about that immobile, deflated *mound,* I couldn't help but feel a twinge of guilt about what we were doing.

"Ms. Hughes?" I whispered.

She didn't stir.

"What does she look like?" whispered Nora anxiously from the doorway. "Is she okay?"

"As okay as a blown-out tire on the side of the highway."

"Seriously. Is she asleep?"

"I think so."

Hopper, who'd moved to the other nightstand, was inspecting the label of a prescription bottle.

"Nembutal," he whispered, shaking it, pills rattling, setting it down. "Very retro."

He wandered over to the chest of drawers along the wall between the windows—concealed under bloated pink curtains, which looked like faded bridesmaid dresses from the early eighties. He pulled open the top drawer, staring inside, and pulled out a piece of paper.

" 'My dear Miss Hughes,' " he read quietly. " 'Let me start out by saying I am your number-one fan.' "

I moved beside him. Inside the drawer were stacks upon stacks of envelopes, some loose and crumpled, others bound with rubber bands. It was fan mail. I pulled out an envelope. It read BOONVILLE CORRECTIONAL FACILITY C-3 in the return address, the stamp reading MAY 21, 1980. The letter was crudely typed on thin typing paper. *Deer Miss Hughes, On July 4th, 1973, at 1:32 A.M. I shot and killed a man in the parking lot of Joe's Barbecue.* I read through the rest, a plea for her to write to him, signed with a profession of love. I refolded it and pulled out another. *Dear Marlowe, if you ever pass through D'Lo, Mississippi, please visit my restaurant, Villa Italia. I named an entrée after you, the Bellissima Marlowe. It is a capellini dish with white clam sauce.* I put the letter back.

In the corner was a bookshelf crammed with magazines, a folded-up wheelchair in front of it. Stepping toward it, I realized these fan letters had actually infiltrated the room like parasites; they were tucked into every nook and cranny, filling every vacant hole, stashed above piles of *Hello!* magazines, issues of *Star* dating back to the seventies, one with an ugly shot of Marlowe on the cover (WASTED! REHAB FOR MARLOWE was the headline, THE INSIDE SCOOP ON HER SECRET COLLAPSE), a bound stack of papers, which I saw, pulling it out, was a coffee-stained screenplay, *The Intoxicator,* by Paddy Chayefsky. The Oscar-winning screenwriter had actually written Marlowe a handwritten note on the title page. *Miss M—I wrote this with you in mind, P.* I pulled out another stack and saw it was a printout of Google returns.

Marlowe Hughes. About 32,000,000 results.

Hopper was scrutinizing another letter, Nora was bent over the vanity table strewn with old perfume bottles and jewelry boxes, inspecting what looked to be sepia baby pictures tucked along the dappled mirror.

"Let's get moving," I whispered. "You guys check those rooms off of the hall. I'll look around here and keep an eye on her."

They seemed reluctant to leave. The room itself had a sort of barbiturate effect; it'd be easy to browse forever around this Pompeii of lost promise. But Nora nodded, re-tucking a picture into the mirror, and with a last look at me, they filed out, closing the door.

I glanced back at that mound on the bed. It hadn't stirred.

Across the room, beyond the vanity table, was another doorway. I crept over to it, gently pushed it open, switching on the light.

It was a large walk-in dressing room bloated with clothes, warped pumps and stilettos lined up in rows, a door opposite leading into a bathroom.

There was a strong smell of mothballs. The clothes looked to be mostly from the seventies and eighties. Toward the very back of a rack I noticed a set of pale purple garment bags peeking out from a cluster of sequined evening gowns, *as if hoping to remain unseen.* There were nine of them. For the hell of it, I yanked back the dresses, pulled down the first bag, and unzipped it.

To my surprise, it was the chic white suit Hughes wore throughout *Lovechild,* covered in grass stains, the pale purple label of Cordova's costume designer, Larkin, sewn into the inside pocket.

I pulled down the next, unzipping it. It was the same suit. I unzipped the bag behind that. It was identical, though *this* one was splattered in blood. I scratched at the rusty brown streaks. They looked convincingly real.

I unzipped the bag behind it. Again, it was the same suit, covered in even *more blood* and mud, the skirt ripped. The bag behind that was the same suit, only absolutely clean, a pristine white.

Hughes wore only the white suit in the film, which took place over the course of a single day. Larkin had obviously made nine versions of the suit, each one stained with varying amounts of blood, mud, sweat, beer, and grass stains, depending on where Hughes was in the narrative. By the end of the movie, after everything she endures in her hunt for her blackmailer and former pimp—she's raped, beaten, chased through housing projects, across highways and alleys, injected with sedatives—the suit is torn up and brown. She peels it off and torches it in the barbecue grill in her serene suburban backyard before climbing into bed next to her sleeping husband—a pediatrician, who is and will forever remain entirely ignorant of his wife's past and her last twenty-four hours of perdition.

In the film's last chilling shot, he drowsily wraps his arm around her, as she, wide awake, stares out into the darkness of their immaculate bedroom—a picture that seemed to encapsulate Cordova's view on the tenuous bonds between people, the deepest secrets about ourselves that we, in the ultimate act of humanity, will spare those we truly love.

I took out my phone and took a few shots of the costumes, then zipped the garment bags up, returning them to their spot in the back of the closet, and switched off the lights.

As I stepped back into the bedroom, however, I stared in disbelief. *The bed was empty.*

That shriveled *lump* was no longer there. The pink satin sheets had been flung aside.

"Miss Hughes?"

There was no response. *Fuck.*

85 | She had to be hiding somewhere here. The wheelchair remained folded beside the bookshelf, the bedroom door still closed. I lifted up the pink taffeta bed skirt. *Nothing but a few balls of Kleenex.*

I strode to the curtains, jerking them aside, then checked the bathroom. It was empty. Only two working bulbs above a dirty mirror, a counter littered with old makeup—blushes and chalky powders, fake eyelashes in plastic cases—behind the door, a limp red robe. I flung back the shower curtain. A filthy loofah hung from a rusty showerhead, a caddy laden with cruddy bottles. Prell. Breck Silk 'n Hold. *I hope those don't date back to the last time she washed her hair.*

I slipped out into the hall, finding Nora in the next room, which was cluttered with suitcases and old boxes. She'd switched on a lamp and was going through the closet.

"I lost Marlowe."

"What?"

"She slipped out of bed when I wasn't looking."

"But Harold said she needed a wheelchair to move."

"Harold is mistaken. The woman moves like the Vietcong."

I darted out, Nora right behind me. We searched the next room, an ornate living room that looked like a rotten terrarium, then headed into a dated kitchen, where we found Hopper taking pictures of clippings magnetized to the fridge—all of them faded photo spreads of Marlowe.

"She couldn't be in here," he said, after I explained. "I've been here the whole time."

As he said it, I spotted, *right* behind him, the kitchen door *moving.*

"Miss Hughes?" I called out. "Don't be alarmed. We just want to talk."

As I stepped toward the door, it banged forward and a diminutive figure shrouded in black satin, a voluminous hood hiding her face, jumped down from a countertop with a *whoosh* and came lunging at me, wielding a meat cleaver.

I easily deflected it—she had the strength of a dandelion—the knife clattering to the floor. Her shoulder was shockingly brittle—like grabbing a spike in a railing. I instinctively let go as she wheeled around, kicking me hard in the groin before darting out, the kitchen door swinging wildly. We lurched after, Hopper snatching the hood of her robe.

She shrieked as he clamped his arms around her, hauling her, flailing, into the living room and setting her down in a purple velvet chair underneath some fake palms.

"Calm down," he said. "We're not going to hurt you."

Nora switched on the overhead lights, and Marlowe immediately curled up into a fetal position, burying her face in her knees as if she were some light-sensitive night bloom. Her silk robe covered her, the interior tomato red, so she was little more than a heap of fabric lumped on the chair.

"Turn the light off," she whispered in a husky voice. "Turn it *off.*"

I felt an icy chill on the back of my neck. It was *her* voice.

Marlowe had a very distinct one—"a voice that lounges in its bathrobe all day," Pauline Kael had written in her rapturous *New Yorker* review of *Lovechild*. And it was true. Even when Marlowe was running from thugs, hanging off the side of a building, pouring gasoline over her blackmailer and lighting him with a match, her voice still came out slow honey sighs and goo.

After all these years, it sounded the same, if slightly slower and gooier.

I motioned to Nora, and she turned off the lights. I opened the curtains, and the orange neon light along FDR Drive lit the room, softening the décor, transforming the gaudiness into a garden at midnight. Fake roses, gilt chairs, a floral couch became mysterious tree stumps tangled with overgrowth and wildflowers.

Slowly Hughes raised her head and pale light caught the side of her face.

All three of us stared in awe, in shock. The famous cleft chin, the valentine face, the wide-set eyes were still there, yet so eroded as to be nearly unrecognizable. She was a temple in ruins. She'd had terrible plastic surgery, the kind that wasn't a nip and tuck but *vandalism*: bulging cheekbones, her eyes and skin stretched as if life had literally pulled her apart at the seams. Her skin was waxy and ashen, her eyebrows drawn in shaky dark lines with what looked like a felt-tip pen.

If there was ever evidence that nothing lasted, that time ravaged all roses, it was here. My first thought was from a sci-fi movie, that her immense beauty had been an alien thing that had feasted upon her, eaten her alive, and when it had moved on, it left this ravaged skeleton.

"Have you come here to *kill* me?" Marlowe whispered gleefully, maybe even with hope, tilting her head as if posing for a camera, her profile gilded in the light. It had the same slopes and angles of her youth ("a profile you'd love to ski down," Vincent Canby had rhapsodized in his *Times* review), but now it was a sluggish sketch of what it'd once been.

"No," I said calmly, sitting on a chair in front of her. "We're here because we want to know about Cordova."

"*Cordova.*"

She said it with wonder, as if she hadn't intoned the word in years, almost sucking on his name hungrily like a hard candy.

"His daughter's dead as a doornail," she blurted.

"What do you know about it?" I asked, surprised. Obviously we didn't have the full picture of Marlowe's mental state; she knew Ashley was dead.

"Girl never stood a chance," she muttered under her breath.

"What did you say?" Hopper demanded, stepping toward her.

I wanted to kill him for interrupting her. She was gazing at him with a knowing smile as he sat down on an adjacent velvet chair.

"This must be Tarzan, Greystoke, Lord of the *Apes*. You're missing a grunt and a club. Can't wait to see you in your loincloth. Now, who else do we have here?" Enunciating this acidly, she leaned forward to survey Nora. "A chorus girl. You won't be able to fuck your way to the middle, Debbie. And *you*." She turned to me. "A wannabe Warren straight from *Reds*. Every one of you, the farting demeanor of the artfully clueless. You people demand to know about *Cordova*?" She scoffed dramatically, though it sounded like a handful of pebbles rasping in her throat. "And so fleas look up at the sky and wonder *why* stars."

"Drop the crazy actress shtick," Hopper said.

"It's not shtick," whispered Nora, sitting stiffly on the couch.

"We're not leaving until you start talking—"

"Hopper," I cautioned.

"Then I suppose we'll be *shacking up* together. You'll sleep in the guest room. My days of bull riding are *over*. Though I warn you. The sheets haven't been changed since I bedded Hans, so they'll be sticky."

Abruptly, Hopper stood up, strode to a lamp in the corner, and, switching it on, drenched the room suddenly in blue light. It was as if he'd thrown acid on her. Marlowe hunched forward, gasping, burying her face in her knees.

"Turn it off," I said to him, though he didn't appear to hear me. I realized this situation was swiftly eroding, though the more I reprimanded Hopper, the more it seemed to invigorate Marlowe.

"Ashley Cordova. What do you know?" he demanded, looming over her.

"Diddly squatkis! You *deaf*, Romeo?"

"*Hopper.*" I stood up.

"Poop," chirped Marlowe. "Zilch-o. Goose egg. From the day she was born, she was toast."

"She doesn't know what she's saying," said Nora.

"Are you going to shake it out of me? Murder me? *Good.* I'll finally get my postage stamp. Unlike Ashley. No one will remember her. She died for nothing."

Before I could react, Hopper bent over her, roughly shaking her by the shoulders.

"You don't hold a candle to her—"

I leapt forward and wrenched Hopper away from her, shoving him back onto the couch.

"What the hell's the matter with you?" I shouted.

Hopper appeared to be as stunned by what he'd just done as I was. I turned back to Marlowe. She was slumped in the chair, motionless.

Jesus Christ.

It looked like he'd just shaken the last bit of life out of her.

Now we were *all* going to meet Old Sparky.

Nora raced back over to the lamp, switching it off, and the room again melted into dark drowsy vines and sharp rocks, Marlowe a slippery black animal lying wounded in the chair. After a moment, I realized with a wave of horror that Marlowe was whimpering, frail moans that sounded as if they were trickling out of some dark corner inside of her.

"We're sorry," Nora whispered, crouching beside her, putting a hand on her knee. "He didn't mean to hurt you. Can we bring you something to drink? Some water, or . . . ?"

Abruptly, Marlowe stopped crying—like someone had flicked an off switch.

She lifted her head.

"Oh, *yes*, child. There's some, uh, club soda just"—she twisted around the armchair, craning her neck toward the other side of the room—"there, in the bookcase, second shelf; behind *Treasure Island* you'll find some, uh, *water*. If you could just fetch it for me, dearie."

She was pointing emphatically at the shelves lining the far side of the room, around them a painted fresco of trellised roses climbing to the ceiling. Nora ran to it, fumbling behind the rows of books.

"There's just booze here," Nora said, pulling out a large bottle, reading the front. "Heaven Hill Old Style Bourbon."

"*Really?* What a shame. Lucille must have confiscated my Evian. She's always riding me hard about my water drinking. Wants me to go to meetings for it, Hydrated Anonymous or whatever the fuck. I'll have to make due with that, uh, *bourbon*, child. *Bring me my Heaven Hill.* And don't drag your feet."

Nora was reluctant.

"Give it to her," I said.

"What if it mixes with the pills she's taken?"

My gut told me ol' Marlowe wasn't on pills—or *anything* at all. When she'd jumped down from that countertop like a flying monkey out of *The Wizard of Oz* she'd had superb reflexes. Whatever irrational phrases she was spewing seemed purely mental, a side effect of being alone and locked inside this apartment for a couple of years. For all of her feigned terror at our break-in, I could see, too, she was eager for a live audience.

"*Give it to her.*"

Marlowe practically lurched out of the chair to snatch the bottle from Nora. Her hands moving faster than a blackjack dealer's in Vegas, she unscrewed it and chugged. Never before had I seen such thirst except in a Mountain Dew commercial. There was a soft *clink* of metal against the glass, and I noticed her spidery white fingers had slipped out of the long sleeve. She was wearing a single piece of jewelry, a ring with a large black pearl.

It was what her old fiancé Knightly had allegedly given her, the day he'd broken off their engagement. Though I'd fact-checked Beckman's story before, it was startling to see evidence of that emblem of heartbreak, here, now, right in front of me.

Marlowe pulled the bottle from her lips with a gasp, wiping her mouth. She sat back, settling comfortably into the chair. She looked calm now and *oddly lucid,* clutching the bottle like a swaddled child in her arms.

"So, you'd like to know about Cordova, dearies," Marlowe whispered.

"Yes," said Nora.

"You *sure*? Some knowledge, it eats you alive."

"We'll take our chances," I said, sitting in the chair across from her.

She seemed very pleased by this response, gearing up for something, *preparing.*

It was at least two or three minutes before she spoke again, her low voice, rutted with rocks and potholes only moments before, suddenly smoothly paved, winding its way effortlessly through the dark.

"What do you know about The Peak?" she whispered.

86

"IT'S CORDOVA'S LEGENDARY ESTATE," I said. "It sits north of Lows Lake in the wilderness."

"Did you know it was built on a Mohawk massacre site?"

"No. I didn't."

She excitedly licked her lips. "Sixty-eight women and children were slaughtered there, their bodies thrown in a pit on a hill and set fire to. This was where they constructed the foundation for the house. Stanny naturally didn't know that when he bought the place. He told me all he knew was that the couple living there, some British lord and his idiot wife, had gone bankrupt. But they failed to disclose the wife went completely loony living there. When they sold the estate, returning to England, the lord had no choice to put his poor mad wife into an institution. Within days, she stabbed a doctor in the ear with scissors. She was transferred to Broadmoor, hospital for the criminally insane. Shortly thereafter, the lord dropped dead of a heart attack. And *that,* as they say, is a *wrap.*"

Stanny—it was obviously her pet name for Cordova. She paused to take another long drink from the bottle. It was as if with every swig she was resuscitating herself, coming slowly back to life. She even seemed to grow less bony, *filling in.*

"My Stanny," she went on, clearing her throat, "without knowing a thing about any of this, moved right into his lovely mansion with his lovely wife, and his baby son. Now, I'm a cynical old *bitch,* if you haven't noticed. I don't *believe.* Religion? Humans desperate to take out infinity insurance. Death? The great big *nada.* Love? Dopamine released in the brain, which gets depleted over time, leaving contempt. Nevertheless, knowledge of those two simple facts, massacre and madness? It would have kept even *me* away."

She took another swig, wiping her mouth with her sleeve.

"Stanny told me, the very first day they arrived, after the movers had gone, his wife disappeared to take a nap upstairs and he went for one of his long walks. He always walked alone in the woods when he needed an idea for a picture. And he needed one. *Somewhere in an Empty Room* had come out. It was so good it broke hearts. Everyone was dying to see what he'd do next."

She paused, her bony hands crawling out of the sleeves to fiddle with the white Heaven Hill label on the bottle.

"He'd been walking for an hour, following one path and then another deep into the forest when he noticed a knotted red string dangling from a tree branch. A *single red string.* Do you know what it means?"

Nora shook her head. Marlowe nodded with a wave of her hand.

"He untied it, thinking nothing of it, and continued on until the trail opened up into a circular clearing beside a wild rushing river. Within the clearing, *nothing* grew. Not a stray leaf or pinecone or twig. Only dirt in a perfect—*inhuman*—circle. Outside of it on the ground he found a sheet of plastic, letters written backward across it, the words indecipherable. There was a naked, headless doll with its feet nailed to a wooden board, its wrists tied with more red string. Stanny assumed it had been left by local pranksters who frequented his property. He collected the junk and threw it away. But when he checked the *same* area three weeks later, he saw black charred circles on the ground where there had been evident burning. It smelled *recent*. He complained to local police. They wrote up a report and assured him they'd patrol the area and let locals know the house was no longer vacant. Stanny put up no-trespassing signs along the perimeter of his property. A month later, he and his wife woke to piercing screams in the dead of night. They didn't know if they were animal or human. In the morning he went to the area. There, at the center of a perfect circle, was an altar with a newborn fawn on it, its eyes gouged out, its mouth tied shut. Carved into its dappled body with a knife were strange symbols. Stanny was livid. He reported it to the local police. Again they wrote up the report. And yet? There was *something* in their expression, the way they glanced at each other. Stanny realized they not only already *knew* who was doing such things, *they* were in on it *themselves*. They, along with countless people in the town, were using his property for sadistic rituals. Not that Stanny should have been surprised. He was living amongst country *kooks*, after all, white-trash crazies, in-bred *Deliverance* freakazoids."

371 | NIGHT FILM

She grinned impishly, her eyes bright.

"*You* get the idea. And you can imagine what Stanny's dear wife, Genevra, from a swank Milanese family, thought about such backwoods heathens. She pleaded with him to erect a fence around the property for protection, to keep them *out*. So he *did*. He put up a twenty-foot electric fence, spent a fortune on it. The problem was, what he'd actually done was, rather than keeping them *out*, he'd barricaded himself and his family *in*."

She fell silent for a moment.

"I don't know how he fell into experimenting with it," she went on. "He never told me. Stanny wasn't afraid of the unknown. Within the universe. Within ourselves. It was the subject he plumbed endlessly. He took submarines down there. He went down, down into the dark crags and muck of human desire and longing into the ugly unconscious. No one knew when he'd come back, if he ever would. When he was working on a project he disappeared. He breathed it. He'd write all night for days and days until he was so tired he slept for two weeks like a hibernating monster. He could be agony to live with. I, of course, experienced it firsthand, up close and personal."

Visibly proud of this pronouncement, she gulped down the Heaven Hill, a drop sliding off her chin.

"The problem with Stanny," she went on, wiping her mouth, "as with so many *geniuses,* was his insatiable *needs.* For life. For learning. For devouring. For fucking. For understanding why people did the things they did. He never judged, you see. *Nothing* was categorically *wrong.* It was all human in his eyes and thus worthy of inquiry, of examining from all sides."

She squinted at us.

"You're his fans, are you not?"

I couldn't immediately answer. I was too stunned, not just by what she was saying but by her sudden energy and sanity, both of which seemed to increase in direct ratio to the amount of Heaven Hill she guzzled—now almost half the bottle.

"What do you know about his early life?" she demanded.

"He was the only child of a single mother," I said. "Grew up in the Bronx."

"And he was amazing at chess," Nora added. "He used to play for money at the tables in Washington Square Park."

"That was Kubrick. Not Cordova. Get your *geniuses straight,* for fuck's sake." Marlowe surveyed us. "That's *it?*"

When we said nothing, she scoffed.

"That's what I've always found so pathetic about *fans.* They weep when they have a live glimpse of you, frame the fork you touched. Yet they're impervious to *doing* anything with that inspiration, like enriching their own lives. It drove Stanny-boy crazy. He used to say to me, '*Huey*'—it was his nickname for me—'*Huey,* they see the films five times, write me fan letters, but the underlying meaning is lost on them. They take nothing away. Not heroism. Not courage. It's all just *entertainment.*' "

Huey sighed, taking another swig.

"Stanny was raised to be a good Catholic. His mother, Lola, worked two jobs as a maid in one of the big New York hotels. She was from a small village outside of Naples. Yet she knew a great deal about *stregheria.* You've heard of it, I suppose?"

"No," Nora said, shaking her head.

"It's an ancient Italian word for *witchcraft.* A seven-hundred-year-old tradition, passed along mostly in wives' tales, yarns to scare children, make them eat their vegetables and go to bed early. Cordova's father was from the Catalan region of Spain, a blacksmith. The family lived together in a small town outside Barcelona before they were due to immigrate to the States when Stanny was three years old. The day they were meant to leave, the father decided he couldn't go. He didn't want to leave his homeland. So, Lola took her son and set out for America. Within a year the father had a new family. Stanny never spoke to his father again. But he remembered his Spanish grandmother telling him about *bruixeria,* the Catalan tradition of witchcraft. He said she told him on New Year's Eve witches have the utmost power, and that's when they kidnap children. She told him to put the fire tongs in the form of a cross over the embers in the fireplace, sprinkle them with salt, and the boy would prevent a witch's entry via the chimney. So, you see, my dears, Stanny grew up with superstition. Certainly not taken seriously, yet it was nevertheless present on both his mother's and his father's side of the family. And Stanny's imagination on the *worst* of days is stronger than our realities. I think with a background like that, he was sadly predisposed to it . . . *susceptible,* you might say."

She gazed at us, her fingers fiddling with the pearl ring, twisting it around and around her finger.

"He never told me how it happened. But shortly after building the fence around the property, he realized the townspeople were still trespassing."

"How?" I asked.

"They came by boat. The estate is north of Lows Lake. If you leave from the public shore and make your way to the northern side and along a narrow river, eventually it will feed into a lake on The Peak property. When Stanislas found this breach, he had his men build a chain-link patch straight down to the bottom of the riverbed so only a *thimble* could get past. A week later he and his wife woke up to the sound of drumming. Voices. *Screams.* The next morning he went back to the fence and saw that the spot barring the way by the river had been *sawed straight through.* And he could see from the way the wires were cut it'd been done by somebody on the *inside* of the property, not the *out.*"

"Someone living there," I said.

She nodded but didn't elaborate.

"Who? A servant?"

"Every paradise has its viper." She smiled. "If Stanny had one weakness it was his belief that personality was fluid. He didn't believe people could be evil, not in some pure form. He always liked a lot of people around him. Hangers-on, *groupies,* you'd call them, though *he* called them his *allies.* He hadn't been living at The Peak a month when he met in town, quite by accident, a handsome young priest who'd also just moved to Crowthorpe to set up his parish. Stanny needed a religious adviser for a script he was working on, *Thumbscrew,* and the two men became friends. Within weeks, the priest was shacked up at The Peak. Genevra was furious. She loathed the man. He was hot as *hell,* a brawny Tyrone Power type with gold hair, blue eyes. Probably had one hell of a *der Schwanz,* if you catch my drift. He claimed to have been raised in the Iowan cornfields. But something was rancid about the man. Genevra tried to convince Stanny he was dangerous. An impostor. A leech. She was Italian, a staunch Catholic, and had noticed rather *gaping holes* in the man's knowledge of the Church. She also believed he was unnaturally obsessed with her husband. Stanny told her to relax, that the man was fascinating, an inspiration."

Marlowe took another long drink.

"I don't know how it happened," she said. "I suspect one night Stanny went down to the crossroads to confront these townspeople and ended up hiding, watching them. By the time he returned to the mansion at dawn, he had a wildly different perspective on the entire business. I don't know what he saw or what they *did.* Nothing was proven, but Genevra always believed that the priest had everything to do with it. That he'd made some kind of *deal* with these people, was perhaps even one of them."

She sighed.

"So Stanny began his life there. Creatively, he came into his own. Certainly, his previous pictures were electrifying, but this new body of work he was producing at The Peak, it was a different dimension. He began to craft his night films. He explained it once. 'Huey,' he said to me. 'I love to put my characters in the dark. It's only then that I can see exactly who they are.' "

She fumbled with her long satin sleeves, smoothing the fabric over her knees. I didn't say anything, mesmerized by what she was telling us about Cordova, and also by Marlowe herself. She'd grown so lucid and animated, she seemed entirely different from the woman we'd encountered before.

"Eventually there was no need for him ever to leave that property," she continued. "Everything, everyone, came to *him*. He had three hundred acres. He built his sets there, edited his films there. When he had to leave, it was because he'd found a shooting location close to Crowthorpe. It was as if he'd come to believe his power could only be harnessed when he was on those grounds. And it was true. The quality of performances he was able to capture was astounding. His energy had no bounds. He was Poseidon, his actors his school of minnows. When you were working with Stanny on a picture you stayed at The Peak. You ate your meals there, you never left, were allowed no contact with the outside world. You turned your life over to him, handed him the keys to your kingdom. That meant your *mind* as much as your *body*. It was all agreed to beforehand. You showed up on the first day of production, ignorant and blind. You knew nothing about the film, or who your character was, or really anything at all except that your life as you'd known it was over. You were setting off on a new journey down a wormhole into something unknown. When you finally emerged three or four months later and returned home, you were *changed*. You realized before, you'd been asleep."

"Why would anyone agree to such a thing?" Hopper asked, as she took another drink. "Signing away your life, your mind and body, to *one man*? He sounds like Charles Manson."

She looked amused by his vehemence, narrowing her eyes at him.

"There's the human desire to exert free will, yes. But there's an *equally* strong desire to be tied up, gagged, and bound. Naturally, there was the glory that came with appearing in a Cordova picture. You were made. You would get the best roles after working with him. Even when he went underground. It gave you cachet. You were a warrior. Yet the true value of working with Stanny was not money or acclaim, it was the *afterward*. All us actors spoke of it. When you finally returned to your real life after working with Cordova, it was as if all of the colors had been turned way up in your eyes. The reds were redder. Blacks blacker. You felt things profoundly, as if your very heart had grown giant and tender and swollen. You dreamed. And *what dreams*. Working with that irascible man was the most grueling time of my life. I accessed the deepest, most tormented parts of myself, parts I was petrified of opening because I doubted I'd ever get them closed again. Perhaps I never have. But I'd do it again in a heartbeat. You were making a film. Something that would outlast you. Something wild. A powerful piece of art that wasn't a commercial concoction, but something to *slice into* people, make them bleed. Living at The Peak, you were as underground as any resistance, working for the last true rebel. You were also learning how far you could go—in love and fear, in resilience and sex, in euphoria. To throw off what you'd been taught by society and make it all up for yourself. To live from *scratch*. Can you imagine the intoxication of such a thing? You come back from this and you realize the rest of the world is asleep, in a coma, and they don't even know."

"Is that why you fell in love with him?" Nora asked tentatively.

Marlowe sat up, jolted by the question, jutting out her chin. "Everyone fell in love with him, child. *You'd* be mere putty in his hands. That goes for every one of you. Who can resist the man who understands and appreciates your every cell? We married during the production of *Lovechild*." She said it with a sad wave of her hand, staring down at the Heaven Hill bottle, now almost empty.

"Let's just say, when it was over, I saw that our love was a hothouse flower. Thriving and vivid indoors, in very specific conditions; outside the enclave, in the real world, dead. I couldn't live at The Peak, not forever. Because by then Stanny refused to leave it. It was his private dimension, his personal netherworld. He wanted to remain forever on this magical planet. I had to get back to Earth."

"He *really* refused to leave?" Nora whispered, incredulous.

Marlowe stared her down. "*Zeus* was loath to leave *Olympus*, was he not, unless he had mortals to torment? Occasionally during shooting, Stanny would vanish somewhere for weeks at a time and couldn't be found. Not anywhere. So we often wondered if there was some other place he went. The secret place within the secret place. When he *did* finally show up again, he had strange rocky sand in his boots and he reeked of the open sea. He was also especially voracious in the *sack,* if you catch my drift—like he'd sailed away for a time on his pirate ship, invaded villages, burned them to the ground, raped and stole and murdered, and then he came back to The Peak with the salt still encrusting his hair, and all that mist, sweat, and blood soaked into his skin." She smiled dreamily. "Those were the nights he split me in half."

"Hold on," Hopper interjected, sitting forward, elbows on his knees. "These intruders from town. You're saying Cordova *became* one of them?"

Marlowe looked exasperated. "I said I didn't know the *exact nature* of his involvement, Tarzan. But at some point he was doing more than just *observing*. It was the reason for his wife's suicide. Genevra. He never told me exactly what happened. But I imagine that the poor, rather fragile woman found out about his nightly *activities*. You see, that priest—he was still there, hanging on, silently waiting at the perimeter. An oily shadow, always around. It was too much for her mentally. One gray afternoon, she drowned herself in a lake on the property. The police ruled it an accident, but Stanny knew the truth. Genevra hadn't gone swimming. She boarded a small boat, rowed out to the center of the lake, and climbed right in, pockets of her dress filled with stones. They found the boat later, destroyed it. Stanny adored her, of course. But not enough to be ordinary. He couldn't be contained by one woman. Or one man. You'll find that great artists don't love, live, fuck, or even die like ordinary people. Because they always have their art. It nourishes them more than any connection to people. Whatever human tragedy befalls them, they're never *too* gutted, because they need only to pour that tragedy into their vat, stir in the other lurid ingredients, blast it over a fire. What emerges will be even more magnificent than if the tragedy had never occurred."

Marlowe fell silent, abruptly weary. For a minute, she did nothing but fumble with the robe, pinching at the fabric.

"Rumors about what Cordova did at The Peak swirled, of course. Especially among us actors. One story I heard was from Max Hiedelbrau. Max played Father Jinley's father in *Crack in the Window* and that prick of a patriarch in *To Breathe with Kings*."

I remembered Max from both films; he was Australian, a tall, portly actor with a drooping bloodhound face.

"Max is a notorious insomniac. At four in the morning during the shooting of *Crack in the Window,* he was outside, taking a walk through the gardens, rehearsing his lines. He saw a figure hurrying to the front entrance, up the steps, vanishing inside the manor. It was Stanny. He appeared to be coming back from the woods, and he was carrying a black bundle in his arms. When Max followed he noticed on the handle of the front doors there were reddish-brown streaks. It was blood. Tiny droplets trailed through the marble foyer and up the stairs. Max went to bed. By morning the droplets had all been cleaned up."

Marlowe slurped down the last drop of Heaven Hill.

"People did whisper," she went on, eyeing me. "But the Warner Brothers executives who periodically visited the set said nothing. And yet—and *this* is rather telling—even though The Peak was one of the most luxurious private residences they'd ever set foot in, with a full-time staff and a French chef, not one of those slick Hollywood suits ever spent a *single night* at the mansion. No matter how late shooting went, they always retired to a hotel in Tupper Lake well over an hour away."

"They were afraid?" Nora asked.

She smiled wryly. "They didn't have the *der Sacke*. As long as Stanny made them money, produced films the public was dying to see, they didn't give a damn about his personal life. If he drank blood? Chanted? Decapitated animals? They'd dealt with trouble before. There was an incident they had to hush up involving one of the actresses—apparently she went mad working with Stanny. So scared out of her skin, the poor girl climbed out of her fourth-floor bedroom window in the dead of night, scaled to the ground like a centipede, and was never seen again."

"Who was she?" asked Nora.

Marlowe shrugged. "Her name escapes me. You see, whatever he was doing to unleash this creativity, get his actors to hack into their own souls and *bleed out* for the camera so the world could drink it—as long as everyone kept their mouths shut, it was business as usual. They looked the other way. We all did."

"But not Ashley."

Hopper whispered it, his voice so quiet and resolute, it sliced through the room, through Marlowe herself, rendering her silent, even a little unnerved.

"She'd *never* look the other way," he said.

"No," Marlowe answered.

87 | "IT HAPPENED ON A DEVIL'S BRIDGE," Marlowe continued, staring at Hopper, anxiously clutching at her shoulders and chest to make sure she was fully covered by the robe. "You've *heard* of them?"

"No," said Nora.

"They're medieval bridges. Steeped in folklore. Most are in Europe, from England to Slovenia, built between one thousand and sixteen hundred A.D. Though the stories of each bridge vary, the underlying premise is that the devil agrees to help build the bridge in exchange for the first human soul to cross it. I don't know the specifics. But somehow there came to be such a bridge on The Peak property. *They* built it, I imagine."

"You mean the townspeople from Crowthorpe Falls," I said.

She nodded. "From the moment she entered the world, Ashley was an extraordinary child. A glorious image of her father. Fearless, dark-haired, with his pale blue-gray eyes clear as a stream. The intelligence, the unquenchable curiosity, the way she *grasped* life. The two of them were inseparable. Stanny loved his son, Theo. But there was something about Ashley that . . . well, he couldn't help but worship her. *Everyone* did."

She chugged the Heaven Hill bottle with her head thrown back, seemingly oblivious that it was totally empty. She wiped her mouth.

"Stanislas never knew how Ashley came to follow him into the woods that night. Ashley never told anyone. But I have a pretty good hunch who gave her the idea. You see, that priest—he was still *lurking*. He hadn't been with Cordova at The Peak for some time. After Genevra's death, he took off, supposedly traveled throughout Africa doing missionary work, but then, rather suddenly, the old *boy* was back in town, having no place to stay and little money. Cordova didn't object to his old pal *shacking up* at The Peak once again. I don't know for a fact, but I imagine the priest was quite jealous of Ashley. He adored Cordova. He must have hoped that Stanny and he would one day . . . I don't know. Live *happily ever after?* Like a couple of lovesick teenagers?"

Marlowe fell back in the chair. "However it happened, in the middle of the night in June—this was back in 1992; Ashley was five—Stanislas was at this devil's bridge he'd constructed with these townspeople.

When he was partaking in, *whatever* it was they *did*—a ritual of the utmost depravity, I'd imagine—Ashley appeared from out of nowhere.

She stepped right onto the bridge. You can imagine how disturbing such a scene would be for any child. But Ashley wasn't afraid. Stanislas, when he saw her, screamed at her to *stop,* go back. But in the chaos, when she saw her father, she did what any little girl who loved her father would do—she ran to him. Ashley ran the entire length of the bridge, stopping only when she'd reached the other side. *She* was the first human soul to cross it."

Marlowe fell silent, sitting unsteadily forward. A white bony hand had emerged from the voluminous black satin sleeve, resting on her throat.

"Stanislas was appalled. The scene was immediately disbanded. Fires put out. *Whoever* and *whatever* these people were, they were ordered to leave the property. Stanislas led Ashley back to the house. To his relief, she seemed fine. She was herself. Wasn't even afraid of what she'd just seen. Her family home was a veritable *movie set,* after all. She'd watched bonfires, cars exploding, men and women declaring their undying love, their undying hate, fight scenes, love scenes, chase scenes, women hanging for dear life off the sides of buildings, men falling out of the sky—all in her own backyard. He tucked her into bed and read aloud to her, a chapter from one of her favorite fairy tales, *The Mysterious World of Bartho Lore.* She fell asleep that night with a smile on her face—just as she always did. Stanny decided not to tell his wife. I don't know the extent of Astrid's—Stanny's third wife's—knowledge of what he'd been up to in the middle of the night, but there seemed to be an understanding that he was free to do what he liked, so long as he didn't involve the children. When Stanny went to bed that night, he prayed to God. An interesting *choice,* given how he'd been spending his free time. But it was to God. Even then, he didn't *quite* believe in the things he'd been doing. Now he hoped none of it was real. It couldn't be. The idea's really absurd. Is it not?"

She asked this with cynical delight, taking another long swig from the empty Heaven Hill bottle. *Maybe she was guzzling the fumes.*

"Within a week, Stanislas began to notice a difference. Ashley was always a watchful, *gifted* child, but now her gifts started having *ferocious* tendencies. He'd invited some Chinese soldiers and a former ambassador to live at the house while he worked on his next picture. Within two weeks of their arrival, Ashley was entirely fluent in the language. She also began staring, staring *right into* people, as if she could read their thoughts, see their fates unspooled before her like a roll of thirty-five-millimeter. She still laughed, of course, was still so beautiful, but there was a gravity in her now that had never been there before. And then there was the *piano.*"

Marlowe shuddered at the thought.

"Astrid was a trained pianist. Since Ashley was four, she had a teacher from Juilliard travel up to the estate twice a week to give the girl private lessons. At five, Ashley was good for her age but never had real passion for the instrument. She preferred to be outdoors, riding horses and bikes, climbing trees. Now she sat down, shut herself inside for hours, and played until her fingers swelled with blisters. Within weeks, the girl could master any piece put before her, Beethoven, Bartók, in *mere hours,* the whole thing memorized. More and more, this shift in Ashley was palpable. Stanny was too devastated to believe it. Yet he began to do research. Throughout history, *alliances* with the *devil* often manifest themselves in virtuosic mastery of an instrument. In eighteenth-century Italy, there was Paganini—still believed to be the finest violinist ever to have lived. The same was true for Robert Johnson, the blues musician. He went to a crossroads in Tunica, Mississippi, and gave the devil his soul in exchange for total music mastery."

She paused, her breathing shallow, nervous.

"Astrid was still ignorant of what had occurred. She thought her daughter was simply growing up with a rabid intelligence. But then she began noticing Ashley was oddly *cold* to the touch, and when she took her temperature, rather than the normal ninety-eight-point-six degrees, Ashley was consistently around ninety-seven, ninety-*six.* She took her to New York City to visit various hospitals. Doctors found nothing wrong. Astrid worried, especially when Ashley began showing signs of behavioral problems. She'd stopped laughing. And when she became angry she had a temper that was *frightening.* Stanislas finally had to tell his poor wife. He showed Astrid what he believed to be the devil's mark on Ashley. Something called the toad's footprint. A sizable freckle in the iris close to the pupil. Ashley had it in her left eye."

I stared at her. Marlowe had just described what Lupe, the house-keeper at the Waldorf had talked about. *Huella del mal. Evil's footprint.*
Nora turned to me, clearly remembering how she'd pointed out the freckle in the medical examiner's photo.

"Astrid naturally didn't want to believe it. But then there was a terrifying incident that changed her perspective. In the middle of the night, the whole house woke up to a man screaming in his bed. It was the priest. The pajamas the man was wearing, as well as the black clerical clothes in his closet, were *on fire*. *He* was on fire. The family managed to snuff out the flames, and Astrid put the man, barely conscious, into the back of her car, so she could drive him to the hospital, because Cordova, of course, could no longer drive. He refused to leave the property. They didn't want to call an ambulance for fear of the terrible publicity. So, in Astrid's frenzied state, driving like hell, she rounded a hairpin turn, lost control, and hit a tree, totaling her car. Theo rescued the man in a van, as this priest, drifting in and out of consciousness, moaning from the pain, inched toward death. He dropped him off at a rural hospital outside of Albany and took off. The priest was admitted under the name John Doe, third-degree burns covering his entire body. Ashley had seemingly slept through the entire incident. But the next morning, Astrid noticed her daughter had a terrible burn mark on her left hand. Astrid knew she was responsible. It was the moment she started to believe Stanny, that this devil's curse was real." Marlowe shook her head. "The priest survived, though I heard he vanished from the hospital a month after his admittance and was never seen again, not at The Peak, not anywhere else."

I could hardly believe it. Marlowe had described in immaculate detail the incident I'd unearthed five years ago when I was researching Cordova. The motel desk clerk, Kate Miller, had witnessed a car accident in the early hours of a late-May morning. Astrid Cordova was behind the wheel. Astrid claimed to be alone in the car, but Kate had sworn there was someone else, a man in the backseat dressed in black clothing, his face covered in bandages—a man she claimed was Cordova.

It had been the priest, burned alive.

"How old was Ashley at the time of this incident?" I asked.

Marlowe shrugged. "Fifteen? Sixteen? Afterward, they sent her away."

"Where?"

"Some camp for unruly teens. It was a final, rather *futile* attempt to pretend the problem with Ashley was ordinary."

I turned to Hopper. He was slumped down in the chair, ankle crossed on his knee, watching Marlowe intently.

"Astrid was irate, demanded her husband *fix it*. He *did* have an idea. He believed it just might be possible to reverse this curse if they exchanged Ashley's soul for another's. A swap. With another child. This led to the rift between Ashley and her family. Because when it was finally explained to her, Ashley wanted to accept her fate. But Cordova was always searching for a way out. He did until the very end. He became consumed with it. To make another film was out of the question. There was only *this*. It ate him alive, cannibalized the family. There would be times when Ashley was perfectly normal, when they'd hope that whatever darkness she was succumbing to was entirely in their heads. But then something would happen and they'd know it was happening. He'd be coming for her."

"He?" Hopper demanded suddenly. *"Who?"*

Marlowe turned to him.

"Why, the devil, of course."

He chuckled. *"Right."*

She stared him down, her masklike face immobile.

"Iblis in Islam," she whispered. *"Mara* in Buddhism. *Set* in Ancient Egypt. *Satan* in Western civilizations. It's surprising when you take the time to look at history how universally accepted he *actually is.*"

Marlowe thoughtfully tilted her head, turning toward me.

"Stanislas believed it would happen when she was twenty-four, *twenty-five*—some calculation of the full moons and all that. I don't know the nature of what went on, but at some point the entire family became complicit in this design to transfer the promise onto some other child. Sadly, it wasn't that outlandish a concept. These cults prey on runaways, children who wouldn't be missed if they went missing. Many of these people get pregnant for the purpose of sacrificing the infant child on an altar. Occult crimes are very *real* in this country, only they're shoved under the rug by police because it's nearly impossible to convict in a court of law. *Not* because there isn't evidence. Oh, no. These people can't help but leave evidence of their terrifying rituals. It's hard to clean up after yourself, if you *spill blood weekly.* No. It's because juries can never *quite believe.* It's a fantastical leap that they can't make. It sounds like something out of a night film. Not real life."

She fell silent. In a mechanical reflex she fastidiously unscrewed the bottle, put it to her lips, but at last noticed, stunned, that there was nothing left in there, not a drop.

"How do *you* know so much about all of it?" asked Nora quietly.

Marlowe turned, seemingly about to berate her, but then lost steam, only gazed down at her hands, crumpled on her knees. She considered them as if they weren't part of her, but strange insects that'd crawled up her legs and she was too weary to brush them away.

"Stanny trusted me. He told me everything. He knew I'd understand the pain. Once I experienced such loss, it gutted me. It left me just my skin. When you love like that and lose, you never recover. Stanny knew I'd know how it felt. I'd spent time with Ashley. I certainly didn't believe any of it when he first told me. But then I took her with me on vacation when she was about eight. We were sitting on the beach near Côté Plongée in Antibes and I'd catch her *staring* at me. It was as if she saw my past and my future—even my soul where it was headed when I died, writhing forever in limbo. It was as if she saw it all and she pitied me."

This *gutting loss* had to be a reference to Marlowe's dashing fiancé, Knightly, dumping her for her sister, Olivia.

"This priest," I said, after a moment. "Do you remember his name?"

"People just called him *Priest,* sort of playfully sarcastic. I remember him during the shooting of *Lovechild.* He liked to spend his day fishing. I'd spot him from a distance standing on the shore by the lake all in black, like an accidental inkblot seeping into the bright landscape of sky and blue lakes and trees. I wouldn't know what he was doing until I was near him and noticed his long fishing rod and tackle box, that he was standing there so immobile, patiently waiting for a fish. He looked like he had the self-control to wait forever. Genevra gave him the nickname *Ragno.* The spider."

"*What?*" I asked.

"S—spider." She slurred the word. "How he moved. So *silent.*"

"Was his real name Hugo Villarde?"

"I . . . I don't really know."

Marlowe was slipping away again, growing feeble, hunched back in the chair so no light hit her and she was little more than a ghostly white face floating in the dark. When she'd started talking, I'd had little confidence that what she told us would be *sentient,* much less the honest truth. Yet again and again she'd surprised me, disclosing details that corroborated everything I'd uncovered.

And now: this revelation about the Spider.

"Did you ever meet Cordova's assistant, Inez Gallo?" I asked.

Marlowe shuddered with distaste. *"Coyote?* But of course. Wherever Cordova went, his little Coyote followed. She loved him, of course. Did his every bidding, every menial chore, no matter how cruel. All she asked of him in return was to breathe his air. It was Stanny who came up with the title *To Breathe with Kings,* after *her,* Coyote's, sheer *pathetic*-ness. I think she actually wished he'd eat her alive, so at last *she'd* be the closest to him of everyone, living out the rest of her days huddled in the darkest corners of his belly."

"Where is he now?" Nora asked after a moment. "Cordova, I mean."

"The jackpot question. No one has ever answered it right."

She mumbled this distractedly and didn't speak again for such a long time, her chin lowered to her chest, that I wondered if she'd actually dozed off.

"I imagine he's still there," she croaked at last. "Or he's sailed away on his pirate ship out into the sea, never to return. With Ashley dead, I imagine, whatever last bit of humanity he had, my Stanny, he's let go of it. Let it fly. There's nothing holding him back now. Not anymore."

Marlowe made an odd choking noise and, bending over, began to cough, a violent hacking sound.

"My bed," she whispered. "Take me to my bed. I'm so . . . so very tired."

Nora glanced at me. It was my cue to assist Marlowe, though I hesitated. It was the fear of seeing her ravaged face close-up, the worry she was too fragile to touch. She'd retreated again, gone far away, folded up like an old deck chair, so weathered it seemed possible she'd come apart in raw splintered beams in my hands. Nora gently took the Heaven Hill bottle from her—Marlowe was reluctant to let it go, like a child unwilling to part with a doll—and then, bending over her, she gave her a hug.

"Everything's going to be okay," Nora whispered.

I stepped beside her, and as carefully as I could, gathered Marlowe into my arms. She clamped her elbows tightly around my neck as I carried her out and down the hall, her face hidden deep inside the hood. When I set her down in her bed, Nora and Hopper stepping in behind me, instantly she buried herself under the covers like a beetle hiding in the sand.

"Don't leave me yet," Marlowe whispered hoarsely from under the sheet. "You must read to me so I can sleep. Oh. *Swallow*. That was it."

"*Read* to you?" asked Nora.

"I have a boy who comes. Every night at eight he comes and reads me asleep. There's *The Count*. Read me just a little little . . ."

"What book?" whispered Nora.

"In the drawer. There, there. *The Count of Cristo*. He's waiting."

Glancing at me uncertainly, Nora reached for the handle of the bedside table. And I found myself hoping that Marlowe was telling the truth. She seemed to be referring to the *drug dealer* both Harold and Olivia had mentioned. It was a fantastic misreading of the world, that someone mistaken for a drug dealer was simply coming up here to read books aloud to an old woman, lightness mistaken for dark, heaven mistaken for hell.

But when Nora pulled open the drawer, there was nothing inside, no book, nothing but wads of Kleenex and fan mail.

Hopper and I searched some of the other drawers, but we could find no copy of *The Count of Monte Cristo*—no books in her bedroom at all, only celebrity magazines and rubber-banded stacks of hundreds of fan letters addressed to *Miss Marlowe Hughes*. Hopper asked if she wanted him to read one of *those* aloud, but she didn't answer.

At last she was asleep.

88

"I CAN ACTUALLY UNDERSTAND IT," I said, downing the rest of my scotch, pacing beside the living-room couch. "Cordova confined himself to a claustrophobic compound in the wilderness. He never *left*. He was king of a three-hundred-acre kingdom. He surrounded himself with people who idolized him, those hangers-on, *allies,* people who doubtlessly reminded him every day he was a god. He comes to buy into it, this so-called power. He cavorts in the woods in the middle of the night with locals who worship the devil. It's only logical that eventually the entire family, including Ashley, comes to believe in it. And that belief destroys them."

"What if it *is* real?" asked Nora quietly from the couch. Hopper was at the other end, pensively smoking a cigarette.

"You mean the powers Cordova harnessed on the property?"

"Yes."

"In the forty-three years I've been alive, I've never seen a ghost. Never had a *cold chill* pass through me. Never seen a miracle. Every time my mind wanted to jump to some mystical conclusion, I've always found that inclination was simply born of fear and there was a rational explanation behind it."

"For someone who *investigates,* you're blind," Nora said.

I didn't know what had gotten into her. From the moment we'd left Marlowe's apartment and come back here, ordering Chinese takeout and hashing it out, she'd been utterly convinced that everything Marlowe had told us, including this curse of the devil, was categorically true, and any suggestion otherwise, including simple skepticism, infuriated her.

"It all makes sense, don't you see?" Her face was turning red. "Ashley came to the city to track down this Spider. We don't know why. But she knew it was finally happening. This transformation. She knew the devil was coming for her at last."

"Ashley *believed* it was happening, but it was only in her head."

"Then how do you explain that maid at the Waldorf seeing evil's footprint in her eye? How Ashley magically made Morgan Devold break her out of Briarwood? Peter at Klavierhaus said the way she moved was otherworldly. Even Hopper's story about her with the rattlesnake fits in with this. And what about the couple who lived at The Peak before Cordova arrived?"

"Countless British aristocrats are eccentric. They marry their cousins. They're inbred."

"How do you explain what happened to Olivia?"

"She had a stroke. People have them every day."

She sighed. "How much evidence do you need before you wonder if it *just might* be real?"

"There will never be hard evidence that people get *sold* to the devil."

"You don't know that."

"This is New York. If people found out worshipping the devil *actually* worked, every ambitious type A would be practicing it in their studio apartments."

She glared at me. "You're an *idiot.*"

"All of a sudden I'm an idiot?"

"Not all of a sudden. You've been one for a *while.*"

"Because I don't buy into the power of some ceremony performed by a couple of country bumpkins? Because I ask questions? Need proof?"

"You think you know everything. But you don't. Life and people are right in front of you and you act superior and make jokes but it's just a cover for the fact that you're scared. If you were a child in first grade and a teacher gave you a crayon and asked you to draw yourself? You'd draw yourself *this big!*" She indicated a millimeter with her thumb and forefinger.

"And *you* at *nineteen,* you know everything. Back in Saint Cloud near Kissimmee you figured it all out. Maybe I should shack up with Moe and Old Grubby Bill and that parakeet—which, by the way, doesn't have magical powers unless you call shitting all day *magic!*"

"*You* wouldn't know magic if it kicked you in the ass."

"The answer's simple," Hopper said.

I turned to him. "What?"

"We have to break into The Peak."

He announced it calmly, inhaling his cigarette.

"What you guys are arguing. It's irrelevant. We don't *know* where people's belief ends and what's real begins. Is there even a difference? But we do know three things."

"What?" asked Nora.

"One. Ash was tracking down this Spider, and that makes at least some of what Hughes told us sound right. Ash wouldn't let that guy off the hook, not if he was responsible for the devil's curse. So if *one* thing Hughes said is right, logically the other stuff should at least be *considered.* Two. If Cordova was involved in that black magic, whether it's real or not, Ash got sucked into it because of him. And that makes me want to kill him. Three. If any of this is true, people will want to know about it. That doesn't make any difference to me. I care about Ash and nothing else. She sent me that monkey because I think she wanted me to find out the truth about her family. It was her way of confiding in me, the way she knew about Orlando."

Of course, he was right. In some ways, I'd known from the beginning where this was all heading: back to The Peak.

"We'll find a way to break in," Hopper went on. "And whatever evidence we find, whatever truth we uncover about the Cordovas, however fucked up or however innocent, afterward, all three of us will decide together what to do with the knowledge. We'll take a vote, and that'll be it."

He eyed me with obvious mistrust as he said this, exhaling cigarette smoke in a fast stream.

"But first we find the Spider," I said.

89 THE FOLLOWING DAY, we planned to be at Hugo Villarde's antiques shop, The Broken Door, when it opened at 4:00 P.M.

But in the mayhem of the past week, I'd forgotten one crucial detail: *Santa Barbara.* I had custody of Sam for the long weekend. Cynthia called me early, telling me that Sam's new nanny—a woman named Staci Dillon—was going to pick up Sam from school at three-fifteen and bring her straight to my apartment. Cynthia had given the woman a set of my keys, so this wasn't a problem; I figured she could let herself in and wait with Sam until we returned from the antiques shop.

But the entire morning passed, then the early afternoon, and there was no word from this new nanny. I called her every half-hour, wondering *how in the hell* my ex-wife decided to trust a woman who ended her name in *i. She might as well have hired someone named Ibiza or Tequila.* Finally, at two-thirty, Staci called. She'd had an emergency; her seventeen-year-old son had been in a car accident on the Bruckner Expressway. He was okay, but she was coming from a Bronx hospital and running about an hour late. The earliest she could be at my apartment was five. I assured her it was no problem for me to pick Sam up from school. This meant, however, I'd have to bring Sam with me to The Broken Door—an unpleasant prospect.

"Call Cynthia," said Nora. "She might have a backup nanny."

"I can't do that. She's about to get on a plane."

"What about some 1-800 emergency nanny service?" asked Hopper, sitting on the couch's armrest.

"I can't send a stranger to pick up Sam."

"Hopper and I can go to the shop," said Nora.

"And I sit this one out?"

She nodded. It wasn't a mystery where *that* suggestion was coming from; she was still stonewalling me after last night's heated discussion about what was real and what wasn't.

"Just take her with us," said Hopper. "If it's sketchy? Leave."

I said nothing, thinking it over. We were close to something. I could feel it. If I left such a critical confrontation in the hands of Hopper and Nora, the lead could be blown entirely. Villarde could be tipped off, and he'd slip right through our fingers. But to put Sam in any kind of danger was inconceivable.

"Better decide soon," said Hopper. "We need to go."

90

THERE WAS NO OBVIOUS STOREFRONT and no sign, only a closed garage door with peeling red paint.

Dead vines clung to the brick façade in long coils, like coarse strands of hair left on tiles after a shower. The upper floors were derelict, the windows broken or boarded up. The building had once been quite elegant, probably—detailed pilaster Corinthian columns flanked the garage; there was a row of yellow-and-blue stained-glass windows along the ground floor—but now it was all encrusted with dirt and washed out, as if the building had been buried for years and excavated only days ago.

I stepped up to one of the doors, checking to see if there were apartment buzzers, and was amazed to see the name *right there*—VILLARDE—written neatly by hand in black pen beside a buzzer for the second floor.

"He must live above the shop," Hopper said quietly, staring up at the building.

The second floor was the only one with windows that weren't blown out. They were tall and narrow, the glass filthy, though in one I could see long yellow curtains hanging there, and a terra-cotta pot with a small green plant.

"Scott." Sam was yanking my hand. *"Scott."*

"Yes, sweetheart."

"Who's that man?"

She was pointing at Hopper.

"I told you, honey. That's Hopper."

She squinted up at me. "He's your friend?"

"Yes."

She considered this seriously, scrunching her mouth to the side. She then frowned at Nora, who'd moved toward the other door, trying the handle.

"It's locked," Nora whispered, shading her eyes as she looked in the window.

Sam was wearing her Spence uniform—white blouse, green-and-blue plaid jumper—though Cynthia had naturally added her Merchant Ivory touches: black coat with puffed sleeves, velvet barrette in her ringlets, black patent-leather shoes. From the moment we'd picked Sam up, she'd been shy and watchful—toward Hopper, in particular. She was also extremely squirmy, shuffling her feet, bouncing on my arm, putting her head *way, way back* to ask me something—all of which signaled she was coming down off some serious *sugar* and needed a snack.

"It's dark inside," said Nora, still peering in the window.

"What time is it?" I asked.

Hopper checked his phone. "Ten after four."

"Let's give it fifteen minutes."

We left, heading west down the block to Lexington Avenue and into the East Harlem Café. I bought Sam a granola bar, again explaining that we were on a field trip and afterward we'd go to Serendipity 3 for hot-fudge sundaes. She barely paid attention and only pretended to nibble the granola bar, transfixed, instead, by *Hopper.* I didn't know what this intense fascination meant until he was standing in line to order another coffee.

"Do you want to watch me jump from there to right there?" Sam asked him, pointing at the floor.

Hopper glanced at me, uncertain. "Uh, sure."

Sam readied herself, feet together at the edge of one of the orange floor tiles, and then, making sure Hopper was watching attentively, she jumped the length of the café, stopping at the display of coffee mugs.

"That was awesome," Hopper said.

"Do you want to watch me jump there to there and through *there*?"

"Absolutely."

She took a deep breath, holding it—as if she were about to plunge underwater—and then she toad-hopped, square to square, in the other direction. She stopped and looked back at him.

"Amazing," Hopper said.

Sam swiped her curls from her eyes and took off hopping again.

If worse came to worst, I could wait with her outside. It was a bustling street with trees and sun, a constant stream of cars. Even if the Spider was a maniacal presence, there was nothing he could do *now*—not in the light of day.

Ten minutes later, we headed back to The Broken Door. Nothing appeared to have changed. The garage door was still closed, the windows dark.

Hopper tried the narrow wooden door, turning the handle—and this time, it *opened*. I stepped behind him.

It was a dim warehouse filled with antiques so densely heaped, chairs on top of tables on top of wagon wheels, that the way into the store wasn't obvious. The door didn't even open all the way, and the entrance was crowded with a birdbath encrusted with birdshit, a rusty sundial, banged-up steamer trunks, and piled on top of *those,* an Eisenhower-era radio, faded brass lamps with yellowed shades, stacks of old newspapers.

Hopper and Nora crept through the narrow opening, disappearing inside. I bent down, scooping up Sam in my arms.

"No," Sam protested. "I'm too big."

"It's just for a minute, sweetheart." I put my finger to my lips and widened my eyes—going for the hard sell that this was an incredible game—and we stepped inside.

Overhead, fluorescent lights sizzled with blued, greasy light. Hopper and Nora were far ahead, quickly making their way single-file down what looked to be the only discernible pathway in—a constricted gorge through piles of junk. The place was cavernous, an entire block deep, though the light gave up on reaching the outer reaches of the store, let-ting it wallow in dirty shadow. There were tables and wardrobes, a cracked suitcase labeled ASBESTOS FIRE SUIT, Sherlock Holmes pipes, a carafe with a coiled preserved *cobra* inside it, a red bottle reading CHAM-PION EMBALMING FLUID. Comic books rose in piles all around us like red rock formations in Arizona. I held my breath due to the overwhelm-ing stench—something between mothballs and an old man's halitosis.

I had to proceed carefully because the store looked *rigged*, as if it was hoping you accidentally elbowed something so the whole place came crashing down and you were charged a couple hundred thousand bucks for the damage.

As Sam and I went deeper inside, squeezing past a sewing machine, an antique train set, a wooden Quaker chair with what looked to be a mummified dog resting stiffly against the seat, we reached a section packed with barbaric-looking old medical equipment.

I moved Sam to my other side so she wouldn't see it: toddler-sized hospital cots with grayed mattresses, blemished basins that had prob-ably held leeches, rubber tourniquets and crusty yellow vials, pumps and syringes, a wooden case featuring silver tongs, large and small. Dented tin lockers stood stiffly along the back wall. Hundreds of brown medicine bottles—every one with a white label, too far away to read—were clustered on a stainless-steel table, which had worn-out leather restraints dangling off the sides. *To restrain someone during their lo-botomy.* I glanced apprehensively at Sam. Thankfully, she was staring clear in the opposite direction, at Hopper.

He was wandering toward the back, where there appeared to be a long wooden table piled with papers and an antique cash register.

"Hello?" he called out loudly. "Anybody here?"

Nora, wading through the store far on the other side, looked capti-vated. I wasn't surprised. The place was right up *her* alley—especially the vintage clothing hanging along the walls like scarecrows: old '40s dirt-brown dresses, fluffy pink strapless gowns worn to some 1950s prom. She stopped beside a hat tree, carefully plucked a purple felt hat off—a crispy black feather glued to the side—lifted her chin, and put it on, then set about climbing through the junk to get to the speckled mirror propped against a black wagon wheel.

"Hello?" Hopper shouted.

Frowning, he picked up what looked to be a *real* bayonet, the end rusty and pointed.

"I don't want to be carried anymore." Sam was kicking like a colt.

"You *have* to. This place is enchanted."

She stared. "What's enchanted?"

"*This place.*" I stepped around an African drum—it looked to be made out of human skin, cured and dried—heading after Hopper.

Suddenly, I accidentally kicked the leg of a wooden table and it collapsed at the center. It was piled with tarnished skeleton keys, chrome car-hood ornaments, a dirty crystal chandelier, and it all started to spill off, a loud cascade of crystal drops, chains, hundreds of metal keys clattering stridently onto the floor. Clutching Sam—who mashed her face against my shoulder—I managed to catch the chandelier with one hand and right the table legs with my knee.

Hopper snapped his fingers.

He pointed at the back wall, where there was a cruddy skylight and a narrow door with frosted glass.

A *human shadow* had just moved *directly* behind it, though, as if sensing we'd spotted it, it *froze.*

It looked like a man, elongated head, broad shoulders.

"Anybody there?" Hopper called out again.

After a slight hesitation, the door opened and a man poked his head out. It was too dark to see his face, but he had a full head of orange-blond hair.

"I'm *sorry.* I didn't hear anyone come in."

The voice was husky yet delicate—oddly so. With a sharp intake of breath, the man stepped inside, closing the door behind him. And yet, facing us, he remained *exactly* where he was, his arm tucked behind him, his hand probably on the doorknob, as if considering escaping back through there in a matter of seconds.

It had to be him. The Spider.

He was a massive presence—at least 6'6"—with a hulking, muscular build. He wore all black, the only interruption in his black attire a priest's white clerical collar.

"How may I help you?" His voice came out in a rush, followed by silence, almost as if the words accumulated in his mouth like pebbles in a drain, then suddenly burst out, giving him this strange, jarring cadence. "Are you looking for something in particular?"

"Yes," said Hopper, stepping slowly toward him. "Hugo Villarde."

The man went absolutely still.

"I *see.*"

He said nothing else, didn't move a muscle for at least half a minute. Yet I could see, even from where I was standing a fair distance behind Hopper and Nora, his shoulders rising and falling.

He was afraid.

"Don't bother making a run for it," Hopper said, stepping toward him. "We know who you are. We just want to talk."

The man lowered his head in submission, his hair—an unnatural bronze color—catching the light.

"You're police, I take it?" he asked.

None of us responded. I was surprised by the assumption. I *was,* after all, holding a *child* in my arms.

Yet perhaps he hadn't noticed me. He was staring at the floor.

"I—I actually knew you'd come," he whispered. "*Eventually.* So you found it all up there, is that it? At long last, it's all *coming out.*"

He whispered this with evident *fear*—again, in that low, eerily female voice.

"How many were there?" he asked.

"How many *what?*" I demanded, stepping toward him.

He raised his head, noticing me for the first time.

He then turned to stare pointedly at Nora and then Hopper, slowly gathering that he'd misjudged the situation: We were *not* police. And though he *did* nothing specific, I was somehow aware that as this dawned on him, his shoulders relaxed, his head rose an inch, as if he no longer was deflating himself or tucking himself away.

When he finally looked back at me a chill of unease shivered through me. I was certain he was an even *blacker* form hovering there by the door, as if extreme confidence were slowly returning to him and it made him *swell* slightly, come more darkly into being.

What was it Marlowe Hughes had said?

You see, that priest—he was still there, hanging on, silently waiting at the perimeter. An oily shadow always around.

Though the man's face remained immobile, his eyes—what I could see of them—flicked curiously around Sam.

I needed to get Samantha away from him. *Now.*

91

I MOVED WITH HER back down the narrow pathway toward the front of the shop. I needed a safe enough distance but close enough where I could keep an eye on her. About ten yards away I found a large, plum-colored velvet armchair, the seat worn white. Beside it was a table with a stack of magazines and a yellow plastic horse, nothing of any danger.

"Noooooo," Sam whined as I placed her in the chair. "I don't want to."

"Honey, I need you to wait right here."

"It's *enchanted.*" She stared up at me, her face distraught and crumpled. She was on the verge of tears.

"Not anymore, honey. It's *fun.*"

She shook her head and clamped her arms around my leg, burying her face against my knee. I picked up the horse.

"Great *Scott.* Do you know who this is?"

Keeping her forehead glued to my thigh, she craned her face back an inch to eye the toy sideways.

"It's Hi Ho Silver. *Incredible.* He's a thousand years old, and if you're nice to him he'll tell you his secrets. Now, I'll be *right* over there. Do not touch anything. I'll be right back. And then you and I are going to have huge ice-cream sundaes, okay?"

There must have been something intriguing about the horse—he looked to date back to the forties, his saddle and reins painted on—because she took him, sullenly turning him over in her tiny hands.

Unfortunately, they'd all been listening to this interaction, Nora and Hopper apprehensively, Hugo Villarde with what I took to be a faint *smile* on his face. But as I moved toward him he immediately lowered his head, as if he didn't like anyone staring directly at him.

I stepped between him and Sam so he wouldn't have a view of her. *Just a few more minutes and then I'll get her the hell out of here.*

"Let's start with Ashley Cordova," Hopper said. "How do you know her?"

He didn't answer.

"Why was she looking for you?" pressed Hopper.

"Looking for me?" the man repeated. "You mean *hunting* me."

"*Why?*"

He took a few cautious steps away from the door, reaching down to grab a metal stool hidden beneath a table. He dragged it slowly toward him across the concrete floor—it made a loud grating, *rasping* sound, which he seemed to enjoy—then he slipped around it and perched on the very *edge*, facing us. He hooked the heel of his shoe—a black cowboy boot with elaborate white stitching—on the top rung.

He sat there like that, staring at us like a muscular old swan, once majestic, now barely alive, so unnervingly graceful for such a towering presence. He was in a bit more light now, and I could see his face was deeply wrinkled, though on the right side, from his eye down into his neck, the skin was blistered and scarred. *Marlowe Hughes must have been telling the truth.* Because that scarring had to be from the night she'd told us about, when Ashley had allegedly burned the Spider alive.

"What were you doing on the thirtieth floor of the Waldorf Towers?" I asked.

He looked surprised.

"I—I was meeting somebody," he said.

"Who?" demanded Hopper.

"*My Deformed Unreal.*" He smiled. "That's what he called himself. We met on the Internet."

"Who was paying who?" Hopper demanded rudely.

Villarde inclined his head in acceptance. "*I* was paying *him*."

"What happened?" I asked.

"I followed his very specific directions. I obtained the room. Put it under my *real* name. I stripped down to nothing but a bathrobe. And when I heard the knock, three times, I opened the door. I expected a beautiful *boy* to be standing there." He paused, swallowing. "Certainly not that *thing*."

"You mean Ashley?" I asked.

His eyes met mine. He seemed to find the simple mention of her name repellant.

"She set you up," I said.

He nodded. "I've never been so horrified. I shoved her aside. Ran screaming down the hall into the elevator, shaking, *convulsing* from the shock. I ran through the lobby out onto the street wearing nothing but a bathrobe. No keys. No wallet. I'd left thousands of dollars in the room. But I had to get out of there. My life depended on it."

From his breathy, saccharine voice you'd have thought he was a nervous fifteen-year-old *girl* sitting there—not a hulking man in his late sixties. I couldn't get used to this disconnect between his lilting voice and his physical self. In fact, the more he talked the more unnerving it became.

Something else about the man was *off.*

For one thing, I hadn't expected him to pull up a chair, sitting down to *chat* without any evident discomfort or resistance. Marlowe Hughes—I understood *her* desire to talk, an isolated and neglected fallen star, so eager to bathe in the attention of a captive audience. But this gnarled human bird? Why tell us the truth so easily? *There had to be something he wanted from us.*

Uneasy, I looked back at Sam. She'd put the horse down on the table and was closely inspecting him.

"Where did you see Ashley again?" I asked, turning back. *"Oubliette?"*

Villarde was visibly astonished by the mention of the club. He shifted on the stool, hunching his shoulders and back before going still.

"My, my. You *have* done your homework. That's right."

"How did she know you'd be there?" Hopper asked him.

"I assume she found my member's card in my wallet, which I'd left back in the Waldorf hotel room when I'd fled. On the back there's a private number to call in order to arrange for your captivity. I found out later that Ashley had called and made arrangements to come as my guest."

He paused, heavily breathing in and out, a sensuous, nauseating sound.

"I—I was with my defeater in my cell when she stepped out of the dark. As if from the stone walls themselves. I screamed. I ran away.

Alerted security. They went right after her, chasing her down along the beach by the cliffs, a whole fleet of guards. But they came back empty-handed. They said her footprints *simply cut out*, as if she'd flown away like a bird. Or she'd walked right into the waves and drowned." He lowered his head, gazing at his lap. "The following day, there was no sign of her. But I knew it was just a matter of time. She was coming."

"And did she?" I asked.

"Oh, *yes*. Most definitely."

"Where?"

"*Right here*." He held out his arm, indicating his own shop. "I was doing inventory in the back, when suddenly I was aware that all light had retreated from the store, as if the sun had fled, cowering behind a cloud. Alarmed, I glanced up. *And she was right there*."

He pointed toward the front of the store, where light from the street streamed in through the stained-glass windows and the cracked door.

"She hadn't seen me yet, so I crouched down, crawled across the floor on my hands and knees, trying to be as silent as I could. I reached the back corner and hid inside there."

He turned to his right, gesturing toward a huge double-door wooden wardrobe in the far corner.

"I heard every step she took, coming closer and closer toward my hiding place. As if she was the devil coming. There was a long stretch of silence. I heard her reach for the handle on the door. Very slowly it creaked open. And I knew that was it. That I'd come face-to-face with my own death."

He fell silent and shivered, hunching his shoulders.

Trying to ignore the repulsion flooding through me, I turned, again checking on Sam. Thankfully, she and the horse were now the best of friends. She was explaining something of great importance to him, whispering in his ear.

"Why'd she come after you?" asked Hopper suddenly.

Villarde said nothing, only guiltily lowered his head.

"You worked with the townspeople from Crowthorpe Falls?" asked Nora gently, taking a step toward Villarde. "You helped them access The Peak property?"

"I did," Villarde said, smiling wanly, grateful for her kindness.

"How did it work, exactly?" I asked. "You made a deal with them?"

"I did," he whispered meekly.

"With *who*?"

He shook his head. "I never knew. There were so many of them. I—I'd just moved to Crow. I met Stanislas for the first time, quite by accident, at the General Store. His wife had sent him into town to buy her gardening gloves. He asked me what I thought of the selection. 'Which of these gloves are fit for a fairy queen?' It was the first thing he said to me. We had an instant attraction. When men desire each other, they crash together like wrecking balls, quenching their need right then and there, as if the world were about to end. We began to meet around town, and within the month he invited me to his estate. He gave me my own suite in the top tower, mahogany with red damask curtains, the most beautiful room I'd ever seen. Several weeks later, I was back in town, having lunch at a diner, when a bearded man in overalls slid into the seat right across from me, a toothpick in his mouth. He asked if I had any interest in a mutually beneficial arrangement. I didn't have any money at the time. I felt that if I built up some goodwill with the locals it would help me setting up my ministry."

"But you're not *technically* a priest," I muttered.

"I attended two years of seminary. But yes, I dropped out."

"Yet you wear the outfit. Isn't that sacrilegious?"

He only smiled weakly, slowly rubbing his palms together.

"Why'd you drop out?" asked Nora.

"I didn't have what it takes to make it in the Catholic Church."

"Funny, I've noticed *scum* flourishes with surprising ease through the top dioceses," I said.

Villarde didn't answer, and I turned to check on Sam. She was dancing the plastic horse along the surface of the table.

"So, what was this *mutually beneficial arrangement*?" Hopper asked.

"I'd help them get onto the property," said Villarde. "It was simple. All I had to do was cut open a bit of the wire military fencing on the southern perimeter of the property, which would allow access to The Peak by canoe via a narrow rivulet which emptied into one of the lakes on the property. I was also asked to open up the tunnels."

"The tunnels?" I asked.

"A labyrinth of underground passageways exists beneath the entire Peak property. They've been there since the mansion's construction, so servants could move easily throughout the grounds, avoiding bad weather. Stanislas didn't know they existed when he purchased the estate. The British couple who lived at The Peak before Stanislas had sealed them off, and the realtor had no clue of their existence. I was asked by this bearded stranger to *unseal* them. It was fairly easy to do, took me no more than a few nights' work. They were crudely barricaded with random bits of wood and nails, snippets of poetry and odd verse scribbled backward on the brick, almost as if the person who'd done the job had been totally insane. The other thing I was asked to do was open the front gate. Every Wednesday night at midnight, I'd walk down the tunnel that led to the property's gatehouse—about two miles—and unlock the gate. Then I'd simply go back to bed. The tunnels are vast, laid out like a spider's web. There is a central point where one can see the many different tunnels diverging to other secret parts of the property. I didn't know what they all were. I always stuck to the tunnel leading to the gatehouse. It was the only one I dared go down. And that was *it*. Certainly, what I did to Cordova was a betrayal. But honestly I really didn't see the harm. The property was immense. Why not let these poor locals, who had nothing, use the grounds for their pagan rituals if it made them happy?"

"Did you participate in the rituals?" asked Hopper.

Villarde seemed insulted. "Of course not."

"But Cordova did," I suggested bluntly.

Villarde closed his eyes for a moment, as if in pain.

"The night he discovered the tunnels, he caught a lone woman running through them on her way to the site they used. Stanislas followed her, the idea being he'd confront them all. Instead, he somehow became involved." He smiled feebly. " 'For every man there exists bait he cannot resist swallowing.' "

"What did these rituals entail?" I asked.

"I don't know. Stanislas refused to tell me."

"What exactly was the nature of your friendship with Stanislas?"

The question made him shy. "We had a . . . a bond."

"According to *you*," muttered Hopper. "It's funny how one-sided those can be."

Villarde bristled. "*I* didn't do anything to Cordova. *He* was the vampire. He made you feel like he loved you, like you were the dearest person in the world to him; all the while he was sucking you dry, leeching your life out of you. You'd spend an hour with him. Afterward you were a carcass. You lost all sense of yourself, all dimension, as if there were no difference between you and the chair you were sitting in. *He'd be more alive, of course, invigorated for a week, writing, filming, insatiable, so wildly alive.* Art, language, food, men, women—they had to be constantly fed to him as if he were a ravenous beast that could barely be contained within human walls. There was no end to his appetites."

He blurted all of this heatedly and was about to go on but caught himself, abruptly falling silent.

"How long did you live with Cordova at The Peak?" I asked.

"Not long. Our friendship became strained after the death of his first wife. Genevra. She was so jealous of our bond. I thought it best to leave. I traveled abroad. But when you flee someone, no matter *how far* you roam, that person will follow you as doggedly as the stars. In fact, their grip on you grows even *stronger.* I was gone for fifteen years. When I returned to Crow, I went to The Peak and asked Stanislas if I might stay with him again. I hoped we could turn over a new leaf, go back to how things had been before the death of his first wife. But he had a *new* one now, Astrid, and a beautiful child. Ashley. Also a new *film* he was hacking out of nothingness into wild being. There were a great many people living there, writers, artists, scientists. Yet after a month he pulled *me* aside and said I should think about my future, where I was finally going to set up the church I'd always dreamed of. Surely it would be far away from *him. 'Time to let the vines take over,'* he was fond of saying, which meant there was no use keeping parts of the house manicured and well lit, not when he had no intention of ever entering those rooms again. He lived his life like that. *He* was the sprawling mansion of grown-over chambers, trees winding through the broken ceiling, plants twisting up through the floors. I understood what he meant. He'd done it so many times before me. He was dismissing me. Giving me my orders to *dissolve.* Fade to black. Stanislas was always moving on, always warring, always loving, galloping toward the next mysterious stranger, the next island, the next sea. And what he left behind was always ruins. But he never turned around to *see* it. He never looked *back.* I was deeply wounded. He was at once the kindest and the most barbaric man. He shifted between these traits arbitrarily, when it suited him. With Cordova you felt as if you were following a beautiful twinkling light, luring you into the woods. As soon as you lost all sense of direction, were unable to find the way back, it turned on you viciously, exposed your nakedness, blinded you, burned you. I couldn't move on. I hadn't moved on from Stanislas in fifteen years. *I don't know why the fuck he thought I would then.*"

He snarled this, spitting, unable to control himself, but then just as quickly silenced himself. He took a breath to regain his composure.

I could only stare. Marlowe Hughes had called him *oily*—such a strange description. But he *was* an insidious trickle of *oil* oozing out of a loosened pipe, dripping silently, relentlessly, to the floor. The stain it made barely visible at first, but over time immense, repugnant.

And yet for all his pathetic self-pity, I sensed a very real and very deep gash of pain inside him, which had never healed.

"Shortly after his dismissal of me," he went on, "I slipped into his little girl's room in the middle of the night. It was *so absurdly easy. Ironic,* really, that he'd done nothing to protect his most cherished creation—*Cordova,* of all people, Cordova who always warned us we *should* be afraid of our own shadow, that there was nothing scarier in the world." He smiled. "She wasn't afraid when I shook her awake. She sat up, rubbed her eyes, and asked if I'd had a bad dream. *Quite* the *understatement.* I told her something terrible had happened. I needed her help. I said her father had been kidnapped by trolls and we had to travel deep, deep down into the darkest wood to rescue him. I pulled her roughly out of bed, telling her that she had to be silent or they'd come for her mother and her brother and they'd kill them. She didn't say a word. I took her straight to the basement and down the steps, right down into the tunnels. I didn't even bother to put her little shoes on or give her a coat. But Ashley wasn't afraid. Oh, *no.* She was Cordova's daughter, after all. Five years old and she was so *certain,* so devoid of all fear. I can still remember the sound of her bare feet, how soft and *clean* they were, padding along the filthy ground next to mine, how my flashlight touched the hem of her white nightgown, *scalding* it as we followed that passage. It was like a black vein that twisted on and on in front of us. When we reached the central area she told me she hurt her foot. It was bleeding. I think she'd stepped on a nail. But I pulled her on and down the narrow tunnel that would lead us to the clearing. And the *crossroads*. I'd never been there before. I'd never *dared* go."

He shook his head, clasping his hands, interlacing his fingers as if in prayer. I turned to check on Sam. She'd placed the horse atop the stack of magazines and was quietly chatting with him and stroking his mane. *Just a few minutes longer.*

"*At last,*" Villarde whispered almost inaudibly, "*just* when I started to imagine we'd descended not into the woods but to the very core of the Earth, we reached the end. There was only a dirt wall with a metal ladder. I climbed up first and unfastened the hatch. It opened up into a dense section of woods, and far to my right, beyond what appeared to be a bridge over a rushing river, I could *see* them. A crowd. And a bonfire. Orange light like a strobe on their pitch-black robes. And yet the *sound* they were making—like nothing I'd ever heard before. It was like animals, but no animal I could identify. Like a goat, a pig, and a man, all in one *beast*. I was petrified. I couldn't go farther. I reached down and grabbed that little girl roughly by the arm, hauling her up the ladder. She cried out from the pain. I shoved her out of the hole. And I told her now was her only chance to save her father from burning in hell. I pointed toward the fire and I said her daddy was right *there,* at the end of that bridge. All she had to do was run to him, run as fast as her little feet could carry her, and she'd save him. She listened with such wisdom in her eyes, gray eyes that were really *his eyes*. It was as if she knew what I was doing, as if she understood completely."

He paused to catch his breath. "I couldn't watch her do it. I didn't dare. I descended the ladder, pulled the hatch into place, locking it so she wouldn't be able to get back in. Then I sprinted back through the tunnel. I hadn't gone two minutes when I heard the most gutting *screaming*. I recognized the voice. It was his. My love's. *Cordova*. It sounded as if he were being mauled, as if his beloved dogs were ripping him apart, tearing off his arms and legs. It was his *love* destroying him. I didn't stop. I ran back through the tunnel to the house, all the way upstairs to my room. I hid under the covers all night, my heart pounding in horror over what I'd done. I was waiting for him to come for me. I knew he wouldn't hesitate to kill me for retribution. And yet . . . I was wrong. Dawn came. It was *sunny*. The sky was blue, the clouds like candy, as if nothing had happened at all. As if it'd all been a dream."

He took another beleaguered breath, moved his other foot to the top rung of the stool, tucking his arms into his lap, hunching over, as if he were trying to collapse himself.

"The transformation that started taking place . . ."

His voice cut out in apparent incredulity.

"Before, I never *believed,* you see. Of *course* not. Yet I couldn't help it now. There could be no other explanation. Stanislas was devastated. Yet he had no idea about my role in the whole thing. Ashley, for some reason, did not tell him. And yet, if I found myself in the same room with her, I'd catch that little girl watching me. I knew she was thinking about that night and what I'd done to her. But Stanislas, entirely ignorant, was desperate for me to stay on. He needed me because he wanted to cling to God now. *God,* the boring relative everyone ignores—no one calls, no one writes—until they need a serious *favor.*"

He smiled.

"I made myself indispensable. For the next ten years, I lived with the family. I gave my life to him. I educated Stanislas on Catholic theology. I helped him study and pray, pray for his own soul, but especially Ashley's, which was slowly, inveterately turning *dark.* I suggested an exorcist. But then, it *wasn't* possession, was it? No. It was a *promise.* A deal. After researching legendary pacts made with the devil throughout history, I came across a potential solution. If Stanislas found another child to take Ashley's end of the bargain. An *even exchange.* One pure soul for another. Ashley might go free. And I'd read that if one were to try such a thing, a *simple transfer* of *debt,* one needed not harm the other child in the process. One needed only an article of clothing or object that had *belonged exclusively* to this new child. I told Cordova about the idea quite arbitrarily, not thinking he'd actually try such a thing. Cordova, for all his flaws, *loved* children. But he began to leave The Peak in the middle of the night. He had his chauffeur drive him to different schools in the area, where he'd wander the playgrounds and the athletic fields and the hallways, looking for some child's small lost belonging. When he returned to the house with his loot of little shirts and little shoes, plastic soldiers and teddy bears, he'd stick them in a bag and take them down to the crossroads. And there he tried to exchange her, night after night, week after week. I was the only one who knew. But it wouldn't work. *Nothing did.*"

I was too stunned to speak. It was, of course, exactly what the anonymous caller, John, had described to me years ago.

It had been real, after all. I had not been set up. The man had been telling me the truth.

I felt dizzying exhilaration at the realization that I had *not* been *deceived. There's something he does to the children,* John had claimed. And it was true. The reason Cordova had visited those schools in the middle of the night was that he was hoping to use them, exchange them, save Ashley's soul by condemning theirs.

"It was because he could find no equal to Ashley," Villarde continued. "The devil had been promised a child of such perfection, such intelligence, depth, and beauty, it was proving impossible to find her replacement. Like finding a stand-in for an archangel. But Stanislas wouldn't give up. He'd try and fail and try yet again. He'd do whatever it took to save her. No matter what amount of guilt and horror was left on his hands. He knew he was already beyond salvation. But *she* wasn't."

Villarde swallowed, lowering his head, his breath shallow. "A few months after I made this suggestion for a *swap,* I woke up in the middle of the night to the most unbearable pain. My bed was on fire. *I* was on fire. So were the clerical clothes in my closet, the curtains in my room. They were ablaze, writhing as if alive. I screamed, bumbling around, tried to get out to the bathroom, to *water,* but Ashley was blocking the doorway. Her left hand was on *fire*—and yet it wasn't hurting her—a wild look in her eyes. *Triumph.* It was the last thing I remembered. When I regained consciousness, I was in a hospital and learned I'd been dropped off anonymously at an emergency room in Albany. I didn't know who had driven me or how, but I had third-degree burns on eighty percent of my body. I received blood transfusions, skin grafts, and, months later, when I was at last allowed to leave, I knew I'd never go back. That *thing* she was turning into wanted me dead. She *owned* me, after all. I couldn't save them anymore. But I could save myself. I disappeared. And so it remained, for eight years, until a few weeks ago, when she found me."

So, everything Marlowe told us was true. Villarde was the burn victim in Astrid's car, and Ashley was sent to Six Silver Lakes for what she'd done.

"When we arrived, why did you think we were the police?" Nora asked.

Villarde glanced at her. "I thought that . . . I thought you'd found evidence up on the property."

"Evidence of *what*?" I asked.

"What Cordova did. Trying to save her. When the clothing and the toys didn't work, I thought . . . no, I *panicked* that he'd grown so desperate, he'd moved on to using the children themselves. I think they might be up there somewhere. Buried. Unless they were all burned, incinerated in the mill ovens to nothing." He closed his eyes in anguish. " 'I will show you fear in a handful of dust,' " he whispered.

The implication of what he was saying rendered me mute.

The entire shop and everything in it seemed to freeze from the revulsion of it, darkening, sinking deeper into shadow, holding its breath. I was stunned by his mention of a single word: *burned*. It triggered a memory of something I had in my old notes, what Nelson Garcia, Cordova's next-door neighbor in Crowthorpe Falls, had told me years ago.

Now they set fire to all their garbage, he'd told me. *You can smell it when it's hot at night. Burning. And sometimes when the wind's blowing southeast I can even see the smoke.*

"What did she do to you?" asked Hopper suddenly.

Villarde glanced up at him, uneasy.

"When she opened up that closet and found you cowering in the corner, *what* did she *do*? You're still *alive,* aren't you? You're still wearing that sacrilegious getup. What did Ashley do that you were so fucking afraid of?"

Villarde only lowered his head.

"You can't even *say* it, can you?"

Villarde opened his mouth, but no sound came out. Then he gasped, a bizarre gagging sound that prompted disgust to flood through me. He was, without doubt, one of the most wretched beings I'd ever laid eyes on.

"She pulled me to my feet," he whispered. "And she . . ."

"*She what*?" shouted Hopper.

"She . . ." Villarde was crying. "There's really nothing more *terrifying*—"

"*WHAT*?"

"She told me she . . . forgave me."

The words were so fragile and unexpected, no one spoke.

Villarde remained frozen on the stool, his shoulders hunched as if waiting for divine retribution, for God or even the devil to strike him from the world. I was about to break the silence, but abruptly, the man jerked his head up and *stared right at me.*

It was such a penetrating look it *stunned* me.

His eyes were completely dry.

For seconds, all I could think was that I'd misjudged his despair and self-loathing because his aged, carved-up face was unmistakably thrilled now, excited, his eyes pricked with light.

It was too quiet.

There was no whispering, nothing behind me. I whipped around.

The chair where Sam had been sitting was *empty.*

"Samantha!"

I lurched down the narrow passageway, knocking over stacks of magazines, a wooden walking stick clattering to the ground. I wheeled around, my heart pounding, staring into the hat racks and banker's lamps, rocking chairs and vintage radios, and *none of it was Sam.*

"Samantha!" I shouted.

Suddenly, there was a rustling noise.

To my relief, Sam poked her head out of the junk. She'd been hiding under a dining-room table laden with animal taxidermy, elk heads with antlers, bobcats and lizards, monkey skulls. She was clutching the plastic horse tightly against her chest.

"Samantha! Get over here *now!*"

She blinked in alarm and obediently started toward me. But then there was a loud *scraping sound.*

A wooden Art Deco floor lamp with a wide crystal shade standing beside her—it was shuddering, tipping forward, drunken and *alive.*

"Sam! Don't move!"

I scrambled over a steamer trunk, comic books, a bird skeleton under a glass dome smashing to the floor, but I knew I was too late.

Sam pitched forward, falling, and the lamp crashed right beside her, the shade exploding over her onto the floor seconds before her piercing screams. I climbed over a rolling stretcher, pushed aside globes and dolls to get to her, *my Sam, my dearest Sam,* barely aware of the chaos behind me, shouts and echoing footsteps of someone racing out of the shop.

92

THE NEON LIGHTS of the hospital washed out Cynthia's face, made it pale and soft as she stared back at me as if she were underwater.

"The doctor said she'll have bruising and black eyes for six weeks," she said. "Some swelling under her chin."

"What about the stitches?"

"Four on her hand where they removed some glass. But it will heal."

I numbly stared down the hall to Sam's curtained cubicle, fighting the lump in my throat.

Bruce was in there with her. Though he'd pulled the curtains, I could still see Sam through a crack between them. She was snug in bed under a mound of blue blankets, her face puffy and red, a square white piece of gauze taped to her chin. The hospital emergency room attending physician stood beside her, talking to Bruce.

The doctor was more comfortable speaking to *him*. I didn't blame her. When I'd come running in here, shouting for *help*, Sam crying in my arms, the nurses had doubtlessly thought the worst, that I had hurt her.

And I had. Even when I was reassured that she'd be all right, I was still racked with the terrible understanding that I was responsible, bringing Sam into that hideous shop. Even more gutting was my growing certainty that Villarde had somehow orchestrated it. I didn't know *how* and I didn't *understand* it, but I sensed that he'd sat down and willingly talked to us only in order to put us under the black spell of his story, and all the while he was working on a way to hurt Samantha. I wondered if he'd done it as a means to distract us, make his escape, because in the chaos of her fall, Villarde had sprinted clear out of the shop. Hopper instantly took off after him, but when he reached Third Avenue, the man was gone.

The emergency room staff sensed from my agitation I hadn't told them the whole story and thus were understandably relieved when Cynthia and Bruce arrived. I'd called Cynthia from the cab, and their private plane, minutes from taking off at Teterboro Airport in New Jersey, headed back to the terminal. She showed up within an hour and a half, and I'd been gently ushered by a nurse into the hallway.

Or was I wrong? Had it been a simple accident? It was possible I'd been sucked so deeply into Villarde's story, the horror of what he'd done to Ashley, that I was no longer thinking clearly.

"She was playing," I said to Cynthia. "She tripped on the electrical cord."

"It doesn't matter."

She said it in a monotone. I stared at her, bewildered, but there was nothing to see. Her face was so drained of feeling, it was startling to behold, as if a room I'd lived in all my life was suddenly without furniture, barren; piece by tiny piece, it had been dismantled, carted away, such a gradual progression into emptiness I hadn't noticed it until now.

She shook her head, her bloodshot eyes electric green. "The doctors said you ran in here, shouting about someone hurting her? A *priest?* Have you lost your mind?"

I didn't have a response.

"We're finished with visitation."

"I understand."

"No. I'm going to the judge so it's official. You're not going to see her anymore. *Ever.*"

"Cynthia—"

"*Stay. Away.*"

She shouted it angrily, causing a nurse who'd just walked past to turn and frown at me.

Cynthia smoothed down the front of her blouse and started back toward the curtains, but then she turned back.

"Almost forgot." She fumbled in the pocket of her blazer. "The nurse found *this* in Sam's coat pocket."

She held out a small figurine. I took it.

It was a black wood carving of a serpent. I realized, after a dazed moment, that I'd seen it before; it was the same figurine that had belonged to the deaf child back at 83 Henry Street.

He'd dropped it down the stairwell. I'd found it, given it back.

And now Sam had it.

"*This* is a toy that you consider fit for your five-year-old daughter? I can't *wait* to show this one to the judge."

The sounds in the hospital, the intercoms, the clicks and phones ringing, the squeaks of a gurney wheel, footsteps on the floor—they all grew deafeningly loud in my ears, then, almost as quickly, *silent.*

Again, I could feel the sucking back of that black tidal wave rising over me. It was *still* rising, growing stronger.

Bruce had pulled the curtain aside, and I could see Sam staring up at a doctor, her tiny bandaged hand lying atop the blankets like a lost mitten.

I turned and suddenly sprinted down the hall.

"Come back here!" Cynthia yelled after me. "I want to keep that!"

I raced past an old man lying on a gurney, blinking at the ceiling, a doctor in a white coat. I pushed open the doors to the waiting room. Hopper and Nora, sitting on the seats under the TV, glanced up at me.

"Scott?" shouted Nora.

I didn't stop, racing through the revolving doors, emptying me back into the night.

93 | I REACHED ENCHANTMENTS five minutes after closing time. The door was locked, but a handful of customers were still browsing inside.

I pounded loudly on the glass. A woman stepped out from behind the register.

"We're closed!"

"I need to see Cleopatra! *It's an emergency!*"

She shook her head and stepped to the door, unlocking it.

"Dude, I'm *sorry,* but—"

I barged right past her, racing by the few remaining customers to the counter in the back.

"Is she here?"

A punky blond kid on the stool only stared in confused alarm. I dashed past him, yanking aside the black velvet curtain.

"Hey! You can't go in there!"

I stepped inside, finding Cleo seated at the round table, conferring with a young couple.

"This is an emergency. I need your help."

"He barged right in," said the blond kid hurrying in behind me.

Cleo looked unruffled by the intrusion.

"It's all right," she said. "We're pretty much finished."

The couple scrambled to their feet, grabbing the plastic bag of herbs off the table, and nervously filed past—*giving me a wide berth*—stepping after the blond kid through the velvet curtains, leaving me alone with Cleo.

I reached into my coat pocket and pulled out the figurine. It felt strangely heavy in my hand, heavier than before.

"My daughter had this in her pocket. What the hell is it?"

Cleo rose, stepping toward me. She was wearing a white embroidered peasant blouse, jeans, her red Doc Martens, her hands and wrists laden with the same silver bracelets and rings as before. She scrutinized the serpent without getting too close to it and then turned, stepping to the cluttered shelves in the back, returning with a pair of latex gloves.

She snapped them on, carefully took the figurine—as if it were a dangerous explosive—and took it over to the table.

"You *just* found this?"

"Yes." I pulled up a metal folding chair, sitting across from her. "But I've seen it once before. Another child I encountered recently had it."

She turned it over in her hands, shaking it, listening to the interior.

I could see now, in the strong red light overhead, the wood was intricately carved, every scale, fin, and tooth polished and pointed. The beast's leering expression looked lecherous, lips curled back, tongue protruding.

"Could it be used to mark a person?" I asked. "Give them some type of, I don't know, *devil's* marking? Have you heard of something called *huella del mal*? Evil's footprint?"

Cleo didn't seem to hear me, setting the serpent down at the center of the table. Bending forward, with great concentration, she grabbed it by the tail—which coiled up and over the body—sliding the figurine in a slow counterclockwise circle. She did this three times, the only sound in the room the figurine's jarring *rasping* on the wood.

Suddenly she whipped her hand away as if she'd been scalded, the snake falling onto its side.

"What?" I asked quickly.

She looked disconcerted. "You didn't see that?"

"No. *What?*"

With a deep breath, Cleo reached out again, grabbing the tail.

"Watch the shadow," she whispered.

I was so flooded with adrenaline, I could hardly bring myself to focus on the deliberate movement.

And then I saw what she meant.

The shadow—*resolutely black* on the table—did not naturally follow the object. Instead, it froze as if snagged on something invisible, quivering with tension, the shadow's tongue elongating, *pulling far out behind the figurine* before swiftly snapping back into place and moving normally. Amazed, I blinked, leaning in, certain my eyes were playing tricks on me, but within seconds, it happened again.

And again.

She reversed the direction, moving the figurine clockwise, and the shadow behaved ordinarily.

"How is it possible?" I asked.

"I don't know." She set down the figurine. "I told you I'm not proficient in black magic. I've never seen anything like this."

"But you've *read* something about it. In your extensive witch education."

She looked at me. "I can't help you. You need to visit a real practitioner of black magic."

"I don't *know* a real practitioner of black magic. I only know *you,* so *you're* getting to the bottom of this, even if it means we sit here for two weeks figuring it out."

I leapt to my feet, the folding chair falling backward with a *crack* as I raced to the back of the room. The counters were disordered, burnt candles and ashtrays, scraps of paper scribbled with recipes for spells, battered notebooks, plastic sachets of powders marked YES and NO, jars of black ashes. The shelves were crammed to the ceiling with musty texts.

Book of the Sacred Magic of Abramelin the Mage. 777 and Other Qabalistic Writings of Aleister Crowley.

Cleo was suddenly beside me. "Calm down."

The Evil Eye. Book of Tobit. The Essential Nostradamus. I yanked down *Encyclopedia of Popular 19th Century Spells* from the top shelf, black paperbacks showering the floor, a red pentagram on the cover.

"You'll make it *worse,*" Cleo said. "Potent black magic around an unstable mind is like enriched uranium near a fuse."

I opened the encyclopedia, scanning the contents page.

"There *might* be another option," Cleo said. "But it's a long shot."

I looked at her. "What the hell are you waiting for?"

She looked grudgingly at her watch, sighed, and moved to the back corner, where there was a small sink, stacks of notebooks, and a bulletin board propped on the counter laden with papers. She lifted the pages, looking for *something,* riffling through hand-drawn maps of Witch Country, Pennsylvania, a pamphlet from The Crystal Science League, the timeline of John the Conqueror, photographs of Enchantments employees, the *Magical Practitioner's Code of Ethics.* She inspected a small scrap tacked underneath a postcard of a demonic-looking man and took it down, grabbing the cordless phone off the counter.

I stepped beside her.

It was a faded classified ad circled in red pen and torn from a newspaper. It read simply FOR THE GRIMMEST SITUATION ONLY, followed by a phone number, the area code 504.

"*That's* your expert? Are you kidding?"

"I said it was a long shot," Cleo snapped, dialing the number.

I took the paper. On the reverse side there was a half-torn headline that read FLOODING SUSPENDS, and above that, *The Lafourche Gazette,* November 8, 1983.

"No answer," Cleo said.

"Try again."

Sighing, she pressed *redial.*

After another three tries, she shook her head.

"I'm sorry. I don't even know what the number *is.* The paper's been here forever. No one knows where it came from. Come back tomorrow and we'll try—"

I grabbed the phone, pressed *redial,* pacing, my heart pounding with every unanswered ring.

It can't end like this, not with my daughter vulnerable to some dark hell I'd unwittingly unleashed on her. As I silently repeated this, I realized with a wave of sickened understanding that Cordova must have chanted the very same thing when he'd learned Ashley had run over the devil's bridge.

This truth I'd been chasing, slowly it was becoming my own.

Suddenly, the ringing stopped. There was a *click* on the line.

I thought for a moment it had gone dead, but then I heard faint *wheezing.*

"Hello?" The connection was full of static. "Anyone there?"

"Who's calling?"

The voice was a prehistoric gasp. If it was a man, woman, or *creature*—I had no idea.

Cleo, frowning, grabbed the phone.

"Hello?"

She cleared her throat, her eyes widening in surprise.

"Yes. This is Cleopatra at Enchantments in New York City. I hope it's not too late to be calling. We have the grimmest situation."

She fell silent, seemingly being reprimanded, but then she smiled at me, relieved, and hurried back to the table.

"I understand. Yes, ma'am. Thank you. If you want to check the stove I'll wait." Cleo paused, taking a deep breath, staring at the black figurine. After a minute, in a bland, clinical voice, she succinctly explained the situation.

"And the inverse shadow is totally misbehaving," she added.

She fell silent, listening, her face grave.

After ten minutes or so, she put a hand over the receiver.

"Go to the bookshelf," she whispered. "See if you can find a book called *Symbols of Black Alchemy Animal and Mineral.* Should be on the top shelf." She listened for a moment, frowning. "Green cover."

I raced to the back. It took me just a minute to find it, a thick hardback by C.T. Jaybird Fellows. I yanked it down, carrying it back to the table.

"We need to identify the animal before she can help," Cleo whispered.

I flipped open the book, scanning the musty pages, the drawings of animals discolored, the type old-fashioned and faded.

Dragon. Heart. Liver. Deer.

"I understand." Cleo squinted at the figurine. "Fins, a tail with a small suction on the end. Like something between a snake and a fish."

Pig. Goat. Tiger. Worm.

"Look up *leviathan*," Cleo whispered heatedly.

Owl. Pillar. Pine Tree. Leviathan.

The colored picture on the page for leviathan was nearly identical to the figurine. It had the same leering face, the distended tongue.

"That's what it is," announced Cleo happily into the phone, sliding the book toward herself, gazing down at the entry. "Out loud?" She cleared her throat. " 'The leviathan is a primordial sea serpent and one of the Dukes of Hell,' " she read. " 'Dante designated the creature the incarnation of total evil. Saint Thomas Aquinas described him as one of the Seven Deadly Sins, *envy*—the monstrous craving for that which you don't have. In the Middle East, he represents chaos. In Satanism, he's a demon of the inferno, which can be harnessed by the witch or warlock and discharged into the natural world for destructive means.' "

She paused, listening.

"Let me ask him." She eyed me. "How many children did you see with this?"

"Two."

"Did they have anything *linking* them? Did they go to the same school, have the same hobby, were they distantly related by blood? Anything like that?"

I couldn't answer. My mind was spinning. Because I'd suddenly re-called Morgan Devold's house, when his daughter, wearing that cherry-covered nightgown, had tiptoed after me down the drive. She'd been holding something in her fist, something small and black. *It was this figurine.*

"No," I said. "There were *three*. Three children."

"What did they have in common?"

I rubbed my eyes, trying to calm down, to *think*.

"They were between four and six years old. They had contact with a certain woman. The one who laid down the killing curse on our shoes. Ashley." I'd said this, really only considering Devold's daughter and the deaf child at Henry Street. But then the conclusion of my own words hit me: *That meant Sam had encountered Ashley.*

But that was impossible.

Cynthia never allowed Sam to talk to strangers. Yet she'd found me at the Reservoir. It wasn't so vast a leap, then, that she'd found my child.

"How did they act?" Cleo asked. "Any strange behaviors? Whispering? Twitching or tics? Trancelike countenances? Any talk of death or violence?"

I couldn't answer her. The horror of what I'd unknowingly done made me feel as if the room were caving in on me.

I'd brought the Cordovas right to Sam.

It's a tapeworm that's eaten its own tail. There's no end to it. All it will do is wrap around your heart and squeeze all the blood out.

"Hello?" Cleo prompted.

Why in hell didn't I turn away when I had the chance?

"*Excuse* me, but we have a *real live black witch* on the line," Cleo hissed, clamping her hand over the receiver. "We interrupted her while she was gutting a milk snake for an *intranquillity* spell. And she sounds like she's three breaths from going tits up. If I were you, I'd *focus. How did the children behave?*"

"I didn't see my daughter with it. My ex-wife found it in her coat pocket. But she seemed normal."

"What about the others?"

"One child was deaf. He was upset when he dropped it. He nearly had a tantrum, but calmed down when I returned it to him."

"Irrepressible imprinting," Cleo whispered hastily into the phone, then glanced at me. "The third?"

Devold's daughter.

"I wasn't around her," I said.

"You saw nothing out of the ordinary?"

I thought back to that night, the dark yard strewn with forgotten toys, shivering trees, the dog barking in the distance, baby screaming.

"Her favorite doll was found decomposing in a kiddie pool," I blurted. Cleo was startled. "A *baby* doll?"

"It'd been missing for a few weeks. They'd looked for it everywhere."

"*And?*"

"Her father fished it out, gave it back to his daughter, even though the thing looked *demonic,* eyes missing, clumps of hair falling out."

Cleo waved me on impatiently. "What happened when he gave it back?"

"She was very upset. She cried. But later she chased me down the driveway, cradling the doll, and attempted to give *me* the figurine."

"Definitive evidence of doll magic," Cleo blurted excitedly into the receiver, relaying what I'd just explained. She listened for a minute.

"All right. I'll try it."

She stood up, hurried to the back of the room, scribbling something on a yellow slip of paper. "I'll tell him. Thank you."

She hung up. Without a word, her face somber with concentration, she crouched down, rummaging through the cabinets, pulling out books, candles, and balled-up newspaper. She returned carrying a pair of electrician's pliers, a red bowl, a black-and-white reversing candle—the same kind she'd given us during our last visit—and some tweezers.

She meticulously laid out the items on the table like a doctor preparing a makeshift surgery.

"We're dealing with doll magic," she announced flatly, lighting the candle.

"What's that?"

"Poppets. Voodoo dolls stuck with pins. It's a doll connected by magic to a person to control their behavior. They're pretty common. This leviathan was bound by sympathetic magic to each child, which explains why the boy didn't want to let go of it. And we're about to find out why."

She sat down stiffly, closed her eyes, whispering something. She picked up the figurine and placed the head between the pliers. With one hand covering the serpent's body, she squeezed the handle, *hard.* It didn't budge. Cleo's face began to turn bright red, the bracelets and pendants clanging louder on her arms the harder she squeezed, her face wincing as if in pain, gnashing her teeth.

Suddenly, there was a *loud sucking pop.* Something flew past my face, hitting the wall, and fell to the floor with a sharp crack.

Right beside my feet, there was now a small black rock wrapped in copper wire.

"Don't touch it," Cleo shouted.

A strong smell of sulfur filled the air. The figurine was not solid wood as I'd thought, but a thin shell. Using the tweezers, Cleo was cautiously emptying the contents—a gold-brown liquid, bits of dark hair and mud—into the bowl.

The sight of it, knowing this had been intended for Sam, made a wave of nausea rise in my throat. I'd been so arrogant believing Ashley had been a viable way to get to Cordova, to avenge myself, get my life back, when I hadn't realized that I had my own fragile corridor. *Sam.*

He'd reversed my own plan back onto me. It was as if the man had had access to my head. *Now there would be no end to it.*

"Is my daughter cursed?" I asked.

Cleo blew out the candle.

"What do we do?" I pressed. "Tell me."

"Nothing," she answered flatly.

"Nothing?"

"This figurine contains a *protection spell.* It's not malignant. Quite the opposite." She smiled at my bewildered face, standing and moving to the back, returning with one of the volumes of *Hoodoo—Conjuration—Witchcraft—Rootwork.* She sat down, flipping through the index.

" 'Compelling oil,' " she read after paging to the entry. " 'Commanding oil, calamus, a piece of obsidian rock,' which is volcanic glass wrapped in copper wire—that's what flew onto the floor." She glanced at me sternly. "It's a molten wall of protection." She grabbed the bowl, swirling the contents. "The leviathan was used to ward off any evil that tried to advance upon the child. The spell inside protected the carrier. Any child given this toy would play exclusively with it for the heyday of the spell. About a hundred and one days. Any other deeply loved toy would have to be confiscated and hidden, so as not to compromise the potency. To submerge it out of sight in a body of water is ideal. *That* was the first hint this was domination through doll magic. This person—*Ashley*—must have stolen the doll, hiding it in the pool so as not to compromise the effect of the figurine on the child. But when the doll was returned to the little girl, she reclaimed her beloved toy and could no longer play with the leviathan. The protection was broken." She frowned. "There's one slightly *weird* detail that the witch mentioned."

"What's that?"

"In magic, you fight *like* with *like,* so using the form of the leviathan, the symbol of envy—*thou shall not covet*—Ashley seemed to believe these three children would be envied and coveted. Any idea why?"

I could only stare at her, incredulous.

The exchange. A simple transfer of debt. Ashley knew her father, Cordova, and her brother, Theo, would come looking for her after she escaped from Briarwood. Encountering the children in her path as she tracked down the Spider, she must have been concerned Cordova might try to use them, one soul for another, in a final attempt to save her life. *This led to the rift between Ashley and her family,* Marlowe had said. *Because when it was finally explained to her, Ashley wanted to accept her fate. But Cordova was always searching for a way out. He did until the very end.*

"My daughter . . . ?" I managed to ask, my voice hoarse.

"She'll probably be fine."

"Probably? You're not sure?"

Cleo stared at me. "A tornado knocks a house down, killing the owner, and it's a tragedy. Then you learn a *serial killer* lived there and the same act becomes a miracle. The truth about what happens to us in this world keeps changing. Always. It never stops. Sometimes not even after death." She stood up, grabbing the yellow scrap of paper she'd scribbled on, handing it to me. "This is where you send payment to the witch. Any amount you think is fair. She prefers cash."

It was a P.O. box in Larose, Louisiana.

"What do I owe you?" I asked.

She shook her head. "Just go home."

I gazed down at the beheaded leviathan, capsized on the table. It *actually* looked as if it had faded to a slightly lighter shade of black, as if it'd started to wilt like a flower clipped from its life-sustaining branch—though perhaps it was just my imagination. I'd walked into this room with a belief that I could distinguish between what was factual and what was an invention of the mind. Now I wasn't sure I knew the difference.

I stood up, the chair shrilly scraping the floor.

"Thank you," I said to Cleo.

She nodded, and I stepped back through the black curtain, leaving her staring after me.

All of the customers were gone, the lights switched off so the scarred wooden floors were doused in orange light spilling in from the street. Two workers waited behind the register, speaking in low, worried voices, though they fell silent as I walked past them and unlocked the door.

"WHERE YOU GUYS FROM?" the woman asked me.

She was plump, with a round friendly face. She'd been behind the desk the night before, when her husband had checked us in.

"Saratoga," I answered.

"Not *too* bad a drive. You guys're up here to go paddlin'?"

She must have noticed my car had a canoe strapped to the roof.

"It's gonna be cold the next few days, so be sure to dress in layers."

"About that extra key?" I asked.

"*Right.* You're in room . . . ?"

"Nineteen."

She unhooked the keychain, handing it to me. "Need any maps or directions?"

"No, thanks," I said, grabbing the shopping bag at my feet.

"Our restaurant serves supper till eleven. Everything's home-cooked. We got a mean apple pie. You should check it out."

"Thanks for the recommendation."

I exited through the glass door. As it dinged closed behind me, I turned back and saw the woman's friendliness had been erased from her face and she was inspecting me carefully over her bifocals.

I waved and took off down the covered walkway.

Last night, after sizing up every roadside motel along NY Route 3 between the Adirondack towns of Fine and Moody, I chose Evening View Motel & Restaurant because of its anonymity. It was in Childwold, forty miles north of Crowthorpe Falls, and sat sulking right off the side of the road: twenty dreary rooms, each rationed one cruddy window and a brown door. The motel had a popular eatery, the parking lot crowded with cars, license plates from Michigan to Vermont. Across the street was a busy RV campground—Green Meadows, THE NORTH WOODS' FRIENDLIEST COMPOUND, read the wood sign—so I'd guessed Evening View saw enough traffic for the proprietors not to pay close attention to any *particular* guest.

I was way off on that one. The woman had stared at me as if she knew within a matter of days she'd be picking me out of a police lineup.

I made my way along the walkway, scanning the parking lot. It had cleared out after lunch, leaving only a handful of cars, nothing suspicious, no one watching. A bald man exited a white sedan, stretching and yawning as he made his way toward the motel office.

I stopped outside #19—second to last on the end—and knocked once.

Hopper opened it. I slipped inside.

"How'd you make out?" He locked the door behind me.

"Fine. I had to go all the way to Tupper Lake." I handed him the shopping bag, and he pulled out the new camera battery—this morning he'd discovered his wouldn't charge, so I'd gone out for a replacement. "She only has one extra room key. Who wants it?"

"Give it to Nora."

I walked over to the far double bed, where Nora was sitting, eating a protein bar, and handed it to her. She smiled wanly, her eyes lingering a moment too long on my face.

I knew what she was thinking, what we were *all* thinking: What if this plan we'd methodically prepared over the past twelve days was a mistake?

We had weighed the possibilities. There was no other option. If I called Sharon Falcone and told her that I suspected occult crimes had been taking place at The Peak, she'd tell me what I already knew: Police would need hard evidence for a warrant, evidence I did not have.

The one thing I *did* have was knowledge of a covert way to access the property. The Spider had claimed he'd cut open the fence for the townspeople along a narrow stream. Marlowe had mentioned it originated from Lows Lake.

Inspecting detailed maps of the area, I could find no such river. It was only after finding an Adirondack geological map that dated back to 1953 that we uncovered where it just might be—a frail, nameless rivulet that twisted off the lake's north shore, meandering through dense forest, right onto The Peak grounds.

If we managed to locate this stream and covertly enter that way after nightfall, we could see what was at The Peak, once and for all—if there was evidence not just of occult practices but what the Spider had suggested, actual child killings. We'd gather what proof we could, exit the way we'd come before dawn, then get it into the hands of authorities.

The plan was a blind risk—not to mention illegal, immoral, crossing the line of even the *slackest ethics* of investigative reporting, totally outrageous. It could very well get one of us arrested—or injured. For me, it could mean a new low of professional disgrace. I could only imagine the headlines. *Back for More: Fallen Journalist Caught Breaking Into Cordova Estate. Judge Orders Comprehensive Psychiatric Evaluation.*

I'd explained all of this to Nora and Hopper, emphasizing that it was my decision, one that was personal, not professional, and they'd be better off remaining behind. But Hopper was as resolute as I was. He said grimly, *"I'm in,"* as if it were something he'd resolved long ago. Nora was also adamant.

"I'm *coming,*" she announced.

And so it was decided.

Over the course of the past week, however, as we'd memorized the plan, assembled supplies, even as we'd driven the seven hours to the Adirondacks, a bleak landscape of gray sky, roads smothered with trees—the reality of what we were doing seemed to swell exponentially in magnitude. It was a mountain we'd started climbing, which grew beneath us into a rambling skyscraping ridge, pushing us back, the summit snowcapped, lost in clouds.

Every word Nora chirped in her singsong voice—*Mind if we stop at that gas station? I'll have the French toast with maple syrup*—sounded *doomed,* made me regret that I'd even allowed her to come along.

I was concerned that as much as we'd uncovered about Ashley and her father, I still didn't have the complete picture. Cleo had warned me of this: *The truth about what happens to us in this world keeps changing . . . it never stops.*

It was possible The Peak—and Cordova himself—was like that locked hexagonal Chinese box of Beckman's I'd tried to pry open years ago: something that should remain forever sealed, its contents hidden from the light of day for good reason.

Though Cleo had assured me the spell inside the leviathan was *not* malevolent, there was little solace in this. Even if Ashley had meant to protect Sam, even if Hopper had loved Ashley, she was still a shifting cipher, her movements that night at the Central Park Reservoir impossible to fathom. The mystery of how Sam came to have the figurine in her coat pocket, the idea that Ashley had once approached her, shook me awake in the middle of the night, filled me with anxiety made all the more acute by the knowledge that it was my fault.

I'd put her in harm's way. I couldn't help but wonder if it had shown me my true nature, a raw view as infinite and irrefutable as two facing mirrors, the selfish blind man I was and always would be. My countless phone calls to Cynthia to check on Sam went ignored.

And then there was the question of the Spider and The Broken Door.

I went back to the antiques shop after leaving Enchantments, the same day of Samantha's fall. I found the store locked, windows black. Nora and Hopper returned with me the next day, and two days after that, every day after. We monitored the building from the shadows of the stoop across the street, waiting for a light in an upstairs window, a curtain gently pulled aside.

Yet the building remained inscrutable and silent.

The Spider had obviously come back, packed a suitcase, and vanished into the night—perhaps forever. It wasn't hard to imagine; his past had caught up with him, after all, first with Ashley, then the three of us. Yet The Broken Door's red crumbling façade, the mystery of his absence, and even more chilling, what exactly had happened to Sam in his shop—all left questions that ate away at me, exhausting me, like a fever that wouldn't break.

I wasn't even confident I was thinking lucidly. Sam was a line that had been crossed. Staying so nimbly out of sight, letting us view only the twisted shadows he made on the wall, Cordova still existed primarily in my mind—the most powerful place for any enemy to hide. His very films told you that. The suspected but unseen *threat*, fueled by the imagination, was punishing and all-powerful. It'd devastate before you even left your room, your bed, before you even opened your eyes and took a breath.

That leviathan figurine with its quivering shadow, sliding along the table with a mind of its own—it was proof of a hidden world beyond the one I'd taken for granted all my life, the reality that science and logic assured me was ever constant and changing only within a fixed set of laws. That *misbehaving shadow* was the edge of the unknown. The world's certainty and truth had revealed a fault line. It was a minute tear in the wallpaper, which could be ignored, chalked up to my mind playing tricks on me. Or it could be torn back, farther and farther, into an ever larger and grotesque piece, eventually tearing off completely—exposing *what* type of wall? And if that wall were knocked down, what lay beyond it?

The only way to handle these uncertainties was to shove them aside and concentrate on a concrete plan.

Hopper had finished lacing up his boots. He stood up, zipping his jacket. Nora was in front of the mirror, applying, for mysterious reasons, red lipstick fit for a Parisian jazz club. Smacking her lips, she crouched down, pulling up her army fatigues and thermo-underwear to rearrange the hunting knife strapped to her ankle, which I'd bought her yesterday at a Walmart in Saratoga Springs.

The least I could do was make sure she could defend herself.

"Okay, troops. Let's go over this one last time."

I unzipped the backpack, removed the map.

Our carefully hatched *plan*—it was the rope for us to hold on to.

And yet I couldn't help but wonder if, fumbling along that cord into the dark, we'd find out that the end was tied to nothing.

WE DROVE TO LOWS LAKE the long way, keeping away from the center of Crowthorpe Falls.

It was a tangle of meandering side roads, every one deserted.

We were in a rental—a black Jeep—but there was no way of knowing who in Crowthorpe was involved in what took place on The Peak property, and I didn't want to risk drawing any attention. We'd monitored Perry Street, not to mention every car behind us during the drive upstate, and we didn't appear to be followed.

I'd forgotten in the five years since I'd been here how impenetrable the wilderness was, how suffocating. Evergreens, maples, and beech trees swarmed the hills, massive branches reaching out over the road as if to smother us, soaking up what little daylight there was. Log cabins, groceries, out-of-business video stores stood forlornly in one crumbling lot after the next.

"It's the next left," said Nora.

Within a few yards I saw the sign: WELLER'S LANDING.

I slowed, made the left into the parking lot. There were two other cars, a blue pickup and a station wagon—probably other paddlers already out on the lake. I inched into a distant spot in the farthest corner, half hidden by a large hemlock, and cut the engine.

"We're clear," said Hopper, looking out the back windshield.

"Any last-minute concerns?" I asked. I looked at Hopper in the rearview mirror. His pointed stare back at me told me everything. *Nothing would stop him now.*

"Bernstein?" I asked.

Nora was yanking a black knit cap onto her head, tucking in the loose strands of hair.

"Oh, shoot. Can't believe I almost forgot." She reached into her vest pocket, pulling out two small plastic packets. She opened one, removing a thin gold necklace. Beckoning me to lean forward, she unclasped the chain and fastened it around my neck.

"This is Saint Benedict."

It was a crude piece of jewelry, the pendant emblazoned with a gaunt, robed Jesus type.

"He's the napalm of Catholic saints," Nora said, reaching back to put Hopper's around his neck. "You drop Benedict into a situation, you don't *need* anything else. He'll protect us from what's up there."

"Thanks," said Hopper.

"You have one, too?" I asked her.

"Of *course*."

"Then let's move."

We unloaded the car rapidly—to minimize risk of a witness noticing us. But also I knew that to hesitate now in *any* way would only let serious doubt flood in, like water in a rowboat full of holes.

Hopper carried the paddles to the load-in area. I unhitched the Souris River canoe from the roof. Nora grabbed the lifejackets, the backpacks. I hid the car key under a rock by the hemlock, in case we became separated and one of us made it back before the others. Hopper and I picked up the canoe, and with a final look back at the Jeep, we took off across the parking lot.

We lowered the canoe into the water, and Hopper stepped in, heading to the bow, shoving his backpack behind his seat. Nora clambered in after him, binoculars swinging from her neck. I grabbed my paddle, threw in my backpack, was just about to climb in, when I noticed my cellphone vibrating in my jacket.

I thought of ignoring it, but then realized it could be Cynthia. I pulled off my glove, unzipped the pocket. It was a blocked number.

"Hello?"

"McGrath."

I recognized the voice. It was Sharon Falcone.

"Shit, this connection's *crap*. Sounds like you're halfway around the world. Let me call you back—"

"No, *no*," I blurted, flooded with an ominous feeling that something was wrong. "What's the matter?"

"Nothing. Just wanted to get back to you on that tip you gave us."

"Tip?"

"For child services."

The landlord and her deaf nephew back at 83 Henry Street.

I'd forgotten that I'd called Sharon about them.

"Sure you gave me the right address? Eighty-three Henry?"

"That's right."

"They checked it out. There's no certificate of occupancy for the building."

"What?"

"There was no one living there. No tenants in—"

Abruptly, her voice cut out. Loud metallic echoing filled the line.

"Hello?"

". . . illegal . . . a couple times last week . . ."

"Sharon."

". . . knee-deep in major . . ."

Her voice cut out into wild static.

"Hello?"

". . . thing was okay. McGrath, you still *there?*"

"Yes. Hello?"

A clanging screeched across the line and it went dead.

I tried calling her back, but it wouldn't connect. I waited another minute, in the off chance she'd manage to get through again, but the phone had no service. I zipped it back into my jacket pocket, explaining to Hopper and Nora what she'd just told me.

"What do you mean empty?" asked Nora.

"There were no tenants."

"But that's impossible."

"Is it?"

"*No,*" said Hopper. "Maybe they were illegal aliens. When *we* showed up, it was too much attention."

"But Ashley's neighbor," interjected Nora. "Iona. *She* wasn't illegal. She had an American accent, and she told us she'd lived there for a year. Why would she take off?"

"To avoid arrest for prostitution."

Nora was unconvinced. "It doesn't seem right."

They fell silent, waiting for me to weigh in. I recognized the moment for what it was, the chance not to go ahead, to reconsider everything, and go back.

The sky had faded from white to gray, the surrounding forest hushed and still. I climbed in and grabbed the paddle.

"We'll look into it when we get back," I said.

THERE WASN'T A STREAM—only a swamp.

We'd spent the last hour crossing Lows Lake, Hopper and I paddling in silent tandem. Battered by shifting currents and a cold, unrelenting wind, we sailed past deserted islands crowded with pines and a ghost tree growing straight out of the water, its gaunt trunk and scrawny branches raised heavenward like an outcast pleading for his life. Now, having reached the north shore, we were doggedly searching for the hidden rivulet that would take us into The Peak. We were trapped in muddy water barbed with grasses and covered with thick green algae, which broke apart in clumps, then, after we'd edged through, resealed, erasing all signs of our passing.

The wind had dissipated—*strange,* as it'd been so turbulent minutes ago out on the lake. Dense trees surrounded us, packed like hordes of stranded prisoners. There wasn't a single bird, not a scuttle through the branches, not a cry—as if everything alive had fled.

"This can't be right," said Nora, turning around.

I hadn't realized, sitting behind her, how worried she'd become.

"Let me see the map."

She handed it to me along with the compass.

"We should go back," she blurted, staring into the reeds.

"*What?*" asked Hopper irritably, turning.

"We can't get stuck in this in the dark. We can't sleep here."

"Who said anything about *sleeping* here?"

"We're supposed to be following a *stream*. Where's the stream?"

"We'll give it a little while longer," I said.

Within minutes, we were stuck on a submerged log. Hopper, without hesitation, clambered out and, standing thigh-deep in the muck, shoved us loose. Climbing back in, his jeans were coated with mud and that strange neon algae, though he didn't seem to notice or care. He stared resolutely ahead as if in a trance, beating the grasses with his oar. I couldn't help but imagine he was thinking about Ashley, because out here, the stark emptiness of the wilderness seemed to naturally summon regrets and fear.

Our progress remained slow. The swamp reeked of decay, a smell that seemed to be coming off the algae, which only grew thicker the deeper into this bog we drifted. We had to shove the paddles straight down to wrestle the canoe even an inch past the sludge and yellow reeds rising around us, forming a suffocating corridor.

I checked my watch. It was already after five. It'd be nightfall in less than an hour. Our plan had been to be on The Peak property by now.

Suddenly Nora gasped, clamping a hand over her mouth and pointing at something to her left.

A faded piece of red string had been knotted to one of the reeds, the end dangling in the water. I recognized it immediately. Marlowe had claimed Cordova discovered such strings when he'd first moved to The Peak. They'd led him to the clearing where the townspeople performed their rituals.

"We're going the right way," said Hopper.

We pushed on, the swamp suddenly deepening, the mud thinning. A frail but discernible current appeared, seemingly out of nowhere. The only sounds were the laps of the water, the grasses bending around us, whispering against the sides of the boat.

"I can see the fence," said Hopper.

Sure enough—far ahead, I could make out the dark silhouette of

Cordova's military fence cutting across the stream, marking the southern edge of his property.

When we were twelve feet away, we extended the paddles to the bank. The fence looked like something surrounding a defunct prison, the chain links rusted, the top looped with razor wire. Where the water passed underneath, the wires had been brutally hacked—*exactly* as Marlowe had described, the ends gnarled and twisted back, leaving a triangular hole about a foot wide.

"See any cameras?" I asked.

Nora, looking through the binoculars, shook her head.

I unzipped my backpack, removed the fluorescent bulb, and climbed out, heading to the fence. Immediately I spotted three wires running horizontally across the distorted chain links. They hung loosely, and on the closest metal fencepost they'd twisted free of the casings.

I tapped the metal end of the bulb against the wires. It remained dim touching the first two. But on the third, the one closest to the ground, the bulb glowed orange and blew out.

After all these years, *it was still a live wire.* I stepped closer to the stream, following the cable's path as it hung slackly between the severed links, dangling across the top, continuing on the other side.

"There's an electric current in the wire," I said, stepping back to them. "It just blew out the bulb."

"Killer security system," Hopper said. "No pun intended."

"It's not funny," said Nora, looking at me uncertainly.

"There's enough room to pass," I said. "We each lie down. Go through one at a time."

The other option was to *swim* through—without the boat, it'd be easy to get by unscathed—but for us all to be soaked from the neck down in temperatures about to fall below twenty degrees would be a major handicap, making a systematic search of the property difficult. Passing under the wire *inside* the canoe was our best bet, so long as we each stayed lower than the boat's rim. The canoe was fiberglass, but there was aluminum detailing along the outer edges. I wasn't an electrician, but it seemed possible it might conduct current if the wire grazed it.

"Hopper," I said, "you're first."

He shoved his backpack into the center of the canoe and, lying down in the hull, crossed his arms.

Pulling away, we took a moment to reposition ourselves, angling the bow toward the mangled opening. It was probably just my eyes adjusting to the fading light, but as we glided forward, I swore the fence's wires seemed to constrict, *squirm* like plants sensitive to movement.

When we were two feet away, suddenly we slipped into a strong current and were whipped sideways, crashing against the opening, the wire lowering from the impact.

"It's about to *touch*," whispered Nora.

"Keep your arms off the metal," I ordered.

She raised her paddle as I shoved mine in, forcing the bow through, the chain links scraping the boat. We eased in another few inches, and I realized the wire was lowering again—as if it were a *rigged trap*. Before I could react, it struck the rim of the canoe. I waited for a white blast of electricity.

Nothing.

I thrust the paddle into the water, keeping the canoe steady in the undercurrent. I propelled us forward another foot or so. Hopper was on the opposite side, the wire in front of Nora, the chain links rasping.

"You're clear," I said.

Hopper sat up. Nora slid the oar to him, and she inched forward, curling up into a fetal position in the hull.

"If I get zapped and it's my time to go, I just want to say I love you both and these times have been the best in my life."

"It's not your time quite *yet,* Bernstein," I said.

We jostled forward. There was no sound but the water, the screech of the wires as they curved, protesting against the boat. Suddenly, we hit something submerged and the wire dipped, tapping the sides. I swore I heard a faint sizzle of voltage charging around us, though as soon as I did, the wire raised, we slid through, and it was my turn.

I lay down in the hull, the water rumbling around me.

"Any last words?" Hopper asked.

"Try not to kill me."

The canoe lurched, that thin wire striking the sides inches from my nose. It slipped over my head and was gone.

"We're *in*," whispered Hopper.

I sat up, checking behind us, surprised to see the fence was already quickly retreating. The current had increased, the water pooling, as if excited by the prospect of delivering us to—what? *But that fence wasn't actually a fence. It was a booby trap.* Maybe Marlowe hadn't mentioned this secret entrance so innocuously, but to plant a *seed* in our heads, so we'd try to enter exactly this way. *Why?* To annihilate us on that wire? Or was it to get us securely inside Cordova's property, trapping us in here?

As WE PADDLED ON, the night descended around us like a black tide coming in.

Before, the forest had been blanketed with an unsettling stillness. Now noises echoed from every direction. Branches snapped. Leaves rustled. Trees shuddered—as if all the wild animals that hid during the day were rousing now, crawling out of their holes.

My eyes gave up trying to discern anything beyond Hopper's silhouette at the bow and Nora's hunched shoulders in front of me. I recalled, with a twinge of anxiety, the feeling of suffocation Olivia Endicott had described when visiting The Peak. I wondered if *I* was experiencing it, a vague sense of disorientation, detachment, *drowning.* I assumed it was just adrenaline and nerves, but then I felt, very clearly, a marked heaviness, as if after inhaling all of this moist air, it was now suffused inside me, slowing my limbs, suppressing my thoughts.

Hopper motioned ahead. Visible at the end of this black tunnel of trees was a shimmering surface.

Graves Pond—where Genevra, Cordova's first wife, had drowned.

We reached the mouth in less than a minute, pulling over to the bank, listening. Nora pulled the binoculars away, nodding, and we silently eased the canoe out, veering right, keeping tight to the perimeter under the cover of overhanging branches.

Far to our left on the opposite side, a wooden dock became visible.

It looked abandoned, a crude wooden ladder hanging over the side and into the water. Steps led onto a stone path that twisted up a steep hill gradually coming into view.

Suddenly, Hopper and Nora jolted upright.

And then *I* saw what was coming, what was slowly rising over the crest of that hill like a dark sun.

THE PEAK.

It sat in moonlight, a hulking mansion of such absolute darkness it made the surrounding night gray. Its grandeur looked straight out of the European countryside, a lost world of horse-drawn carriages and candlelight. Spiked gabled roofs pitched upward, lancing the sky. I could discern an ornate entrance pavilion, a colonnade across the front drive, three stories of windows, every one unlit—all of it fortified with shadow, as if shadows were the very mortar that kept it standing. In fact, the house seemed to challenge the laws of the physical world, the inevitable slide of man's grandest constructions into decay and ruin, boasting instead that it would be rising over that hill for centuries to come.

A wild overgrown lawn raced breathlessly up to it from Graves Pond. There was no sign of life, no movement. My feeling was the mansion had been abandoned for some time.

We extended the paddles ashore, the canoe beaching in the mud, and the three of us climbed out, pulling on our backpacks. Hopper and I carried the canoe up the bank and into the trees, set it down behind a fallen log, covering it with leaves and branches. Nora shoved a stick into the mud to use as a marker, so later we'd know where to find the boat. Then we took a moment to survey one another. Hopper looked invigorated, his face toughened by the dark. Nora looked disconcertingly *blank*. I squeezed her shoulder for reassurance, but she only fumbled with her jacket zipper so it was zipped all the way to her chin.

"Remember the emergency plan," I whispered. "Anything happens, we meet back here."

With a nod of mutual agreement, we took off. The plan was to check the house first, see if we could get in, and from there find the clearing in the woods where they performed the rituals. We walked due north, keeping to the perimeter of the pond, and then proceeded single-file up a steep knoll through the woods, heading in the general direction of the house. We reached the summit, staying hidden along the tree line, overlooking the eastern wing of The Peak.

Up close, the mansion was palatial, yet I could see how weathered the façade was, the limestone streaked and discolored. I could make out elaborate detailing on pediments and corners, black ironwork and carved stones along the roof. Perched on window ledges and above doorways, what at first glance looked like real birds roosting there were gargoyles in the form of crows. There was a domed glass solarium on the ground floor that led out onto a columned loggia, so soaked in darkness it was as if a black vapor had leaked out of the house and fermented.

A stone pathway led away from the terrace steps, winding through tall grass to an enormous wall of neglected privet at the rear of the house, vanishing somewhere beyond it. I knew from aerial photographs it led into the estate's sprawling gardens, which had featured prominently in Cordova's *To Breathe with Kings*. A check of Google Earth had revealed that hints of the elaborate landscaping were still there—pebbled pathways and sculpture—though most of it was shrouded under wild greenery.

"I'll see if anyone's home," Hopper said.

"What? *No*. We're waiting here."

But before I could stop him, he stepped right out onto the lawn, jogging nonchalantly down the hill. Reaching the steps to the terrace, he ducked and slipped right up them, out of sight.

My shock over what he'd just done quickly turned to outrage. I should have *known* he'd be reckless, follow his own private agenda. I had every intention of going after him, dragging him back, when I froze.

A dog was barking. It sounded *close*.

Nora turned to me, horrified. I held up my hand. We'd considered the possibility of dogs and had bought clothing with scent elimination, which supposedly masked our smell from animals.

The dog barked again, angry and insistent.

And then a single faint *light* appeared in a gabled window along the roof. It was shrouded with a heavy curtain but unmistakable.

Someone *was* home.

The dog went silent as a sudden gust of wind whipped through the trees. There was no sign of Hopper. Presumably he was hiding somewhere on the terrace, waiting for the chance to make his way back. But then I heard the unmistakable thud of a *heavy door* heaving open, followed by staccato thumping and the jingling of a *dog collar*.

I unzipped Nora's backpack, groping through the clothing, finding the pepper spray. I shoved it into her hands just as a massive hound, barking furiously, came bounding across the mansion's front entrance.

It looked like something between a Russian wolfhound and a coyote, its mangy coat splotched gray and white, a long curled tail.

The dog froze and howled another warning bark as it stared down the grassy hill toward Graves Pond, ears pricked.

A second dog appeared, this one bigger and all black. It loped around the house exactly in our direction, stopping some twenty yards from the terrace where Hopper was hiding. It growled ominously. Then, nose to the ground, the dog loped up the hill toward us, zigzagging through the grass.

"Get back to the canoe and wait for me there," I whispered.

Nora hesitated.

"Do it."

Petrified, she took off, barking exploding around us, as I ran in the other direction out onto the lawn. I headed straight down the incline, racing past the terrace and along the stone path, making a beeline for the privet. When I glanced over my shoulder I saw what I expected: Both dogs were chasing me now, plowing through the tall grass.

I tore along the hedge, finding an opening, and barreled blindly through, careening down a white-pebbled path overrun with weeds.

The dogs sounded close behind me, paws ricocheting across the stones.

I appeared to be running through a garden maze, tall walls of privet growing high around me, birdbaths scarred with lichen, plants clinging to trellises. I could make out crumbling statuary—a headless girl, a man's naked torso entwined with a snake. Colossal shrubs—probably once topiaries—rose around me, their animal shapes long melted away.

I tripped down some steps and raced into a narrow alcove with a dried-up fountain, a wrought-iron gate.

I stopped, listening.

The dogs sounded as if they'd multiplied, coming from every direction.

I crept over to the wrought-iron gate.

Suddenly a dog leapt up on the opposite side, snarling. I lurched away, expecting, at any moment, its jaws to sink into my arm, but only frustrated yowls exploded behind me. I swung back out, instantly spotted another dog bounding toward me at the opposite end of the corridor.

I bent down, finding a hole in the hedge, and scrambled through, running out into an open yard, a large swimming pool at the center covered with a plastic tarp.

I sprinted to the farthest corner and bent down, yanking off my gloves, groping at the nylon strings.

I could hear the dogs whimpering, searching for the way in. I managed to undo a few knots, pulled back the tarp, and almost gagged when I saw what was inside.

IT WAS PUTRID BLACK WATER.

I yanked off my backpack, plunged my boots in first, and then, gritting my teeth, slipped inside, the icy water seeping into my clothes, swallowing me up to my neck. I pulled my backpack in—doing my best to keep it dry, though there was only about a foot of space between the tarp and water. I removed the camera from the front pocket, yanked the corner of the tarp back into place, and, blinking in the sudden darkness, floated away from the opening.

Instantly, I heard that insidious *jingling*. The dogs had found me, barking, racing around the perimeter, whining, their paws clicking rhythmically across the flagstones.

I fumbled my way along the perimeter as quietly as I could, groping at the broken tiles covered in slime, the coldness starting to eat away at me.

I kept my eyes on the ribbon of light cutting between the tarp and the side of the pool, my left foot striking something underneath me. *A drowned deer?* I'd reached the next corner, kicking my way around it, a ripple of water splashing a little *too* loudly. I froze.

I could hear footsteps, heavy-set. *Someone was coming,* striding along a paved path and entering the yard.

"What is it, boys?" It was a man's low voice.

The dogs whimpered as they continued to race around the pool, the man coming closer. Then he stopped.

Cordova?

Suddenly—the powerful beam of a flashlight danced across the tarp, sending a spasm of panic through me, the gold circle gliding to the corner where I'd crawled in.

I pressed my back against the tiles, trying to remain motionless.

I heard faster footsteps, the whisk of the tarp being flung back.

The flashlight sliced across the water, illuminating blackened leaves and branches, disembodied shapes—frogs, maybe squirrels—floating deep inside the pool.

The beam hovered a few feet from my backpack, slipping closer. I tucked the camera under the tarp on the ledge, took a deep breath, and carefully sank all the way underwater, pulling my backpack in behind me. I fell a few feet and then opened my eyes, trying to ignore the searing sting, watching the beam of light slip over my head.

I waited, my lungs feeling like they were going to explode, trying to remain calm. We'd been fine, the three of us, *just a few goddamn minutes ago.* How had it all unraveled so quickly?

The beam hovered over me for a few more seconds, then at last slipped away to inspect another corner. I floated back to the surface, gasping for air.

Suddenly a sharp scream pierced the night. It sounded like a woman. *Nora?*

The dogs erupted into vicious barking, their paws thumping, flashlight streaking away. I heard fumbling, then footsteps striding across the stones.

Soon there was only silence around me. *They were gone.*

I grabbed the camera, then kicked back toward the opening, but when I reached the corner, I saw the tarp had been pulled back into place. Ignoring my alarm—my mind instantly killing me off, evoking my corpse wafting through here with the other debris—I reached out, my fingers groping underneath the plastic.

The strings had been retied.

I set the camera on the ledge, pulled my backpack over, fumbling inside the front pocket, found the pocket knife, yanked it open with my teeth, and, gripping the knife awkwardly in my frozen fingers, began to saw at the ties.

I managed to sever a few. I shoved the backpack out first, then blindly heaved myself onto the pool's edge, freezing wind instantly pummeling me. I lifted my head and saw with relief—I was alone.

I crawled to my feet, dragging my backpack up over my shoulder. I grabbed the camera and staggered across the yard, heading toward the arched opening in the hedge, rancid water squelching from my boots with every step.

I hoped Nora was safe and Hopper was with her. I'd meet them back at the canoe and we'd come up with a new plan.

The dogs—and the man with the flashlight—appeared to have gone quite far, because the night was still again.

I stepped outside the enclosure, finding myself on another stone path, what had to be the garden's western boundary. To my right, beyond a stretch of overgrown lawn, loomed a forest of dense pines, vast and black, and to my left, sitting high on the hill, beyond tangled greenery, the mansion.

It remained in darkness.

I took off across the grass and into the cover of the forest, following the tree line southward, back around the hill toward Graves Pond. A dank cold was shuddering through me, but I ignored it, trying to break into a jog. My legs wouldn't respond. I stumbled over branches and tree trunks, cutting east when I could see a clearing to my left—shimmering water through the trunks. Within minutes, I reached the same mouth of the stream by which we'd entered the pond and lurched across it, thigh-deep in the water and mud, moving as fast as I could up onto the bank.

I reached the western side, traipsing along the shoreline, and saw with relief—and *amazement*—the small branch Nora had stuck in the mud.

"*Nora,*" I whispered, walking straight into the woods.

When I found the fallen log, I stopped dead.

The branches and dirt had been thrown aside.

And the canoe was gone.

I LOOKED AROUND THE TREES seemingly locking me in an infinite jail.

I stepped back to the lake's edge, staring out at the moonlit water.

It was deserted.

Hopper and Nora must have been caught. Or they took off, leaving me stranded. Or they'd been chased, escaped, planned to make their way back when the coast was clear. Or someone else had found the boat and confiscated it, someone waiting for me, *watching.*

I listened intently for footsteps but heard nothing.

I couldn't stay here. And I couldn't use a flashlight for fear someone in the distance would notice it. I took off around the perimeter of the lake, following the general direction the three of us had originally taken.

A dog barked.

It sounded miles away. But I picked up my pace and headed directly up the hill, feeling the last bit of warmth somewhere in my gut flickering, as if seconds from going out.

I stopped, staring far off to my right. There was some type of structure standing beyond the trees, glowing faintly blue in the dark. I took off toward it.

It was a gigantic warehouse, a flat roof, no evident windows. I rounded the first corner, finding a set of steel doors, a rusted chain looped through the handles, secured with a padlock. I quickly searched the ground, found a suitable rock, carried it back, and smashed the lock a few times until it twisted off. At this point, I didn't care if the world heard me.

I slung the chain to the ground, pulled the door open, and stumbled inside.

The moonlight flooding in behind me illuminated a crude beamed wall, a concrete floor, the back of a brown couch farther ahead, a blanket folded neatly over the back—all of it retreating into pitch darkness as the metal door closed behind me with a resounding *thud.*

I slung off my backpack, untied my boots, stripped down to my boxers, and, nearly tripping over a raised step, collapsed on the couch. I fumbled for the blanket, pulling it over me. And I huddled there, shivering uncontrollably, willing my mind to thaw. I realized after a dazed moment that all I *really* wanted to do was *sleep,* which made me figure I had mild hypothermia, but I shoved that idea away as soon as it came.

Sleep will kill you. It's the drug your body gives you before closing up shop.

Minutes passed. I didn't know how long, as I couldn't move my arm to check my watch. My thoughts kept slipping out of reach, tiny deflating buoys I was trying to grab ahold of to stay afloat. I imagined myself sitting in my bed at Perry Street, staring up at the ceiling. I wondered if we'd gotten into a car accident on the way to Weller's Landing and this was what it felt like to be unconscious, detached from the world, bobbing between life and death, the Earth and the unknown.

Maybe I was still in that rancid swimming pool.

Maybe I'd never climbed out.

But after a while, I realized my eyes had adjusted to the dark. I was staring at an open newspaper sitting on a coffee table in front of me.

The Doverville Sentinel.

POLICE PROBE BOY DEATHS.

I BLINKED. I was sitting in a modest furnished living room. There was a white shag carpet on a wooden floor, and modern chairs, curtained windows, a brick fireplace.

I'd been here before.

I'd been *inside* this room.

Hanging on the wall opposite were three framed pictures beside a tiny kitchenette. A floor lamp with a cream shade hung over the couch. I reached up and tried the switch.

Instantly, pale light illuminated the room.

A wicker chair stood beside the front door, a man's herringbone overcoat slung over the back. To my right, atop an end table, there was an Art Deco bronze statue of a woman balancing a crystal ball on her head. Emily, weeping in terror, grabs that statue to use as a weapon before dashing down the hall, hiding in a bedroom closet. This couch I was on, Emily sat *right here* in the opening scene, reading the newspaper about the latest child murder, as Brad entered, slinging his coat and briefcase on that chair beside the door.

I looked up. There was no ceiling, only scaffolding some forty feet overhead. Lights had been rigged up there, a few pointing down at me.

It was a film set.

I was in Brad and Emily Jackson's living room from *Thumbscrew—*

"an ominous tale of suspicion, paranoia, marriage, and the inscrutability of the human psyche," according to Beckman.

Brad, a handsome professor of medieval studies at a small liberal arts college in rural Vermont, is newly married to Emily, a young woman with a lurid imagination. She becomes preoccupied with a string of local unsolved murders of young boys, every one eight years old, and begins to suspect her husband is the killer. *Thumbscrew* ends without a definitive conclusion as to whether or not Brad is guilty. *I* felt he *was,* though the Internet and almost certainly the Blackboards were rife with arguments for both sides. Beckman devoted an entire chapter to the film in his book *American Mask*: Chapter 11: The Brief Case. He wrote that the truth, which will set both Emily *and* the audience free, ultimately exists in Brad's beaten-up leather Samsonite briefcase, which Brad fastidiously locks away in a safe along with his thumbscrews—the medieval torture device—every night when he returns home from teaching at the college.

Brad's briefcase dominates the film so entirely—Emily becomes obsessed with it, desperate to steal it, break the locks, see what her husband was stowing inside—it was actually a main character, featured in more shots than Brad himself. Neither Emily nor the audience is ever allowed to see the inside, a narrative device Tarantino used in *Pulp Fiction* fifteen years later.

In the film's third act, during the confrontation between Emily and Brad, when they fight each other—Emily convinced she must fend off a psychopath; Brad convinced his wife has gone crazy—the briefcase inadvertently slips down onto the floor between the bed and the wall. It remains there, unnoticed, tucked inside this tiny Vermont cottage, which, with Emily—an orphan—taken away to a mental hospital and Brad *dead,* will remain deserted for an unknown period of time.

The final shot of *Thumbscrew* is the briefcase, a slow tracking shot pulling out from under the bed, winding down the hall, out the front door past the police, into the woods, fading to black.

I rolled off the couch—some feeling had returned to my legs—and stepped across the room to the fireplace.

I walked over to the bookshelves. *Thumbscrew,* I remembered, had been made in 1978, and the worn-out paperbacks were from that time: *Looking for Mr. Goodbar, Salem's Lot, The Gemini Contenders.* So was the geometric brown-and-mustard-yellow wallpaper, the lacquered furniture, the orange swag lamp hanging by the front door, the orange-tiled kitchenette, an old GE waffle maker on the counter.

The place had a frozen-in-time feel, as if life had stopped here mid-conversation. No one seemed to have set foot here in decades.

I stepped through the doorway, heading down the narrow corridor. It was dim. I fumbled my way, opening two false doors—they opened back into the warehouse—though the one at the end led into another room.

It was the Jacksons' master bedroom. I moved to the closet and slid aside the door. Emily's clothing hung along the racks, housedresses, a pair of bell-bottom jeans, pairs of platform sandals and go-go boots. I stepped to the other end, which had Brad's clothes, wool slacks, tweed jackets.

I grabbed a pair of the brown corduroy trousers from the top shelf, and a yellow polyester button-down. And I put them on *rapidly,* because I didn't want to even *attempt* to get my mind around the fact that I was donning Brad Jackson's seventies-era clothes, that I was *literally* rummaging through *Thumbscrew.*

The slacks were a few inches short in the leg, but they fit well enough. So Ray Quinn Jr., who played Brad Jackson, unlike *most* Hollywood leading men, wasn't a homunculus. I pulled on a red sweater far too tight in the sleeves, found a pair of argyle socks in the chest of drawers, an orange portable Philips record player on top, James Brown's *The Payback* on the turntable. After putting them on, I was about to head back to the living room to regroup, when I stopped in the doorway.

I had a sudden vision of Wolfgang Beckman—how he'd shout at me, eyes bulging: "You stumbled, by *accident,* into Brad and Emily Jackson's Vermont ranch house and it didn't occur to you to look under the bed for the *briefcase?* You're dead to me now."

Indulging this hallucination, I crouched down, squinting under the bed.

It was too dark to see anything, so I stood back up, stepped to the bedside table, switched on the lamp, and yanked the bed away from the wall to get a better view.

Immediately, there was a clattering thump. *It was there.*

I stared at it in disbelief.

The infamous Samsonite fawn-colored briefcase.

It had been wedged against the wall and the other bedside table in the corner. I was shocked, and yet—what did Emily say in the film? *Wherever the briefcase goes, Brad follows.* I found myself looking over my shoulder to the empty doorway, half wondering if I was going to see Brad's warped shadow projected on the hallway wall.

I grabbed the case by the handle—it was surprisingly heavy—and set it down on the bed.

I tried the latches. *Locked.* I realized then I *knew* the combination. Emily goes to great lengths to figure it out. It was the date that marked the sacking of Rome, the final blow in the decline of the Roman Empire, marking the onset of the Dark Ages.

410.

I spun the numbers into place. The locks popped open.

I lifted the lid.

It was piled with papers. I went through them, pulling out an issue of *Time* dated July 31, 1978, "The Test-Tube Baby" on the cover. Under *that* was a stack of student term papers, graded with handwritten comments. *Marcie, you make a very nice argument that the Dark Ages were a natural rotation of history, but you need to go deeper.*

When I saw what was underneath that, I froze.

Neatly folded in the corner was a boy's plaid button-down shirt.

I picked it up, feeling a wave of revulsion as the shriveled rigid sleeves unfolded in front of me, as if they had a fragile will of their own.

The front of the shirt was stiff, covered in deep brown stains.

It looked harrowingly *real,* a real souvenir from a real murder. The fabric itself seemed beaten, as if residue of unimaginable violence had soaked and dried into the fabric.

It was a hell of a lot of effort to go through for a prop that never appears in the film. I recalled the ravaged white suits I'd found in Marlowe's closet. *I accessed the deepest, most tormented parts of myself,* she'd said. *Parts I was petrified of opening because I doubted I'd ever get them closed again.*

Maybe Cordova's films were real. The terrors on-screen, real terrors, the murders, real murders. *Was it possible?*

It would explain Cordova's popularity—nothing moved people, made them gawk, like the truth. It also explained why none of the people who worked with Cordova ever spoke of the experience. Perhaps they were complicit—to disclose what horrors occurred during filming would only incriminate themselves. It was feasible that at the end of shooting, Cordova had something on every one of his actors, something that guaranteed their silence. I recalled a remark of Olivia Endicott's, which at the time had struck me as rather strange—Cordova's interrogation of her when she visited him for a potential role in *Thumbscrew*: *I began to suspect the underlying purpose of the questions wasn't so much to know me or see if I was right for the part, but to learn how isolated a person I was, who would notice if I ever vanished or changed in some way.*

Undoubtedly, Cordova looked for people he could manipulate. He had an obsession with capturing what was real; he'd forced his son, Theo, to appear in *Wait for Me Here,* rather than sending him to the emergency room so they could reattach his severed fingers. I also knew from the Blackboards—and Peg Martin—that Cordova used a film crew of illegal immigrants, a complicit squad of men and women who would never speak of what they'd seen.

I suddenly felt wild exhilaration over the thought. How easily it fit in with everything I'd learned about the man, following in his daughter's final footsteps.

Cordova obviously took great care in assembling his players, every one from different backgrounds, some with no acting experience at all. He brought them here to live in his remote world, locking them inside it, allowing them no contact with the outside. Who would willingly agree to such a thing, signing away their life to one man?

Hopper had asked Marlowe this. Yet did he need to? Millions of people walked through their lives numb, dying to feel something, to feel alive. To be chosen by Cordova for a film was an opportunity for just *that,* not simply for fame and fortune, but to leave their old selves behind like discarded clothes.

What exactly did Cordova make them endure? Everything his characters did? Then his night films were documentaries, live horrors, not fiction.

He was even more depraved than I'd realized. A madman. *The devil himself.* Maybe he hadn't always been, but it was what he'd become living here. But if his films were real, how easy it would be for the man to slip into harming real children, in order to save Ashley.

I rummaged through the remaining papers in the briefcase. There were only lectures and notes, a typewritten letter from Simon & Schuster, dated January 13, 1978. *Dear Mr. Jackson: I regret to inform you that your novel,* Murder in the Barbican, *will not fit within our current list of fiction titles.* I remembered Brad had a wall safe he was always unlocking, but it was in his home office, which didn't appear to be attached to this set. There was a door off the bedroom, which in the film opened into a bathroom, but when I opened it, there was only the black wall of the soundstage.

I locked the briefcase, returning it to its infamous spot under the bed, and then rolled up the child's blood-soaked shirt, tucked it into my back pants pocket; I didn't want to lose it, so it was safest to keep it on me. I switched off the lamp and headed back down the hall.

I rooted through my sodden clothes scattered beside the couch, finding my camera in the jacket. Thankfully I'd had the forethought to keep it dry, because it still worked, unlike my cellphone and flashlight. Both were dead. I took a few shots of the living room and kitchenette—fully stocked with seventies-era food: Velveeta cheese (still edible after thirty years), Dr Pepper, Swift Sizzlean Pork Strips—then stepped to the edge of the living room, staring out.

From the lamp, I could see the soundstage extended far in front of me. Beyond the couch, a wall of steel pipe scaffolding was supporting something—*probably another set*—constructed on the opposite side.

I realized, after a dazed moment, that I was still shivering. My jacket was still soaked, so after lacing up my boots, I strode to the front door, grabbed Brad Jackson's herringbone overcoat off the chair, and put the thing on—again, not letting my mind consider the absurdity of it, that I was donning the coat of a probable psychopath.

Hopefully, it wasn't contagious.

I checked my watch but saw it had stopped after being submerged in the pool. It read 7:58, which couldn't be right. It had to be later.

And then, heaving my backpack over my shoulder, I stepped out of *Thumbscrew,* following along the scaffolding to see what else was in this massive soundstage, what other worlds plucked from Cordova's treacherous head I could sift through like an archaeologist searching for bones.

✶

WHEN IT BECAME TOO DARK to see anything, I took a picture, looking at it in the camera's screen.

An enormous red bird had been crudely spray-painted across the concrete wall to my left. I'd seen it in articles about Cordova. *It was what Cordova's fans used as a way to invoke the man's presence, an anonymous sign calling for him to return.* I moved on, stepping around the end of the scaffolding, entering what appeared to be a vast room. I could dimly make out an enormous mountain in front of me strewn with boulders. I took another photo and realized the mountain was *garbage,* the boulders corroded gasoline barrels, sprouting like giant mushrooms across the expanse.

I took off across it, knocking right into a wooden sign.

MILFORD GREENS LANDFILL
DO NOT ENTER
HAZARDOUS

I was in *La Douleur*—French for *the pain.*

The film's meek and mousy heroine, Leigh—receptionist at a car dealership by day, community college student by night—agrees to spy on her best friend's husband and not only becomes smitten with him—a native German named Axel—but gets dangerously entangled in his gangland dealings.

The first night, she follows his maroon Mercury Grand Marquis all over town, eventually ending up here sometime around dawn, the Milford Greens Landfill. Leigh watches Axel park his car and take off on foot across the junkyard, flocks of seagulls wafting off the trash like a screeching exhaust.

He carries a small bag, its color the unmistakable robin's-egg blue of *Tiffany*—the jewelry store. Spellbound, Leigh tiptoes after him, her hair going fizzy, her frumpy blouse untucking from her skirt. She climbs inside an old funeral hearse to spy on the man as he scales the

hill to an overturned school bus. After removing a paper bag from behind the front wheel, Axel sticks the Tiffany bag in its place. Leigh
waits for him to drive away, then makes her *own way* to the school bus,
skidding and sliding through the debris. She pulls out the Tiffany bag,
and inside finds a small blue Tiffany *ring box*—a box commonly used
for engagement rings. Leigh is about to open it, when, noticing a black
car pulling into the junkyard parking lot, she loses her balance and
slips, the blue Tiffany box clattering through an open window into the
derelict bus. Leigh goes after it. Within minutes, the thug known simply as Y shows up to collect the Tiffany bag. It doesn't take him long to
discover the bag empty, Leigh cowering inside the bus. And that's the
moment *La Douleur* morphs from voyeuristic suspense into a spellbinding *wrong man* nightmare.

The landfill didn't *smell* hazardous. There was a musty dampness in
the air, as if this were a subterranean basement sealed for years, and
faintly within it, a smell of gasoline. I stopped to check behind me and
saw with surprise that it looked as if I were actually outside. Colossal
screens mounted along the scaffolding gave the impression of wide-
open sky. I could discern ghostly clouds painted there, though at least
twenty feet above, the screens cut out to the empty black soundstage.
The effect was dizzying, seemed to suggest some truth about the inherently blinkered nature of human perception. *If only you looked a little
farther, McGrath, you'd see it all gave way to . . . nothing.*

I hadn't noticed it before, but down along the section where I'd entered was a small gravel parking lot fringed with bushes, a lone car
parked there, beneath an unlit streetlight. With a chill of unease, I
realized it was Leigh's boxy blue Chevy Citation, straight from the
1980s. It looked as if it were waiting for her to come back.

Maybe she never had. Maybe Leigh had never left this warehouse—
or The Peak. I couldn't recall if I'd heard of the actress ever appearing
in another film.

I turned, squinting far ahead at the indistinct smudge on the hill,
realizing as I stumbled toward it, it was the overturned school bus, the
very one Leigh gets trapped inside. In the final minutes of *La Douleur*,
she's forced in there by the gangsters, blindfolded and bound. Though
she struggles courageously, determined to untie her hands using a
metal spike jutting out of a derelict seat, the question of her fate is left

unanswered. As she whimpers and flails, the film fades to black—though her cries can be heard throughout the end credits, barely

drowned by the Beastie Boys song "Posse in Effect."

The incline was surprisingly steep, and I began to trip and slide in the plastic bags, blown-out tires, mattresses, and cracked TVs. I'd gone a few yards when I realized not just that the incline was growing even more vertical, but that my movement was dislodging the trash beneath me. I could feel it shifting, and within minutes the *entire mountain* was dislodging around me. I froze but found myself falling backward, nearly submerged in an avalanche of rusted cans and garbage bags. I scrambled upright, untangling myself from a biohazard suit, surfing toward the perimeter of the set as the entire hill continued to loosen, including that bus. *It was impossible to get up there.* I groped my way to the scrim of sky, lifted the fabric, and scrambled through the scaffolding as the landfill continued to crash behind me. I'd had enough of *La Douleur.* I'd be damned if I was going to die buried alive in Cordova's trash.

I lurched to my feet and took off down the dark corridor. Far ahead, at the very end—what looked to be a *mile* away—was an opening with pale red light. I hoped it was the way out of here.

EVERY NOW AND THEN I stopped to listen, hearing only the wind yowling across the soundstage roof high overhead. The longer I walked, the more that red light remained doggedly, *persistently* far-off. I couldn't help but wonder if I was hallucinating, or if this warehouse's concrete floor was somehow a treadmill and I was running in place. At one point I smelled, rather bizarrely, *salt water.* It was strong, intermixed with the scents of seaweed and sand. It had to be another film set, built behind the scaffolding rising up to my left, but it was too high to see anything.

I could see the red light getting closer and felt sudden nerve-racking curiosity about what it was. Marlowe Hughes's suburban McMansion in *Lovechild*? The brothel where Annie looks for her father in *At Night All Birds Are Black*? Archer's boxcar clubhouse from *The Legacy*?

I stepped around the corner.

It was the greenhouse from *Wait for Me Here.*

What was it Beckman had said about it? "If there was one setting that perfectly evoked the treacherous mind of a psychopath, it *isn't* the Bates Motel, but the Reinhart family greenhouse, with its domes of moldy glass and corroded iron, tropical plants growing inside like insidious thoughts run amok, the frail sand pathway snaking through the foliage like the last vestige of humanity shrinking out of sight."

The greenhouse was a domed rectangular structure, built out of glass panes and pale green oxidized iron, the architecture mimicking the Royal Greenhouses in Brussels. It sat in serene seclusion in a dense medieval forest of Douglas firs—the effect created by more screens rigged around the set. The intense red light was emanating from inside the greenhouse and then, I remembered—*of course*—from the film.

It was the crimson plant lights.

I waited to be sure I was alone and stepped out onto the lawn, the silvered grass crunching under my boots. I stared down at it, unsettled, because it looked so real, bathed even in a morning dew. I bent down to touch it. It was *plastic,* the *dew* actually shiny iridescent paint sprayed across every blade.

I reached the stone path, following it to the greenhouse's single steel door—the *back* door, if I remembered correctly. The glass had become opaque from dirt and decades of condensation. Shadows of dark leaves pressed against the panes like the hands and faces of a trapped crowd, frantic to get out.

I grabbed the iron doorknob—noticing it was in the form of an elegant and *rather sinister* R for Reinhart—and heaved the door open.

A BOILING BLAST of humidity hit my face.

It had to be at least ninety-five degrees inside.

A pathway of immaculate white sand led away from the door, though within a few feet, the dark knots of plants mushrooming from every direction buried it from view. Suspended overhead were green iron barrels lit up with row upon row of cherry-red and blue lights, giving the greenhouse the look of a gigantic oven set on *broil.*

In *Wait for Me Here,* the Reinharts' longtime deaf-mute gardener, Popcorn—prime suspect in the Leadville killings, later found to be innocent—lovingly tended these plants. Glancing around, I realized with unease that they looked *exactly* as they had in the film. I grabbed a giant shiny black leaf beside my shoulder, rubbing the surface to make sure it was real. It was.

Wait for Me Here, I recalled, had been shot in 1992. The bulbs of these plant lights wouldn't have lasted twenty years.

Someone must come here regularly to tend these plants.

A chill inched down my spine, but I stepped resolutely inside, shoving back the door, trying to keep it propped open to let some of the heat out.

I wasn't *thrilled* with the idea of getting trapped inside here, either, roasted alive by these lights. But even when I wedged in the rubber doorstopper, found buried in the sand just inside, the heavy iron door kept *thudding* determinedly *closed* right behind me, so I gave up, letting it slam. I checked to make sure it would still open, then headed down the path, shoving aside the foliage.

It was like the Amazon. Stems as solid and twisted as water pipes laden with white tubular flowers, trees at least eight feet tall, limbs barbed with thistle, black star-shaped blooms, buds with tiny red berries—all of it clutched at my face and arms like swarming orphans desperate for a handout, for human contact. Their aromas were overpowering and pungent, sweet as honeysuckle, though as soon as I inhaled them they seemed to turn earthen and foul. Given that I was wearing three layers of Brad Jackson's wool clothing suitable for a brutal winter in *Vermont,* I was already sweating profusely. But I did my best to ignore the heat, jostling past a cluster of verdant trees leaden with drooping yellow blossoms as big as my hands. They collided with my face, getting into my nose and mouth, the pollen tart and acidic.

I spit, left with an acrid aftertaste. Within a few yards, I saw with relief something I recognized: *the koi pond.*

The pond was a perfect circle made of stones, filled to the brim with black water. In *Wait for Me Here,* giant Amazonica lily pads floated across the surface. *And when Special Agent Fox nearly drowned in there, held underwater by the killer, he clawed at them for dear life, but they only dissolved feebly in his hands.*

Now the pool was devoid of plants, the black water so slick and smooth it looked to be made of *plastic,* though as I shoved my way past the foliage to reach the stone perimeter, I saw perfectly well it was real. I dipped my finger in to make sure. Lazy circular ripples marred the reflection of the red lights and the hulking glass and iron dome overhead.

I assumed there'd be no koi left, not twenty years after the film was shot. *But no*—in the murky water, I glimpsed a white and orange streak through the murk. As quickly as it appeared, it vanished.

Someone must come here regularly to feed the fish.

In the film, Popcorn notoriously fed them Cracker Jacks from a box he kept in the front pocket of his filthy dirt-streaked Levi's overalls.

Maybe he *still* did.

Maybe the poor man worked in here, lived in here.

The thought made me turn, my eyes scanning the twisted leaves for some sign of that old gardener, his black face wrinkled and glistening, the bright gold tooth in his smile. "The Reinharts' glorious greenhouse is Popcorn's holy sanctuary," I remembered Beckman intoning one night to his students. "It's his refuge from ridicule—the one place in the world he doesn't feel afraid."

I took a moment to recalibrate my mind, to assure myself I was alone and whatever I found in here was a narrative plucked from Cordova's head. I was not and never had been in *Wait for Me Here*—though as I noted this, I realized the very fact that I needed to reassure myself of such a thing was horrifying in itself.

Had I already lost my head? Not yet.

I wiped the sweat off my face and headed around the pond's perimeter, staring into the red-soaked greenery.

Within minutes, I found what I was looking for: *Popcorn's work shed.*

The old blue wooden door was ajar, the same crooked sign nailed to the outside: PRIVATE KEEP OUT. I gently pushed it open.

Popcorn wasn't home.

It was no bigger than a walk-in closet, filled with meticulously organized shelving, cubbyholes housing envelopes of seeds, plastic trays, terra-cotta pots, bags of mulch and fertilizer. Directly in front of me, facing the greenhouse's glass walls—too dirty to see through—sat a desk and tall stool, where Popcorn could always be found smoking his cigars, reading his comic books, and listening to the Beatles. A small wire cage—some kind of trap for catching raccoons—stood atop the desk beside a faded comic called *Mikey's Friend* and a half-smoked cigar in an ashtray.

I stepped inside to pick it up. It smelled *recent.*

Next to the desk on the wall was an old bulletin board, jumbled with poorly written directions for tending the soil and plants, a tattered postcard of colored shacks standing on stilts along the edge of a dark bay.

I tugged it loose and checked the reverse side. There was no address, only four scribbled words on the back.

Someday soon you'll come.

I put it back, turning. Various gardening tools had been mounted along the walls using old spikes: hand sickles, Austrian scythes, pruning saws, axes of all different sizes. I moved over to inspect them—*the same way Special Agent Fox had inspected them.*

In *Wait for Me Here,* the eleven teenage bodies of the Leadville killings had been mutilated in ways mimicking accidents that occurred at an old paper mill—chemical burns, boiler explosions, industrial roller entrapment. But there was *another* constant: Each victim was a high-school student killed by a stab through the left ventricle of the heart using a pair of hedge shears, the pointed blades exactly nine and a half inches long.

Special Agent Fox sneaks in here in the dead of night to examine Popcorn's gardening tools—every saw, snip, and clipper—trying to find a blade with that exact measurement. He comes up empty-handed. Because the hedge shears *weren't* hidden in the work shed, as he'd suspected.

Now where in the hell were they?

My eyes were stinging, and I was drenched in sweat, getting steamed alive in here like a lobster. The heat was so overpowering I could hardly think, hardly remember that pivotal scene at the end, when Popcorn accidentally finds the shears buried somewhere in here, in one of his beloved flower beds.

I remembered they were encrusted in blood and the look on the poor man's face when he came across them planting a new set of seeds, seeds with a bizarre name. His look was of such horror.

Real horror?

Was it my imagination or was it actually getting *hotter* in here?

I shrugged off my backpack, yanked off Brad Jackson's herringbone coat and the sweater, leaving them on the wire trap. I wrenched a hoe off the wall and exited the shed, slipping around the koi pond.

Popcorn was the only person in the film to know the truth behind the murders. "Sometimes only the silent man can see the full picture." Beckman had said it, or was it someone in the film?

I needed to get my hands on those shears.

I stepped into the flower bed, traipsing through plants growing so thickly I couldn't see the ground.

I bent down, noticing a white handwritten sign stuck into the dirt.

EYE-PRICKLES, it read.

I stepped forward a few feet, spotting another.

DEATH CHERRIES.

There were countless similar signs arranged under the leaves.

BLUE ROCKET. TONGUE TACKS. SORCERER'S VIOLET. MAD SEEDS.

That one sounded familiar. Pushing up my sleeves, I raked the hoe through the dirt and immediately felt something hard in the loose soil. I bent down, seeing something shiny.

It was a brass compass, the glass face cracked.

It had belonged to Popcorn. The compass was a source of ridicule throughout the film. The whole town mocked the way he constantly pulled it out of his overalls, closely inspecting it as if to make sure he was still on course on his very important journey around the world, the joke being that the poor man had been born in Leadville and had never set foot outside the tiny town.

I pocketed the compass and shoved the hoe deeper into the dirt, the blade catching on something else.

I crouched down to inspect it. It was a half-decomposed cardboard box, sodden and limp, though I could make out the letters on the front. *Cracker Jack.*

I threw it aside, ignoring the unease flooding through me, doggedly digging into the soil again. And I felt something else there, something bulky. I bent down to it.

Something was buried deep in the dirt.

Fighting a wave of nausea—it had to be the oppressive heat, the red lights making every plant and flower, *even my own hands,* look blood-soaked—I stabbed the hoe directly downward. It caught in some roots.

Crouching, I brutally tore out some of the plants, leaves and limbs shuddering in my face as if in protest.

I could feel it with my hands, something hidden here, something *hard.*

Something human-sized. Popcorn?

It made no sense. At the end of the film, Popcorn was in the clear, *safe.* He was keeping the killer's secret, and if anyone could keep a secret it was a mute man. *Then what the hell was buried here?* Why were his compass and box of Cracker Jack—the two items the gardener was famously never without—hidden here? Had the killer decided to finish him off? Had Cordova?

As my mind spun, suddenly I was aware of, somewhere far away, a *dull thud. It sounded like a door banging closed.* I scrambled to my feet.

I could hear faint footsteps of more than one person—two, maybe *three.* They echoed through the warehouse, moving quickly, probably hurrying down those narrow corridors between the film sets.

I was no longer alone. I tried to ignore this reality for a few seconds, frantically digging through the flower bed with my bare hands.

I just needed one glimpse of what was here. I uprooted plants, throwing them aside, tunneling through the soil, my fingers feeling *something.*

It felt like denim. *Popcorn's overalls.*

I fumbled to take the camera from my pocket, but realized, *idiotically,* I'd left it back in Brad's herringbone coat. To excavate whatever it was buried here would require clearing away the entire flower bed.

I paused, listening.

Those footsteps were getting louder. They had to know I was here.

I'd have to come back.

I stepped out of the foliage, racing back around the pond to the work shed. I grabbed Brad's coat, pulled it on, throwing the backpack over my shoulder. I fought my way through the plants to reach the back door.

I OPENED IT A CRACK, staring out at the deserted lawn. I darted out, gulping down the freezing air, relieved to be out of that gory crimson light, that tropical *heat,* barreling into the crisp darkness of the sound-stage.

I froze. The entire building was hiccoughing with footsteps, seemingly coming down the same passage where I'd entered *Wait for Me Here.*

I took off in the opposite direction, moving down a stone path out of the set straight into a vast desolate beach of white sand dunes and bristling sea grass. In the distance, an angular beach house rose high in the sky on stilts.

It was Kay Glass's house from *A Small Evil.*

I headed across the sand toward the house and beyond it, the moonlit ocean. My sense was *this* set would take me back to the Jacksons', and hopefully the exit *out* of here.

Suddenly—far ahead, a dark figure with a flashlight streaked over the dunes, heading straight for me.

I whipped around, stumbling back out, careening through the *next* opening I could find, finding myself racing down the middle of a deserted street.

It was the Main Street of a small town, a ghost town that I didn't recognize, though I could *see* fairly well, due to the blinking red and green Christmas lights strewn up over the road.

Dark storefronts slipped past.

SILVER DOLLAR SALOON.

SUNSHINE GROCERY.

PASTIME GENTLEMAN'S CLUB. MEMBERS ONLY.

Sprinting footsteps ricocheted behind me. I leapt up onto the sidewalk to Dream-a-lot Movie House, heaved the door open, and sprinted past candy and soda counters and down a narrow hall, theaters advertising *Distortion* at eleven-thirty, *Chasing the Red* at twelve.

I yanked open the first door and it dumped me, thank Christ, *back* into the warehouse and smack into something hard, a concrete wall. I charged along it, looking behind, and saw the flashlight was there again, and another one was heading straight toward me. I grabbed the bars of some scaffolding and began to climb. I'd gone ten, twelve feet, when I reached a wooden platform. I scrambled up onto it.

"See anything?" I heard a male say below.

"He headed the other way."

I waited several minutes, and, when the lights were farther off, cautiously stood up. The platform was sturdy, the rigging supporting tungsten lights pointing downward into some kind of stone interior. A pillar stood about four feet across from me with a banner reading—I could barely make out the words—STIR THE WATERS. It was Father Jinley's church from *A Crack in the Window.* Just beneath me along the wall were stained-glass windows, a three-inch ledge. I bent down, sliding down onto it, and with a silent Hail Mary, leapt across the divide—*intending* to grab the pillar and slide down.

I missed. I reached out, seizing some sort of mounted wood plaque to break my fall. It wrenched loose, tiles clattering around me as I crashed to the floor, the plaque skidding across the stones.

Fuck. I scrambled to my feet, seeing a flashlight slipping down the arched passageway in front of me, illuminating a vaulted ceiling, alcoves with statues. I hurried away from it down the rows of pews, heading to the back portal, spotting the confessional in the back corner. The simple sight of it made my stomach plunge, but I unlatched the ornate door—it emitted a faint moan—and climbed inside.

It was tight with my backpack on, pitch-black.

I crouched down to the floor, waiting.

Within seconds, I heard someone enter the church and *stop*—no doubt inspecting the smashed hymn board I'd pried off the wall.

I waited, my heart pounding, noticing a stench. *Vomit? Urine?* The footsteps resumed, the flashlight edging closer, illuminating the confessional door, which I could see was a carved wood screen of vines and flowers. I recognized the pattern and could hardly believe now *I* was staring out of it with dread, *exactly* as Father Jinley had stared out—albeit for somewhat different reasons.

The film's opening scene took place *right in here,* when Jinley was conducting his first confessional duties. He was fresh out of seminary school and believed, with the arrogant optimism of the young and inexperienced, that he would lead the depraved to the righteous path. After waiting for more than an hour without a single penitent sinner showing up, a mysterious figure at last enters the other side in a rush, sitting down on the seat with an *ominous thud.*

The memory made me inadvertently crane my neck to inspect that confessional window only a few inches above my head, the dark latticed smoke screen ensuring total anonymity.

This enigmatic stranger, as the priest soon realizes, knows Jinley's dark secret, that he put his three-year-old bastard daughter on a Brooklyn rooftop, allowing her to teeter along the edge while chasing the roosting pigeons, and then, losing her balance, fall to her death on a sidewalk far below—all the while, Jinley watched from a crack in the window and did nothing. Jinley had his reasons, of course—he believed his little girl to be the devil incarnate. But as for who was watching him that afternoon, who this mysterious person *was* poised behind the screen, someone who vows in a knowing whisper to *tear him apart and make him renounce God*—it takes Jinley the whole film to figure it out, the identity of the person even more terrifying than his secret.

I realized the footsteps sounded as if they were retreating down some other passage, the faint light now gone.

I rose a few inches, sitting on the wooden seat just behind me, listening. I appeared to be alone. Had it been *this side* of the box Father Jinley had been sitting on or the other? Was I on the good guy's side or the side of evil? *Where was that goddamn smell coming from?* I leaned forward, staring through the screen, the latticed openings in the form of minute crosses.

I froze in horror. *Someone was there.*

There was a person sitting on the other side.

I hardly believed my eyes, yet I could hear breathing, the shifting of heavy fabric, and then—as if aware that he was now being observed—he slowly turned to face me.

I was barely able to make out a face shadowed by a dark hood.

The next few moments happened so swiftly, I was hardly aware of what I did: I blasted out of the box, racing past the transept, passing the entrance to Jinley's office and through a door, which if I remembered correctly led into an underground crypt. It was too dark to see. I reached out, waiting for the feel of cold stones, then realized I'd been emptied back into the soundstage.

I heard pounding, a chorus of neon lights moaning above. *The lights were coming on.* Suddenly I was drenched in bright light, half-blinded.

I stumbled forward, feeling a door handle, pulled it, wheeling out into another freezing room.

But it wasn't a room.

Real leaves crunched under my feet. Real wind rushed my face. And looking up, I swore that was a real moon over my head.

I DIDN'T LET MYSELF BELIEVE IT, that I'd actually escaped that soundstage. But after running a few yards, I looked back and saw the warehouse sitting quietly in the woods behind me. It looked innocuous, so wan and blank-faced—no hint of the levels of hell that lay inside.

I was back in cold, hard reality, thank Christ. I ran back down the hill, heading toward Graves Pond. The men must not have realized I'd escaped, because no one was running after me anymore. *Who the hell were they? And what had I seen on the other side of that confessional?*

I checked my watch, forgetting it was broken: 7:58.

I fumbled in my pockets, taking a quick inventory of what I had— *the child's blood-soaked shirt and Popcorn's compass.* They were there; so was my pocket knife, but my camera was gone. It had been deep inside the pocket but must have fallen out when I'd yanked the coat back on. Berating myself for such sloppiness, fighting the urge to go back for it, I broke into a sprint, the wind hissing punitively in my ears, the moon lighting the way.

A dog barked. It sounded like one of the hounds that had chased me, but frustrated now, tied up, though it was probably just a matter of time until it was set loose again.

I'd come to Graves Pond. I crept to the water's edge, staring through the foliage to its shimmering surface. There was still no sign of Hopper, Nora, *or* the canoe—not of anyone. Hopper and Nora. I realized with amazement those names seemed to come at me from far away, deep in my past. *How long had I been inside that soundstage? Years?* Was it some sort of wormhole, a dimension away from time? I hadn't thought about them, not their well-being or the mystery of where they'd gone. I hadn't been aware of anything except Cordova. Those sets were narcotics, dominating my head so entirely there'd been no space for any other thought.

They must have gone for help. They were paddling back the way we'd come, safe. I needed to believe this so I wouldn't worry, instead devising a new plan. But I knew in my gut Hopper wouldn't give up on Ashley so easily. Neither would Nora. They must both be here somewhere, then, wandering, running in desperate circles.

Squinting out at the opposite shoreline, the black hill, I spotted another one of the flashlights moving over the crest. The person seemed to be hurrying down the path to the wooden dock. Something was running through the grass. *It had to be one of the dogs.*

I stepped away from the lake's perimeter, breaking into a jog, heading east. I could gage my direction from what I knew of the lake's position. East was the shortest distance to the property's perimeter and the closest public road, Country Road 112. It was my best bet for help. My priorities had changed. Lives might be at stake now, if Nora and Hopper were trapped somewhere inside here, possibly hurt—*or worse.*

Considering this as I ran, I'd unconsciously taken Popcorn's compass from my pocket, clasping it as if it were a prized possession, *a last hope.* I saw in surprise that though the glass face was cracked, the needle was trembling due north.

I turned in a circle to check its bearings. *They were spot-on.*

The thing actually worked.

I raced on, every now and then checking the compass to make sure I was on course—*just as old Popcorn had checked it,* much to the entertainment of the entire town.

When in hell was I going to have the chance to go back to that greenhouse? I'd given up too soon. Popcorn, if he was actually buried there, would remain an entombed secret. My mind spinning, I forced myself to keep moving. The forest seemed to parade past in a cruel loop, like the synthetic backdrop in an old movie where the characters chat and drive but never look at the road. *Were these real trees?* Every trunk of every spruce was elongated and bare, identical to the others, *every one.*

And then, staring off to my left, I saw it again, *the warehouse.*

I froze, horrified.

I'd run in a complete circle.

Popcorn's compass had been playing tricks on me, deliberately leading me astray. But no—taking a few steps toward the hulking structure, I realized this one was cylindrical, a silo, the exterior painted yellow.

I turned my back to it, breaking into a sprint.

Within fifteen minutes, I'd reached a paved road. *It had to be the lower section of The Peak's driveway,* which meant I *was* going in the right direction. Reassured, I veered away from it, keeping under the cover of forest but following its general direction. Within minutes, I could discern far ahead the dark blur of the military fence.

I sprinted toward it, flooded with relief.

There were no discernible electrical wires. I took a chance, running my hands along the rusted links, waiting for a shock.

I felt nothing.

I grabbed the chain link and began to climb. I was six feet off the ground when I noticed, far off to my right, two roofs protruding through the foliage, each with a blackened spike.

The Peak gatehouses.

I recognized them because I'd driven up here years ago. I'd climbed out of my car and took a snapshot of the entrance, so desperate to get inside here. *Now so desperate to get out.* I recalled what the Spider had told us, how he'd taken that underground tunnel, which linked the mansion to a gatehouse, in order to help the Crowthorpe townspeople enter the property.

It meant—*if* the Spider had been telling the truth—access to that maze of tunnels underneath the property was *right there, yards away, so goddamn close.* I could see it with my own eyes.

After a split second's hesitation, I was clambering back down the fence and *back into The Peak,* my mind screaming in protest. I leapt into the overgrown grass, moving along the fence, heading straight for those two cottages flanking the wrought-iron gate.

The first one had no entrance. The second had a narrow black door, a window at the top. There was no discernible light inside, no evident camera, the paint was flaking, the glass too filthy to see through.

I needed one quick look at the entrance to those tunnels, to substantiate Villarde's story—*and then I'd get the hell out of here.*

It was locked, so I smashed the window with a rock, unlocked it, and slipped inside. It was a minuscule room, with a window overlooking the approach to the gate, a desk with an old computer, an office chair glazed with dust. The floor was bare—except for a small black carpet in the corner.

I walked over to it and pulled back the rug.

There it was: a small wooden hatch. I slid aside the metal bars, grabbed the rings, and heaved it open, staring into the raw black hole.

Concrete stairs, barely a foot wide, led sharply downward. I moved down a few, crouching to take a look.

The tunnel extending in front of me was *black.* Only a few feet of brick walls were visible before cutting out into a darkness so absolute it looked as if this part of the world had been left unfinished—a raw edge of the Earth, which gave way not to simple darkness, but to *outer space.*

Staring into it, my head urged me to *get the hell out now,* close the hatch, climb back over that fence while I still had the chance.

But what *did* I have on Cordova? What did I actually know?

I tried to mentally grab hold of a few hard facts to stay afloat. I had in my pocket a few items, which *might* incriminate the man, but could very well amount to nothing as far as the law was concerned. I had stories, eyewitness accounts, testimonies, the truth that Ashley was dead. But was it enough to bury him? I'd hardly speared Cordova, my great white whale. He could go on with his black magic, his live horrors. Ashley was dead, so there was no need for an exchange, but had he stopped? What had I seen with my own eyes?

As I considered this, the decaying brick walls of the tunnel seemed to constrict imperceptibly around me.

Just *what,* exactly, was I escaping unscathed back *to?*

An empty apartment. No one would be waiting for me when I made it back to Perry Street. Life would go on as before. *I'd* go on as before. Simply to think this was suddenly unbearable.

What in the hell was I waiting for? When in life was the truth right in front of you? Because it was here, beyond the pitch darkness. Even if I couldn't see it now, it was somewhere in front of me.

Do I dare? I took three more steps down. The air was frigid, an iciness that ate at my bones. I yanked off my backpack, rummaged in the pocket for my flashlight, tried turning it on, but it still didn't work. I removed a Ziploc bag containing a box of matches, heaved my backpack on, and lit a match.

The tiny orange flame trembled as I held it out before me.

I almost laughed out loud. The dark was shoved back just a few inches. The redbrick walls were crumbling, the ceiling low, thick with mold. It looked like a shriveled artery to hell. I checked my watch.

Seven-fifty-eight. I was making incredible time.

I moved back up, grabbing the hatch. I pulled it closed over my head with an irrevocable *thud. Had I just sealed myself inside my own coffin?*

THE MATCH ABRUPTLY BLEW OUT. I lit another and began to walk.

When that one extinguished, I slipped on through the darkness as quickly as I could. There were a hundred matches in the box. I had to ration them. I remembered the Spider mentioning the distance between the gatehouse and the mansion was two miles. *If I walked four miles an hour, within fifteen minutes I'd be halfway.* I waited for my eyes to adjust, but after a time I realized the swirling black liquid I was staring into *was* my eyes adjusted.

My footsteps were a metronome for my breathing.

Beyond that, my hiking boots crunching down the grimy floor, there were no other sounds, just a marked pressure—of being *sealed,* as if this passage were cutting under a body of water.

When I couldn't stand the dark any longer, when I actually began to feel confused as to whether or not I was actually moving, I stopped and lit another match.

The constricted corridor had shrunken around me, and was now less than four feet wide, extending identically in both directions. I realized that seeing the fragile light was infinitely more disturbing than just plunging forward in total darkness. *I might as well put my head all the way under. Just don't stop swimming.* When that light burned out, I dropped the match and kept on, my right hand running along the crumbling bricks as a guide. It kept me tethered to the world, to *reality,* because this darkness was so total it became physical, a thick black curtain. It turned me upside down, made me wonder if I was actually submerged in black water and I'd forgotten which was the way to air and light. Gravity seemed to be frail down here.

I tripped on something bulky, instantly gripped with an irrational dread. *It was a body, a severed limb.* I kicked it a second time. It sounded like a bed sheet.

I fumbled to light another match.

A red piece of silk lay on the ground, covered in dust.

I picked it up. It was a woman's dress—cranberry red, old-fashioned—with long sleeves and a black plastic belt. Nearly all of the front buttons were missing. I studied the neck and glimpsed the pale purple label of Cordova's longtime costume designer—*Larkin*—seconds before the match burned out.

I unzipped my backpack, stuffed the dress inside, zipped it back up, and shuffled on. After a time, I worried that I'd accidentally turned around and was blindly rushing back to the gatehouse, but I didn't stop. *It was just disorientation, the dark bullying the mind.* How flimsy was a single person's authority, his confidence about his place in the world. Give him fifteen minutes of this, even Einstein would start to doubt the laws of the physical world, who he was, where he was, if he were alive or dead.

To my horror, I kicked something *again*. It scuttled noisily across the floor, something hard. It sounded like a piece of wood.

No. It was a bone. I lit another match.

It was a woman's black leather *pump* with a square scuffed heel, covered in dust.

I checked my watch without thinking: 7:58.

I stood up again, holding the match out in front of me.

The view was a carbon copy of the one from before—a wizened brick corridor disappearing infinitely in both directions.

It looked like I hadn't moved.

I continued on, trying to remain calm. *Why was the dress down here? A woman had tried to escape?* Very much like the boy's blood-soaked plaid shirt in my pocket, the dress looked like the vestiges of violence. To die here, alone and cold, to never be found, never be loved again. Sam would think I'd abandoned her. I tried to wrench my mind away from these thoughts, chuck my attention onto something cheerful, but this place, so black and cold, extinguished levity within seconds.

I stepped on something.

Pebbles.

I stopped, feeling so many of them—hard and round—rolling underneath my boot. *Children's teeth? Molars, sprinkled here like crumbs?*

I fumbled with another match, lighting it.

They weren't teeth, but the red round plastic buttons of the dress.

I bent down to inspect them. A few feet away, lying along the wall, was the other black shoe. I grabbed a handful of the buttons, shoved them into Brad's overcoat pocket, and stood up again.

It was *exactly* the same view—a black tunnel extending in front of me and behind me, eternal. I was on a treadmill, running in place. I was trapped in a fourth dimension, purgatory, where there was no time or progression, only inert floating.

The match, I realized, was burning my fingers.

I let go of it, lurched forward, faster now. I could feel my mind faltering as if on a tightrope, threatening to lose its balance. I lit another match and saw with relief only a few yards ahead—a break in the tunnel. In my haste to get there, the match blew out. I hurried on. When I felt the wall open up to my right, I lit another.

I was in a small circular alcove, gaping mouths of more tunnels fanning out, seemingly in all directions. I slipped past them, seeing faint words scrawled above each opening in crude white paint.

GATEHOUSE. MANSION. LAKE. STABLES. WORKSHOP. LOOKOUT. TROPHY. PINCOYA NEGRO. CEMETERY. MRS. PEABODY'S. LABORATORY. THE Z. CROSSROADS.

Pincoya Negro? Laboratory? The Z? I remembered the Spider had mentioned there existed at this central point other secret passageways, which led to other hidden parts of the estate. I lit another match, holding it up to the word painted on the wood right in front of me.

Crossroads.

It was what the Spider had called the clearing where he'd taken Ashley.

Crudely nailed planks, once blocking the passage, had been hacked away with an ax. *It was what Villarde had done for the townspeople.* Only bits of splintered wood and twisted nails had been left, some strewn on the ground.

This corridor was cruder than the others, barely three feet wide, and looked as if it cut straight through granite, the walls slick from water seeping in from somewhere. Taking a step down it, I could see more words had been scrawled on the rocks in the same white paint. Farther down, there were drawings of stick figures with protruding noses and screaming mouths.

I stepped forward to read some of it. *If y go father leave all your love right HERE at the floor. WARNING: ye will leav this path neither amimal, vegetabl, or mineral. Say goodbi to ye lamb. May the Lord help y*

The match flickered out.

I lit another and forced myself to take one more step inside, holding the flame out. It swiftly extinguished, a subzero wind blasting my face, swelled and quickly dispersed. Then, I heard *sizzling* in my ears, so deafening and close, I lurched backward, stumbled on the uneven floor back into the alcove, dropping the box of matches.

Fuck. My heart pounding, I knelt down, groping for it along the floor. It had disappeared.

Something was with me here, standing behind me, toying with me.

Trying not to panic, I wheeled around unsteadily, getting down on my hands and knees, fumbling for the matches in the dirt.

Calm down, McGrath. The box has to be here.

The side of my left hand hit something. *Matches.* I grabbed them. But somehow, impossibly, the box had been tossed far behind me, wedged against the opposite wall between two passageways. *It was like the leviathan's shadow. It had a mind of its own.*

I got to my feet, ignoring that thought, lit a match, and stepped back to the opening.

Crossroads. The tunnel twisted sharply left and out of sight.

I took another step down the passage, the flame burning calmly now. Just for the hell of it, I groped in my pocket and removed the compass, curious to see what direction I'd be heading in.

I could only stare down at it, incredulous.

The red needle was going berserk, spinning madly counterclockwise.

I shook it, but the needle wouldn't stop rotating, around and around.

It was too much for my mind to compute, so I dropped it back into Brad Jackson's herringbone coat pocket and, trying to forget I'd ever looked at the thing, I took off down the corridor.

I DIDN'T KNOW HOW LONG I WALKED.

I had the distinct feeling I wasn't alone.

It was a bone-chilling understanding that I was in close proximity to something *alive* and was seconds from running headlong into it. And yet when I shoved the flickering flame in front of me, expecting to see a face, *animal eyes*—there was only darkness in every direction.

The Spider's insidious voice began to worm its way into my head, growing louder with every step, as if that day at The Broken Door, he'd been narrating not his own secret, but the future, this walk, *my walk. I can still remember the sound of her bare feet, how soft and* clean *they were, padding along the filthy ground next to mine.*

Was that what I was hearing, what I sensed beside me? Ashley?

I kept walking, listening, but there was only my own boots, trudging on.

After a time, the Spider's voice faded and my mind became blank, a dirty chalkboard, smeared with half-erased thoughts.

Ashley had come this way.

And Cordova. He walked this, every time he had a new child to try and barter with the devil. Anything to save his daughter.

I could discern a strong smell of *metal* mixed into the heavy moisture and mud. At one point, I heard distant *rumbling,* as if, overhead, animals were thundering in a stampede across the property, *fleeing in terror.* I touched the slippery rocks, warm water trickling through my fingers. The walls felt as if they were vibrating. Pebbles came loose from the ceiling, rattling to the ground. But then the noise was gone, the tunnel as silent as before, and I was left wondering if my anxiety, needing some type of outlet, had conjured the whole thing.

I plodded on, noticing that my brain felt loose inside my skull, as if it were melting. I noted with a stab of horror that I was sweating as if I were back inside that greenhouse, as if I'd never escaped, never gotten out from under the blood-splattered lights. Yet I shivered, riddled with chills, the feeble flame I was holding revealing what I already knew: The black tunnel unspooled in front of me, on and on.

The moment I accepted it, understood I could very well die wandering here, I'd reached the end.

A few feet ahead, a bent and rusted metal ladder extended to the ceiling.

I paused, listening, hearing nothing but the wails of powerful wind. I grabbed the rungs and climbed up, my arms and legs oddly weakened and slack as if filled with sand. When I reached the top, I could feel another wooden hatch above me, seemingly identical to the one I'd entered at the gatehouse. I slipped back the rails, shoved my shoulder against it, and opened the hatch.

I was in a dense forest of birch trees, the entire *world* in razor focus. I could make out every leaf and branch, rock and weed bathed in green moonlight. It had to be a side effect of being submerged for so long underground in blackness, as if my eyes, ecstatic to be granted one last chance to see, were doing their best.

I climbed out.

I TOOK OFF down a rutted dirt path, noticing, tied to an overhanging branch, a red string dancing in the wind.

A few yards ahead, I saw a bridge. *The devil's bridge.*

Simply thinking it sucked the breath from my lungs.

There was no one here. I was alone. The wind was howling furiously, shoving the coattails of my coat so far out, it felt as if a crowd were grasping at it.

The bridge was arched, made of dark gray stone. The construction looked meticulous, as if every piece had been laid by a master's hand, a delicate curved structure diving up and over a deep ravine, where, I saw as I stepped closer, a river was raging, icy and black. I noticed the water didn't flow freely but dammed around the rocks, then rolled over them in lumps like tar. Yet the sound of an ordinary river surged in my ears.

Or was that the wind?

The bridge was long, ending in another grove of trees.

Ashley ran the entire length of this bridge.

She was the first human soul to cross it.

I stepped onto the first laid stones. I had nothing to fear. The curse was finished. *The devil had what he wanted. Ashley.* Yet I found myself whipping around to stare behind me into those skeletal trees to make sure no one was there, that Sam hadn't somehow followed me, believing *I'd* been kidnapped by trolls.

When I was halfway across, I was hit by a rush of vertigo. It was as if the bridge had been rising imperceptibly under my feet, because I could see great distances, high over the branches of an immense forest, stretching out for miles, churning in the wind like a mad sea. A roof with black spikes protruded from the treetops, *so far away.*

A nauseating dizziness suddenly overtook me, and I had to turn away, staring ahead to the bridge's end.

Something was there.

I felt myself go numb. It was only half human. What the *other* half was, I didn't know. It was tall, seven or eight feet, with gaunt arms and a round, wide face so coarse it looked like bark. I could see its eyes, round red eyes, like two fire holes in the dirt, a mouth of thorns.

I had to be hallucinating. Or I was asleep, in a coma. *Dead.*

What in the hell was happening to me? How flimsy sanity was.

I waited for my eyes to tell me it was an illusion, a hoax of the birch trees and the shadows falling in dark piles across the bridge as if they'd been severed from the objects that had created them. I reached for my pocket knife, realizing I was holding Popcorn's compass.

How had it snuck into my hand again? The red needle had stopped spinning and was now pointing straight ahead.

The wind launched into another shrieking fit. I blinked, staring back to the end of the bridge and saw in disbelief that *that thing* wasn't a trick of my eyes. It was still there, yet beginning to slink away, its bony limbs gyrating as if caught in some invisible eddy before vanishing into the trees.

Get off this bridge, a voice screamed in my head. I tore down the incline, slipping on the leaves plastering the stones, stumbling blindly off, barreling down a dirt path, which led me into a circular clearing.

It was deserted.

That strange vision, whatever it was, had to be hiding somewhere. *It was here they performed the rituals, where Cordova became one of them.* I stepped forward, the movement making me so off balance I fell to the ground, staring up at the night sky, a sky so smooth it looked like black liquid had been poured between the trees. *What was happening to me?* My limbs were melting.

I willed myself to sit upright. I wasn't sitting in ordinary dirt, but fine black powder glittering with minerals, a few feet away, a charred log. I reached for it, astounded that even though it looked like the ordinary remnants of a bonfire, it was as heavy as iron and I couldn't lift it.

A ripped piece of white fabric was caught underneath it. *It looked like it'd been torn off a child's blouse.*

I pulled it loose, but a blast of wind whipped it out of my hand, sending it tripping like a stray white leaf across the clearing, vanishing into the trees. I stumbled after it. When I saw where it had escaped to, what had just sucked it down, I could only stare in horror.

It was a trench filled with children's belongings.

I could make out every item lying there, some fifteen feet below: tiny slippers and T-shirts, baby dolls and trains, undershirts and sneakers, all of it decomposed and sodden, some blackened as if burned. It was here where Cordova had thrown it all, the stolen objects, his attempts at an exchange. I could see it so vividly, a clarity that seared my eyes— his mania, his desperation, his willingness to let every corner of his soul go black so that his daughter might live.

I realized in shock that I was lying facedown in the dirt.

How long had I been lying here? Hours? Days?

I lifted my head, which was throbbing, the dark ground and spindly trees swinging drunkenly away from me.

I wasn't alone.

Black robed figures were standing farther off, all around me, silent, hidden by the dark, as if they'd grown off of the shadows themselves. One suddenly streaked between the trees, wearing a hooded black cloak, and then another beside him. And then another.

They were moving toward me. I scrambled to my feet.

"Stay where you are," I said. "Don't come any closer."

Was that me shouting? The voice sounded miles away. I fumbled for my pocket knife. It was gone.

It wasn't normal, how fast they moved, faces missing inside those black hoods, and then I felt hands gripping me as I was pulled backward.

There was the night sky and then a bag over my head, smells of dirt and sweat and my herringbone coat—*no, no, it was my backpack*—wrenching off of me, my arms pulled as if to tear them off. I heard one man's terrible screaming. When the cries didn't stop and I felt myself hoisted into the air, I realized they were my own.

WHEN I OPENED MY EYES I was aware of nothing but a *moth*.

It was small, pale white in the dim light. It appeared to be injured. One of its wings would not fold over its back. Just a few inches from my nose, it was trying to climb a dark wall. It walked up the wood and kept falling off, trying again, falling. Ruffling its wings, it moved straight toward me. It had a furry head and brown legs, antennae working in apparent consternation. Sensing I was alive and large, it shifted directions, away from me and back to the wall.

It was cold. The air was subzero. My hands were numb.

Where the hell was I? I was flying. The draft on my face was the wind pummeling me as I swerved to avoid a cluster of black clouds, atmospheric particles, ice and dust and sharp snowflakes spraying my face. A shrill note was ringing in my ears, a painful sound like a long needle stitching my brain.

I tried to sit up, but my head hit something.

I reached out. It was a smooth wooden wall.

I was *inside* something, a capsule spinning upside down, vibrating with velocity. *But it was only a dream.* I let go of my fear. I stretched out my legs—I was still wearing boots—and they encountered another wall on both sides. This enclosure I was inside, this spaceship, was tight, yet a good foot or two larger than I was.

I opened my eyes, blinking, but there was nothing to see, as if I were suspended high above the Earth, between layers of atmosphere and outer space. The ringing in my ears went silent.

I had nothing to worry about, because eventually I'd wake up. That was what dreams were for, the waking, the floods of relief, shock that the mind could be so easily deceived, tangled sheets, sunlight streaming through a window. But then, *what was the hurry?* If the dream was born of my subconscious fears and desires, why not remain inside here a little while longer, soaring through space, to explore the dream, ransack it, find out its laws and parameters and what I'd been so afraid of.

My arms reached out around me, groping at the sides.

Aha. Same as below and above. The coffin. I am in my coffin.

I opened my eyes. This *wasn't* a dream, I realized with sudden horror.

I couldn't wake. I *was* awake.

The pale white moth—somehow it had made it onto the ceiling and it was crawling in circles, as if it, too, were realizing it was trapped, that there was absolutely nowhere to go.

I began to shout, banging on the walls with my fists, pummeling and kicking.

It sounded as if I were only calling into an empty hole in the earth.

Oh, God, no. This couldn't be right. This couldn't be real.

Suddenly, I understood. I was *meant* to know where I was. *To see.* The fresh air would keep me alive for days, *even weeks,* as I struggled and fought the inevitable, so I could lucidly consider everything I was about to be ripped away from.

My mind froze as I tried to remember where I'd been only moments ago. I had the feeling I'd traveled miles. My arms felt as if they'd rowed across an ocean. Maybe I *was* dreaming, then, because dreams had so many layers, so many slippery departures and ends of ends I couldn't find footing or the slightest edge for my fingers to grasp hold of.

I reached out, feeling the space around me.

Odd. The coffin appeared to have more than four sides. I maneuvered myself around on my back, using the heels of my boots to propel myself in a circle, counting the walls. But I had no endpoint, and when I'd counted *twelve,* I was certain I'd done more than one rotation.

I leaned down to my right foot, untied the laces around the metal hooks of my boot, and wrenched it off. I turned onto my stomach, inched myself close to a wall, feeling for a corner, leaving the shoe there as a marker, and then I slipped along the floor counterclockwise, my hands counting.

One. Two.

I spun on like this, a captive animal inspecting the boundaries of his cage.

Three. Four. Five. Six.

I touched the boot again. *Six sides.*

A hexagon.

Horror gripped me once again. It actually had a face and legs, a massive beast with skin of black rubber, a bony spine, and it was perched right beside me, waiting for me to give up hope so it could feast upon me. I struggled and kicked, banging my head multiple times, screaming for help—*someone, anyone*—though after a while, when there was no answer, when that shrill noise had returned, ricocheting inside my skull like a lazy bullet without the strength to make its way out, I could only lie back down, wheezing, in my six-sided coffin.

I closed my eyes, letting my fear wash over me. I had to bathe in it, accept it, drink it down, let it cover me like sludge, so it became nothing so extraordinary, nothing so fearsome—*and I could think.*

Images wafted through my head. Sam was there, playing hopscotch across a checkered floor. The Peak came into view, dark and colossal, rising up on its overgrown hill, and then I saw myself in an overcoat, running across a bridge, figures like a black fog overtaking me, blotting me out.

They must have dumped me in here, my *oubliette.* Why couldn't I remember? My memories, they'd been hacked into, tinkered with, cut away, because there was nothing in my immediate past—nothing at all.

But if there was a way *in,* there was a way *out.*

I opened my eyes, realizing, in my wild flailing, I must have accidentally brushed the moth off the ceiling. It seemed to have sought refuge in a corner, and once again, fluttering its wings, it was trying to climb the wall.

Taking care not to squash the thing, I managed to put my boot back on, then spun on my back like the rotating minute hand of a clock. Each foot that I moved, I pounded downward on the walls with my feet. On and on I went, the beating noises oddly muffled, so much despair flooding through me it felt as if it were splashing off my elbows and feet.

When I heard the fifth panel crack, I struck it a second time. The wood buckled right in half, splintering, falling through. I looked down at my feet, my heart pounding.

A gray rectangular hole stared back at me.

I immediately twisted around, staring out the opening, my euphoria quickly sliding back into horror.

There was nowhere to go—only *another* wooden panel just two feet away.

It appeared to be another box.

I pulled myself through. There was incrementally more light and more space, though my old coffin took up most of it, sitting in the center. I couldn't sit up in here, either, the ceiling just a few inches higher. I crawled on my stomach along the outside perimeter and when I scrambled past the hole I'd just crawled out of, I knew I was right, I was inside yet another hexagonal box.

What the hell was this? A hell of coffins built like Russian Matryoshka dolls, one inside the next, on and on, toward infinity? Or was it a mind game built from an M. C. Escher print? A scene from a Cordova film—I tried to think back through every scene of every film, but I knew I'd never seen anything like this.

If I broke out of the first, I could break out of the second. Wedging my back against the first hexagon, positioning my feet on the outer walls, I bashed each panel as I had before, making my way around the perimeter.

I did it once, twice, *three* times. Not one wall gave way.

I inspected the first coffin and could make out in the faint light smooth wood, the side panels painted black. The sight suddenly triggered a memory deep in the storm-flooded cellars of my head.

And then it hit me, exactly where I'd seen this before.

The realization was such a shock, I could feel myself falling away from whatever flimsy reality I'd just been grasping, and I dropped backward, spinning through cold, black space.

"There it is," Beckman had said. "The mysterious threshold between reality and make-believe . . . Because every one of us has our box, a dark chamber stowing the thing that lanced our heart. It contains what you do everything for, *strive* for, *wound* everything around you. And if it were opened, would anything be set free? *No.* For the impenetrable prison with the impossible lock is your own head."

Right now, a box like this was sitting on top of Beckman's coffee table in Beckman's living room, beside piles of faded newspapers and a tray of tea. It was the infamously locked box that had belonged to the killer in *Wait for Me Here,* his prized possession containing the thing that had destroyed him as a child, a box that had never been opened. Beckman had caught me trying to pick the lock. And just a few weeks ago when I'd visited him, I'd held it in my hands, shaking it, amused to hear the same old mysterious thumps inside, wondering what in the hell they could be.

They were me. Those rattles were my own bones. *What I'd wanted to see inside, I was now locked in.*

I heard myself gasp out loud at the irony of it. I could feel tears welling in my eyes, sliding off my face. It was too cruel an ending to fathom, a punishment that was pure Cordova. The man was showing me that some mysteries were best left untouched, that the truth of them *was* the unknown. To try and wrestle them open, letting their contents come to light, was only to destroy oneself.

Suddenly filled with such rage, I began to pound every wall around me, over and over again, like a reptile trying to hatch. I shoved my back against the ceiling, heard it crack, and, thrusting my shoulder against it again, felt it give way. I climbed up, emerging onto a floor, blinking in the increased light at a third black hexagon boxing me in. *How long would it go on? How many cages were there?* I pounded every panel until another gave way, and another. I kept on escaping, crawling through walls that broke down, one box giving way to another, clambering forward and backward, up and down, so disoriented at times, I had to sit, letting my legs and arms settle on the ground, feel which direction gravity was coming from, so I'd know which way was up and which was down.

I didn't know how many boxes I'd crawled through—it felt like dozens, the light increasing with each one, inching ever closer—when, pressing against a ceiling, abruptly the floor gave way.

Bright light, and *I was plummeting, plummeting straight down—*

I reached out, grabbed the edge of the box seconds before it flew past, desperately hanging on as the panel I'd just smashed struck the ground.

I looked down, blinking.

Maybe it was just my faltering vision, my eyes unable any longer to register great depths or space, because it appeared as if I were hanging off the top of a skyscraper, the concrete ground about *a mile* below.

Bright light was pouring in from somewhere, through a window out of sight. Craning my neck upward, I could see that I was inside a vast metal tower, dangling like a bit of *snagged thread* out of a hole in the bottom of a large wooden structure, which appeared to be suspended from the ceiling.

There was nothing else here except *a single metal ladder,* which extended from the ground, up the steel wall, disappearing from view over the top of this box.

I had to get up there. I couldn't go around the outside. *The only way to climb out was to climb back in.* I swung myself up onto my elbows, the entire structure swaying dangerously from the movement. The cables or ropes, which were keeping this thing suspended in the air, emitted off-putting *creaks,* as if the whole thing were literally hanging by a thread—as if *I* were hanging by a thread.

I managed to heave myself back inside the box, and then, trying to keep my movements easy so as not to dislodge the entire structure, I crawled back through every hole in every hexagon that I'd made. It felt nauseating to do this, to be breaking *back* inside the boxes from which I'd just liberated myself, my mind protesting as the light around me fell away, as if, with it went my every hope for escape. For life.

I spent the next few hours searching for another way out, pounding the other panels in the other hexagons, trying to find the walls that would take me up to the top—to that ladder.

But no matter how hard I pounded, nothing gave way.

I couldn't help but suspect in my brutish demolition, my fury, I'd inadvertently destroyed the *correct* way out of here, the *only* way, and all I could do now was wait for the inevitable.

Time became a milky liquid I let myself float on, drifting away from this box on its lazy current, back and forth.

Then I realized I was lying on my right side, gazing through the hole I'd made in that very first coffin. A sudden sound of fluttering caught my attention, waking me from a dream.

The moth.

I'd forgotten about it. I was overwhelmed with relief at the simple sight, the understanding that I wasn't alone. It was crawling on the ceiling, but fell off, and then calmly righting itself, took off again for one of the walls. I leaned in, gently brushed it into my hand. Working its antennae, it began walking around, exploring the boundaries of its new cage, which was, of course, the palm of my hand.

So I would die in here. *I'd leave my little life.*

I'd barely worn it out. Life had been a suit I'd only put on for special occasions. Most of the time I kept it in the back of my closet, forgetting it was there. We were meant to die when it was barely stitched anymore, when the elbows and knees were stained with grass and mud, shoulder pads uneven from people hugging you all the time, downpours and blistering sun, the fabric faded, buttons gone.

Sam came into my head.

She came the way she always did, padding over to me with her brown bare feet and her wise face, staring down at me, wrinkling her nose. *What would she think when Cynthia told her I'd disappeared?* I'd become a mystery she'd have to give life to. I'd become a hero, a world explorer who'd gone missing searching for buried treasure on the high seas, more courageous than I'd ever been in real life. Or *no*—I'd be a cavern in her heart she'd brick up and wallpaper over, hang paintings in front of and potted plants, so no one would ever know that dank and hollow passage was even there.

I could hear Beckman, as if he were suddenly here, staring dubiously at the walls enclosing me before downing the vodka in the shot glass in his hand. *Did I not warn you, McGrath, that to capture Cordova was to try and trap shadows in a jar? You wanted the truth. Here it is. It's boxes inside of boxes. What made you so certain you could ever figure him out? That his questions even had answers?*

But what had Beckman shouted, when he'd caught me drunkenly trying to pick the lock on that hexagon box? "Traitor!" "Philistine!" And yet, before he'd slammed the door in my face, he'd said *something else.*

"You couldn't even see where it opened."

It was a hint that I *wasn't* seeing all of it, not the full picture, that I was blind to something, that the way out wasn't the way out.

I had it wrong.

I noticed the moth had managed to fly even with its injured wing. It was crawling again across the ceiling of that first box. I stuck my head inside, watching it move in circles, and then, working its antennae and legs, it paused, then slipped through a hole in the wood, vanishing from sight.

I reached out, running my hands across the ceiling, feeling where the moth had disappeared, an opening the size of a grain of rice. Tracing my fingers along it, I could feel something else, *an indentation.* I fumbled through my own clothing, which felt strangely foreign and detached from me, as if I were riffling through the pockets of *another man,* a man who was passed out or dead. I groped, hoping to find some type of tool to use, yet the only hard object I could find was some type of pendant around my neck.

It was the Saint Benedict necklace Nora had given me. I yanked it from my neck and, wedging the metal into the crack, inched it along the trench. After I'd gone all the way around it, I could see it was some type of circular door. I managed to lift up the wood a few centimeters, enough to wedge my fingers underneath. The door, a circular panel, came loose in my hands, falling away.

I was staring into a black pipe entirely devoid of light, nothing visible at the end. I reached out, running my hands along the smooth metal sides, accidentally grazing that moth.

It fell out onto my cheek.

I rolled over, collecting the insect into my hand, and then, making sure it was all right, tucked it in the inside pocket of my coat, where I hoped it'd remain safe and alive. Then I wedged myself up inside the pipe. It was tight, horrifyingly so, like being trapped in an old air vent. There were no rungs to climb, nothing to grab hold of. All I could do was inch blindly up into the thing by pressing against the sides as hard as I could, bracing myself with the soles of my boots. Within a few yards I encountered a wall.

I pressed against it. It opened easily and I shoved it back, blinking in the bright light.

The metal ladder was directly over my head, bolted to the ceiling.

I pulled myself out onto the top of the wooden hexagon, staring around me. *This box I was standing on was a perfect replica of the box back at Beckman's.* Light was flooding in through narrow windows in the ceiling, though there were no trees visible and no sky, only white light. I couldn't tell if it was artificial light or from the sun.

I took another step. Suddenly there was a jolt and a sharp *snap*.

I reached up, tightening my grip on the ladder's rung just as the entire hexagon box swung out from under my feet, dangling for a moment by a piece of thread before breaking loose. And then the entire box was plunging, a spinning black box tumbling out of the sky. There was a sucking noise and then an explosion as the boxes shattered on the ground below.

I didn't wait, and I didn't look down. I swung from rung to rung, heading toward that wall in front of me where the ladder twisted downward. As I moved, I noticed with amazement that the tiny white moth had managed to escape my coat pocket. It was now crawling down my arm, over the cuff of my sleeve, slipping over my watch.

It was still only 7:58.

Reaching the tower wall, I started my descent, the metal bars slipping eagerly into my hands and under my boots. But then, I began to realize in horror, the ground with its piles of demolished wood, it wasn't getting any closer, no matter how long I went on. I was never going to reach the ground, never feel it hard under my feet, never wake up.

Suddenly I was no longer on a metal ladder.

I was tripping frantically down another black corridor. It looked exactly like the one leading to the crossroads. *Had I been walking it for days and, reaching no end, simply lay down on the ground and fallen asleep?*

Or was I passed out on the living-room couch back in *Thumbscrew?*

Abruptly I reached a wall with a ladder, at the top, another wooden hatch. I climbed up, sliding aside the rails, and opened it.

I was in an abandoned factory surrounded by hulking machinery with rusted blades, piles of stripped logs and rubble. I scrambled out, racing across a floor strewn with wood chips and sawdust, heading for the small door—

What the hell was happening? I was outside, racing through a field of grasses up to my waist, across old railroad tracks. I was sprinting past a derelict caboose on which someone had spray-painted another red bird, when I realized in shock I'd been running the entire time with my eyes closed.

I opened them.

BLINDING SUN CRASHED INTO MY EYES.

"I think he's *dead*."

"Dude. Can you hear me?"

Something sharp poked my shoulder.

"Oh, my God. Don't touch him. He's covered in maggots."

"That's not a maggot. That's a moth."

I opened my mouth to speak, but I couldn't. My throat felt like it'd been burned. Sight slowly came back into my eyes. I was lying on my side in a muddy ditch. Two teenagers, a boy and a girl, were staring down at me. The boy appeared to have been prodding me with a long branch. Behind them, a blue station wagon was parked on the shoulder of the road.

"Want us to call you an ambulance?" the girl asked.

I rolled upright, my head throbbing. I stared down at myself, dimly taking an inventory. I was wearing a heavy overcoat, corduroy slacks, hiking boots, argyle socks, all of which were caked in black mud. My right hand, covered with dirt, was clasping something. My fingers felt dead, as if the bones had been broken, the flesh swollen stiff around them, because they refused to loosen their grip on what they clutched so resolutely, what I realized was a brass compass with a shattered face.

And I was alive.

94 "You were gone for *three* days," Nora said.

I could only stare back at her, unable to speak.

I'd been lost inside The Peak for three days. How was it possible?

And the fact that all three of us were *together* now, alive, unhurt, huddled in an isolated booth in the back of a country restaurant called Dixie's Diner, was also bizarre. The last four hours had transpired in such a haze, I wondered if there was a minute's delay between what was happening in the world and my brain perceiving it.

Struggling to my feet in that ditch, I'd managed to convince the two teenagers *not* to call the police but to give me a ride back to the Evening View Motel in Childwold. They seemed rather *enthusiastic* to oblige, probably due to their suspicion I could very well be the top developing story on the local news, themselves star witnesses. As we drove, they cheerfully informed me they'd been partaking in a cleanup project for their high school, picking up trash along the side of the road, when they'd found me.

"We thought you were dead," said the boy.

"What day is it?" I managed to ask.

"Saturday," the girl answered with a shocked glance at the boy.

Saturday? Jesus Christ. We'd broken into The Peak on a Wednesday night.

They'd found me along Mount Arab Road, close to New York Route 3 and Tupper Lake, which I knew from poring over so many maps of the area was about fourteen driving miles to Lows Lake, some twenty miles from The Peak. *Had I been running through the wilderness and passed out? Or had someone driven me there, left me like a sack of garbage on the side of the road?*

I had no idea. My memories seemed to have been trashed, ripped and crumpled, strewn haphazardly around my head.

When the teenagers asked me what had happened, I managed to put together an excuse about drinking too much the night before during a bachelor party, losing my friends. Yet the longer we drove, my confusion over where I'd just woken up and what in the hell had happened to me quickly slid into paranoia over my *present,* including these two kids who'd randomly found me. There was something about them that was a little too *vivid*—from the peace sign scribbled in blue ink on his arm, her bare feet propped up on the glove compartment, toenails painted yellow, the way he turned the radio way up, playing Dylan's "Tangled Up in Blue." They looked like brightly painted characters from another Cordova film. The suspicion made my heart begin to pound in alarm as I sat in the backseat, watching the marijuana leaf ornament swinging from the rearview mirror.

I didn't fully believe that I *just might* be free of The Peak until we barreled into the Evening View parking lot. I thanked the kids and climbed out, waiting for them to swing back onto the main road, accelerating away, before I walked up to the room, #19.

I did nothing but gaze at the door for a moment, wondering what I was going to find on the other side.

An empty room, untouched since we'd left it? Or was a stranger staying there now, someone who'd claim he'd been there for weeks, no sign of Hopper or Nora? Or would my knock be answered by one of those figures in a black cloak, the nightmare only beginning again?

I knocked. There was a long pause.

And then the door, chained from the inside, opened just a crack— someone peering out. It closed again, the chain slid back, and suddenly Nora was flinging her arms around my neck. Hopper appeared right behind her, silently hastening us inside, taking a suspicious look at the parking lot before closing and locking the door.

The first thing we decided to do was check out of the motel, get into the car, get the hell out of here. Nora was agitated and had, I noticed, terrible scratches down her cheeks. She kept saying, "What happened to you? We thought they *got* you. We *thought*—" But Hopper only snapped that we should get out of here *now* and we could talk when we were away from this place, his terse explanation being that he'd noticed a banged-up maroon Pontiac loitering around the parking lot.

"It has to be *them*," he muttered, zipping up his gray hoodie, grabbing his canteen off the bed. "The windows are tinted black. It looks like it's from the seventies. *And* it's missing a headlight."

As I watched the two of them darting around the room, hastily stuffing clothing and toiletries and snacks into their backpacks, I remembered that I no longer had my own.

Where had I left the bag? Those figures had pulled it off of me.

I stepped dazedly in front of the mirror beside one of the beds and saw I was still wearing Brad Jackson's herringbone coat. Its extreme heaviness was due to not just the dampness and mud but the *pockets*—they were stuffed with *objects*, one of which I noticed, as I pulled it out with a wave of revulsion, I didn't even recall *seeing*, much less *taking* with me.

And then I saw my *face*. I understood the teenagers' shock, even Nora's and Hopper's worried sideways glances.

I looked *crazy*. There was no other word to describe it.

I rinsed the smeared mud off in the bathroom, watching the thick sludge spinning down the drain.

We left the motel quickly, Hopper climbing behind the wheel.

They had the Jeep but not the canoe. I meant to ask them about it but was abruptly so tired I couldn't muster the strength. Hopper drove as if we were being tailed, careening down deserted roads, pines and maples and empty fields spinning past, eyeing the rearview mirror. Nora, in the passenger seat beside him, was subdued, her hands clasped in her lap.

"You see the Pontiac?" she whispered.

He shook his head.

We'd been driving for about three hours when Nora pointed out a white farmhouse perched on the side of the road—*Dixie's Diner, Homemade Food That's Doggone Good!*—the parking lot packed. Only *then* did I feel I just might return to normal. My right arm was showing signs of life, tingling as if filled with needles. My fingers were moving again, though the palm of my hand, where I'd been holding that compass, was swollen. The horror of The Peak seemed to be drying on me, as if it were black water I'd been swimming through and now it was evaporating from my skin, leaving the faintest film.

The three of us filed into the restaurant and Hopper asked the hostess for the booth in the back.

"What happened to your *arms*?" Nora blurted out as we made our way to the back.

I didn't know what she meant. I'd taken off the coat, rolled up my sleeves, and saw now that my arms were covered with a horrific-looking rash. As we slipped into the booth, Nora said, "We've been waiting for you for three days."

"*Christ*," said Hopper. "Let him *eat*."

We ordered food, and I was able to piece together from their disjointed and strung-out commentary that in the three days I'd been missing, apart from a few searches along the roads around The Peak, they'd been too paranoid and worried about me to leave the motel. They hadn't left The Peak together. Nora had been the first to make it back, arriving at the room at five in the morning the same night we'd broken in. It wasn't until after six that evening, Thursday, that Hopper showed up, driving the Jeep.

"I thought I was going to have to go to the police," said Nora. "I didn't know what I'd *say*. 'We broke illegally into this estate and now my accomplices are being held hostage.' I got the number of your police friend, Sharon Falcone. She didn't pick up."

"Can I interest you guys in any dessert?" the waitress asked, suddenly beside our table.

"I'll have a slice of apple pie," I said hoarsely.

"Anyone else?"

Nora and Hopper stared at me in surprise. *I* was surprised *myself.* It was the first time I'd managed to speak with a normal voice.

They ordered pie and coffee, and then, after the waitress brought the food, Nora, who'd been so jittery and talkative as she ate, fell silent, touching the scrapes on her cheek as if to check that they were still there. Hopper looked lost in thought. It was obvious then, the two of them weren't simply upset over *my* three-day disappearance. They'd each had their own strange experiences up there.

I *also* noticed uneasily, glancing around, that Dixie's Diner, so cheery and bustling only *minutes* ago, had unexpectedly cleared out.

It was just the three of us now and, hunched over the counter, an elderly man in a green-and-black checked flannel shirt, who looked as gnarled and spindly as the walking stick propped beside him. It was as if whispers of what we were about to tell one another, about The Peak, were already suffused in the air here, already drifting out of our mouths, darkening the place, and any innocent soul or carefree person couldn't help but subconsciously sense that the time had come to leave.

"Let's start with the canoe," I said.

"WE DON'T KNOW what happened to it," Nora answered. "We think they took it."

"They?"

"Those people living there."

She glanced uncertainly at Hopper. He added nothing to this, only hooked his index finger through the handle of his coffee mug, frowning.

"I told you to wait for me at the pond," I said to her.

"I *meant* to. But when I ran down the hill, I got mixed up, and went too far north. When I backtracked, I was heading toward the canoe, when someone grabbed my shoulder from behind. I screamed, sprayed him with the pepper spray, and then I just *ran*."

"Did you see the man's face?" *That scream I'd heard, it had been Nora.*

She shook her head. "He had a flashlight. *Blinded* me with it. I kept running and running, until I realized there was no one behind me. After an hour I came to this dirt road winding through the woods. I took off down it, hoping it'd lead me off the property and I'd be able to go for help."

Abruptly she fell silent, glancing apprehensively at Hopper again.

"Did it lead you off the property?" I asked.

She shook her head.

"Where did it *lead* you?" I prompted, when she didn't go on.

"To this concrete lot. An old-fashioned truck was parked there. At the center were these gigantic metal *boxes*. Five in a row. At *first* I thought it had to be an electrical plant used for powering the estate. Or maybe they were *traps* for wild animals. They looked cruel. But then I smelled smoke. I got closer and, shining my flashlight on them, I saw each one had a rusty door and a chimney sticking up into the air. Strewn all over the ground was a pale gray powder. I didn't realize until I'd walked through it that it was *ashes*. The boxes were incinerators. And they'd been used recently, because I could still feel heat coming off them."

Incinerators.

The word made me suddenly recall those tunnels originating from the underground alcove, those blackened entryways and the rudimentary words scrawled above the openings in white paint. I couldn't believe it and I didn't know how, but I remembered every one, as if they were the refrain of a nursery rhyme I'd sung as a child, the lyrics lodged in my head forever.

Gatehouse. Mansion. Lake. Stables. Workshop. Lookout. Trophy. Pincoya Negro. Cemetery. Mrs. Peabody's. Laboratory. The Z. Crossroads.

Nora frowned. "I remembered the next-door neighbor in the trailer that you'd interviewed, Nelson Garcia, how he told you the Cordovas set fire to all their garbage. I went up to one and unlatched the door. There was nothing but black walls, piles and piles of ashes. The smell was awful. Synthetic, but *sweet.* I opened the other doors, raked a tree branch through the ashes to see if there was anything left. There was nothing, not one hair. I started combing the ground, trying to find some piece of evidence of what they were going to so much trouble to destroy. It wasn't until I inspected the truck that I found something."

"What?"

"A glass vial used for drawing blood at a doctor's office. It was wedged along the side in the rear bed. It looked empty, but there was a tiny pink label on the side with a *biohazard* symbol. They must use the truck to transport medical waste or toxic garbage from somewhere at The Peak to burn in those ovens. The vial must have accidentally fallen out."

She took a breath. "It made me wonder if the whole area was contaminated. I began to feel sick, so I ran." She stared at the table in front of her. "I had the feeling someone was following me, but every time I looked around, there was no one. When I reached the fence, I didn't even think about it, I went right over it. I didn't care if I died or got electrocuted or cut up. I climbed right through the razor wire, didn't feel a *thing.* I just wanted to *get out,* and nothing would stop me."

"How'd you get back to the motel?"

"I reached this paved road—this was about four in the morning—and a red station wagon pulled up, a tiny old lady behind the wheel. She offered me a ride. I was petrified. I thought for sure she was one of the townspeople. She even *looked* like a witch, with a green blouse and all these rings on her fingers. But I was so tired and she looked so fragile, I got in. She drove me straight back to the motel and said, 'Take care of yourself, girl.' And that was it. Nothing happened. I staggered into the room and slept for thirteen hours."

I stared at her. I could feel the outskirts of another headache coming on, but I tried to focus, to think. *A glass vial used for drawing blood? Medical waste?* Why would Cordova have such things—for use in another film?

Her mention of Nelson Garcia made me remember the other incident he'd told me about, the UPS delivery of medical equipment intended for The Peak, but accidentally arriving at his own trailer. Nothing we'd learned over the course of the investigation, no one we'd interviewed had mentioned a detail that validated this story or Garcia's suspicion, that there was someone injured or ill up at The Peak—except perhaps now, Nora and these incinerators she'd just described.

Hopper had been listening to her with annoyed detachment, occasionally glaring at her over some specific detail she mentioned—the word *incinerators,* the glass vial labeled *biohazard.*

"What about you?" I asked him. "What happened?"

"Hopper got inside the mansion," blurted Nora excitedly. "He found Ashley's *room*—"

"I don't know it was her room for sure," Hopper countered.

"But—of course you do." Clearly surprised by his sudden reticence, she turned to me, leaning in. "He found *letters* that he'd written Ashley, ones she'd never answered. They were kept safe, in order, right beside her bed. It looked like she'd read through them a million times. And there were pictures of them together on top of her desk. Then he found her practice room—"

"I *don't know* it was her practice room—"

"But you found a piece on the piano she'd written, called *Tiger Foot.*"

"*Tiger Foot?*" I asked, puzzled.

"Hopper's tribe name from Six Silver Lakes."

Hopper looked livid. "I don't know *what* I found up there, okay. I don't know."

"How did you get inside the house?" I asked him.

"Climbed up onto the roof. Found a window unlatched."

"What was it like inside? Abandoned?"

"No. It was . . . *nice.*" He brushed his hair out of his eyes and seemed unwilling to elaborate, but, as I was waiting expectantly, he sighed. "It was a castle. Gigantic. Gloomy as fuck. Mahogany walls. Tapestries with unicorns. Snarling bear heads. Paintings depicting floods and mayhem and people in pain. Wooden chairs, big as thrones. Knights' swords hanging on the wall, and an iron chandelier with burned white candles covered in wax. *Not* that I had much time to *browse*. Someone let the dogs back in. I found a back staircase, headed to the basement, ducked inside the first room I found that was unlocked. I hid in there for hours."

"It was filled with *thousands* of *filing cabinets*," added Nora.

"Filing cabinets?" I asked. "Containing what?"

"Actors' head shots. *Millions* of pictures and résumés with weird notes written on the back." She waited for Hopper to explain it to me, but, again, he looked infuriated by her candor.

"What kind of notes?" I pressed when neither of them spoke.

"Personal details," said Hopper.

"Such as?"

"Background. Phobias. Secrets."

"They had to be actors Cordova had considered for roles," said Nora. "It reminded me of the audition Olivia Endicott described. Remember how he asked her those weird personal questions?" She glanced at Hopper. "What was the one you told me about? That woman named Shell Baker?"

"Her picture looked like it dated back to the seventies," he said. "Someone had written on the back of it, 'No family except a brother in the Navy, hates cats, diabetic, doesn't like to be alone, sexually inexperienced.' Another was, like, 'Raised in Texas, car accident as a five-year-old child, left her in a back brace for a year, painfully shy.' "

"Did you take anything with you?" I asked.

He seemed irritated by the question. "Why?"

"For evidence?"

"*No.* I put it back and got the hell out of there."

"Then Hopper found a *torture* chamber," Nora blurted.

"It *wasn't* a torture chamber," he countered angrily. He looked at me. "Another room in the basement just had a bunch of wooden stretchers and planks, metal bridles, antiques—I didn't know what half the shit was. I slipped out, snuck upstairs to the third floor. I found what I think was Ashley's room, was looking around when I accidentally knocked over a lamp. Someone must have heard me, because I could hear someone coming up the stairs. I darted into a closet while this person, it sounded like a woman, wandered around. She righted the lamp and then she *left*. Only she locked me *in*. I couldn't unlock the door from the *inside*. I was going to unscrew the doorknob, but then I heard one of the dogs outside the door. He had to have known I was in there. But he didn't bark. There were giant bay windows in the room, overlooking the hill and Graves Pond, but when I climbed out, there was a sheer drop. I stayed in the room all night, silent, waiting for the dog to leave. About five in the morning someone whistled and it ran downstairs. I unscrewed the doorknob, managed to get out of the house without encountering anyone. I made a beeline for the canoe, but naturally it was gone. So I just followed the same stream that we'd come in on. I got lost, though. I wandered deep into a swamp, ended up in mud chest-high. I came upon a group of campers who looked at me like they thought I was the Loch Ness Monster. They told me I was in a section called the Hitchins Pond Primitive Area, which is all the way east of Lows Lake. It was about six at night when I made it back to the Jeep."

"Any sign of one of the Cordovas living at the house?" I asked.

"No. The top floor was where the family had their bedrooms. No one slept there all night. I think the other people with the dogs were caretakers. Not that I saw any of them up close."

"You didn't enter any other room in the basement?"

"No. They were all locked."

"What about upstairs? Anything unusual?"

He nodded, his face somber. "I found a closed-off wing toward the back of the house. Up a flight of spiral stairs into this tower was a bedroom suite. Half of it was brand-new. Brand-new beams of wood on the floors. You could see where the old met the new. I wondered if it'd been remodeled after a fire. And maybe that had been the Spider's room. There was nothing there, though. Not a photograph, not a *clerical collar*. Nothing."

"What about this Pontiac you saw in the Evening View parking lot?"

"I think it's one of the caretakers. I had to leave Ashley's doorknob unbolted, so they know someone entered her room."

"Any sign she'd been there in the days before her death?"

"Yeah," he admitted quietly. "I don't know how, but . . ." A smile flickered across his face, went out. "She was still in the air."

Expressly avoiding eye contact, he took a sip of coffee.

"Now it's your turn," Nora whispered eagerly, leaning in.

96 | *What had happened to me? Did I even know?*

I told them everything I remembered, beginning with the dogs chasing me all the way to my return to the Evening View Motel. I didn't consciously choose to tell them in such detail—Nora looked stricken, Hopper slightly infuriated, which made me wonder if it was wise to be so uncensored—but each word I uttered seemed to wrench loose the next, until all the confusion and horror came tumbling out in a landslide.

When I'd finished, they said nothing for a moment, speechless. And I was relieved. I don't think in all of my days of reporting, I'd ever so much needed to tell someone exactly what had happened, as if to do so was to finally walk out of there, pull myself out of those tunnels and shadows, once and for all.

"What do you mean you found something you didn't remember taking in Brad's coat pockets?" Nora whispered.

Before answering, I looked around to make sure our waitress was still back inside the kitchen. We were the only ones left in the restaurant. Even the elderly man who'd been seated at the counter was now shuffling out the door, leaning heavily on his cane, his every step an effort.

Brad Jackson's mud-soaked coat sat folded on the seat beside me.

I pulled it over and, object by object, emptied the pockets, placing each item on the table in front of us. *Popcorn's compass. The child's blood-soaked shirt.* They looked odd here in the neon lights, out of place, souvenirs from a nightmare.

"*These* I remember taking," I said. "But not *this.*"

I fumbled in the pocket and pulled out the final object lying at the bottom. It was a three-jointed set of bones, weathered and dirty, about five inches long.

"What *is* that?" asked Nora.

"It looks to me like a portion of a child's foot. But I don't know."

"Where did it come from?"

"I'm guessing I came across it somewhere and took it, thinking it could be evidence. But I really don't remember."

Nora's alarmed gaze left the bones on the table and moved to me. "You don't remember if those people *did* anything to you, or . . ."

"No."

"What about how you got into that hexagon?"

I shook my head.

"It's obvious you were drugged," said Hopper.

Nora anxiously bit her lip. "Now what do we do?"

"We'll have some of this analyzed," I said. "Find out if it's human blood on the shirt or human bones. If it is, we need to find out whom they belong to. Was the Spider correct in his suspicions? Is there a mother out there, waiting for news of her missing child? I can't prove what I saw up there was real, but I *can* prove Cordova believed in the curse. How far did he go in his work and in his hope to save Ashley? The man blurred fiction and fact. His art and his life were the same."

"That's not what we decided," Hopper muttered. "We made a deal before we broke into The Peak *all three* of us would decide what to do with the information. Not just *you.*"

"But we don't know what we have yet."

"What do you want to *gain* from all of this?" He stared at me accusingly. "Your name in *friggin' lights?* The glory of stripping the great Cordova naked so you can parade him on a leash in front of the world for everyone to look at? So you can gloat that this is really what he is? And he wasn't *so great?* You think that's what Ash would've wanted?"

"I don't know what she wanted."

"This isn't your lottery ticket. This is her *life*. I'm not going to let you turn it into some cheap tabloid story—"

"No one's suggesting that—"

"We *know* what she went through," he went on angrily. "We know the kind of madhouse she grew up in, what sort of family she had. How she lived her life. We know why she climbed to the top of that elevator shaft by herself in the middle of the night and *jumped*. It was to put an *end* to it. *We know.* You even saw that ditch filled with the shoes and gloves. So, when is it enough? How much more *truth* do you need to *suck down* until you're *fucking full?*" He furiously shoved back his plate, fork clattering to the floor, and stalked out of the restaurant, the door slamming behind him.

"He saw something up there," whispered Nora. "Don't know what. He'll probably never tell anyone."

It had started to rain, and Hopper, zipping up his jacket, gazing at the ground, ducked away from the window, out of sight.

"Whatever he was looking for," she said, "whatever he wanted from her, he found it."

97 THE DRIVE BACK to the city was tense and mostly silent. I stopped at River Rentals Inc. in Pine Lake to pay in full for the missing Souris River canoe, explaining to the kid with dreadlocks behind the counter that it'd been destroyed.

"*Seriously?* What happened, man?"

I could only hand him a credit card. *He definitely didn't want to know.*

We pulled onto the highway, and immediately Nora fell sound asleep in the seat beside me. I thought Hopper had, too, but every time I glanced in the rearview mirror, he was only staring out the window, his face unreadable, his thoughts probably somewhere back at The Peak.

Nora was absolutely right. Hopper had admitted he'd spent the night in Ashley's room, and I couldn't help but suspect something he'd seen there or encountered had changed his view of what had happened between them. It had somehow set him free. And he'd let it fly, that gorgeous blackbird of a love he'd been keeping in a cage. What was it like for him, every day standing outside in the wind and rain to stare at the ocean, yearning for some sign of her, never giving up hope? At The Peak perhaps she'd finally come into view, a ship coming neither toward him nor away, only riding that perfect line between heaven and earth, long enough for him to know that she had loved him, that what they had was real, before slipping out of sight, probably forever.

I certainly understood his anger toward me *and* his desire to protect Ashley. I'd even anticipated it, that the deeper we got into the investigation, the more disturbing the truth about her family, Hopper and I would inevitably clash over what to do with the information. But for me to let it rest *here, not* to go all the way, was not an option.

Hours later, at dusk, we were back in Manhattan, driving down its battered blocks of pedestrians and potholes. Hopper asked me to drop him off at his apartment on Ludlow, the only words he'd said during the entire ride.

He climbed out of the Jeep, pulling his backpack over his shoulder.

"I'll see you guys," he said curtly and slammed the door.

"Wait," said Nora.

She hastily scrambled out and threw her arms around his neck, hugging him right on the sidewalk. He chucked her affectionately on the chin and moved up the steps to his building. When she climbed back in, I was surprised to see that she was crying.

"Bernstein. Hey. What's the matter?"

"You don't get it." She wiped her eyes. "We're never going to see him again."

"What? Don't be silly."

She shook her head in disagreement, watching him disappear inside.

I was surprised by the pronouncement, to say the least, certain it couldn't be true. It couldn't end like this, not here, when so much was still unanswered, but then I remembered his apartment, the bare walls and the bag from South Dakota, the lyrics from "Ramble On." Had he found all the answers he needed and he was finished with us—simple as that?

I didn't know *what* to say, because abruptly Nora was heartbroken. She silently wept all the way out of the Lower East Side, down Houston Street, and well into the West Village. I tried comforting her, but ultimately was too drained to do more than concentrate on the simple task of getting the rental Jeep back to Hertz.

A hot Saturday night in the Village was detonating around us. As we walked back to Perry Street, negotiating the dense crowds and honking cars, Nora didn't say a word. When I let us back into the apartment, she ignored my question about whether or not she wanted any dinner, fleeing upstairs to Sam's room.

I headed to my office. It looked solemn, untouched. Gazing at the windows, the night, I actually wished Septimus was there on the windowsill to greet me. I could've used the company; he might be a *parakeet,* but he was *reasonable.* But we'd taken him to a kennel to be looked after. There was nothing and no one here.

I tried calling Cynthia—I had the overwhelming desire to hear Sam's low voice, to hear that she was all right—but she didn't pick up. I left a message. I went upstairs and took a shower, locked everything I'd taken out of The Peak in my safe, and climbed into bed. I'd stuck Brad Jackson's coat on a hanger, hanging it on the back of my closet door. It looked oddly limp there, oddly lifeless. *Had I gone far enough up there? Seen enough at The Peak to get to the bottom of it?*

98

I WOKE UP GASPING and lurched upright, expecting to hit my head on the ceiling of yet another hexagon, only to realize I really was at home. Nora was perched on the edge of my bed.

"Christ. You scared me."

"I'm sorry," she said.

"Everything all right?" I sat up, propping myself up on the pillows. I was relieved to see she was no longer crying. "Are you upset about what happened? I'm sure you're wrong about Hopper."

"No. *Yes.* It's just . . ."

"What?"

"When we were tracking Ashley before, she was *alive.* Now I can feel she's gone. And when Hopper said goodbye it reminded me of Terra Hermosa. There, the endings hit you hard because they're *sudden.* Like, one day Amelia who loves flowers is there in the dining hall with her oxygen tank ordering the fruit plate, and the next? She's *nowhere.* All they leave out is this memorial and what it *is* depends on what hallway you lived on. Like, if you lived on the *first* floor they put up an easel with a laminated picture of you smiling and knitting with your glasses around your neck. But if you lived on the *fourth* floor, they put this guestbook out to sign with flowers and a poem about loss printed off the Internet. And *that's* it. After two weeks they take it down, the poster and the guestbook, and it's like you were never there. I *hate* it so much."

"*I* hate it so much."

"It's not fair."

"It's not. But then, that's the game. It makes life great. The fact that it ends when we don't want it to. The ending gives it meaning. But now that you *mention* it, will you promise to off me when I'm ninety and never leave home without an oxygen tank? Make a day of it. Just roll me and my wheelchair off the George Washington Bridge and call it a life. Deal?"

The request seemed to make her smile. "Deal."

"They should really tack that on to the marriage ceremony. 'Do you promise to love, honor, obey me, and also to kill me when I can no longer stand in a shower?' "

"I really love you, Scott."

She blurted the words. They took me so off guard, I wasn't certain I'd heard her correctly, but then she slid forward in the dark, kissed me on the mouth, then sat back, studying me intently, as if she'd just added a key ingredient to a new science experiment.

"What'd you do that for?"

"I told you. I love you. And not as a friend or a boss, but real love. I've known it for twenty-four hours."

"Sounds like a stomach bug that will pass."

"I'm serious." She scrambled on top of me, sitting Indian-style on my shins, and before I could stop her, the girl leaned in and planted another kiss on me, her hands clasping the sides of my head. I was almost too tired to do anything about it, but managed to grab her shoulders and pull her away.

"You need to go back to bed."

"You don't think I'm pretty?"

"You're gorgeous."

She was inches from my face, really *squinting,* as if it were a section of a globe she'd never closely inspected before, an ocean filled with strings of unnamed islands.

"So what's the matter?"

"To my knowledge, Woodward and Bernstein never took it this far. I'd prefer we didn't, either."

"You're making a *joke?*"

"You have your life in front of you. You're *young,* and I'm . . . an old bicycle." I had no idea where *that* unfortunate metaphor came from— maybe I was half asleep—but I suddenly had a very unpleasant vision of myself as a rusty junkyard ten-speed, no front wheel, stuffing bulging out of the torn seat.

"You're not. You're *amazing.*"

"*You're* amazing."

"Well, two people who feel that way should be together right now this second and not think." She scrambled eagerly right alongside me, as if we were together in a compact camping tent. She felt bony and light, and as she rolled over me, her hair and a smell of soap fell around my head, a waterfall I was drenched inside.

"Nora. Please. Go to *bed.*" I shoved her back, a little more forcefully this time. "I love you, too," I went on. "You *know* I do—but, *not like* that."

I was aware of how shoddily stitched together the words were—suddenly I was a kid in the hall standing outside my locker about to head to *Math.* But that was how it went sometimes, the English language, when you really needed it, crumbled to clay in your mouth. That's when all the real things were said.

"Why are you treating me like I don't know my own feelings?"

"Experience. I'm forty-three. Maybe even forty-four."

"In olden days people only lived to thirty, so I'd be *ancient.*"

"And I'd be dead."

"Why do you have to joke? Why can't you just *be?*"

I didn't answer, only held out my hand, waiting for her to take it.

"You know I'll always be on the sidelines," I said, "cheering you on. You're a powerful woman. And you're going to *go on* being powerful, for miles. For *years.* I'd only slow you down."

"Maybe I *want* to be slow. Why do people have to keep moving away from each other all the time?" She was on the verge of tears again. She wrenched her hand away. "Hopper's right. You're not attached to anyone. You love only yourself."

She waited for me to disagree, but I didn't. Maybe it was the effect of the last three days. I was spent, had no more will to exert on my own life. I could only keep watching it now, in all its gory glory, as it twisted and bucked in front of me.

"You're going to ruin everything. Like Hopper said. You don't care about me. *Or* Ashley. She means nothing to you. Even *now.* All you care about is the hunt."

She struggled off the bed, white comet shooting through the room.

"Nora," I called out.

But she was gone.

99

My alarm went off at seven. By seven-thirty, I was out the door.

I took the 1 train up the West Side to Barney Greengrass—the famed hundred-year-old Jewish deli—arriving when it opened, and then, bags of bagels and fresh lox in hand, I rode the M train to its very last stop, Metropolitan Avenue in Middle Village, Queens. If I was going to pay an unannounced visit to Sharon Falcone on a Sunday morning, I could only come bearing gifts, and Sharon had a weak spot for poppy-seed bagels, Nova Scotia salmon, and a Yiddish delicacy called schmaltz herring, a cured whitefish that to me tasted like leather encrusted in salt. To Sharon, it was heaven.

She lived in a mug shot of a house: redbrick, sobered, bleary-eyed, square. More than a decade ago, I'd once dropped her off at home when we were working late on the same case—her father had just died, leaving her the house—and I'd quietly made note of her address, in the off chance I ever needed to find her.

There was no answer when I rang the bell, so I sat down on the leaf-strewn steps to wait, wondering if she'd already headed into the city to the station or if she'd moved. But then I noticed the empty dog's water dish and the bald tennis ball in the yard under the single bush, and within fifteen minutes I spotted Sharon speed-walking down the side-walk. She was wearing her maroon North Face jacket and carrying two large deli coffees. In true Falcone fashion, she wasn't surprised to see me.

"If you're selling Bibles, I got twelve already," she said, skipping past me up the stairs.

"I'm peddling another powerful religion. Barney Greengrass."

Thankfully, her gaze couldn't help but dart curiously down to the plastic bag in my hands. But she said nothing and then, nimbly balancing one coffee cup atop the other, opened the screen, unlocked her door, and, fast as a burrowing mole, darted inside. She was furious I'd shown up, that was clear, but she also didn't slam the door and bolt it.

"Some girl left me a voicemail the other day, claiming you were in mortal danger." She was shrugging off her jacket, hanging it on a hook.

"That'd be my assistant, Nora. She can be *dramatic*—"

"I don't know *why* she thought that'd be anything other than *wonderful* news."

"I'm sorry," I said through the screen, Sharon quickly disappearing down a hallway. "I'm sorry I'm here. But I need your advice, and if I didn't think that you would absolutely care, I wouldn't bother you. Just hear me out. Then *throw* me out. And as far as we're concerned, we never met."

This must have had its satisfying prospects, because not a minute later, she was escorting me into her dining room, or perhaps her living room. *Whatever* it was, it was empty, apart from a yellow carpet, a wobbly folding table, two chairs, and a pillow bed in the corner covered in dog hair.

I unzipped my pockets and pulled out two plastic bags, one containing the child's blood-soaked shirt, the other the bones. Obviously I didn't volunteer where I'd stumbled upon them, though based on Sharon's silently fuming face, she had her suspicions. But the moment she saw the shirt on the table, her demeanor changed. And I knew then that I wasn't off-base or crazy, because if that shirt could take *Sharon Falcone* by surprise, even if it *was* simply a prop, it was a realistic one. Without taking her eyes off it, she set aside her two coffees—it was clear now both were hers—examining the shirt through the plastic. She zeroed in on it like a microscope, squarely considering it, going very still.

"Is it blood?" I asked.

"Hard to say. If it *is,* it's an old stain. Ten years at least. Must have been kept somewhere dry or the cotton fibers would have degraded. Or there's an inorganic blend in the shirt. It *acts* like blood, though, because of the stiffness. Another substance wouldn't cause such rigidity."

"What about the bones?"

She removed them from the plastic bag, testing the weight in her hands.

"No idea. I'd have to have an anthropologist take a look."

"Could it be part of a child's foot?"

"The human foot is long and narrow, weight largely borne on the heel. A nonhuman foot is broader, weight borne on the toes. But it gets more confusing the younger the bones, as they're not fully developed. Infant ribs can look like a small creature's even at a macrostructural level. Cranial bones of children often resemble turtle shells."

Saying nothing more, she set aside the bag and, grabbing one of her coffees, took a sip, watching me closely.

"Some heads are rolling, by the way, over that suicide you're so interested in."

She meant Ashley. "Whose head?"

"You remember a lawyer was lobbying against an autopsy, the Jewish faith against desecration of the body and so on. The ME can overrule it. And he was planning to. Only her body disappeared in the middle of the night. It's also why those pictures were missing. Someone was paid off."

"Pictures?" I repeated, not following her.

"I told you. Some body shots were missing from her file. They never appeared on record. There's a departmental witch hunt going on, trying to get to the bottom of the whole thing. It's a mess. And I'm sure they'll come up empty-handed. Those types of tracks tend to dissolve before they're even laid. The girl's family's got power."

I remembered, then, Sharon mentioning the missing pictures in the file, Ashley's front and back torso.

"Our phone call the other day," I said, after a moment, "about the child services case. It wasn't the best connection—"

"There was no certificate of occupancy for the building. No sign of anyone living there."

"Any idea who owns the building?"

"It was registered to an LLC. Something Chinese. I have it in my notes. I'll call you with it. *And* I will *quietly* look into this"—she picked up the plastic bags off the table, shooting me a penetrating look—"even though I *should* have you booked for being a royal pain in my ass. It'll take a month to process, at *least*. Lab's backed up. Don't ever show up here again. You look like crap, by the way."

She slipped out of the room with the bags.

"Thank you," I called after her.

"You need to get that right hand checked out," she shouted from the depths of her house. "You got something lodged in there, and it's about to turn into staph."

I had no idea what she was talking about, until I stared down at my hand. She was absolutely right. The swelling and redness had gotten worse. What I'd *thought* to be encrusted dirt in the palm appeared to be a splinter embedded deep in the skin under my thumb. Seeing it gave me a sudden stab of paranoia. *Had those people in black cloaks marked me? Put another curse on me? Was it a dart steeped in poison? A rusted, tetanus-yielding nail?*

I had to get home. "How can I repay you?" I called out after a minute, when I realized Sharon, preoccupied with something else now, wasn't ever returning to the living room. "Can I get you another German shepherd, a yacht, an island in the South Pacific?"

"You can get out of my house," she called from somewhere.

100 BACK IN MANHATTAN, I stopped at the emergency care clinic on Thirteenth Street. The waiting room was crowded and it took nearly three hours for a doctor to see me. I explained I'd just come back from a camping trip.

"I can see that," he stated cheerfully, pulling the curtain closed. He was a chipper, quick-talking young man with overcaffeinated energy and Scotch tape accidentally stuck to the back of his white coat. "You have *contact dermatitis*. You did a fair amount of hiking through heavy foliage? Looks like you came into contact with something you're allergic to."

I was about to clarify that I'd been in the Adirondacks—when I realized, stupidly, that that was hardly the case. What about the swimming pool? An animal might have been decomposing in that water for months. *And the Reinhart family greenhouse?*

"What type of plants in the greenhouse?" the doctor asked after I sketchily explained some of this.

"One was called Mad Seeds. I can't remember the others."

"Mad Seeds," the doctor repeated, tilting his head. *And that didn't make you want to run screaming out of there?* he seemed to be thinking.

"I've also gotten stuck with something, a bad splinter."

I showed him. Within minutes, a nurse was cleaning my hand with water and a topical antiseptic and the doctor, wielding a scalpel and a long pair of tweezers, was slicing into the palm, whitened pus oozing out as he took hold of something embedded inside and pulled it out.

When I saw what it was, I was too stricken to speak, though the doctor chucked it on the stainless-steel table beside us.

"Looks like you had quite a camping trip," he said, smiling. "Maybe next time try the beach."

It was a black thorn off some type of plant, though my first thought was that it was a sharp twisted fingernail, crooked and two inches long.

101 | BY THE TIME I made it back to Perry Street, it was after four. I was looking forward to seeing Nora, filling her in about Sharon, showing her the blackened spike I'd just had extracted from my hand. And we could get back to work. But the moment I entered my apartment, I heard an odd banging upstairs.

Racing into Sam's room, it looked as if Moe Gulazar's closet—maybe Moe himself—had exploded all over the carpet. Sequined gold leggings, a mink stole (suffering from mange), silk blouses, and striped neckties were draped everywhere. Nora, in a pair of black jodhpurs and a tuxedo shirt, sleeves rolled up, was packing up the clothes. I noticed Jesus and Judy Garland were no longer taped to the wall.

"What's going on?" I asked.

She glanced at me over her shoulder and then turned away, folding a pair of purple hot pants and shoving them into one of the Duane Reade bags.

"I'm moving out."

"What?"

"I'm moving *out*. I found an amazing sublet."

"When?"

"Just now. I'm finished with the case."

"Okay. *First* of all, you don't find amazing sublets *just now* in New York City. It takes months. Years, sometimes."

"Not for me."

"And where did this amazing sublet come from? Angel Gabriel?"

"Craigslist."

"Okay. Let me explain something. People who use Craigslist tend to be hookers, homicidal maniacs, and massage therapists who give happy endings."

"I already checked it out."

"When?"

"This morning. It's a huge room in the side of a townhouse in the East Village with a bay window. *Tons* of light. All I have to pay is five hundred a month and share a bathroom with this really cool old hippie."

I took a deep breath. "Let me tell you about cool old hippies in the East Village. They're nuts. They study tarot cards and eat soy. Sometimes they *eat* tarot cards and study soy. Most haven't left this island since Nixon was president and have identifiable plant life growing under their toenails. Trust me on this one."

"We just had lunch. She's super-nice."

"*Super-nice?*"

She nodded. "She grows organic tomatoes."

"Fertilized with the carcasses of her thirty cats."

"She was a photographer's assistant for Avedon for years."

"That's what they all say."

"She had an affair with Axl Rose. He wrote a song about her."

"It was probably 'Welcome to the Jungle.' "

"I don't know *why* you're freaking out. It'll be *cool*."

It'll be cool. I felt as if a rug were being yanked out from under me when I'd been standing on hardwood floors in bare feet.

"This is because of last night," I said.

She only raised her chin, grabbing her Harmony High School yearbook, frowning dramatically as she paged through it.

"You're angry because I was a gentleman? *Respected* the boundaries of our working relationship?"

She snapped the book closed, sticking it inside the bag. "*No.*"

"No?"

"*No,* it's because of *Hamlette* auditions at the Flea Theater."

"*Hamlette* auditions at the Flea Theater."

She nodded triumphantly. "They're reversing the genders of all the roles, so there are finally good parts for females. I'm going to try for Ham*lette,* so I have to practice my monologues night and day. It'd drive you crazy because you hate my acting."

"That's not true. I've grown quite fond of your acting."

She was folding an old gray cardigan with a sequin flying bird pin on the shoulder and a massive gaping hole in the left elbow that resembled a silently screaming mouth.

"*You yourself* said last night that I have to go hurling forward into space and you'll be my cheerleader on the sidelines. So that's what I'm *doing*."

"Why would you take my advice?"

"I *said* it was temporary. That it was until we found out about Ashley. And we *did*. And I have money now."

I'd paid Nora before we'd gone to The Peak, including a very sizable bonus that I was now sort of regretting.

"Plus, you're going to be busy publicizing everything and making money off of Ashley for your own benefit, just like Hopper said."

I let that remark sail past me like a grenade blowing up inches from my face. She wouldn't stop zipping around the room like some insect with ten thousand eyes, folding, tucking, packing it all away.

"The investigation is not over," I said. "You're quitting in the end zone, fourth quarter, five seconds left, three downs."

She glared at me. "You still don't *get* it."

"What don't I *get*? I'd be fascinated to find out."

"You don't see that if Cordova had ever done something that'd hurt anyone, Ashley wouldn't have allowed it. I trust her. And so does Hopper. You obviously don't trust anyone. Here's your coat back." She'd brutally yanked Cynthia's black coat off a closet hanger and chucked it over the bed. It sagged onto the floor. I'd given it to her weeks ago, so she'd have something without feathers to wear to Olivia Endicott's. She'd loved it, announcing with unabashed joy that it made her feel like *a French person,* whatever that meant.

"I gave it to you," I said.

She put on the coat, stepped in front of Sam's Big Bird mirror, and took a very long time fixing a bright green scarf around her neck. She then grabbed a black fedora off the bedpost, setting it delicately atop her head like a lost queen crowning herself. I followed her downstairs in a sort of daze. She set down her bags, heading into my office. She'd picked up Septimus from the kennel. She crouched beside his cage.

"When Grandma Eli gave me Septimus, she gave me the directions that went with him," she said. "You have to give him away to someone who needs him. That's part of his magic. You're supposed to know the right time to give him away, and it's when it hurts the most. I want you to have him."

"I don't want a bird."

"But you *need* a bird."

She unlatched the door, and the blue parakeet fluttered into her palm. She whispered something into his invisible ear, returned him to his swing, and then she was moving again, slipping past me down the hall. She didn't stop until we were outside on my stoop.

"I'll go with you. Interview the hippie. Make sure this person wasn't part of the Symbionese Liberation Army—"

"No. I'm handling it."

"So that's *it*? I'll never see you again?"

She wrinkled her nose as if I'd said something idiotic. *"Course* you're going to see me again." She reached up onto her tiptoes and hugged me. The girl gave the most premium of hugs—skinny arms clamped around your neck like zip ties, bony knees bumping yours. It was like she was trying to get an indelible impression of you to take away with her forever.

She grabbed her bags and took off down the steps.

I waited until she rounded the corner, then took off after her. I knew she'd kill me if she saw me, but thankfully the sidewalks were mobbed with shoppers, so I was able to stay out of sight, tailing her all the way into the subway, where she hopped on a 1 train, transferred to the L and then the 6, finally exiting at Astor Place.

Emerging from the packed station, I lost sight of her. I looked everywhere, even began to panic, worried *that* was *it*, I'd never know what happened to her, if she was safe—Bernstein, the precious gold coin slipping out of my fumbling hands, disappearing into New York's millions.

But then I spotted her. She'd crossed Saint Marks Place, was walking with her usual corkscrew gait past the pizza parlor, the racks of magazines. I followed her down East Ninth, coming to a small triangular garden where the street intersected Tenth. She skipped up the steps of a shabby brownstone. I held back, slipping into a doorway.

Nora set down her bags and rang the bell.

As I'd tailed her, I'd mapped the various rescue scenarios—barging in the front door, kicking aside the nine cats, the raccoon, four decades' worth of *Village Voices*, racing past the stoners making out on the couch and the psychedelic poster for the *Human Be-In*, all the way upstairs to Nora's room: rat-friendly, stench of old sponge. Nora, perched on the edge of a futon, would spring to her feet, throwing her arms around my neck.

Woodward? I made a huge mistake.

And yet. Though the building was certainly dodgy—rusty air conditioners, window boxes with dead plants—I noticed on the first and second floors there were not one but *two* bay windows, and they *did* appear to get *tons of light.*

But no one had answered the door. Nora rang the buzzer a second time.

Let no one be home. Let the super-nice hippie have had a family emergency back in Woodstock. Or if someone answered, let it be a half-naked singer-songwriter with a tattoo on his chest that read WELCOME TO THE RAINBOW. *Let me just rescue her one more time.*

The door opened, and a plump woman with frizzy gray hair appeared, wearing a striped apron streaked with dirt from a flower bed or clay from a potter's wheel. She *was* unquestionably into tarot cards and soy, though I might have been wrong about everything else. Nora said something, and the woman smiled, taking a Duane Reade bag as they disappeared inside, the door closing.

I waited for something—music turning on, a light. But there was nothing, nothing for me, not anymore, only a soft breeze coursing down the block, pushing the stray yellow leaves and the bits of trash caught along the curb.

I walked home.

102 I'D DECIDED it'd be wise to take a few days to recover from The Peak and clear my head before organizing my thoughts, wrapping up the investigation. I had that persistent sense again of having swum through leagues of blackened water, my insides still leaden, my mind streaked with mud.

Yet real life was calling. I had unpaid bills, voicemails, month-old emails I hadn't bothered to open, quite a few from friends who'd writ-

ten *I'm worried* and *You OK* and *WTF???* in the subject lines. I wrote
them all back—I'd bought a replacement HP laptop a week before we
left for The Peak—but to do even this simple task seemed pointless
and irritating.

I began to realize, with a sort of morbid fascination, that I hadn't
actually *left* The Peak—not entirely. Because the moment I was in bed,
lights off, I needed only to close my eyes and I was back there. That
property, maybe it was an unrequited time I'd always be returning to
now, the way others returned in their dreams to golden childhood
dances or battlefields, weekends at a lake house with some girl in a red
bikini. Half awake, half dreaming, I plunged back inside that estate,
wandering its dark gardens and statues hacked to pieces, past the dogs,
the blinding flashlights manned by shadows. I backtracked through the
tunnels, no longer searching for evidence to incriminate Cordova, but
some crucial part of myself I'd accidentally lost up there—like an arm,
or my soul.

And that *fear* I'd felt, the disembodying confusion, seemed to be a
drug I was now addicted to, because moving through the ordinary
world—watching CNN, reading the *Times,* walking to Sant Ambroeus
to have a coffee at the bar—made me feel exhausted, even depressed.
Perhaps I was suffering from the same problem as the man who'd
sailed around the world and now on land, facing his farmhouse, his
wife and kids, understood that the constancy of *home* stretching out
before him like a dry flat field was infinitely more terrifying than any
violent squall with thirty-foot swells.

Why did I assume that I'd be fine, be able to process The Peak as if
it were a trip to Egypt or the time in Mitú I'd been held for eleven days
in a jail cell—a harrowing experience to digest and get over? Not *this*
thing. No, The Peak and the truth about what the man had done were
still sitting in my stomach very much *alive,* pulsing and drooling and
intact, making me increasingly sick, maybe even killing me.

This restlessness was made all the more worse by the fact that I was
alone. Everyone was gone. Nora was right. Hopper was as finished as
she was. I called him twice, heard nothing. I didn't understand it—that
they could both be done with the case and me, simple as that, that they
could so ignorantly conclude that it all ended here. Didn't they want to
know if those were real human bones I'd found up there, that there

were no other children hurt in Cordova's mad attempts to save Ashley's life? Weren't they curious about the obvious remaining question—where was Cordova now?

I drew all sorts of scathing conclusions—that they'd finally shown me their true colors; they were young and shallow; it was a larger indicator of the problems of today's youth; raised by the Internet, they flitted from one fixation to the next with all the gravity of a mouse-click—but the truth was, I missed them. And I was furious I cared.

It made me remember Cleo's pronouncement all those weeks ago when she'd found the killing curse on the soles of our shoes.

It pulls apart the closest friends, isolates you, pits you against the world so you're driven to the margins, the periphery of life. It'll drive you mad, which in some ways is worse than death.

I hadn't taken it seriously. Now I couldn't help but note how accurate it was turning out to be, the isolation and fractured friendships, the sense of being pushed to the outer margins of life.

Unless that was just *Cordova.* Maybe he was a virus: contagious, destructive, mutating constantly so you never quite *grasped* what you were dealing with, silently sewing himself into your DNA. Those with even the barest exposure contracted a fascination and a fear that replicated to the point that it overtook your entire life.

There was no cure. You could only learn to live with it.

After three days of wandering my apartment, avoiding the box of the remaining Cordova research, taking antibiotics and steroids for my hand and rash, I realized that to try and relax was making me so uncomfortable, I had little choice but to let it remain murky.

At eleven o'clock on Wednesday night I hailed a taxi and told the driver to take me to 83 Henry. Falcone, unsurprisingly, was right. When I stepped across the street, staring at the shabby walk-up nestled by Manhattan Bridge, it appeared that every tenant, for whatever reason, had vacated. Now every window was dark, though I could make out the ruffled pink gauzy curtains on the fifth floor. I tried the front entrance. It was locked, of course; yet, staring through the small window, I noticed that the names had been removed from all the mailboxes.

I took off toward Market Street, and within two blocks, passed Hao Hair Salon, where I'd taped up Ashley's flier in the window all those weeks ago. I was surprised to see that it was still there, only faded by the sun.

Ashley was little more than a ghostly face, the words HAVE YOU SEEN THIS GIRL? barely legible. Seeing it gave me a nagging feeling that time was running out—or maybe it was simply moving on.

Hopper and Nora were gone, and now, so was Ashley.

| PARKING | CORDOVA | FILMS | FREAK | RED BAND | STRANGERS | CLIMB IN |

SEARCH RESULTS FOR "LEIGH" "LA DOULEUR"   *Result 1 of 643 results*

THE NATURAL HUNTSMAN

AMERICAN HUNTING NEWS   *Vol. 102   No. 1223   MAY 2007*

FAMED FEMALE HUNTER GOES MISSING IN NEPAL

RACHEL DEMPSEY, 41, REPORTED MISSING

DOLPA, Nepal – An American hunter went missing in the Dhorpatan Hunting Reserve in western Nepal last month. Authorities are seeking information on her whereabouts.

Rachel Dempsey, 41, of Woonsocket, R.I., flew to Nepal on March 30 for a 10-day blue sheep and wild boar hunting expedition. She was last seen by a Sherpa in her trekking party, when she abruptly left the campground in the early hours of April 2. Dempsey's camping gear and radio set were recovered miles away, but there was no sign of Dempsey.

On April 11, Dempsey's satellite phone was turned on in Santiago, Chile, and a 15-second phone call was made to the port city of Puerto Montt. No subsequent activity has been recorded.

Dempsey was a skilled tracker, known for her expertise in stalking the most elusive of targets across difficult high-altitude terrain. In 2005 she was a finalist for the Carlo Caldesi Award for her Kashmir Markhor trophy taken in Pakistan, with a CSI score of 113.

Dempsey came to her hunting career late in life, having enjoyed a previous life as a successful film actress. She appeared on the

DEMPSEY WITH A MARCO POLO TROPHY ON A 2005 TRIP TO TAJIKISTAN

police drama *Reasonable Doubts* and played Leigh in the cult thriller *La Douleur*.

Dempsey is 5 feet 9 inches tall with chin-length light brown hair and a dime-sized birthmark on the back of her left shoulder. She was last seen wearing a white Gore-Tex jacket, gray windbreaker pants,

a fur hat, and carrying binoculars, a skinning knife, and a .300 Winchester Short Magnum rifle.

Anyone with additional information should contact the Woonsocket Police Department or SAFARI BONGO DENMARK EXPEDITIONS at: mads@safaribongoexpeditions.dk.

POSTED BY KAY GLASS XIV   12/12/2007 1:02 P.M.

NEXT >>

| PARKING | CORDOVA | FILMS | FREAK | RED BAND | STRANGERS | CLIMB IN |

SEARCH RESULTS FOR "POPCORN"　　　*Result 5,233 of 14,392 results*

POSTED BY Sustained Arguments　　　　5/15/1996 2:26 A.M.

Popcorn in *Wait for Me Here* was played by a Cuban man named
Fernando Ponti. I traveled from my home in Cologne, Germany,
to Crowthorpe Falls in early 1996 hoping for a Cordova
sighting. After six days there with no luck, I came across
this man wandering through town. It was Popcorn. I followed
him. When he noticed me, he ducked inside this Trophy Washing
Machines store toward the end of Main Street. When I entered
after him, seconds later—it was a store where you can buy
washing machines, but also rent formalwear—there was no sign
of him. I assumed Popcorn had slipped out the back door. But
when I looked, it opened out into a long alleyway. There was
no sign of him anywhere and nowhere to hide in the store.　It
was like he had evaporated into thin air.

NEXT >>

103

I'D TRIED CYNTHIA COUNTLESS TIMES, hoping for an up-date on Sam, but I'd still heard nothing. As much as her stonewalling drove me crazy, I did sense it meant that Sam was okay; if anything was seriously wrong, she'd phone me. At least, this was what I told myself.

As Sharon Falcone had explained, it was going to take at least a month until I knew if those were human bones I'd found up at The Peak, so in the meantime, there were a few critical leads to follow up on.

I logged on to the Blackboards, checking out rumors about the real-world fates of Rachel Dempsey and Fernando Ponti, the actors who'd played Leigh and Popcorn in the Cordova films. Cross-checking the Blackboards, I was surprised to learn that *The Natural Huntsman*—some kind of macho pro-NRA hunting newsletter—was accurate re-garding Rachel Dempsey.

Dempsey, who played Leigh in *La Douleur* when she was only twenty, was never seen or heard from again after vanishing in Nepal on April 2, 2007. There were two articles about the disappearance in her hometown newspaper, though there were no further developments and no record of any husband or children she'd left behind. I did find on the Internet existence of a Marion Dempsey living in Woonsocket—Rachel's mother or sister, I hoped. I called the public directory, found the number, and after it rang interminably, an exasperated woman who curtly identified herself as "Mrs. Dempsey's nurse" picked up. When I asked if her employer had a daughter named Rachel, I was told, "Mrs. Dempsey doesn't trouble with that anymore"—which I took as a *yes*—and the woman hung up.

Fernando Ponti, on the other hand—the charismatic elderly Cuban man who'd played Popcorn—had been spotted by three different indi-viduals on three different occasions around Crowthorpe Falls between October 1994 (a year after *Wait for Me Here* was released) and August 1999. When I'd been inside the greenhouse, I'd had the distinct feeling that Popcorn was somehow *still there,* tending his plants and fish, and these three sightings seemed to suggest that I was right.

Had the man never left? Had he loved his time at The Peak so much—or been so brainwashed—that he'd chosen to stay on as Pop-corn, preferring his character to real life? Was he dead now, eternally buried in his fictitious gardens? I couldn't find any records of Ponti's family or where he'd come from beyond *Cuba*—which was mentioned only by the Blackboards. However, I was even more startled by the posting that detailed his disappearance inside Trophy Washing Machines, a store on the outskirts of Crowthorpe Falls.

I'd come across the word *Trophy* back at The Peak. It'd been scrawled above one of the entrances to the underground tunnels.

Had *that* particular corridor led to *Trophy Washing Machines,* clandestinely linking Crowthorpe Falls to the estate? It was too specific a word to be a coincidence. And it explained how Popcorn could have evaporated into thin air. He'd disappeared through a hidden hatch inside the store and headed home along this passage.

I checked up on quite a few more actors on the Blackboards, those with the largest parts who'd probably resided at The Peak during shooting. I uncovered only one *true* constant: After working with Cordova, they all entered new phases of their lives, which tended to scatter them to the outer reaches of the globe.

In not one case did the person remain the same, take up where they'd left off, go back to where they began.

Rachel Dempsey, who'd played Leigh, had become an international hunter, which, oddly enough, made perfect sense; after playing the gullible and vulnerable Leigh, gagged and hog-tied in that buried bus, upon leaving The Peak, she appeared to have transformed herself from *prey* to *predator.* The rumor about Lulu Swallow, the woman who played Emily Jackson in *Thumbscrew,* was that she ended up living in a remote part of Nova Scotia and penning a series of dark-themed children's books—the Lucy Straye orphan series—using the pen name E. Q. Nightingale. The debonair man who played Axel in *La Douleur*—Diane's mysterious husband, with whom Leigh falls in love as she shadows him—ended up going to veterinary school and becoming a prominent Thoroughbred horse doctor; it was he who euthanized Eight Belles at the 2008 Kentucky Derby. The actor who played Brad Jackson—originally from England—supposedly moved to Thailand, where he was spotted by a Cordovite in 2002 in the red-light district *Soi Cowboy* with a teenage girl on the back of his motorbike.

These people had scattered into the wind like ashes tossed in the air, all around the globe—one traveling as far as Tristan da Cunha in the South Atlantic. I couldn't tell if they were fleeing something by disappearing into new lives. Had they uncovered the truth about Cordova, seen the man up close, and that horror was what made them run? Or was it the opposite—had they been set free? Had they *slaughtered the lamb,* as they called it on the Blackboards—no longer restrained by anything; after working with Cordova, were they able to design the wildest life they could fathom for themselves and set about fiercely living it?

From my vantage point, it was impossible to know if it was freedom or fear that drove them—or perhaps it was neither of these things and they'd been unleashed by Cordova onto the world, his devoted disciples, sent out to do his bidding, his work, which was God knew what.

Whatever their motivations, I wondered if they felt anything similar to what I was feeling—the exhaustion, the nightmares, the sense of dislocation—as if somehow I'd swollen beyond ordinary life and could no longer fit back down into it.

I was looking into this, searching the Blackboards not so facetiously for "aftereffects of Cordova" and "known symptoms," when I was abruptly ejected from the site.

No matter how many times I unplugged my laptop, restarted the settings, got a new IP address, tried a new user name—it resulted in the same exit page. Had I been banned, shut out—or *found out?*

http://tunnelstaircase8903–5493r89jidfj9w0129e61)??)*#(((sovereigndeadlyperfect.blackboards.onion/interlope

| PARKING | CORDOVA | FILMS | FREAK | RED BAND | STRANGERS | CLIMB IN |

WHOEVER YOU ARE,
YOU SHOULDN'T BE HERE.
GET OUT.

ENTER >

I turned my attention to looking into those plants that I'd hacked through inside the Reinhart greenhouse. The emergency room doctor's last words had been that I'd encountered a potent irritant and it'd be helpful to know what it was, in case the rash didn't improve. It *was* improving, had practically vanished within twenty-four hours of my taking the steroid medication. Yet one search for *Mad Seeds* was enough to set off alarm bells.

Mad Seeds was one of many nicknames for *Datura stramonium,* or jimsonweed, a plant so poisonous one cup of the tea could kill a grown man. According to Wikipedia, side effects of either sucking the juice or eating the seeds produced "an inability to differentiate reality from fantasy, delirium and hallucinations, bizarre and possibly violent behavior, severe *mydriasis*"—dilation of the pupils—"resulting in painful *photophobia*"—intolerance to light—"that can last several days." It gave men a sense of their upcoming deaths, turned ordinary people to "natural fools."

It was possible that, under the heat of those oppressive lights, sweating like a goddamn pig, I'd gotten drenched with the pollen and had unwittingly ingested it.

I looked up every other name that I remembered: *Tongue Tacks, Death Cherries, Blue Rocket, Eye-Prickles.* I couldn't find tongue tacks or eye-prickles anywhere, but blue rocket was *aconitum*—one of the deadliest plants on Earth. It could be "absorbed through the skin, resulting in convulsions, and within an hour, a prolonged and excruciating death similar to strychnine poisoning." Death Cherries was *belladonna,* also lethal and known for its fantastic hallucinatory properties, many of which came from one's hopes and mental wishes, turning them to wild reality.

I hadn't realized it, but when I'd unwittingly wandered into that Reinhart greenhouse, it was akin to stepping inside a nuclear waste plant with a *slight leak* in one of the reactors or swimming blindly into a reef of great white sharks. It was a wonder that I wasn't *dead,* hadn't passed out somewhere on the property, fallen down a gorge—even jumped off the devil's bridge, imagining I could fly. Beyond the obvious horror of my safety—it now called into question everything I'd seen and experienced up there. I could no longer trust a single recollection after I'd entered that greenhouse.

Had I *actually seen* that stick man or been trapped inside those hexagons? Had I seen that deep ditch in the ground, or had my own overpowering hope to find tangible evidence up there conjured it right before my eyes? Those people in black cloaks who'd swarmed me— one of them waiting inside that church confessional—had they been real? Or a drug-induced incarnation of my fear?

Now I couldn't prove it either way. *I might as well have smoked a goddamn crack pipe.* It was an infuriating development, to say the least.

Disgusted, vaguely enraged at myself for not being more careful, I decided to turn my attention instead to something concrete, something *categorically real*—researching missing persons in the Adirondacks.

Within a few hours, using the database from the National Center for Missing & Exploited Children, I'd compiled a list of individuals who'd gone missing within a three-hundred-mile radius of The Peak between 1976—the year Cordova had moved into the estate—and the present day.

There was a markedly higher incidence of missing persons *after* 1992, the year of Ashley traversing the bridge and the devil's curse.

There was also a young boy who went missing in Rome, New York (114 miles from The Peak), on May 19, 1978, the year that *Thumbscrew* had been shot at the estate. The four children reported killed in *Thumbscrew* were between the ages of six and nine. It was a flimsy lead, but if Falcone got back to me with confirmation that it *was* human blood, Brian Burton was a worthwhile place to start. He was six years old when his mother, a waitress at Yoder Motel and Restaurant, parked illegally on the curb and popped inside the restaurant to pick up a check, leaving her son alone in the backseat. She'd locked the car but left the back windows cracked. When she returned less than ten minutes later, the car was unlocked and her son was gone. He was never seen again.

S. McGrath

Missing Persons
within a 300 mile radius of The Peak and Crowthorpe Falls, NY

1976 - Present

NAME	AGE	STATUS	LAST SEEN
Kate Gonzalez	28	Endangered Runaway	8/8/1977
Brian Burton	6	Non-family Abduction	5/19/1978
Madonna Clyde	15	Endangered Runaway	12/3/1981
Lacey Robertson	17	Endangered Runaway	10/1/1990
Kevin Tsui	9	Family Abduction	11/21/1997
Vincent Giovanelli	24	Missing	9/30/2000
Laura Belle Helmsley	15	Runaway	3/13/2001
Valerie Lorraine-Luca	3	Abduction	6/3/2004
Sophie Hecta	8	Endangered Missing	3/13/2005
Vanessa Mills	52	Missing	7/16/2005
Kurt Sullivan	9	Endangered Missing	9/13/2009
Jessica Ann Carr	5	Non-family Abduction	8/13/2011

Post "Devil's Curse"

Around the time that
Thumbscrew was shot at The Peak!

Ashley Cordova Timeline

Born: 12/30/1986
Devil's Bridge Incident: Sometime in 1992

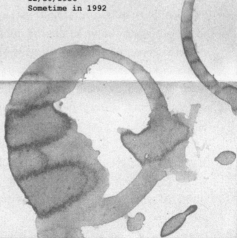

The other incidents were similarly haunting—so many last-seens and symbolic details: Sophie Hecta's locket necklace, Jessica Carr's crayon drawing of a black fish discovered in her bed when she was found missing by her parents. Unfortunately (and *unsurprisingly,* given that Cordova would probably know how to obscure his tracks), no detail I read overtly linked any of these cases to the director—no parallels to his films, no sighting of a mysterious man wearing black lenses that stamped out his eyes.

Nothing—but then, one tenuous clue.

Laura Helmsley's locker had been ransacked a week before she ran away from home, and she'd reported her journal stolen to the school office. This detail was vaguely reminiscent of the incidents John, the anonymous caller, had described. Had Cordova stolen the girl's journal, hoping she might serve as an equal exchange for Ashley? Police believed Laura had simply run off with her older boyfriend. They'd been caught on camera at a White Castle drive-thru two days after she disappeared.

But there'd been no word from her in more than ten years.

Before I'd read about the hallucinogenic plants, I might have believed in an *alternate* possibility, that the world had simply opened up and swallowed these people whole. It actually seemed the only logical explanation in the case of Kurt Sullivan, who disappeared across thirty yards of an easy hiking trail in the Moose River Plains Wild Forest (ninety-four miles from The Peak). He left his family, skipping around the bend back to the campsite to put on longer socks—and was never seen again. A six-hundred-man search, which included help from the U.S. Air Force, elicited not one clue as to what had happened to the boy.

Shadows with wills of their own, killing curses and devil's curses, rivers that ran black and beasts with bark for skin, a world with invisible fissures that anyone could accidentally fall down into at any time—I could have actually considered it after what had happened to me at The Peak. Hadn't this investigation of Cordova been hinting at the outskirts of such a reality—a world that was infinitely mysterious, shrouded with the questions that were impossible to explain? Cordova might very well be a madman, have fatally erased all boundaries between fantasy and reality in his life and work, but hadn't he been legitimately able to harness some kind of power up there, whatever it was? Hadn't that been true? Hadn't I witnessed it with my own eyes?

Now I didn't know what I believed. It was logical I'd simply been exposed to too many *Mad Seeds*. And anyway, what was Cordova—or Popcorn—doing, keeping that greenhouse thriving with enough toxic plants to wipe out an army?

The more missing-persons cases I read, the more those mysteries seemed to fray into a million threads. Still, I jotted down the various details, vague developments mentioned by local newspapers and missing-person blogs. Then, my mind overloaded, I tore myself away from the computer—deciding to head uptown to Klavierhaus.

If Ashley had frequented the shop as a child, as Hopper had told us, I wanted to talk to someone who knew her from those early days. The manager we'd spoken to, Peter Schmid, might be helpful finding such a person.

When I arrived, however, I was shocked to learn something *odd* had happened—or else, it wasn't odd *at all,* given what I'd been researching the past three days.

Peter Schmid was gone.

104

"WHAT DO YOU MEAN?" I asked.

"He quit," said the young man behind the Klavierhaus counter.

"When?"

"Two weeks ago."

"Where did he go?"

"No clue. It was pretty sudden. Mr. Reisinger, our owner, was *pissed* 'cuz we're short-staffed now. I'm just an intern. But Peter had been having some problems, so."

"Do you have his phone number?"

The kid looked it up and I dialed it, heading out of the shop—the Fazioli piano that Ashley had played still in the window.

I stopped on the sidewalk in disbelief. A recording announced that the number had been disconnected.

I didn't know what it meant—only that something was wrong.

I hailed a cab, and minutes later was striding into the lobby of The Campanile—Marlowe Hughes's building. I recognized the chubby-faced doorman as the second one who'd been on duty the day I'd approached Harold.

"I'm looking for Harold," I said, stepping toward him.

"He doesn't work here anymore. Got a brand-new gig on Fifth. Some swank white-glove building—"

"*Which one? I need the address.*"

"He didn't say."

"I need to go upstairs to see Marlowe." I handed him my business card. "I'm a friend of Olivia Endicott's."

"*Marlowe?*"

"Marlowe Hughes. Apartment 1102."

He looked uncomfortable. "Yeah, Miss Hughes isn't exactly . . . *home.*"

"Where is she?"

"I can't discuss the particulars."

Alarm flooding through me, I handed the man a hundred bucks, which he cheerfully pocketed.

"They packed her off to rehab," he said quietly. "She had an incident. But she's all right."

"Could you still let me into her apartment?"

He shook his head. "Sorry, *no.* No one's been up there since—"

"I know Olivia's out of the country, but call her assistant. She'll authorize it."

He looked doubtful, but waited patiently while I found the number.

"Yeah, hi," he said into the phone after I dialed for him. "This is The Campanile. I got a gentleman here." He squinted down at my business card. "*Scott McGrath.*" He went on to explain the situation, falling silent.

And then, abruptly, his face—so amiable before—sobered. He glanced at me, visibly startled, then hung up without a word. He stood up, coming around the side of the desk, his arm out to escort me toward the door.

"You're gonna have to be on your way, mister."

"Just tell me what she said."

"If you harass any of the people here again, I'm gonna call the cops. You don't have any connection to Olivia Endicott."

Outside, I turned back—speechless—but he was standing staunchly in the door, glaring at me.

I headed swiftly down the sidewalk. When I reached the corner, I dialed Olivia's assistant's number myself. She picked up immediately.

"This is Scott McGrath. What the hell just happened?"

"I beg your pardon, sir? I don't know what you're talking—"

"Cut the bullshit. What'd you tell the doorman?"

She said nothing, seemingly deciding whether or not to feign ignorance. Then, in a cold, clipped voice:

"Mrs. du Pont would prefer it if you did not contact her or any member of her family."

"Mrs. du Pont and I are working together."

"Not anymore. She wants no further connection to your activities."

I hung up, seething, and phoned The Campanile's management company to get Harold's home phone number.

It was disconnected.

105 I RETURNED TO PERRY STREET and systematically tried contacting every witness we'd encountered during the investigation.

Iona, the *bachelor party entertainer* who'd tipped us off to Ashley heading to Oubliette—I called the number on her business card and was informed by the automated recording that her voicemail box was *full*.

This didn't change, not even after four days.

I dialed Morgan Devold. I no longer had the page torn out of the phone book—that had been stolen when my office was broken into—but found it after calling directory assistance for Livingston Manor, New York.

There was only a busy signal. I tried the number every hour for the next *six hours*. It remained busy.

After learning from the assistant director of housekeeping at the Waldorf Towers that Guadalupe Sanchez was no longer an employee at the hotel, I decided to track down the strawberry-haired young nurse who'd run out in front of our car at Briarwood. I remembered her name had been Genevieve Wilson; Morgan Devold had mentioned it.

"Genevieve Wilson was a student nurse in our central administration for three months," a man in the nursing department explained.

"Can I speak to her?"

"Her last day was November third."

That was more than three weeks ago.

"Is there a number where I can reach her? A home address?"

"That's not available."

Was this somehow *my* doing? *Had I lost my mind?* The primary symptom of madness was near-constant amazement at the world and a suspicion of all people from strangers to family and friends. I had both symptoms in spades. *Why wouldn't I?* Every witness, every stranger and bystander who'd encountered Ashley, was extinct now. They'd silently receded like a fog I hadn't noticed was lifting until it was gone. It was what had actually happened to my anonymous caller, John, years ago.

Or did I have it all wrong? Had these people run for their lives, going missing, absconding to the outer reaches of the world—like Rachel Dempsey and the countless other actors who'd worked and lived with Cordova—because they were fleeing something? Were they afraid of him, Cordova, because they'd talked to me about his daughter? With my notes stolen, there was no record of what they'd told me about Ashley. Their testimony now existed solely in my head—and Hopper's and Nora's.

But even they were gone now.

Then, it existed solely in *my head.*

Filled with sudden worry that Nora and Hopper might have vanished in the same way as the others, I called both of them, leaving messages to call me back. I then phoned Cynthia, suddenly wanting to hear Sam's voice, irrationally worried she, too, was gone. It went to voicemail. I left a terse message, threw on my coat, and left the apartment.

106 | IN THE FADING DAYLIGHT, Morgan Devold's driveway looked so different from the night the three of us drove up here, I hardly recognized it. I pulled over to the shoulder, cut the engine, and climbed out.

Immediately I was hit by a smell: *smoke.*

I started up the drive. Some overgrown branches had been split backward and broken in half—*as if a large truck had driven up here.* The charred smell grew stronger, and when I crested the top I stopped, staring out at the lawn in front of me.

Morgan Devold's ramshackle house had burned to the ground.

I headed toward it, light-headed with shock. Both cars were gone. All that remained was a charred air conditioner and half a splintered swing.

My guess was the fire had happened a week ago, maybe longer, and it wasn't an accident. I climbed through it, looking for evidence, but the only identifiable objects I found were a blackened ceramic bathtub, the burnt base of a La-Z-Boy, and a plastic doll's arm reaching out from the rubble. Seeing it made me wonder if it belonged to Baby, the doll Morgan had fished out of the kiddie pool. Immediately, I made my way across the overgrown grass toward the far corner of the yard.

I spotted it exactly where it'd been before, still partially inflated yet turned upside down. I flung it upright and saw, apart from the encrusted leaves, a sizable black splotch stained the bottom.

It had to be where Ashley had hidden the doll, so her spell inside the leviathan figurine would work. It was oddly overwhelming to see—as if that black mark was the last confirmation that what we'd learned about her life and death had been real.

Who had torched the house? Had Morgan and his family been inside when it happened or long gone, like every other witness Ashley had met?

I spent a half-hour roaming the debris trying to find answers, at once disbelieving and angered by the finality of it. It felt as if this scorched devastation *wasn't simply* Devold's house, but the entire investigation. Because all of it was gone, wasted, and me, the last man, too late, trawling through it, digging for an underlying truth now gone.

Starting back to my car, I spotted lying in the tall grass, something small and white.

It was a cigarette butt.

There were four. I picked up one and saw the strange, minute brand printed by the filter. I hastily collected all four butts and then, my head spinning, sprinted down the driveway.

Murad.

107 | BECKMAN, DRESSED IN BLACK CORDUROYS and a blue plaid flannel shirt, was speaking in front of a packed lecture hall. There were at least three hundred students, every one hanging on his every word.

"The film keeps the tension *skin tight* deep into the final minutes," Beckman was saying, "when Mills learns the contents sealed inside the FedEx-delivered box—his wife's *severed head*. The film ends on a cliffhanger and we're left to wonder what the poor detective's fate is. He was once so brash, so confident. Now he's come face-to-face with the horrors that he was chasing. He has the chance to turn into horror himself. Will Mills be *savaged* or *saved*? We have to evaluate the story's moral universe, everything that's come before, to know the answer. Does he make it out alive?"

Rather dramatically, Beckman turned on his heel, raising the remote—like a sorcerer pointing a magic wand—and a film clip appeared on the gigantic screen behind him. It was the final minutes of *Se7en*, which featured Morgan Freeman and Brad Pitt as Somerset and Mills, and Kevin Spacey as John Doe in the back of the police car.

I knocked a second time on the window, and this time Beckman heard me, jolted in evident surprise, glanced back at his students, and scurried over.

"McGrath, what the *hell*," he hissed, opening the door a crack.

"I need to talk to you."

"Can't you see I'm in the middle of something?"

"This is an emergency."

His dark eyes blinked at me behind his glasses. He glanced over his shoulder. His students remained transfixed watching the clip, so he quickly darted out into the hall, silently closing the door behind him.

"What in *Christ's*—you *know* I don't like to be interrupted while I'm teaching. There's a little *something* called *creative flow*—"

"I need the names of your cats."

"Excuse me?"

"Your *cats,* your *fucking cats*. What are their names?"

A female student walking past turned, eyeing me warily.

"My fucking *cats*?" Beckman repeated, glaring at me. "This is why I've never liked you, McGrath. Not only are you rude and demanding, but *cats* you've been introduced to fifteen, *sixteen* times you don't have any recollection of, as if they're somehow beneath you." He opened his mouth, on the verge of berating me further, but must have noticed I was frantic, because he pushed his glasses farther onto the bridge of his nose.

"Their *full birth* names or their nicknames?"

"Full birth names. Start with the one you told me about the other day. Something about Murad Turkish cigarettes."

Beckman cleared his throat. "Murad Cigarettes. Boris the Burglar's Son. One-Eyed Pontiac. The Peeping Tom Shot. The Know Not What. Steak Tartare." He kneaded his eyebrows. "How many's that?"

"Six." I was writing them down.

"Evil King. Phil Lumen. And last but not least, The Shadow. There you have it. *Enjoy.*" With a matador's *olé,* he started for the door.

"These are *what,* Cordova's trademarks?"

He sighed. "McGrath, I've *explained* it to you countless times—"

"How do they work, exactly? Where do they appear?"

He closed his eyes. "In every story Cordova constructs, rain or shine, at least one or two, sometimes up to *five* of these trademarks—signatures, if you will—show up *unannounced,* like long lost family members on Christmas Eve. Naturally they cause a great deal of drama." He squinted at me, observing my scribbling. "What's this *about,* anyway?"

I reached into my pocket, holding out the cigarette butts. Beckman, frowning, picked up one, scrutinizing it, and then, probably reading the brand printed by the filter, stared at me in alarm.

"Where in *God's name* did you find—"

"In the country. At the scene of a house fire."

"But they don't *exist* except in a Cordova film."

"I'm in one."

"Excuse me?"

"I think I'm *inside* a Cordova film. One of his narratives. And it's not over."

"What are you *talking*—?"

"He set me up. *Cordova.* Maybe Ashley, too. I don't know *why* or *how.* All I know is that I tried to uncover the circumstances around Ashley's death and every person I spoke to, everyone who met her, has disappeared. The man had a penchant for working with reality—manipulating his actors, pushing them to the brink. Now he's done it with me."

Beckman's mouth was open, his eyes wide with disbelief. He appeared to have entered some kind of unresponsive fugue state.

"Just tell me about the cigarettes," I said.

He took a breath. "McGrath, this is really not good."

"Can you be a little more *specific*?"

"Didn't I *tell* you to leave him alo—?"

"The cigarettes!"

He tried to collect himself. "If you're the first character who appears in the scene *after* the Murad cigarettes have been smoked, it means you're marked, McGrath. You're fated. You're doomed."

"But there's *some way out*—"

"No." He arched an eyebrow. "There *is* a very slim chance if you manage to make a huge and improbable leap of faith you *will* survive, but it's like jumping from the top of one skyscraper to the next. It almost always ends with you splat on the sidewalk, either dead or caught forever in a sticky hell, struggling in your cocoon like Leigh at the end of *La Douleur*."

I jotted it down. "What about Boris the Burglar's Son?"

"Cordova's longtime stuntman. His full name is Boris Dragomirov. He's a diminutive but brawny Russian. His father was a notorious gangster known back in the motherland simply as The Black *Eye*. The man managed to successfully escape every gulag they ever locked him in and he taught his only son, *Boris*, all of his techniques. Cordova used Boris in every film. He did all the dirty work, the cons, the beat-ups, the breaking and entering, the car wrecks, the cliff dives. His largest role was playing the blackmailer in *A Crack in the Window*, the one who appears on the other side of that confessional screen, scaring the bejesus out of Jinley. He runs as fast as a supercharged Maserati and can escape *anything* at *any time*."

It took only a second for me to know where I'd encountered him.

"I chased him," I said. "I spoke to him."

"You *spoke* to Boris the Burglar's Son?"

Quickly I explained how he'd broken into my apartment, hightailed it across the West Side Highway out onto the pier, posing as a cruising gay man and then vanishing in the blink of an eye.

"McGrath, how could you miss it? He used the Horny Geezer on you, one of his most legendary cons."

"What about One-Eyed Pontiac?"

Beckman thoughtfully interlaced his fingers. "There's always a dark-colored Pontiac, black, blue, or deep maroon, with a single headlight. Whatever object or person it illuminates in its single glaring light will be annihilated."

I remembered it immediately: Hopper had claimed to see such a car in the parking lot of the Evening View, when they'd been waiting for me to return from The Peak. I hastily made a note of it, Beckman eyeing my scribbles.

"You saw the One-Eyed Pontiac?" he gasped. *"Don't* tell me you were in its *headli—"*

"I wasn't. Someone else saw it. The Peeping Tom Shot?"

He blinked in flustered exasperation. "It's Cordova's trademark shot. Much like Tarantino's signature *trunk shot,* the Peeping Tom is a single extended shot of another person who doesn't know he or she is being closely observed. It's always framed by a pulled curtain, venetian blinds, the muddy backseat window of a car, or a cracked door."

I thought it over, but it didn't seem to shed any light on what I'd encountered over the course of the investigation.

"The Know Not What?" I went on.

Beckman shrugged. "He's the henchman, the right-hand man, the *face*-man, the flunky. He appears when his boss will not, passively carrying out his orders with no judgment, thereby releasing a dark, malevolent force upon the world. The phrase comes from the Bible, of course, Luke, chapter twenty-three: 'Father, forgive them, for they know not what they do.' "

It took me a moment of racking my brain, and then the answer hit me. It was so obvious I nearly laughed out loud. I scribbled down his name.

"Theo Cordova?" said Beckman, reading over my shoulder. "What do you want with Theo Cordova?"

"He's been following me."

"Cordova's son? But how did you know it was he?"

"He's missing three fingers on his left hand."

Beckman looked startled. "That's right. Theo was always a strange, silent young man. Badgered by his father, lovesick for the same older woman for years."

I hastily made a note of it. *"Steak Tartare?"*

Beckman eagerly licked his lips. "In every Cordova film someone, often an extra, can be seen eating finely chopped raw meat. Well. The *very next person* who appears on-screen in either a medium or close-up shot *after* this uncooked consumption? He or she will be *malignant*. He or she has secretly—usually off-screen—become a turncoat, a whore, a *defector*, a deserter, and can *no longer be trusted*. It's Cordova reminding us of our omnipresent inner cannibal, a reminder that we all are, in the end, ravenous beasts who will satisfy our ugliest desires when the timing is right. They say it's his favorite meal."

I wasn't sure I'd noticed anyone eating the dish. I wrote a question mark beside it.

"Evil King?"

"Evil King," Beckman announced officially, clearing his throat. "He's the villain. A universally terrifying character of both myth and the real world. He can look outwardly repellant or totally innocuous. Usually it's someone in a position of great power. The smarter and more conniving the Evil King, the more turbulent and satisfying the tempest he creates."

That one was easy. *Cordova.*

"Phil Lumen?"

Beckman nodded. "A small detail. The Phil Lumen Company is the manufacturer of all light sources in a Cordova film. Lightbulbs, flashlights, headlamps, strobes, lava lamps, and streetlights—they *all* come from the Phil Lumen Company, which is Latin for *love of light*. Occasionally the name is called out in airport or store intercoms. 'Paging Mr. Phil Lumen. Please report to United Airlines Terminal B.' "

I didn't recall hearing anything of the kind—not that I would have noticed.

"The Shadow?"

Beckman paused, smiling sadly. "My favorite. The Shadow is what people are hunting throughout the tale. Or else it can dog the hero, refusing to leave him alone. It's a potent force that bewitches as much as it torments. It can lead to hell or heaven. It's the hollow forever inside you, never filled. It's everything in life you can't touch, hold on to, so ephemeral and painful it makes you gasp. You might even glimpse it for a few seconds before it's gone. Yet the image will live with you. You'll never forget it as long as you live. It's what you're terrified of and paradoxically what you're looking for. We are nothing without our shadows. They give our otherwise pale, blinding world definition. They allow us to see what's right in front of us. Yet they'll haunt us until we're dead."

It was Ashley. Beckman had seamlessly described my encounter with her at the Reservoir. As he watched me write down her name, his black beady eyes moved from the word to my face.

"What else?" I asked.

"What else about *what?*"

"Cordova's mind. His stories."

After a moment, Beckman shrugged, a wistful expression on his face. "Those constants festering inside Cordova's brain are all I've ever been able to come up with. The rest, as they say, is—not *history,* I've never liked that phrase—but *revolution.* Constant upheaval. Conversion. Rotation. Oh, dear." He jolted upright, struck by an idea. "One thing, McGrath."

"What?"

"Often, at *some* point in a Cordova narrative, the hero encounters a character who is life and death itself. He or she will be sitting at the intersection of the two, the beginning of one, the end of another." Beckman took a short breath, pointing at me. "It will be a decoy, a substitute to grant freedom to the *real thing.* He's Cordova's favorite character. He's always there, when Cordova's mind is at work, no matter what, do you understand?"

I wasn't sure I did, but hastily made note of it.

"And what about his endings?"

"Endings?" Beckman looked startled.

"How does it *all end?*"

He nervously scratched his chin, too troubled to continue.

"You know as well as I do, McGrath. His endings are seismic jolts to the psyche. Parting shots that keep you awake and wondering *for days,* for the rest of your life. You just *never know* with *Cordova*. His ends can be as full of hope and salvation as the tiny green-white bud of a new flower. Or they can be devastating charred-black battlefields strewn with lost legs and tongues."

I made a note of it, feeling an insidious wave of dread as I did, folding the scrap of paper into my pocket.

"Thank you," I said to Beckman—abruptly he appeared to be in too ruminating a mood to speak. "I'll explain when I have more time," I added, starting down the hall.

"McGrath."

I stopped, turning. He was staring after me.

"I need to give you a last bit of advice in the off chance this rather extraordinary and *enviable* situation in which you find yourself is actually *true*—that somehow you've fallen deep down into a Cordova story."

I stared back at him.

"Be the *good guy*," he said.

"How do I know I'm the good guy?"

He pointed at me, nodding. "A very wise question. You don't. Most bad guys think they're good. But there are a few signifiers. You'll be miserable. You'll be hated. You'll fumble around in the dark, alone and confused. You'll have little insight as to the true nature of things, not until the *very last minute,* and only if you have the stamina and the madness to go to the very, very end. But most importantly—and *critically*—you will act without regard for yourself. You'll be motivated by something that has *nothing* to do with the ego. You'll do it for justice. For grace. For love. Those large rather heroic qualities only the *good* have the strength to carry on their shoulders. And you'll *listen.*"

He licked his lips again, frowning.

"*If* you're the good guy, you *just might* survive, McGrath. But of course, there are no guarantees with Cordova."

"I understand."

"Good luck to you," he said, then spun quickly on his heel and, without looking at me again, vanished back inside his classroom.

108

I CASED THE TOWNHOUSE on East Seventy-first Street—the one Hopper had broken into—for the next eleven days. I returned home to fitfully sleep, of course, leaving a small thread clandestinely strung across the base of the front door, secured with a microscopic piece of tacking putty, so I'd know if anyone entered while I was away.

But the thread remained intact.

At this point, all that I accepted as the truth was that *somehow* I'd been artfully set up, beginning, I sensed, with Ashley appearing that night at the Reservoir. But why or how it had been planned and executed, whether or not the witnesses we'd tracked down had even been telling the truth about Ashley's behavior, what was *real,* what *wasn't*—I didn't know anymore. Could something be real when all evidence of it was gone? Was something categorically true if it lived on only in your head, same as your dreams?

Cordova, in his life and art, had blended fantasy and reality, and so he seemed to be flagrantly showing off to me, much to my chagrin, such an intermingling of truth and fiction. Perhaps it was his way of underscoring for me not just his superiority—that he was beyond unmasking, that I'd never catch him—but that, in some cases, the biggest truth about a family, about a person's life, was the fantasy and it was only a simple man's mind that craved one being tidily distinguished from the other.

Hopper and Nora, shortly after I'd interrupted Beckman's lecture, had both called me back within a few hours of each other, worriedly asking if I was all right. It seemed, then, that the two of them had *not* disappeared like all the others, but were only preoccupied with getting on with their lives. Nora was in the midst of practicing Al Pacino's opening monologue from *Glengarry Glen Ross,* which she was planning to do for her *Hamlette* audition at the Flea Theater. My conversation with Hopper, though civil, was stilted, part of which was because we were constantly interrupted by his incoming calls and he hadn't exactly forgiven me for my choice to keep stripping away the truth about Ashley. They both asked me if I was still working on the investigation, but didn't seem to want to hear the answer. I sensed that Ashley was something in their pasts now, a dusky beautiful day they wanted to remember in a certain moody light, with a certain haunting theme song, and they didn't want to hear another experience that would tarnish this image. I hung up with both of them, mentioning nothing about the disappearances of every one of our witnesses *or* anything about the Murad cigarettes, the Cordova trademarks that seemed to have peppered the real-life investigation.

There *was* one crucial person, however, who remained *exactly* where I'd found her.

I went back to Enchantments, stepping unannounced through the black curtain into the back room, expecting to see someone new sitting at the round table who'd duly inform me Cleo had moved to the Louisiana bayou.

But to my shock—and relief—Cleo was there. She was surprised to see me, and after a few awkward pleasantries, which involved me asking her if she knew Cordova ("That director? No," she answered, visibly confused) or ate steak tartare ("I'm vegan," she said blankly), also checking the red bulb in the light overhanging the table to see if by chance it was manufactured by Phil Lumen (it was GE)—I thanked her and swiftly left, my mind obsessively replaying the last time I'd seen her, when she'd showed me how the leviathan's tail moved with a mind of its own.

That had been real.

It couldn't be explained away by my having ingested Mad Seeds. It was a hint of the reality of black magic, of dark and invisible fractures cutting through our ordinary world.

Wasn't it? Thinking all of this over for days, finally I received the phone call I'd been waiting for.

"McGrath. Sharon Falcone."

I felt uneasy hearing her voice. Something told me I was not going to like what she said about the stained shirt I'd given her and the bones.

"We were able to take a look at what you gave me."

"And?"

"There's nothing there."

She paused, as if sensing I'd be distressed by the news.

"There's no blood, animal or otherwise, in the sample. What they found was trace glucose, maltose, some oligosaccharides."

"What's that?"

"Corn syrup. It might have been soda, some canned or bottled beverage that spilled on the shirt. How it was stored over the years must have created the stiffness. But it's such a degraded sample, it's hard to say."

"There's absolutely *no chance* it's human blood?"

"No chance."

I closed my eyes. *Corn syrup.*

"And the bones?" I asked.

"They were traced to family *Ursidae,* probably *Ursus Americanus.*"

"What's that?"

"A black bear. It's probably the foot of a cub."

A black bear.

"You need a vacation," Sharon said. "Leave town for a couple weeks. The city can screw with your head. Like all toxic love affairs, you need to take a break before you go back in for more pain and heartbreak."

I had nothing to say, because it couldn't be right. *I'd been so certain,* certain of the film sets, that they had contained real human suffering. It couldn't end like this.

"You still there?" Sharon asked.

"I'm sorry to have bothered you with this," I managed to say.

She cleared her throat. "You need to move on. I understand, *believe* me, how this stuff gets to you, that there's nothing more important than finding that hidden door which will lead to the underground bunker where the truth is sitting there behind bars. But sometimes the truth just isn't there. Even if you can smell it and hear it. Or there just *isn't* a way in anymore. It's grown over. Rocks have shifted. Shafts caved in. There's no human way to *get* to it, not even with all the dynamite in the world. So you leave it at that. And you move on."

As she said this, a phone began to bleat on her end, though she ignored it.

"The dark side of life has a way of finding us all *anyway,* so stop chasing it."

"Thank you, Sharon. For everything."

"Forget it. Now, would you go to the beach, get a girlfriend, a *tan, something?*"

"Sure."

"Take care."

"You, too."

The line went dead. *A black bear's foot.*

I went about the rest of my day, trying to get my mind off the sheer disappointment, telling myself to accept it, that Hopper and Nora were right. I'd come to the end of the road. And found an undeniable dead end. *There was no evidence of any crime.*

But then, I realized, there *was* one last stone to turn over. There was *one person* left who might shed light on the situation, who could explain from an insider's point of view what it all meant—and that person was Cordova's longtime assistant, Inez Gallo.

I needed only to wait for her to return to the townhouse. I'd wait as long as it took. And when that woman *finally* appeared—whether it was tomorrow or three years from now—I'd be ready.

109

IT HAPPENED THE TWELFTH DAY I'd been watching. Just after five o'clock in the evening, I was returning from a deli on Lex when I noticed a petite woman in a black coat walking swiftly down the sidewalk, half a block in front of me.

It was Inez Gallo. I recognized her immediately: the hastily cropped gray hair, hunched, stalwart bearing like a tiny bull poised to charge. As if she didn't want to be seen, she hurried up the steps, disappearing inside.

I waited for a few minutes, and when the street remained deserted, I grabbed the wrought-iron grate spanning the townhouse's first-floor window and began to climb. I needed Gallo off her guard, and I remembered how Hopper had done it: wedging his feet between the bars, bracing his right foot on the old-fashioned lamp over the front door. Seizing the latticed railing along the second floor high over my head, I managed to hoist myself up to the balcony, hooking my right leg over the side, climbing up, and collapsing onto the leaf-strewn floor. I headed to the window on the right, the one that Ashley had disabled from the house alarm.

Gallo had turned on quite a few lights in the entrance hall below, because light was shining through the doorway opposite, allowing me to see. It was an ornate wood-paneled library, every piece of furniture covered in white sheets. It was empty.

I took out a credit card, wedged it under the window's sash, lifting it just enough to get my fingers underneath, slid it open, and climbed inside.

Hopper had said, the night he'd broken in, that the townhouse looked frozen in time. He found every object to be sitting precisely where it'd been seven years before—the day Ashley and he were due to leave for Brazil and she'd stood him up. *Same exact sheets tossed randomly over the furniture*, he'd said, *the same Chopin music on Ashley's piano*. Now everything was meticulously covered and put away; when I lifted the sheet over the massive Steinway, positioned in the far corner by the bookshelves, there was no music. It seemed to me someone— Inez Gallo, perhaps—had packed up the house more carefully now, maybe as a result of Hopper breaking in. Or else the family had asked her to do it after Ashley's body had been found.

There was an armchair facing the library's entrance, which overlooked the lit-up landing and a spiral staircase. I sat down, waiting, and within minutes I could hear footsteps rapidly coming up the steps.

Suddenly, there she was—Inez Gallo, in baggy gray wool slacks and a white blouse, hurrying across the landing, headed for the next flight.

"Miss Gallo."

She froze, stunned, and whipped around, staring in at me, though probably couldn't see much beyond my silhouette.

"Or do you prefer to be called *Coyote*?"

She lurched furiously to the doorway, sliding her hand over a light switch, and suddenly the library was bathed in dim gold light from the overhead lamp.

When she saw me, she sized me up with enough scorn for me to know she knew precisely who I was.

"Sorry to drop in like this."

"You people just can't take a *hint*. I hope you like sleeping in jail." It was a deep, throaty voice, which sounded better suited for a truck driver or a six-foot bouncer, not such a hefty yet diminutive woman. She was barely five feet but shaped like a cinder block. She strode into the library and snatched a cordless phone off the counter, started to dial.

"I wouldn't do that."

"*No?*"

"*Coyote* is an intriguing nickname. Personally, I'd have wanted *my* term of endearment to be a little less incriminating. *Human trafficking for forced labor?* My friend at ICE tells me there used to be quite a racket originating from your hometown. *Puebla,* isn't it? Apparently, a mysterious woman arrived in an empty minivan once a year and left with it chock-full of *people*—stacked in the back like firewood. I've spoken to a few. They gave a *startling* description of the woman behind the wheel. The punishment per offense is a minimum of three to seven years. How many films did they work up there? *Ten?* That's thirty to seventy years. After The Peak, I expect federal prison will be quite a culture shock."

As I said this, I'd been watching Gallo's face. The second I'd said *human trafficking,* I knew I'd hit the bull's-eye.

And *thank Christ*—because I was bluffing: I had no friend at the ICE, and not a single witness. For the last few days, I'd pored over my hastily rewritten notes, trying to nail down something, *anything,* to use against Gallo. I kept returning to her nickname, mentioned by both Peg Martin and Marlowe Hughes: *Coyote.* A *coyote* was a wild prairie dog, but it was also slang for anyone who escorts illegal aliens over the Mexican-U.S. border. They could range from makeshift mom-and-pop organizations to those sponsored by billion-dollar drug cartels.

Peg Martin had specifically mentioned the film crew had used the nickname, and thus I wondered if it was because Gallo had been their actual coyote. *That,* combined with her birthplace in Mexico and Marlowe's assertion that Gallo did Cordova's dirty work, I made the theoretical leap that it just might be Gallo who had transported all of the illegal aliens to The Peak. The arrangement probably was that they worked crew on his film for three months, witnessing any number of appalling acts, and then, after being sufficiently threatened so they'd never spill the beans, were free to go. It *was* unquestionably a long shot, and I hadn't expected it to work—until now, when I'd watched the color drain out of Gallo's face.

She'd transformed considerably in the years since her bright-eyed teenage wedding photo—even since the day she'd accepted Cordova's Academy Award for *Thumbscrew.* It was as if all those decades serving the director, standing in such close proximity to him, had petrified her, made her gray hair grow coarser and wirier, her low brow heavier, her lips tighten as pulled string. There seemed nothing left in her that was light or carefree. But perhaps that was what happened when one decided to forever orbit a hulking planet with a mass that dwarfed one's own.

She hadn't moved a muscle, only watched me intently. She put down the phone.

"What do you want, Mr. McGrath?"

"To have a heart-to-heart."

"We've nothing to discuss."

"I *disagree*. We can start with Ashley Cordova being dead at twenty-four, then I have another problem, the fact that everyone I've talked to about Ashley has gone missing, including a man's house burned to the ground. If you talk to me, maybe my friend at ICE will *let slide* your slave-labor operation."

She looked furious but bit her tongue, striding deliberately to the bar in the corner and pouring herself a drink.

"If that was *slave labor*, then *millions* would die to be slaves," she muttered. "They lived like *kings*."

"They couldn't leave. So technically they were prisoners."

"It was how they *paid* for the crossing—all agreed to ahead of time. There was no coercion and no lies. At the end of production, we could hardly get them to go. They wanted to stay on forever."

"Like children not wanting to leave Epcot. *Touching*."

She narrowed her eyes. "What do you hope to gain out of all this?"

"The truth."

"*The truth*." She smirked, quick as a spark off a defunct lighter, then looked serious. I could see she was genuinely shocked by my showing up here—of *that* I was certain—and seemed now to be deciding how best to handle the situation, the quickest way to be rid of me. She must have decided to play along, at least for *now*, because she cocked her head to the side and smiled stiffly.

"Can I get you a drink?"

"So long as it's not poured over arsenic."

She fixed me a glass of Jameson from the same bottle she'd served herself, and hurried over, thrust the glass at me.

I noticed, as she sat down on the couch adjacent, she actually had a small wheel tattoo on the back of her left hand—exactly as I'd read weeks ago on the Blackboards. The anonymous poster had claimed it was evidence Gallo and Cordova were the same person. Staring at her rigid profile now, I considered the possibility that the director and his assistant were one and the same, that *this* was Cordova. But there was something about the woman, in her stocky lieutenant's bearing, in her flitting eyes, so subservient and unfulfilled—as if the eternal object of her attention was not present, but standing somewhere in the wings.

No, she was most certainly *not* Cordova. I was positive. And she was stalling.

"Before you demand to see the scaffolding, Mr. McGrath," she said, staring me down, "make sure it *is* what you actually want to *see*. The cranks and the ropes and the metal supports. The rust and the heavy chains. Lights painstakingly positioned overhead. It's a different reality than what's on-screen. And much less thrilling."

She tilted her head, as if struck by a new thought, closely scrutinizing my face and smiling thinly.

"It's funny. I'd have thought *you* of all people would have been on to her. You *really* never saw it?"

"Saw what?"

"Surely you must have noticed *hints,* here and there, clues—"

"Hints of *what*?" Suddenly I sensed I no longer had the upper hand in this situation, that Inez Gallo had *recovered*—or I'd never had her in a corner in the first place.

She raised an eyebrow. "You really never figured it out?"

"Figured out *what*?"

"Ashley was *sick.*"

"From the devil's curse."

She chuckled. "I can *assure* you, and so can an *army* of doctors and specialists around the world, Ashley never suffered from a *devil's curse.* Or any other type of curse. She had *cancer.* Acute lymphoblastic leukemia. She had it off and on all her life."

I stared at her, stunned.

My first infuriated inclination was to tell her I knew what she was doing, force-feeding me another lie so I'd trust her. It was a preposterous assertion and I knew it wasn't true.

It couldn't be.

But then, almost as quickly, I wondered if I'd missed something—*if*

Hopper had—if this, a real-life illness, had been there all the time, written in the sand, and we'd been straining our eyes, staring far out to sea, never once looking at our feet.

"Call Sloan-Kettering if you don't believe me," Gallo added petulantly. "Find someone to *bribe* in the records department, and they'll tell you. Ashley was treated there *three times,* registered under Goncourt, her mother's maiden name. The first time when she was *five,* the second when she was fourteen, and finally when she was seventeen, also at the University of Texas at Houston."

She looked at me with triumph. "You'll *see* I'm *right.*"

I said nothing, going through the dates in my head. Ashley had been only five years old when she'd crossed the devil's bridge, condemning her to the curse. At fourteen, she'd abruptly abandoned her classical music career, and at seventeen—I felt a rush of disbelief: At seventeen Ashley had called Hopper, crying. *She was desperate,* he'd told us. *She couldn't live with her parents anymore. She wanted to go where they couldn't find her.* Had she wanted to escape her illness?

"It isn't your fault," Gallo announced flatly, as if reading my mind. "Whatever wild nonsense you've come to believe, curses and Satan, the bogeyman—though *honestly,* I'd have expected a grown man, a *veteran reporter,* to be a little more skeptical. But give yourself a break. Ashley was a charismatic girl. You'd be *surprised* what she's convinced people of over the years. She was quite proficient in making people believe the impossible. Like *her father.* They had a knack, the *both* of them, for taking you by the hand, looking deep into your eyes, so you'd follow them down into the passageways of the absurd and unbelievable and live there forever, a total convert. *I* know. I *did* it. For forty-six years. Gave up everything. My husband. My kids. But now that it's over I can see. Probably because I'm not one of them. I don't have trouble distinguishing make-believe from reality. I live in the real world. And so do *you.*"

She said it insistently, even angrily, crossing her arms.

"Her sickness tore the family apart. For young children the prognosis for ALL is good. After the first round of treatment, most have remissions that last a lifetime. It wasn't the case with Ashley. Every time we thought she was out of the woods, that she would at last be granted the gift of a life without round after round of shots and steroids, spinal taps, and stem-cell transplants, a few years would pass, she'd be tested, and the doctors would give us the terrible news again. *Matilde* had returned."

"*Matilde?*" I repeated.

She nodded, eyeing me. "It was Ashley's name for her illness. She *nicknamed* it, the way other children nickname imaginary friends, which will give you a good sense of the way her mind worked. When she was five, one morning she came into the kitchen, and as she ate her bowl of Cheerios she cheerfully announced to her mother that she had a new friend. *Who?* Astrid asked her. *Matilde,* she answered. Matilde. It was a strange name. No one knew where she'd heard it. *Matilde is going to kill me,* Ashley said. Everyone was startled, but then, she *was* her father's daughter. *Dramatic.* Blessed—you might even say *cursed*—with the most graphic of imaginations. The very next day, Ashley became sick with a high fever. Tiny red spots covered her arms and her back. Astrid took her to the hospital, and the doctors gave us the terrible news."

"But wasn't *Matilde* meant to be the title of Cordova's next film? A film that was never released."

Gallo nodded. "He wanted to write about it. But he couldn't. To write directly about something so gutting is like staring at the sun, day after day. You can't really make it out, no matter how hard you try. You're sure to go blind." She sighed. "He didn't want to work on another film, wanted only to save his daughter. It's excruciating for a parent to lose a child. But it's even worse to watch your child suffer, day in, day out, teetering interminably between life and death, living a life of death. But you go through with it, continue to fight, because you hope one day it won't be like this. Life can be so cruel. It doles out just enough hope to keep you going, like a small cup of water and one slice of bread to someone on the verge of starvation."

She paused to sip her drink. "Ashley made the decision not to tell anyone outside of the family," Gallo continued. "Against her doctors' advice. But she was adamant. She didn't want to be pitied. She said— and she was only six at the time—it would hurt much more to be tiptoed around, treated as if she were a fragile butterfly with a ripped-off wing, than to suffer at the hands of Matilde. We all made a pact with her, swearing never to tell anyone. And if Ashley wasn't well enough to go out into the world to experience life, her father arranged for the most fascinating and outrageous of lives to come to *her.* In between her hospital visits to the city four, sometimes five, times a week, she was homeschooled at The Peak, and the estate became a backdrop, a hostel, a secret hidden *lodging,* populated around the clock with philosophers and actors and artists and scientists, all of them teaching Ashley how to live and think and dream, teaching all of us, really."

I was immediately reminded of the afternoon picnic Peg Martin had described. Ashley had been six years old. It would have been around the time she was finishing treatment—*if* Gallo was telling the truth.

Ashley took my hand and brought me down to a deserted part of the lake where there was a willow tree and tall grass, the water emerald green. She asked me if I could see the trolls.

"Astrid had a concert pianist from Juilliard come to the house three times a week to give Ashley lessons. Doctors had warned us, some of the very potent drugs used in treatment could have long-term effects on her nervous system, weakening her motor skills and dexterity, making something like playing the piano *difficult,* if not *impossible.* Her hands and fingers might go numb, have increased sensitivity. She might experience dizzy spells. In Ashley, however, the drugs had the *opposite* effect. She was able to play with astounding speed. Her memory, her ability to master even the most complicated of pieces went into overdrive, became *superhuman.* It was at the piano she began to live again, escape death, sailing over continents and mountain ranges and seas. She'd been in remission when she won first place in the International Tchaikovsky Competition in Moscow. But three years later, when she was fourteen, we all learned the horrible news again. *Matilde* had come *back.* Ashley was strong, but it would be logistically impossible for her to travel to her concerts *and* undergo another round of treatment. She had to give it all up. And she did."

Gallo fell silent.

My mind was spinning from the symmetry of this equation I suddenly faced: magical on one side, scientific on the other, a dark pulsing myth and an acceptable reality. Cordova was desperate to save his daughter, as any father would be—but from a devil's curse or terminal cancer? Ashley's sudden musical genius at the piano—caused by her traversing the devil's bridge or a side effect from the chemotherapy drugs she'd taken as a child?

I thought back to what Beckman had told me, describing Ashley in concert. *She had knowledge of darkness in the most extreme form.* But what had given her this knowledge, staring the devil in the face, knowing he'd take her soul, or turning corner after corner of an endless illness, wondering if Death was waiting for her on the other side?

The explanations were like two sides of the same coin, and the side that I favored revealed something essential about the person I was. Prior to investigating Ashley, with little hesitation I'd have believed the side most others would, the side that was logical, rational, exact. But now, much to my own shock, like a man who suddenly realized he was no longer a person he recognized, that other impossible, illogical, *mad* side still had a very firm grip on me.

I didn't want to believe it, didn't want to accept that Ashley—such a fierce presence in every story I'd ever heard about her—could be singlehandedly struck down by real life. I wanted a wilder explanation for her death, something darker, bloodier, more insane—*a devil's curse.*

"Things became difficult when Ashley underwent treatment that *second time,*" Gallo continued sternly. "She'd always had a strong personality. As strong as her father's. The two of them began to fight constantly—*war,* really. Doctors warned us that the steroids Ashley was taking could produce volatility—explosions of temper, even violence. No one could control either of them. Not Astrid. Not me. It was like living with two dragons and the rest of us were bluebirds, taking cover in closets and under stairs, hoping not to be incinerated by the crossfire."

"What did they fight about?" I asked.

She arched an eyebrow. "I don't know if you know much about the *temperament* of *geniuses,* but they have hungers unknown to ordinary men. If you're going to commit to such a person, you have to accept it or there'll be no end to your suffering. To survive such a person you must bend and twist all the time like a thin piece of wire, making allowances. It's always changing, the shape you're in. There were always other women. *Other men.* Other *everything.* Astrid accepted it. But Ashley, when she was old enough to understand, thought it unconscionable—a sort of gluttony on his part, a lack of integrity, a total betrayal of the family. One of his longtime lovers came to town and moved back into The Peak, a man Ashley did *not like*. One night, while I happened to be away, she went to his bedroom, and as he slept, she set his bed on fire. Astrid, not wanting the negative publicity, drove the man, screaming in pain, off the property in the dead of night. Along the way she was in an accident. Theo rescued the man before an ambulance arrived and managed to get him to an emergency room without being spotted. But Ashley got her wish. The man disappeared." She shot me a look. "I suspect you know most of this already."

I nodded. "The man was Hugo Villarde. The Spider. A sham priest."

"It was *my* suggestion to send Ashley to that camp," she announced. "Six Silver Lakes."

"The place came well recommended. When we were notified an accidental death had occurred there, some young boy drowning during a rainstorm, you can imagine how we felt. Yet when I picked up Ashley she was . . . *different*." She shrugged, a faintly cynical expression on her face. "She'd met a *boy*. The loneliest boy in the world, she called him. She described him as a beautiful red maple leaf that had detached prematurely from its tree. And it floated through wind and rain, scuttled down drains and across fields, absolutely alone, connected to nothing. Yet there was something fundamentally *good* about him, she believed. Shortly afterward she tracked him down and they began whatever—a correspondence. I don't know what they wrote or said to each other, only that she was vital and alive again. Her father was relieved. We all were. Ashley wanted to leave The Peak, be around ordinary people, an ordinary life. He bought this place for Ashley."

She paused to glance tiredly around the room, as if recalling how warm and bustling it had once been, how alive with voices and music, before it had been buried like a lost civilization under the white sheets.

"It felt like the beginning of something. We enrolled her in school here. I prayed he'd return to his work."

"Making another film."

Gallo nodded, draining the rest of her drink.

"The prognosis for cancer gets worse after more relapses. The window for long-term survival begins to close. Toxicities have been building in the body, which is being demolished from the inside out. Early that May, Ashley was due for a checkup. She didn't want to go. Because she knew the truth, of course. She always did. Her doctors recommended a treatment involving clinical trials, an experimental program in Houston. Shortly after that, Astrid discovered, hidden inside Ashley's bedroom, a packed suitcase. And two one-way tickets to *Brazil.* When Astrid confronted Ashley, she said she was running away with Hopper and there was nothing anyone could do to stop her. She didn't want treatment. But, of course, her life was at stake. She was just a teenager. This boy she claimed was the love of her life, some juvenile delinquent—none of us took it seriously. Who really *loves* at that age?"

"Romeo and Juliet," I said.

"*And* Hopper and Ashley. Ashley and her father fought horribly over it. He threw her into the car, locked the doors, and told her she was going to Houston whether she liked it or not. She could tell the boy the *truth or not.* But Ashley decided not to. She said to love someone who is dying is torture. She'd rather the boy hate her, because within that hate is the motivation to move on, to forget, to vanquish—better that than be gutted by loss, to long for something that can never be. And for that deep love to turn into something else, like pity or revulsion—Ashley couldn't bear it. She cut all ties with the boy. And went to Houston. She almost died there, but it was more from a broken heart than the disease."

Gallo fell silent, her hardened profile softened, ever so slightly.

"Ashley got better?" I asked, after a moment.

"Yes. She went to Amherst. She had to leave early spring semester due to dizzy spells and fatigue, but after she rested at The Peak she was able to return her sophomore year. And she was all right. She graduated. And then, six months ago, it began again."

"*Matilde.*"

Gallo nodded thoughtfully, staring at the coffee table. My mind was spinning because two things she'd said struck me: First, the detail about Ashley leaving early her freshman year at Amherst. It had actually been mentioned in the *Vanity Fair* article. Reading it, I'd wondered about the reason behind her mysterious departure, and now here it was, explained.

Second, there was a question of timing.

"How long was Ashley treated at the University of Texas?" I asked.

"Eight months? Why?"

"And then she returned to The Peak?"

She nodded slowly, puzzled. "She did the maintenance therapy back in New York. Why?"

"Did the family order medical equipment for her? A wheelchair? Or something from a company called Century Scientific?"

"I ordered everything for her. The Peak was outfitted like the Mayo Clinic. Everything to keep Ashley comfortable, so she wouldn't be needlessly disturbed. She had round-the-clock nurses monitoring her."

"And the garbage at The Peak is burned at night?"

"Crowthorpe Falls is always swarming with Cordovites. It's their Mecca. They migrate there from around the world, hoping for a sighting. The last thing he wanted was a fan trawling through his trash, discovering a prescription revealing that Ashley was sick and jabbering about it on the Internet. We had to protect her. Though in the end, protection is just another cage."

It had all come together. The incinerators Nora had seen up at The Peak, the glass vial marked *biohazard*, Nelson Garcia's accidental UPS delivery back in December 2004—it all made sense now, in light of Ashley's illness. But the rush of solving these last few mysteries was almost immediately replaced with something else, a sense of hollowness, even grief.

I felt *let down.* I always did, slightly, when I'd come to the end of an investigation, when, looking around, I realized there were no more dark corners to plumb.

And yet—this was different. The desolation came from the realization that all of the *kirin* were dead. They'd never existed in the first place. Because, however much I might not want to face it, wanting something larger than life for Ashley, some other tempestuous reality that defied reason, alive with trolls and devils, shadows that had minds of their own, black magic as powerful as H-bombs—I knew Inez Gallo was telling me the truth.

And her truth razed everything, clear-cut that magical and dark jungle I'd wandered into following Ashley's footprints, revealing that I was actually standing on flat dry land, which was blindingly lit, but barren.

110

"THE BUSINESS WITH YOU STARTED because she was sick again," Gallo blurted with evident contempt.

I drained my drink, feeling the scalding whiskey course down my throat.

"How's *that*?" I muttered.

She turned to me, exasperated. "I *told* you. Ashley was a charismatic girl. Thanks to her inventive upbringing, her solitary life at The Peak, *her sickness*, she had trouble distinguishing made-up stories from real life. When Ashley was ten, Astrid made the mistake of inviting a witch doctor from Haiti to reside for four months at the house for *fun*. She didn't realize it would permanently uproot Ashley's imagination, like running along a coastline filled with quietly roosting flamingos, displacing them. Suddenly, everything in Ashley's head became riotous and squawking and in motion, all pink feathers and screeching and flapping wings everywhere. She came to believe in it all, voodoo. Witchcraft." She shook her head. "I found spells she'd laid for me in my own *room*, protection from evil, or so she claimed. She was certain she'd been marked by something evil, that the devil was causing her illness. It was heartbreaking. And *delusional*. Ashley was terrified to be in close physical proximity to people she cared about, because she believed she'd harm them. She claimed this darkness growing inside her due to her—*I* don't even know how to put it—her *soul* slowly being overtaken by the devil—that it made her dangerous. *Lethal*. The idea was, of course, absurd."

Gallo sighed. "Six months ago, when we learned she was sick again, her mental state became *especially* precarious. She had periods of not knowing where she was. Or *who* she was. Not that it was her fault, after what she'd withstood as a child, having those staring contests with Death, over and over again. She made it clear she didn't want to be in a hospital bed anymore, plugged into tubes and monitors, weak with morphine. Astrid refused to accept it. She took Ashley, against her will, to a clinic, hoping it'd bring her to her senses, that she'd agree to another round of treatment."

"And that clinic was Briarwood Hall."

Gallo nodded. "She escaped, as you know, thanks to some horny half-wit working in security. Ashley was a master at manipulation, especially men. They melted and sweated and went weak in front of her like a bunch of idiot iced teas. She vanished into thin air. It was horrifying for all of us. We'd no clue where she'd gone. Theo and Boris searched everywhere for her, but she was clever. She knew how to remain invisible. We found out later she'd shacked up in a tenement slum on the Lower East Side."

"Eighty-three Henry Street."

"Astrid went out of her mind with worry. By then Ashley had grown quite sick. Astrid wanted her to die at home with her family around her. Still, we had a few inklings as to where she'd go. There wasn't a day that went by that she didn't think about that boy. *Hopper.* She'd kept track of him over the years, knew he'd gotten into trouble with the law, was making a mess of his life. We sensed she'd seek him out in some way. The other option, of course, was *you.*"

"Me?"

"She'd been interested in you ever since her *father* dealt with you snooping into his life the only way he knew how. Fighting fire with fire."

"*Dealt* with me? Is that what Cordova called it?"

A challenging look flickered across her face, but she remained silent.

"Was it a setup? Who in hell was the man who contacted me, then? *John.*"

She shrugged. "Someone paid to lead you astray."

"But what he told me, Cordova visiting all of those schools in the middle of the night—"

"A juicy *fabrication.* And one just salacious enough for you to blurt it out and hang yourself by your own hubris. I'm sure it was a painful lesson for you to learn, Mr. McGrath, but an artist like *him* needs just one fundamental thing in order to thrive. And he'll do anything to keep it."

"And what's that?"

"*Darkness.* I know it's hard to fathom *today,* but a true artist needs darkness in order to create. It gives him his power. His invisibility. The less the world knows about him, his whereabouts, his origins and secret methods, the more *strength* he has. The more inanities about him the world eats, the smaller and drier his art until it shrinks and shrivels into a Lucky Charms marshmallow to be consumed in a little bowl with milk for *breakfast.* Did you really think *he'd* ever let that *happen?*"

As she said this, her still-very-much-alive reverence for Cordova took up in her voice, tossed it high into the air, made it swoop in figure-eights, trailing wild red ribbons—a voice otherwise limp, lying in a dull heap on the ground. I'd also noticed that during the entire conversation Inez Gallo hadn't actually *said* the word *Cordova,* not a single time—referring to him only as *he* or *Ashley's father.*

It had to be her private superstition or she didn't like cavalierly intoning the word, as if it were akin to *God.*

As she stood up, stalking over to the bar and returning with the whiskey bottle, hastily splashing it into our glasses, I considered what she said. If there was no devil's curse, there could be no reason for Cordova to obsess over an exchange, no reason to visit those schools at night, no pit filled with children's belongings. *Had I been hallucinating after all, thanks to the Mad Seeds?*

"To comprehend the force that was Ashley," Gallo said, sitting back against the couch, clutching her drink, "you must understand, she was her father's daughter. The family's favorite fairy tale was *Rumpelstiltskin.* That's what they *did,* what they were, fantastical creatures spinning the ordinary, dreary straw around them into gold. They won't stop until they're dead. And so Ashley reconceived her illness to be a devil's curse."

"But it wasn't just Ashley who believed it. Marlowe Hughes and Hugo Villarde were also pretty convinced."

She scoffed. "Marlowe Hughes is a drug addict. She'd believe the sky was hot-pink polka dots if you told it to her. *Especially* if you wrote it in a fan letter. She spent time with Ashley. Became swept up in her tales. And Villarde, after what Ashley did to *him?* The man went out of his mind. He believed her to be the devil's queen, trembling at the sight of a flea."

I suddenly recalled how Villarde had described, without shame, crawling on his hands and knees across his shop to hide from Ashley, cowering in a wardrobe like a terrified child.

"What about how Cordova worked?" I asked. "The horrors on the screen—they were *real,* weren't they? The actors aren't acting."

She looked me over, her stare challenging. "It was nothing they didn't ask for."

"I've heard serial killers say the same thing."

"Everyone who stayed at The Peak *knew* full well what they were getting into. They were *dying* to work with him. But if you're asking me if he ever crossed the line into pure insanity, if he jumped headfirst into hell, he didn't. He knew his limits."

"What are they, exactly?"

She narrowed her eyes. "He was never a murderer. He loves life. But believe what you want. You'll never find any evidence."

You'll never find any evidence. It was an odd thing to say. It sounded almost like an admission—*almost.* I thought back to the boy's tiny shriveled shirt, caked not in blood but corn syrup, according to Falcone. What Gallo was saying certainly backed up the results Sharon had given me, whether I wanted to accept it or not.

"Why has everyone I've talked to about Ashley disappeared?"

"I took care of them," Inez said with a hint of pride.

"What does that mean? They're all lying in an unmarked grave?"

She ignored this, sitting up stiffly. "I also took care of the coroner's photos of Ashley's body, and then the body itself—before she was cut open in front of strangers like a lab rat. I've paid everyone off handsomely and sent them on their merry way."

"How did you know who I talked to?"

She looked surprised. "Why, your *own notes,* Mr. McGrath. Surely you remember the break-in at your apartment. They were very helpful for tying up loose ends."

Of course: the break-in.

"We were *desperate,*" she went on. "We didn't know where Ashley had gone, what had happened to her in the time she'd vanished from Briarwood and ended up in that warehouse dead. The only thing we did know was that she came *here* one night, broke in, took money from a safe. I suspected *you'd* know more. Briarwood, after all, informed us that you'd showed up there, snooping. We broke in to find out what you knew."

"Any chance I can have my laptop back?"

"It's been a costly enterprise, in the wake of her death, getting rid of each witness. But it's all in keeping our promise to her, never letting anyone know the truth. It's what *he* wanted. Ashley's history will now forever remain where she wished it, where she believed in her heart it always was—beyond reason, between heaven and earth, land and sky, suspended much closer to legend than ordinary life—ordinary life where the *rest* of us, including *you,* Mr. McGrath, must remain."

"Where the mermaids sing," I added quietly, reminded of the Prufrock poem. As Hopper had explained it, the mermaids were the one thing the family was always seeking out, always fighting for—life's most stunning and precarious razor edge. *Where there was danger and beauty and light. Only* the now. *Ashley said it was the only way to live.*

Inez Gallo, I noticed, was staring at me, her mouth open in shock—seemingly surprised I knew such an intimate detail about the family. She decided not to delve further into it, however, taking a long sip of her drink.

"Marlowe Hughes suffered an overdose," I said. "Did you have anything to do with that?"

"I asked her drug dealer to *scare* her a little. I didn't expect him to nearly bump her off."

"Your compassion is very moving."

She glared at me. "It was the best thing that could happen. It got her out of that apartment. Right now she's sitting in an oceanview suite at Promises in Malibu, climbing up onto that first, very high, very worn-out step of all twelve-step sobriety programs."

"And what did you say to Olivia Endicott?"

She shrugged. "Nothing. She's out of the country. But I *did* speak to her secretary. I paid the girl a small fortune to avoid you like the plague and not to pass along any of your messages to her employer."

"And Morgan Devold? Why did his house burn down?"

"He needed the insurance money. He was in dire financial straits, two kids, no job. When I explained who I was, that I was there to offer a *helping hand,* he was quite receptive. If you ever approach him again, he'll swear he's never seen you or Ashley before in his life." She lifted her chin, satisfied. "Everyone in this world has a price, Mr. McGrath. Even *you.*"

"You're wrong. Some of us aren't for sale. Who set the house on fire?"

"Theo and Boris. Boris is a longtime friend of the family."

"Who smokes Murad cigarettes?"

She was visibly irritated by the question. "Theo. It was his father's favorite brand."

Again, she deliberately said *his father*, rather than simply *Cordova*. She was taking the long way to avoid a certain hazardous stretch of road.

"Years ago," she went on, "he cleaned out the world's supply. *Murad.* The brand's been discontinued since the mid-thirties. It's very rare. But he bought up every last pack from every obscure tobacco collector across the globe. He liked the caramel smell, the gorgeous packaging, *and* the fact that it was the only detail he remembered about his natural born father, a Spaniard, whom he'd last seen when he was three. But he especially liked the way they *burned*. It's like nothing else. There are hundreds of shots of it in the films. The smoke spirals through the air like it's alive. 'Like a swarm of white snakes were struggling to be free,' he once said to me."

She'd gone on with strange, unchecked fervor, her eyes bright and raised to the ceiling, her mouth twitching in excitement. But then, remembering *me*, she stopped herself.

"I don't see why it's so important to you, these *details*," she muttered in annoyance.

"It's where the devil is. Haven't you heard?"

She eyed me disdainfully. "You've done a lifetime's worth of *mining*, Mr. McGrath. Maybe it's time to come back to the surface and go home with whatever lumps of coal you've managed to dig loose."

"And be on my *merry way*. Like all the others."

She shrugged, unperturbed. "Do whatever you like with the information. Of course, now there's no one in the world to back up your story. You're alone again with your wild claims."

Staring at the woman, I couldn't help but marvel at her smug meticulousness, the way she'd managed to get rid of each and every witness, one by one.

"What happened to Ashley's mother? Astrid?"

"Gone. Somewhere in Europe. With her precious child now *dead,* there's nothing keeping her here. Too many black memories."

"But you don't mind them."

She smiled. "My memories are all I have left. And when I'm gone? They're gone."

I frowned, suddenly doubtful again of what she'd been telling me, suddenly struck by something. Maybe it was the last dying whisper of *magic*—the *kirins* and devils, the supernatural powers of one startling woman—before it was all laid to rest.

"But I went up to The Peak," I said. "I broke in—"

"*Did* you?" Gallo interrupted excitedly. "What did you find?"

Her reaction was puzzling, to say the least. She actually looked thrilled by my admission.

"A perfect circular clearing in which nothing grows," I went on. "A maze of underground tunnels. Soundstages. Film sets entirely intact. Everything is overgrown and black. I walked over the devil's bridge. And I saw . . ."

Gallo was hanging on my words so excitedly, waiting for me to continue, I fell silent, bewildered.

"Who lives there?" I went on. "Who are the watchmen with the dogs?"

She shook her head. "I've no idea."

"*What*—you . . . you no longer work for the family?" I asked.

"You really don't understand. The Peak's been left to the fans."

"What?"

"The Cordovites. It belongs to them now. They've overtaken it. Quite a few squat there year-round. It's a dangerous theme park, left, free of charge, to his most dedicated. It's become a secret rite of passage, a cult expedition to be there, wander the work or get swallowed inside it. They can fight over it, tend it, destroy it, rule it as they see fit. *He* hasn't set foot there in years. It's finished for him. His work is done."

I wondered if it could actually be true—the men who'd chased me, the mongrels, the spray-painted red birds. I'd been terrorized by *fans*? I'd hardly managed to get my mind around this, when I had no choice but to reach for the other question she'd just left dangling in front of me.

"Where is he?" I asked.

"I was wondering when you might ask me that." She turned away, staring somewhere in front of us, her expression like a truck driver looking out at a lonely road twisting interminably in front of her.

I had a sudden vision of that drunken South African journalist years ago, cautioning me that some stories are infected, that they're like tapeworms. *A tapeworm that's eaten its own tail. No use going after it. Because there's no end. All it will do is wrap around your heart and squeeze all the blood out.*

For the first time since I'd met her, Inez Gallo smiled warmly at me. And I knew then I had it wrong. Because *here it was*. The end. The tail. I'd found it, after all.

111

I WAS SHOCKED there was no security.

I expected something miserable. *How couldn't it be?* A place where men and women were tucked out of sight so they could bumble around the end of their lives—a place like Terra Hermosa. I thought about phoning Nora for this very reason, asking her to come, but then, sensing she'd say no, left it alone. But once I'd turned off the highway and pulled into the place, following the neatly paved driveway to the series of cream-colored signs and stucco buildings with red tile roofs, I saw Enderlin Estates Retirement Community was trying its best to bring to mind a Spanish hacienda taking a very long siesta. There were plantings and courtyards and chirping birds, a twisting stone path that led promisingly toward the main entrance nestled behind a wrought-iron gate.

I checked the paper where I'd written the address Gallo had given me. *Enderlin Estates. Apartment 210.*

I walked into the deserted lobby, took an elevator to the second floor, encountering a redheaded nurse behind a front desk.

"I'm looking for Apartment Two-ten."

"Last room at the end of the hall."

I headed down the carpeted hallway, passing a young nurse helping an elderly woman with a walker. The door marked 210 was closed, and the name—the beautifully generic *Bill Smith*—was mounted on a tiny blue plaque beside the door.

I knocked and, when there was no answer, turned the knob. It opened into a large sitting room, sparsely furnished, awash with sunlight. There was a bedroom on the left with a single bed, a dresser, a bedside table—entirely bare except for a lamp and a figurine of the Virgin Mary, her hands together in prayer. No photos, no personal items of any kind, but Gallo had doubtlessly seen to this, so there would be total anonymity or, as she put it, no more dark memories. "*What he needs now is peace,*" she'd said with a look of warning.

"You looking for Bill?" a cheerful voice asked behind me.

I turned. A nurse stood in the open doorway.

"I just took him to the morning room."

She explained how to find it. I made my way back down the elevator and along the main hall, passing Activity calendars, an advertisement for Movie Night—*Bogart and Bacall together again!*—stepping through the double wooden doors into an old-fashioned glass-walled solarium. The room was bright and cheerful, filled with potted palms and flowers, white wicker chairs, a gray stone floor. Classical piano music played feebly from somewhere—an old stereo beside a bookshelf packed with paperbacks.

It was crowded. Elderly men and women, moving as if they were underwater, hair that looked like a few wisps off a cloud, sat at tables with jigsaw puzzles and checkerboards. A few nurses sat among them, quietly reading aloud, one pinning a pink carnation to an old man's lapel.

Yet my eyes were pulled away from the activity to one man.

He sat alone on the farthest side of the room in the corner, his back to me. He was in front of the windows, staring out. And even though he was in a wheelchair, wearing an old gray sweater and old-man shoes, there was something sturdy about him, something oddly immobile.

I stepped toward him.

He gave no indication he was aware of my approach. In fact, he seemed unaware of anything at all in the room. His gaze—stripped of those ink-black circular lenses he'd allegedly worn all his life—remained fixed out the window, where a vast lawn ringed by woods stretched out like an empty lake, its surface gold-green and hard in the afternoon sun. He had a dense head of silver-white hair, which showed no sign of relenting, a sizable stomach, which seemed more imperial, even threatening, rather than fat—as if, like some Greek god with explosive moods and appetites, he had swallowed a boulder and it hadn't killed him, just kept him brutally secured to the ground. He was sitting back easily in the chair, his hands—massive workman's hands—loosely hanging off the armrests, the way an exhausted king might relax on his throne. His face was different from how I'd pictured it, less certain somehow, slightly more drooping and crude.

Yet I was certain it was he.

Cordova.

I could even see the faded wheel tattoo on his left hand, exactly where Gallo's had been. His gaze remained somewhere out on the lawn like an anchor that'd been thrown there. It was as if he was picturing something, a final scene for a film he'd never made—or a scene he'd intended for his life. Maybe he was imagining himself walking across the grass with the sun on his back, the wind pressing against his face. Perhaps he was thinking of his family, of Ashley, wherever and everywhere she was.

Gallo had warned me he'd be aware of nothing.

"A day or two after Ashley learned she was sick again, this last time, he went to bed early," Gallo had told me. "He was always up at four A.M. working, living. But he didn't come down. Alarmed, I went upstairs. I found him in his bed, propped upright in his pillows as if a ghost had come in the middle of the night to talk something over. His eyes were wide open, staring out at nothing. He was catatonic—a television turned *on,* but one single channel, only static." To my shock, Gallo had gone on to explain it all in great detail: His doctors, certain he'd suffered a stroke, transferred him to a nursing facility for the elderly in Westchester—Enderlin Estates, outside of Dobbs Ferry—the decision to use the alias Bill Smith, so he wouldn't be hounded or hunted, but left to live out his final days in peace.

I told Gallo it was a wild coincidence, this prevalence of death, two vibrant lives drawing to an abrupt close—first Ashley, now Cordova. Granted, he wasn't *technically* dead, but given the kind of life he'd lived, he *was*—unresponsive, his spirit locked forever inside him, or else, it had already fled.

"It's not a *coincidence*," Gallo snapped, as if she found the word insulting. "He was *finished,* don't you see? Men and women who have fulfilled what they meant to, those who have found answers to a few grave questions about life—not *all* of the answers, but *a few*—they end their lives when they choose. They're ready. And he *was.* He'd lived exactly as he wanted—wildly, *insanely*—and now he's ready for the *next.* He's wrung every drop of life out of himself, leaving only dried-up piles of nerves and bones. I know as sure as I know my own name he'll be dead within a matter of months."

I'd found Gallo's demeanor startlingly efficient and brisk for a woman who'd just lost the focus of her life, the sun that had ordered her days. But then she lifted her head and I saw there were tears in her eyes— waiting for me to leave, so they could slide freely down her sunken cheeks. Silently she led me downstairs to the front door, extended her hand with a brusque *"I'll see you"*—a statement we both knew was false. And though I didn't especially *like* Inez Gallo and she hadn't exactly *warmed* to me, we'd come to a sort of unspoken understanding, found on a surprising patch of common ground: both of us spectators swept up in the wild squall that was Cordova.

And now here he was, less than two feet away.

And he was a fragile old man.

I'd been fighting no one. The crimes, the horrors I'd tried and found Cordova guilty of, seemed laughable now, considering the fact that, all those moments I'd been so certain he was outmaneuvering me, he'd been right *here—probably sitting peacefully like this in front of this very window.*

I couldn't help but be awed by the shock of it.

Even like this he was having the last word.

Strange emotion abruptly swelled in my throat. It might have been a laugh or just as easily a sob. Because I realized, staring at this man, that I was actually just staring at myself, at what I'd become much sooner and more suddenly than I'd ever know. Life was a freight train barreling toward just one stop, our loved ones streaking past our windows in blurs of color and light. There was no holding on to any of it, and no slowing it down.

It was so calm standing next to him, so lonely. I swore I could hear his breathing, every breath he borrowed from the world then set free. It wasn't the simple lungs of an ordinary man, but the faint howl of a gust of wind as it snagged the rocks of some far-off bluff by the sea. I wondered—another unchecked wave of feeling rising in my chest— what in the hell I was going to *say* to him after all this, all I'd done and come to see—if I had the nerve to say anything at all.

Or maybe, like a child encountering the reassembled bones of a dangerous species of dinosaur he'd dreamed about, read about with a flashlight under a comforter for nights and days, maybe I was going to simply reach out and touch his shoulder, wondering if in that touch I could get a sense of what he must have been like when he was alive, in his prime, roaming the Earth, a force of nature, when he wasn't silent grayed bones on display, but something splendid to behold.

In the end, all I did was pull up a chair and sit down beside him.

And together, for what seemed like hours, we did nothing but stare out at that empty lawn, which seemed to hold in its strict boundaries and flawless green, the empty space in which we could pile our memories and questions, what we'd once loved but let go of, taking silent inventory of it all. When I became aware of the music again, piano music, a pale, listless approximation of what Ashley would have played, I realized then that all I was going to say to the man was "thank you."

I did. Then I rose and left, not looking back.

112 WHAT CAN I SAY about the ensuing weeks?

Marlowe Hughes said it best: "When you finally returned to your real life after working with Cordova, it was as if all of the colors had been turned way up in your eyes. The reds were redder. *Blacks blacker.* You felt things profoundly, as if your very heart had grown giant and tender and swollen. You *dreamed.* And *what dreams.*"

I drove home from Enderlin Estates, pulled the curtains, and slept for twenty hours, a sleep as blacked-out and resolute as death. I woke up around nightfall the following day, shadows streaked across the ceiling, the dying light outside making the street blush with the elegance of a memory.

My old life took me back, the old faithful mutt that it was.

I was somewhat shocked to learn it was December. I spent a few evenings at dinners with friends, most of whom assumed I'd been away, traveling. I let them believe it. In a way it was true.

"You look *good,*" quite a few of them remarked, though certain lingering stares seemed to suggest this wasn't exactly true, that there was something else altered about me, something they sensed best left alone. I wondered, half seriously, if it was residue from the devil's curse—if, even though it had turned out *not* to be true, perhaps one never recovered from having *once believed.* Maybe certain far-flung attic rooms in the brain had been violently broken into—doors bashed in, lamps broken, desks flipped upside down, curtains left dancing strangely by open windows—rooms that would never be reached again or ever reordered.

But I was thankful for the company, for friends, for light conversation forgotten as soon as it began. I joined in wholeheartedly, I laughed, I ordered wine and duck and dessert, and people slapped me on the back and said they were happy to see me, that I'd been away too long. But occasionally I slipped, unseen, outside all the talk and stared in at it, wondering if I'd stumbled back to the wrong table, the wrong life. I felt at once rested and relieved the investigation was over, but also vague regret, even a dulled longing to go back, to return to something I couldn't pinpoint—a woman I hadn't realized had bewitched me until she was gone.

Lines of laughter on a face, rude waitresses with bony arms, dark figures hurrying along sidewalks eager to get somewhere, nearby voices filled with dusk, cabs and panhandlers and one drunken girl screeching like a wounded bird—all of it flushed with a warmth and sad beauty I'd never noticed before.

Maybe it was a consequence of reaching the end of the end, finding out the dark, mad, gleaming tale had concluded the only way it *could* in the real world—with mortal people doing mortal things, a father and daughter, facing their deaths.

Because there could be no doubt about what Gallo told me: I'd phoned Sloan-Kettering Hospital, posing as a health insurance agent from a disorganized HR department. After telling a few half-truths to three different assistant department heads, and giving Ashley's Social Security number taken from the missing-person's report—one of the few documents left behind—three different people confirmed it on two different days. Ashley Goncourt had been treated in the pediatric oncology department in 1992 and 1993, 2001 and 2002, and finally in 2004 in conjunction with the University of Texas at Houston, exactly as Gallo had said.

At night I strolled home on the crooked sidewalks, past silent brownstones with lit-up windows filled with lives. Glasses clinking, the street gasping with laughter as the door of a bar was shoved open—these sounds seemed to follow me longer than they ever had before.

I hadn't returned to the Reservoir after seeing Ashley there, but in the aftermath of learning about her sickness, I went back.

There was no hint of her—not in the water or the green lamplight or the biting wind, the shadows that threw themselves at my feet. I ran, lap after lap, and could think only of how she'd gone to the warehouse and what a lonely walk it must have been, up the steps to the edge of the elevator, which was the edge of her life, staring it down.

She'd been dying when she'd appeared here. It made sense, given the way she'd walked. She'd been weak, *in an especially precarious mental state,* according to Inez Gallo.

Even accepting this, still, something gnawed at me. I'd come to believe Ashley had sought me out because she wanted to tell me something—something crucial and real—her circumstances preventing a direct approach. Now even this had an explanation: Gallo had mentioned Ashley's fear, that she might cause physical harm to anyone she came in close proximity to—a fear that could very well have begun when she learned what had happened to Olivia Endicott or the tattoo artist, Larry, when they'd been in her presence.

It had to have been why she stayed away from me.

In all the stories I'd heard, Ashley stood for the truth. She was the antithesis of weak. Even hunting the Spider, she'd sought him only to forgive. To accept now that it'd been delusions that brought Ashley out here, *spinning her straw into gold, a master of manipulation,* as Gallo put it, felt *off.*

What had Ashley wanted me to know?

I took so many laps around the track I lost count, and then, lungs burning, exhausted, I left, jogging down East Eighty-sixth to the subway, and boarded the train, exactly as I had the night I'd seen her.

Staring across the platform, the neon light flat and bright, I wondered if I could manifest through *sheer will* her boots, her red-and-black coat—if she might come one last time, so I could get a clear glimpse of her face—decode, once and for all, the truth behind her.

But there was no one.

Even the sci-fi movie poster that had been there before—the sprinting man with his eyes scribbled out—even he was gone now, replaced with an ad for a romantic comedy starring Cameron Diaz.

She just doesn't get it, read the tagline.

Maybe I should take the hint.

113 | Days later, I packed away the Cordova research—what was *left* of it, anyway—shoved it back inside the cardboard box and the box inside the closet, Septimus quietly looking on.

I took a mountain of dirty clothes to the dry cleaner, including Brad Jackson's herringbone coat. But then, eyeing the sad thing slumped over the counter under piles of my button-downs, I had the sudden paranoid thought that it was the last shred of evidence, my last tie to the insanity of The Peak, and if Brad's coat were cleaned and steam-pressed, encased in plastic with a paper draped over the shoulders reading, *We Love Our Customers!*—gone, too, would be my recollections. So I awkwardly pulled the filthy thing *back out* of the pile, and, returning home, shoved it in the closet behind Ashley's red one, and shut the door.

I wanted to see Sam. I wanted to hear her voice, have her hang heavily on my arm and squint up at me—but Cynthia never returned my calls, not once. I wondered if her silence meant she was working with her lawyers to petition for a new custody arrangement, as she'd threatened to do in the emergency room. Finally, my old divorce attorney called with this very news.

"They set a court date. She wants to restrict visitation."

"Whatever she wants." This appeared to jolt him, as simple acts of kindness *did* to attorneys.

"But you might never see your daughter."

"I want Sam to be safe and happy. We'll leave it at that."

I did secretly go uptown to check on her, one late December afternoon. The day was graying from the cold, giant snowflakes drifting, bewildered, through the air, forgetting to fall. I didn't want Sam to see me, so I remained behind a few parked cars and a FreshDirect truck, watching the gleaming black doors of her school opening, the bundled-up children in coats spilling out onto the sidewalks. To my surprise, Cynthia was there waiting, and after she tucked Sam's hands into black mittens, they took off.

Sam was wearing a new blue coat. Her hair was longer than I remembered, secured in a ponytail under a black velvet hat. She looked more mature, too, quite seriously informing Cynthia of something about her day. I was overcome. Because I saw, suddenly, how it would always be for me, Sam's life unfolding like slides in an old projector I'd always be clicking through in the dark, stunning leaps forward in time—but never the uncut reel.

But she was happy. I could see that. She was perfect.

When they crossed the street, I could make out only their blue and black coats. A surge of yellow cabs and buses flooded Fifth Avenue, and then I couldn't see them anymore.

114 IT ARRIVED ON JANUARY 4: an email from Nora inviting me to her New York theatrical debut at the Flea Theater in that gender-bending off-off-Broadway production of *Hamlette.* She'd done well in her audition and had won the lottery for all New York actors—an actual *paying part.* Granted, she was only *Bernarda,* one of two Elsinore castle guards (renamed from *Bernardo*) who appeared solely in act one, scene one, and she received just $30 per performance—*but still.*

"I'm a real actress now," she wrote.

I went opening night, in a small theater. As soon as the lights went down and the heavy black curtain was noisily hauled aside, there was Nora in blue light, her blond hair in two long braids, climbing up to a rickety castle lookout tower made out of plywood. She was surprisingly good—infusing all of her lines with the comical, wide-eyed guilelessness I'd heard so many times. When she encountered Hamlette's mom's ghost (who in a strange costume choice was wearing a garter belt and white teddy and thus came off as a strung-out spirit who'd sauntered in from not purgatory but the Crazy Horse in Vegas) and Nora tripped and stumbled backward, naïvely announcing, *"'Tis here!"* and *"It was about to speak, when the cock crew!"* the audience erupted with delighted laughter.

The play ran without intermission. When it was finally over—after Ophelio offed himself by throwing back too many Xanax, Hamlette finally had the nerve to off her bitchy stepmom, *and,* at long last, Fortinbrassa and her army of gal pals arrived fashionably late at Elsinore wearing nylon miniskirts straight from the Ice Capades—I remained in my seat.

When the theater emptied, I was surprised to see someone else had remained behind, too.

Hopper. Of course.

He was sitting in the last row in the very back. He must have snuck in after the lights went down.

"McGrath."

Like me, he'd brought Nora a bouquet of flowers, red roses. He'd gotten a haircut. And though he was still wearing his gray wool coat and Converse sneakers, he had on a white button-down shirt, which looked as if he hadn't found it on the floor of his apartment, the circles no longer carved so deeply under his eyes.

"How've you been?" I asked.

He smiled. "Pretty good."

"You *look* good. Have you quit smoking?"

"Not yet." He was about to add something, but his gaze moved behind me, and I turned to see Nora stepping out from the curtain. I was relieved to see she was still sporting the old transvestite's wardrobe—black leggings, one of Moe's purple tuxedo shirts—that she hadn't changed. Because New York could do that to you in no time, streamlining and sanding, polishing and buffing you into something that looked *good,* but like everyone else.

Nora gave us the tightest of hugs and waved goodbye to her cast mates.

"Bye, Riley! You were *amazing* tonight!" (Riley, a pretty bleached blonde, had played Hamlette and delivered "To Be or Not to Be" with all the gravitas of wondering, "To Text or Not to Text.") "Drew, you left your hat on the prop table."

Nora, beaming, amped up on theater energy, pulled on her coat and suggested we all go grab a bite. As we exited the theater, she linked her arms through ours, striding down the sidewalk—Dorothy reunited with Scarecrow and Tin Man.

"Woodward, how've you been? I *missed* you. Oh, wait. How's Septimus?"

"Immortal, as usual."

"You both brought *flowers*? You guys got chivalrous all of a sudden?"

We went to The Odeon, a French brasserie on West Broadway open late. We piled into the booth, Nora staring at our faces like they were foreign newspapers she'd finally got her hands on, filled with the latest news from home.

"You both look *good*. *Oh*." She yanked off a glove to display the inside of her right wrist, across it a small tattoo of three words.

Do I Dare?

"So I never forget her." She bit her bottom lip, glancing nervously at Hopper. "You don't mind, do you?"

He shook his head. "Ash would have loved it."

"I went to Rising Dragon for the tattoo. But that guy we talked to, Tommy? He moved back to Vancouver, so this *other* guy did it. It hurt like *nothing*. But it was worth it."

I'd completely forgotten Tommy, the tattoo artist. *Then Gallo had sent him on his merry way, too.*

Nora took my startled look for disapproval. "I knew you wouldn't like it. But it's *tiny*. And I can cover it up with makeup. And before my wedding I can always get it lasered."

"What wedding?" I demanded.

"*One* day. *If* I have one. But Woodward, will you give me away? I was thinking that I didn't have anyone to do it."

"*Yes*. Provided it's twenty years from now."

We ended up staying out until five in the morning, getting drunk and loud, leaving Odeon for some unmarked speakeasy in a Chinatown Laundromat where Hopper was a regular; leaving that for an after-hours club where Nora's friend Maxine was a hostess; leaving that for some dive bar on Essex Street to play pool and take over the jukebox—playing Joy Division's "Love Will Tear Us Apart" ("This is our anthem," Nora said, as Hopper, displaying remarkable dancing skills, spun her around the room). They told me what had happened in their lives since those two months we'd spent holed up together, chasing the truth about Ashley—and Cordova.

Nora was fully committed to conquering off-off-Broadway—fitting in auditions posted in *Backstage* with a full-time job at Healthy Bakes. (Healthy Bakes, the brainchild of Josephine, Nora's hippie landlord, was a highly appetizing vegan, sugar-and-gluten-free, macrobiotic cupcake shop in the East Village.) Nora showed us her new head shots, which featured her eyeing us over her shoulder, her hair straightened and cascading. *Nora Edge Halliday,* the picture announced in elaborate cursive. If the headshot had a voice, it would be a husky British whisper on *Masterpiece Theatre.*

"Do you *really* need the Edge?" I asked her. "Nora Halliday is more than enough."

"The Edge gives it an edge," said Hopper.

Nora lifted her chin. "You're outnumbered, Woodward. As usual."

She leaned over the pool table and, squinting with concentration, shot the cue ball. Three solids ricocheted into opposite pockets. Apparently, there was a billiards room at Terra Hermosa she'd never told me about.

"I figure I'll give it a good ten years to try and make it big," she went on, moving around the table to line up her next shot. "Then I'm getting out while I *still can.* I'm going to buy a farm with hills and donkeys. Have some kids. You'll both come visit. We could have reunions. Wherever in the world we are, we'll come together this one amazing day."

"I like it," said Hopper.

"I have a boyfriend named Jasper," she added.

"Jasper?" I said. "He sounds like he highlights his hair."

"He's a first-class person. You'd like him."

"How old?"

"Twenty-two."

"But an *old* twenty-two?"

She nodded and glanced away, suddenly shy, and stepped around the table so I couldn't see her face.

Hopper, as it turned out, had been about to leave New York altogether when he'd received Nora's email, so he delayed his departure by a week to have this last chance to see the two of us. He'd given up his apartment. He was heading to South America.

"South *America?"* asked Nora, as if he'd said he was going to the moon.

"Yeah. I'm going to find my mom."

In typical Hopper fashion, he chose not to elaborate further on this tantalizing premise, though I remembered something he'd said about his mom, that she was involved in some strange missionary work, the afternoon I'd first talked to him in his apartment.

Nora nibbled her thumbnail, perched on the corner of the pool table.

"And after that what are you going to do?" she asked.

"After that . . ." He smiled. "Something really good."

We ordered shots of Patrón and danced and reloaded the jukebox— my *old man vintage music,* as Nora called it, The Doors, Harry Nilsson's "Everybody's Talkin'," and Elvis Costello's "Beyond Belief" interspersed with Hopper's hip selections like Beach House's "Real Love" and M83's "Skin of the Night."

At every moment, I felt Ashley was with us, the invisible fourth member of our little party. I sensed we were all acutely aware of her, though we didn't need to mention her by name. It was obvious Nora and Hopper had resolved her life and death in their heads. They believed in her without question, without doubt. She'd made the world all right for them, even better. *They still believed the myth,* I reasoned, *the myth of the devil's curse. They were still living in an enchanted world— Ashley, not struck with cancer, but a wild avenging angel, and Cordova, not catatonic in a nursing home, but an evil king who'd fled to the unknown.* For the rest of their lives, they'd have this magical reality to turn to when their car keys inexplicably moved across the room, when they read stories about children who went missing without a trace, when someone broke their heart for no good reason.

But of course, they'd think. *It's the magic.*

It felt as if we'd been to war together. Deep in a jungle, alone, I had relied on them, these strangers. They'd held me up in ways only people could. When it was over, an ending that never felt like an ending, only an exhausted draw, we went our separate ways. But we were bonded forever by the history of it, the simple fact they'd seen the raw side of me and me of them, a side no one, not even closest friends or family had ever seen before, or probably ever would.

And in between the laughter and the jokes, the music, a long stretch of silence fell over us. We were sitting side by side on a wooden bench underneath a dartboard and a Coors Light neon sign. I saw the moment for what it was—the chance to tell them the truth.

I stared at Hopper's profile, his head tipped way back against the wall, the gold strands of Nora's hair stuck to her flushed cheek, the words shouting in my head.

You can't imagine what she hid from us. It was the ultimate triumph of life over death—never to give in to her illness, never to stop living.

It suddenly occurred to me that perhaps Ashley had not been so delusional in the last days of her life, a truth Inez Gallo had been so eager that I accept. Maybe she, displaying that searing intuition for people and a heart not even Gallo could take away from her—maybe she'd somehow intended this moment. Perhaps she'd planned with her death, the three of us would find each other. *It was why she chose the warehouse. She knew I'd go there looking for clues—and encounter Hopper who'd be wondering about the return address on the envelope. And why else would she leave Nora her coat?*

I realized the moment had drifted away. Hopper rolled off the bench, shuffling across the bar to put another song on the jukebox, which had gone silent, and Nora went off in search of the bathroom.

I remained where I was. *That had to be it.*

I'd tell them both the truth one day. But now, tonight, they could keep their myth.

Hours later, the bar was closing, turning up glaring lights, erasing the mirage of forever. It was time to go. I was bombed. Outside, on the sidewalk, I embraced the two of them, announcing to the empty city— New York City *finally* a little drowsy and at a loss for words—they were two of the best people I'd ever met.

"We're family!" I shouted at the walk-ups, my voice half swallowed by the deserted street.

"We heard ya, Aretha," said Hopper.

"But we *are*," Nora said. "We always will be."

"With you two in it?" I went on. "This world has nothing to worry about! You hear me?" Nora, giggling, put her arm around me, trying to pry me off the telephone pole I was hugging like Gene Kelly in *Singin' in the Rain.*

"You're wasted," she said.

"Of course I'm wasted."

"It's time to go home."

"Woodward *never* goes home."

Filing down the sidewalk, we fell silent, knowing it was coming within minutes, our parting, knowing we might not see each other for a long time.

We hailed a cab. That's what you did in New York at the close of a night, cramming together into your filthy yellow stagecoach with the faceless chauffeur, who delivered you, one by one, relatively unscathed, to your quiet street. The night would be filed away somewhere, one day brought out and dusted off, remembered as one of the best moments. We piled in, Nora in the middle, her now-exhausted roses slung over her knees. Hopper was crashing on a friend's couch on Delancey Street.

"Right here," he said to the driver, tapping the glass.

The cab pulled over, and he turned to me, extending his hand.

"Keep looking for the mermaids," he told me in a hoarse voice. He lowered his head so I wouldn't see the tears in his eyes. "Keep fighting for them."

I nodded and hugged him as hard as I could. He then kissed Nora gently on her forehead and climbed out. He didn't immediately go inside, but stood on the sidewalk watching us drive away, a dark figure drenched in orange streetlight. Nora and I watched out the back windshield—the moving picture we had to keep our eyes on, reluctant to blink or breathe, as it'd become only a memory in seconds.

He held up his left hand to us, a wave and a salute. And the taxi rounded the corner.

"Now we're heading to Stuyvesant Street where it intersects East Tenth," I told the driver. "Close to Saint Marks."

Nora turned to me, eyes wide.

"You told me where you live," I said.

"I didn't. I purposefully *didn't*."

"But you *did*, Bernstein. You're getting absentminded in your old age."

She huffed, crossing her arms. "You spied on me."

"Nope."

"You did. I can tell."

"Please. I have *better* things to do with my time than worry about Bernsteins."

She scowled, but when the taxi pulled over in front of the brownstone she didn't move, only stared ahead.

"You won't forget me?" she whispered.

"It'd be physically impossible."

"You promise?"

"You should really think about coming with a warning Do-Not-Remove-This-Tag. You'll fall for her against your will, like it or not."

"You'll be *all right*?"

She turned to me, really asking it, worried.

"Of course. And so will you."

She nodded, as if trying to convince herself, and then suddenly she smiled as if thinking of an old joke I'd made, one she was finding funny only now. She leaned forward and kissed my cheek. And then, as if some spell were about to break, she streaked out of the cab, door slamming, up the stoop with her leaden purse and arms full of roses.

She unlocked the door and stepped inside. But then, she slowly turned back, her hair gilded by some hidden light behind her.

She smiled one last time. The door closed and the street went still.

"That's it," I whispered, more to myself than the cabdriver. I turned around, sitting back against the seat, pale yellow light washing over me as we pulled away.

115 It was a fluke. But then, life *is*.

It was a few days after my night out with Hopper and Nora, when I'd just started recovering from my hangover. I was cleaning my office. I let Septimus out of his cage, so he might fly around for a little exercise. I yanked the leather couch away from the wall and noticed, wedged along the floor, the three black-and-white reversing candles Cleo had given us.

I'd forgotten all about them. They must have fallen there, unseen, when the room was ransacked.

We'd barely burned them, preoccupied with everything else. *But why not finish the job?* I set them on a plate and lit all three. Hours later, when I was on the couch with a scotch and *The Wall Street Journal,* I glanced up and saw they'd burned down to nothing, just a sliver of white wax. The first and then the second extinguished, as if waiting for my full attention, the wicks flaring orange for a moment before going out. The third held on, the flame twisting as if refusing to let go, to die, but then it went dark, too.

I realized my cell was ringing.

"Hello?" I answered, not bothering to check the caller ID. My accountant was due to call back to inform me my life savings was on its last leg and it was time to either apply for a new teaching position or consider another investigation, one that actually paid money.

"Scott? It's Cynthia."

Fear instantly gripped me. "Is Sam all right?"

"Yes. She's wonderful. Well, no, actually, that's not true." She took a deep breath. "Is this a good time to talk?"

"What's the matter?"

She sounded upset. "I'm sorry. Not returning your calls. I thought it was the right thing to do. But she's inconsolable. Scott this, Scott that. *Crying*. I can't take it." Cynthia herself seemed on the verge of tears. "Does this Saturday work for you to spend some time with her?"

"Saturday works."

She sniffed. "Maybe she can stay the night."

"I'd like that."

"Good. How are you, by the way?"

"I'm great *now*. How are you?"

"Good." She laughed gently. "So, Saturday, then? Jeannie's back. She's recovered from mono."

"Saturday."

We hung up. I was unable to take my eyes off those candles.

They were smoking rather innocently, three long gray threads embroidering the air.

116 It was with the acute sense that a miracle had been worked, when on Saturday, Sam arrived on my doorstep with Jeannie in tow.

It was a clear winter day with all the bounce and bright-eyed resilience of a teenager, sky blue, sun blinding, the two-day-old snow crunching like cake icing under our boots. I pulled out the stops: lemon and ricotta pancakes at Sarabeth's; an expedition through FAO Schwarz where Sam was quite taken with a twelve-hundred-dollar life-sized African elephant from the Safari Collection (*his coat meticulously hand cut by seasoned craftsmen,* according to the tag), which Jeannie promptly nanny-nixed me from purchasing. We lost Jeannie after ice cream at the Plaza; crashing from a sugar high, she opted to skip the day's crown jewel—ice-skating at Wollman Rink in Central Park—meeting us back at my place.

"Please be careful," Jeannie said, giving me a hard, knowing look before collapsing into a taxi.

But it was smooth sailing, with just one rough patch: fitting Sam's left foot into her skate. It seemed to get chewed up somewhere around the ankle and she screwed up her face, which prompted me to whisk it off and wrestle the skate *wide* open, doing a bit of phony straining like I was a prime contender for Mr. Universe—Sam giggled quite a bit— and then we hit the ice, father and daughter, hand in hand. It was packed with tourists—they were too giddy to be native New Yorkers— but once we were swallowed by the mob, it was as if we were inside a sea of joy. Everywhere—it was colored parkas and laughter, sizzling *woosh* noises as Central Park South and Fifth Avenue towered over us.

It was when we walked down the cobblestone sidewalk along Fifth that the good stuff happened. Sam disclosed the name of her best friend: Delphine. The girl sounded *beyond chic* at six, born in Paris.

"Delphine comes to school in a limousine," Sam noted.

"Good for Delphine. How do *you* get to school?"

"Mommy walks me."

Thank Christ, Bruce was keeping his Bentley under wraps. I made a mental note to keep an eye on old *Delphine.* It sounded like she'd be climbing out of bedroom windows in no time.

Sam wanted to show me her new shin guards and soccer cleats and had recently learned the difference between Fahrenheit and Celsius. She also very much liked her new PE teacher, a young woman named Lucy who was happily married to Mr. Lucas, who taught earth science. Sam spoke quietly and categorically on each of these subjects, explaining them with senior official authority, me the cheerful ignorant underling. She also mentioned quite a few proper names—*Clara,* a dog (or very unfortunate boy) named *Maestro, Mr. Frank,* something called *The Tall Tale Circle*—as if I knew precisely who and what each of these things were. And I was moved by this, because it meant Sam sensed there'd never been a moment I *wasn't* with her, that I was always seeing what she saw.

After we greeted two passing dachshunds, Sam announced she was ready to go home. In the taxi, I asked if she'd had a good day. She nodded.

"And honey?"

She was yawning.

"Remember the toy Mom found in your coat pocket?"

It was an intriguing enough question for Sam to stare at me.

"The, uh, black snake?" I clarified, as casually as I could.

"The dragon Mommy got mad about?" asked Sam.

"Yes, the *dragon* Mommy got mad about. Where'd you get it?"

"Ashley."

I did my best to look nonchalant. "And where did you meet Ashley?"

"With Jeannie in the playground."

With Jeannie in the playground. "When was this?"

"A long time ago." Sam yawned again, her eyes comically heavy.

"Did you speak to her?"

She shook her head. "She was too far away."

"How far away?"

"She was by cars and I was on the swing."

"But how did she give you the dragon?"

"She left it." She said it with a teacher's exasperation, as if it'd already been explained many times.

"When? The next day?"

She nodded vaguely.

"Okay. You're the most astute judge of character I've ever met, and I greatly value your opinion. What'd you think of her? Ashley."

She smiled faintly at the mention of the name. But her eyes were closing.

"She was a magical . . ." she whispered.

"What? Sam?"

But she was out, head lolling against my arm, hands on her lap as if holding an invisible clump of violets. At Perry Street I carried her upstairs so she could sleep, though Jeannie woke her up at seven to put her in her cloud pajamas. We watched *Finding Nemo.* I made eggwhite omelets. When Jeannie went upstairs to take out her contacts, which seemed to be code for calling a boyfriend, Sam sat eating quietly at the kitchen table.

It was the chance to ask her more about Ashley, to fathom how on earth it had happened, but then, taking the seat beside her, she looked at me, chewing slowly with her mouth tightly closed, as if she knew very well what I was about to ask and she found it sad that I still did not understand. Swallowing, she set down her fork and took my right hand, patting it like it was a lonely rabbit in a pet store, before reaching for her glass of milk.

And I realized—*of course*—Sam had told me everything.

117 | SHE WAS A MAGICAL.

When I said goodbye to Sam the following day, I gave her the tightest hug and kissed her cheek, and then her hot head.

"I love you more than—how much again?" I asked her.

"The sun plus the *moon*."

I embraced Cynthia. She wasn't expecting it.

"You're glorious," I whispered into her hair. "And you always were. I'm sorry I never said it."

She stared after me in shock as I made my way out of the lobby, smiling at the two doormen, blatantly eavesdropping.

"Did you get that? *This woman is glorious.*"

The moment I got home, I pulled out the old sagging cardboard box again, spreading the few papers out on the floor.

What had I learned when I'd been trapped inside that hexagon box—about myself? *You couldn't even see where it opened.* It was a hint that I *wasn't* seeing all of it, not the full picture.

Maybe I still had it all wrong. Maybe I still wasn't seeing something that even Sam had seen. And Nora. And Hopper.

All three of them believed in Ashley. And I didn't.

But what if I did believe as blindly as Hopper, Nora—and Sam? Was it blindness, or did they all see in a way that I didn't? What if I punted reason and common sense into the air, let them soar dumbly out of sight, and believed in witchcraft, in black magic, in Ashley? Burning the reversing candles had brought Sam back into my life. Yes, one could argue it was simply a coincidence that the moment they'd extinguished, Cynthia within a matter of seconds had called—but what if it wasn't?

Maybe it was the black magic again rearing its head, insisting it was real.

What if I took a leap of faith and simply accepted that the truth behind this entire investigation resided *not* with Inez Gallo, but with Ashley? What if she hadn't been in an especially precarious mental state? The truth about her illness meant nothing. Why couldn't cancer be yet another symptom of the devil's curse, as Ashley herself had believed? I might not have collected sufficient evidence up at The Peak— the stained boy's shirt and those animal bones—but that did not vindicate Cordova from what I'd suspected, that he practiced black magic with the townspeople, that his night films weren't fictions, but real live horrors, that he'd used children to try and free his daughter from the curse, possibly even crossing the line into hurting one of them, as the Spider had hinted.

There's nothing Gallo won't do to protect him. I'd read it on the Blackboards. Yet, oddly enough, she'd chosen *not* to protect him from me. She'd directed me straight toward him.

Or *had* she?

Beckman had warned me that I might encounter a figure stationed at the intersection between life and death. *It will be a decoy. A substitute to grant freedom to the* real thing. *He's Cordova's favorite character. He's always there, when Cordova's mind is at work, no matter what.*

That figure could very well have been that man back at the nursing home, the stranger I'd sat down beside.

Bill Smith.

He could have been anyone—anyone with a hefty enough frame and build, just senile and soundless enough not to be aware he was passing for Cordova. That wheel tattoo wasn't definitive proof. It could have been drawn there—even tattooed by Gallo into the man's hand in the middle of the night, when no nurse was watching. There was no security at Enderlin Estates, nothing stopping Gallo from doing what she wanted to whatever elderly stranger she chose, so he might serve as a feasible stand-in for her lord and master—*thereby granting freedom to the real thing.*

She'd wanted him to go free.

Perhaps Gallo was Cordova's paid executioner, waiting for anyone who got too close to his whereabouts, who knew too much. Maybe she'd been waiting for me to come clamoring up onto that final wooden platform, and it was her job to tuck the burlap bag over my head and then the noose, ruthlessly heaving the ground out from under me, sending me flying, kicking, gasping back to *reality,* where she was so certain I'd stay.

"I live in the real world," she'd announced flatly. "And so do *you.*"

She'd meant it as an order, a directive. She was giving me instructions, certain I'd follow them on my own accord, because I was a realist, a skeptic, a practical man. And yet I'd noticed, too, there was something faintly scathing about the way she'd said *real world,* as if it were the most miserable of life sentences.

Ashley's history will now forever remain where she wished it, where she believed in her heart it always was—beyond reason, between heaven and earth, land and sky, suspended much closer to legend than ordinary life— where the rest of us, including you, Mr. McGrath, must remain.

Where the mermaids sing, I'd muttered.

Mermaids. There was something about that word that had bothered Gallo. And if it unnerved her, it could only mean one thing: It was too close for her comfort to the real Cordova.

It took me all night, all day, and one more night after that to find the connection. I didn't sleep. I didn't need to. I retyped the notes that had been stolen, detailing every witness we'd tracked down who'd encountered Ashley, everything I'd encountered at The Peak, every word I'd heard whispered about Cordova.

When I did see it, I realized, it had been right in front of me, all along.

Gatehouse. Mansion. Lake. Stables. Workshop. Lookout. Trophy. Pincoya Negro. Cemetery. Mrs. Peabody's. Laboratory. The Z. Crossroads.

The word had been scribbled above one of the thirteen blackened doorways down in the underground tunnels at The Peak.

Pincoya. It was a kind of mermaid.

"Long blond hair, incomparable beauty, luscious and sensual, she rises from the depths of the sea," read the entry on Wikipedia. "She bestows riches or choking scarcity, and all of the mortals on land live in answer to her whims." The creature had been spotted in one remote place on Earth and only one—an isolated island off the coast of South America called Chiloé.

La Pincoya was just one of a throng of mythical creatures that haunted the island's land and shores, which remained shrouded in heavy mist and rain eleven months of the year. It was a bleak and inhospitable place, one of the remotest islands on Earth, an island with a legendary history of witchcraft.

I suddenly remembered, a detail Cleo had mentioned back at Enchantments the first time we'd gone to see her, when she was inspecting the materials we'd given her of Ashley's Black Bone killing curse.

I see some dark brown sand in here, some seaweed, too, she'd told us. *She must have picked this up someplace exotic.*

There wasn't much information about this island, Chiloé, but when I was reading a Spanish backpacker's blog, I came across another connection.

Puerto Montt.

It was the last city on Chile's mainland, before the country breaks up like a cookie into hundreds of crumbled islands. The backpacker had traveled from Puerto Montt to *another* town, Pargua, and from Pargua took the ferry to Chiloé. The only way to access the island was by boat, apart from a few rudimentary airfields.

I knew I'd recently read about the city and after an hour of searching, I found where: in *The Natural Huntsman,* the article posted on the Blackboards about Rachel Dempsey's vanishing from Nepal—Rachel Dempsey, who'd played Leigh in *La Douleur.* Although there'd been no sign of her after she'd disappeared from her hunting expedition, nine days after she was reported missing, her satellite phone had been turned on in Santiago, Chile, and she'd made a brief phone call to a number that was traced to Puerto Montt.

I'd retyped the interview with Peg Martin in Washington Square Park and recalled Martin had mentioned that Theo Cordova had been carrying on an affair with a woman ten years older than he, a woman named Rachel who had appeared in one of Cordova's films.

Checking the dates, I saw Rachel Dempsey would have been twenty-seven in the spring of 1993, the year Peg Martin attended the picnic. Theo would have been only sixteen, an eleven-year age difference.

It was close enough. So Rachel and Theo had seemingly been together. But what, exactly, had Rachel Dempsey planned for her hunting expedition in Nepal—to vanish off the face of the Earth? Disappear without a trace so she might resurface somewhere on that island in order to—*what*? Reunite in paradise with her lover, Theo? What was on that island?

The houses there had a singular style of architecture. Called *palafitos,* they were modest cottages built atop rickety stilts and painted vibrant pinks, blues, and reds, so they resembled long-legged water bugs swarming the coastline, which was not a tropical paradise, but thorny and gray, with sharp rocks and dark water that seeped across the beach.

I'd seen those stilt houses before.

It was when I'd been inside *Wait for Me Here,* in the Reinhart family greenhouse, in Popcorn's work shed. I'd noticed a postcard tacked to a bulletin board—those very same stilt houses pictured on the front of it. Thankfully I'd the prescience to take it down and read the back, where someone had scribbled four words.

Someday soon you'll come.

There was more: The churches on Chiloé looked like no others in the world, a combination of European Jesuit culture and the native traditions of the indigenous people on the island. They were austere, covered in wooden tiles like flaking dragon scales and jutting steeples topped with a spindly cross. Like the *palafitos,* they, too, were painted wild colors, though this brightness evoked not jubilation, but the sinister cheer of a clown's face.

I'd seen one somewhere before. I raced back over to the floor, trawling the papers until I found it.

In the *Vanity Fair* article, Ashley's freshman-year roommate had mentioned, when Ashley abruptly moved out with no word, all she'd left were *three Polaroids,* which had slipped, forgotten, behind her dresser. The snapshots had been included in the article—artifacts of Ashley's lost existence, portholes into her world. I'd barely glanced at them.

Now, staring down at the first one, I felt light-headed with shock.

It featured a small, morose-looking church. It wasn't an exact match, but it had the same architecture as all the others on the island.

The second Polaroid featured a massive black boulder on a beach, seagulls circling overhead. The boulder had a mystical hole through the center, as if God had punched his thumb through it, making an impish void in the world. I didn't recognize it.

But the *third* featured a flock of black-necked swans, one of them carrying a cygnet on its back. *Black-necked swans,* I read on Wikipedia, were prevalent in South America. Yet they bred and hatched their young only in a few specific areas, one of which was Chile's Zona Sur, which included Chiloé.

Ashley could very well have been on the island. It seemed to have been where she'd taken the Polaroids.

I opened up Google Earth, staring at a satellite view. Parts of the main island, *Isla Grande,* and almost all of the smaller islands around it freckling the blue sea were concealed by silvered clouds.

Had all this evidence been silently leading me there?

Gallo had been so adamant about keeping me down in the *real world, ordinary life,* making sure that I didn't keep chasing Cordova— into what?

Warning voices echoed resoundingly through my head, one of the loudest of which was that old grizzled alcoholic reporter back at the bar in Nairobi. Slumped over his drink, wearing his stained khaki jacket and fatigues, he'd warned me about the fates of the three reporters who'd worked the cursed case, the case without an end, the tapeworm.

One had gone mad. Another quit the story and a week later, hanged himself in a Mombasa hotel room. The third simply disappeared into thin air, leaving his family and a prime post at an Italian newspaper.

"It's infected," the man had mumbled. "*The story.* Some are, you know."

I sat back thoughtfully in my desk chair. Septimus, I saw with disbelief, had chosen to fly as I'd never seen him do before. He was crashing drunkenly into the ceiling and windows, the *Le Samouraï* poster, his wings fluttering against the glass in excitement—or was it alarm at what I was about to do, where I was about to go?

Because I noticed now, the fates of those three reporters were not unlike the actors who'd worked alongside Cordova, those who, once they left The Peak, never returned to ordinary lives, but scattered to the outer reaches of the world, most never heard from again, becoming unfathomable and unseen, beyond reach.

It was happening to me now.

Wasn't it? I was following in their footsteps, sending myself to the outer reaches of the world. Was I fleeing something or had I been set free?

I wouldn't know until I saw what was there, if anything at all.

118 FOUR DAYS LATER, I took a flight to Santiago, Chile, and another to Puerto Montt.

I strode through *El Tepual* airport to the baggage claim, brimming with children, families embracing, signs for INFORMACION and Eurocar. I found my army duffel sitting alone on the revolving carousel, as if it'd been awaiting me for months.

I took a taxi to the bus station and boarded the first one to Pargua. It was packed, half the seats occupied by rowdy boys in white kneesocks, some madrigal singing group manned by a sweaty-faced director who looked ready to quit. An old woman took the seat beside me, giving me a wary look, but once she dozed off, her head bobbed gently against my shoulder like a buoy in choppy seas. Our bus, an old yellowed beast with dirty rainbows emblazoned up its sides, slung and bumped its way through the streets, past Bavarian A-frame chalets and busy cafés out into the countryside.

The ferry to Chiloé Island left every twenty minutes. It cost a dollar. As we took off across the wind-chopped sea, I was surrounded by a large and boisterous group of tourists crowding the top deck. An Italian woman was trying to keep her thrashing hair out of her face as her boyfriend took a picture. He noticed me and motioned with a grin if I'd take one of them together. As I obliged, I couldn't help but wonder if someday someone might track them down and show them my photo as I'd showed Ashley's.

Do you recognize him? Did he speak to you? What was he wearing? What was his demeanor? Did he strike you as strange?

Standing along the railing, staring out, I could see the island far ahead. It was revealing itself like a woman stepping out from behind a curtain, unhurried and deliberate: deep-green rolling hills, white mist streaking the shoreline, soft lights twinkling through the vegetation, telephone poles with tangled wires, a homely beach. For a minute, a large black-and-white bird, some type of stormy petrel, flew alongside the ferry, very close to where I stood, diving up and down, calling out in one shattering screech before veering away on a new gust of wind, swallowed by the sky.

We unloaded in Chacao, a frazzled village with the neglected countenance of a place people were constantly leaving. There, with many of the same people from the ferry, I boarded another bus to Castro, the largest town on the island, where I checked into the hotel, the *Unicornio Azul*. It was hard to miss: bright pink building on a wet gray street. I'd read it was lively, popular with locals and tourists traveling cheap, known for good food and English conversation. My room had faded blue wallpaper, a cot only *slightly* larger than the massive Santiago telephone book provided on the bedside table. I took a shower standing beside the toilet (the bathroom the size of a telephone booth), and then, clean-shaven, went downstairs to find the dining room. I ordered a pisco sour, what the waitress explained was the local drink, and when she lingered, asking if I was Australian, I took out the *Vanity Fair* article and inquired if, by some small chance, she recognized the landmarks in the pictures.

My question caused a great deal of intrigue.

It wasn't a minute before two fellow diners, as well as the Dutch bartender, were crowded around my table, hashing over the Polaroids—and probably *me*—in Spanish. The consensus was that, though no one recognized the tiny church, one of the locals—a petulant dark little man who, at the waitress's urging, waddled awkwardly over to us, hinting he did better in water—claimed to have seen the black boulder with the hole somewhere along the coast south of Quicaví when he was a little boy. (The man, it should be noted, looked to be in his late seventies.)

"Quicaví? How do I get there?" I asked.

But the man only jutted out his chin, grimacing as if I'd just insulted him, and shuffled back over to his table.

The waitress leaned in with an apologetic look. "The *Chilote,* locals, we're *muy superticiosa* about Quicaví. It's north. About an hour's drive."

"Why are you superstitious about Quicaví?"

"That's where the man arrives."

"What man?"

She widened her eyes, as if unsure how to begin to answer, and swiftly moved off. "Just don't go at night," she offered over her shoulder.

The Dutch bartender suggested I rent a car from his friend down the road to reach Quicaví before nightfall—*before nightfall* seemed the most crucial part of the directions—which was why, not an hour later, I was behind the wheel of a green four-wheel-drive Suzuki Samurai dating back to the eighties, heading down a twisting road with no shoulder and a width that barely fit two cars. I had my passport on me, all of my money, both dollars and Chilean pesos, my cell, a switchblade, and Popcorn's compass.

As I drove, checking the map and the compass, indicating I was driving northeast, the island seemed to shake loose around me. Undulating hills, horses galloping alone in fields—I passed an unmanned goat procession and two young boys escorting a sheep. I kept picturing my abandoned room back at the Unicornio Azul, as if it were a newly minted crime-scene photo imprinted in my head: my army duffel unzipped on the bed, clothes hastily thrown inside, the itinerary from Expedia in the inside pocket, red toothbrush on the edge of the sink, tube of Colgate Total indented from my hand, and, finally, the cruddy mirror that had held the last known sighting of my face. I wondered, suddenly, if I should have left a note, something for Sam, a small clue—*just in case.* I'd left Septimus with her, assuring Cynthia I'd be traveling only for a few weeks, so Sam would know I was coming back.

And I was.

The Suzuki began to gripe about some of the hills, and when we faced a particularly steep one—the road's pavement had given out long ago, now it was dirt and rocks—I switched on the four-wheel drive, flooring it. This killed the engine. I pushed it to the shoulder of the road and began to walk.

As if by black magic, a boy in a truck passed me, backed up, and offered me a ride. He spoke no English, the radio playing Rod Stewart. Reaching the apparent edge of Quicaví, a thin sloping road splintering with dark houses—all of them leaning downhill as if desperate to reach the ocean, visible at the end—the boy dropped me off and continued on.

It *was* beginning to get dark, spitting light rain. I made a right onto another road, which led me into the heart of Quicaví. There was nothing overtly sinister about the town—cafés advertised free Internet and Pepsi; a large pig grazed in front of a grocery store. And yet every shop at ten minutes after six had dark windows, signs on the doors reading CERRADO. All that appeared to be open was a restaurant called Café Romeo, a few people hunched over the tables inside, and when I reached the beach, a shack at the very end, what looked to be some sort of cantina, its sharply pitched roof lit with lights.

I headed toward it across the sand, which was rocky and black, the water sluggishly lapping the shore. I realized with surprise I was alone out here. I ran through the last forty hours in my head, noting that starting with JFK airport at five A.M. some two days ago, until *now*, the number of people around me had been gradually dwindling—as if I'd walked into a roaring party and now, looking around, I saw I was the last guest left.

I reached the shack, and when I looked up, reading the weathered sign over the dark door, I stopped dead, stunned.

La Pincoya Negro. Black mermaid. That exact phrase had been scribbled above one of the doorways in the underground tunnels at The Peak. *If I'd walked through it, would it have taken me here?*

"*Quiere barquito?*"

I turned. A scrawny old man was standing far behind me, close to the water beside a stake in the sand, a trio of weathered boats tied to it. He was the only other person out here. He started toward me and I could see he had a kind smile, missing a few teeth, oil-splattered slacks rolled to his shins, and wisps of gray hair strung across his tanned head, as if a bit of sea mist still clung there.

I unfolded the *Vanity Fair* article, showing him the Polaroids.

The man nodded with obvious recognition at the church, saying something I couldn't understand, which sounded like, "*Buta Chauques. Isla Buta Chauques.*" When he saw the boulder with the hole, he grinned.

"*Sí, sí, sí. La trampa de sirena.*"

He repeated the phrase, his parched lips twitching in excitement. I did the rudimentary translation in my head. *The trap for the mermaids?* The trap *of* the mermaids? I nodded in my confusion and he, taking it for some kind of agreement, grinned and lurched back over to his boats. He untied the largest and began to drag it toward the water.

"No!" I called out to him. "You misunderstood."

But he was jerking it with surprising strength by the bow, the boat's propeller digging into the sand as if trying to resist.

"Hey, forget it! *Mañana!*"

The man made no sign of having heard me. Knee-deep in the water now, he was stooped over, yanking the starter cord.

I fell silent, watching him, and then found myself turning, staring back at the way I'd come.

There were a few lights, back at the end of that road. They looked lively and soft, and suddenly I was filled with longing, as if around the corners of those dark houses I might find Perry Street and my old life, all that was known to me and familiar, all that I loved, if only I had the inclination to walk back there. Yet as close as they appeared, they seemed also to be receding, warm rooms I'd already passed through, the doorways gone.

The man had managed to turn over the motor, thick smoke streaming out, a deep rumble tearing through the wind clattering across the rooftops of the shops behind me.

I walked to the boat and climbed in. An inch of seawater slurped in the hull, but the old man was unconcerned. Taking his position beside the engine, he unfolded a blue cap from his shirt pocket, pulled it low over his eyes, and with a single nod at me of evident pride, he began to steer us away from the shore.

We hadn't gone two minutes when I spotted deep green, seemingly uninhabited islands surfacing like giant whales to my left. I assumed we'd stop at one, but the man kept driving us past, one after the other, until I saw there was absolutely nothing left in front of us, not a single landmass, nothing—only a black churning ocean and a sky, equally empty.

"How much longer?" I shouted, turning around.

But the man only held up a grizzled hand, muttering something voided by the wind, which seemed to charge his dirty gray shirt with volts of current, revealing a frame as withered as an old tree.

Maybe he was Charon, ferryman of the River Styx, transporting all newly dead souls into the underworld.

I turned back, staring ahead, trapped in the feeling that something was about to appear and the horror that nothing ever would. We con-

swarming not only around the boulder but most of the shoreline, feasting on something scattered across the rocks. The rain began to fall harder, so I took off, taking refuge under the foliage fringing the beach.

I noticed, just a few yards away, a plank jutting across the sand.

A series of boards had been flung over a muddy path leading straight back into the forest. I checked the compass, the needle resolutely pointing east, and then stepped onto the wood, the mud underneath belching from my weight. I followed it, instantly hit with stagnant air, humid and thick, but also something else—a rush, a sensation that I was sliding toward something, being funneled into a hole I couldn't climb out of and shouldn't try. Twisted branches wound around one another growing so dense all that was left of the rain was the sound of it, like a crowd whispering overhead. I began to walk faster, and the walk became a run, the run a sprint, the uneven planks hitting my feet, some snapping in half, sending me knee-deep in mud. I didn't stop, streaking past spider ferns and bobbing flowers, waist-thick tree roots climbing out on either side of the path, as if trying to escape. My only company appeared to be a single bird, which dogged me like a final warning, fluttering, chirping in the overgrowth until it flew right at me, black wings grazing my cheek, emitting a sharp cry before diving again into the dark. The pathway was becoming an incline, growing steeper as if trying to shake me off, but I didn't stop, ascending so rapidly, after a while I couldn't feel the ground under my feet.

There was a house ahead. Nestled in the trees, it looked like so many others I'd seen on the main island, battered, covered in wooden shingles, a splintered shutter dangling from a window. Gasping to catch my breath, I slung myself up onto the porch, grabbed the rusted knob, and opened the door.

It was a deserted room—stark wooden furniture, dim light, an old ceiling fan whirling overhead.

A large oil painting hung directly across from me on the wall. It was a man's portrait, his warped and chalky face retreating into a black background as if melting. I stepped inside, then froze, my eyes drawn to movement in the far corner. There, by a wall of dark windows, sat two leather-and-wood mission chairs like waiting thrones. On a small table beside one, a *cigarette* was burning—*Murad,* no doubt—white ribbons of smoke uncoiling off the end.

tinued on, I didn't know how long. I couldn't release
sides of the boat to check my watch or the compass, the
violent, ocean spray soaking me as they turned upon the
ing the boat. Slowly I began to surrender to the possibilit
on and on like this, until the gas ran out, and when it d
motor would clear its throat like an exhausted opera singe
stage, and I'd turn to find that even the old man was gone.

But when I did turn, he was still hunched there, squintii
our left, steering us toward another massive green-black isla
out of the horizon, this one with a narrow beach fringed w
and beyond that, immense cliffs rising like muscular should
the sea. The man grinned as if recognizing an old friend and
were some twenty yards offshore, abruptly he cut the engine,
me expectantly as the boat pitched and jerked. I realized, a
tended one oil-blackened index finger toward the water, still sn
was my cue to *jump*.

I shook my head. "What?"

He only jabbed that finger toward the water, and when I wav
arm, trying to tell him to *forget it,* a heavy swell blasted the boat. I
I could brace myself, I was abruptly tossed forward.

I was spinning upside down in the freezing waves. I broke the
face, gasping, seawater filling my mouth, but as the ground found
feet I realized it was shallow. I kicked my way to shore, strugglin
stand, bending over, coughing. But then I whipped around, horrifi
I'd neither paid the man nor made any arrangements to *get back.*

He'd already restarted the motor and was circling the boat around

"Hey!" I shouted, but again, the wind erased my voice. "*Wait!* Com
back!"

He didn't react or didn't hear me. Shoulders hunched, bracing himself against the wind, he was speeding across the water, motor screeching, and within minutes he was nothing but a speck of black on the sea.

I looked around. There was just enough light left to see, farther
down the beach, where the sand narrowed as if brutally shoved aside
by the cliffs, a giant boulder. It had a hole through it.

The trap of the mermaids.

Stunned, I stumbled toward it, then quickly realized that an immense flock of seagulls, their cries extinguished by the ocean, were

I moved toward it and spotted a pair of folded wire glasses, the lenses round and pitch black. Beside them was a bottle of Macallan scotch— *my scotch,* I noted with astonishment—and two empty glasses.

I turned, sensing someone watching me.

He was there, a hulking dark silhouette in the doorway.

Cordova.

A hundred things went through my head in that moment. Hunters stare their prey in the eyes and what do they see? I hadn't known I'd ever find him, and, if I did, whether I'd have the impulse to kill him, condemn him, or weep. Perhaps I'd pity him, brought to my knees by the vulnerable child inside every man. But I had a feeling he'd been expecting me, that we were going to do nothing more than sit down in those empty chairs, one father with another, and as the rain fell and the smoke coiled around us, weaving another hypnotic spell, he'd tell me. There would be unimaginable darkness and streaks of blood inside it, this tale he told, which would probably last for days, screams and bright red birds, and astounding hints of hope, as the sun, in an instant, can christen the blackest sea. I'd learn more about the lengths people went to feel something than I ever thought possible and I'd hear Sam's laughter inside of Ashley's.

I didn't know the end or what I'd find when it was over—if I'd stare at the rubble and recognize his story as one of evil or fallen grace, or if I'd see myself in all he'd done, trying to save his daughter, in his insatiable need to stretch life as far as it would go, risking it breaking.

Somehow, I sensed as soon as he told me, he'd find a way to be gone, faster than the wind across a field. I'd wake up somewhere far away, wondering if I'd imagined it, if he'd been here at all, inside this quiet house poised at the edge of the world.

The one thing I did know, as I stepped toward him, was that he was going to sit down beside me and tell me his truth.

And I would listen.

ISSUE NUMBER 255   DECEMBER 29, 1977 $1.90€ UK 17p

RollingStone

STANISLAS CORDOVA
To the Edge and Back
By R.S. Miles

PROJECT MKULTRA
The CIA's Secret Attempts at Mind Control
By Susannah Steinberg

APPLE II
The World's First Personal Computer Will It Change the Way We Live?
By George R. Harvey

A PLACE CALLED STUDIO 54
By Matthew Nash

CORDOVA

TO THE EDGE AND BACK

BY R.S. MILES

That this meeting is happening at all is a miracle. I'd been lobbying for years to get Cordova on the cover of *Rolling Stone.* Every time we extended the invitation, we heard nothing. Then, out of the blue, a note from his assistant, Inez Gallo: *Mr. Cordova would like to have the interview take place in four days at the Ritz-Carlton.*

Now, the man himself was sitting in front of me in the presidential suite, waiting for me to ask him a question. He was tall, wearing a black overcoat and round black-lensed glasses, which gave his head the alarming appearance of having two drilled holes in it.

What inspires you?

SC: The breath of a woman on my shoulder, the sunrise on a snowy mountain that is pink as a rose, my son.

All of the articles I have read about your work suggest that you must be an exacting eccentric, a ferocious dictator, even a sadist. The *Times* said in its review of *Somewhere in an Empty Room* that the ending—when we have no idea if the hero makes it out alive—indicates you have such a chilling view of humanity, your childhood must have been straight out of a horror movie. What was it like?

SC: I was raised by a single mother in the Bronx. We were poor. I often cut school, taking the subway into the city where I sat in cafés and bus stations and strip clubs. It was at this time I learned that the human mind is a blackened, overgrown place. Society tries to mow the lawn and trim back the plants, but every one of us is just days away from a wild jungle. And it's the jungle that interests me.

There's an impenetrable force field around you when it comes to talking about what it was like to be in your film. Why is that?

SC: Can married couples explain what happens when the guests go home, the

The edge of the end? That sounds a little dangerous.

SC: Mortal fear is as crucial a thing to our lives as love. It cuts to the core of our being and shows us what we are. Will you step back and cover your eyes? Or will you have the strength to walk to the precipice and look out? Do you want to know what is there or live in the dark delusion that this commercial world insists we remain sealed inside like blind caterpillars in an eternal cocoon? Will you curl up with your eyes closed and die? Or can you fight your way out of it and fly?

"THE HUMAN MIND IS A BLACKENED, OVERGROWN PLACE"

plates are cleared, the bedroom door closes, the lights go off? What goes on between the people I have chosen to tell a story remains between myself and them. They give themselves over to the work because they know I'll be careful, that I'll lead them, sometimes against their will, to the edge of the end. It's up to them to decide if they want to close their eyes after they get there and run away—or keep looking.

"Sovereign, deadly, and perfect"

What is your favorite shot out of all your films?

SC: The extreme close-up of the eye in *Figures*. It's actually my eye used in the shot. It's sovereign, deadly, and perfect.

What do you regret?

SC: That we can destroy those we love.

Why are your films thematically so disturbing?

SC: You have to walk for a time on the shaded side of the street to feel the sun when it hits your shoulders.

Your wife, Genevra, accidentally drowned in a lake on your property a few months ago.

SC: Yes.

13

How did such a terrible tragedy affect you?

SC: I can only describe it with an image—a racehorse with a shattered front leg, struggling to stand. The creature eventually realizes there can be nothing different, that he must remain on the ground, suffering because of what he did. He ran too hard, held nothing back, saved nothing for later, for going home. It's the price we pay for that kind of living. Our lives are flowers that bloom brightly and then they're gone.

My films are just stories. But that's all we have. The stories we tell others and the stories we tell ourselves. When you talk to the elderly, men and women at the end of their lives, you see that's what's left behind as the body disintegrates. Our stories. Our children will decide whether or not to keep telling them.

What's next for you—in your life, in work, in love?

SC: I'm going to step outside for a moment, if you don't mind.

"OUR LIVES ARE FLOWERS THAT BLOOM BRIGHTLY AND THEN THEY'RE GONE."

Of course.

I turned off the tape recorder, catching

The only publicity still released from the set of Treblinka

a fleeting glimpse of Cordova darting behind the door—then silence. I sat there reviewing my notes, deciding I'd ask him more about his fascination with the jungles of the mind—and who was he, exactly? After fifteen minutes, I rode the elevator down to the lobby, looking for him in the restaurant, in the crowds on the street, but he was gone like a shadow dissolved in daylight.

Repeated phone calls to his assistant elicited no response. Neither did a submission of this interview a week before it went to press. Had I said something to offend him? What had made him flee?

For now, he remains a mystery—until his next film, his next sound bite, an exclusive appearance on *60 Minutes* or *The Mike Douglas Show*. Until then, we'll go on wondering. Maybe some of us will even happen upon that mysterious edge of the end that he speaks of, lifting up our eyes, staring out. Is it hell or heaven that we will see? Maybe just life in its infinite spectacle.

Wherever it is, Cordova is there.

A Note about the Interactive Elements of *Night Film*

DEAR READER,

If you want to continue the *Night Film* experience, interactive touch points buried throughout the text will unlock extra content on your smartphone or tablet. These hidden Easter eggs include new images and audio. If you have a device with a rear-facing camera (connected to WiFi or a cellular network), please follow these steps to access the bonus content:

1. Visit NightFilmDecoder.com to learn how to download the free app.

2. Install the *Night Film* Decoder app on your device.

3. Search for the bird image below in select illustrations throughout *Night Film*. When you see it, launch the app on your device and scan the illustration with the camera until a Play button appears on the screen. *Hint*: Not every one hides a secret.

4. Press the Play button and enjoy.

   If you experience any issues with the *Night Film* Decoder app, please email support@randomhousedigital.com.

ACKNOWLEDGMENTS

NIGHT FILM would not have been possible if not for the guidance and support of a world-class group of people.

Binky Urban: Your reality is even better than your myth. Thank you for your sage advice, friendship, huge heart, and always telling me like it is. Many thanks to the team at ICM who are the best at what they do: Margaret Southard, Molly Atlas, Daisy Meyrick, Karolina Sutton, Rachel Clements, and Ron Bernstein.

Kate Medina: Your editorial insight and passion for Ashley's story continually challenged me as a writer, pushing this book to new heights and depths. Thank you for giving me the courage to tread even deeper down those dark corridors (and for Alexander McQueen).

Lindsey Schwoeri: Your close and perceptive reading of that early draft led me in an entirely new direction, cracking new and unexpected doors for me to open. Thanks for pointing them out or I might never have known they were there.

Anna Pitoniak: Your enthusiasm and creative suggestions were a breath of fresh air. The way you juggled with Ginger Rogers–style aplomb so many of the different elements that it took to assemble this book was awe-inspiring. Thank you for never missing a beat.

ACKNOWLEDGMENTS

To my Dream Team at Random House who worked round the clock with such fearless passion on my behalf:

Gina Centrello, thank you for being my fervent champion.

To Sally Marvin and Karen Fink—thank you for your zeal, your outside-the-box ideas, and being so totally cool.

Many thanks to Debbie Aroff for dreaming up the many ways in which to merge the *Night Film* universe with the real world. Thank you, too, to Maggie Oberrender for your behind-the-scenes contributions.

To Paolo Pepe, Barbara Bachman, and Simon M. Sullivan—I am so grateful for your willingness to push book design in a new direction. You put together a stunning package that even Cordova would approve of.

Many thanks to my digital team, the tech prophets Ken Wohlrob and Matt Schwartz—you help me to push the envelope and reimagine what's possible.

Laura Goldin—thank you for taking the time from your hectic schedule to be my advocate.

Thank you to Richard Elman, Benjamin Dreyer, and Lisa Feuer, who somehow made the production of this book happen on time and ahead of schedule.

Thank you to the stellar copy editor Amy Brosey and a huge thank you to Loren Noveck, whose Mensa-level Sherlock Holmes–like powers of deduction were amazing and invaluable. (They could use you at the C.I.A.)

Thank you to Jocasta Hamilton and the rest of the team at Hutchinson in London for their support, enthusiasm, and the House of Wolf.

Cordova's world never would have come to life with such dark vibrancy if it weren't for the inimitable Tristan Woods-Scawen, whose enthusiasm, wild creativity, and outstanding art direction for the illustrations transcended time zones and exploded expectations. Cordova never would have stepped out of the shadows without you. I'm indebted to the entire team of visionaries at Kennedy Monk: Stuart Monk, Bruce Kennedy, Jolyon Meldrum, Steven Harrison, Colin Taylor, Charlotte Kelly, and Michelle Thomas. It was a joy to work with you.

Thank you to my beautiful characters who have faces that whisper questions and glances that sear the brain: Sophie Blackbrough, Seb Castang, Verona Edo, Samantha Englebrecht, and Steven Harrison. I couldn't have come up with a more mesmerizing cast if I'd invented you myself.

Thank you to the photographer, Paul Archer, who made art out of evidence. Much gratitude to Lucy Flower, David Wadlow, and Lisa Jahovic, whose attention to detail made every photo look timely, rich, and real.

A host of medical experts were generous enough to take time out of their busy days to answer my questions: Lawrence Levin, M.D., one of the most caring and insightful physicians in New York City, and Leonard H. Wexler, M.D., who educated and humbled me with the incredible work he does for children.

An eternal thank you to my assistant and right-hand man, Seth D. Rabinowitz. You're my trusted confidant and partner-in-crime.

Thank you to my beloved family, friends, and other compatriots who contributed to this book in ways great and greater: James Rosow, Robert Strent, Nicole Caruso, Adam Weber (your twenty-two hours incarcerated in Brooklyn Central Booking was worth it for *the Tombs*), Nic Caiano, Noriel Abdon, Josh Thomas, Elke Pessl, and Don Marvel.

I will forever be grateful to my amazing mom and first reader, Anne, who teaches me that the true meaning of success is someone who leaves much love and light in her wake. So often you know what I'm trying to say before I do.

Finally I want to thank my late grandmother, Ruth, who lived with true grace. Her favorite quote was "The day shall not be up so soon as I / To try the fair adventure of to-morrow."

Let's keep living it.

IMAGE CREDITS

IMAGE CREDITS

NIGHT FILM

Marisha Pessl

A READER'S GUIDE

Questions and Topics for Discussion

1. Professor Wolfgang Beckman accuses Scott of having "no respect for *murk*. For the blackly unexplained. The un-nail-downable." How does Scott's perspective on mystery and the "blackly unexplained" change over the course of the novel?

2. Nora asks Scott, "How much evidence do you need before you wonder if it *just might* be real?" Do you think Scott's skepticism is a mark of pride as well as rationality, as Nora suggests? Why does he wish to believe in Ashley's curse after his conversation with Inez Gallo? How ready were you to believe in the curse?

3. Scott is relentless in his pursuit of the truth about Cordova. How far would you have gone in his situation? Is there a point at which you would have stopped pursuing the truth?

4. Cordova's films are filled with such horror and violence that in many cases, they were banned from theaters. What is your perspective on violence—its role and its effects—in movies today?

5. Cordova's philosophy is in many ways antithetical to our modern world, where transparency, oversharing, and social media are the

norms. Did you feel drawn to Cordova's philosophy or repelled by it, or both? Why?

6.   Discuss how Scott advertently or inadvertently involved his daughter, Samantha, in his investigation. What did you think of the role she wound up playing in his discovery?

7.   How does your perception of Scott change from the beginning to the end of the novel?

8.   What did you think of the evolution of Nora and Scott's relationship?

9.   Both Scott and Nora reflect on the power of memory and story to alter the way we relate to our experiences. Scott says: "It was never the act itself but our own understanding of it that defeated us, over and over again." Nora says: "The bad things that happen to you don't have to mean anything at all." Do you agree with either of them?

10.   Beckman says "Every one of us has our box, a dark chamber stowing the thing that lanced our heart." Consider Nora, Hopper, Ashley, Cordova, and Scott. What do their boxes contain, and in what ways do these secrets motivate them? Imprison them?

11.   What do you think helped Hopper come to peace with Ashley's memory?

12.   New York City is just as much a character in the novel as any one person. How does your personal experience of—or relationship with—the city affect your reading?

13.   How did the visual elements throughout the book enhance or impact your reading experience?

MARISHA PESSL grew up in Asheville, North Carolina, and now lives in New York City. *Special Topics in Calamity Physics,* her debut novel, was a best seller in both hardcover and paperback. It won the 2006 John Sargent Sr. First Novel Prize (now the Center for Fiction's Flaherty-Dunnan First Novel Prize), and was selected as one of the 10 Best Books of the Year by *The New York Times Book Review.*

ABOUT THE TYPE

This book was set in Fairfield, the first typeface from the hand
of the distinguished American artist and engraver Rudolph
Ruzicka (1883–1978). Ruzicka was born in Bohemia and came to
America in 1894. He set up his own shop, devoted to wood en-
graving and printing, in New York in 1913 after a varied career
working as a wood engraver, in photoengraving and banknote
printing plants, and as an art director and freelance artist. He
designed and illustrated many books, and was the creator of a
considerable list of individual prints—wood engravings, line engravings on copper, and aquatints.